HMS ULYSSES
FORCE TEN FROM NAVARONE
WHEN EIGHT BELLS TOLL

HMS ULYSSES

FORCE TEN FROM NAVARONE

WHEN EIGHT BELLS TOLL

by

Alistair MacLean

COLLINS
8 Grafton Street, London W1
1987

William Collins Sons & Co. Ltd
London · Glasgow · Sydney · Auckland
Toronto · Johannesburg

BRITISH LIBRARY CATALOGUING IN PUBLICATION DATA

MacLean, Alistair, *1922-1987*
    HMS Ulysses; Force Ten from Navarone,
    When eight bells toll.
    I. Title   II. MacLean, Alistair. *1922-1987*
    Force ten from Navarone   III. MacLean,
    Alistair, 1922-1987   When eight bells toll
    823'.914[F]   PR6063.A248

    ISBN 00-00-223324-X

Made and printed in Great Britain
by William Collins Sons and Co Ltd., Glasgow

HMS ULYSSES

To Gisela

I wish to acknowledge my debt to my elder brother, Ian L. MacLean, Master Mariner, for the considerable technical help and advice on matters maritime given me in the preparation of this book.

To avoid possible confusion it must be clearly stated that there is no connection whatsoever between the H.M.S. *Ulysses* of this book and the Ulster-class destroyer—now fully converted to a frigate—of the same name which entered operational service in the early part of 1944, some 12 months after the events described in this book. Nor is there any connection between any ship herein mentioned as being in Scapa Flow or participating in the convoy and any naval ship of the same name that has served, or is serving, in the Royal Navy.

A. M.

CHAPTER ONE

PRELUDE: SUNDAY AFTERNOON

SLOWLY, deliberately, Starr crushed out the butt of his cigarette. The gesture, Captain Vallery thought, held a curious air of decision and finality. He knew what was coming next, and, just for a moment, the sharp bitterness of defeat cut through that dull ache that never left his forehead nowadays. But it was only for a moment—he was too tired really, far too tired to care.

" I'm sorry, gentlemen, genuinely sorry." Starr smiled thinly. " Not for the orders, I assure you—the Admiralty decision, I am personally convinced, is the only correct and justifiable one in the circumstances. But I do regret your—ah—inability to see our point of view."

He paused, proffered his platinum cigarette case to the four men sitting with him round the table in the Rear-Admiral's day cabin. At the four mute headshakes the smile flickered again. He selected a cigarette, slid the case back into the breast pocket of his double-breasted grey suit. Then he sat back in his chair, the smile quite gone. It was not difficult to visualise, beneath that pin-stripe sleeve, the more accustomed broad band and golden stripes of Vice-Admiral Vincent Starr, Assistant Director of Naval Operations.

" When I flew north from London this morning," he continued evenly, " I was annoyed. I was very annoyed. I am—well, I am a fairly busy man. The First Sea Lord, I thought, was wasting my time as well as his own. When I return, I must apologise. Sir Humphrey was right. He usually is . . ."

His voice trailed off to a murmur, and the flint-wheel of his lighter rasped through the strained silence. He leaned forward on the table and went on softly.

9

"Let us be perfectly frank, gentlemen. I expected—I surely
had a right to expect—every support and full co-operation from
you in settling this unpleasant business with all speed. Unpleasant business?" He smiled wryly. "Mincing words won't
help. Mutiny, gentlemen, is the generally accepted term for it—
a capital offence, I need hardly remind you. And yet what do I
find?" His glance travelled slowly round the table. "Commissioned officers in His Majesty's Navy, including a Flag
Officer, sympathising with—if not actually condoning—a lower-
deck mutiny!"

He's overstating it, Vallery thought dully. He's provoking
us. The words, the tone, were a question, a challenge inviting
reply.

There was no reply. The four men seemed apathetic, indifferent. Four men, each an individual, each secure in his own
personality—yet, at that moment, so strangely alike, their faces
heavy and still and deeply lined, their eyes so quiet, so tired, so
very old.

"You are not convinced, gentlemen?" he went on softly.
"You find my choice of words a trifle—ah—disagreeable?" He
leaned back. "Hm... 'mutiny.'" He savoured the word slowly,
compressed his lips, looked round the table again. "No, it
doesn't sound too good, does it, gentlemen? You would call
it something else again, perhaps?" -He shook his head, bent
forward, smoothed out a signal sheet below his fingers.

"'Returned from strike on Lofotens,'" he read out: "'1545
—boom passed: 1610—finished with engines: 1630—provisions,
stores lighters alongside, mixed seaman-stoker party detailed
unload lubricating drums: 1650—reported to Captain stokers
refused to obey C.P.O. Hartley, then successively Chief Stoker
Hendry, Lieutenant (E) Grierson and Commander (E): ringleaders apparently Stokers Riley and Petersen: 1705—refused
to obey Captain: 1715—Master at Arms and Regulating P.O.
assaulted in performance of duties.'" He looked up. "What
duties? Trying to arrest the ringleaders?"

Vallery nodded silently.

"'1715—seaman branch stopped work, apparently in sympathy: no violence offered: 1725—broadcast by Captain, warned

of consequences : ordered to return to work : order disobeyed :
1730—signal to C.-in-C. *Duke of Cumberland*, for assistance.' "

Starr lifted his head again, looked coldly across at Vallery.

" Why, incidentally, the signal to the Admiral ? Surely your
own marines——"

" My orders," Tyndall interrupted bluntly. " Turn our own
marines against men they've sailed with for two and a half years ?
Out of the question ! There's no matelot—boot-neck antipathy
on *this* ship, Admiral Starr : they've been through far too much
together. . . . Anyway," he added dryly, " it's wholly possible
that the marines would have refused. And don't forget that
if we had used our own men, and they had quelled this—
ah—mutiny, the *Ulysses* would have been finished as a fighting
ship."

Starr looked at him steadily, dropped his eyes to the signal
again.

" ' 1830—Marine boarding party from *Cumberland* : no resistance offered to boarding : attempted to arrest six, eight
suspected ringleaders : strong resistance by stokers and seamen,
heavy fighting poop-deck, stokers' mess-deck and engineers' flat
till 1900 : no firearms used, but 2 dead, 6 seriously injured, 35-40
minor casualties.' " Starr finished reading, crumpled the paper
in an almost savage gesture. " You know, gentlemen, I believe
you have a point after all." The voice was heavy with irony.
" ' Mutiny ' is hardly the term. Fifty dead and injured : ' pitched
battle ' would be much nearer the mark."

The words, the tone, the lashing bite of the voice provoked
no reaction whatsoever. The four men still sat motionless,
expressionless, unheeding in a vast indifference.

Admiral Starr's face hardened.

" I'm afraid you have things just a little out of focus, gentlemen. You've been up here a long time and isolation distorts
perspective. Must I remind senior officers that, in wartime,
individual feelings, trials and sufferings are of no moment at all ?
The Navy, the country—they come first, last and all the time."
He pounded the table softly, the gesture insistent in its restrained
urgency. " Good God, gentlemen," he ground out, " the future
of the world is at stake—and you, with your selfish, your in-

excusable absorption in your own petty affairs, have the colossal
effrontery to endanger it ! "

Commander Turner smiled sardonically to himself. A pretty
speech, Vincent boy, very pretty indeed—although perhaps a
thought reminiscent of Victorian melodrama : the clenched teeth
act was definitely overdone. Pity he didn't stand for Parliament
—he'd be a terrific asset to any Government Front Bench.
Suppose the old boy's really too honest for that, he thought in
vague surprise.

" The ringleaders will be caught and punished—heavily
punished." The voice was harsh now, with a biting edge to it.
" Meantime, the 14th Aircraft Carrier Squadron will rendezvous
at Denmark Strait as arranged, at 1030 Wednesday instead of
Tuesday—we radioed Halifax and held up the sailing. You will
proceed to sea at 0600 to-morrow." He looked across at Rear-
Admiral Tyndall. " You will please advise all ships under your
command at once, Admiral."

Tyndall—universally known throughout the Fleet as Farmer
Giles—said nothing. His ruddy features, usually so cheerful and
crinkling, were set and grim : his gaze, heavy-lidded and troubled,
rested on Captain Vallery and he wondered just what kind of
private hell that kindly and sensitive man was suffering right then.
But Vallery's face, haggard with fatigue, told him nothing : that
lean and withdrawn asceticism was the complete foil. Tyndall
swore bitterly to himself.

" I don't really think there's more to say, gentlemen," Starr
went on smoothly. " I won't pretend you're in for an easy trip
—you know yourselves what happened to the last three major
convoys—P.Q.17, FR71 and 74. I'm afraid we haven't yet found
the answer to acoustic torpedoes and glider bombs. Further, our
intelligence in Bremen and Kiel—and this is substantiated by
recent experience in the Atlantic—report that the latest U-boat
policy is to get the escorts first. . . . Maybe the weather will save
you."

You vindictive old devil, Tyndall thought dispassionately.
Go on, damn you—enjoy yourself.

" At the risk of seeming rather Victorian and melodramatic,"
—impatiently Starr waited for Turner to stifle his sudden fit of

coughing—" we may say that the *Ulysses* is being given the opportunity of—ah—redeeming herself." He pushed back his chair. " After that, gentlemen, the Med. But first—FR77 to Murmansk, come hell or high water 1 " His voice broke on the last word and lifted into stridency, the anger burring through the thin veneer of suavity. " The *Ulysses* must be made to realise that the Navy will never tolerate disobedience of orders, dereliction of duty, organised revolt and sedition 1 "

" Rubbish 1 "

Starr jerked back in his chair, knuckles whitening on the arm-rest. His glance whipped round and settled on Surgèon-Commander Brooks, on the unusually vivid blue eyes so strangely hostile now under that magnificent silver mane.

Tyndall, too, saw the angry eyes. He saw, also, the deepening colour in Brooks's face, and moaned softly to himself. He knew the signs too well—old Socrates was about to blow his Irish top. Tyndall made to speak, then slumped back at a sharp gesture from Starr.

" What did you say, Commander ? " The Admiral's voice was very soft and quite toneless.

" Rubbish," repeated Brooks distinctly. " Rubbish. That's what I said. ' Let's be perfectly frank,' you say. Well, sir, I'm being frank. ' Dereliction of duty, organised revolt and sedition ' my foot 1 But I suppose you have to call it something, preferably something well within your own field of experience. But God only knows by what strange association and sleight-of-hand mental transfer, you equate yesterday's trouble aboard the *Ulysses* with the only clearly-cut code of behaviour thoroughly familiar to yourself." Brooks paused for a second : in the silence they heard the thin, high wail of a bosun's pipe—a passing ship, perhaps. " Tell me, Admiral Starr," he went on quietly, " are we to drive out the devils of madness by whipping—a quaint old medieval custom—or maybe, sir, by drowning—remember the Gaderene swine ? Or perhaps a month or two in cells, you think, is the best cure for tuberculosis ? "

" What in heaven's name are you talking about, Brooks ? " Starr demanded angrily. " Gaderene swine, tuberculosis—what *are* you getting at, man ? Go on—explain." He drummed his fingers impatiently on the table, eyebrows arched high into his furrowed brow. " I hope, Brooks," he went on silkily, " that you can justify this—ah—insolence of yours."

" I'm quite sure that Commander Brooks intended no insolence, sir." It was Captain Vallery speaking for the first time. " He's only expressing——"

" Please, Captain Vallery," Starr interrupted. " I am quite capable of judging these things for myself, I think." His smile was very tight. " Well, go on, Brooks."

Commander Brooks looked at him soberly, speculatively.

" Justify myself ? " He smiled wearily. " No, sir, I don't think I can." The slight inflection of tone, the implications, were not lost on Starr, and he flushed slightly. " But I'll try to explain," continued Brooks. " It may do some good."

He sat in silence for a few seconds, elbow on the table, his hand running through the heavy silver hair—a favourite mannerism of his. Then he looked up abruptly.

" When were you last at sea, Admiral Starr ? " he inquired.

" Last at sea ? " Starr frowned heavily. " What the devil has that got to do with you, Brooks—or with the subject under discussion ? " he asked harshly.

" A very great deal," Brooks retorted. " Would you please answer my question, Admiral ? "

" I think you know quite well, Brooks," Starr replied evenly, " that I've been at Naval Operations H.Q. in London since the outbreak of war. What are you implying, sir ? "

" Nothing. Your personal integrity and courage are not open to question. We all know that. I was merely establishing a fact." Brooks hitched himself forward in his chair.

" I'm a naval doctor, Admiral Starr—I've been a doctor for over thirty years now." He smiled faintly. " Maybe I'm not a very good doctor, perhaps I don't keep quite so abreast of the latest medical developments as I might, but I believe I can claim to know a great deal about human nature—this is no time for modesty—about how the mind works, about the wonderfully intricate interaction of mind and body.

" ' Isolation distorts perspective '—these were your words, Admiral Starr. ' Isolation ' implies a cutting off, a detachment from the world, and your implication was partly true. But—and this, sir, is the point—there are more worlds than one. The Northern Seas, the Arctic, the black-out route to Russia—these are another world, a world utterly distinct from yours. It is a world, sir, of which you cannot possibly have any conception. In effect, you are completely isolated from *our* world."

Starr grunted, whether in anger or derision it was difficult to say, and cleared his throat to speak, but Brooks went on swiftly.

" Conditions obtain there without either precedent or parallel in the history of war. The Russian Convoys, sir, are something entirely new and quite unique in the experience of mankind."

He broke off suddenly, and gazed out through the thick glass of the scuttle at the sleet slanting heavily across the grey waters and dun hills of the Scapa anchorage. No one spoke. The Surgeon-Commander was not finished yet : a tired man takes time to marshal his thoughts.

" Mankind, of course, can and does adapt itself to new conditions." Brooks spoke quietly, almost to himself. " Biologically and physically, they have had to do so down the ages, in order to survive. But it takes time, gentlemen, a great deal of time. You can't compress the natural changes of twenty centuries into a couple of years : neither mind nor body can stand it. You can try, of course, and such is the fantastic resilience and toughness of man that he can tolerate it—for extremely short periods. But the limit, the saturation capacity for adaptation is soon reached. Push men beyond that limit and anything can happen. I say ' anything ' advisedly, because we don't yet know the precise form the crack-up will take—but crack-up there always is. It may be physical, mental, spiritual—I don't know. But this I do know, Admiral Starr—the crew of the *Ulysses* has been pushed to the limit—and clear beyond."

" Very interesting, Commander." Starr's voice was dry, sceptical. " Very interesting indeed—and most instructive. Unfortunately, your theory—and it's only that, of course—is quite untenable."

Brooks eyed him steadily.

" That, sir, is not even a matter of opinion."

" Nonsense, man, nonsense ! " Starr's face was hard in anger.

" It's a matter of fact. Your premises are completely false." Starr leaned forward, his forefinger punctuating every word. " This vast gulf you claim to lie between the convoys to Russia and normal operational work at sea—it just doesn't exist. Can you point out any one factor or condition present in these Northern waters which is not to be found somewhere else in the world ? Can you, Commander Brooks ? "

" No, sir." Brooks was quite unruffled. " But I can point out a frequently overlooked fact—that differences of degree and association can be much greater and have far more far-reaching effects than differences in kind. Let me explain what I mean.

" Fear can destroy a man. Let's admit it—fear is a natural thing. You get it in every theatre of war—but nowhere, I suggest, so intense, so continual as in the Arctic convoys.

" Suspense, tension can break a man—any man. I've seen it happen too often, far, far too often. And when you're keyed up to snapping point, sometimes for seventeen days on end, when you have constant daily reminders of what may happen to you in the shape of broken, sinking ships and broken, drowning bodies —well, we're men, not machines. Something has to go—and does. The Admiral will not be unaware that after the last two trips we shipped nineteen officers and men to sanatoria—mental sanatoria ? "

Brooks was on his feet now, his broad, strong fingers splayed over the polished table surface, his eyes boring into Starr's.

" Hunger burns out a man's vitality, Admiral Starr. It saps his strength, slows his reactions, destroys the will to fight, even the will to survive. You are surprised, Admiral Starr ? Hunger, you think—surely that's impossible in the well-provided ships of to-day ? But it's not impossible, Admiral Starr. It's inevitable. You keep on sending us out when the Russian season's over, when the nights are barely longer than the days, when twenty hours out of the twenty-four are spent on watch or at action stations, and you expect us to feed well ! " He smashed the flat of his hand on the table. " How the hell can we, when the cooks spend nearly all their time in the magazines, serving the turrets, or in damage control parties ? Only the baker and butcher are excused—and so we live on corned-beef sandwiches. For weeks on end! Corned-beef sandwiches!" Surgeon-Commander Brooks almost spat in disgust.

Good old Socrates, thought Turner happily, give him hell. Tyndall, too, was nodding his ponderous approval. Only Vallery was uncomfortable—not because of what Brooks was saying, but because Brooks was saying it. He, Vallery, was the captain : the coals of fire were being heaped on the wrong head.

"Fear, suspense, hunger." Brooks's voice was very low now. "These are the things that break a man, that destroy him as surely as fire or steel or pestilence could. These are the killers.

"But they are nothing, Admiral Starr, just nothing at all. They are only the henchmen, the outriders, you might call them, of the Three Horsemen of the Apocalypse—cold, lack of sleep, exhaustion.

"Do you know what it's like up there, between Jan Mayen and Bear Island on a February night, Admiral Starr ? Of course you don't. Do you know what it's like when there's sixty degrees of frost in the Arctic—and it still doesn't freeze ? Do you know what it's like when the wind, twenty degrees below zero, comes screaming off the Polar and Greenland ice-caps and slices through the thickest clothing like a scalpel ? When there's five hundred tons of ice on the deck, where five minutes' direct exposure means frostbite, where the bows crash down into a trough and the spray hits you as solid ice, where even a torch battery dies out in the intense cold ? Do you, Admiral Starr, do you ? " Brooks flung the words at him, hammered them at him.

"And do you know what it's like to go for days on end without sleep, for weeks with only two or three hours out of the twenty-four ? Do you know the sensation, Admiral Starr ? That fine-drawn feeling with every nerve in your body and cell in your brain stretched taut to breaking point, pushing you over the screaming edge of madness. Do you know it, Admiral Starr ? It's the most exquisite agony in the world, and you'd sell your friends, your family, your hopes of immortality for the blessed privilege of closing your eyes and just letting go.

"And then there's the tiredness, Admiral Starr, the desperate weariness that never leaves you. Partly it's the debilitating effect of the cold, partly lack of sleep, partly the result of incessantly

bad weather. You know yourself how exhausting it can be to
brace yourself even for a few hours on a rolling, pitching deck :
our boys have been doing it for months—gales are routine on
the Arctic run. I can show you a dozen, two dozen old men, not
one of them a day over twenty."

Brooks pushed back his chair and paced restlessly across the
cabin. Tyndall and Turner glanced at each other, then over at
Vallery, who sat with head and shoulders bowed, eyes resting
vacantly on his clasped hands on the table. For the moment,
Starr might not have existed.

"It's a vicious, murderous circle," Brooks went on quickly.
He was leaning against the bulkhead now, hands deep in his
pockets, gazing out sightlessly through the misted scuttle. "The
less sleep you have, the tireder you are : the more tired you
become, the more you feel the cold. And so it goes on. And then,
all the time, there's the hunger and the terrific tension. Everything interacts with everything else : each single factor conspires
with the others to crush a man, break him physically and mentally,
and lay him wide open to disease. Yes, Admiral—disease." He
smiled into Starr's face, and there was no laughter in his smile.
"Pack men together like herring in a barrel, deprive 'em of every
last ounce of resistance, batten 'em below decks for days at a
time, and what do you get ? T.B. It's inevitable." He shrugged.
"Sure, I've only isolated a few cases so far—but I *know* that
active pulmonary T.B. is rife in the lower deck.

"I saw the break-up coming months ago." He lifted his
shoulders wearily. "I warned the Fleet Surgeon several times.
I wrote the Admiralty twice. They were sympathetic—and that's
all. Shortage of ships, shortage of men . . .

"The last hundred days did it, sir—on top of the previous
months. A hundred days of pure bloody hell and not a single
hour's shore leave. In port only twice—for ammunitioning : all
oil and provisions from the carriers at sea. And every day an
eternity of cold and hunger and danger and suffering. In the
name of God," Brooks cried, "we're not machines ! "

He levered himself off the wall and walked over to Starr,
hands still thrust deep in his pockets.

"I hate to say this in front of the Captain, but every officer in the ship—except Captain Vallery—knows that the men would have mutinied, as you call it, long ago, but for one thing—Captain Vallery. The intense personal loyalty of the crew to the Captain, the devotion almost to the other side of idolatry is something quite unique in my experience, Admiral Starr."

Tyndall and Turner both murmured approval. Vallery still sat motionless.

"But there was a limit even to that. It had to come. And now you talk of punishing, imprisoning these men. Good God above, you might as well hang a man for having leprosy, or send him to penal servitude for developing ulcers!" Brooks shook his head in despair. "Our crew are equally guiltless. They just couldn't help it. They can't see right from wrong any more. They can't think straight. They just want a rest, they just want peace, a few days blessed quiet. They'll give anything in the world for these things and they *can't* see beyond them. Can't you see that, Admiral Starr? Can't you? Can't you?"

For perhaps thirty seconds there was silence, complete, utter silence, in the Admiral's cabin. The high, thin whine of the wind, the swish of the hail seemed unnaturally loud. Then Starr was on his feet, his hand stretching out for his gloves : Vallery looked up, for the first time, and he knew that Brooks had failed.

"Have my barge alongside, Captain Vallery. At once, please." Starr was detached, quite emotionless. "Complete oiling, provisioning and ammunitioning as soon as possible. Admiral Tyndall, I wish you and your squadron a successful voyage. As for you, Commander Brooks, I quite see the point of your argument—at least, as far as you are concerned." His lips parted in a bleak, wintry smile. "You are quite obviously overwrought, badly in need of some leave. Your relief will be aboard before midnight. If you will come with me, Captain . . ."

He turned to the door and had taken only two steps when Vallery's voice stopped him dead, poised on one foot.

"One moment, sir, if you please."

Starr swung round. Captain Vallery had made no move to rise. He sat still, smiling. It was a smile compounded of deference, of understanding—and of a curious inflexibility. It made Starr feel vaguely uncomfortable.

"Surgeon-Commander Brooks," Vallery said precisely, "is a quite exceptional officer. He is invaluable, virtually irreplaceable and the *Ulysses* needs him badly. I wish to retain his services."

"I've made my decision, Captain," Starr snapped. "And it's final. You know, I think, the powers invested in me by the Admiralty for this investigation."

"Quite, sir." Vallery was quiet, unmoved. "I repeat, however, that we cannot afford to lose an officer of Brooks's calibre."

The words, the tone, were polite, respectful; but their significance was unmistakable. Brooks stepped forward, distress in his face, but before he could speak, Turner cut in smoothly, urbanely.

"I assume I wasn't invited to this conference for purely decorative purposes." He tilted back in his chair, his eyes fixed dreamily on the deck-head. "I feel it's time I said something. I unreservedly endorse old Brooks's remarks—every word of them."

Starr, white-mouthed and motionless, looked at Tyndall. "And you, Admiral?"

Tyndall looked up quizzically, all the tenseness and worry gone from his face. He looked more like a West Country Farmer Giles than ever. He supposed, wryly, that his career was at stake; funny, he thought, how suddenly unimportant a career could become.

"As Officer Commanding, maximum squadron efficiency is my sole concern. Some people *are* irreplaceable. Captain Vallery suggests Brooks is one of these. I agree."

"I see, gentlemen, I see," Starr said heavily. Two spots of colour burned high up on his cheekbones. "The convoy has sailed from Halifax, and my hands are tied. But you make a great mistake, gentlemen, a great mistake, in pointing pistols at the head of the Admiralty. We have long memories in Whitehall. We shall—ah—discuss the matter at length on your return. Good day, gentlemen, good day."

Shivering in the sudden chill, Brooks clumped down the ladder to the upper deck and turned for'ard past the galley into the Sick Bay. Johnson, the Leading Sick Bay Attendant, looked out from the dispensary.

"How are our sick and suffering, Johnson?" Brooks inquired. "Bearing up manfully?"

Johnson surveyed the eight beds and their occupants morosely.

"Just a lot of bloody chancers, sir. Half of them are a damned sight fitter than I am. Look at Stoker Riley there—him with the broken finger and whacking great pile of *Reader's Digests*. Going through all the medical articles, he is, and roaring out for sulph., penicillin and all the latest antibiotics. Can't pronounce half of them. Thinks he's dying."

"A grievous loss," the Surgeon-Commander murmured. He shook his head. "What Commander Dodson sees in him I don't know. . . . What's the latest from hospital?"

The expression drained out of Johnson's face.

"They're just off the blower, sir," he said woodenly. "Five minutes ago. Ordinary Seaman Ralston died at three o'clock."

Brooks nodded heavily. Sending that broken boy to hospital had only been a gesture anyway. Just for a moment he felt tired, beaten. "Old Socrates," they called him, and he was beginning to feel his age these days—and a bit more besides. Maybe a good night's sleep would help, but he doubted it. He sighed.

"Don't feel too good about all this, Johnson, do you?"

"Eighteen, sir. Exactly eighteen." Johnson's voice was low, bitter. "I've just been talking to Burgess—that's him in the next bed. Says Ralston steps out across the bathroom coaming, a towel over his arm. A mob rushes past, then this bloody great ape of a bootneck comes tearing up and bashes him over the skull with his rifle. Never knew what hit him, sir—and he never knew why."

Brooks smiled faintly.

"That's what they call—ah—seditious talk, Johnson," he said mildly.

"Sorry, sir. Suppose I shouldn't—it's just that I——"

"Never mind, Johnson. I asked for it. Can't stop anyone from thinking. Only, don't think out loud. It's—it's prejudicial to naval discipline. . . . I think your friend Riley wants you. Better get him a dictionary."

He turned and pushed his way through the surgery curtains. A dark head—all that could be seen behind the dentist's chair— twisted round. Johnny Nicholls, Acting Surgeon Lieutenant, rose quickly to his feet, a pile of report cards dangling from his left hand.

" Hallo, sir. Have a pew."

Brooks grinned.

" An excellent thing, Lieutenant Nicholls, truly gratifying, to meet these days a junior naval officer who knows his place. Thank you, thank you."

He climbed into the chair and sunk back with a groan, fiddling with the neck-rest.

" If you'll just adjust the foot-rest, my boy . . . so. Ah— thank you." He leaned back luxuriously, eyes closed, head far back on the rest, and groaned again. " I'm an old man, Johnny, my boy, just an ancient has-been."

" Nonsense, sir," Nicholls said briskly. " Just a slight malaise. Now, if you'll let me prescribe a suitable tonic . . ."

He turned to a cupboard, fished out two tooth-glasses and a dark-green, ribbed bottle marked " Poison." He filled the glasses and handed one to Brooks. " My personal recommendation. Good health, sir ! "

Brooks looked at the amber liquid, then at Nicholls.

" Heathenish practices they taught you at these Scottish Universities, my boy . . . Admirable fellers, some of these old heathens. What is it this time, Johnny ? "

" First-class stuff," Nicholls grinned. " Produce of the Island of Coll."

The old surgeon looked at him suspiciously.

" Didn't know they had any distilleries up there."

" They haven't. I only said it was made in Coll. . . . How did things go up top, sir ? "

" Bloody awful. His nibs threatened to string us all from the yard-arm. Took a special dislike to me—said I was to be booted off the ship instanter. Meant it, too."

" You ! " Nicholl's brown eyes, deep-sunk just now and red- rimmed from sleeplessness, opened wide. " You're joking, sir, of course."

" I'm not. But it's all right—I'm not going. Old Giles, the skipper and Turner—the crazy idiots—virtually told Starr that if I went he'd better start looking around for another Admiral, Captain and Commander as well. They shouldn't have done it, of course—but it shook old Vincent to the core. Departed in high dudgeon, muttering veiled threats . . . not so veiled, either, come to think of it."

" Damned old fool ! " said Nicholls feelingly.

" He's not really, Johnny. Actually, he's a brilliant bloke. You don't become a D.N.O. for nothing. Master strategist and tactician, Giles tells me, and he's not really as bad as we're apt to paint him ; to a certain extent we can't blame old Vincent for sending us out again. Bloke's up against an insoluble problem. Limited resources at his disposal, terrific demand for ships and men in half a dozen other theatres. Impossible to meet half the claims made on him ; half the time he's operating on little better than a shoe-string. But he's still an inhuman, impersonal sort of cuss—doesn't understand men."

" And the upshot of it all ? "

" Murmansk again. Sailing at 0600 to-morrow."

" What ! Again ? This bunch of walking zombies ? " Nicholls was openly incredulous. " Why, they can't do that, sir ! They—they just can't ! "

" They're doing it anyway, my boy. The *Ulysses* must—ah—redeem itself." Brooks opened his eyes. " Gad, the very thought appals me. If there's any of that poison left, my boy . . ."

Nicholls shoved the depleted bottle back into the cupboard, and jerked a resentful thumb in the direction of the massive battleship clearly visible through the porthole, swinging round her anchor three or four cable-lengths away.

" Why always us, sir ? It's always us. Why don't they send that useless floating barracks out once in a while ? Swinging round that bloody great anchor, month in, month out——"

" Just the point," Brooks interrupted solemnly. " According to the Kapok Kid, the tremendous weight of empty condensed milk cans and herring-in-tomato sauce tins accumulated on the ocean bed over the past twelve months completely defeats all attempts to weigh anchor."

Nicholls didn't seem to hear him.

"Week in, week out, months and months on end, they send the *Ulysses* out. They change the carriers, they rest the screen destroyers—but never the *Ulysses*. There's no let-up. Never, not once. But the *Duke of Cumberland*—all it's fit for is sending hulking great brutes of marines on board here to massacre sick men, crippled men, men who've done more in a week than——"

"Easy, boy, easy," the Commander chided. "You can't call three dead men and the bunch of wounded heroes lying outside there a massacre. The marines were only doing their job. As for the *Cumberland*—well, you've got to face it. We're the only ship in the Home Fleet equipped for carrier command."

Nicholls drained his glass and regarded his superior officer moodily.

"There are times, sir, when I positively love the Germans."

"You and Johnson should get together sometime," Brooks advised. "Old Starr would have you both clapped in irons for spreading alarm and . . . Hallo, hallo! " He straightened up in his chair and leaned forward. "Observe the old *Duke* there, Johnny! Yards of washing going up from the flag-deck and matelots running—actually running—up to the fo'c'sle head. Unmistakable signs of activity. By Gad, this *is* uncommon surprising! What d'ye make of it, boy? "

"Probably learned that they're going on leave," Nicholls growled. "Nothing else could possibly make that bunch move so fast. And who are we to grudge them the just reward for their labours? After so long, so arduous, so dangerous a spell of duty in Northern waters . . ."

The first shrill blast of a bugle killed the rest of the sentence. Instinctively, their eyes swung round on the crackling, humming loudspeaker, then on each other in sheer, shocked disbelief. And then they were on their feet, tense, expectant : the heart-stopping urgency of the bugle-call to action stations never grows dim.

"Oh, my God, no ! " Brooks moaned. "Oh, no, no ! Not again ! Not in Scapa Flow ! "

"Oh, God, no ! Not again—*not in Scapa Flow* ! "
These were the words in the mouths, the minds, the hearts of

727 exhausted, sleep-haunted, bitter men that bleak winter evening in Scapa Flow. That they thought of, and that only could they think of as the scream of the bugle stopped dead all work on decks and below decks, in engine-rooms and boiler-rooms, on ammunition lighters and fuel tenders, in the galleys and in the offices. And that only could the watch below think of—and that with an even more poignant despair—as the strident blare seared through the bliss of oblivion and brought them back, sick at heart, dazed in mind and stumbling on their feet, to the iron harshness of reality.

It was, in a strangely indefinite way, a moment of decision. It was the moment that could have broken the *Ulysses*, as a fighting ship, for ever. It was the moment that bitter, exhausted men, relaxed in the comparative safety of a land-locked anchorage, could have chosen to make the inevitable stand against authority, against that wordless, mindless compulsion and merciless insistence which was surely destroying them. If ever there was such a moment, this was it.

The moment came—and passed. It was no more than a fleeting shadow, a shadow that flitted lightly across men's minds and was gone, lost in the rush of feet pounding to action stations. Perhaps self-preservation was the reason. But that was unlikely —the *Ulysses* had long since ceased to care. Perhaps it was just naval discipline, or loyalty to the captain, or what the psychologists call conditioned reflex—you hear the scream of brakes and you immediately jump for your life. Or perhaps it was something else again.

Whatever it was, the ship—all except the port watch anchor party—was closed up in two minutes. Unanimous in their disbelief that this could be happening to them in Scapa Flow, men went to their stations, silently or vociferously, according to their nature. They went reluctantly, sullenly, resentfully, despairingly. But they went.

Rear-Admiral Tyndall went also. He was not one of those who went silently. He climbed blasphemously up to the bridge, pushed his way through the port gate and clambered into his high-legged armchair in the for'ard port corner of the compass platform. He looked across at Vallery.

" What's the flap, in heaven's name, Captain ? " he demanded
testily. " Everything seems singularly peaceful to me."

" Don't know yet, sir." Vallery swept worried eyes over the
anchorage. " Alarm signal from C.-in-C., with orders to get
under way immediately."

" Get under way ! But why, man, why ? "

Vallery shook his head.

Tyndall groaned. " It's all a conspiracy, designed to rob old
men like myself of their afternoon sleep," he declared.

" More likely a brainwave of Starr's to shake us up a bit,"
Turner grunted.

" No." Tyndall was decisive. " He wouldn't try that—
wouldn't dare. Besides, by his lights, he's not a vindictive man."

Silence fell, a silence broken only by the patter of sleet and
hail, and the weird haunting pinging of the Asdic. Vallery
suddenly lifted his binoculars.

" Good lord, sir, look at that ! The *Duke's* slipped her
anchor ! "

There was no doubt about it. The shackle-pin had been
knocked out and the bows of the great ship were swinging slowly
round as it got under way.

" What in the world—— ? " Tyndall broke off and scanned
the sky. " Not a plane, not a paratrooper in sight, no radar
reports, no Asdic contacts, no sign of the German Grand Fleet
steaming through the boom——"

" She's signalling us, sir ! " It was Bentley speaking, Bentley
the Chief Yeoman of Signals. He paused and went on slowly :
" Proceed to our anchorage at once. Make fast to north buoy."

" Ask them to confirm," Vallery snapped. He took the
fo'c'sle phone from the communication rating.

" Captain here, Number One. How is she ? Up and down ?
Good." He turned to the officer of the watch. " Slow ahead
both : Starboard 10." He looked over at Tyndall's corner,
brows wrinkled in question.

" Search me," Tyndall growled. " Could be the latest in
parlour games—a sort of nautical musical chairs, you know. . . .
Wait a minute, though ! Look ! The *Cumberland*—all her 5.25's
are at maximum depression ! "

Vallery's eyes met his.

" No, it can't be ! Good God, do you think—— ? "

The blare of the Asdic loudspeaker, from the cabinet immediately abaft of the bridge, gave him his answer. The voice of Leading Asdic Operator Chrysler was clear, unhurried.

" Asdic—bridge. Asdic—bridge. Echo, Red 30. Repeat, Red 30. Strengthening. Closing."

The captain's incredulity leapt and died in the same second.

" Alert Director Control ! Red 30. All A.A. guns maximum depression. Underwater target. Torps "—this to Lieutenant Marshall, the Canadian Torpedo Officer—" depth charge stations."

He turned back to Tyndall.

" It can't be, sir—it just can't ! A U-boat—I presume it is—in Scapa Flow. Impossible ! "

" Prien didn't think so," Tyndall grunted.

" Prien ? "

" Kapitan-Leutnant Prien—gent who scuppered the *Royal Oak*."

" It couldn't happen again. The new boom defences—— "

" Would keep out any normal submarines," Tyndall finished. His voice dropped to a murmur. " Remember what we were told last month about our midget two-man subs—the chariots ? The ones to be taken over to Norway by Norwegian fishing-boats operating from the Shetlands. Could be that the Germans have hit on the same idea."

" Could be," Vallery agreed. He nodded sardonically. " Just look at the *Cumberland* go—straight for the boom." He paused for a few seconds, his eyes speculative, then looked back at Tyndall. " How do you like it, sir ? "

" Like what, Captain ? "

" Playing Aunt Sally at the fair." Vallery grinned crookedly. " Can't afford to lose umpteen million pounds worth of capital ship. So the old *Duke* hares out to open sea and safety, while we moor near her anchor berth. You can bet German Naval Intelligence has the bearing of her anchorage down to a couple of inches. These midget subs carry detachable warheads and if there's going to be any fitted, they're going to be fitted to us."

Tyndall looked at him. His face was expressionless. Asdic reports were continuous, reporting steady bearing to port and closing distances.

" Of course, of course," the Admiral murmured. " We're the whipping boy. Gad, it makes me feel bad ! " His mouth twisted and he laughed mirthlessly. " Me ? This is the final straw for the crew. That hellish last trip, the mutiny, the marine boarding party from the *Cumberland*, action stations in harbour—and now this ! Risking our necks for that—that . . ." He broke off, spluttering, swore in anger, then resumed quietly :

" What are you going to tell the men, Captain ? Good God, it's fantastic ! I feel like mutiny myself . . ." He stopped short, looked inquiringly past Vallery's shoulder.

The Captain turned round.

" Yes, Marshall ? "

" Excuse me, sir. This—er—echo." He jerked a thumb over his shoulder. " A sub, sir—possibly a pretty small one ? " The transatlantic accent was very heavy.

" Likely enough, Marshall. Why ? "

" Just how Ralston and I figured it, sir." He grinned. " We have an idea for dealing with it."

Vallery looked out through the driving sleet, gave helm and engine orders, then turned back to the Torpedo Officer. He was coughing heavily, painfully, as he pointed to the glassed-in anchorage chart.

" If you're thinking of depth-charging our stern off in these shallow waters——"

" No, sir. Doubt whether we could get a shallow enough setting anyway. My idea—Ralston's to be correct—is that we take out the motor-boat and a few 25-lb. scuttling charges. 18-second fuses and chemical igniters. Not much of a kick from these, I know, but a miniature sub ain't likely to have helluva—er—very thick hulls. And if the crews are sitting on top of the ruddy things instead of inside—well, it's curtains for sure. It'll kipper 'em."

Vallery smiled.

" Not bad at all, Marshall. I think you've got the answer there. What do you think, sir ? "

" Worth trying, anyway," Tyndall agreed. " Better than waiting around like a sitting duck."

" Go ahead then, Torps." Vallery looked at him quizzically. " Who are your explosives experts ? "

" I figured on taking Ralston——"

" Just what I thought. You're taking nobody, laddie," said Vallery firmly. " Can't afford to loose my torpedo officer."

Marshall looked pained, then shrugged resignedly.

" The Chief T.G.M. and Ralston—he's the senior L.T.O. Good men both."

" Right. Bentley—detail a man to accompany them in the boat. We'll signal Asdic bearings from here. Have him take a portable Aldis with him." He dropped his voice. " Marshall ? "

" Sir ? "

" Ralston's young brother died in hospital this afternoon." He looked across at the Leading Torpedo Operator, a tall, blond, unsmiling figure dressed in faded blue overalls beneath his duffel. " Does he know yet ? "

The Torpedo Officer stared at Vallery, then looked round slowly at the L.T.O. He swore, softly, bitterly, fluently.

" Marshall ! " Vallery's voice was sharp, imperative, but Marshall ignored him, his face a mask, oblivious alike to the reprimand in the Captain's voice and the lashing bite of the sleet.

" No, sir," he stated at length, " he doesn't know. But he did receive some news this morning. Croydon was pasted last week. His mother and three sisters live there—lived there. It was a land-mine, sir—there was nothing left." He turned abruptly and left the bridge.

Fifteen minutes later it was all over. The starboard whaler and the motor-boat on the port side hit the water with the *Ulysses* still moving up to the mooring. The whaler, buoy-jumper aboard, made for the buoy, while the motor-boat slid off at a tangent.

Four hundred yards away from the ship, in obedience to the flickering instructions from the bridge, Ralston fished out a pair of pliers from his overalls and crimped the chemical fuse. The

Gunner's Mate stared fixedly at his stop-watch. On the count of twelve the scuttling charge went over the side.

Three more, at different settings, followed it in close succession, while the motor-boat cruised in a tight circle. The first three explosions lifted the stern and jarred the entire length of the boat, viciously—and that was all. But with the fourth, a great gout of air came gushing to the surface, followed by a long stream of viscous bubbles. As the turbulence subsided, a thin slick of oil spread over a hundred square yards of sea. . . .

Men, fallen out from Actions Stations, watched with expressionless faces as the motor-boat made it back to the *Ulysses* and hooked on to the falls just in time : the Hotchkiss steering-gear was badly twisted and she was taking in water fast under the counter.

The *Duke of Cumberland* was a smudge of smoke over a far headland.

Cap in hand, Ralston sat down opposite the Captain. Vallery looked at him for a long time in silence. He wondered what to say, how best to say it. He hated to have to do this.

Richard Vallery also hated war. He always had hated it and he cursed the day it had dragged him out of his comfortable retirement. At least, " dragged " was how he put it ; only Tyndall knew that he had volunteered his services to the Admiralty on 1st September, 1939, and had had them gladly accepted.

But he hated war. Not because it interfered with his life-long passion for music and literature, on both of which he was a considerable authority, not even because it was a perpetual affront to his æstheticism, to his sense of rightness and fitness. He hated it because he was a deeply religious man, because it grieved him to see in mankind the wild beasts of the primeval jungle, because he thought the cross of life was already burden enough without the gratuitous infliction of the mental and physical agony of war, and, above all, because he saw war all too clearly as the wild and insensate folly it was, as a madness of the mind that settled nothing, proved nothing—except the old, old truth that God was on the side of the big battalions.

But some things he had to do, and Vallery had clearly seen that this war had to be his also. And so he had come back to the service, and had grown older as the bitter years passed, older and frailer, and more kindly and tolerant and understanding. Among Naval Captains, indeed among men, he was unique. In his charity, in his humility, Captain Richard Vallery walked alone. It was a measure of the man's greatness that this thought never occurred to him.

He sighed. All that troubled him just now was what he ought to say to Ralston. But it was Ralston who spoke first.

"It's all right, sir." The voice was a level monotone, the face very still. "I know. The Torpedo Officer told me."

Vallery cleared his throat.

"Words are useless, Ralston, quite useless. Your young brother—and your family at home. All gone. I'm sorry, my boy, terribly sorry about it all." He looked up into the expressionless face and smiled wryly. "Or maybe you think that these are all words—you know, something formal, just a meaningless formula."

Suddenly, surprisingly, Ralston smiled briefly.

"No, sir, I don't. I can appreciate how you feel, sir. You see, my father—well, he's a captain too. He tells me he feels the same way."

Vallery looked at him in astonishment.

"Your father, Ralston? Did you say——"

"Yes, sir." Vallery could have sworn to a flicker of amusement in the blue eyes, so quiet, so self-possessed, across the table. "In the Merchant Navy, sir—a tanker captain—16,000 tons."

Vallery said nothing. Ralston went on quietly:

"And about Billy, sir—my young brother. It's—it's just one of these things. It's nobody's fault but mine—I asked to have him aboard here. I'm to blame, sir—only me." His lean brown hands were round the brim of his hat, twisting it, crushing it. How much worse will it be when the shattering impact of the double blow wears off, Vallery wondered, when the poor kid begins to think straight again?

"Look, my boy, I think you need a few days' rest, time to think things over." God, Vallery thought, what an inadequate, what a futile thing to say. " P.R.O. is making out your travelling warrant just now. You will start fourteen days' leave, as from to-night."

" Where is the warrant made out for, sir ? " The hat was crushed now, crumpled between the hands. " Croydon ? "

" Of course. Where else——" Vallery stopped dead ; the enormity of the blunder had just hit him.

" Forgive me, my boy. What a damnably stupid thing to say ! "

" Don't send me away, sir," Ralston pleaded quietly. " I know it sounds—well, it sounds corny, self-pitying, but the truth is I've nowhere to go. I belong here—on the *Ulysses*. I can do things all the time—I'm busy—working, sleeping—I don't have to talk about things—I can do things . . ." The self-possession was only the thinnest veneer, taut and frangible, with the quiet desperation immediately below.

" I can get a chance to help pay 'em back," Ralston hurried on. " Like crimping these fuses to-day—it—well, it was a privilege. It was more than that—it was—oh, I don't know. I can't find the words, sir."

Vallery knew. He felt sad, tired, defenceless. What could he offer this boy in place of this hate, this very human, consuming flame of revenge ? Nothing, he knew, nothing that Ralston wouldn't despise, wouldn't laugh at. This was not the time for pious platitudes. He sighed again, more heavily this time.

" Of course you shall remain, Ralston. Go down to the Police Office and tell them to tear up your warrant. If I can be of any help to you at any time——"

" I understand, sir. Thank you very much. Good night, sir."

" Good night, my boy."

The door closed softly behind him.

CHAPTER TWO

MONDAY MORNING

"CLOSE ALL water-tight doors and scuttles. Hands to stations for leaving harbour." Impersonally, inexorably, the metallic voice of the broadcast system reached into every farthest corner of the ship.

And from every corner of the ship came men in answer to the call. They were cold men, shivering involuntarily in the icy north wind, swearing pungently as the heavy falling snow drifted under collars and cuffs, as numbed hands stuck to frozen ropes and metal. They were tired men, for fuelling, provisioning and ammunitioning had gone on far into the middle watch : few had had more than three hours' sleep.

And they were still angry, hostile men. Orders were obeyed, to be sure, with the mechanical efficiency of a highly-trained ship's company ; but obedience was surly, acquiescence resentful, and insolence lay ever close beneath the surface. But Divisional Officers and N.C.O.s handled the men with velvet gloves : Vallery had been emphatic about that.

Illogically enough, the highest pitch of resentment had not been caused by the *Cumberland's* prudent withdrawal. It had been produced the previous evening by the routine broadcast, " Mail will close at 2000 to-night." Mail ! Those who weren't working non-stop round the clock were sleeping like the dead with neither the heart nor the will even to think of writing. Leading Seaman Doyle, the doyen of " B " mess-deck and a venerable three-badger (thirteen years undiscovered crime, as he modestly explained his good-conduct stripes) had summed up the matter succinctly : " If my old Missus was Helen of Troy and Jane Russell rolled into one—and all you blokes wot have seen the old dear's photo know that the very idea's a shocking libel on either of them ladies—I still wouldn't send her even a bleedin' postcard. You gotta draw a line somewhere. Me, for my scratcher." Whereupon he had dragged his hammock from the rack, slung it with milli-metric accuracy beneath a hot-air louvre—seniority carries its privileges—and was asleep in two minutes. To a man, the port watch did likewise : the mail bag had gone ashore almost empty. . . .

At 0600, exactly to the minute, the *Ulysses* slipped her moorings and steamed slowly towards the boom. In the grey half-light, under leaden, lowering clouds, she slid across the anchorage like an insubstantial ghost, more often than not half-hidden from view under sudden, heavy flurries of snow.

Even in the relatively clear spells, she was difficult to locate. She lacked solidity, substance, definition of outline. She had a curious air of impermanence, of volatility. An illusion, of course, but an illusion that accorded well with a legend—for a legend the *Ulysses* had become in her own brief lifetime. She was known and cherished by merchant seamen, by the men who sailed the bitter seas of the North, from St. John's to Archangel, from the Shetlands to Jan Mayen, from Greenland to far reaches of Spitz-bergen, remote on the edge of the world. Where there was danger, where there was death, there you might look to find the *Ulysses*, materialising wraith-like from a fog-bank, or just, miraculously, being there when the bleak twilight of an Arctic dawn brought with it only the threat, at times almost the certainty, of never seeing the next.

A ghost-ship, almost, a legend. The *Ulysses* was also a young ship, but she had grown old in the Russian Convoys and on the Arctic patrols. She had been there from the beginning, and had known no other life. At first she had operated alone, escorting single ships or groups of two or three : later, she had operated with corvettes and frigates, and now she never moved without her squadron, the 14th Escort Carrier group.

But the *Ulysses* had never really sailed alone. Death had been, still was, her constant companion. He laid his finger on a tanker, and there was the erupting hell of a high-octane detonation ; on a cargo liner, and she went to the bottom with her load of war supplies, her back broken by a German torpedo ; on a destroyer, and she knifed her way into the grey-black depths of the Barents Sea, her still-racing engines her own executioners ; on a U-boat, and she surfaced violently to be destroyed by gunfire, or slid down gently to the bottom of the sea, the dazed, shocked crew hoping for a cracked pressure hull and merciful, instant extinction, dreading the endless gasping agony of suffocation in their iron tomb on the ocean floor. Where the *Ulysses* went, there also went death. But death never touched her. She was a lucky ship. A lucky ship and a ghost ship and the Arctic was her home.

Illusion, of course, this ghostliness, but a calculated illusion. The *Ulysses* was designed specifically for one task, for one ocean, and the camouflage experts had done a marvellous job. The special Arctic camouflage, the broken, slanting diagonals of grey and white and washed-out blues merged beautifully, imperceptibly into the infinite shades of grey and white, the cold, bleak grimness of the barren northern seas.

And the camouflage was only the outward, the superficial indication of her fitness for the north.

Technically, the *Ulysses* was a light cruiser. She was the only one of her kind, a 5,500-ton modification of the famous *Dido* type, a forerunner of the *Black Prince* class. Five hundred and ten feet long, narrow in her fifty-foot beam with a raked stem, square cruiser stern and long fo'c'sle deck extending well abaft the bridge —a distance of over two hundred feet, she looked and was a lean, fast and compact warship, dangerous and durable.

" Locate : engage : destroy." These are the classic requirements of a naval ship in wartime, and to do each, and to do it with maximum speed and efficiency, the *Ulysses* was superbly equipped.

Location, for instance. The human element, of course, was indispensable, and Vallery was far too experienced and battle-wise a captain to underestimate the value of the unceasing vigil of look-outs and signalmen. The human eye was not subject to blackouts, technical hitches or mechanical breakdowns. Radio reports, too, had their place and Asdic, of course, was the only defence against submarines.

But the *Ulysses's* greatest strength in location lay elsewhere.

She was the first completely equipped radar ship in the world. Night and day, the radar scanners atop the fore and main tripod masts swept ceaselessly in a 360° arc, combing the far horizons, searching, searching, searching. Below, in the radar rooms—eight in all—and in the Fighter Direction rooms, trained eyes, alive to the slightest abnormality, never left the glowing screens. The radar's efficiency and range were alike fantastic. The makers, optimistically, as they had thought, had claimed a 40-45 mile operating range for their equipment. On the *Ulysses's* first trials after her refit for its installation, the radar had located a Condor, subsequently destroyed by a Blenheim, at a range of eighty-five miles.

Engage—that was the next step. Sometimes the enemy came to you, more often you had to go after him. And then, one thing alone mattered—speed.

The *Ulysses* was tremendously fast. Quadruple screws powered by four great Parsons single-reduction geared turbines —two in the for'ard, two in the after engine-room—developed an unbelievable horse-power that many a battleship, by no means obsolete, could not match. Officially, she was rated at 33.5 knots. Off Arran, in her full-power trials, bows lifting out of the water, stern dug in like a hydroplane, vibrating in every Clyde-built rivet, and with the tortured, seething water boiling whitely ten feet above the level of the poop-deck, she had covered the measured mile at an incredible 39.2 knots—the nautical equivalent of 45 m.p.h. And the ' Dude '—Engineer-Commander Dobson— had smiled knowingly, said he wasn't half trying and just wait till the *Abdiel* or the *Manxman* came along, and he'd show them something. But as these famous mine-laying cruisers were widely believed to be capable of 44 knots, the wardroom had merely sniffed " Professional jealousy " and ignored him. Secretly, they were as proud of the great engines as Dobson himself.

Locate, engage—and destroy. Destruction. That was the be-all, the end-all. Lay the enemy along the sights and destroy him. The *Ulysses* was well equipped for that also.

She had four twin gun-turrets, two for'ard, two aft, 5.25 quick-firing and dual-purpose—equally effective against surface targets and aircraft. These were controlled from the Director Towers, the main one for'ard, just above and abaft of the bridge, the auxiliary aft. From these towers, all essential data about bearing, wind-speed, drift, range, own speed, enemy speed, respective angles of course were fed to the giant electronic computing tables in the Transmitting Station, the fighting heart of the ship, situated, curiously enough, in the very bowels of the *Ulysses*, deep below the water-line, and thence automatically to the turrets as two simple factors—elevation and training. The turrets, of course, could also fight independently.

These were the main armament. The remaining guns were purely A.A.—the batteries of multiple pom-poms, firing two-pounders in rapid succession, not particularly accurate but producing a blanket curtain sufficient to daunt any enemy pilot, and isolated clusters of twin Oerlikons, high-precision, high-velocity weapons, vicious and deadly in trained hands.

Finally, the *Ulysses* carried her depth-charges and torpedoes—36 charges only, a negligible number compared to that carried by many corvettes and destroyers, and the maximum number that could be dropped in one pattern was six. But one depth-charge carries 450 lethal pounds of Amatol, and the *Ulysses* had destroyed two U-boats during the preceding winter. The 21-inch torpedoes, each with its 750-pound warhead of T.N.T., lay, sleek and menacing, in the triple tubes on the main deck, one set on either side of the after funnel. These had not yet been blooded.

This, then, was the *Ulysses*. The complete, the perfect fighting machine, man's ultimate, so far, in his attempt to weld science and savagery into an instrument of destruction. The perfect fighting machine—but only so long as it was manned and serviced by a perfectly-integrating, smoothly-functioning team. A ship—any ship—can never be better than its crew. And the crew of the *Ulysses* was disintegrating, breaking up : the lid was clamped on the volcano, but the rumblings never ceased.

The first signs of further trouble came within three hours of clearing harbour. As always, minesweepers swept the channel ahead of them, but, as always, Vallery left nothing to chance. It was one of the reasons why he—and the *Ulysses*—had survived thus far. At 0620 he streamed paravanes—the slender, torpedo-shaped bodies which angled out from the bows, one on either

side, on special paravane wire. In theory, the wires connecting
mines to their moorings on the floor of the sea were deflected
away from the ship, guided out to the paravanes themselves and
severed by cutters : the mines would then float to the top to be
exploded or sunk by small arms.

At 0900, Vallery ordered the paravanes to be recovered. The
Ulysses slowed down. The First Lieutenant, Lieutenant-Commander Carrington, went to the fo'c'sle to supervise operations :
seamen, winch drivers, and the Subs. in charge of either side
closed up to their respective stations.

Quickly, the recovery booms were freed from their angled
crutches, just abaft the port and starboard lights, swung out and
rigged with recovery wires. Immediately, the three-ton winches
on " B " gun-deck took the strain, smoothly, powerfully; the
paravanes cleared the water.

Then it happened. It was A.B. Ferry's fault that it happened.
And it was just ill-luck that the port winch was suspect, operating
on a power circuit with a defective breaker, just ill-luck that
Ralston was the winch-driver, a taciturn, bitter-mouthed Ralston
to whom, just then, nothing mattered a damn, least of all what
he said and did. But it was Carslake's responsibility that the
affair developed into what it did.

Sub-Lieutenant Carslake's presence there, on top of the Carley
floats, directing the handling of the port wire, represented the
culmination of a series of mistakes. A mistake on the part of his
father, Rear-Admiral, Rtd., who had seen in his son a man of his
own calibre, had dragged him out of Cambridge in 1939 at the
advanced age of twenty-six and practically forced him into the
Navy : a weakness on the part of his first C.O., a corvette captain
who had known his father and recommended him as a candidate
for a commission : a rare error of judgment on the part of the
selection board of the *King Alfred*, who had granted him his
commission ; and a temporary lapse on the part of the Commander, who had assigned him to this duty, in spite of Carslake's
known incompetence and inability to handle men.

He had the face of an overbred racehorse, long, lean and
narrow, with prominent pale-blue eyes and protruding upper
teeth. Below his scanty fair hair, his eyebrows were arched in a

perpetual question mark : beneath the long, pointed nose, the supercilious curl of the upper lip formed the perfect complement to the eyebrows. His speech was a shocking caricature of the King's English : his short vowels were long, his long ones interminable : his grammar was frequently execrable. He resented the Navy, he resented his long overdue promotion to Lieutenant, he resented the way the men resented him. In brief, Sub-Lieutenant Carslake was the quintessence of the worst by-product of the English public-school system. Vain, superior, uncouth and illeducated, he was a complete ass.

He was making an ass of himself now. Striving to maintain balance on the rafts, feet dramatically braced at a wide angle, he shouted unceasing, unnecessary commands at his men. C.P.O. Hartley groaned aloud, but kept otherwise silent in the interests of discipline. But A.B. Ferry felt himself under no such restraints.

"'Ark at his Lordship," he murmured to Ralston. "All for the Skipper's benefit." He nodded at where Vallery was leaning over the bridge, twenty feet above Carslake's head. "Impresses him no end, so his nibs reckons."

"Just you forget about Carslake and keep your eyes on that wire," Ralston advised. "And take these damned great gloves off. One of these days——"

"Yes, yes, I know," Ferry jeered. "The wire's going to snag 'em and wrap me round the drum." He fed in the hawser expertly. "Don't you worry, chum, it's never going to happen to me."

But it did. It happened just then. Ralston, watching the swinging paravane closely, flicked a glance inboard. He saw the broken strand inches from Ferry, saw it hook viciously into the gloved hand and drag him towards the spinning drum before Ferry had a chance to cry out.

Ralston's reaction was immediate. The foot-brake was only six inches away—but that was too far. Savagely he spun the control wheel, full ahead to full reverse in a split second. Simultaneously with Ferry's cry of pain as his forearm crushed against the lip of the drum came a muffled explosion and clouds of acrid smoke from the winch as £500 worth of electric motor burnt out in a searing flash.

Immediately the wire began to run out again, accelerating momentarily under the dead weight of the plunging paravane. Ferry went with it. Twenty feet from the winch the wire passed through a snatch-block on the deck : if Ferry was lucky, he might lose only his hand.

He was less than four feet away when Ralston's foot stamped viciously on the brake. The racing drum screamed to a shuddering stop, the paravane crashed down into the sea and the wire, weightless now, swung idly to the rolling of the ship.

Carslake scrambled down off the Carley, his sallow face suffused with anger. He strode up to Ralston.

" You bloody fool ! " he mouthed furiously. " You've lost us that paravane. By God, L.T.O., you'd better explain yourself ! Who the hell gave you orders to do anything ? "

Ralston's mouth tightened, but he spoke civilly enough.

" Sorry, sir. Couldn't help it—it had to be done. Ferry's arm——"

" To hell with Ferry's arm ! " Carslake was almost screaming with rage. " I'm in charge here—and I give the orders. Look ! Look ! " He pointed to the swinging wire. " Your work, Ralston, you—you blundering idiot ! It's gone, gone, do you understand, *gone* ? "

Ralston looked over the side with an air of large surprise.

" Well, now, so it is." The eyes were bleak, the tone provocative, as he looked back at Carslake and patted the winch. " And don't forget this—it's gone too, and it costs a ruddy sight more than any paravane."

" I don't want any of your damned impertinence ! " Carslake shouted. His mouth was working, his voice shaking with passion. " What you need is to have some discipline knocked into you, and, by God, I'm going to see you get it, you insolent young bastard ! "

Ralston flushed darkly. He took one quick step forward, his fist balled, then relaxed heavily as the powerful hands of C.P.O. Hartley caught his swinging arm. But the damage was done now. There was nothing for it but the bridge.

Vallery listened calmly, patiently, as Carslake made his outraged report. He felt far from patient. God only knew, he thought wearily, he had more than enough to cope with already. But the unruffled, professional mask of detachment gave no hint of his feelings.

"Is this true, Ralston?" he asked quietly, as Carslake finished his tirade. "You disobeyed orders, swore at the Lieutenant and insulted him?"

"No, sir." Ralston sounded as weary as the Captain felt. "It's not true." He looked at Carslake, his face expressionless, then turned back to the Captain. "I didn't disobey orders—there were none. Chief Petty Officer Hartley knows that." He nodded at the burly impassive figure who had accompanied them to the bridge. "I didn't swear at him. I hate to sound like a sea-lawyer, sir, but there are plenty of witnesses that Sub-Lieutenant Carslake swore at me—several times. And if I insulted him "—he smiled faintly—" it was pure self-defence."

"This is no place for levity, Ralston." Vallery's voice was cold. He was puzzled—the boy baffled him. The bitterness, the brittle composure—he could understand these ; but not the flickering humour. "As it happens, I saw the entire incident. Your promptness, your resource, saved that rating's arm, possibly even his life—and against that a lost paravane and wrecked winch are nothing." Carslake whitened at the implied rebuke. "I'm grateful for that—thank you. As for the rest, Commander's Defaulters to-morrow morning. Carry on, Ralston."

Ralston compressed his lips, looked at Vallery for a long moment, then saluted abruptly and left the bridge.

Carslake turned round appealingly.

"Captain, sir . . ." He stopped at the sight of Vallery's upraised hand.

"Not now, Carslake. We'll discuss it later." He made no attempt to conceal the dislike in his voice. "You may carry on, Lieutenant. Hartley—a word with you."

Hartley stepped forward. Forty-four years old, C.P.O. Hartley was the Royal Navy at its best. Very tough, very kindly and very competent, he enjoyed the admiration of all, ranging from the vast awe of the youngest Ordinary Seaman to the warm respect of the Captain himself. They had been together from the beginning.

" Well, Chief, let's have it. Between ourselves."

" Nothing to it really, sir." Hartley shrugged. " Ralston did a fine job. Sub-Lieutenant Carslake lost his head. Maybe Ralston *was* a bit sassy, but he was provoked. He's only a kid, but he's a professional—and he doesn't like being pushed around by amateurs." Hartley paused and looked up at the sky. " Especially bungling amateurs."

Vallery smothered a smile.

" Could that be interpreted as—er—a criticism, Chief ? "

" I suppose so, sir." He nodded forward. " A few ruffled feathers down there, sir. Men are pretty sore about this. Shall I—— ? "

" Thanks, Chief. Play it down as much as possible."

When Hartley had gone, Vallery turned to Tyndall.

" Well, you heard it, sir ? Another straw in the wind."

" A straw ? " Tyndall was acid. " Hundreds of straws. More like a bloody great cornstack. . . . Find out who was outside my door last night ? "

During the middle watch, Tyndall had heard an unusual scraping noise outside the wardroom entry to his day cabin, had gone to investigate himself : in his hurry to reach the door, he'd knocked a chair over, and seconds later had heard a clatter and the patter of running feet in the passage outside ; but, when he had thrown the door open, the passage had been empty. Nothing there, nothing at all—except a file on the deck, below the case of Navy Colt .445s ; the chain on the trigger guards was almost through.

Vallery shook his head.

" No idea at all, sir." His face was heavy with worry. " Bad, really bad."

Tyndall shivered in an icy flurry. He grinned crookedly.

" Real Captain Teach stuff, eh ? Pistols and cutlasses and black eye-patches, storming the bridge . . ."

Vallery shook his head impatiently.

" No, not that. You know it, sir. Defiance, maybe, but—well, no more. The point is, a marine is on guard at the keyboard—

just round the corner of that passage. Night and day. Bound to have seen him. He denies——"

" The rot has gone that far ? " Tyndall whistled softly. " A black day, Captain. What does our fire-eating young Captain of Marines say to that ? "

" Foster ? Pooh-poohs the very idea—and just about twists the ends of his moustache off. Worried to hell. So's Evans, his Colour-Sergeant."

" So am I ! " said Tyndall feelingly. He glared into space. The Officer of the Watch, who happened to be in his direct line of vision, shifted uncomfortably. " Wonder what old Socrates thinks of it all, now ? Maybe only a pill-roller, but the wisest head we've got. . . . Well, speak of the devil ! "

The gate had just swung open, and a burly, unhappy-looking figure, duffel-coated, oilskinned and wearing a Russian beaver-skin helmet—the total effect was of an elderly grizzly bear caught in a thunderstorm—shuffled across the duckboards of the bridge. He brought up facing the Kent screen—an inset, circular sheet of glass which revolved at high speed and offered a clear view in all weather conditions—rain, hail, snow. For half a minute he peered miserably through this and obviously didn't like what he saw.

He sniffed loudly and turned away, beating his arms against the cold.

" Ha ! A deck officer on the bridge of H.M. Cruisers. The romance, the glamour ! Ha ! " He hunched his oil skinned shoulders, and looked more miserable than ever. " No place this for a civilised man like myself. But you know how it is, gentlemen —the clarion call of duty. . . ."

Tyndall chuckled.

" Give him plenty of time, Captain. Slow starters, these medics, you know, but——"

Brooks cut in, voice and face suddenly serious.

" Some more trouble, Captain. Couldn't tell it over the phone. Don't know how much it's worth."

" Trouble ? " Vallery broke off, coughed harshly into his handkerchief. " Sorry," he apologised. " Trouble ? There's nothing else, old chap. Just had some ourselves."

" That bumptious young fool, Carslake ? Oh, I know all right. My spies are everywhere. Bloke's a bloody menace. . . . However, my story.

" Young Nicholls was doing some path. work late last night in the dispensary—on T.B. specimens. Two, three hours in there. Lights out in the bay, and the patients either didn't know or had forgotten he was there. Heard Stoker Riley—a real trouble-maker, that Riley—and the others planning a locked-door, sit-down strike in the boiler-room when they return to duty. A sit-down strike in a boiler-room ! Good lord, it's fantastic ! Anyway, Nicholls let it slide—pretended he hadn't heard."

" What ! " Vallery's voice was sharp, edged with anger. " And Nicholls ignored it, didn't report it to me ! Happened last night, you say. Why wasn't I told—immediately ? Get Nicholls up here—now. No, never mind." He reached out to pick up the bridge phone. " I'll get him myself."

Brooks laid a gauntleted hand on Vallery's arm.

" I wouldn't do that, sir. Nicholls is a smart boy—very smart indeed. He knew that if he let the men know they had been overheard, they would know that he must report it to you. And then you'd have been bound to take action—and open provocation of trouble is the last thing you want. You said so yourself in the wardroom last night."

Vallery hesitated. " Yes, yes, of course I said that, but—well, Doc., this is different. It could be a focal point for spreading the idea to——"

" I told you, sir," Brooks interrupted softly. " Johnny Nicholls is a very smart boy. He's got a big notice, in huge red letters, outside the Sick Bay door : ' Keep clear : Suspected scarlet fever infection.' Kills me to watch 'em. Everybody avoids the place like the plague. Not a hope of communicating with their pals in the Stokers' Mess."

Tyndall guffawed at him, and even Vallery smiled slightly.

" Sounds fine, Doc. Still, I should have been told last night."

" Why should you be woken up and told every little thing in the middle of the night ? " Brooks's voice was brusque. " Sheer selfishness on my part, but what of it ? When things get bad, you damn, well carry this ship on your back—and when we've all got to depend on you, we can't afford to have you anything less than as fit as possible. Agreed, Admiral ? "

Tyndall nodded solemnly. " Agreed, O Socrates. A very complicated way of saying that you wish the Captain to have a good night's sleep. But agreed."

Brooks grinned amiably. " Well, that's all, gentlemen. See you all at the court-martial—I hope." He cocked a jaundiced eye over a shoulder, into the thickening snow. " Won't the Med. be wonderful, gentlemen ? " He sighed and slid effortlessly into his native Galway brogue. " Malta in the spring. The beach at Sliema—with the white houses behind—where we picnicked, a hundred years ago. The soft winds, me darlin' boys, the *warm* winds, the blue skies and Chianti under a striped umbrella——"

" Off ! " Tyndall roared. " Get off this bridge, Brooks, or I'll——"

" I'm gone already," said Brooks. " A sit-down strike in the boiler-room ! Ha ! First thing you know, there'll be a rash of male suffragettes chaining themselves to the guard-rails ! " The gate clanged shut behind him.

Vallery turned to the Admiral, his face grave.

" Looks as if you were right about that cornstack, sir."

Tyndall grunted, non-committally.

" Maybe. Trouble is, the men have nothing to do right now except brood and curse and feel bitter about everything. Later on it'll be all right—perhaps."

" When we get—ah—busier, you mean ? "

" Mmm. When you're fighting for your life, to keep the ship afloat—well, you haven't much time for plots and pondering over the injustices of fate. Self-preservation is still the first law of nature. . . . Speaking to the men to-night, Captain ? "

" Usual routine broadcast, yes. In the first dog, when we're all closed up to dusk action stations." Vallery smiled briefly. " Makes sure that they're all awake."

" Good. Lay it on, thick and heavy. Give 'em plenty to think about—and, if I'm any judge of Vincent Starr's hints, we're going to *have* plenty to think about this trip. It'll keep 'em occupied."

Vallery laughed. The laugh transformed his thin sensitive face. He seemed genuinely amused.

Tyndall lifted an interrogatory eyebrow. Vallery smiled back at him.

" Just passing thoughts, sir. As Spencer Faggot would have said, things have come to a pretty pass. . . . Things are bad indeed, when only the enemy can save us."

CHAPTER THREE

MONDAY AFTERNOON

ALL DAY long the wind blew steadily out of the nor'-nor'-west. A strong wind, and blowing stronger. A cold wind, a sharp wind full of little knives, it carried with it snow and ice and the strange dead smell born of the forgotten ice-caps that lie beyond the Barrier. It wasn't a gusty, blowy wind. It was a settled, steady kind of wind, and it stayed fine on the starboard bow from dawn to dusk. Slowly, stealthily, it was lifting a swell. Men like Carrington, who knew every sea and port in the world, like Vallery and Hartley, looked at it and were troubled and said nothing.

The mercury crept down and the snow lay where it fell. The tripods and yardarms were great, glistening Xmas trees, festooned with woolly stays and halliards. On the mainmast, a brown smear appeared now and then, daubed on by a wisp of smoke from the after funnel, felt rather than seen : in a moment, it would vanish. The snow lay on the deck and drifted. It softened the anchor-cables on the fo'c'sle deck into great, fluffy ropes of cotton-wool, and drifted high against the breakwater before " A " turret. It piled up against the turrets and superstructure, swished silently into the bridge and lay there slushily underfoot. It blocked the great eyes of the Director's range-finder, it crept unseen along passages, it sifted soundlessly down hatches. It sought out the tiniest unprotected chink in metal and wood, and made the mess-decks dank and clammy and uncomfortable : it defied gravity and slid effortlessly up trouser legs, up under the skirts of coats and oilskins, up under duffel hoods, and made men thoroughly miserable. A miserable world, a wet world, but always and pre-dominately a white world of softness and beauty and strangely muffled sound. All day long it fell, this snow, fell steadily and persistently, and the *Ulysses* slid on silently through the swell, a ghost ship in a ghost world.

But not alone in her world. She never was, these days. She had companionship, a welcome, reassuring companionship, the company of the 14th Aircraft Carrier Squadron, a tough, experienced and battle-hardened escort group, almost as legendary now as that fabulous Force 8, which had lately moved South to take over that other suicide run, the Malta convoys.

Like the *Ulysses*, the squadron steamed NNW. all day long. There were no dog-legs, no standard course alterations. Tyndall abhorred the zig-zag, and, except on actual convoy and then only in known U-boat waters, rarely used it. He believed —as many captains did—that the zig-zag was a greater potential source of danger than the enemy. He had seen the *Curaçoa*, 4,200 tons of cockle-shell cruiser, swinging on a routine zig-zag, being trampled into the grey depths of the Atlantic under the mighty forefoot of the *Queen Mary*. He never spoke of it, but the memory stayed with him.

The *Ulysses* was in her usual position—the position dictated by her role of Squadron flagship—as nearly as possible in the centre of the thirteen warships.

Dead ahead steamed the cruiser *Stirling*. An old Cardiff class cruiser, she was a solid reliable ship, many years older and many knots slower than the *Ulysses*, adequately armed with five single six-inch guns, but hardly built to hammer her way through the Arctic gales : in heavy seas, her wetness was proverbial. Her primary role was squadron defence : her secondary, to take over the squadron if the flagship were crippled or sunk.

The carriers—*Defender, Invader, Wrestler* and *Blue Ranger*—were in position to port and starboard, the *Defender* and *Wrestler* slightly ahead of the *Ulysses*, the others slightly astern. It seemed *de rigueur* for these escort carriers to have names ending in -er, and the fact that the Navy already had a *Wrestler*—a Force 8 destroyer (and a *Defender*, which had been sunk some time previously off Tobruk)—was blithely ignored. These were not the 35,000-ton giants of the regular fleet—ships like the *Indefatigable* and the *Illustrious*—but 15-20,000 ton auxiliary carriers, irreverently known as banana boats. They were converted merchantmen, American-built : these had been fitted out at Pascagoula, Mississippi, and sailed across the Atlantic by mixed British-American crews.

They were capable of eighteen knots, a relatively high speed for a single-screw ship—the *Wrestler* had two screws—but some of them has as many as four Busch-Sulzer Diesels geared to the one shaft. Their painfully rectangular flight-decks, 450 feet in length, were built up above the open fo'c'sle—one could see right under the flight-deck for'ard of the bridge—and flew off about thirty fighters—Grummans, Seafires or, most often, Corsairs— or twenty light bombers. They were odd craft, awkward, un-gainly and singularly unwarlike ; but over the months they had done a magnificent job of providing umbrella cover against air attack, of locating and destroying enemy ships and submarines : their record of kills, above, on and below the water was im-pressive and frequently disbelieved by the Admiralty.

Nor was the destroyer screen calculated to inspire confidence among the naval strategists at Whitehall. It was a weird hodge-podge, and the term " destroyer " was a purely courtesy one.

One, the *Nairn*, was a River class frigate of 1,500 tons : another, the *Eager*, was a Fleet Minesweeper, and a third, the *Gannet*, better known as *Huntley and Palmer*, was a rather elderly and very tired Kingfisher corvette, supposedly restricted to coastal duties only. There was no esoteric mystery as to the origin of her nickname—a glance at her silhouette against the sunset was enough. Doubtless her designer had worked within Admiralty specifications : even so, he must have had an off day.

The *Vectra* and the *Viking* were twin-screwed, modified " V " and " W " destroyers, in the superannuated class now, lacking in speed and fire-power, but tough and durable. The *Baliol* was a diminutive early Hunt class destroyer which had no business in the great waters of the north. The *Portpatrick*, a skeleton-lean four-stacker, was one of the fifty lend-lease World War I destroyers from the United States. No one even dared guess at her age. An intriguing ship at any time, she became the focus of all eyes in the fleet and a source of intense interest whenever the weather broke down. Rumour had it that two of her sister ships had overturned in the Atlantic during a gale ; human nature being what it is, everyone wanted a grandstand view whenever weather conditions deteriorated to an extent likely to afford early confirmation of these rumours. What the crew of the *Portpatrick* thought about it all was difficult to say.

These seven escorts, blurred and softened by the snow, kept their screening stations all day—the frigate and minesweeper ahead, the destroyers at the sides, and the corvette astern. The eighth escort, a fast, modern "S" class destroyer, under the command of the Captain (Destroyers), Commander Orr, prowled restlessly around the fleet. Every ship commander in the squadron envied Orr his roving commission, a duty which Tyndall had assigned him in self-defence against Orr's continual pestering. But no one objected, no one grudged him his privilege : the *Sirrus* had an uncanny nose for trouble, an almost magnetic affinity for U-boats lying in ambush.

From the warmth of the *Ulysses's* wardroom—long, incongruously comfortable, running fifty feet along the starboard side of the fo'c'sle deck—Johnny Nicholls gazed out through the tumbled grey and white of the sky. Even the kindly snow, he reflected, blanketing a thousand sins, could do little for these queer craft, so angular, so graceless, so obvious outdated.

He supposed he ought to feel bitter at My Lords of the Admiralty, with their limousines and armchairs and elevenses, with their big wall-maps and pretty little flags, sending out this raggle-taggle of a squadron to cope with the pick of the U-boat packs, while they sat comfortably, luxuriously at home. But the thought died at birth : it was, he knew, grotesquely unjust. The Admiralty would have given them a dozen brand-new destroyers —if they had them. Things, he knew, were pretty bad, and the demands of the Atlantic and the Mediterranean had first priority.

He supposed, too, he ought to feel cynical, ironic, at the sight of these old and worn-out ships. Strangely, he couldn't. He knew what they could do, what they had done. If he felt anything at all towards them, it was something uncommonly close to admiration—perhaps even pride. Nicholls stirred uncomfortably and turned away from the porthole. His gaze fell on the somnolent form of the Kapok Kid, flat on his back in an armchair, an enormous pair of fur-lined flying-boots perched above the electric fire.

The Kapok Kid, Lieutenant the Honourable Andrew Carpenter, R.N., Navigator of the *Ulysses* and his best friend—he was the one to feel proud, Nicholls thought wryly. The most glorious extrovert Nicholls had ever known, the Kapok Kid was equally at home anywhere—on a dance floor or in the cockpit of a racing yacht at Cowes, at a garden party, on a tennis court or at the wheel of his big crimson Bugatti, windscreen down and the loose ends of a seven-foot scarf streaming out behind him. But appearances were never more deceptive. For the Kapok Kid, the Royal Navy was his whole life, and he lived for that alone. Behind that slightly inane façade lay, besides a first-class brain, a deeply romantic streak, an almost Elizabethan love for sea and ships which he sought, successfully, he imagined, to conceal from all his fellow-officers. It was so patently obvious that no one ever thought it worth the mentioning.

Theirs was a curious friendship, Nicholls mused. An attraction of opposites, if ever there was one. For Carpenter's hail-fellow ebullience, his natural reserve and reticence were the perfect foil : over against his friend's near-idolatry of all things naval stood his own thorough-going detestation of all that the Kapok Kid so warmly admired. Perhaps because of that over-developed sense of individuality and independence, that bane of so many highland Scots, Nicholls objected strongly to the thousand and one pin-pricks of discipline, authority and bureaucratic naval stupidity which were a constant affront to his intelligence and self-respect. Even three years ago, when the war had snatched him from the wards of a great Glasgow hospital, his first year's internship barely completed, he had had his dark suspicions that the degree of compatibility between himself and the Senior Service would prove to be singularly low. And so it had proved. But, in spite of this antipathy—or perhaps because of it and the curse of a Calvinistic conscience—Nicholls had become a first-class officer. But it still disturbed him vaguely to discover in himself something akin to pride in the ships of his squadron.

He sighed. The loudspeaker in the corner of the wardroom had just crackled into life. From bitter experience, he knew that broadcast announcements seldom presaged anything good.

" Do you hear there ? Do you hear there ? " The voice was metallic, impersonal : the Kapok Kid slept on in magnificent oblivion " The Captain will broadcast to the ship's company at 1730 to-night. Repeat. The Captain will broadcast to the ship's company at 1730 to-night. That is all."

Nicholls prodded the Kapok Kid with a heavy toe. " On your feet, Vasco. Now's the time if you want a cuppa char before getting up there and navigating." Carpenter stirred, opened a red-rimmed eye : Nicholls smiled down encouragingly. "Besides, it's lovely up top now—sea rising, temperature falling and a young blizzard blowing. Just what you were born for, Andy, boy ! "

The Kapok Kid groaned his way back to consciousness, struggled to a sitting position and remained hunched forward, his straight flaxen hair falling over his hands.

" What's the matter now ? " His voice was querulous, still slurred with sleep. Then he grinned faintly. " Know where I was, Johnny ? " he asked reminiscently. " Back on the Thames, at the Grey Goose, just up from Henley. It was summer, Johnny, late in summer, warm and very still. Dressed all in green, she was——".

" Indigestion," Nicholls cut in briskly. " Too much easy living. . . . It's four-thirty, and the old man's speaking in an hour's time. Dusk stations at any time—we'd better eat."

Carpenter shook his head mournfully. " The man has no soul, no finer feelings." He stood up and stretched himself. As always, he was dressed from head to foot in a one-piece overall of heavy, quilted kapok—the silk fibres encasing the seeds of the Japanese and Malayan silk-cotton tree : there was a great, golden " J " embroidered on the right breast pocket : what it stood for was anyone's guess. He glanced out through the porthole and shuddered.

" Wonder what's the topic for to-night, Johnny ? "

" No idea. I'm curious to see what his attitude, his tone is going to be, how he's going to handle it. The situation, to say the least, is somewhat—ah—delicate." Nicholls grinned, but the smile didn't touch his eyes. "Not to mention the fact that the crew don't know that they're off to Murmansk again—although they must have a pretty good idea."

"Mmm." The Kapok Kid nodded absently. "Don't suppose the old man'll try to play it down—the hazards of the trip, I mean, or to excuse himself—you know, put the blame where it belongs."

"Never." Nicholls shook his head decisively. "Not the skipper. Just not in his nature. Never excuses himself—and never spares himself." He stared into the fire for a long time, then looked up quietly at the Kapok Kid. "The skipper's a very sick man, Andy—very sick indeed."

"What !" The Kapok Kid was genuinely startled. "A very sick . . . Good lord, you're joking ! You must be. Why——"

"I'm not," Nicholls interrupted flatly, his voice very low. Winthrop, the padre, an intense, enthusiastic, very young man with an immense zest for life and granitic convictions on every subject under the sun, was in the far corner of the wardroom. The zest was temporarily in abeyance—he was sunk in exhausted slumber. Nicholls liked him, but preferred that he should not hear—the Padre would talk. Winthrop, Nicholls had often thought, would never have made a successful priest—confessional reticence would have been impossible for him.

"Old Socrates says he's pretty far through—and he knows," Nicholls continued. "Old man phoned him to come to his cabin last night. Place was covered in blood and he was coughing his lungs up. Acute attack of hæmoptysis. Brooks has suspected it for a long time, but the Captain would never let him examine him. Brooks says a few more days of this will kill him." He broke off, glanced briefly at Winthrop. "I talk too much," he said abruptly. "Getting as bad as the old padre there. Shouldn't have told you, I suppose—violation of professional confidence and all that. All this under your hat, Andy."

"Of course, of course." There was a long pause. "What you mean is, Johnny—he's dying ? "

"Just that. Come on, Andy—char."

Twenty minutes later, Nicholls made his way down to the

Sick Bay. The light was beginning to fail and the *Ulysses* was pitching heavily. Brooks was in the surgery.

"Evening, sir. Dusk stations any minute now. Mind if I stay in the bay to-night?"

Brooks eyed him speculatively.

"Regulations," he intoned, "say that the Action Stations position of the Junior Medical Officer is aft in the Engineer's Flat. Far be it from me——"

"Please."

"Why? Lonely, lazy or just plain tired?" The quirk of the eyebrows robbed the words of all offence.

"No. Curious. I want to observe the reactions of Stoker Riley and his—ah—confederates to the skipper's speech. Might be most instructive."

"Sherlock Nicholls, eh? Right-o, Johnny. Phone the Damage Control Officer aft. Tell him you're tied up. Major operation, anything you like. Our gullible public and how easily fooled. Shame."

Nicholls grinned and reached for the phone.

When the bugle blared for dusk Action Stations, Nicholls was sitting in the dispensary. The lights were out, the curtains almost drawn. He could see into every corner of the brightly lit Sick Bay. Five of the men were asleep. Two of the others—Petersen, the giant, slow-spoken stoker, half-Norwegian, half-Scots, and Burgess, the dark little cockney—were sitting up in bed, talking softly, their eyes turned towards the swarthy, heavily-built patient lying between them. Stoker Riley was holding court.

Alfred O'Hara Riley had, at a very early age indeed, decided upon a career of crime, and beset, though he subsequently was, by innumerable vicissitudes, he had clung to this resolve with an unswerving determination: directed towards almost any other sphere of activity, his resolution would have been praiseworthy, possibly even profitable. But praise and profit had passed Riley by.

Every man is what environment and heredity makes him. Riley was no exception, and Nicholls, who knew something of his upbringing, appreciated that life had never really given the big stoker a chance. Born of a drunken, illiterate mother in a filthy, overcrowded and fever-ridden Liverpool slum, he was an outcast from the beginning : allied to that, his hairy, ape-like figure, the heavy, prognathous jaw, the twisted mouth, the wide flaring nose, the cunning black eyes squinting out beneath the negligible clearance between hairline and eyebrows that so accurately reflected the mental capacity within, were all admirably adapted to what was to become his chosen vocation. Nicholls looked at him and disapproved without condemning ; for a moment, he had an inkling of the tragedy of the inevitable.

Riley was never at any time a very successful criminal—his intelligence barely cleared the moron level. He dimly appreciated his limitations, and had left the higher, more subtle forms of crime severely alone. Robbery—preferably robbery with violence—was his *métier*. He had been in prison six times, the last time for two years.

His induction into the Navy was a mystery which baffled both Riley and the authorities responsible for his being there. But Riley had accepted this latest misfortune with equanimity, and gone through the bomb-shattered " G " and " H " blocks in the Royal Naval Barracks, Portsmouth, like a high wind through a field of corn, leaving behind him a trail of slashed suitcases and empty wallets. He had been apprehended without much difficulty, done sixty days cells, then been drafted to the *Ulysses* as a stoker.

His career of crime aboard the *Ulysses* had been brief and painful. His first attempted robbery had been his last—a clumsy and incredibly foolish rifling of a locker in the marine sergeants' mess. He had been caught red-handed by Colour-Sergeant Evans and Sergeant MacIntosh. They had preferred no charges against him and Riley had spent the next three days in the Sick Bay. He claimed to have tripped on the rung of a ladder and fallen twenty feet to the boiler-room floor. But the actual facts of the case were common knowledge, and Turner had recommended his discharge. To everyone's astonishment, not least that of Stoker Riley, Dodson, the Engineer Commander, had insisted that he be given a last chance, and Riley had been reprieved.

Since that date, four months previously, he had confined his activities to stirring up trouble. Illogically but understandably, his brief encounter with the marines had swept away his apathetic tolerance of the Navy : a smouldering hatred took its place. As an agitator, he had achieved a degree of success denied him as a criminal. Admittedly, he had a fertile field for operations ; but credit—if that is the word—was due also to his shrewdness, his animal craft and cunning, his hold over his crew-mates. The husky, intense voice, his earnestness, his deep-set eyes, lent Riley a strangely elemental power—a power he had used to its maximum effect a few days previously when he had precipitated the mutiny which had led to the death of Ralston, the stoker, and the marine —mysteriously dead from a broken neck. Beyond any possible doubt, their deaths lay at Riley's door ; equally beyond doubt, that could never be proved. Nicholls wondered what new devilment was hatching behind these lowering, corrugated brows, wondered how on earth it was that that same Riley was continually in trouble for bringing aboard the *Ulysses* and devotedly tending every stray kitten, every broken-winged bird he found.

The loudspeaker crackled, cutting through his thoughts, stilling the low voices in the Sick Bay. And not only there, but throughout the ship, in turrets and magazines, in engine-rooms and boiler-rooms, above and below deck everywhere, all conversation ceased. Then there was only the wind, the regular smash of the bows into the deepening troughs, the muffled roar of the great boiler-room intake fans and the hum of a hundred electric motors. Tension lay heavy over the ship, over 730 officers and men, tangible, almost, in its oppression.

" This is the Captain speaking. Good evening." The voice was calm, well modulated, without a sign of strain or exhaustion. " As you all know, it is my custom at the beginning of every voyage to inform you as soon as possible of what lies in store for you. I feel that you have a right to know, and that it is my duty. It's not always a pleasant duty—it never has been during recent months. This time, however, I'm almost glad." He paused, and the words came, slow and measured. " This is our last operation as a unit of the Home Fleet. In a month's time, God willing, we will be in the Med."

Good for you, thought Nicholls. Sweeten the pill, lay it on, thick and heavy. But the Captain had other ideas.

"But first, gentlemen, the job on hand. It's the mixture as before—Murmansk again. We rendezvous at 1030 Wednesday, north of Iceland, with a convoy from Halifax. There are eighteen ships in this convoy, big and fast—all fifteen knots and above. Our third Fast Russian convoy, gentlemen—FR77, in case you want to tell your grandchildren about it," he added dryly. "These ships are carrying tanks, planes, aviation spirit and oil —nothing else.

"I will not attempt to minimise the dangers. You know how desperate is the state of Russia to-day, how terribly badly she needs these weapons and fuel. You can also be sure that the Germans know too—and that her Intelligence agents will already have reported the nature of this convoy and the date of sailing." He broke off short, and the sound of his harsh, muffled coughing into a handkerchief echoed weirdly through the silent ship. He went on slowly. "There are enough fighter planes and petrol in this convoy to alter the whole character of the Russian war. The Nazis will stop at nothing—I repeat, nothing—to stop this convoy from going through to Russia."

"I have never tried to mislead or deceive you. I will not now. The signs are not good. In our favour we have, firstly, our speed, and secondly—I hope the element of surprise. We shall try to break through direct for the North Cape.

"There are four major factors against us. You will all have noticed the steady worsening of the weather. We are, I'm afraid, running into abnormal weather conditions—abnormal even for the Arctic. It may—I repeat 'may'—prevent U-boat attacks : on the other hand it may mean losing some of the smaller units of our screen—we have no time to heave to or run before bad weather. FR77 is going straight through. . . . And it almost certainly means that the carriers will be unable to fly off fighter cover."

Good God, has the skipper lost his senses, Nicholls wondered. He'll wreck any morale that's left. Not that there *is* any left. What in the world——

"Secondly," the voice went on, calm, inexorable, " we are

taking no rescue ships on this convoy. There will be no time to
stop. Besides, you all know what happened to the *Stockport* and
the *Zafaaran*. You're safer where you are.[1]

"Thirdly, two—possibly three—U-boat packs are known to
be strung out along latitude seventy degrees and our Northern
Norway agents report a heavy mustering of German bombers
of all types in their area.

"Finally, we have reason to believe that the *Tirpitz* is preparing to move out." Again he paused, for an interminable time,
it seemed. It was as if he knew the tremendous shock carried in
these few words, and wanted to give it time to register. "I need
not tell you what that means. The Germans may risk her to stop
convoy. The Admiralty hope they will. During the latter part
of the voyage, capital units of the Home Fleet, including possibly
the aircraft-carriers *Victorious* and *Furious* and three cruisers will
parallel our course at twelve hours' steaming distance. They have
been waiting a long time, and we are the bait to spring the
trap. . . .

"It is possible that things may go wrong. The best-laid plans
. . . or the trap may be late in springing shut. This convoy must
still get through. If the carriers cannot fly off cover, the *Ulysses*
must cover the withdrawal of FR77. You will know what that
means. I hope this is all perfectly clear."

There was another long bout of coughing, another long pause,
and when he spoke again the tone had completely changed. He
was very quiet.

"I know what I am asking of you. I know how tired, how
hopeless, how sick at heart you all feel. I know—no one knows
better—what you have been through, how much you need, how
much you deserve a rest. Rest you shall have. The entire ship's
company goes on ten days' leave from Portsmouth on the
eighteenth, then for refit in Alexandria." The words were casual,
as if they carried no significance for him. "But, before that—
well, I know it seems cruel, inhuman—it must seem so to you—
to ask you to go through it all again, perhaps worse than you've

---

[1] Rescue ships, whose duties were solely what their name implies, were a feature
of many of the earlier convoys. The *Zafaaran* was lost in one of the war's worst
convoys. The *Stockport* was torpedoed. She was lost with all hands, including all
those survivors rescued from other sunken ships.

ever gone through before. But I can't help it—no one can help it." Every sentence, now, was punctuated by long silences : it was difficult to catch his words, so low and far away.

"No one has any right to ask you to do it, I least of all . . . least of all. I know you *will* do it. I know you will not let me down. I know you will take the *Ulysses* through. Good luck. Good luck and God bless you. Good night."

The loudspeakers clicked off, but the silence lingered on. Nobody spoke and nobody moved. Not even the eyes moved. Those who had been looking at the 'speakers still gazed on, unseeingly ; or stared down at their hands ; or down into the glowing butts of forbidden cigarettes, oblivious to the acrid smoke that laced exhausted eyes. It was strangely as if each man wanted to be alone, to look into his own mind, follow his thoughts out for himself, and knew that if his eyes caught another's he would no longer be alone. A strange hush, a supernatural silence, the wordless understanding that so rarely touches mankind : the veil lifts and drops again and a man can never remember what he has seen but knows that he has seen something and that nothing will ever be quite the same again. Seldom, all too seldom it comes : a sunset of surpassing loveliness, a fragment from some great symphony, the terrible stillness which falls over the huge rings of Madrid and Barcelona as the sword of the greatest of the matadors sinks inevitably home. And the Spaniards have the word for it—" the moment of truth."

The Sick Bay clock, unnaturally loud, ticked away one minute, maybe two. With a heavy sigh—it seemed ages since he had breathed last—Nicholls softly pulled to the sliding door behind the curtains and switched on the light. He looked round at Brooks, looked away again.

"Well, Johnny ? " The voice was soft, almost bantering.

"I just don't know, sir, I don't know at all." Nicholls shook his head. " At first I thought he was going to—well, make a hash of it. You know, scare the lights out of 'em. And good God ! " he went on wonderingly, " that's exactly what he did do. Piled it on—gales, *Tirpitz*, hordes of subs.—and yet . . ." His voice trailed off.

" And yet ? " Brooks echoed mockingly. " That's just it. Too much intelligence—that's the trouble with the young doctors to-day. I saw you—sitting there like a bogus psychiatrist, analysing away for all you were worth at the probable effect of the speech on the minds of the wounded warriors without, and never giving it a chance to let it register on yourself." He paused and went on quietly.

" It was beautifully done, Johnny. No, that's the wrong word —there was nothing premeditated about it. But don't you see ? As black a picture as man could paint : points out that this is just a complicated way of committing suicide : no silver lining, no promises, even Alex. thrown in as a casual afterthought. Builds 'em up, then lets 'em down. No inducements, no hope, no appeal—and yet the appeal was tremendous. . . . What was it, Johnny ? "

" I don't know." Nicholls was troubled. He lifted his head abruptly, then smiled faintly. " Maybe there *was* no appeal. Listen." Noiselessly, he slid the door back, flicked off the lights. The rumble of Riley's harsh voice, low and intense, was unmistakable.

"—just a lot of bloody clap-trap. Alex.? The Med.? Not on your —— life, mate. You'll never see it. You'll never even see Scapa again. Captain Richard Vallery, D.S.O.! Know what that old bastard wants, boys ? Another bar to his D.S.O. Maybe even a V.C. Well, by Christ, he's not going to have it ! Not at my expense. Not if I can —— well help it. ' I know you won't let me down,' " he mimicked, his voice high-pitched. " Whining old bastard ! " He paused a moment, then rushed on.

" The *Tirpitz* ! Christ Almighty ! The *Tirpitz* ! We're going to stop it—us ! This bloody toy ship ! Bait, he says, bait ! " His voice rose. " I tell you, mates, nobody gives a damn about us. Direct for the North Cape ! They're throwing us to the bloody wolves ! And that old bastard up top——"

" Shaddap ! " It was Petersen who spoke, his voice a whisper, low and fierce. His hand stretched out, and Brooks and Nicholls in the surgery winced as they heard Riley's wrist-bones crack under the tremendous pressure of the giant's hand. " Often I wonder about you, Riley," Petersen went on slowly. " But not now, not any more. You make me sick ! " He flung Riley's hand down and turned away.

Riley rubbed his wrist in agony, and turned to Burgess.

" For God's sake, what's the matter with him ? What the hell . . ." He broke off abruptly. Burgess was looking at him steadily, kept looking for a long time. Slowly, deliberately, he eased himself down in bed, pulled the blankets up to his neck and turned his back on Riley.

Brooks rose quickly to his feet, closed the door and pressed the light switch.

" Act 1, Scene 1. Cut ! Lights ! " he murmured. " See what I mean, Johnny ? "

" Yes, sir." Nicholls nodded slowly. " At least, I think so."

" Mind you, my boy, it won't last. At least, not at that intensity." He grinned. " But maybe it'll take us the length of Murmansk. You never know."

" I hope so, sir. Thanks for the show." Nicholls reached up for his duffle-coat. " Well, I suppose I'd better make my way aft."

" Off you go, then. And, oh—Johnny——"

" Sir ? "

" That scarlet-fever notice-board of yours. On your way aft you might consign it to the deep. I don't think we'll be needing it any more."

Nicholls grinned and closed the door softly behind him.

CHAPTER FOUR

MONDAY NIGHT

Dusk Action Stations dragged out its interminable hour and was gone. That night, as on a hundred other nights, it was just another nagging irritation, a pointless precaution that did not even justify its existence, far less its meticulous thoroughness. Or so it seemed. For although at dawn enemy attacks were routine, at sunset they were all but unknown. It was not always so with other ships, indeed it was rarely so; but then, the *Ulysses* was a lucky ship. Everyone knew that. Even Vallery knew it, but he also knew why. Vigilance was the first article of his sailor's creed.

Soon after the Captain's broadcast, radar had reported a contact, closing. That it was an enemy plane was certain: Commander Westcliffe, Senior Air Arm Officer, had before him in the Fighter Direction Room a wall-map showing the operational routes of all Coastal and Ferry Command planes, and this was a clear area. But no one paid the slightest attention to the report, other than Tyndall's order for a 45° course alteration. This was as routine as dusk Action Stations themselves. It was their old friend Charlie coming to pay his respects again.

" Charlie "—usually a four-engined Focke-Wulf Condor—was an institution on the Russian Convoys. He had become to the seamen on the Murmansk run very much what the albatross had been the previous century to sailing men, far south in the Roaring Forties: a bird of ill-omen, half-feared but almost amicably accepted, and immune from destruction—though with Charlie, for a different reason. In the early days, before the advent of cam-ships and escort carriers, Charlie frequently spent the entire day, from first light to last, circling a convoy and radioing to base pin-point reports of its position.[1]

Exchanges of signals between British ships and German reconnaissance planes were not unknown, and apocryphal stories were legion. An exchange of pleasantries about the weather was almost commonplace. On several occasions Charlie had plaintively asked for his position and been given highly-detailed latitude and longitude bearings which usually placed him somewhere in the South Pacific ; and, of course, a dozen ships claimed the authorship of the story wherein the convoy Commodore sent the signal, " Please fly the other way round. You are making us dizzy," and Charlie had courteously acknowledged and turned in his tracks.

Latterly, however, amiability had been markedly absent, and Charlie, grown circumspect with the passing of the months and the appearance of ship-borne fighters, rarely appeared except at dusk. His usual practice was to make a single circle of the convoy at a prudent distance and then disappear into the darkness.

That night was no exception. Men caught only fleeting glimpses of the Condor in the driving snow, then quickly lost it in the gathering gloom. Charlie would report the strength, nature and course of the Squadron, although Tyndall had little hope that the German Intelligence would be deceived as to their course. A naval squadron, near the sixty-second degree of latitude, just east of the Faroes, and heading NNE. wouldn't make sense to them—especially as they almost certainly knew of the departure of the convoy from Halifax. Two and two, far too obviously, totted up to four.

No attempt was made to fly off Seafires—the only plane with a chance to overhaul the Condor before it disappeared into the night. To locate the carrier again in almost total darkness, even on a radio beam, was difficult : to land at night, extremely

[1] Cam-ships were merchant ships with specially strengthened fo'c'sles. On these were fitted fore-and-aft angled ramps from which fighter planes, such as modified Hurricanes, were catapulted for convoy defence. After breaking off action, the pilot had either to bale out or land in the sea. "Hazardous" is rather an inadequate word to describe the duties of this handful of very gallant pilots : the chances of survival were not high.

dangerous ; and to land, by guess and by God, in the snow and blackness on a pitching, heaving deck, a suicidal impossibility. The least miscalculation, the slightest error of judgment and you had not only a lost plane but a drowned pilot. A ditched Seafire, with its slender, torpedo-shaped fuselage and the tremendous weight of the great Rolls-Royce Merlin in its nose, was a literal death-trap. When it went down into the sea, it just kept on going.

Back on to course again, the *Ulysses* pushed blindly into the gathering storm. Hands fell out from Action Stations, and resumed normal Defence Stations—watch and watch, four on, four off. Not a killing routine, one would think : twelve hours on, twelve hours off a day—a man could stand that. And so he could, were that all. But the crew also spent three hours a day at routine Action Stations, every second morning—the forenoon watch—at work (this when they were off-watch) and God only knew how many hours at Action Stations. Beyond all this, all meals—when there were meals—were eaten in their off-duty time. A total of three to four hours' sleep a day was reckoned unusual : forty-eight hours without sleep hardly called for comment.

Step by step, fraction by menacing fraction, mercury and barograph crept down in a deadly dualism. The waves were higher now, their troughs deeper, their shoulders steeper, and the bone-chilling wind lashed the snow into a blinding curtain. A bad night, a sleepless night, both above deck and below, on watch and off.

On the bridge, the First Lieutenant, the Kapok Kid, signalmen, the Searchlight L.T.O., look-outs and messengers peered out miserably into the white night and wondered what it would be like to be warm again. Jerseys, coats, overcoats, duffels, oilskins, scarves, balaclavas, helmets—they wore them all, completely muffled except for a narrow eye-slit in the woollen cocoon, and still they shivered. They wrapped arms and forearms round, and rested their feet on the steam pipes which circled the bridge, and froze. Pom-pom crews huddled miserably in the shelter of their multiple guns, stamped their feet, swung their arms and swore incessantly. And the lonely Oerlikon gunners, each jammed in his lonely cockpit, leaned against the built-in " black " heaters and fought off the Oerlikon gunner's most insidious enemy—sleep.

The starboard watch, in the mess-decks below, were little happier. There were no bunks for the crew of the *Ulysses*, only hammocks, and these were never slung except in harbour. There were good and sufficient reasons for this. Standards of hygiene on a naval warship are high, compared even to the average civilian home : the average matelot would never consider climbing into his hammock fully dressed—and no one in his senses would have dreamed of undressing on the Russian Convoys. Again, to an exhausted man, the prospect and the actual labour of slinging and then lashing a hammock were alike appalling. And the extra seconds it took to climb out of a hammock in an emergency could represent the margin between life and death, while the very existence of a slung hammock was a danger to all, in that it impeded quick movement. And finally, as on that night of a heavy head sea, there could be no more uncomfortable place than a hammock slung fore and aft.

And so the crew slept where it could, fully clothed even to duffel coats and gloves. On tables and under tables, on narrow nine-inch stools, on the floor, in hammock racks—anywhere. The most popular place on the ship was on the warm steel deck-plates in the alleyway outside the galley, at night-time a weird and spectral tunnel, lit only by a garish red light. A popular sleeping billet, made doubly so by the fact that only a screen separated it from the upper-deck, a scant ten feet away. The fear of being trapped below decks in a sinking ship was always there, always in the back of men's minds.

Even below decks, it was bitterly cold. The hot-air systems operated efficiently only on " B " and " C " mess-decks, and even there the temperature barely cleared freezing point. Deckheads dripped constantly and the condensation on the bulkheads sent a thousand little rivulets to pool on the corticene floor. The atmosphere was dank and airless and terribly chill—the ideal breeding ground for the T.B., so feared by Surgeon-Commander Brooks. Such conditions, allied with the constant pitching of the ship and

the sudden jarring vibrations which were beginning to develop
every time the bows crashed down, made sleep almost impossible,
at best a fitful, restless unease.

Almost to a man, the crew slept—or tried to sleep—with heads
pillowed on inflated lifebelts. Blown up, bent double then tied
with tape, these lifebelts made very tolerable pillows. For this
purpose, and for this alone, were these lifebelts employed,
although standing orders stated explicitly that lifebelts were to
be worn at all times during action and in known enemy waters.
These orders were completely ignored, not least of all by those
Divisional Officers whose duty it was to enforce them. There
was enough air trapped in the voluminous and bulky garments
worn in these latitudes to keep a man afloat for at least three
minutes. If he wasn't picked up in that time, he was dead anyway.
It was shock that killed, the tremendous shock of a body at 96° F.,
being suddenly plunged into a liquid temperature some 70°
lower—for in the Arctic waters, the sea temperature often falls
below normal freezing point. Worse still, the sub-zero wind
lanced like a thousand stilettos through the saturated clothing of
a man who had been submerged in the sea, and the heart, faced
with an almost instantaneous 100° change in body temperature,
just stopped beating. But it was a quick death, men said, quick
and kind and merciful.

At ten minutes to midnight the Commander and Marshall
made their way to the bridge. Even at this late hour and in the
wicked weather, the Commander was his usual self, imperturbable
and cheerful, lean and piratical, a throw-back to the Elizabethan
buccaneers, if ever there was one. He had an unflagging zest for
life. The duffel hood, as always, lay over his shoulders, the braided
peak of his cap was tilted at a magnificent angle. He groped for
the handle of the bridge gate, passed through, stood for a minute
accustoming his eyes to the dark, located the First Lieutenant and
thumped him resoundingly on the back.

"Well, watchman, and what of the night?" he boomed
cheerfully. "Bracing, yes, decidedly so. Situation completely
out of control as usual, I suppose? Where are all our chickens
this lovely evening?" He peered out into the snow, scanned the

horizon briefly, then gave up. "All gone to hell and beyond, I suppose."

"Not too bad," Carrington grinned. An R.N.R. officer and an ex-Merchant Navy captain in whom Vallery reposed complete confidence, Lieutenant-Commander Carrington was normally a taciturn man, grave and unsmiling. But a particular bond lay between him and Turner, the professional bond of respect which two exceptional seamen have for each other. "We can see the carriers now and then. Anyway, Bowden and his backroom boys have 'em all pinned to an inch. At least, that's what they say."

"Better not let old Bowden hear you say that," Marshall advised. "Thinks radar is the only step forward the human race has taken since the first man came down from the trees." He shivered uncontrollably and turned his back on the driving wind. "Anyway, I wish to God I had his job," he added feelingly. "This is worse than winter in Alberta!"

"Nonsense, my boy, stuff and nonsense!" the Commander roared. "Decadent, that's the trouble with you youngsters nowadays. This is the only life for a self-respecting human being." He sniffed the icy air appreciatively and turned to Carrington. "Who's on with you to-night, Number One?"

A dark figure detached itself from the binnacle and approached him.

"Ah, there you are. Well, well, 'pon my soul, if it isn't our navigating officer, the Honourable Carpenter, lost as usual and dressed to kill in his natty gent's suiting. Do you know, Pilot, in that outfit you look like a cross between a deep-sea diver and that advert for Michelin tyres?"

"Ha!" said the Kapok Kid aggrievedly. "Sniff and scoff while you may, sir." He patted his quilted chest affectionately. "Just wait till we're all down there in the drink together, everybody else dragged down or frozen to death, me drifting by warm and dry and comfortable, maybe smoking the odd cigarette——"

"Enough. Be off. Course, Number One?"

"Three-twenty, sir. Fifteen knots."

"And the Captain?"

"In the shelter." Carrington jerked his head towards the reinforced steel circular casing at the after end of the bridge.

This supported the Director Tower, the control circuits to which ran through a central shaft in the casing. A sea-bunk—a spartan, bare settee—was kept there for the Captain's use. " Sleeping, I hope," he added, " but I very much doubt it. Gave orders to be called at midnight."

" Why ? " Turner demanded.

" Oh, I don't know. Routine, I suppose. Wants to see how things are."

" Cancel the order," Turner said briefly. " Captain's got to learn to obey orders like anybody else—especially doctor's orders. I'll take full responsibility. Good night, Number One."

The gate clanged shut and Marshall turned uncertainly towards the Commander.

" The Captain, sir. Oh, I know it's none of my business, but "—he hesitated—" well, is he all right ? "

Turner looked quickly around him. His voice was unusually quiet.

" If Brooks had his way, the old man would be in hospital." He was silent for a moment, then added soberly. " Even then, it might be too late."

Marshall said nothing. He moved restlessly around, then went aft to the port searchlight control position. For five minutes, an intermittent rumble of voices drifted up to the Commander. He glanced up curiously on Marshall's return.

" That's Ralston, sir," the Torpedo Officer explained. " If he'd talk to anybody, I think he'd talk to me."

" And does he ? "

" Sure—but only what *he* wants to talk about. As for the rest, no dice. You can almost see the big notice round his neck— ' Private—Keep Off.' Very civil, very courteous and completely unapproachable. I don't know what the hell to do about him."

" Leave him be," Turner advised. " There's nothing anyone can do." He shook his head. " My God, what a lousy break life's given that boy ! "

Silence fell again. The snow was lifting now, but the wind still strengthening. It howled eerily through masts and rigging, blending with a wild and eldritch harmony into the haunting pinging of the Asdic. Weird sounds both, weird and elemental and foreboding, that rasped across the nerves and stirred up nameless, atavistic dreads of a thousand ages past, long buried under the press of civilisation. An unholy orchestra, and, over years, men grew to hate it with a deadly hatred.

Half-past twelve came, one o'clock, then half-past one. Turner's thoughts turned fondly towards coffee and cocoa. Coffee or cocoa? Cocoa, he decided, a steaming potent brew, thick with melted chocolate and sugar. He turned to Chrysler, the bridge messenger, young brother of the Leading Asdic Operator.

"W.T.—Bridge. W.T.—Bridge." The loudspeaker above the Asdic cabinet crackled urgently, the voice hurried, insistent. Turner jumped for the hand transmitter, barked an acknowledgment.

"Signal from *Sirrus*. Echoes, port bow, 300, strong, closing. Repeat, echoes, port bow, strong, closing."

"Echoes, W.T.? Did you say 'echoes'?"

"Echoes, sir. I repeat, echoes."

Even as he spoke, Turner's hand cut down on the gleaming phosphorescence of the Emergency Action Stations switch.

Of all sounds in this earth, there is none so likely to stay with a man to the end of his days as the E.A.S. There is no other sound even remotely like it. There is nothing noble or martial or blood-stirring about it. It is simply a whistle pitched near the upper limit of audio-frequency, alternating, piercing, atonic, alive with a desperate urgency and sense of danger: knife-like, it sears through the most sleep-drugged brain and has a man—no matter how exhausted, how weak, how deeply sunk in oblivion—on his feet in seconds, the pulse-rate already accelerating to meet the latest unknown, the adrenalin already pumping into his bloodstream.

Inside two minutes, the *Ulysses* was closed up to Action Stations. The Commander had moved aft to the After Director Tower, Vallery and Tyndall were on the bridge.

The *Sirrus*, two miles away to port, remained in contact for half an hour. The *Viking* was detached to help her, and, below-deck in the *Ulysses*, the peculiar, tinny clanging of depth-charging was clearly heard at irregular intervals. Finally, the *Sirrus* reported. "No success: contact lost: trust you have not been disturbed." Tyndall ordered the recall of the two destroyers, and the bugle blew the stand-down.

Back on the bridge, again, the Commander sent for his long overdue cocoa. Chrysler departed to the seamen's for'ard galley —the Commander would have no truck with the wishy-washy liquid concocted for the officers' mess—and returned with a steaming jug and a string of heavy mugs, their handles threaded on a bent wire. Turner watched with approval the reluctance with which the heavy, viscous liquid poured glutinously over the lip of the jug, and nodded in satisfaction after a preliminary taste. He smacked his lips and sighed contentedly.

"Excellent, young Chrysler, excellent! You have the gift. Torps., an eye on the ship, if you please. Must see where we are."

He retired to the chart-room on the port side, just aft of the compass platform, and closed the black-out door. Relaxed in his chair, he put his mug on the chart-table and his feet beside it, drew the first deep inhalation of cigarette smoke into his lungs. Then he was on his feet, cursing: the crackle of the W.T. loud-speaker was unmistakable.

This time it was the *Portpatrick*. For one reason and another, her reports were generally treated with a good deal of reserve, but this time she was particularly emphatic. Commander Turner had no option; again he reached for the E.A.S. switch.

Twenty minutes later the stand-down sounded again, but the Commander was to have no cocoa that night. Three times more during the hours of darkness all hands closed up to Action Stations, and only minutes, it seemed, after the last stand-down, the bugle went for dawn stations.

There was no dawn as we know it. There was a vague, imperceptible lightening in the sky, a bleak, chill greyness, as the men dragged themselves wearily back to their action stations. This, then, was war in the northern seas. No death and glory heroics, no roaring guns and spitting Oerlikons, no exaltation of the spirit, no glorious defiance of the enemy: just worn-out, sleepless men, numbed with cold and sodden duffels, grey and drawn and stumbling on their feet with weakness and hunger and lack of rest, carrying with them the memories, the tensions, the cumulative physical exhaustion of a hundred such endless nights.

Vallery, as always, was on the bridge. Courteous, kind and considerate as ever, he looked ghastly. His face was haggard, the colour of putty, his bloodshot eyes deep-sunk in hollowed sockets, his lips bloodless. The severe hæmorrhage of the previous night and the sleepless night just gone had taken terrible toll of his slender strength.

In the half-light, the squadron came gradually into view. Miraculously, most of them were still in position. The frigate and minesweeper were together and far ahead of the fleet—during the night they had been understandably reluctant to have their tails tramped on by a heavy cruiser or a carrier. Tyndall appreciated this and said nothing. The *Invader* had lost position during the night, and lay far outside the screen on the port quarter. She received a very testy signal indeed, and came steaming up to resume station, corkscrewing violently in the heavy cross seas.

Stand-down came at 0800. At 0810 the port watch was below, making tea, washing, queueing up at the galley for breakfast trays, when a muffled explosion shook the *Ulysses*. Towels, soap, cups, plates and trays went flying or were left where they were: blasphemous and bitter, the men were on their way before Vallery's hand closed on the Emergency switch.

Less than half a mile away the *Invader* was slewing round in a violent half-circle, her flight-deck tilted over at a crazy angle. It was snowing heavily again now, but not heavily enough to obscure the great gouts of black oily smoke belching up for'ard of the *Invader's* bridge. Even as the crew of the *Ulysses* watched, she came to rest, wallowing dangerously in the troughs between the great waves.

" The fools, the crazy fools ! " Tyndall was terribly bitter, unreasonably so ; even to Vallery, he would not admit how much he was now feeling the burden, the strain of command that sparked off his now almost chronic irritability. " This is what happens, Captain, when a ship loses station ! And it's as much my fault as theirs—should have sent a destroyer to escort her back." He peered through his binoculars, turned to Vallery.

" Make a signal, please : ' Estimate of damage—please inform.'
. . . That damned U-boat must have trailed her from first light,
waiting for a line-up."

Vallery said nothing. He knew how Tyndall must feel to see
one of his ships heavily damaged, maybe sinking. The *Invader*
was still lying over at the same unnatural angle, the smoke rising
in a steady column now. There was no sign of flames.

" Going to investigate, sir ? " Vallery inquired.

Tyndall bit his lip thoughtfully and hesitated.

" Yes, I think we'd better do it ourselves. Order squadron
to proceed, same speed, same course. Signal the *Baliol* and the
Nairn to stand by the *Invader*."

Vallery, watching the flags fluttering to the yardarm, was
aware of someone at his elbow. He half-turned.

" That was no U-boat, sir." The Kapok Kid was very sure
of himself. " She can't have been torpedoed."

Tyndall overheard him. He swung round in his chair, glared
at the unfortunate navigator.

" What the devil do you know about it, sir ? " he growled.
When the Admiral addressed his subordinates as " sir," it was
time to take to the boats. The Kapok Kid flushed to the roots
of his blond hair, but he stood his ground.

" Well, sir, in the first place the *Sirrus* is covering the *Invader's*
port side, though well ahead, ever since your recall signal. She's
been quartering that area for some time. I'm sure Commander
Orr would have picked her up. Also, it's far too rough for any
sub. to maintain periscope depth, far less line up a firing track.
And if the U-boat did fire, it wouldn't only fire one—six more
likely, and, from that firing angle, the rest of the squadron must
have been almost a solid wall behind the *Invader*. But no one
else has been hit. . . . I did three years in the trade, sir."

" I did ten," Tyndall growled. " Guesswork, Pilot, just
guesswork."

" No, sir," Carpenter persisted. " It's not. I can't swear to
it "—he had his binoculars to his eyes—" but I'm almost sure
the *Invader* is going astern. Could only be because her bows
—below the waterline, that is—have been damaged or blown off.
Must have been a mine, sir, probably acoustic."

"Ah, of course, of course ! " Tyndall was very acid. "Moored in 6,000 feet of water, no doubt ? "

" A *drifting* mine, sir," the Kapok Kid said patiently. " Or an old acoustic torpedo—spent German torpedoes don't always sink. Probably a mine, though."

" Suppose you'll be telling me next what mark it is and when it was laid," Tyndall growled. But he was impressed in spite of himself. And the *Invader was* going astern, although slowly, without enough speed to give her steerage way. She still wallowed helplessly in the great troughs.

An Aldis clacked acknowledgment to the winking light on the *Invader*. Bentley tore a sheet off a signal pad, handed it to Vallery.

"'*Invader* to Admiral,'" the Captain read. "'Am badly holed, starboard side for'ard, very deep. Suspect drifting mine. Am investigating extent of damage. Will report soon.'"

Tyndall took the signal from him and read it slowly. Then he looked over his shoulder and smiled faintly.

" You were dead right, my boy, it seems. Please accept an old curmudgeon's apologies."

Carpenter murmured something and turned away, brick-red again with embarrassment. Tyndall grinned faintly at the Captain, then became thoughtful.

" I think we'd better talk to him personally, Captain. Barlow, isn't it ? Make a signal."

They climbed down two decks to the Fighter Direction room. Westcliffe vacated his chair for the Admiral.

" Captain Barlow ? " Tyndall spoke into the hand-piece.

" Speaking." The sound came from the loudspeaker above his head.

" Admiral here, Captain. How are things ? "

" We'll manage, sir. Lost most of our bows, I'm afraid. Several casualties. Oil fires, but under control. W.T. doors all holding, and engineers and damage control parties are shoring up the cross-bulkheads."

" Can you go ahead at all, Captain ? "

" Could do, sir, but risky—in this, anyway."

" Think you could make it back to base ? "

" With this wind and sea behind us, yes. Still take three-four days."

" Right-o, then." Tyndall's voice was gruff. " Off you go. You're no good to us without bows ! Damned hard luck, Captain Barlow. My commiserations. And oh ! I'm giving you the *Baliol* and *Nairn* as escorts and radioing for an ocean-going tug to come out to meet you—just in case."

" Thank you, sir. We appreciate that. One last thing— permission to empty starboard squadron fuel tanks. We've taken a lot of water, can't get rid of it all—only way to recover our trim."

Tyndall sighed. " Yes, I was expecting that. Can't be helped and we can't take it off you in this weather. Good luck, Captain. Good-bye."

" Thank you very much, sir. Good-bye."

Twenty minutes later, the *Ulysses* was back on station in the squadron. Shortly afterwards, they saw the *Invader*, not listing quite so heavily now, head slowly round to the south-east, the little Hunt class destroyer and the frigate, one on either side, rolling wickedly as they came round with her. In another ten minutes, watchers on the *Ulysses* had lost sight of them, buried in a flurrying snow squall. Three gone and eleven left behind ; but it was the eleven who now felt so strangely alone.

CHAPTER FIVE

TUESDAY

THE *Invader* and her troubles were soon forgotten. All too soon, the 14th Aircraft Carrier Squadron had enough, and more than enough to worry about on their own account. They had their own troubles to overcome, their own enemy to face—an enemy far more elemental and far more deadly than any mine or U-boat.

Tyndall braced himself more firmly against the pitching, rolling deck and looked over at Vallery. Vallery, he thought for the tenth time that morning, looked desperately ill.

" What do you make of it, Captain ? Prospects aren't altogether healthy, are they ? "

" We're for it, sir. It's really piling up against us. Carrington has spent six years in the West Indies, has gone through a dozen hurricanes. Admits he's seen a barometer lower, but never one so low with the pressure still falling so fast—not in these latitudes. This is only a curtain-raiser."

" This will do me nicely, meantime, thank you," Tyndall said dryly. " For a curtain-raiser, it's doing not so badly."

It was a masterly understatement. For a curtain-raiser, it was a magnificent performance. The wind was fairly steady, about Force 9 on the Beaufort scale, and the snow had stopped. A temporary cessation only, they all knew—far ahead to the northwest the sky was a peculiarly livid colour. It was a dull glaring purple, neither increasing nor fading, faintly luminous and vaguely menacing in its uniformity and permanence. Even to men who had seen everything the Arctic skies had to offer, from pitchy darkness on a summer's noon, right through the magnificent displays of Northern Lights to that wonderfully washed-out blue that so often smiles down on the stupendous calms of the milk-white seas that lap the edge of the Barrier, this was something quite unknown.

But the Admiral's reference had been to the sea. It had been building up, steadily, inexorably, all during the morning. Now, at noon, it looked uncommonly like an eighteenth-century print of a barque in a storm—serried waves of greenish-grey, straight, regular and marching uniformly along, each decoratively topped with frothing caps of white. Only, here, there were 500 feet between crest and crest, and the squadron, heading almost directly into it, was taking heavy punishment.

For the little ships, already burying their bows every fifteen seconds in a creaming smother of cascading white, this was bad enough, but another, a more dangerous and insidious enemy was at work—the cold. The temperature had long sunk below freezing point, and the mercury was still shrinking down, close towards the zero mark.

The cold was now intense : ice formed in cabins and mess-decks : fresh-water systems froze solid : metal contracted, hatch-covers jammed, door hinges locked in frozen immobility, the oil in the searchlight controls gummed up and made them useless. To keep a watch, especially a watch on the bridge, was torture : the first shock of that bitter wind seared the lungs, left a man fighting for breath : if he had forgotten to don gloves—first the silk gloves, then the woollen mittens, then the sheepskin gauntlets —and touched a handrail, the palms of the hands seared off, the skin burnt as by white-hot metal : on the bridge, if he forgot to duck when the bows smashed down into a trough, the flying spray, solidified in a second into hurtling slivers of ice, lanced cheek and forehead open to the bone : hands froze, the very marrow of the bones numbed, the deadly chill crept upwards from feet to calves to thighs, nose and chin turned white with frostbite and demanded immediate attention : and then, by far the worst of all, the end of the watch, the return below deck, the writhing, excruciating agony of returning circulation. But, for all this, words are useless things, pale shadows of reality. Some things lie beyond the knowledge and the experience of the majority of mankind, and here imagination finds itself in a world unknown.

But all these things were relatively trifles, personal inconveniences to be shrugged aside. The real danger lay elsewhere. It lay in the fact of ice.

There were over three hundred tons of it already on the decks of the *Ulysses*, and more forming every minute. It lay in a thick, even coat over the main deck, the fo'c'sle, the gun-decks and the bridges : it hung in long, jagged icicles from coamings and turrets and rails : it trebled the diameter of every wire, stay and halliard, and turned slender masts into monstrous trees, ungainly and improbable. It lay everywhere, a deadly menace, and much of the danger lay in the slippery surface it presented—a problem much more easily overcome on a coal-fired merchant ship with clinker and ashes from its boilers, than in the modern, oil-fired warships. On the *Ulysses*, they spread salt and sand and hoped for the best.

But the real danger of the ice lay in its weight. A ship, to use technical terms, can be either stiff or tender. If she's stiff, she has a low centre of gravity, rolls easily, but whips back quickly and is extremely stable and safe. If she's tender, with a high centre of gravity, she rolls reluctantly but comes back even more reluctantly, is unstable and unsafe. And if a ship were tender, and hundreds of tons of ice piled high on its decks, the centre of gravity rose to a dangerous height. It could rise to a fatal height. . . .

The escort carriers and the destroyers, especially the *Portpatrick*, were vulnerable, terribly so. The carriers, already unstable with the great height and weight of their reinforced flight-decks, provided a huge, smooth, flat surface to the falling snow, ideal conditions for the formation of ice. Earlier on, it had been possible to keep the flight-decks relatively clear—working parties had toiled incessantly with brooms and sledges, salt and steam hoses. But the weather had deteriorated so badly now that to send out a man on that wildly pitching, staggering flight-deck, glassy and infinitely treacherous, would be to send him to his death. The *Wrestler* and *Blue Ranger* had modified heating systems under the flight-decks—modified, because, unlike the British ships, these Mississippi carriers had planked flight-decks : in such extreme conditions, they were hopelessly inefficient.

Conditions aboard the destroyers were even worse. They had to contend not only with the ice from the packed snow, but with ice from the sea itself. As regularly as clockwork, huge clouds of spray broke over the destroyer's fo'c'sles as the bows crashed solidly, shockingly into the trough and rising shoulder of the next wave : the spray froze even as it touched the deck, even before it touched the deck, piling up the solid ice, in places over a foot thick, from the stem aft beyond the breakwater. The tremendous weight of the ice was pushing the little ships down by their heads ; deeper, with each successive plunge ever deeper, they buried their noses in the sea, and each time, more and more sluggishly, more and more reluctantly, they staggered laboriously up from the depths. Like the carrier captains, the destroyer skippers could only look down from their bridges, helpless, hoping.

Two hours passed, two hours in which the temperature fell to zero, hesitated, then shrank steadily beyond it, two hours in which the barometer tumbled crazily after it. Curiously, strangely, the snow still held off, the livid sky to the north-west was as far away as ever, and the sky to the south and east had cleared completely. The squadron presented a fantastic picture now, little toy-boats of sugar-icing, dazzling white, gleaming and sparkling in the pale, winter sunshine, pitching crazily through the ever-lengthening, ever-deepening valleys of grey and green of the cold Norwegian Sea, pushing on towards that far horizon, far and weird and purply glowing, the horizon of another world. It was an incredibly lovely spectacle.

Rear-Admiral Tyndall saw nothing beautiful about it. A man who was wont to claim that he never worried, he was seriously troubled now. He was gruff, to those on the bridge, gruff to the point of discourtesy and the old geniality of the Farmer Giles of even two months ago was all but gone. Ceaselessly his gaze circled the fleet; constantly, uncomfortably, he twisted in his chair. Finally he climbed down, passed through the gate and went into the Captain's shelter.

Vallery had no light on and the shelter was in semi-darkness. He lay there on his settee, a couple of blankets thrown over him. In the half-light, his face looked ghastly, corpse-like. His right hand clutched a balled handkerchief, spotted and stained: he made no attempt to hide it. With a painful effort, and before Turner could stop him, he had swung his legs over the edge of the settee and pulled forward a chair. Tyndall choked off his protest, sank gratefully into the seat.

"I think your curtain's just about to go up, Dick. . . . What on earth ever induced me to become a squadron commander?"

Vallery grinned sympathetically. "I don't particularly envy you, sir. What are you going to do now?"

"What would *you* do?" Tyndall countered dolefully.

Vallery laughed. For a moment his face was transformed, boyish almost, then the laugh broke down into a bout of harsh, dry coughing. The stain spread over his handkerchief. Then he looked up and smiled.

"The penalty for laughing at a superior officer. What would I do? Heave to, sir. Better still, tuck my tail between my legs and run for it."

Tyndall shook his head.

"You never were a very convincing liar, Dick."

Both men sat in silence for a moment, then Vallery looked up.
"How far to go, exactly, sir?"

"Young Carpenter makes it 170 miles, more or less."

"One hundred and seventy." Vallery looked at his watch. "Twenty hours to go—in this weather. We *must* make it!"

Tyndall nodded heavily. "Eighteen ships sitting out there—nineteen, counting the sweeper from Hvalfjord—not to mention old Starr's blood pressure . . ."

He broke off as a hand rapped on the door and a head looked in.

"Two signals, Captain, sir."

"Just read them out, Bentley, will you?"

"First is from the *Portpatrick*: 'Sprung bow-plates: making water fast: pumps coping: fear further damage: please advise.'"

Tyndall swore. Vallery said calmly: "And the other?"

"From the *Gannet*, sir. 'Breaking up.'"

"Yes, yes. And the rest of the message?"

"Just that, sir. 'Breaking up.'"

"Ha! One of these taciturn characters," Tyndall growled.

"Wait a minute, Chief, will you?" He sank back in his chair, hand rasping his chin, gazing at his feet, forcing his tired mind to think.

Vallery murmured something in a low voice, and Tyndall looked up, his eyebrows arched.

"Troubled waters, sir. Perhaps the carriers——"

Tyndall slapped his knee. "Two minds with but a single thought. Bentley, make two signals. One to all screen vessels—tell 'em to take position astern—close astern—of the carriers. Other to the carriers. Oil hose, one each through port and starboard loading ports, about—ah—how much would you say, Captain?"

"Twenty gallons a minute, sir?"

"Twenty gallons it is. Understand, Chief? Right-o, get 'em off at once. And Chief—tell the Navigator to bring his chart here." Bentley left, and he turned to Vallery. "We've got to fuel later on, and we can't do it here. Looks as if this might be the last chance of shelter this side of Murmansk. . . . And if the next twenty-four hours are going to be as bad as Carrington forecasts, I doubt whether some of the little ships could live through it anyway. . . . Ah! Here you are, Pilot. Let's see where we are. How's the wind, by the way?"

"Force 10, sir." Bracing himself against the wild lurching of the *Ulysses*, the Kapok Kid smoothed out the chart on the Captain's bunk. "Backing slightly."

"North-west, would you say, Pilot?" Tyndall rubbed his hands. "Excellent. Now, my boy, our position?"

"12.40 west. 66.15 north," said the Kapok Kid precisely. He didn't even trouble to consult the chart. Turner lifted his eyebrows but made no comment.

"Course?"

"310, sir."

"Now, if it were necessary for us to seek shelter for fuelling——"

"Course exactly 290, sir. I've pencilled it in—there. Four and a half hours' steaming, approximately."

"How the devil——!" Tyndall exploded. "Who told you to—to——" He spluttered into a wrathful silence.

"I worked it out five minutes ago, sir. It—er—seemed inevitable. 290 would take us a few miles inside the Langanes peninsula. There should be plenty shelter there." Carpenter was grave, unsmiling.

"Seemed inevitable!" Tyndall roared. "Would you listen to him, Captain Vallery? Inevitable! And it's only just occurred to me! Of all the . . . Get out! Take yourself and that damned comic-opera fancy dress elsewhere!"

The Kapok Kid said nothing. With an air of injured innocence he gathered up his charts and left. Tyndall's voice halted him at the door.

"Pilot!"

"Sir?" The Kapok Kid's eyes were fixed on a point above Tyndall's head.

"As soon as the screen vessels have taken up position, tell Bentley to send them the new course."

"Yes, sir. Certainly." He hesitated, and Tyndall chuckled. "All right, all right," he said resignedly. "I'll say it again—I'm just a crusty old curmudgeon . . . and shut that damned door! We're freezing in here."

The wind was rising more quickly now and long ribbons of white were beginning to streak the water. Wave troughs were deepening rapidly, their sides steepening, their tops blown off and flattened by the wind. Gradually, but perceptibly to the ear now, the thin, lonely whining in the rigging was climbing steadily up the register. From time to time, large chunks of ice, shaken loose by the increasing vibration, broke off from the masts and stays and spattered on the deck below.

The effect of the long oil-slicks trailing behind the carriers was almost miraculous. The destroyers, curiously mottled with oil now, were still plunging astern, but the surface tension of the fuel held the water and spray from breaking aboard. Tyndall, justifiably, was feeling more than pleased with himself.

Towards half-past four in the afternoon, with shelter still a good fifteen miles away, the elation had completely worn off. There was a whole gale blowing now and Tyndall had been compelled to signal for a reduction in speed.

From deck level, the seas now were more than impressive. They were gigantic, frightening. Nicholls stood with the Kapok Kid, off watch now, on the main deck, under the port whaler, sheltering in the lee of the fo'c'sle deck. Nicholls, clinging to a davit to steady himself, and leaping back now and then to avoid a deluge of spray, looked over to where the *Defender*, the *Vectra* and *Viking* tailing behind, was pitching madly, grotesquely, under that serene blue sky. The blue sky above, the tremendous seas below. There was something almost evil, something literally spine-chilling, in that macabre contrast.

"They never told me anything about this in the Medical School," Nicholls observed at last. " My God, Andy," he added in awe, " have you ever seen anything like this ? "

"Once, just once. We were caught in a typhoon off the Nicobars. I don't think it was as bad as this. And Number One says this is damn all compared to what's coming to-night —and he knows. Gad, I wish I was back in Henley ! "

Nicholls looked at him curiously.

"Can't say I know the First Lieutenant well. Not a very— ah—approachable customer, is he ? But everyone—old Giles, the skipper, the Commander, yourself—they all talk about him with bated breath. What's so extra special about him ? I respect him, mind you—everyone seems to—but dammit to hell, he's no superman."

"Sea's beginning to break up," the Kapok Kid murmured absently. "Notice how every now and again we're beginning to get a wave half as big again as the others ? Every seventh wave, the old sailors say. No, Johnny, he's not a superman. Just the greatest seaman you'll ever see. Holds two master's-tickets— square-rigged and steam. He was going round the Horn in Finnish barques when we were still in our prams. Commander could tell you enough stories about him to fill a book." He paused, then went on quietly :

"He really is one of the few great seamen of to-day. Old Blackbeard Turner is no slouch himself, but he'll tell anyone that he can't hold a candle to Jimmy. . . . I'm no hero-worshipper, Johnny. You know that. But you can say about Carrington what they used to say about Shackleton—when there's nothing left and all hope is gone, get down on your knees and pray for him. Believe me, Johnny, I'm damned glad he's here."

Nicholls said nothing. Surprise held him silent. For the Kapok Kid, flippancy was a creed, derogation second nature : seriousness was a crime and anything that smacked of adulation bordered on blasphemy. Nicholls wondered what manner of man Carrington must be.

The cold was vicious. The wind was tearing great gouts of water off the wave-tops, driving the atomised spray at bullet speed against fo'c'sle and sides. It was impossible to breathe without turning one's back, without wrapping layers of wool round mouth and nose. Faces blue and white, shaking violently with the cold, neither suggested, neither even thought of going below. Men hypnotised, men fascinated by the tremendous seas, the towering waves, 1,000, 2,000 feet in length, long, sloping on the lee side, steep-walled and terrifying on the other, pushed up by a sixty knot wind and by some mighty force lying far to the north-west. In these gigantic troughs, a church steeple would be lost for ever.

Both men turned round as they heard the screen door crashing behind them. A duffel-coated figure, cursing fluently, fought to shut the heavy door against the pitching of the *Ulysses*, finally succeeded in heaving the clips home. It was Leading Seaman Doyle, and even though his beard hid three-quarters of what could be seen of his face, he still looked thoroughly disgusted with life.

Carpenter grinned at him. He and Doyle had served a commission together on the China Station. Doyle was a very privileged person.

"Well, well, the Ancient Mariner himself ! How are things down below, Doyle ? "

"Bloody desperate, sir ! " His voice was as lugubrious as his face. " Cold as charity, sir, and everything all over the bloody place. Cups, saucers, plates in smithereens. Half the crew——"

He broke off suddenly, eyes slowly widening in blank disbelief. He was staring out to sea between Nicholls and Carpenter.

"Well, what about half the crew ? . . . What's the matter, Doyle ? "

"Christ Almighty!" Doyle's voice was slow, stunned: it was almost a prayer. "Oh, Christ Almighty!" The voice rose sharply on the last two syllables.

The two officers twisted quickly round. The *Defender* was climbing—all 500 feet of her was literally climbing—up the lee side of a wave that staggered the imagination, whose immensity completely defied immediate comprehension. Even as they watched, before shocked minds could grasp the significance of it all, the *Defender* reached the crest, hesitated, crazily tilted up her stern till screw and rudder were entirely clear of the water, then crashed down, down, down. . . .

Even at two cable-lengths' distance in that high wind, the explosive smash of the plummeting bows came like a thunderclap. An æon ticked by, and still the *Defender* seemed to keep on going under, completely buried now, right back to the bridge island, in a sea of foaming white. How long she remained like that, arrowed down into the depths of the Arctic, no one could afterwards say: then slowly, agonisingly, incredibly, great rivers of water cascading off her bows, she broke surface again. Broke surface, to present to frankly disbelieving eyes a spectacle entirely without precedent, anywhere, at any time. The tremendous, instantaneous, up-thrusting pressure of unknown thousands of tons of water had torn the open flight-deck completely off its mountings and bent it backwards, in a great, sweeping "U," almost as far as the bridge. It was a sight to make men doubt their sanity, to leave them stupified, to leave them speechless—all, that is, except the Kapok Kid. He rose magnificently to the occasion.

"My word!" he murmured thoughtfully. "That *is* unusual."

Another such wave, another such shattering impact and it would have been the end for the *Defender*. The finest ships, the stoutest, most powerful vessels, are made only of thin, incredibly thin, sheets of metal, and metal, twisted and tortured as was the *Defender's*, could never have withstood another such impact.

But there were no more such waves, no more such impacts. It had been a freak wave, one of these massive, inexplicable contortions of the sea which have occurred, with blessed infrequency, from time immemorial, in all the great seas of the world whenever Nature wanted to show mankind, an irreverent, over-venturesome mankind, just how puny and pitifully helpless a thing mankind really is. . . . There were no more such waves and, by five o'clock, although land was still some eight to ten miles away, the squadron had moved into comparative shelter behind the tip of the Langanes peninsula.

From time to time, the captain of the *Defender*, who seemed to be enjoying himself hugely, sent reassuring messages to the Admiral. He was making a good deal of water, but he was managing nicely, thank you. He thought the latest shape in flight-decks very fashionable, and a vast improvement on the old type ; straight flight-decks lacked imagination, he thought, and didn't the Admiral think so too. The vertical type, he stated, provided excellent protection against wind and weather, and would make a splendid sail with the wind in the right quarter. With his last message, to the effect that he thought that it would be rather difficult to fly off planes, a badly-worried Tyndall lost his temper and sent back such a blistering signal that all communications abruptly ceased.

Shortly before six o'clock, the squadron hove-to under the shelter of Langanes, less than two miles offshore. Langanes is low-lying, and the wind, still climbing the scale, swept over it and into the bay beyond without a break ; but the sea, compared to an hour ago, was mercifully calm, although the ships still rolled heavily. At once the cruisers and the screen vessels—except the *Portpatrick* and the *Gannet*—moved alongside the carriers, took oil hoses aboard. Tyndall, reluctantly and after much heart-searching, had decided that the *Portpatrick* and *Gannet* were suspect, a potential liability : they were to escort the crippled carrier back to Scapa.

Exhaustion, an exhaustion almost physical, almost tangible, lay heavily over the mess-decks and the wardroom of the *Ulysses*. Behind lay another sleepless night, another twenty-four hours with peace unknown and rest impossible. With dull tired minds, men heard the broadcast that the *Defender*, the *Portpatrick* and the *Gannet* were to return to Scapa when the weather moderated. Six gone now, only eight left—half the carrier force gone. Little wonder that men felt sick at heart, felt as if they were being deserted, as if, in Riley's phrase, they were being thrown to the wolves.

But there was remarkably little bitterness, a puzzling lack of resentment which, perhaps, sprung only from sheer passive acceptance. Brooks was aware of it, this inaction of feeling, this unnatural extinction of response, and was lost for a reason to account for it. Perhaps, he thought, this was the nadir, the last extremity when sick men and sick minds cease altogether to function, the last slow-down of all vital processes, both human and animal. Perhaps this was just the final apathy. His intellect told him that was reasonable, more, it was inevitable. . . . And all the time some fugitive intuition, some evanescent insight, was thrusting upon him an awareness, a dim shadowy awareness of something altogether different ; but his mind was too tired to grasp it.

Whatever it was, it wasn't apathy. For a brief moment that evening, a white-hot anger ran through the ship like a flame, then resentment of the injustice which had provoked it. That there had been cause for anger, even Vallery admitted ; but his hand had been forced.

It had all happened simply enough. During routine evening tests, it had been discovered that the fighting lights on the lower yardarm were not working. Ice was at once suspected as being the cause.

The lower yardarm, on this evening dazzling white and heavily coated with snow and ice, paralleled the deck, sixty dizzy feet about it, eighty feet above the waterline. The fighting lights were suspended below the outer tip : to work on these, a man had either to sit on the yardarm—a most uncomfortable position as the heavy steel W.T. transmission aerial was bolted to its upper length—or in a bosun's chair suspended from the yardarm. It was a difficult enough task at any time : to-night, it had to be done with the maximum speed, because the repairs would interrupt radio transmission—the 3,000-volt steel " Safe-to-Transmit " boards (which broke the electrical circuits) had to be withdrawn and left in the keeping of the Officer of the Watch during the repair : it had to be done—very precise, finicky work had to be done—in that sub-zero temperature : it had to be done on that slippery, glass-smooth yardarm, with the *Ulysses* rolling regularly through a thirty-degree arc : the job was more than ordinarily difficult—it was highly dangerous.

Marshall did not feel justified in detailing the duty L.T.O. for the job, especially as that rating was a middle-aged and very much overweight reservist, long past his climbing prime. He asked for volunteers. It was inevitable that he should have picked Ralston, for that was the kind of man Ralston was.

The task took half an hour—twenty minutes to climb the mast, edge out to the yardarm tip, fit the bosun's chair and life-line, and ten minutes for the actual repair. Long before he was finished, a hundred, two hundred tired men, robbing themselves of sleep and supper, had come on deck and huddled there in the bitter wind, watching in fascination.

Ralston swung in a great arc across the darkening sky, the gale plucking viciously at his duffel and hood. Twice, wind and waves flung him out, still in his chair, parallel to the yardarm, forcing him to wrap both arms around the yardarm and hang on for his life. On the second occasion, he seemed to strike his face against the aerial, for he held his head for a few seconds after-wards, as if he were dazed. It was then that he lost his gauntlets —he must have had them in his lap, while making some delicate adjustment : they dropped down together, disappeared over the side.

A few minutes later, while Vallery and Turner were standing amidships examining the damage the motor-boat had suffered in Scapa Flow, a short, stocky figure came hurriedly out of the after screen door, made for the fo'c'sle at an awkward stumbling run. He pulled up abruptly at the sight of the Captain and the Com-mander : they saw it was Hastings, the Master-at-Arms.

" What's the matter, Hastings ? " Vallery asked curtly. He always found it difficult to conceal his dislike for the Master-at-Arms, his dislike for his harshness, his uncalled-for severity.

" Trouble on the bridge, sir," Hastings jerked out breath-lessly. Vallery could have sworn to a gleam of satisfaction in his eye. " Don't know exactly what—could hardly hear a thing but the wind on the phone. . . . I think you'd better come, sir."

They found only three people on the bridge : Etherton, the gunnery officer, one hand still clutching a phone, worried, unhappy : Ralston, his hands hanging loosely by his sides, the palms raw and torn, the face ghastly, the chin with the dead pallor of frostbite, the forehead masked in furrowed, frozen blood : and, lying in a corner, Sub-Lieutenant Carslake, moaning in agony, only the whites of his eyes showing, stupidly fingering his smashed mouth, the torn, bleeding gaps in his prominent upper teeth.

" Good God ! " Vallery ejaculated. " Good God above ! " He stood there, his hand on the gate, trying to grasp the significance of the scene before him. Then his mouth clamped shut and he swung round on the Gunnery Officer.

" What the devil's happened here, Etherton ? " he demanded harshly. " What *is* all this ? Has Carslake——"

" Ralston hit him, sir," Etherton broke in.

" Don't be so bloody silly, Guns ! " Turner grunted.

" Exactly ! " Vallery's voice was impatient. " We can see that. Why ? "

" A W.T. messenger came up for the ' Safe-to-Transmit ' boards. Carslake gave them to him—about ten minutes ago, I— I think."

" You think ! Where were you, Etherton, and why did you permit it ? You know very well . . ." Vallery broke off short, remembering the presence of Ralston and the M.A.A.

Etherton muttered something. His words were inaudible in the gale.

Vallery bent forward. " What did you say, Etherton ? "

" I was down below, sir." Etherton was looking at the deck. " Just—just for a moment, sir."

" I see. You were down below." Vallery's voice was controlled now, quiet and even ; his eyes held an expression that promised ill for Etherton. He looked round at Turner. " Is he badly hurt, Commander ? "

" He'll survive," said Turner briefly. He had Carslake on his feet now, still moaning, his hand covering his smashed mouth.

For the first time, the Captain seemed to notice Ralston. He looked at him for a few seconds—an eternity on that bitter, storm-lashed bridge—then spoke, monosyllabic, ominous, thirty years of command behind the word.

" Well ? "

Ralston's face was frozen, expressionless. His eyes never left Carslake.

" Yes, sir. I did it. I hit him—the treacherous, murdering bastard ! "

" Ralston ! " The M.A.A.'s voice was a whiplash.

Suddenly Ralston's shoulders sagged. With an effort, he looked away from Carslake, looked wearily at Vallery.

" I'm sorry. I forgot. He's got a stripe on his arm—only ratings are bastards." Vallery winced at the bitterness. " But he——"

" Rub your chin, man ! " Turner interrupted sharply. " You've got frostbite."

Slowly, mechanically, Ralston did as he was told. He used the back of his hand. Vallery winced again as he saw the palm of the hand, raw and mutilated, skin and flesh hanging in strips. The agony of that bare-handed descent from the yardarm. . . .

" He tried to murder me, sir. It was deliberate." Ralston sounded tired.

" Do you realise what you are saying ? " Vallery's voice was as icy as the wind that swept over Langanes. But he felt the first, faint chill of fear.

" He tried to murder me, sir," Ralston repeated tonelessly. " He returned the boards five minutes before I left the yardarm. W.T. must have started transmitting just as soon as I reached the mast, coming down."

" Nonsense, Ralston. How dare you——"

" He's right, sir." It was Etherton speaking. He was replacing the receiver carefully, his voice unhappy. " I've just checked."

The chill of fear settled deeper on Vallery's mind. Almost desperately he said :

" Anyone can make a mistake. Ignorance may be culpable, but——"

" Ignorance ! " The weariness had vanished from Ralston as

if it had never been. He took two quick steps forward. "Ignorance! I gave him these boards, sir, when I came to the bridge. I asked for the Officer of the Watch and he said *he* was—I didn't know the Gunnery Officer was on duty, sir. When I told him that the boards were to be returned only to me, he said: 'I don't want any of your damned insolence, Ralston. I know my job—you stick to yours. Just you get up there and perform your heroics.' He *knew*, sir."

Carslake burst from the Commander's supporting arm, turned and appealed wildly to the Captain. The eyes were white and staring, the whole face working.

"That's a lie, sir! It's a damned, filthy lie!" He mouthed the words, slurred them through smashed lips. "I never said . . ."

The words crescendoed into a coughing, choking scream as Ralston's fist smashed viciously, terribly into the torn, bubbling mouth. He staggered drunkenly through the port gate, crashed into the chart house, slid down to lie on the deck, huddled and white and still. Both Turner and the M.A.A. had at once leapt forward to pinion the L.T.O.'s arms, but he made no attempt to move.

Above and beyond the howl of the wind, the bridge seemed strangely silent. When Vallery spoke, his voice was quite expressionless.

"Commander, you might phone for a couple of our marines. Have Carslake taken down to his cabin and ask Brooks to have a look at him. Master-At-Arms?"

"Sir?"

"Take this rating to the Sick Bay, let him have any necessary treatment. Then put him in cells. With an armed guard. Understand?"

"I understand, sir." There was no mistaking the satisfaction in Hastings's voice.

Vallery, Turner and the Gunnery Officer stood in silence as Ralston and the M.A.A. left, in silence as two burly marines carried Carslake, still senseless, off the bridge and below. Vallery moved after them, broke step at Etherton's voice behind him.

"Sir?"

Vallery did not even turn round. "I'll see you later, Etherton."

"No, sir. Please. This is important."

Something in the Gunnery Officer's voice held Vallery. He turned back, impatiently.

"I'm not concerned with excusing myself, sir. There's no excuse." The eyes were fixed steadily on Vallery. "I was standing at the Asdic door when Ralston handed the boards to Carslake. I overheard them—every word they said."

Vallery's face became very still. He glanced at Turner, saw that he, too, was waiting intently.

"And Ralston's version of the conversation?" In spite of himself, Vallery's voice was rough, edged with suspense.

"Completely accurate, sir." The words were hardly audible. "In every detail. Ralston told the exact truth."

Vallery closed his eyes for a moment, turned slowly, heavily away. He made no protest as he felt Turner's hand under his arm, helping him down the steep ladder. Old Socrates had told him a hundred times that he carried the ship on his back. He could feel the weight of it now, the crushing burden of every last ounce of it.

Vallery was at dinner with Tyndall, in the Admiral's day cabin, when the message arrived. Sunk in private thought, he gazed down at his untouched food as Tyndall smoothed out the signal.

The Admiral cleared his throat.

"On course. On time. Sea moderate, wind freshening. Expect rendezvous as planned. Commodore 77."

He laid the signal down. "Good God! Seas moderate, fresh wind! Do you reckon he's in the same damned ocean as us?"

Vallery smiled faintly.

"This is it, sir."

"This is it," Tyndall echoed. He turned to the messenger.

"Make a signal. 'You are running into severe storm. Rendezvous unchanged. You may be delayed. Will remain at rendezvous until your arrival.' That clear enough, Captain?"

"Should be, sir. Radio silence?"

"Oh, yes. Add 'Radio silence. Admiral, 14th A.C.S.' Get it off at once, will you? Then tell W.T. to shut down themselves."

The door shut softly. Tyndall poured himself some coffee, looked across at Vallery.

"That boy still on your mind, Dick?"

Vallery smiled non-committally, lit a cigarette. At once he began to cough harshly.

"Sorry, sir," he apologised. There was silence for some time, then he looked up quizzically.

"What mad ambition drove me to become a cruiser captain?" he asked sadly.

Tyndall grinned. "I don't envy you. . . . I seem to have heard this conversation before. What are you going to do about Ralston, Dick?"

"What would *you* do, sir?" Vallery countered.

"Keep him locked up till we return from Russia. On a bread-and-water diet, in irons if you like."

Vallery smiled.

"You never were a very good liar, John."

Tyndall laughed. "*Touché!*" He was warmed, secretly pleased. Rarely did Richard Vallery break through his self-imposed code of formality. "A heinous offence, we all know, to clout one of H.M. commissioned officers, but if Etherton's story is true, my only regret is that Ralston didn't give Brooks a really large-scale job of replanning that young swine's face."

"It's true, all right, I'm afraid," said Vallery soberly. "What it amounts to is that naval discipline—oh, how old Starr would love this—compels me to punish a would-be murderer's victim!" He broke off in a fresh paroxysm of coughing, and Tyndall looked away: he hoped the distress wasn't showing in his face, the pity and anger he felt that Vallery—that very perfect, gentle knight, the finest gentleman and friend he had ever known—should be coughing his heart out, visibly dying on his feet, because of the blind inhumanity of an S.N.O. in London, two thousand miles away. "A victim," Vallery went on at last, "who has already lost his mother, brother and three sisters. . . . I believe he has a father at sea somewhere."

" And Carslake ? "

" I shall see him to-morrow. I should like you to be there, sir.
I will tell him that he will remain an officer of this ship till we
return to Scapa, then resign his commission. . . . I don't think
he'd care to appear at a court-martial, even as a witness," he
finished dryly.

" Not if he's sane, which I doubt," Tyndall agreed. A sudden
thought struck him. " Do you think he *is* sane ? " he frowned.

" Carslake," Vallery hesitated. " Yes, I think so, sir. At
least, he was. Brooks isn't so sure. Says he didn't like the look
of him to-night—something queer about him, he thinks, and in
these abnormal conditions small provocations are magnified out
of all proportion." Vallery smiled briefly. " Not that Carslake
is liable to regard the twin assaults on pride and person as a small
provocation."

Tyndall nodded agreement. " He'll bear watching. . . . Oh,
damn ! I wish the ship would stay still. Half my coffee on the
tablecloth. Young Spicer "—he looked towards the pantry—
" will be as mad as hell. Nineteen years old and a regular tyrant.
. . . I thought these would be sheltered waters, Dick ? "

" So they are, compared to what's waiting for us. Listen ! "
He cocked his head to the howling of the wind outside. " Let's
see what the weather man has to say about it."

He reached for the desk phone, asked for the transmitting
station. After a brief conversation he replaced the receiver.

" T.S. says the anemometer is going crazy. Gusting up to
eighty knots. Still north-west. Temperature steady at ten below."
He shivered. " Ten below ! " Then looked consideringly at
Tyndall. " Barometer almost steady at 27.8."

" What ! "

" 27.8. That's what they say. It's impossible, but that's
what they say." He glanced at his wrist-watch. " Forty-five
minutes, sir. . . . This is a very complicated way of committing
suicide."

They were silent for a minute, then Tyndall spoke for both
of them, answering the question in both their minds.

" We must go, Dick. We must. And by the way, our fire-
eating young Captain (D), the doughty Orr, wants to accompany

us in the *Sirrus*. . . . We'll let him tag along a while. He has things to learn, that young man."

At 2020 all ships had completed oiling. Hove to, they had had the utmost difficulty in keeping position in that great wind; but they were infinitely safer than in the open sea. They were given orders to proceed when the weather moderated, the *Defender* and escorts to Scapa, the squadron to a position 100 miles ENE. of rendezvous. Radio silence was to be strictly observed.

At 2030 the *Ulysses* and *Sirrus* got under way to the East. Lights winked after them, messages of good luck. Fluently, Tyndall cursed the squadron for the breach of darken-ship regulations, realised that, barring themselves, there was no one on God's earth to see the signals anyway, and ordered a courteous acknowledgment.

At 2045, still two miles short of Langanes point, the *Sirrus* was plunging desperately in mountainous seas, shipping great masses of water over her entire fo'c'sle and main deck, and, in the darkness, looking far less like a destroyer than a porpoising submarine.

At 2050, at reduced speed, she was observed to be moving in close to such slight shelter as the land afforded there. At the same time, her six-inch Aldis flashed her signal: " Screen doors stove in : ' A ' turret not tracking : flooding port boiler-room intake fans." And on the *Sirrus's* bridge Commander Orr swore in chagrin as he received the *Ulysses's* final message: " Lesson without words, No. 1. Rejoin squadron at once. You can't come out to play with the big boys." But he swallowed his disappointment, signalled: " Wilco. Just you wait till I grow up," pulled the *Sirrus* round in a madly swinging half-circle and headed thankfully back for shelter. Aboard the flagship, it was lost to sight almost immediately.

At 2100, the *Ulysses* moved out into the Denmark Strait.

CHAPTER SIX

TUESDAY NIGHT

It was the worst storm of the war. Beyond all doubt, had the records been preserved for Admiralty inspection, that would have proved to be incomparably the greatest storm, the most tremendous convulsion of nature since these recordings began. Living memory aboard the *Ulysses* that night, a vast accumulation of experience in every corner of the globe, could certainly recall nothing even remotely like it, nothing that would even begin to bear comparison as a parallel or precedent.

At ten o'clock, with all doors and hatches battened shut, with all traffic prohibited on the upper deck, with all crews withdrawn from gun-turrets and magazines and all normal deck watchkeeping stopped for the first time since her commissioning, even the taciturn Carrington admitted that the Caribbean hurricanes of the autumns of '34 and '37—when he'd run out of sea-room, been forced to heave-to in the dangerous right-hand quadrant of both these murderous cyclones—had been no worse than this. But the two ships he had taken through these—a 3,000-ton tramp and a superannuated tanker on the New York asphalt run—had not been in the same class for seaworthiness as the *Ulysses*. He had little doubt as to her ability to survive. But what the First Lieutenant did not know, what nobody had any means of guessing, was that this howling gale was still only the deadly overture. Like some mindless and dreadful beast from an ancient and other world, the Polar monster crouched on its own doorstep, waiting. At 2230, the *Ulysses* crossed the Arctic Circle. The monster struck.

It struck with a feral ferocity, with an appalling savagery that smashed minds and bodies into a stunned unknowingness. Its claws were hurtling rapiers of ice that slashed across a man's face and left it welling red : its teeth were that sub-zero wind, gusting over 120 knots, that ripped and tore through the tissue paper of Arctic clothing and sunk home to the bone : its voice was the devil's orchestra, the roar of a great wind mingled with the banshee shrieking of tortured rigging, a requiem for fiends : its weight was the crushing power of the hurricane wind that pinned a man helplessly to a bulkhead, fighting for breath, or flung him off his feet to crash in some distant corner, broken-limbed and senseless. Baulked of prey in its 500-mile sweep across the frozen wastes of the Greenland ice-cap, it goaded the cruel sea into homicidal alliance and flung itself, titanic in its energy, ravenous in its howling, upon the cockleshell that was the *Ulysses*.

The *Ulysses* should have died then. Nothing built by man could ever have hoped to survive. She should just have been pressed under to destruction, or turned turtle, or had her back broken, or disintegrated under these mighty hammer-blows of wind and sea. But she did none of these things.

How she ever survived the insensate fury of that first attack, God only knew. The great wind caught her on the bow and flung her round in a 45° arc and pressed her far over on her side as she fell—literally fell—forty heart-stopping feet over and down the precipitous walls of a giant trough. She crashed into the valley with a tremendous concussion that jarred every plate, every Clyde-built rivet in her hull. The vibration lasted an eternity as overstressed metal fought to re-adjust itself, as steel compressed and stretched far beyond specified breaking loads. Miraculously she held, but the sands were running out. She lay far over on her starboard side, the gunwales dipping : half a mile away, towering high above the mast-top, a great wall of water was roaring down on the helpless ship.

The "Dude" saved the day. The "Dude," alternatively known as "Persil," but officially as Engineer-Commander Dodson, immaculately clad as usual in overalls of the most dazzling white, had been at his control position in the engine-room when that tremendous gust had struck. He had no means of knowing what had happened. He had no means of knowing that the ship was not under command, that no one on the bridge had as yet recovered from that first shattering impact : he had no means of knowing that the quartermaster had been thrown unconscious into a corner of the wheelhouse, that his mate, almost a child in years, was too panic-stricken to dive for the madly-spinning wheel. But he did know that the *Ulysses* was listing crazily, almost broadside on, and he suspected the cause.

His shouts on the bridge tube brought no reply. He pointed to the port controls, roared " Slow " in the ear of the Engineer W.O.—then leapt quickly for the starboard wheel.

Fifteen seconds later and it would have been too late. As it was, the accelerating starboard screw brought her round just far enough to take that roaring mountain of water under her bows, to dig her stern in to the level of the depth-charge rails, till forty feet of her airborne keel lay poised above the abyss below. When she plunged down, again that same shuddering vibration enveloped the entire hull. The fo'c'sle disappeared far below the surface, the sea flowing over and past the armoured side of " A " turret. But she was bows on again. At once the "Dude" signalled his W.O. for more revolutions, cut back the starboard engine.

Below decks, everything was an unspeakable shambles. On the mess-decks, steel lockers in their scores had broken adrift, been thrown in a dozen different directions, bursting hasps and locks, spilling their contents everywhere. Hammocks had been catapulted from their racks, smashed crockery littered the decks : tables were twisted and smashed, broken stools stuck up at crazy angles, books, papers, teapots, kettles and crockery were scattered in insane profusion. And amidst this jumbled, sliding wreckage, hundreds of shouting, cursing, frightened and exhausted men struggled to their feet, or knelt, or sat, or just lay still.

Surgeon-Commander Brooks and Lieutenant Nicholls, with an inspired, untiring padre as good as a third doctor, were worked off their feet. The veteran Leading S.B.A. Johnson, oddly enough, was almost useless—he was violently sick much of the time, seemed to have lost all heart : no one knew why—it was just one of these things and he had taken all he could.

Men were brought in to the Sick Bay in their dozens, in their scores, a constant trek that continued all night long as the *Ulysses* fought for her life, a trek that soon overcrowded the

meagre space available and turned the wardroom into an
emergency hospital. Bruises, cuts, dislocations, concussion,
fractures—the exhausted doctors experienced everything that
night. Serious injuries were fortunately rare, and inside three
hours there were only nine bed-patients in the Sick Bay, including
A.B. Ferry, his already mangled arm smashed in two places—a
bitterly protesting Riley and his fellow-mutineers had been unceremoniously turfed out to make room for the more seriously
injured.

About 2330, Nicholls was called to treat the Kapok Kid.
Lurching, falling and staggering in the wildly gyrating ship, he
finally found the Navigator in his cabin. He looked very unhappy. Nicholls eyed him speculatively, saw the deep, ugly gash
on his forehead, the swollen ankle peeping out below the Kapok
Kid's Martian survival suit. Bad enough, but hardly a border-
line case, although one wouldn't have thought so from the
miserable, worried expression. Nicholls grinned inwardly.

" Well, Horatio," he said unkindly, " what's supposed to be
the matter with you ? Been drinking again ? "

The Hon. Carpenter groaned piteously.

" It's my back, Johnny," he muttered. He turned face-down
on the bunk. " Have a look at it, will you ? "

Nicholls's expression changed. He moved forward, then
stopped short.

" How the hell can I," he demanded irritably, " when
you're wearing that damned ugly suit of yours ? "

" That's what I mean," said the Kapok Kid anxiously. " I
was thrown against the searchlight controls—all knobs and nasty,
sharp projections. Is it torn ? Is it ripped, cut in any way ? Are
the seams—— ? "

" Well, for God's sake ! Do you mean to tell me—— ? "
Nicholls sank back incredulously on a locker.

The Kapok Kid looked at him hopefully.

" Does that mean it's all right ? "

" Of course it's all right ! If it's a blasted tailor you want
why the hell—— "

" Enough ! " The Kapok Kid swung briskly on to the side
of his bunk, lifting an admonitory hand. " There is work for you

sawbones." He touched his bleeding forehead. " Stitch this up and waste no time about it. A man of my calibre is urgently needed on the bridge. . . . I'm the only man on this ship who has the faintest idea where we are."

Busy with a swab, Nicholls grinned. " And where are we ? "

" I don't know," said the Kapok Kid frankly. " That's what's so urgent about it. . . . But I do know where I was ! Back in Henley. Did I ever tell you . . . ? "

The *Ulysses* did not die. Time and again that night, hove to with the wind fine on her starboard bow, as her bows crashed into and under the far shoulder of a trough, it seemed that she could never shake free from the great press of water. But time and again she did just that, shuddering, quivering under the fantastic strain. A thousand times before dawn officers and men blessed the genius of the Clyde shipyard that had made her : a thousand times they cursed the blind malevolence of that great storm that put the *Ulysses* on the rack.

Perhaps " blind " was not the right word. The storm wielded its wild hate with an almost human cunning. Shortly after the first onslaught, the wind had veered quickly, incredibly so and in defiance of all the laws, back almost to the north again. The *Ulysses* was on a lee shore, forced to keep pounding into gigantic seas.

Gigantic—and cunning also. Roaring by the *Ulysses*, a huge comber would suddenly whip round and crash on deck, smashing a boat to smithereens. Inside an hour, the barge, motor-boat and two whalers were gone, their shattered timbers swept away in the boiling cauldron. Carley rafts were broken off by the sudden hammer-blows of the same cunning waves, swept over the side and gone for ever : four of the Balsa floats went the same way.

But the most cunning attack of all was made right aft on the poop-deck. At the height of the storm a series of heavy explosions, half a dozen in as many seconds, almost lifted the stern out of the water. Panic spread like wildfire in the after mess-decks : practically every light abaft the after engine-room smashed or failed. In the darkness of the mess-decks, above the clamour, high-pitched cries of " Torpedoed ! " " Mined ! " " She's breaking up ! "

galvanised exhausted, injured men, even those—more than half
—in various degrees of prostration from seasickness, into frantic
stampeding towards doors and hatches, only to find doors and
hatches jammed solid by the intense cold. Here and there, the
automatic battery lamps had clicked on when the lighting circuits
failed : glowing little pin-points, they played on isolated groups
of white, contorted faces, sunken-eyed and straining, as they
struggled through the yellow pools of light. Conditions were ripe
for disaster when a voice, harsh, mocking, cut cleanly through the
bedlam. The voice was Ralston's : he had been released before
nine o'clock, on the Captain's orders : the cells were in the very
forepeak of the ship, and conditions there were impossible in a
head sea : even so, Hastings had freed him only with the worst
possible grace.

" It's our own depth charges ! Do you hear me, you bloody
fools—it's our own depth charges ! " It was not so much the
words as the biting mockery, that stopped short the panic, halted
dazed, unthinking men in their tracks. " They're *our* depth
charges, I tell you ! They must have been washed over the side ! "

He was right. The entire contents of a rack had broken adrift,
lifted from their cradles by some freak wave, and tumbled over
the side. Through some oversight, they had been left set at their
shallow setting—those put on for the midget submarine in Scapa
—and had gone off almost directly under the ship. The damage,
it seemed, was only minor.

Up in " A " mess-deck, right for'ard, conditions were even
worse. There was more wreckage on the decks and far more
seasickness—not the green-faced, slightly ludicrous malaise of
the cross-channel steamer, but tearing rending convulsions, dark
and heavy with blood—for the bows had been rearing and
plunging, rearing and plunging, thirty, forty, fifty feet at a time
for endless, hopeless hours ; but there was an even more sinister
agent at work, rapidly making the mess-deck untenable.

At the for'ard end of the capstan flat, which adjoined the mess-
deck, was the battery-room. In here were stored, or on charge, a
hundred and one different batteries, ranging from the heavy lead-
acid batteries weighing over a hundred pounds to the tiny
nickel-cadmium cells for the emergency lighting. Here, too, were

stored earthenware jars of prepared acid and big, glass carboys of undiluted sulphuric. These last were permanently stored : in heavy weather, the big batteries were lashed down.

No one knew what had happened. It seemed likely—certain, indeed—that acid spilt from the batteries by the tremendous pitching had eaten through the lashings. Then a battery must have broken loose and smashed another, and another, and another, and then the jars and carboys until the entire floor—fortunately of acid-resisting material—was awash to a depth of five or six inches in sulphuric acid.

A young torpedoman, on a routine check, had opened the door and seen the splashing sea of acid inside. Panicking, and recalling vaguely that caustic soda, stored in quantities just out-side, was a neutraliser for sulphuric, he had emptied a forty-pound carton of it into the battery-room : he was in the Sick Bay now, blinded. The acid fumes saturated the capstan flat, making entry impossible without breathing equipment, and was seeping back, slowly, insidiously, into the mess-deck : more deadly still, hundreds of gallons of salt water from sprung deck-plates and broken capstan speaking tubes were surging crazily around the flat : already the air was tainted with the first traces of chlorine gas. On the deck immediately above, Hartley and two seamen, belayed with ropes, had made a brief, hopelessly gallant attempt to plug the gaping holes : all three, battered into near senselessness by the great waves pounding the fo'c'sle, were dragged off within a minute.

For the men below, it was discomfort, danger and desperate physical illness : for the bare handful of men above, the officers and ratings on the bridge, it was pure undiluted hell. But a hell not of our latter-day imagining, a strictly Eastern and Biblical conception, but the hell of our ancient North-European ancestors, of the Vikings, the Danes, the Jutes, of Beowulf and the monster-haunted meres—the hell of eternal cold.

True, the temperature registered a mere 10° below zero—42° of frost. Men have been known to live, even to work in the open, at far lower temperatures. What is not so well known, what is barely realised at all, is that when freezing point has been passed, every extra mile per hour of wind is *equivalent*, in terms of

pure cold as it reacts on a human being, to a 1° drop in temperature. Not once, but several times that night, before it had finally
raced itself to destruction, the anemometer had recorded gusts of
over 125 m.p.h., wave-flattening gusts that sundered stays and
all but tore the funnels off. For minutes on end, the shrieking,
screaming wind held steady at 100 m.p.h. and above—the total
equivalent, for these numbed, paralysed creatures on the bridge,
of something well below a 100° below zero.

Five minutes at a time was enough for any man on the bridge,
then he had to retire to the Captain's shelter. Not that manning
the bridge was more than a gesture anyway—it was impossible
to look into that terrible wind : the cold would have seared the
eyeballs blind, the ice would have gouged them out. And it was
impossible even to see through the Kent Clear-view windscreens.
They still spun at high speed, but uselessly : the ice-laden storm,
a gigantic sand-blaster, had starred and abraded the plate glass
until it was completely opaque.

It was not a dark night. It was possible to see above, abeam
and astern. Above, patches of night-blue sky and handfuls of
stars could be seen at fleeting intervals, obscured as soon as seen
by the scudding, shredded cloud-wrack. Abeam and astern, the
sea was an inky black, laced with boiling white. Gone now were
the serried ranks of yesterday, gone, too, the decorative whitecaps : here now were only massive mountains of water, broken
and confused, breaking this way and that, but always tending
south. Some of these moving ranges of water—by no stretch of
the imagination, only by proxy, could they be called waves—
were small, insignificant—in size of a suburban house : others
held a million tons of water, towered seventy to eighty feet,
looming terrifyingly against the horizon, big enough to drown a
cathedral. . . . As the Kapok Kid remarked, the best thing to do
with these waves was to look the other way. More often than
not, they passed harmlessly by, plunging the *Ulysses* into the
depths : rarely, they curled over and broke their tops into the
bridge, soaking the unfortunate Officer of the Watch. He had
then to be removed at once or he would literally have frozen
solid within a minute.

So far they had survived, far beyond the expectation of any

man. But, as they were blind ahead, there was always the worry of what would come next. Would the next sea be normal—for that storm, that was—or some nameless juggernaut that would push them under for ever ? The suspense never lifted, a suspense doubled by the fact that when the *Ulysses* reared and crashed down, it did so soundlessly, sightlessly. They could judge its intensity only by movement and vibration : the sound of the sea, everything, was drowned in the Satanic cacophony of that howling wind in the upper works and rigging.

About two in the morning—it was just after the depth-charge explosions—some of the senior officers had staged their own private mutiny. The Captain, who had been persuaded to go below less than a hour previously, exhausted and shaking uncontrollably with cold, had been wakened by the depth-charging and had returned to the bridge. He found his way barred by the Commander and Commander Westcliffe, who bundled him quietly but firmly into the shelter. Turner heaved the door to, switched on the light. Vallery was more puzzled than angry.

"What—what in the world does this mean ? " he demanded.

"Mutiny ! " boomed Turner happily. His face was covered in blood from flying splinters of ice. "On the High Seas, is the technical term, I believe. Isn't that so, Admiral ? "

"Exactly," the Admiral agreed. Vallery swung round, startled : Tyndall was lying in state on the bunk. "Mind you, I've no jurisdiction over a Captain in his own ship ; but I can't see a thing." He lay back on the bunk, eyes elaborately closed in seeming exhaustion. Only Tyndall knew that he wasn't pretending.

Vallery said nothing. He stood there clutching a hand-rail, his face grey and haggard, his eyes blood-red and drugged with sleep. Turner felt a knife twist inside him as he looked at him. When he spoke, his voice was low and earnest, so unusual for him that he caught and held Vallery's attention.

"Sir, this is no night for a naval captain. Danger from any quarter except the sea itself just doesn't exist. Agreed ? "

Vallery nodded silently.

" It's a night for a seaman, sir. With all respect, I suggest that neither of us in the class of Carrington—he's just a different breed of man."

" Nice of you to include yourself, Commander," Vallery murmured. " And quite unnecessary."

" The First Lieutenant will remain on the bridge all night. So will Westcliffe here. So will I."

" Me, too," grunted Tyndall. " But I'm going to sleep." He looked almost as tired, as haggard as Vallery.

Turner grinned. " Thank you, sir. Well, Captain, I'm afraid it's going to be a bit overcrowded here to-night. . . . We'll see you after breakfast."

" But——"

" But me no buts," Westcliffe murmured.

" Please," Turner insisted. " You will do us a favour."

Vallery looked at him. " As Captain of the *Ulysses* . . ." His voice tailed off. " I don't know what to say."

" I do," said Turner briskly, his hand on Vallery's elbow. " Let's go below."

" Don't think I can manage by myself, eh ? " Vallery smiled faintly.

" I do. But I'm taking no chances. Come along, sir."

" All right, all right." He sighed tiredly. " Anything for a quiet life . . . and a night's sleep ! "

Reluctantly, with a great effort, Lieutenant Nicholls dragged himself up from the mist-fogged depths of exhausted sleep. Slowly, reluctantly, he opened his eyes. The *Ulysses*, he realised, was still rolling as heavily, plunging as sickeningly as ever. The Kapok Kid, forehead swathed in bandages, the rest of his face pocked with blood, was bending over him. He looked disgustingly cheerful.

" Hark, hark, the lark, etcetera," the Kapok Kid grinned. " And how are we this morning ? " he mimicked unctuously. The Hon. Carpenter held the medical profession in low esteem.

Nicholls focused blurred eyes on him.

" What the matter, Andy ? Anything wrong ? "

" With Messrs. Carrington and Carpenter in charge," said the

Kapok Kid loftily, " nothing could be wrong. Want to come up top, see Carrington do his stuff? He's going to turn the ship round. In this little lot, it should be worth seeing!"

" What! Dammit to hell! Have you woken me just——"

" Brother, when this ship turns, you would wake up anyway —probably on the deck with a broken neck. But as it so happens, Jimmy requires your assistance. At least, he requires one of these heavy plate-glass squares which I happen to know you have in great numbers in the dispensary. But the dispensary's locked— I tried it," he added shamelessly.

" But what—I mean—plate glass——"

" Come and see for yourself," the Kapok Kid invited.

It was dawn now, a wild and terrible dawn, fit epilogue for a nightmare. Strange, trailing bands of misty-white vapour swept by barely at mast-top level, but high above the sky was clear. The seas, still gigantic, were shorter now, much shorter, and even steeper: the *Ulysses* was slowed right down, with barely enough steerage way to keep her head up—and even then, taking severe punishment in the precipitous head seas. The wind had dropped to a steady fifty knots—gale force: even at that, it seared like fire in Nicholls'a lungs as he stepped out on the flag-deck, blinded him with ice and cold. Hastily he wrapped scarves over his entire face, clambered up to the bridge by touch and instinct. The Kapok Kid followed with the glass. As they climbed, they heard the loudspeakers crackling some unintelligible message.

Turner and Carrington were alone on the twilit bridge, swathed like mummies. Not even their eyes were visible—they wore goggles.

" Morning, Nicholls," boomed the Commander. " It *is* Nicholls, isn't it? " He pulled off his goggles, his back turned to the bitter wind, threw them away in disgust. " Can't see damn all through these bloody things. . . . Ah, Number One. he's got the glass."

Nicholls crouched in the for'ard lee of the compass platform. In a corner, the duckboards were littered with goggles, eye-shields and gas-masks. He jerked his head towards them.

" What's this—a clearance sale ? "

" We're turning round, Doc." It was Carrington who
answered, his voice calm and precise as ever, without a trace of
exhaustion. " But we've got to see where we're going, and as the
Commander says all these damn' things there are useless—mist
up immediately they're put on—it's too cold. If you'll just hold
it—so—and if you would wipe it, Andy ? "

Nicholls looked at the great seas. He shuddered.

" Excuse my ignorance, but why turn round at all ? "

" Because it will be impossible very shortly," Carrington
answered briefly. Then he chuckled. " This is going to make
me the most unpopular man in the ship. We've just broadcast a
warning. Ready, sir ? "

" Stand by, engine-room : stand by, wheelhouse. Ready,
Number One."

For thirty seconds, forty-five, a whole minute, Carrington
stared steadily, unblinkingly through the glass. Nicholls's hands
froze. The Kapok Kid rubbed industriously. Then :

" Half-ahead, port ! "

" Half-ahead, port ! " Turner echoed.

" Starboard 20 ! "

" Starboard 20 ! "

Nicholls risked a glance over his shoulder. In the split
second before his eyes blinded, filled with tears, he saw a huge
wave bearing down on them, the bows already swinging
diagonally away from it. Good God ! Why hadn't Carrington
waited until that was past ?

The great wave flung the bows up, pushed the *Ulysses* far over
to starboard, then passed under. The *Ulysses* staggered over the
top, corkscrewed wickedly down the other side, her masts, great
gleaming tree trunks thick and heavy with ice, swinging in a great
arc as she rolled over, burying her port rails in the rising shoulder
of the next sea.

" Full ahead port ! "

" Full ahead port ! "

" Starboard 30 ! "

" Starboard 30 ! "

The next sea, passing beneath, merely straightened the

Ulysses up. And then, at last, Nicholls understood. Incredibly, because it had been impossible to see so far ahead, Carrington had known that two opposing wave systems were due to interlock in an area of comparative calm : how he had sensed it, no one knew, would ever know, not even Carrington himself : but he was a great seaman, and he had known. For fifteen, twenty seconds, the sea was a seething white mass of violently disturbed, conflicting waves—of the type usually found, on a small scale, in tidal races and overfalls—and the *Ulysses* curved gratefully through. And then another great sea, towering almost to bridge height, caught her on the far turn of the quarter circle. It struck the entire length of the *Ulysses*—for the first time that night—with tremendous weight. It threw her far over on her side, the lee rails vanishing. Nicholls was flung off his feet, crashed heavily into the side of the bridge, the glass shattering. He could have sworn he heard Carrington laughing. He clawed his way back to the middle of the compass platform.

And still the great wave had not passed. It towered high above the trough into which the *Ulysses*, now heeled far over to 40°, had been so contemptuously flung, bore down remorselessly from above and sought, in a lethal silence and with an almost animistic savagery, to press her under. The inclinometer swung relentlessly over—45°, 50°, 53°, and hung there an eternity, while men stood on the side of the ship, braced with their hands on the deck, numbed minds barely grasping the inevitable. This was the end. The *Ulysses* could never come back.

A lifetime ticked agonisingly by. Nicholls and Carpenter looked at each other, blank-faced, expressionless. Tilted at that crazy angle, the bridge was sheltered from the wind. Carrington's voice, calm, conversational, carried with amazing clarity.

" She'd go to 65° and still come back," he said matter-of-factly. " Hang on to your hats, gentlemen. This is going to be interesting."

Just as he finished, the *Ulysses* shuddered, then imperceptibly, then slowly, then with vicious speed lurched back and whipped through an arc of 90°, then back again. Once more Nicholls found himself in the corner of the bridge. But the *Ulysses* was almost round.

The Kapok Kid, grinning with relief, picked himself up and tapped Carrington on the shoulder.

" Don't look now, sir, but we have lost our mainmast."

It was a slight exaggeration, but the top fifteen feet, which had carried the after radar scanner, were undoubtedly gone. That wicked, double whip-lash, with the weight of the ice, had been too much.

" Slow ahead both ! Midships ! "

" Slow ahead both ! Midships ! "

" Steady as she goes ! "

The *Ulysses* was round.

The Kapok Kid caught Nicholls's eye, nodded at the First Lieutenant.

" See what I mean, Johnny ? "

" Yes." Nicholls was very quiet. " Yes, I see what you mean." Then he grinned suddenly. " Next time you make a statement, I'll just take your word for it, if you don't mind. These demonstrations of proof take too damn' much out of a person ! "

Running straight before the heavy stern sea, the *Ulysses* was amazingly steady. The wind, too, was dead astern now, the bridge in magical shelter. The scudding mist overhead had thinned out, was almost gone. Far away to the south-east a dazzling white sun climbed up above a cloudless horizon. The long night was over.

An hour later, with the wind down to thirty knots, radar reported contacts to the west. After another hour, with the wind almost gone and only a heavy swell running, smoke plumes tufted above the horizon. At 1030, in position, on time, the *Ulysses* rendezvoused with the convoy from Halifax.

CHAPTER SEVEN

WEDNESDAY NIGHT

THE CONVOY came steadily up from the west, rolling heavily in cross seas, a rich argosy, a magnificent prize for any German wolf-pack. Eighteen ships in this argosy, fifteen big, modern cargo ships, three 16,000-ton tankers, carrying a freight far more valuable, infinitely more vital, than any fleet of quinqueremes or galleons had ever known. Tanks, planes and petrol —what were gold and jewels, silks and the rarest of spices compared to these ? £10,000,000, £20,000,000—the total worth of that convoy was difficult to estimate : in any event, its real value was not to be measured in terms of money.

Aboard the merchant ships, crews lined the decks as the *Ulysses* steamed up between the port and centre lines. Lined the decks and looked and wondered—and thanked their Maker they had been wide of the path of that great storm. The *Ulysses*, seen from another deck, was a strange sight : broken-masted, stripped of her rafts, with her boat falls hauled taut over empty cradles, she glistened like crystal in the morning light : the great wind had blown away all snow, had abraded and rubbed and polished the ice to a satin-smooth, transparent gloss : but on either side of the bows and before the bridge were huge patches of crimson, where the hurricane sand-blaster of that long night had stripped off camouflage and base coats, exposing the red lead below.

The American escort was small—a heavy cruiser with a sea-plane for spotting, two destroyers and two near-frigates of the coastguard type. Small, but sufficient : there was no need of escort carriers (although these frequently sailed with the Atlantic convoys) because the Luftwaffe could not operate so far west, and the wolf-packs, in recent months, had moved north and east of

Iceland : there, they were not only nearer base—they could more easily lie astride the converging convoy routes to Murmansk.

ENE. they sailed in company, freighters, American warships and the *Ulysses* until, late in the afternoon, the box-like silhouette of an escort carrier bulked high against the horizon. Half an hour later, at 1600, the American escorts slowed, dropped astern and turned, winking farewell messages of good luck. Aboard the *Ulysses*, men watched them depart with mixed feelings. They knew these ships had to go, that another convoy would already be mustering off the St. Lawrence. There was none of the envy, the bitterness one might expect—and had indeed been common enough only a few weeks ago—among these exhausted men who carried the brunt of the war. There was instead a careless accept-ance of things as they were, a quasi-cynical bravado, often a queer, high nameless pride that hid itself beneath twisted jests and endless grumbling.

The 14th Aircraft Carrier Squadron—or what was left of it— was only two miles away now. Tyndall, coming to the bridge, swore fluently as he saw that a carrier and minesweeper were missing. An angry signal went out to Captain Jeffries of the *Stirling*, asking why orders had been disobeyed, where the missing ships were.

An Aldis flickered back its reply. Tyndall sat grim-faced and silent as Bentley read out the signal to him. The *Wrestler's* steering gear had broken down during the night. Even behind Langanes the weather position had been severe, had worsened about mid-night when the wind had veered to the north. The *Wrestler*, even with two screws, had lost almost all steering command, and, in zero visibility and an effort to maintain position, had gone too far ahead and grounded on the Vejle bank. She had grounded on the top of the tide. She had still been there, with the minesweeper *Eager* in attendance, when the squadron had sailed shortly after dawn.

Tyndall sat in silence for some minutes. He dictated a W.T. signal to the *Wrestler*, hesitated about breaking radio silence, countermanded the signal, and decided to go to see for himself. After all, it was only three hours steaming distance. He signalled the *Stirling* : "Take over squadron command : will rejoin in the morning," and ordered Vallery to take the *Ulysses* back to Langanes.

Vallery nodded unhappily, gave the necessary orders. He was worried, badly so, was trying hard not to show it. The least of his worries was himself, although he knew, but never admitted to anyone, that he was a very sick man. He thought wryly that he didn't have to admit it anyway—he was amused and touched by the elaborate casualness with which his officers sought to lighten his load, to show their concern for him.

He was worried, too, about his crew—they were in no fit state to do the lightest work, to survive that killing cold, far less sail the ship and fight her through to Russia. He was depressed, also, over the series of misfortunes that had befallen the squadron since leaving Scapa : it augured ill for the future, and he had no illusions as to what lay ahead for the crippled squadron. And always, a gnawing torment at the back of his mind, he worried about Ralston.

Ralston—that tall throwback to his Scandinavian ancestors, with his flaxen hair and still blue eyes. Ralston, whom nobody understood, with whom nobody on the ship had an intimate friendship, who went his own unsmiling, self-possessed way. Ralston, who had nothing left to fight for, except memories, who was one of the most reliable men in the *Ulysses*, extraordinarily decisive, competent and resourceful in any emergency—and who again found himself under lock and key. And for nothing that any reasonable and just man could call fault of his own.

Under lock and key—that was what hurt. Last night, Vallery had gladly seized the excuse of bad weather to release him, had intended to forget the matter, to let sleeping dogs lie. But Hastings, the Master-At-Arms, had exceeded his duty and returned him to cells during the forenoon watch. Masters-At-Arms—disciplinary Warrant Officers, in effect—had never been particularly noted for a humane, tolerant and ultra-kindly attitude to life in general or the lower deck in particular—they couldn't afford to be. But even amongst such men, Hastings was an exception—a machine-like, seemingly emotionless creature, expressionless, unbending, strict, fair according to his lights, but utterly devoid of heart and sympathy. If Hastings were not careful,

Vallery mused, he might very well go the same way as Lister, until recently the highly unpopular Master-At-Arms of the *Blue Ranger*. Not, when he came to think of it, that anyone knew what had happened to Lister, except that he had been so misguided as to take a walk on the flight-deck on a dark and starless night. . . .

Vallery sighed. As he had explained to Foster, his hands were tied. Foster, the Captain of Marines, with an aggrieved and incensed Colour-Sergeant Evans standing behind him, had complained bitterly at having his marines withdrawn for guard duty, men who needed every minute of sleep they could snatch. Privately, Vallery had sympathised with Foster, but he couldn't afford to countermand his original order—not, at least, until he had held a Captain's Defaulters and placed Ralston under open arrest. . . . He sighed again, sent for Turner and asked him to break out grass lines, a manilla and a five-inch wire on the poop. He suspected that they would be needed shortly, and, as it turned out, his preparations were justified.

Darkness had fallen when they moved up to the Vejle bank, but locating the *Wrestler* was easy—her identification challenge ten minutes ago had given her approximate position, and now her squat bulk loomed high before them, a knife-edged silhouette against the pale afterglow of sunset. Ominously, her flight-deck raked perceptibly towards the stern, where the *Eager* lay, apparently at anchor. The sea was almost calm here—there was only a gentle swell running.

Aboard the *Ulysses*, a hooded, pinhole Aldis started to chatter. " Congratulations I How are you fast ? "

From the *Wrestler*, a tiny light flickered in answer. Bentley read aloud as the message came.

" Bows aft 100 feet."

" Wonderful," said Tyndall bitterly. " Just wonderful I Ask him, ' How is steering-gear ? ' "

Back came the answer : " Diver down : transverse fracture of post : dockyard job."

" My God ! " Tyndall groaned. " A dockyard job I That's handy. Ask him, ' What steps have you taken ? ' "

"All fuel and water pumped aft. Kedge anchor. *Eager* towing. Full astern, 1200-1230."

The turn of the high tide, Tyndall knew. "Very successful, very successful indeed," he growled. "No, you bloody fool, don't send that. Tell him to prepare to receive towing wire, bring own towing chain aft."

"Message understood," Bentley read.

"Ask him, 'How much excess squadron fuel have you?'"

"800 tons."

"Get rid of it."

Bentley read, "Please confirm."

"Tell him to empty the bloody stuff over the side!" Tyndall roared.

The light on the *Wrestler* flickered and died in hurt silence.

At midnight the *Eager* steamed slowly ahead of the *Ulysses*, taking up the wire that led back to the cruiser's fo'c'sle capstan: two minutes later, the *Ulysses* began to shudder as the four great engines boiled up the shallow water into a seething mudstained cauldron. The chain from the poop-deck to the *Wrestler's* stern was a bare fifteen fathoms in length, angling up at 30°. This would force the carrier's stern down—only a fraction, but in this situation every fraction counted—and give more positive buoyancy to the grounded bows. And much more important—for the racing screws were now aerating the water, developing only a fraction of their potential thrust—the proximity of the two ships helped the *Ulysses's* screws reinforce the action of the *Wrestler's* in scouring out a channel in the sand and mud beneath the carrier's keel.

Twenty minutes before high tide, easily, steadily, the *Wrestler* slid off. At once the blacksmith on the *Ulysses's* bows knocked off the shackle securing the *Eager's* towing wire, and the *Ulysses* pulled the carrier, her engines shut down, in a big half-circle to the east.

By one o'clock the *Wrestler* was gone, the *Eager* in attendance and ready to pass a head rope for bad weather steering. On the bridge of the *Ulysses*, Tyndall watched the carrier vanish into the night, zig-zagging as the captain tried to balance the steering on the two screws.

"No doubt they'll get the hang of it before they get to Scapa," he growled. He felt cold, exhausted and only the way an Admiral can feel when he has lost three-quarters of his carrier force. He sighed wearily and turned to Vallery.

"When do you reckon we'll overtake the convoy?"

Vallery hesitated: not so the Kapok Kid.

"0805," he answered readily and precisely. "At twenty-seven knots, on the intersection course I've just pencilled out."

"Oh, my God!" Tyndall groaned. "That stripling again. What did I ever do to deserve him. As it so happens, young man, it's imperative that we overtake before dawn."

"Yes, sir." The Kapok Kid was imperturbable. "I thought so myself. On my alternative course, 33 knots, thirty minutes before dawn."

"I thought so myself! Take him away!" Tyndall raved. "Take him away or I'll wrap his damned dividers round . . ." He broke off, climbed stiffly out of his chair, took Vallery by the arm. "Come on, Captain. Let's go below. What the hell's the use of a couple of ancient has-beens like us getting in the way of youth?" He passed out the gate behind the Captain, grinning tiredly to himself.

The *Ulysses* was at dawn Action Stations as the shadowy shapes of the convoy, a bare mile ahead, lifted out of the greying gloom. The great bulk of the *Blue Ranger*, on the starboard quarter of the convoy, was unmistakable. There was a moderate swell running, but not enough to be uncomfortable: the breeze was light, from the west, the temperature just below zero, the sky chill and cloudless. The time was exactly 0700.

At 0702, the *Blue Ranger* was torpedoed. The *Ulysses* was two cable-lengths away, on her starboard quarter: those on the bridge felt the physical shock of the twin explosions, heard them shattering the stillness of the dawn as they saw two searing columns of flame fingering skywards, high above the *Blue Ranger's* bridge and well aft of it. A second later they heard a signalman shouting something unintelligible, saw him pointing forwards and downwards. It was another torpedo, running astern of the carrier, trailing its evil phosphorescent wake across the heels of the convoy, before spending itself in the darkness of the Arctic.

Vallery was shouting down the voice-pipe, pulling round the *Ulysses*, still doing upwards of twenty knots, in a madly heeling, skidding turn, to avoid collision with the slewing carrier. Three sets of Aldis lamps and the fighting lights were already stuttering out the " Maintain Position " code signal to ships in the convoy. Marshall, on the phone was giving the stand-by order to the depth-charge L.T.O.: gun barrels were already depressing, peering hungrily into the treacherous sea. The signal to the *Sirrus* stopped short, unneeded : the destroyer, a half-seen blur in the darkness, was already knifing its way through the convoy, white water piled high at its bows, headed for the estimated position of the U-boat.

The *Ulysses* sheered by parallel to the burning carrier, less than 150 feet away ; travelling so fast, heeling so heavily and at such close range, it was impossible to gather more than a blurred impression, a tangled, confused memory of heavy black smoke laced with roaring columns of flame, appalling in that near-darkness, of a drunkenly listing flight-deck, of Grummans and Corsairs cartwheeling grotesquely over the edge to splash icy clouds of spray in shocked faces as the cruiser slewed away ; and then the *Ulysses* was round, heading back south for the kill.

Within a minute, the signal-lamp of the *Vectra*, up front with the convoy, started winking. " Contact, Green 70, closing : Contact, Green 70, closing."

" Acknowledge," Tyndall ordered briefly.

The Aldis had barely begun to clack when the *Vectra* cut through the signal.

" Contacts, repeat contacts. Green 90, Green 90. Closing. Very close. Repeat contacts, contacts."

Tyndall cursed softly.

" Acknowledge. Investigate." He turned to Vallery. " Let's join him, Captain. This is it. Wolf-pack Number One—and in force. No bloody right to be here," he added bitterly. " So much for Admiralty Intelligence ! "

The *Ulysses* was round again, heading for the *Vectra*. It should have been growing lighter now, but the *Blue Ranger*, her squadron fuel tanks on fire, a gigantic torch against the eastern horizon, had the curious effect of throwing the surrounding sea into heavy darkness. She lay almost athwart of the flagship's course for the *Vectra*, looming larger every minute. Tyndall had his night glasses to his eyes, kept on muttering : " The poor bastards, the poor bastards ! "

The *Blue Ranger* was almost gone. She lay dead in the water, heeled far over to starboard, ammunition and petrol tanks going up in a constant series of crackling reports. Suddenly, a succession of dull, heavy explosions rumbled over the sea : the entire bridge island structure lurched crazily sideways, held, then slowly, ponderously, deliberately, the whole massive body of it toppled majestically into the glacial darkness of the sea. God only knew how many men perished with it, deep down in the Arctic, trapped in its iron walls. They were the lucky ones.

The *Vectra*, barely two miles ahead now, was pulling round south in a tight circle. Vallery saw her, altered course to intercept. He heard Bentley shouting something unintelligible from the fore corner of the compass platform. Vallery shook his head, heard him shouting again, his voice desperate with some nameless urgency, his arm pointing frantically over the windscreen, and leapt up beside him.

The sea was on fire. Flat, calm, burdened with hundreds of tons of fuel oil, it was a vast carpet of licking, twisting flames. That much, for a second, and that only, Vallery saw : then with heart-stopping shock, with physically sickening abruptness, he saw something else again : the burning sea was alive with swimming, struggling men. Not a handful, not even dozens, but literally hundreds, soundlessly screaming, agonisingly dying in the barbarous contrariety of drowning and cremation.

" Signal from *Vectra*, sir." It was Bentley speaking, his voice abnormally matter-of-fact. " ' Depth-charging. 3, repeat 3 contacts. Request immediate assistance.' "

Tyndall was at Vallery's side now. He heard Bentley, looked a long second at Vallery, followed his sick, fascinated gaze into the sea ahead.

For a man in the sea, oil is an evil thing. It clogs his movements, burns his eyes, sears his lungs and tears away his stomach in uncontrollable paroxysms of retching ; but oil on fire is a hellish thing, death by torture, a slow, shrieking death by drowning, by burning, by asphyxiation—for the flames devour all the life-giving oxygen on the surface of the sea. And not even in the bitter Arctic is there the merciful extinction by cold, for the insulation of an oil-soaked body stretches a dying man on the rack for eternity, carefully preserves him for the last excruciating refinement of agony. All this Vallery knew.

He knew, too, that for the *Ulysses* to stop, starkly outlined against the burning carrier, would have been suicide. And to come sharply round to starboard, even had there been time and room to clear the struggling, dying men in the sea ahead, would have wasted invaluable minutes, time and to spare for the U-boats ahead to line up firing-tracks on the convoy; and the *Ulysses's* first responsibility was to the convoy. Again, all this Vallery knew. But, at that moment, what weighed most heavily with him was common humanity. Fine off the port bow, close in to the *Blue Ranger*, the oil was heaviest, the flames fiercest, the swimmers thickest : Vallery looked back over his shoulder at the Officer of the Watch.

" Port 10 ! "

" Port 10, sir."

" Midships ! "

" Midships, sir."

" Steady as she goes ! "

For ten, fifteen seconds the *Ulysses* held her course, arrowing through the burning sea to the spot where some gregariously atavistic instinct for self-preservation held two hundred men knotted together in a writhing, seething mass, gasping out their lives in hideous agony. For a second, a great gout of flame leapt up in the centre of the group, like a giant, incandescent magnesium flare, a flame that burnt the picture into the hearts and minds of the men on the bridge with a permanence and searing clarity that no photographic plate could ever have reproduced : men on fire, human torches beating insanely at the flames that licked, scorched and then incinerated clothes, hair and skin : men flinging themselves almost out of the water, backs arched like tautened bows, grotesque in convulsive crucifixion : men lying dead in the water, insignificant, featureless little oil-stained mounds in an oil-soaked plain : and a handful of fear-maddened men, faces inhumanly contorted, who saw the *Ulysses* and knew what was coming, as they frantically thrashed their way to a safety that offered only a few more brief seconds of unspeakable agony before they gladly died.

" Starboard 30 ! " Vallery's voice was low, barely a murmur, but it carried clearly through the shocked silence on the bridge.

" Starboard 30, sir."

For the third time in ten minutes, the *Ulysses* slewed crazily round in a racing turn. Turning thus, a ship does not follow through the line of the bows cutting the water ; there is a pronounced sideways or lateral motion, and the faster and sharper the turn, the more violent the broadside skidding motion, like a car on ice. The side of the *Ulysses*, still at an acute angle, caught the edge of the group on the port bow : almost on the instant, the entire length of the swinging hull smashed into the heart of the fire, into the thickest press of dying men.

For most of them, it was just extinction, swift and glad and merciful. The tremendous concussion and pressure waves crushed the life out of them, thrust them deep down into the blessed oblivion of drowning, thrust them down and sucked them back into the thrashing vortex of the four great screws. . . .

On board the *Ulysses*, men for whom death and destruction had become the stuff of existence, to be accepted with the callousness and jesting indifference that alone kept them sane—these men clenched impotent fists, mouthed meaningless, useless curses over and over again and wept heedlessly like little children. They wept as pitiful, charred faces, turned up towards the *Ulysses* and alight with joy and hope, petrified into incredulous staring horror, as realisation dawned and the water closed over them : as hate-filled men screamed insane invective, both arms raised aloft, shaking fists white-knuckled through the dripping oil as the *Ulysses* trampled them under : as a couple of young boys were sucked into the mælstrom of the propellors, still giving the thumbs-up sign : as a particularly shocking case, who looked as if he had been barbecued on a spit and had no right to be alive, lifted scorified hand to the blackened hole that had been his mouth, flung to the bridge a kiss in token of endless gratitude ;

and wept, oddly, most of all, at the inevitable humorist who lifted his fur cap high above his head and bowed gravely and deeply, his face into the water as he died.

Suddenly, mercifully, the sea was empty. The air was strangely still and quiet, heavy with the sickening stench of charred flesh and burning Diesel, and the *Ulysses's* stern was swinging wildly almost under the black pall overhanging the *Blue Ranger* amidships, when the shells struck her.

The shells—three 3.7s—came from the *Blue Ranger*. Certainly, no living gun-crews manned these 3.7s—the heat must have ignited the bridge fuses in the cartridge cases. The first shell exploded harmlessly against the armour-plating : the second wrecked the bosun's store, fortunately empty : the third penetrated No. 3 Low Power Room via the deck. There were nine men in there—an officer, seven ratings and Chief Torpedo Gunner's Mate Noyes. In that confined space, death was instantaneous.

Only seconds later a heavy rumbling explosion blew out a great hole along the waterline of the *Blue Ranger* and she fell slowly, wearily right over on her starboard side, her flight-deck vertical to the water, as if content to die now that, dying, she had lashed out at the ship that had destroyed her crew.

On the bridge, Vallery still stood on the yeoman's platform, leaning over the starred, opaque windscreen. His head hung down, his eyes were shut and he was retching desperately, the gushing blood—arterial blood—ominously bright and scarlet in the erubescent glare of the sinking carrier. Tyndall stood there helplessly beside him, not knowing what to do, his mind numbed and sick. Suddenly, he was brushed unceremoniously aside by the Surgeon Commander, who pushed a white towel to Vallery's mouth and led him gently below. Old Brooks, everyone knew, should have been at his Action Stations position in the Sick Bay : no one dared say anything.

Carrington straightened the *Ulysses* out on course, while he waited for Turner to move up from the after Director tower to take over the bridge. In three minutes the cruiser was up with the *Vectra*, methodically quartering for a lost contact. Twice the ships regained contact, twice they dropped heavy patterns. A heavy oil slick rose to the surface : possibly a kill, probably a ruse, but in any event, neither ship could remain to investigate further. The convoy was two miles ahead now, and only the *Stirling* and *Viking* were there for its protection—a wholly inadequate cover and powerless to save the convoy from any determined attack.

It was the *Blue Ranger* that saved FR77. In these high latitudes, dawn comes slowly, interminably : even so, it was now more than half-light, and the merchant ships, line ahead through that very gentle swell, lifted clear and sharp against a cloudless horizon, a U-boat Commander's dream—or would have been, had he been able to see them. But, by this time, the convoy was completely obscured from the wolf-pack lying to the south : the light westerly wind carried the heavy black smoke from the blazing carrier along the southern flank of the convoy, at sea level, the perfect smoke-screen, dense, impenetrable. Why the U-boats had departed from their almost invariable practice of launching dawn attacks from the north, so as to have their targets between themselves and the sunrise, could only be guessed. Tactical surprise, probably, but whatever the reason it was the saving of the convoy. Within an hour, the thrashing screws of the convoy had left the wolf-pack far behind—and FR77, having slipped the pack, was far too fast to be overtaken again.

Aboard the flagship, the W.T. transmitter was chattering out a coded signal to London. There was little point, Tyndall had decided, in maintaining radio silence now ; the enemy knew their position to a mile. Tyndall smiled grimly as he thought of the rejoicing in the German Naval High Command at the news that FR77 was without any air cover whatsoever : as a starter, they could expect Charlie within the hour.

The signal read : " Admiral, 14 A.C.S.: To D.N.O., London. Rendezvoused FR77 1030 yesterday. Weather conditions extreme. Severe damage to Carriers : *Defender, Wrestler* unserviceable, returning base under escort : *Blue Ranger* torpedoed 0702, sunk 0730 to-day : Convoy Escorts now *Ulysses, Stirling, Sirrus, Vectra, Viking* : no minesweepers—*Eager* to base, minesweeper from Hvalfjord failed rendezvous : Urgently require air support :

Can you detach carrier battle squadron : Alternatively, permission return base. Please advise immediately."

The wording of the message, Tyndall pondered, could have been improved. Especially the bit at the end—probably sounded sufficiently like a threat to infuriate old Starr, who would only see in it pusillanimous confirmation of his conviction of the *Ulysses's*—and Tyndall's—unfitness for the job. . . . Besides, for almost two years now—since long before the sinking of the *Hood* by the *Bismarck*—it had been Admiralty policy not to break up the Home Fleet squadrons by detaching capital ships or carriers. Old battleships, too slow for modern inter-naval surface action— vessels such as the *Ramillies* and the *Malaya*—were used for selected Atlantic convoys : with that exception, the official strategy was based on keeping the Home Fleet intact, containing the German Grand Fleet—and risking the convoys. . . . Tyndall took a last look round the convoy, sighed wearily and eased himself down to the duckboards. What the hell, he thought, let it go. If it wasted his time sending it, it would also waste old Starr's time reading it.

He clumped his way heavily down the bridge ladders, eased his bulk through the door of the Captain's cabin, hard by the F.D.R. Vallery, partly undressed, was lying in his bunk, between very clean, very white sheets : their knife-edged ironing crease-marks contrasted oddly with the spreading crimson stain. Vallery himself, gaunt-cheeked and cadaverous beneath dark stubble of beard, red eyes sunk deep in great hollow sockets, looked corpse-like, already dead. From one corner of his mouth blood trickled down a parchment cheek. As Tyndall shut the door, Vallery lifted a wasted hand, all ivory knuckles and blue veins, in feeble greeting.

Tyndall closed the door carefully, quietly. He took his time, time and to spare to allow the shock to drain out of his face. When he turned round, his face was composed, but he made no attempt to disguise his concern.

" Thank God for old Socrates ! " he said feelingly. " Only man in the ship who can make you see even a modicum of sense." He parked himself on the edge of the bed. " How do you feel, Dick ? "

Vallery grinned crookedly. There was no humour in his smile.

" All depends what you mean, sir. Physically or mentally? I feel a bit worn out—not really ill, you know. Doc says he can fix me up—temporarily anyway. He's going to give me a plasma transfusion—says I've lost too much blood."

" Plasma? "

" Plasma. Whole blood would be a better coagulant. But he thinks it may prevent—or minimise—future attacks. . . ." He paused, wiped some froth off his lips, and smiled again, as mirthlessly as before. " It's not really a doctor and medicine I need, John—it's a padre—and forgiveness." His voice trailed off into silence. The cabin was very quiet.

Tyndall shifted uncomfortably and cleared his throat noisily. Rarely had he been so conscious that he was, first and last, a man of action.

" Forgiveness? What on earth do you mean, Dick? " He hadn't meant to speak so loudly, so harshly.

" You know damn' well what I mean," Vallery said mildly. He was a man who was rarely heard to swear, to use the most innocuous oath. " You were with me on the bridge this morning."

For perhaps two minutes neither man said a word. Then Vallery broke into a fresh paroxysm of coughing. The towel in his hand grew dark, sodden, and when he leaned back on his pillow Tyndall felt a quick stab of fear. He bent quickly over the sick man, sighed in soundless relief as he heard the quick, shallow breathing.

Vallery spoke again, his eyes still closed.

" It's not so much the men who were killed in the Low Power Room." He seemed to be talking to himself, his voice a drifting murmur. " My fault, I suppose—I took the *Ulysses* too near the *Ranger*. Foolish to go near a sinking ship, especially if she's burning. . . . But just one of these things, just one of the risks . . . they happen. . . ." The rest was a blurred, dying whisper. Tyndall couldn't catch it.

He rose abruptly to his feet, pulling his gloves on.

" Sorry, Dick," he apologised. " Shouldn't have come

—shouldn't have stayed so long. Old Socrates will give me hell."

" It's the others—the boys in the water." Vallery might never have heard him. " I hadn't the right—I mean, perhaps some of them would. . . ." Again his voice was lost for a moment, then he went on strongly : " Captain Richard Vallery, D.S.O.—judge, jury and executioner. Tell me, John, what am I going to say when *my* turn comes ? "

Tyndall hesitated, heard the authoritative rap on the door and jerked round, his breath escaping in a long, inaudible sigh of thankfulness.

" Come in," he called.

The door opened and Brooks walked in. He stopped short at the sight of the Admiral, turned to the white-coated assistant behind him, a figure weighed down with stands, bottles, tubing and various paraphernalia.

" Remain outside, Johnson, will you ? " he asked. " I'll call you when I want you."

He closed the door, crossed the cabin and pulled a chair up to the Captain's bunk. Vallery's wrist between his fingers, he looked coldly across at Tyndall. Nicholls, Brooks remembered, was insistent that the Admiral was far from well. He looked tired, certainly, but more unhappy than tired. . . . The pulse was very fast, irregular.

" You've been upsetting him," Brooks accused.

" Me ? Good God, no ! " Tyndall was injured. " So help me, Doc, I never said——"

" Not guilty, Doc." It was Vallery who spoke, his voice stronger now. " He never said a word. *I'm* the guilty man— guilty as hell."

Brooks looked at him for a long moment. Then he smiled, smiled in understanding and compassion.

" Forgiveness, sir. That's it, isn't it ? " Tyndall started in surprise, looked at him in wonder.

Vallery opened his eyes. " Socrates ! " he murmured. " You would know."

" Forgiveness," Brooks mused. " Forgiveness. From whom —the living, the dead—or the Judge ? "

Again Tyndall started. " Have you—have you been listening outside ? How can you——— ? "

" From all three, Doc. A tall order, I'm afraid."

" From the dead, sir, you are quite right. There would be no forgiveness : only their blessing, for there is nothing to forgive. I'm a doctor, don't forget—I saw these boys in the water . . . you sent them home the easy way. As for the Judge—you know, ' The Lord giveth, the Lord taketh away. Blessed be the name of the Lord '—the Old Testament conception of the Lord who takes away in His own time and His own way, and to hell with mercy and charity." He smiled at Tyndall. " Don't look so shocked, sir. I'm not being blasphemous. If that were the Judge, Captain, neither you nor I—nor the Admiral—would ever want any part of him. But you know it isn't so. . . ."

Vallery smiled faintly, propped himself up on his pillow. " You make good medicine, Doctor. It's a pity you can't speak for the living also."

" Oh, can't I ? " Brooks smacked his hand on his thigh, guffawed in sudden recollection. " Oh, my word, it was magnificent ! " He laughed again in genuine amusement. Tyndall looked at Vallery in mock despair.

" Sorry," Brooks apologised. " Just fifteen minutes ago a bunch of sympathetic stokers deposited on the deck of the Sick Bay the prone and extremely unconscious form of one of their shipmates. Guess who ? None other than our resident nihilist, our old friend Riley. Slight concussion and assorted facial injuries, but he should be restored to the bosom of his mess-deck by nightfall. Anyway, he insists on it—claims his kittens need him."

Vallery looked up, amused, curious.

" Fallen down the stokehold again, I presume ? "

" Exactly the question I put, sir—although it looked more as if he had fallen into a concrete mixer. ' No, sir,' says one of the stretcher-bearers. ' He tripped over the ship's cat.' ' Ship's cat ? ' I says. ' What ship's cat ? ' So he turns to his oppo and says : ' Ain't we got a ship's cat, Nobby ? ' Whereupon the stoker yclept Nobby looks at him pityingly and says : ' 'E's got it all wrong, sir. Poor old Riley just came all over queer—took a weak turn, 'e did. I 'ope 'e ain't 'urt 'isself?' He sounded quite anxious."

" What had happened ? " Tyndall queried.

" I let it go at that. Young Nicholls took two of them aside, promised no action and had it out of them in a minute flat. Seems that Riley saw in this morning's affair a magnificent opportunity for provoking trouble. Cursed you for an inhuman, cold-blooded murderer and, I regret to say, cast serious aspersions on your immediate ancestors—and all of this, mind you, where he thought he was safe—among his own friends. His friends half-killed him. . . . You know, sir, I envy you . . ."

He broke off, rose abruptly to his feet.

" Now, sir, if you'll just lie down and roll up your sleeve . . . Oh, damn ! "

" Come in." It was Tyndall who answered the knock. " Ah, for me, young Chrysler. Thank you."

He looked up at Vallery. " From London—in reply to my signal." He turned it over in his hand two or three times. " I suppose I have to open it some time," he said reluctantly.

The Surgeon Commander half-rose to his feet.

" Shall I——"

" No, no, Brooks. Why should you ? Besides, it's from our mutual friend, Admiral Starr. I'm sure you'd like to hear what he's got to say, wouldn't you ? "

" No, I wouldn't." Brooks was very blunt. " I can't imagine it'll be anything good ? "

Tyndall opened the signal, smoothed it out.

" D.N.O. to Admiral Commanding 14 A.C.S.," he read slowly. " *Tirpitz* reported preparing to move out. Impossible detach Fleet carrier : FR77 vital : proceed Murmansk all speed : good luck : Starr." Tyndall paused, his mouth twisted. " Good luck ! He might have spared us that ! "

For a long time the three men looked at each other, silently, without expression. Characteristically, it was Brooks who broke the silence.

" Speaking of forgiveness," he murmured quietly, " what I want to know is—who on God's earth, above or below it, is ever going to forgive that vindictive old bastard ? "

CHAPTER EIGHT

THURSDAY NIGHT

It was still only early afternoon, but the grey Arctic twilight was already thickening over the sea as the *Ulysses* dropped slowly astern. The wind had died away completely; again the snow was falling, steadily, heavily, and visibility was down to a bare cable length. It was bitterly cold.

In little groups of three and four, officers and men made their way aft to the starboard side of the poop-deck. Exhausted, bone-chilled men, mostly sunk in private and bitter thought, they shuffled wordlessly aft, dragging feet kicking up little puffs of powdery snow. On the poop, they ranged themselves sound-lessly behind the Captain or in a line inboard and aft of the long, symmetrical row of snow-covered hummocks that heaved up roundly from the unbroken whiteness of the poop.

The Captain was flanked by three of his officers—Carslake, Etherton and the Surgeon Commander. Carslake was by the guard-rail, the lower half of his face swathed in bandages to the eyes. For the second time in twenty-four hours he had waylaid Vallery, begged him to reconsider the decision to deprive him of his commission. On the first occasion Vallery had been adamant, almost contemptuous: ten minutes ago he had been icy and abrupt, had threatened Carslake with close arrest if he annoyed him again. And now Carslake just stared unseeingly into the snow and gloom, pale-blue eyes darkened and heavy with hate.

Etherton stood just behind Vallery's left shoulder, shivering uncontrollably. Above the white, jerking line of compressed mouth, cheek and jaw muscles were working incessantly: only his eyes were steady, dulled in sick fascination at the curious

126

mound at his feet. Brooks, too, was tight-lipped, but there the resemblance ended : red of face and wrathfully blue of eye, he fumed and seethed as can only a doctor whose orders have been openly flouted by the critically ill. Vallery, as Brooks had told him, forcibly and insurbordinately, had no bloody right to be there, was all sorts of a damned fool for leaving his bunk. But, as Vallery had mildly pointed out, somebody had to conduct a funeral service, and that was the Captain's duty if the padre couldn't do it. And this day the padre couldn't do it, for it was the padre who lay dead at his feet. . . . At his feet, and at the feet of Etherton—the man who had surely killed him.

The padre had died four hours ago, just after Charlie had gone. Tyndall had been far out in his estimate. Charlie had not appeared within the hour. Charlie had not appeared until mid-morning, but when he did come he had the company of three of his kind. A long haul indeed from the Norwegian coast to this, the 10th degree west of longitude, but nothing for these giant Condors—Focke-Wulf 200s—who regularly flew the great dawn to dusk half-circle from Trondheim to Occupied France, round the West Coast of the British Isles.

Condors in company always meant trouble, and these were no exception. They flew directly over the convoy, approaching from astern : the barrage from merchant ships and escorts was intense, and the bombing attack was pressed home with a marked lack of enthusiasm : the Condors bombed from a height of 7,000 feet. In that clear, cold morning air the bombs were in view almost from the moment they cleared the bomb-bays : there was time and to spare to take avoiding action. Almost at once the Condors had broken off the attack and disappeared to the east, impressed, but apparently unharmed, by the warmth of their reception.

In the circumstances, the attack was highly suspicious. Circumspect Charlie might normally be on reconnaissance, but on the rare occasions that he chose to attack he generally did so with courage and determination. The recent sally was just too timorous, the tactics too obviously hopeless. Possibly, of course, recent entrants to the Luftwaffe were given to a discretion so signally lacking in their predecessors, or perhaps they were under strict orders not to risk their valuable craft. But probably, almost certainly, it was thought, that futile attack was only diversionary and the main danger lay elsewhere. The watch over and under the sea was intensified.

Five, ten, fifteen minutes passed and nothing had happened. Radar and Asdic screens remained obstinately clear. Tyndall finally decided that there was no justification for keeping the entire ship's company, so desperately in need of rest, at Action Stations for a moment longer and ordered the stand-down to be sounded.

Normal Defence Stations were resumed. All forenoon work had been cancelled, and officers and ratings off watch, almost to a man, went to snatch what brief sleep they could. But not all. Brooks and Nicholls had their patients to attend to : the Navigator returned to the chart-house : Marshall and his Commissioned Gunner, Mr. Peters, resumed their interrupted routine rounds : and Etherton, nervous, anxious, oversensitive and desperately eager to redeem himself for his share in the Carslake-Ralston episode, remained huddled and watchful in the cold, lonely eyrie of the Director Tower.

The sharp, urgent call from the deck outside came to Marshall and Peters as they were talking to the Leading Wireman in charge of No. 2 Electrical Shop. The shop was on the port side of the fo'c'sle deck cross-passage which ran athwartships for'ard of the wardroom, curving aft round the trunking of " B " turret. Four quick steps had them out of the shop, through the screen door and peering over the side through the freshly falling snow, following the gesticulating finger of an excited marine. Marshall glanced at the man, recognised him immediately : it was Charteris, the only ranker known personally to every officer in the ship— in port, he doubled as wardroom barman.

" What is it, Charteris ? " he demanded. " What are you seeing ? Quickly, man ! "

" There, sir ! Look ! Out there—no, a bit more to your right ! It's—it's a sub, sir, a U-boat ! "

" What ? What's that ? A U-boat ? " Marshall half-turned as the Rev. Winthrop, the padre, squeezed to the rail between himself and Charteris. " Where ? Where it it ? Show me, show me ! "

" Straight ahead, padre. I can see it now—but it's a damned funny shape for a U-boat—if you'll excuse the language," Marshall added hastily. He caught the war-like, un-Christian gleam in Winthrop's eyes, smothered a laugh and peered through the snow at the strange squat shape which had now drifted almost abreast of them.

High up in the Tower, Etherton's restless, hunting eyes had already seen it, even before Charteris. Like Charteris, he immediately thought it was a U-boat caught surfacing in a snow-storm—the pay-off of the attack by the Condors : the thought that Asdic or radar would certainly have picked it up never occurred to him. Time, speed—that was the essence, before it vanished. Unthinkingly, he grabbed the phone to the for'ard multiple pom-pom.

" Director—pom-pom ! " he barked urgently. " U-boat, port 60. Range 100 yards, moving aft. Repeat, port 60. Can you see it ? . . . No, no, port 60—70 now ! " he shouted desperately. " Oh, good, good ! Commence tracking."

" On target, sir," the receiver crackled in his ear.

" Open fire—continuous ! "

" Sir—but, sir—Kingston's not here. He went——"

" Never mind Kingston ! " Etherton shouted furiously. Kingston, he knew, was Captain of the Gun. " Open fire, you fools—now ! I'll take full responsibility." He thrust the phone back on the rest, moved across to the observation panel. . . . Then realisation, sickening, shocking, fear, seared through his mind and he lunged desperately for the phone.

" Belay the last order ! " he shouted wildly. " Cease fire ! Cease fire ! Oh, my God, my God, my God ! " Through the receiver came the staccato, angry bark of the two-pounder. The receiver dropped from his hand, crashed against the bulkhead. It was too late.

It was too late because he had committed the cardinal sin— he had forgotten to order the removal of the muzzle-covers— the metal plates that sealed off the flash-covers of the guns when not in use. And the shells were fused to explode on contact. . . .

The first shell exploded inside its barrel, killing the trainer and seriously wounding the communication number : the other three smashed through their flimsy covers and exploded within a second of each other, a few feet from the faces of the four watchers on the fo'c'sle deck.

All four were untouched, miraculously untouched by the flying, screaming metal. It flew outwards and downwards, a red-hot iron hail sizzling into the sea. But the blast of the explosion was backwards, and the power of even a few pounds of high explosive detonating at arm's length is lethal.

The padre died instantly, Peters and Charteris within seconds, and all from the same cause—telescoped occiputs. The blast hurled them backwards off their feet, as if flung by a giant hand, the backs of their heads smashing to an eggshell pulp against the bulkhead. The blood seeped darkly into the snow, was obliterated in a moment.

Marshall was lucky, fantastically so. The explosion—he said afterwards that it was like getting in the way of the driving piston of the Coronation Scot—flung him through the open door behind him, ripped off the heels of both shoes as they caught on the storm-sill : he braked violently in mid-air, described a complete somersault, slithered along the passage and smashed squarely into the trunking of " B " turret, his back framed by the four big spikes of the butterfly nuts securing an inspection hatch. Had he been standing a foot to the right or the left, had his heels been two inches higher as he catapulted through the doorway, had he hit the turret a hair's-breadth to the left or right—Lieutenant Marshall had no right to be alive. The laws of chance said so, over-whelmingly. As it was, Marshall was now sitting up in the Sick Bay, strapped, broken ribs making breathing painful, but other-wise unharmed.

The upturned lifeboat, mute token of some earlier tragedy on the Russian Convoys, had long since vanished into the white twilight.

Captain Vallery's voice, low and husky, died softly away. He stepped back, closing the Prayer Book, and the forlorn notes of the bugle echoed briefly over the poop and died in the blanketing snow. Men stood silently, unmovingly, as, one by one, the thirteen figures shrouded in weighted canvas slid down the tipped plank, down from under the Union Flag, splashed heavily into the Arctic and were gone. For long seconds, no one moved. The unreal, hypnotic effect of that ghostly ritual of burial held tired, sluggish minds in unwilling thrall, held men oblivious to cold and discomfort. Even when Etherton half-stepped forward, sighed, crumpled down quietly, unspectacularly in the snow, the trance-like hiatus continued. Some ignored him, others glanced his way, incuriously. It seemed absurd, but it struck Nicholls, standing in the background, that they might have stayed there indefinitely, the minds and the blood of men slowing up, coagulating, freezing, while they turned to pillars of ice. Then suddenly, with exacerbating abruptness, the spell was shattered : the strident scream of the Emergency Stations whistle seared through the gathering gloom.

It took Vallery about three minutes to reach the bridge. He rested often, pausing on every second or third step of the four ladders that reached up to the bridge : even so, the climb drained the last reserves of his frail strength. Brooks had to half-carry him through the gate. Vallery clung to the binnacle, fighting for breath through foam-flecked lips ; but his eyes were alive, alert as always, probing through the swirling snow.

"Contact closing, closing : steady on course, interception course : speed unchanged." The radar loudspeaker was muffled, impersonal ; but the calm precise tones of Lieutenant Bowden were unmistakable.

"Good, good ! We'll fox him yet ! " Tyndall, his tired, sagging face lit up in almost beaming anticipation, turned to the Captain. The prospect of action always delighted Tyndall.

"Something coming up from the SSW., Captain. Good God above, man, what are you doing here ? " He was shocked at Vallery's appearance. "Brooks ! Why in heaven's name——?"

"Suppose *you* try talking to him ? " Brooks growled wrathfully. He slammed the gate shut behind him, stalked stiffly off the bridge.

"What's the matter with him ? " Tyndall asked of no one in particular. "What the hell am I supposed to have done ? "

"Nothing, sir," Vallery pacified him. "It's all my fault—disobeying doctor's orders and what have you. You were saying——?"

"Ah, yes. Trouble, I'm afraid, Captain." Vallery smiled secretly as he saw the satisfaction, the pleased anticipation creep back into the Admiral's face. "Radar reports a surface vessel approaching, big, fast, more or less on interception course for us."

"And not ours, of course?" Vallery murmured. He looked up suddenly. "By jove, sir, it couldn't be——"

"The *Tirpitz*?" Tyndall finished for him. He shook his head in decision. "My first thought, too, but no. Admiralty and Air Force are watching her like a broody hen over her eggs. If she moves a foot, we'll know. . . . Probably some heavy cruiser."

"Closing. Closing. Course unaltered." Bowden's voice, clipped, easy, was vaguely reminiscent of a cricket commentator's. "Estimated speed 24, repeat 24 knots."

His voice crackled into silence as the W.T. speaker came to life.

"W.T.—bridge. W.T.—bridge. Signal from convoy: *Stirling*—Admiral. Understood. Wilco. Out."

"Excellent, excellent! From Jeffries," Tyndall explained. "I sent him a signal ordering the convoy to alter course to NNW. That should take 'em well clear of our approaching friend."

Vallery nodded. "How far ahead is the convoy, sir?"

"Pilot!" Tyndall called, and leaned back expectantly.

"Six—six and a half miles." The Kapok Kid's face was expressionless.

"He's slipping," Tyndall said mournfully. "The strain's telling. A couple of days ago he'd have given us the distance to the nearest yard. Six miles—far enough, Captain. He'll never pick 'em up. Bowden says he hasn't even picked us up yet, that the intersection of courses must be pure coincidence. . . . I gather Lieutenant Bowden has a poor opinion of German radar."

"I know. I hope he's right. For the first time the question is of rather more than academic interest." Vallery gazed to the South, his binoculars to his eyes: there was only the sea, the thinning snow. "Anyway, this came at a good time."

Tyndall arched a bushy eyebrow.

"It was strange, down there on the poop." Vallery was hesitant. "There was something weird, uncanny in the air. I didn't like it, sir. It was desperately—well, almost frightening. The snow, the silence, the dead men—thirteen dead men—I can only guess how the men felt, about Etherton, about anything. But it wasn't good—don't know how it would have ended——"

"Five miles," the loudspeaker cut in. "Repeat, five miles. Course, speed constant."

"Five miles," Tyndall repeated in relief. Intangibles bothered him. "Time to trail our coats a little, Captain. We'll soon be in what Bowden reckons is his radar range. Due east, I think—it'll look as if we're covering the tail of the convoy and heading for the North Cape."

"Starboard 10," Vallery ordered. The cruiser came gradually round, met, settled on her new course : engine revolutions were cut down till the *Ulysses* was cruising along at 26 knots.

One minute, five passed, then the loudspeaker blared again.

"Radar—bridge. Constant distance, altering on interception course."

"Excellent ! Really excellent ! " The Admiral was almost purring. "We have him, gentlemen. He's missed the convoy. . . . Commence firing by radar ! "

Vallery reached for the Director handset.

"Director ? Ah, it's you, Courtney . . . good, good . . . you just do that."

Vallery replaced the set, looked across at Tyndall.

"Smart as a whip, that boy. He's had ' X ' and ' Y ' lined up, tracking for the past ten minutes. Just a matter of pressing a button, he says."

"Sounds uncommon like our friends here." Tyndall jerked his head in the direction of the Kapok Kid, then looked up in surprise. "Courtney ? Did you say ' Courtney ' ? Where's Guns ? "

"In his cabin, as far as I know. Collapsed on the poop. Anyway, he's in no fit state to do his job. . . . Thank God I'm not in that boy's shoes. I can imagine . . ."

The *Ulysses* shuddered, and the whip-like crash of " X " turret

drowned Vallery's voice as the 5.25 shells screamed away into the
twilight. Seconds later, the ship shook again as the guns of " Y "
turret joined in. Thereafter the guns fired alternately, one shell
at a time, every half-minute : there was no point in wasting
ammunition when the fall of shot could not be observed ; but
it was probably the bare minimum necessary to infuriate the
enemy and distract his attention from everything except the ship
ahead.

The snow had thinned away now to a filmy curtain of gauze
that blurred, rather than obscured the horizon. To the west, the
clouds were lifting, the sky lightening in sunset. Vallery ordered
" X " turret to cease fire, to load with starshell.

Abruptly, the snow was gone and the enemy was there, big
and menacing, a black, featureless silhouette with the sudden
flush of sunset striking incongruous golden gleams from the
water creaming high at her bows.

" Starboard 30 ! " Vallery snapped. " Full ahead. Smoke-
screen ! " Tyndall nodded compliance. It was no part of his
plan to become embroiled with a German heavy cruiser or pocket
battleship . . . especially at an almost point-blank range of four
miles.

On the bridge, half a dozen pairs of binoculars peered aft,
trying to identify the enemy. But the fore-and-aft silhouette
against the reddening sky was difficult to analyse, exasperatingly
vague and ambiguous. Suddenly, as they watched, white gouts
of flame lanced out from the heart of the silhouette : simultaneously, the starshell burst high up in the air, directly above
the enemy, bathing him in an intense, merciless white glare, so
that he appeared strangely naked and defenceless.

An illusory appearance. Everyone ducked low, in reflex
instinct, as the shells whistled just over their heads and plunged
into the sea ahead. Everyone, that is, except the Kapok Kid. He
bent an impassive eye on the Admiral as the latter slowly
straightened up.

" Hipper Class, sir," he announced. " 10,000 tons, 8-inch
guns, carries aircraft."

Tyndall looked at his unsmiling face in long suspicion. He
cast around in his mind for a suitably crushing reply, caught sight

of the German cruiser's turrets belching smoke in the sinking glare of the starshell.

"My oath !" he exclaimed. "Not wasting much time, are they? And damned good shooting !" he added in professional admiration as the shells hissed into the sea through the *Ulysses's* boiling wake, about 150 feet astern. "Bracketed in the first two salvoes. They'll straddle us next time."

The *Ulysses* was still heeling round, the black smoke beginning to pour from the after funnel, when Vallery straightened, clapped his binoculars to his eyes. Heavy clouds of smoke were mushrooming from the enemy's starboard deck, just for'ard of the bridge.

"Oh, well done, young Courtney !" he burst out. "Well done indeed !"

"Well done indeed !" Tyndall echoed. "A beauty ! Still, I don't think we'll stop to argue the point with them. . . . Ah ! Just in time, gentlemen ! Gad, that was close !" The stern of the *Ulysses*, swinging round now almost to the north, disappeared from sight as a salvo crashed into the sea, dead astern, one of the shells exploding in a great eruption of water.

The next salvo—obviously the hit on the enemy cruiser hadn't affected her fire-power—fell a cable length's astern. The German was now firing blind. Engineer Commander Dodson was making smoke with a vengeance, the oily, black smoke flattening down on the surface of the sea, rolling, thick, impenetrable. Vallery doubled back on course, then headed east at high speed.

For the next two hours, in the dusk and darkness, they played cat and mouse with the "Hipper" class cruiser, firing occasionally, appearing briefly, tantalisingly, then disappearing behind a smoke-screen, hardly needed now in the coming night. All the time, radar was their eyes and their ears and never played them false. Finally, satisfied that all danger to the convoy was gone, Tyndall laid a double screen in a great curving " U," and vanished to the south-west, firing a few final shells, not so much in token of farewell as to indicate direction of departure.

Ninety minutes later, at the end of a giant half-circle to port, the *Ulysses* was sitting far to the north, while Bowden and his men tracked the progress of the enemy. He was reported as moving steadily east, then, just before contact was lost, as altering course to the south-east.

Tyndall climbed down from his chair, numbed and stiff. He stretched himself luxuriantly.

" Not a bad night's work, Captain, not bad at all. What do you bet our friend spends the night circling to the south and east at high speed, hoping to come up ahead of the convoy in the morning ? " Tyndall felt almost jubilant, in spite of his exhaustion. " And by that time FR77 should be 200 miles to the north of him. . . . I suppose, Pilot, you have worked out inter-section courses for rejoining the convoy at all speeds up to a hundred knots ? "

" I think we should be able to regain contact without much difficulty," said the Kapok Kid politely.

" It's when he is at his most modest," Tyndall announced, " that he sickens me most. . . . Heavens above, I'm froze to death. . . . Oh, damn ! Not more trouble, I hope ? "

The communication rating behind the compass platform picked up the jangling phone, listened briefly.

"For you, sir," he said to Vallery. "The Surgeon Lieutenant."

" Just take the message, Chrysler."

" Sorry, sir. Insists on speaking to you himself." Chrysler handed the receiver into the bridge. Vallery smothered an exclamation of annoyance, lifted the receiver to his ear.

" Captain, here. Yes, what is it ? . . . What ? . . . *What!* Oh, God, no ! . . . Why wasn't I told ? . . . Oh, I see. Thank you, thank you."

Vallery handed the receiver back, turned heavily to Tyndall. In the darkness, the Admiral felt, rather than saw the sudden weariness, the hunched defeat of the shoulders.

" That was Nicholls." Vallery's voice was flat, colourless. " Lieutenant Etherton shot himself in his cabin, five minutes ago."

At four o'clock in the morning, in heavy snow, but in a calm sea, the *Ulysses* rejoined the convoy.

By midmorning of that next day, a bare six hours later, Admiral Tyndall had become an old, weary man, haggard, haunted by remorse and bitter self-criticism, close, very close, to despair. Miraculously, in a matter of hours, the chubby cheeks had collapsed in shrunken flaccidity, draining blood had left the florid cheeks a parchment grey, the sunken eyes had dulled in blood and exhaustion. The extent and speed of the change wrought in that tough and jovial sailor, a sailor seemingly impervious to the most deadly vicissitudes of war, was incredible : incredible and disturbing in itself, but infinitely more so in its wholly demoralising effect on the men. To every arch there is but one keystone . . . or so any man must inevitably think.

Any impartial court of judgment would have cleared Tyndall of all guilt, would have acquitted him without a trial. He had done what he thought right, what any commander would have done in his place. But Tyndall sat before the merciless court of his own conscience. He could not forget that it was he who had re-routed the convoy so far to the north, that it was he who had ignored official orders to break straight for the North Cape, that it was exactly on latitude 70 N.—where their Lordships had told him they would be—that FR77 had, on that cold, clear and windless dawn, blundered straight into the heart of the heaviest concentration of U-boats encountered in the Arctic during the entire course of the war.

The wolf-pack had struck at its favourite hour—the dawn— and from its favourite position—the north-east, with the dawn in its eyes. It struck cruelly, skilfully and with a calculated ferocity. Admittedly, the era of Kapitan Leutnant Prien his U-boat long ago sent to the bottom with all hands by the destroyer *Wolverine*—and his illustrious contemporaries, the hey-day of the great U-boat Commanders, the high noon of individual brilliance and great personal gallantry, was gone. But in its place—and generally acknowledged to be even more dangerous, more deadly —were the concerted, highly integrated mass attacks of the wolf-packs, methodical, machine-like, almost reduced to a formula, under a single directing command.

The *Cochella*, third vessel in the port line, was the first to go. Sister ship to the *Vytura* and the *Varella*, also accompanying her in FR77, the *Cochella* carried over 3,000,000 gallons of 100-octane petrol. She was hit by at least three torpedoes : the first two broke her almost in half, the third triggered off a stupendous detonation that literally blew her out of existence. One moment she was there, sailing serenely through the limpid twilight of sunrise : the next moment she was gone. Gone, completely, utterly gone, with only a seething ocean, convulsed in boiling white, to show where she had been : gone, while stunned eardrums and stupefied minds struggled vainly to grasp the significance of what had happened : gone, while blind reflex instinct hurled men into whatever shelter offered as a storm of lethal metal swept over the fleet.

Two ships took the full force of the explosion. A huge mass of metal—it might have been a winch—passed clear through the superstructure of the *Sirrus*, a cable-length away on the starboard : it completely wrecked the radar office. What happened to the other ship immediately astern, the impossibly-named *Tennessee Adventurer*, was not clear, but almost certainly her wheelhouse and bridge had been severely damaged : she had lost steering control, was not under command.

Tragically, this was not at first understood, simply because it was not apparent. Tyndall, recovering fast from the sheer physical shock of the explosion, broke out the signal for an emergency turn to port. The wolf-pack, obviously, lay on the port hand, and the only action to take to minimise further losses, to counter the enemy strategy, was to head straight towards them. He was reasonably sure that the U-boats would be bunched —generally, they strung out only for the slow convoys. Besides, he had adopted this tactic several times in the past with a high degree of success. Finally, it cut the U-boats' target to an impossible tenth, forcing on them the alternative of diving or the risk of being trampled under.

With the immaculate precision and co-ordination of Olympic equestrians, the convoy heeled steadily over to starboard, slewed majestically round, trailing curved, white wakes phosphorescently alive in the near-darkness that still clung to the surface of the sea. Too late, it was seen that the *Tennessee Adventurer* was not under command. Slowly, then with dismaying speed, she came round to the east, angling directly for another merchantman, the *Tobacco Planter*. There was barely time to think, to appreciate the inevitable : frantically, the *Planter's* helm went hard over in an attempt to clear the other astern, but the wildly swinging *Adventurer*, obviously completely out of control, matched the *Planter's* tightening circle, foot by inexorable foot, blind malice at the helm.

She struck the *Planter* with sickening violence just for'ard of the bridge. The *Adventurer's* bows, crumpling as they went, bit deeply into her side, fifteen, twenty feet in a chaos of tearing, rending metal : the stopping power of 10,000 tons deadweight travelling at 15 knots is fantastic. The wound was mortal, and the *Planter's* own momentum, carrying her past, wrenched her free from the lethal bows, opening the wound to the hungry sea and hastened her own end. Almost at once she began to fill, to list heavily to starboard. Aboard the *Adventurer*, someone must have taken over command : her engine stopped, she lay almost motionless alongside the sinking ship, slightly down by the head.

The rest of the convoy cleared the drifting vessels, steadied west by north. Far out on the starboard hand, Commander Orr, in the *Sirrus*, clawed his damaged destroyer round in a violent turn, headed back towards the crippled freighters. He had gone less than half a mile when he was recalled by a vicious signal from the flagship. Tyndall was under no illusions. The *Adventurer*, he knew, might remain there all day, unharmed—it was obvious that the *Planter* would be gone in a matter of minutes—but that would be a guarantee neither of the absence of U boats nor of the sudden access of misguided enemy chivalry : the enemy would be there, would wait to the last possible second before dark in the hope that some rescue destroyer would heave to alongside the *Adventurer*.

In that respect, Tyndall was right. The *Adventurer* was torpedoed just before sunset. Three-quarters of the ship's company escaped in lifeboats, along with twenty survivors picked up from the *Planter*. A month later the frigate *Esher* found them, in three lifeboats tied line ahead, off the bitter, iron coast of Bear Island, heading steadily north. The Captain, alert and upright, was still sitting in the stern-sheets, empty eye-sockets searching for some lost horizon, a withered claw locked to the tiller. The rest were sitting or lying about the boats, one actually standing, his arm cradled around the mast, and all with shrunken sun-blackened lips drawn back in hideous mirth. The log-book lay beside the Captain, empty : all had frozen to death on that first night. The young frigate commander had cast them adrift, watched them disappear over the northern rim of the world, steering for the Barrier. And the Barrier is the region of the great silence, the seas of incredible peace, so peaceful, so calm, so cold that they may be there yet, the dead who cannot rest. A mean and shabby end for the temple of the spirit. . . . It is not known whether the Admiralty approved the action of the captain of the frigate.

But in the major respect, that of anticipating enemy dispositions, the Admiral was utterly wrong. The wolf-pack commander had outguessed him and it was arguable that Tyndall should have foreseen this. His tactic of swinging an entire convoy into the face of a torpedo attack was well known to the enemy : it was also well known that his ship was the *Ulysses*, and the *Ulysses*, the only one of her kind, was familiar, by sight or picture silhouette, to every U-boat commander in the German Navy : and it had been reported, of course, that it was the *Ulysses* that was leading FR77 through to Murmansk. Tyndall should have expected, expected and forestalled the long overdue counter.

For the submarine that had torpedoed the *Cochella* had been the last, not the first, of the pack. The others had lain to the south of the U-boat that had sprung the trap, and well to the west of the track of FR77—clear beyond the reach of Asdic. And when the convoy wheeled to the west, the U-boats lined up leisurely firing tracks as the ships steamed up to cross their bows at right angles. The sea was calm, calm as a millpond, an extraordinarily deep, Mediterranean blue. The snow-squalls of the night had passed away. Far to the south-east a brilliant sun was shouldering itself clear of the horizon, its level rays striking a great band of silver across the Arctic, highlighting the ships, shrouded white in snow, against the darker sea and sky beyond. The conditions were ideal, if one may use the word "ideal" to describe the prologue to a massacre.

Massacre, an almost total destruction there must inevitably have been but for the warning that came almost too late. A warning given neither by radar nor Asdic, nor by any of the magically efficient instruments of modern detection, but simply by the keen eyes of an eighteen-year-old Ordinary Seaman—and the God-sent rays of the rising sun.

"Captain, sir! Captain, sir!" It was young Chrysler who shouted. His voice broke in wild excitement, his eyes were glued to the powerful binoculars clamped on the port searchlight control position. "There's something flashing to the south, sir! It flashed twice—there it goes again!"

"Where, boy?" Tyndall shouted. "Come on, where, where?" In his agitation, Chrysler had forgotten the golden rule of the reporting look-out—bearing must come first.

"Port 50, sir—no, port 60. . . . I've lost sight of it now, sir."

Every pair of glasses on the bridge swung round on the given bearing. There was nothing to be seen, just nothing at all. Tyndall shut his telescope slowly, shrugging shoulders eloquent in disbelief.

"Maybe there *is* something," said the Kapok Kid doubtfully. "How about the sea catching a periscope making a quick circle sweep?"

Tyndall looked at him, silent, expressionless, looked away, stared straight ahead. To the Kapok Kid he seemed strange, different. His face was set, stonily impassive, the face of a man with twenty ships and 5,000 lives in his keeping, the face of a man who has already made one wrong decision too many.

"There they go again!" Chrysler screamed. "Two flashes —no, *three* flashes!" He was almost beside himself with excitement, literally dancing in an agony of frustration. "I did see them, sir, I *did*. I *did*. Oh, please, sir, please!"

Tyndall had swung round again. Ten long seconds he gazed at Chrysler, who had left his binoculars, and was gripping the gate in gauntleted hands, shaking it in anguished appeal. Abruptly, Tyndall made up his mind.

"Hard aport, Captain. Bentley—the signal!"

Slowly, on the unsupported word of an eighteen-year-old, FR77 came round to the south, slowly, just too slowly. Suddenly, the sea was alive with running torpedoes—three, five, ten— Vallery counted thirty in as many seconds. They were running shallow and their bubbling trails, evil, ever-lengthening, rose swiftly to the surface and lay there milkily on the glassy sea, delicately evanescent shafts for arrowheads so lethal. Parallel in the centre, they fanned out to east and west to embrace the entire convoy. It was a fantastic sight : no man in that convoy had ever seen anything remotely like it.

In a moment the confusion was complete. There was no time for signals. It was every ship for itself in an attempt to avoid wholesale destruction : and confusion was worse confounded by the ships in the centre and outer lines, that had not yet seen the wakes of the streaking torpedoes.

Escape for all was impossible : the torpedoes were far too closely bunched. The cruiser *Stirling* was the first casualty. Just when she seemed to have cleared all danger—she was far ahead where the torpedoes were thickest—she lurched under some unseen hammer-blow, slewed round crazily and steamed away back to the east, smoke hanging heavily over her poop. The *Ulysses*, brilliantly handled, heeled over on maximum rudder and under the counter-thrusting of her great screws, slid down an impossibly narrow lane between four torpedoes, two of them racing by a bare boat's length from either side : she was still a lucky ship. The destroyers, fast, highly manœuvreable, impeccably handled, bobbed and weaved their way to safety with almost contemptuous ease, straightened up and headed south under maximum power.

The merchant ships, big, clumsy, relatively slow, were less fortunate. Two ships in the port line, a tanker and a freighter, were struck : miraculously, both just staggered under the numbing shock, then kept on coming. Not so the big freighter immediately behind them, her holds crammed with tanks, her decks lined with them. She was torpedoed three times in three seconds : there was no smoke, no fire, no spectacular after-explosion : sieved and ripped from stern to stem, she sank quickly, quietly, still on even keel, dragged down by the sheer weight of metal. No one below decks had even the slightest chance of escaping.

A merchantman in the centre line, the *Belle Isle*, was torpedoed amidships. There were two separate explosions—probably she had been struck twice—and she was instantly on fire. Within seconds, the list to port was pronounced, increasing momentarily : gradually her rails dipped under, the outslung lifeboats almost touching the surface of the sea. A dozen, fifteen men were seen to be slipping, sliding down the sheering decks and hatch-covers, already half-submerged, towards the nearest lifeboat. Desperately they hacked at belly-band securing ropes, piled into the lifeboat in grotesquely comical haste, pushed it clear of the dipping davits, seized the oars and pulled frantically away. From beginning to end, hardly a minute had elapsed.

Half a dozen powerful strokes had them clear beyond their ship's counter : two more took them straight under the swinging bows of the *Walter A. Baddeley*, her companion tank-carrier in the starboard line. The consummate seamanship that had saved the *Baddeley* could do nothing to save the lifeboat : the little boat crumpled and splintered like a matchwood toy, catapulting screaming men into the icy sea.

As the big, grey hull of the *Baddeley* slid swiftly by them, they struck out with insane strength that made nothing of their heavy Arctic clothing. At such times, reason vanishes : the thought that if, by some God-given miracle, they were to escape the guillotine of the *Baddeley's* single great screw, they would do so only to die minutes later in the glacial cold of the Arctic, never occurred to them. But, as it happened, death came by neither metal nor cold. They were still struggling, almost abreast the poop, vainly trying to clear the rushing, sucking vortex of water, when the torpedoes struck the *Baddeley*, close together and simultaneously, just for'ard of the rudder.

For swimming men who have been in the close vicinity of an underwater high explosion there can be no shadow of hope : the effect is inhuman, revolting, shocking beyond conception : in such cases, experienced doctors, pathologists even, can with difficulty bring themselves to look upon what were once human beings. . . . But for these men, as so often in the Arctic, death was kind, for they died unknowing.

The *Walter A. Baddeley's* stern had been almost completely blown off. Hundreds of tons of water were already rushing in the great, gaping hole below the counter, racing through cross-bulkheads fractured by the explosion, smashing open engine-boiler room watertight doors buckled by the blast, pulling her down by the stern, steadily, relentlessly, till her taffrail dipped salute to the waiting Arctic. For a moment, she hung there. Then, in quick succession from deep inside the hull, came a muffled explosion, the ear-shattering, frightening roar of escaping high-pressure steam and the thunderous crash of massive boilers rending away from their stools as the ship upended. Almost immediately the shattered stern lurched heavily, sunk lower and lower till the poop was completely gone, till the dripping forefoot was tilted high above the sea. Foot by foot the angle of tilt increased, the stern plunged a hundred, two hundred feet under the surface of the sea, the bows rearing almost as high against the blue of the sky, buoyed up by half a million cubic feet of trapped air.

The ship was exactly four degrees off the vertical when the end came. It was possible to establish this angle precisely, for it was just at that second, half a mile away aboard the *Ulysses*, that the shutter clicked, the shutter of the camera in Lieutenant Nicholls's gauntleted hands.

A camera that captured an unforgettable picture—a stark, simple picture of a sinking ship almost vertically upright against a pale-blue sky. A picture with a strange lack of detail, with the exception only of two squat shapes, improbably suspended in mid-air : these were 30-ton tanks, broken loose from their fore-deck lashings, caught in midflight as they smashed down on the bridge structure, awash in the sea. In the background was the stern of the *Belle Isle*, the screw out of the water, the Red Duster trailing idly in the peaceful sea.

Bare seconds after the camera had clicked, the camera was blown from Nicholls's hands, the case crumpling against a bulkhead, the lens shattering but the film still intact. Panic-stricken the seamen in the lifeboat may have been, but it wasn't un-reasoning panic : in No. 2 hold, just for'ard of the fire, the *Belle Isle* had been carrying over 1,000 tons of tank ammunition. . . . Broken cleanly in two, she was gone inside a minute : the *Baddeley's* bows, riddled by the explosion, slid gently down behind her.

The echoes of the explosion were still rolling out over the sea in ululating diminuendo when they were caught up and flung back by a series of muffled reports from the South. Less than two miles away, the *Sirrus*, *Vectra* and *Viking*, dazzling white in the morning sun, were weaving a crazily intricate pattern over the sea, depth-charges cascading from either side of their poop-decks. From time to time, one or other almost disappeared behind towering mushrooms of erupting water and spray, reappearing magically as the white columns fell back into the sea.

To join in the hunt, to satisfy the flaming, primitive lust for revenge—that was Tyndall's first impulse. The Kapok Kid looked at him furtively and wondered, wondered at the hunched rigidity, the compressed lipless mouth, the face contorted in white and bitter rage—a bitterness directed not least against himself. Tyndall twisted suddenly in his seat.

" Bentley! Signal the *Stirling*—ascertain damage." The *Stirling* was more than a mile astern now, but coming round fast, her speed at least twenty knots.

" Making water after engine-room," Bentley read eventually. " Store-rooms flooded, but hull damage slight. Under control. Steering gear jammed. On emergency steering. Am all right."

" Thank God for that! Signal, 'Take over: proceed east.' Come on, Captain, let's give Orr a hand to deal with these murdering hounds! "

The Kapok Kid looked at him in sudden dismay.

" Sir! "

" Yes, yes, Pilot! What is it? " Tyndall was curt, impatient.

" How about that first U-boat? " Carpenter ventured. " Can't be much more than a mile to the north, sir. Shouldn't we—— ? "

" God Almighty! " Tyndall swore. His face was suffused with anger. " Are you trying to tell me . . .? " He broke off abruptly, stared at Carpenter for a long moment. " What did you say, Pilot? "

" The boat that sunk the tanker, sir," the Kapok Kid said carefully. " She could have reloaded by now and she's in a perfect position—— "

" Of course, of course," Tyndall muttered. He passed a hand across his eyes, flickered a glance at Vallery. The Captain had his

head averted. Again the hand passed across the tired eyes.
" You're quite right, Pilot, quite right." He paused, then smiled.
" As usual, damn you ! "

The *Ulysses* found nothing to the north. The U-boat that had
sunk the *Cochella* and sprung the trap had wisely decamped. While
they were quartering the area, they heard the sound of gunfire,
saw the smoke erupting from the *Sirrus's* 4.7s.

" Ask him what all the bloody fuss is about," Tyndall demanded irritably. The Kapok Kid smiled secretly : the old man
had life in him yet.

" *Vectra* and *Viking* damaged, probably destroyed U-boat," the
message read. " *Vectra* and self sunk surfaced boat. How about
you ? "

" How about you ! " Tyndall exploded. " Damn his confounded insolence ! How about you ? He'll have the oldest,
bloody minesweeper in Scapa for his next command. . . . This
is all your fault, Pilot ! "

" Yes, sir. Sorry, sir. Maybe he's only asking in a spirit of—
ah—anxious concern."

" How would you like to be his Navigator in his next command ? " said Tyndall dangerously. The Kapok Kid retired to
his charthouse.

" Carrington ! "

" Sir ? " The First Lieutenant was his invariable self, clear-
eyed, freshly shaven, competent, alert. The sallow skin—hallmark of all men who have spent too many years under tropical
suns—was unshadowed by fatigue. He hadn't slept for three
days.

" What do you make of that ? " He pointed to the north-
west. Curiously woolly grey clouds were blotting out the
horizon ; before them the sea dusked to indigo under wandering
catspaws from the north.

" Hard to say, sir," Carrington said slowly. " Not heavy
weather, that's certain. . . . I've seen this before, sir—low,
twisting cloud blowing up on a fine morning with a temperature
rise. Very common in the Aleutians and the Bering Sea, sir—
and there it means fog, heavy mist."

" And you, Captain ? "

"No idea, sir." Vallery shook his head decisively. The plasma transfusion seemed to have helped him. "New to me—never seen it before."

"Thought not," Tyndall grunted. "Neither have I—that's why I asked Number One first. . . . If you think it's fog that's coming up, Number One, let me know, will you? Can't afford to have convoy and escorts scattered over half the Arctic if the weather closes down. Although, mind you," he added bitterly, "I think they'd be a damned sight safer without us!"

"I can tell you now, sir." Carrington had that rare gift—the ability to make a confident, quietly unarguable assertion without giving the slightest offence. "It's fog."

"Fair enough." Tyndall never doubted him. "Let's get the hell out of it. Bentley—signal the destroyers : ' Break off engagement. Rejoin convoy.' And Bentley—add the word ' Immediate.' " He turned to Vallery. "For Commander Orr's benefit."

Within the hour, merchant ships and escorts were on station again, on a north-east course at first to clear any further packs on latitude 70. To the south-east, the sun was still bright : but the first thick, writhing tendrils of the mist, chill and dank, were already swirling round the convoy. Speed had been reduced to six knots : all ships were streaming fog-buoys.

Tyndall shivered, climbed stiffly from his chair as the stand-down sounded. He passed through the gate, stopped in the passage outside. He laid a glove on Chrysler's shoulder, kept it there as the boy turned round in surprise.

"Just wanted a squint at these eyes of yours, laddie," he smiled. "We owe them a lot. Thank you very much—we will not forget." He looked a long time into the young face, forgot his own exhaustion and swore softly in sudden compassion as he saw the red-rimmed eyes, the white, macilated cheeks stained with embarrassed pleasure.

"How old are you, Chrysler?" he asked abruptly.

"Eighteen, sir . . . in two days' time." The soft West Country voice was almost defiant.

"He'll be eighteen—in two days' time!" Tyndall repeated slowly to himself. "Good God! Good God above!" He dropped his hand, walked wearily aft to the shelter, entered, closed the door behind him.

"He'll be eighteen—in two days' time," he repeated, like a man in a daze.

Vallery propped himself up on the settee. "Who? Young Chrysler?"

Tyndall nodded unhappily.

"I know." Vallery was very quiet. "I know how it is. . . . He did a fine job to-day."

Tyndall sagged down in a chair. His mouth twisted in bitterness.

"The only one. . . . Dear God, what a mess!" He drew heavily on a cigarette, stared down at the floor. "Ten green bottles, hanging on a wall," he murmured absently.

"I beg your pardon, sir?"

"Fourteen ships left Scapa, eighteen St. John—the two components of FR77," Tyndall said softly. "Thirty-two ships in all. And now"—he paused—"now there are seventeen—and three of these damaged. I'm counting the *Tennessee Adventurer* as a dead duck." He swore savagely. "Hell's teeth, how I hate leaving ships like that, sitting targets for any murdering . . ." He stopped short, drew on his cigarette again, deeply. "Doing wonderfully, amn't I?"

"Ah, nonsense, sir!" Vallery interrupted, impatient, almost angry. "It wasn't any fault of yours that the carriers had to return."

"Meaning that the rest was my fault?" Tyndall smiled faintly, lifted a hand to silence the automatic protest. "Sorry, Dick, I know you didn't mean that—but it's true, it's true. Six merchant boys gone in ten minutes—six! And we shouldn't have lost one of them." Head bent, elbows on knees, he screwed the heels of his palms into exhausted eyes. "Rear-Admiral Tyndall, master strategist," he went on softly. "Alters convoy course to run smack into a heavy cruiser, alters it again to run straight into the biggest wolf-pack I've ever known—and just where the Admiralty said they would be. . . . No matter what old Starr does to me when I get back, I've no kick coming. Not now, not after this."

He rose heavily to his feet. The light of the single lamp caught his face. Vallery was shocked at the change.

" Where to, now, sir ? " he asked.

" The bridge. No, no, stay where you are, Dick." He tried to smile, but the smile was a grimace that flickered only to die. " Leave me in peace while I ponder my next miscalculation."

He opened the door, stopped dead as he heard the unmistakable whistling of shells close above, heard the E.A.S. signal screaming urgently through the fog. Tyndall turned his head slowly, looked back into the shelter.

" It looks," he said bitterly, " as if I've already made it."

CHAPTER NINE

FRIDAY MORNING

THE FOG, Tyndall saw, was all around them now. Since that last heavy snowfall during the night, the temperature had risen steadily, quickly. But it had beguiled only to deceive : the clammy, icy feathers of the swirling mist now struck doubly chill.

He hurried through the gate, Vallery close behind him. Turner, steel helmet trailing, was just leaving for the After Tower. Tyndall stretched out his hand, stopped him.

" What is it, Commander ? " he demanded. " Who fired ? Where ? Where did it come from ? "

" I don't know, sir. Shells came from astern, more or less. But I've a damned good idea who it is." His eyes rested on the Admiral a long, speculative moment. " Our friend of last night is back again." He turned abruptly, hurried off the bridge.

Tyndall looked after him, perplexed, uncomprehending. Then he swore, softly, savagely, and jumped for the radar handset.

" Bridge. Admiral speaking. Lieutenant Bowden at once ! " The loudspeaker crackled into immediate life.

" Bowden speaking, sir."

" What the devil are you doing down there ? " Tyndall's voice was low, vicious. " Asleep, or what ? We are being attacked, Lieutenant Bowden. By a surface craft. This may be news to you." He broke off, ducked low as another salvo screamed overhead and crashed into the water less than half a mile ahead : the spray cascaded over the decks of a merchantman, glimpsed momentarily in a clear lane between two rolling fog-banks. Tyndall straightened up quickly, snarled into the mouth-piece. " He's got our range, and got it accurately. In God's name, Bowden, where is he ? "

" Sorry, sir." Bowden was cool, unruffled. " We can't seem to pick him up. We still have the *Adventurer* on our screens, and there appears to be a very slight distortion on his bearing, sir—approximately 300. . . . I suggest the enemy ship is still screened by the *Adventurer* or, if she's closer, is on the *Adventurer's* direct bearing."

" How near ? " Tyndall barked.

" Not near, sir. Very close to the *Adventurer*. We can't distinguish either by size or distance."

Tyndall dangled the transmitter from his hand. He turned to Vallery.

" Does Bowden really expect me to believe that yarn ? " he asked angrily. " A million to one coincidence like that—an enemy ship accidentally chose and holds the only possible course to screen her from our radar. Fantastic ! "

Vallery looked at him, his face without expression.

" Well ? " Tyndall was impatient. " Isn't it ? "

" No, sir," Vallery answered quietly. " It's not. Not really. And it wasn't accidental. The U-pack would have radioed her, given our bearing and course. The rest was easy."

Tyndall gazed at him through a long moment of comprehension, screwed his eyes shut and shook his head in short fierce jerks. It was a gesture compounded of self-criticism, the death of disbelief, the attempt to clear a woolly, exhausted mind. Hell, a six-year-old could have seen that. . . . A shell whistled into the sea a bare fifty yards to port. Tyndall didn't flinch, might never have seen or heard it.

" Bowden ? " He had the transmitter to his mouth again.

" Sir ? "

" Any change in the screen ? "

" No, sir. None."

" And are you still of the same opinion ? "

" Yes, sir ? Can't be anything else."

" And close to the *Adventurer*, you say ? "

" Very close, I would say."

" But, good God, man, the *Adventurer* must be ten miles astern by now ! "

" Yes, sir. I know. So is the bandit."

" What ! Ten miles ! But, but——"

" He's firing by radar, sir," Bowden interrupted. Suddenly the metallic voice sounded tired. " He must be. He's also tracking by radar, which is why he's keeping himself in line with our bearing on the *Adventurer*. And he's extremely accurate. . . . I'm afraid, Admiral, that his radar is at least as good as ours."

The speaker clicked off. In the sudden strained silence on the bridge, the crash of breaking ebonite sounded unnaturally loud as the transmitter slipped from Tyndall's hand, fractured in a hundred pieces. The hand groped forward, he clutched at a steam pipe as if to steady himself. Vallery stepped towards him, arms outstretched in concern, but Tyndall brushed by unseeingly. Like an old spent man, like a man from whose ancient bones and muscles all the pith has long since drained, he shuffled slowly across the bridge, oblivious of a dozen mystified eyes, dragged himself up on to his high stool.

You fool, he told himself, bitterly, savagely, oh, you bloody old fool ! He would never forgive himself, never, never, never ! All along the line he had been out-thought, out-guessed and out-manœuvred by the enemy. They had taken him for a ride, made an even bigger bloody fool out of him than his good Maker had ever intended. Radar ! Of course, that was it ! The blind assumption that German radar had remained the limited, elementary thing that Admiralty and Air Force Intelligence had reported it to be last year ! Radar—and as good as the British. As good as the *Ulysses's*—and everybody had believed that the *Ulysses* was incomparably the most efficient—indeed the only efficient—radar ship in the world. As good as our own—probably a damned sight better. But had the thought ever occurred to him ? Tyndall writhed in sheer chagrin, in agony of spirit, and knew the bitter taste of self-loathing. And so, this morning, the pay-off : six ships, three hundred men gone to the bottom. May God forgive you, Tyndall, he thought dully, may God forgive you. You sent them there. . . . Radar !

Last night, for instance. When the *Ulysses* had been laying a false trail to the east, the German cruiser had obligingly tagged behind, the perfect foil to his, Tyndall's genius. Tyndall groaned in mortification. Had tagged behind, firing wildly, erratically each time the *Ulysses* had disappeared behind a smoke-screen. Had done so to conceal the efficiency of her radar, to conceal the fact that, during the first half-hour at least, she must have been tracking the escaping convoy as it disappeared to the NNW.— a process made all the easier by the fact that he, Tyndall, had expressly forbidden the use of the zig-zag !

And then, when the *Ulysses* had so brilliantly circled, first to the south and then to the north again, the enemy must have had her on his screen—constantly. And later, the biter bit with a vengeance, the faked enemy withdrawal to the south-east. Almost certainly, he, too, had circled to the north again, picked up the disappearing British cruiser on the edge of his screen, worked out her intersection course as a cross check on the convoy's, and radioed ahead to the wolf-pack, positioning them almost to the foot.

And now, finally, the last insult, the last galling blow to whatever shattered remnants of his pride were left him. The enemy had opened fire at extreme range, but with extreme accuracy—a dead give-away to the fact that the firing was radar-controlled. And the only reason for it must be the enemy's conviction that the *Ulysses*, by this time, must have come to the inevitable conclusion that the enemy was equipped with a highly-sensitive radar transmitter. The inevitable conclusion ! Tyndall had never even begun to suspect it. Slowly, oblivious to the pain, he pounded his fist on the edge of the windscreen. God, what a blind, crazily stupid fool he'd been ! Six ships, three hundred men. Hundreds of tanks and planes, millions of gallons of fuel lost to Russia : how many more thousands of dead Russians, soldiers and civilians, did that represent ? And the broken, sorrowing families, he thought incoherently, families throughout the breadth of Britain : the telegram boys cycling to the little houses in the Welsh valleys, along the wooded lanes of Surrey, to the lonely reek of the peat-fire, remote in the Western Isles, to the lime-washed cottages of Donegal and Antrim : the empty homes across the great reaches of the New World, from Newfoundland and Maine to the far slopes of the Pacific. These families would never know that it was he, Tyndall, who had so criminally squandered the lives of husbands, brothers, sons—and that was worse than no consolation at all.

" Captain Vallery ? " Tyndall's voice was only a husky whisper. Vallery crossed over, stood beside him, coughing painfully as the swirling fog caught nose and throat, lancinated inflamed lungs. It was a measure of Tyndall's distressed pre-occupation that Vallery's obvious suffering quite failed to register.

" Ah, there you are. Captain, this enemy cruiser must be destroyed."

Vallery nodded heavily. " Yes, sir. How ? "

" How ? " Tyndall's face, framed in the moisture-beaded hood of his duffel, was haggard and grey : but he managed to raise a ghost of a smile. " As well hung for a sheep. . . . I propose to detach the escorts—including ourselves—and nail him." He stared out blindly into the fog, his mouth bitter. " A simple tactical exercise—maybe within even my limited compass." He broke off suddenly, stared over the side then ducked hurriedly : a shell had exploded in the water—a rare thing—only yards away, erupting spray showering down on the bridge.

" We—the *Stirling* and ourselves—will take him from the south," he continued, " soak up his fire and radar. Orr and his death-or-glory boys will approach from the north. In this fog, they'll get very close before releasing their torpedoes. Conditions are all against a single ship—he shouldn't have much chance."

" All the escorts," Vallery said blankly. " You propose to detach *all* the escorts ? "

" That's exactly what I propose to do, Captain."

" But—but—perhaps that's exactly what he wants," Vallery protested.

" Suicide ? A glorious death for the Fatherland ? Don't you believe it ! " Tyndall scoffed. " That sort of thing went out with Langesdorff and Middelmann."

" No, sir ! " Vallery was impatient. " He wants to pull us off, to leave the convoy uncovered."

" Well, what of it ? " Tyndall demanded. " Who's going to find them in this lot ? " He waved an arm at the rolling, twisting fog-banks. "Dammit, man, if it weren't for their fog-buoys, even our ships couldn't see each other. So I'm damned sure no one else could either."

"No?" Vallery countered swiftly. "How about another German cruiser fitted with radar? Or even another wolf-pack? Either could be in radio contact with our friend astern—and he's got our course to the nearest minute!"

"In radio contact? Surely to God our W.T. is monitoring all the time?"

"Yes, sir. They are. But I'm told it's not so easy on the V.H.F. ranges."

Tyndall grunted non-committally, said nothing. He felt desperately tired and confused; he had neither the will nor the ability to pursue the argument further. But Vallery broke in on the silence, the vertical lines between his eyebrows etched deep with worry.

"And why's our friend sitting steadily on our tails, pumping the odd shell among us, unless he's concentrating on driving us along a particular course? It reduces his chance of a hit by 90 per cent—and cuts out half his guns."

"Maybe he's expecting us to reason like that, to see the obvious." Tyndall was forcing himself to think, to fight his way through a mental fog no less nebulous and confusing than the dank mist that swirled around him. "Perhaps he's hoping to panic us into altering course—to the north, of course—where a U-pack *may* very well be."

"Possible, possible," Vallery conceded. "On the other hand, he may have gone a step further. Maybe he wants us to be too clever for our own good. Perhaps he expects us to see the obvious, to avoid it, to continue on our present course—and so do exactly what he wants us to do. . . . He's no fool, sir—we know that now."

What was it that Brooks had said to Starr back in Scapa, a lifetime ago? "That fine-drawn feeling . . . that exquisite agony . . . every cell in the brain stretched taut to breaking point, pushing you over the screaming edge of madness." Tyndall wondered dully how Brooks could have known, could have been so damnably accurate in his description. Anyway, he knew now, knew what it was to stand on the screaming edge. . . . Tyndall appreciated dimly that he was at the limit. That aching, muzzy forehead where to think was to be a blind man wading through a sea of molasses. Vaguely he realised that this must be the first —or was it the last?—symptom of a nervous breakdown. . . . God only knew there had been plenty of them aboard the *Ulysses* during the past months. . . . But he was still the Admiral. . . . He must *do* something, *say* something.

"It's no good guessing, Dick," he said heavily. Vallery looked at him sharply—never before had old Giles called him anything but "Captain" on the bridge. "And we've got to do something. We'll leave the *Vectra* as a sop to our consciences. No more." He smiled wanly. "We must have at least two destroyers for the dirty work. Bentley—take this signal for W.T. 'To all escort vessels and Commodore Fletcher on the *Cape Hatteras* . . .'"

Within ten minutes, the four warships, boring south-east through the impenetrable wall of fog, had halved the distance that lay between them and the enemy. The *Stirling, Viking* and *Sirrus* were in constant radio communication with the *Ulysses*— they had to be, for they travelled as blind men in an invious world of grey and she was their eyes and their ears.

"Radar—bridge. Radar—bridge." Automatically, every eye swung round, riveted on the loudspeaker. "Enemy altering course to south: increasing speed."

"Too late!" Tyndall shouted hoarsely. His fists were clenched, his eyes alight with triumph. "He's left it too late!"

Vallery said nothing. The seconds ticked by, the *Ulysses* knifed her way through cold fog and icy sea. Suddenly, the loudspeaker called again.

"Enemy 180° turn. Heading south-east. Speed 28 knots."

"28 knots? He's on the run!" Tyndall seemed to have gained a fresh lease on life. "Captain, I propose that the *Sirrus* and *Ulysses* proceed south-east at maximum speed, engage and slow the enemy. Ask W.T. to signal Orr. Ask Radar enemy's course."

He broke off, waited impatiently for the answer.

"Radar—bridge. Course 312. Steady on course. Repeat, steady on course."

"Steady on course," Tyndall echoed. "Captain, commence firing by radar. We have him, we have him ! " he cried exultantly. "He's waited too long ! We have him, Captain ! "

Again Vallery said nothing. Tyndall looked at him, half in perplexity, half in anger. "Well, don't you agree ? "

"I don't know, sir." Vallery shook his head doubtfully. "I don't know at all. Why did he wait so long ? Why didn't he turn and run the minute we left the convoy ? "

"Too damn' sure of himself ! " Tyndall growled.

"Or too sure of something else," Vallery said slowly. "Maybe he wanted to make good and sure that we *would* follow him."

Tyndall growled again in exasperation, made to speak then lapsed into silence as the *Ulysses* shuddered from the recoil of " A " turret. For a moment, the billowing fog on the fo'c'sle cleared, atomised by the intense heat and cordite generated by the exploding cordite. In seconds, the grey shroud had fallen once more.

Then, magically, it was clear again. A heavy fog-bank had rolled over them, and through a gap in the next they caught a glimpse of the *Sirrus*, dead on the beam, a monstrous bone in her teeth, scything to the south-east at something better than 34 knots. The *Stirling* and the *Viking* were already lost in the fog astern.

"He's too close," Tyndall snapped. "Why didn't Bowden tell us ? We can't bracket the enemy this way. Signal the *Sirrus* : ' Steam 317 five minutes.' Captain, same for us. 5 south, then back on course."

He had hardly sunk back in his chair, and the *Ulysses*, mist-shrouded again, was only beginning to answer her helm when the W.T. loudspeaker switched on.

"W.T.—bridge. W.T.—bridge——"

The twin 5.25s of " B " turret roared in deafening unison, flame and smoke lancing out through the fog. Simultaneously, a tremendous crash and explosion heaved up the duckboards beneath the feet of the men in the bridge, catapulting them all ways, into each other, into flesh-bruising, bone-breaking metal, into the dazed confusion of numbed minds and bodies fighting to reorientate themselves under the crippling handicap of stunning shock, of eardrums rended by the blast, of throat and nostrils stung by acrid fumes, of eyes blinded by dense black smoke. Throughout it all, the calm impersonal voice of the W.T. transmitter repeated its unintelligible message.

Gradually the smoke cleared away. Tyndall pulled himself drunkenly to his feet by the rectifying arm of the binnacle : the explosion had blown him clean out of his chair into the centre of the compass platform. He shook his head, dazed, uncomprehending. Must be tougher than he'd imagined : all that way—and he couldn't remember bouncing. And that wrist, now—that lay over at a damned funny angle. His own wrist, he realised with mild surprise. Funny, it didn't hurt a bit. And Carpenter's face there, rising up before him : the bandages were blown off, the gash received on the night of the great storm gaping wide again, the face masked with blood. . . . That girl at Henley, the one he was always talking about—Tyndall wondered, inconsequentially, what she would say if she saw him now. . . . Why doesn't the W.T. transmitter stop that insane yammering ? . . . Suddenly, his mind was clear.

"My God ! Oh, God ! " He stared in disbelief at the twisted duckboards, the fractured asphalt beneath his feet. He released his grip on the binnacle, lurched forward into the windscreen : his sense of balance had confirmed what his eyes had rejected : the whole compass platform tilted forward at an angle of 15 degrees.

"What is it, Pilot ? " His voice was hoarse, strained, foreign even to himself. "In God's name, what's happened ? A breech explosion in ' B ' turret ? "

"No, sir." Carpenter drew his forearm across his eyes : the kapok sleeve came away covered in blood. "A direct hit, sir—smack in the superstructure."

"He's right, sir." Carrington had hoisted himself far over the windscreen, was peering down intently. Even at that moment, Tyndall marvelled at the man's calmness, his almost inhuman control. "And a heavy one. It's wrecked the for'ard pom-pom and there's a hole the size of a door just below us. . . . It must be pretty bad inside, sir."

Tyndall scarcely heard the last words. He was kneeling over Vallery, cradling his head in his one good arm. The Captain lay crumpled against the gate, barely conscious, his stertorous breathing interrupted by rasping convulsions as he choked on his own blood. His face was deathly white.

" Get Brooks up here, Chrysler—the Surgeon Commander, I mean ! " Tyndall shouted. " At once ! "

" W.T.—bridge. W.T.—bridge. Please acknowledge. Please acknowledge." The voice was hurried, less impersonal, anxiety evident even in its metallic anonymity.

Chrysler replaced the receiver, looked worriedly at the Admiral.

" Well ? " Tyndall demanded. " Is he on his way ? "

" No reply, sir." The boy hesitated. " I think the line's gone."

" Hell's teeth ! " Tyndall roared. " What are you doing standing there, then ? Go and get him. Take over, Number One, will you ? Bentley—have the Commander come to the bridge."

" W.T.—bridge. W.T.—bridge." Tyndall glared up at the speaker in exasperation, then froze into immobility as the voice went on. " We have been hit aft. Damage Control reports coding-room destroyed. Number 6 and 7 Radar Offices destroyed. Canteen wrecked. After control tower severely damaged."

" The After control tower ! " Tyndall swore, pulled off his gloves, wincing at the agony of his broken hand. Carefully, he pillowed Vallery's head on the gloves, rose slowly to his feet. " The After Tower ! And Turner's there ! I hope to God . . ."

He broke off, made for the after end of the bridge at a stumbling run. Once there he steadied himself, his hand on the ladder rail, and peered apprehensively aft.

At first he could see nothing, not even the after funnel and mainmast. The grey, writhing fog was too dense, too maddeningly opaque. Then suddenly, for a mere breath of time, an icy catspaw cleared away the mist, cleared away the dark, convoluted smoke-pall above the after superstructure. Tyndall's hand tightened convulsively on the rail, the knuckles whitening to ivory.

The after superstructure had disappeared. In its place was a crazy mass of jumbled, twisted steel, with "X" turret, normally invisible from the bridge, showing up clearly beyond, apparently unharmed. But the rest was gone—radar offices, coding-room, police office, canteen, probably most of the after galley. Nothing, nobody could have survived there. Miraculously, the truncated mainmast still stood, but immediately aft of it, perched crazily on top of this devil's scrapheap, the After Tower, fractured and grotesquely askew, lay over at an impossible angle of 60°, its range-finder gone. And Commander Turner had been in there. . . . Tyndall swayed dangerously on top of the steep ladder, shook his head again to fight off the fog clamping down on his mind. There was a heavy, peculiarly dull ache just behind his forehead, and the fog seemed to be spreading from there. . . . A lucky ship, they called the *Ulysses*. Twenty months on the worst run and in the worst waters in the world and never a scratch. . . . But Tyndall had always known that some time, some place, her luck would run out.

He heard hurried steps clattering up the steel ladder, forced his blurred eyes to focus themselves. He recognised the dark, lean face at once : it was Leading Signalman Davies, from the flag deck. His face was white, his breathing short and quick. He opened his mouth to speak, then checked himself, his eyes staring at the handrail.

"Your hand, sir ! " He switched his startled gaze from the rail to Tyndall's eyes. "Your hand ! You've no gloves on, sir ! "

"No ? " Tyndall looked down as if faintly astonished he had a hand. "No, I haven't, have I ? Thank you, Davies." He pulled his hand off the smooth frozen steel, glanced incuriously at the raw, bleeding flesh. "It doesn't matter. What is it, boy ? "

"The Fighter Direction Room, sir ! " Davies's eyes were dark with remembered horror. "The shell exploded in there. It's—it's just gone, sir. And the Plot above . . ." He stopped short, his jerky voice lost in the crash of the guns of "A" turret. Somehow it seemed strangely unnatural that the main armament still remained effective. "I've just come from the F.D.R. and the Plot, sir," Davies continued, more calmly now. "They— well, they never had a chance."

" Including Commander Westcliffe ? " Dimly, Tyndall realised the futility of clutching at straws.

"I don't know, sir. It's—it's just bits and pieces in the F.D.R., if you follow me. But if he was there——"

" He would be," Tyndall interrupted heavily. " He never left it during Actions Stations . . ."

He stopped abruptly, broken hands clenching involuntarily as the high-pitched scream and impact explosion of H.E. shells blurred into shattering cacophony, appalling in its closeness.

" My God ! " Tyndall whispered. " That was close ! Davies ! What the hell ! . . ."

His voice choked off in an agonised grunt, arms flailing wildly at the empty air, as his back crashed against the deck of the bridge, driving every last ounce of breath from his body. Wordlessly, convulsively, propelled by desperately thrusting feet and launched by the powerful back-thrust of arms pivoting on the handrails, Davies had just catapulted himself up the last three steps of the ladder, head and shoulders socketing into the Admiral's body with irresistible force. And now Davies, too, was down, stretched his length on the deck, spreadeagled across Tyndall's legs. He lay very still.

Slowly, the cruel breath rasping his tortured lungs, Tyndall surfaced from the black depths of unconsciousness. Blindly, instinctively he struggled to sit up, but his broken hand collapsed under the weight of his body. His legs didn't seem to be much help either : they were quite powerless, as if he were paralysed from the waist down. The fog was gone now, and blinding flashes of colour, red, green and white were coruscating brilliantly across the darkening sky. Starshells ? Was the enemy using a new type of starshell ? Dimly, with a great effort of will, he realised that there must be some connection between these dazzling flashes and the now excruciating pain behind his forehead. He reached up the back of his right hand : his eyes were still screwed tightly shut. . . . Then the realisation faded and was gone.

" Are you all right, sir ? Don't move. We'll soon have you out of this ! " The voice, deep, authoritative, boomed directly above the Admiral's head. Tyndall shrank back, shook his head in imperceptible despair. It was Turner who was speaking, and

Turner, he knew, was gone. Was this, then, what it was like to be dead, he wondered dully. This frightening, confused world of blackness and blinding light at the same time, a dark-bright world of pain and powerlessness and voices from the past?

Then suddenly, of their own volition almost, his eyelids flickered and were open. Barely a foot above him were the lean, piratical features of the Commander, who was kneeling anxiously at his side.

" Turner ! Turner ? " A questioning hand reached out in tentative hope, clutched gratefully, oblivious to the pain, at the reassuring solidity of the Commander's arm. " Turner ! It *is* you ! I thought——"

" The After Tower, eh ? " Turner smiled briefly. " No, sir— I wasn't within a mile of it. I was coming here, just climbing up to the fo'c'sle deck, when that first hit threw me back down to the main deck. . . . How are you, sir ? "

" Thank God ! Thank God ! I don't know how I am. My legs . . . What in the name of heaven is that ? "

His eyes, focusing normally again, widened in baffled disbelief. Just above Turner's head, angling for'ard and upward to port, a great, white tree-trunk stretched as far as he could see in either direction. Reaching up, he could just touch the massive bole with his hand.

" The foremast, sir," Turner explained. " It was sheered clean off by that last shell, just above the lower yardarm. The back blast flung it on to the bridge. Took most of the A.A. tower with it, I'm afraid—and caved in the Main Tower. I don't think young Courtney could have had much chance. . . . Davies saw it coming—I was just below him at the time. He was very quick——"

" Davies ! " Tyndall's dazed mind had forgotten all about him. " Of course ! Davies ! " It must be Davies who was pinioning his legs. He craned his neck forward, saw the huddled figure at his feet, the great weight of the mast lying across his back. " For God's sake, Commander, get him out of that ! "

" Just lie down, sir, till Brooks gets here. Davies is all right."

" All right ? All right ! " Tyndall was almost screaming, oblivious to the silent figures who were gathering around him.

" Are you mad, Turner ? The poor bastard must be in agony ! "
He struggled frantically to rise, but several pairs of hands held
him down, firmly, carefully.

" He's all right, sir." Turner's voice was surprisingly gentle.
" Really he is, sir. He's all right. Davies doesn't feel a thing.
Not any more." And all at once the Admiral knew and he fell
back limply to the deck, his eyes closed in shocked understanding.

His eyes were still shut when Brooks appeared, doubly
welcome in his confidence and competence. Within seconds,
almost, the Admiral was on his feet, shocked, badly bruised, but
otherwise unharmed. Doggedly, and in open defiance of Brooks,
Tyndall demanded that he be assisted back to the bridge. His
eyes lit up momentarily as he saw Vallery standing shakily on his
feet, a white towel to his mouth. But he said nothing. His head
bowed, he hoisted himself painfully into his chair.

" W.T.—bridge. W.T.—bridge. Please acknowledge signal."

" Is that bloody idiot still there ? " Tyndall demanded
querulously. " Why doesn't someone—— ? "

" You've only been gone a couple of minutes, sir," the Kapok
Kid ventured.

" Two minutes ! " Tyndall stared at him, lapsed into silence.
He glanced down at Brooks, busy bandaging his right hand.
" Have you nothing better to do, Brooks ? " he asked harshly.

" No, I haven't," Brooks replied truculently. " When shells
explode inside four walls, there isn't much work left for a doctor
. . . except signing death certificates," he added brutally. Vallery
and Turner exchanged glances. Vallery wondered if Brooks had
any idea how far through Tyndall was.

" W.T.—bridge. W.T.—bridge. *Vectra* repeats request for
instruction. Urgent. Urgent."

" The *Vectra* ! " Vallery glanced at the Admiral, silent now
and motionless, and turned to the bridge messenger. " Chrysler !
Get through to W.T. Any way you can. Ask them to repeat the
first message."

He looked again at Turner, followed the Admiral's sick gaze
over the side. He looked down, recoiled in horror, fighting down
the instant nausea. The gunner in the sponson below—just
another boy like Chrysler—must have seen the falling mast, must

have made a panic-stricken attempt to escape. He had barely
cleared his cockpit when the radar screen, a hundred square feet
of meshed steel carrying the crushing weight of the mast as it
had snapped over the edge of the bridge, had caught him fairly
and squarely. He lay still now, mangled, broken, something less
than human, spreadeagled in outflung crucifixion across the twin
barrels of his Oerlikon.

Vallery turned away, sick in body and mind. God, the crazi-
ness, the futile insanity of war. Damn that German cruiser, damn
those German gunners, damn them, damn them, damn them !
. . . But why should he ? They, too, were only doing a job—
and doing it terribly well. He gazed sightlessly at the wrecked
shambles of his bridge. What damnably accurate gunnery ! He
wondered, vaguely, if the *Ulysses* had registered any hits. Probably not, and now, of course, it was impossible. It was impossible now because the *Ulysses*, still racing south-east through
the fog, was completely blind, both radar eyes gone, victims to
the weather and the German guns. Worse still, all the Fire
Control towers were damaged beyond repair. If this goes on,
he thought wryly, all we'll need is a set of grappling irons and a
supply of cutlasses. In terms of modern naval gunnery, even
although her main armament was intact, the *Ulysses* was hopelessly crippled. She just didn't have a chance. What was it that
Stoker Riley was supposed to have said—" being thrown to the
wolves ? " Yes, that was it—" thrown to the wolves." But only
a Nero, he reflected wearily, would have blinded a gladiator
before throwing him into the arena.

All firing had ceased. The bridge was deadly quiet. Silence,
complete silence, except for the sound of rushing water, the
muffled roar of the great engine-room intake fans, the mono-
tonous, nerve-drilling pinging of the Asdic—and these, oddly
enough, only served to deepen the great silence.

Every eye, Vallery saw, was on Admiral Tyndall. Old Giles
was mumbling something to himself, too faint to catch. His face,
shockingly grey, haggard and blotched, still peered over the side.
He seemed fascinated by the sight of the dead boy. Or was it
the smashed Radar screen ? Had the full significance of the
broken scanner and wrecked Director Towers dawned on him

yet ? Vallery looked at him for a long moment, then turned away :
he knew that it had.

"W.T.—bridge. W.T.—bridge." Everyone on the bridge
jumped, swung round in nerve-jangled startlement. Everyone
except Tyndall. He had frozen into a graven immobility.

"Signal from *Vectra*. First Signal. Received 0952." Vallery
glanced at his watch. Only six minutes ago ! Impossible !

"Signal reads : ' Contacts, contacts, 3, repeat 3. Amend to 5.
Heavy concentration of U-boats, ahead and abeam. Am en-
gaging.' "

Every eye on the bridge swung back to Tyndall. His, they
knew, the responsibility, his the decision—taken alone, against
the advice of his senior officer—to leave the convoy almost
unguarded. Impersonally, Vallery admired the baiting, the
timing, the springing of the trap. How would old Giles react to
this, the culmination of a series of disastrous miscalculations—
miscalculations for which, in all fairness, he could not justly be
blamed. . . . But he would be held accountable. The iron voice
of the loudspeaker broke in on his thoughts.

"Second signal reads : ' In close contact. Depth-charging.
Depth-charging. One vessel torpedoed, sinking. Tanker tor-
pedoed, damaged, still afloat, under command. Please advise.
Please assist. Urgent. Urgent ! "

The speaker clicked off. Again that hushed silence, strained,
unnatural. Five seconds it lasted, ten, twenty—then everyone
stiffened, looked carefully away.

Tyndall was climbing down from his chair. His movements
were stiff, slow with the careful faltering shuffle of the very old.
He limped heavily. His right hand, startling white in its snowy
sheath of bandage, cradled his broken wrist. There was about
him a queer, twisted sort of dignity, and if his face held any
expression at all, it was the far-off echo of a smile. When he spoke,
he spoke as a man might talk to himself, aloud.

"I am not well," he said. "I am going below." Chrysler,
not too young to have an inkling of the tragedy, held open the
gate, caught Tyndall as he stumbled on the step. He glanced
back over his shoulder, a quick, pleading look, caught and understood Vallery's compassionate nod. Side by side, the old and the

young, they moved slowly aft. Gradually, the shuffling died
away and they were gone.

The shattered bridge was curiously empty now, the men felt
strangely alone.   Giles, the cheerful, buoyant, indestructible
Giles was gone. The speed, the extent of the collapse was not for
immediate comprehension : the only sensation at the moment
was that of being unprotected and defenceless and alone.

"Out of the mouths of babes and sucklings . . ." Inevitably,
the first to break the silence was Brooks. "Nicholls always
maintained that . . ." He stopped short, his head shaking in slow
incredulity. "I must see what I can do," he finished abruptly, and
hurried off the bridge.

Vallery watched him go, then turned to Bentley. The Captain's
face, haggard, shadowed with grizzled beard, the colour of death
in the weird half-light of the fog, was quite expressionless.

"Three signals, chief. First to *Vectra.* 'Steer 360°. Do not
disperse. Repeat, do not disperse. Am coming to your assistance.'" He paused, then went on : "Sign it, 'Admiral, 14
A.C.S.' Got it ? . . . Right. No time to code it. Plain language.
Send one of your men to the W.T. at once."

"Second : To *Stirling, Sirrus* and *Viking.* 'Abandon pursuit
immediate. Course north-east. Maximum speed.' Plain language
also." He turned to the Kapok Kid. "How's your forehead,
Pilot ? Can you carry on ? "

"Of course, sir."

"Thank you, boy. You heard me ? Convoy re-routed north
—say in a few minutes' time, at 1015. 6 knots. Give me an
intersection course as soon as possible."

"Third signal, Bentley : To *Stirling, Sirrus* and *Viking* :
'Radar out of action. Cannot pick you up on screen. Stream
fog-buoys. Siren at two-minute intervals.' Have that message
coded. All acknowledgements to the bridge at once. Commander ! "

"Sir ? " Turner was at his elbow.

"Hands to defence stations. It's my guess the pack will have
gone before we get there. Who'll be off watch ? "

" Lord only knows," said Turner frankly. " Let's call it port."
Vallery smiled faintly. " Port it is. Organise two parties.
First of port to clear away all loose wreckage : over the side with
the lot—keep nothing. You'll need the blacksmith and his mate,
and I'm sure Dodson will provide you with an oxy-acetylene
crew. Take charge yourself. Second of port as burial party.
Nicholls in charge. All bodies recovered to be laid out in the
canteen when it's clear. . . . Perhaps you could give me a full
report of casualties and damage inside the hour ? "

" Long before that, sir. . . . Could I have a word with you
in private ? "

They walked aft. As the shelter door shut behind them,
Vallery looked at the Commander curiously, half-humorously.
" Another mutiny, perhaps, Commander ? "

" No, sir." Turner unbuttoned his coat, his hand struggling
into the depths of a hip-pocket. He dragged out a flat half-
bottle, held it up to the light. " Thank the Lord for that ! " he
said piously. " I was afraid it got smashed when I fell. . . . Rum,
sir. Neat. I know you hate the stuff, but never mind. Come
on, you need this ! "

Vallery's brows came down in a straight line.

" Rum. Look here, Commander, do you——? "

" To hell with K.R.s and A.F.O.s ! " Turner interrupted
rudely. " Take it—you need it badly ! You've been hurt, you've
lost a lot more blood and your almost frozen to death." He un-
corked it, thrust the bottle into Vallery's reluctant hands. " Face
facts. We need you—more than ever now—and you're almost
dead on your feet—and I mean dead on your feet," he added
brutally. " This might keep you going a few more hours."

" You put things so nicely," Vallery murmured. " Very well.
Against my better judgment . . ."

He paused, the bottle to his mouth.

" And you give me an idea, Commander. Have the bosun
break out the rum. Pipe ' Up spirits.' Double ration to each man.
They, too, are going to need it." He swallowed, pulled the bottle
away, and the grimace was not for the rum.

" Especially," he added soberly, " the burial party."

CHAPTER TEN

FRIDAY AFTERNOON

THE SWITCH clicked on and the harsh fluorescent light flooded the darkening surgery. Nicholls woke with a start, one hand coming up automatically to shield exhausted eyes. That light hurt. He screwed his eyes to slits, peered painfully at the hands of his wrist-watch. Four o'clock! Had he been asleep that long? God, it was bitterly cold!

He hoisted himself stiffly forward in the dentist's chair, twisted his head round. Brooks was standing with his back to the door, snow-covered hood framing his silver hair, numbed fingers fumbling with a packet of cigarettes. Finally, he managed to pull one out. He looked up quizzically over a flaring match-head.

"Hallo, there, Johnny! Sorry to waken you, but the skipper wants you. Plenty of time, though." He dipped the cigarette into the dying flame, looked up again. Nicholls, he thought with sudden compassion, looked ill, desperately tired and over-strained; but no point in telling him so. "How are you? On second thoughts, don't tell me! I'm a damned sight worse myself. Have you any of that poison left?

"Poison, sir?" The levity was almost automatic, part of their relationship with each other. "Just because you make one wrong diagnosis? The Admiral will be all right——"

"Gad! The intolerance of the very young—especially on the providentially few occasions that they happen to be right. . . . I was referring to that bottle of bootleg hooch from the Isle of Mull."

"Coll," Nicholls corrected. "Not that it matters—you've drunk it all, anyway," he added unkindly. He grinned tiredly at the Commander's crestfallen face, then relented. "But we do have a bottle of Talisker left." He crossed over to the poison cupboard, unscrewed the top of a bottle marked "Lysol." He heard, rather than saw, the clatter of glass against glass, wondered vaguely, with a kind of clinical detachment, why his hands were shaking so badly.

Brooks drained his glass, sighed in bliss as he felt the grateful warmth sinking down inside him.

"Thank you, my boy, thank you. You have the makings of a first-class doctor."

"You think so, sir? I don't. Not any longer. Not after to-day." He winced, remembering. "Forty-four of them, sir, over the side in ten minutes, one after the other, like—like so many sacks of rubbish."

"Forty-four?" Brooks looked up. "So many, Johnny?"

"Not really, sir. That was the number of missing. About thirty, rather, and God only knows how many bits and pieces. . . . It was a brush and shovel job in the F.D.R." He smiled, mirthlessly. "I had no dinner, to-day. I don't think anybody else in the burial party had either. . . . I'd better screen that porthole."

He turned away quickly, walked across the surgery. Low on the horizon, through the thinly-falling snow, he caught intermittent sight of an evening star. That meant that the fog was gone—the fog that had saved the convoy, had hidden them from the U-boats when it had turned so sharply to the north. He could see the *Vectra*, her depth-charge racks empty and nothing to show for it. He could see the *Vytura*, the damaged tanker, close by, almost awash in the water, hanging grimly on to the convoy. He could see four of the Victory ships, big, powerful, reassuring, so pitifully deceptive in their indestructible permanence. . . . He slammed the scuttle, screwed home the last butterfly nut, then swung round abruptly.

"Why the hell don't we turn back?" he burst out. "Who does the old man think he's kidding—us or the Germans? No air cover, no radar, not the faintest chance of help! The Germans have us pinned down to an inch now—and it'll be easier still for them as we go on. And there's a thousand miles to go!" His voice rose. " And every bloody enemy ship, U-boat and plane in the Arctic smacking their lips and waiting to pick us off at their leisure." He shook his head in despair. " I'll take my chance with anybody else, sir. You know that. But this is just murder— or suicide. Take your pick, sir. It's all the same when your dead."

" Now, Johnny, you're not——"

" *Why* doesn't he turn back ? " Nicholls hadn't even heard the interruption. " He's only got to give the order. What does he want ? Death or glory ? What's he after ? Immortality at my expense, at *our* expense ? " He swore, bitterly. " Maybe Riley was right. Wonderful headlines. ' Captain Richard Vallery, D.S.O., has been posthumously awarded——' "

" Shut up ! " Brooks's eye was as chill as the Arctic ice itself, his voice a biting lash.

" You dare to talk of Captain Vallery like that ! " he said softly. " You dare to besmirch the name of the most honourable . . ." He broke off, shook his head in wrathful wonder. He paused to pick his words carefully, his eyes never leaving the other's white, strained face.

" He is a good officer, Lieutenant Nicholls, maybe even a great officer : and that just doesn't matter a damn. What does matter is that he is the finest gentleman—I say ' gentleman '— I've ever known, that ever walked the face of this graceless, God-forsaken earth. He is not like you or me. He is not like anybody at all. He walks alone, but he is never lonely, for he has company all the way . . . men like Peter, like Bede, like St. Francis of Assisi." He laughed shortly. " Funny, isn't it—to hear an old reprobate like myself talk like this? Blasphemy, even, you might call it—except that the truth can never be blasphemy. And I *know*."

Nicholls said nothing. His face was like a stone.

" Death, glory, immortality," Brooks went on relentlessly. " These were your words, weren't they ? Death ? " He smiled and shook his head again. " For Richard Vallery, death doesn't exist. Glory ? Sure, he wants glory, we all want glory, but all the *London Gazettes* and Buckingham Palaces in the world can't give *him* the kind of glory he wants : Captain Vallery is no longer

a child, and only children play with toys. . . . As for immortality."
He laughed, without a trace of rancour now, laid a hand on
Nicholls's shoulder. " I ask you, Johnny—wouldn't it be damned
stupid to ask for what he has already ? "

Nicholls said nothing. The silence lengthened and deepened,
the rush of the air from the ventilation louvre became oppres-
sively loud. Finally, Brooks coughed, looked meaningfully at
the "Lysol" bottle.

Nicholls filled the glasses, brought them back. Brooks caught
his eyes, held them, and was filled with sudden pity. What was
that classical understatement of Cunningham's during the German
invasion of Crete—"It is inadvisable to drive men beyond a
certain point." Trite but true. True even for men like Nicholls.
Brooks wondered what particular private kind of hell that boy
had gone through that morning, digging out the shattered, torn
bodies of what had once been men. And, as the doctor in charge,
he would have had to examine them all—or all the pieces he
could find. . . .

" Next step up and I'll be in the gutter." Nicholls's voice was
very low. " I don't know what to say, sir. I don't know what
made me say it. . . . I'm sorry."

" Me too," Brooks said sincerely. " Shooting off my mouth
like that ! And I mean it." He lifted his glass, inspected the
contents lovingly. " To our enemies, Johnny : their downfall
and confusion, and don't forget Admiral Starr." He drained the
glass at a gulp, set it down, looked at Nicholls for a long moment.

" I think you should hear the rest, too, Johnny. You know,
why Vallery doesn't turn back." He smiled wryly. " It's not
because there are as many of these damned U-boats behind us as
there are in front—which there undoubtedly are." He lit a fresh
cigarette, went on quietly :

" The Captain radioed London this morning. Gave it as his
considered opinion that FR77 would be a goner—' annihilated '
was the word he used and, as a word, they don't come any
stronger—long before it reached the North Cape. He asked at
least to be allowed to go north about, instead of east for the
Cape. . . . Pity there was no sunset to-night, Johnny," he added
half-humourously. " I would have liked to see it."

" Yes, yes." Nicholls was impatient. " And the answer ? "

" Eh ? Oh, the answer. Vallery expected it immediately."
Brooks shrugged. " It took four hours to come through." He
smiled, but there was no laughter in the eyes. " There's something big, something on a huge scale brewing up somewhere. It
can only be some major invasion—this under your hat, Johnny ? "

" Of course, sir ! "

" What it is I haven't a clue. Maybe even the long-awaited
Second Front. Anyway, the support of the Home Fleet seems to
be regarded as vital to success. But the Home Fleet is tied up—
by the *Tirpitz*. And so the orders have gone out—get the
Tirpitz. Get it at all costs." Brooks smiled, and his face was very
cold. " We're big fish, Johnny, we're important people. We're
the biggest, juiciest bait ever offered up to the biggest, juiciest
prize in the world to-day—although I'm afraid the trap's a trifle
rusty at the hinges. . . . The signal came from the First Sea Lord
—and Starr. The decision was taken at Cabinet level. We go
on. We go east."

" We are the ' all costs,' " said Nicholls flatly. " We are
expendable."

" We are expendable," Brooks agreed. The speaker above his
head clicked on, and he groaned. " Hell's bells, here we go
again ! "

He waited until the clamour of the Dusk Action Stations'
bugle had died away, stretched out a hand as Nicholls hurried
for the door.

" Not you, Johnny. Not yet. I told you, the skipper wants
you. On the bridge, ten minutes after Stations begin."

" What ? On the bridge ? What the hell for ? "

" Your language is unbecoming to a junior officer," said
Brooks solemnly. " How did the men strike you to-day ? " he
went on inconsequently. " You were working with them all
morning. Their usual selves ? "

Nicholls blinked, then recovered.

" I suppose so." He hesitated. " Funny, they seemed a lot
better a couple of days ago, but—well, now they're back to the
Scapa stage. Walking zombies. Only more so—they can hardly
walk now." He shook his head. " Five, six men to stretcher.

Kept tripping and falling over things. Asleep on their feet—eyes not focusing, too damned tired to look where they're going."

Brooks nodded. "I know, Johnny, I know. I've seen it myself."

"Nothing mutinous, nothing sullen about them any more." Nicholls was puzzled, seeking tiredly to reduce nebulous, scattered impressions to a homogenous coherence. "They've neither the energy nor the initiative left for a mutiny now, anyway, I suppose, but it's not that. Kept muttering to themselves in the F.D.R.: 'Lucky bastard.' 'He died easy'—things like that. Or 'Old Giles—off his bleedin' rocker.' And you can imagine the shake of the head. But no humour, none, not even the grisly variety you usually . . ." He shook his own head. "I just don't know, sir. Apathetic, indifferent, hopeless—call 'em what you like. I'd call 'em lost."

Brooks looked at him a long moment, then added gently:

"Would you now?" He mused. "And do you know, Johnny, I think you'd be right. . . . Anyway," he continued briskly, "get up there. Captain's going to make a tour of the ship."

"What!" Nicholls was astounded. "During action stations? Leave the bridge?"

"Just that."

"But—but he can't, sir. It's—it's unprecedented!"

"So's Captain Vallery. That's what I've been trying to tell you all evening."

"But he'll kill himself!" Nicholls protested wildly.

"That's what I said," Brooks agreed wryly. "Clinically, he's dying. He should be dead. What keeps him going God only knows—literally. It certainly isn't plasma or drugs. . . . Once in a while, Johnny, it's salutary for us to appreciate the limits of medicine. Anyway, I talked him into taking you with him. . . . Better not keep him waiting."

For Lieutenant Nicholls, the next two hours were borrowed from purgatory. Two hours, the Captain took to his inspection, two hours of constant walking, of climbing over storm-sills and tangled wreckage of steel, of squeezing and twisting through impossibly narrow apertures, of climbing and descending a hundred ladders, two hours of exhausting torture in the bitter, heart-sapping cold of a sub-zero temperature. But it was a memory that was to stay with him always, that was never to return without filling him with warmth, with a strange and wonderful gratitude.

They started on the poop—Vallery, Nicholls and Chief Petty Officer Hartley—Vallery would have none of Hastings, the Master-At-Arms, who usually accompanied the Captain on his rounds. There was something oddly reassuring about the big, competent Chief. He worked like a Trojan that night, opening and shutting dozens of watertight doors, lifting and lowering countless heavy hatches, knocking off and securing the thousand clips that held these doors and hatches in place, and, before ten minutes had passed, lending a protesting Vallery the support of his powerful arm.

They climbed down the long, vertical ladder to "Y" magazine, a dim and gloomy dungeon thinly lit with pinpoints of garish light. Here were the butchers, bakers and candlestick makers— the non-specialists in the purely offensive branches. "Hostilities only" ratings, almost to a man, in charge of a trained gunner, they had a cold, dirty and unglamorous job, strangely neglected and forgotten—strangely, because so terribly dangerous. The four-inch armour encasing them offered about as much protection as a sheet of newspaper to an eight-inch armour-piercing shell or a torpedo. . . .

The magazine walls—walls of shells and cartridge cases— were soaking wet, dripping constantly, visibly, with icy condensation. Half the crew were leaning or lying against the racks, blue, pinched, shivering with cold, their breath hanging heavily in the chill air : the others were trudging heavily round and round the hoist, feet splashing in pools of water, lurching, stumbling with sheer exhaustion, gloved hands buried in their pockets, drawn, exhausted faces sunk on their chests. Zombies, Nicholls thought wonderingly, just living zombies. Why don't they lie down ?

Gradually, everyone became aware of Vallery's presence, stopped walking or struggled painfully erect, eyes too tired, minds too spent for either wonder or surprise.

"As you were, as you were," Vallery said quickly. "Who's in charge here?"

"I am, sir." A stocky, overalled figure walked slowly forward, halted in front of Vallery.

"Ah, yes. Gardiner, isn't it?" He gestured to the men circling the hoist. "What in the world is all this for, Gardiner?"

"Ice," said Gardiner succinctly. "We have to keep the water moving or it'll freeze in a couple of minutes. We can't have ice on the magazine floor, sir."

"No, no, of course not! But—but the pumps, the drain-cocks?"

"Solid!"

"But surely—this doesn't go on all the time?"

"In flat weather—all the time, sir."

"Good God!" Vallery shook his head incredulously, splashed his way to the centre of the group, where a slight, boyish figure was coughing cruelly into a corner of an enormous green and white muffler. Vallery placed a concerned arm across the shaking shoulders.

"Are you all right, boy?"

"Yes, sir. 'Course Ah am!" He lifted a thin white face racked with pain. "Ah'm fine," he said indignantly.

"What's your name?"

"McQuater, sir."

"And what's your job, McQuater?"

"Assistant cook, sir."

"How old are you?"

"Eighteen, sir." Merciful heavens, Vallery thought, this isn't a cruiser I'm running—it's a nursery!

"From Glasgow, eh?" He smiled.

"Yes, sir," defensively.

"I see." He looked down at the deck, at McQuater's boots half-covered in water. "Why aren't you wearing your seaboots?" he asked abruptly.

"We don't get issued with them, sir."

"But your feet, man! They must be soaking!"

"Ah don't know, sir. Ah think so. Anyway," McQuater said simply, "it doesna matter. Ah canna feel them."

Vallery winced. Nicholls, looking at the Captain, wondered if he realised the distressing, pathetic picture he himself presented with his sunken, bloodless face, red, inflamed eyes, his mouth and nose daubed with crimson, the inevitable dark and sodden hand-towel clutched in his left glove. Suddenly, unaccountably, Nicholls felt ashamed of himself : that thought, he knew, could never occur to this man.

Vallery smiled down at McQuater.

" Tell me, son, honestly—are you tired ? "

" Ah am that—Ah mean, aye, aye, sir."

" Me too," Vallery confessed. " But—you can carry on a bit longer ? "

He felt the frail shoulders straighten under his arm.

" 'Course Ah can, sir ! " The tone was injured, almost truculent. " *'Course* Ah can ! "

Vallery's gaze travelled slowly over the group, his dark eyes glowing as he heard a murmured chorus of assent. He made to speak, broke off in harsh coughing and bent his head. He looked up again, his eyes wandering once more over the circle of now-anxious faces, then turned abruptly away.

" We won't forget you," he murmured indistinctly. " I promise you, we won't forget you." He splashed quickly away, out of the pool of water, out of the pool of light, into the darkness at the foot of the ladder.

Ten minutes later, they emerged from " Y " turret. The night sky was cloudless now, brilliant with diamantine stars, little chips of frozen fire in the dark velvet of that fathomless floor. The cold was intense. Captain Vallery shivered involuntarily as the turret door slammed behind them.

" Hartley ? "

" Sir ? "

" I smelt rum in there ! "

" Yes, sir. So did I." The Chief was cheerful, unperturbed. " Proper stinking with it. Don't worry about it though, sir. Half the men in the ship bottle their rum ration, keep it for action stations."

" Completely forbidden in regulations, Chief. You know that as well as I do ! "

"I know. But there's no harm, sir. Warms 'em up—and if it gives them Dutch courage, all the better. Remember that night the for'ard pom-pom got two Stukas?"

"Of course."

"Canned to the wide. Never have done it otherwise. . . . And now, sir, they *need* it."

"Suppose you're right, Chief. They do and I don't blame them." He chuckled. "And don't worry about my knowing—I've always known. But it smelled like a saloon bar in there. . . ."

They climbed up to "X" turret—the marine turret—then down to the magazine. Wherever he went, as in "Y" magazine Vallery left the men the better for his coming. In personal contact, he had some strange indefinable power that lifted men above themselves, that brought out in them something they had never known to exist. To see dull apathy and hopelessness slowly give way to resolution, albeit a kind of numbed and desperate resolve, was to see something that baffled the understanding. Physically and mentally, Nicholls knew, these men had long since passed the point of no return.

Vaguely, he tried to figure it out, to study the approach and technique. But the approach varied every time, he saw, was no more than a natural reaction to different sets of circumstances as they presented themselves, a reaction utterly lacking in calculation or finesse. There *was* no technique. Was pity, then, the activating force, pity for the heart-breaking gallantry of a man so clearly dying? Or was it shame—if *he* can do it, if *he* can still drive that wasted mockery of a body, if he can kill himself just to come to see if *we're* all right—if he can do that and smile—then, by God, we can stick it out, too? That's it, Nicholls said to himself, that's what it is, pity and shame, and he hated himself for thinking it, and not because of the thought, but because he knew he lied. . . . He was too tired to think anyway. His mind was woolly, fuzzy round the edges, his thoughts disjointed, uncontrolled. Like everyone else's. Even Andy Carpenter, the last man you would suspect of it—he felt that way, too, and admitted it. . . . He wondered what the Kapok Kid would have to say to this. . . . The Kid was probably wandering too, but wandering in his own

way, back as always on the banks of the Thames. He wondered
what the girl in Henley was like. Her name started with " J "—
Joan, Jean—he didn't know : the Kapok Kid had a big golden
" J " on the right breast of his kapok suit—*she* had put it there.
But what was she like ? Blonde and gay, like the Kid himself ?
Or dark and kind and gentle, like St. Francis of Assisi ? St.
Francis of Assisi ? Why in the world did he—ah, yes, old
Socrates had been talking about him. Wasn't he the man of whom
Axel Munthe . . .

"Nicholls ! Are you all right ? " Vallery's voice was sharp
with anxiety.

"Yes, of course, sir." Nicholls shook his head, as if to clear
it. " Just gathering wool. Where to, now, sir ? "

"Engineers' Flat, Damage Control parties, Switchboard,
Number 3 Low Power room—no, of course, that's gone—
Noyes was killed there, wasn't he ? . . . Hartley, I'd appreciate
it if you'd let my feet touch the deck occasionally. . . ."

All these places they visited in turn and a dozen others besides
—not even the remotest corner, the most impossible of access,
did Vallery pass by, if he knew a man was there, closed up to his
action station.

They came at last to the engine and boiler-rooms, to the
gulping pressure changes on unaccustomed eardrums as they
went through the airlocks, to the antithetically breath-taking blast
of heat as they passed inside. In " A " boiler-room, Nicholls
insisted on Vallery's resting for some minutes. He was grey with
pain and weakness, his breathing very distressed. Nicholls
noticed Hartley talking in a corner, was dimly aware of someone
leaving the boiler-room.

Then his eyes caught sight of a burly, swarthy stoker, with
bruised cheeks and the remnants of a gorgeous black eye, stalking
across the floor. He carried a canvas chair, set it down with a
thump behind Vallery.

"A seat, sir," he growled.

"Thank you, thank you." Vallery lowered himself gratefully,
then looked up in surprise. "Riley ? " he murmured, then
switched his glance to Hendry, the Chief Stoker. "Doing his
duty with a minimum of grace, eh ? "

Hendry stirred uncomfortably.

" He did it off his own bat, sir."

" I'm sorry," Vallery said sincerely. " Forgive me, Riley. Thank you very much." He stared after him in puzzled wonder, looked again at Hendry, eyebrows lifted in interrogation.

Hendry shook his head.

" Search me, sir. I've no idea. He's a queer fish. Does things like that. He'd bend a lead pipe over your skull without batting an eyelid—and he's got a mania for looking after kittens and lame dogs. Or if you get a bird with a broken wing—Riley's your man. But he's got a low opinion of his fellowmen, sir."

Vallery nodded slowly, without speaking, leaned against the canvas back and closed his eyes in exhaustion. Nicholls bent over him.

" Look, sir," he urged quietly, " why not give it up ? Frankly, sir, you're killing yourself. Can't we finish this some other time ? "

" I'm afraid not, my boy." Vallery was very patient. " You don't understand. ' Some other time ' will be too late." He turned to Hendry. " So you think you'll manage all right, Chief ? "

" Don't you worry about us, sir." The soft Devon voice was grim and gentle at the same time. " Just you look after yourself. The stokers won't let you down, sir."

Vallery rose painfully to his feet, touched him lightly on the arm. " Do you know, Chief, I never thought you would. . . . Ready, Hartley ? " He stopped short, seeing a giant duffel-coated figure waiting at the foot of the ladder, the face below the hood dark and sombre. " Who's that ? Oh, I know. Never thought stokers got so cold," he smiled.

" Yes, sir, it's Petersen," Hartley said softly. " He's coming with us."

" Who said so ? And—and Petersen ? Wasn't that—— ? "

" Yes, sir. Riley's— er—lieutenant in the Scapa business. . . . Surgeon Commander's orders, sir. Petersen's going to give us a hand."

" Us ? Me, you mean." There was no resentment, no bitterness in Vallery's voice. " Hartley, take my advice—never let

yourself get into the hands of the doctors. . . . You think he's
safe ? " he added half-humorously.

" He'd probably kill the man who looked sideways at you,"
Hartley stated matter-of-factly. " He's a good man, sir. Simple,
easily led—but good."

At the foot of the ladder, Petersen stepped aside to let them
pass, but Vallery stopped, looked up at the giant towering
six inches above him, into the grave, blue eyes below the flaxen
hair.

" Hallo, Petersen. Hartley tells me you're coming with us.
Do you really want to ? You don't have to, you know."

" Please, Captain." The speech was slow and precise, the face
curiously dignified in unhappiness. " I am very sorry for what
has happened——"

" No, no ! " Vallery was instantly contrite. " Ycu misunderstand. It's a bitter night up top. But I would like it very much if
you would come. Will you ? "

Petersen stared at him, then began slowly to smile, his
face darkening with pleasure. As the Captain set foot on
the first step, the giant arm came round him. The sensation,
as Vallery described it later, was very much like going up in a
lift.

From there they visited Engineer Commander Dodson in his
engine-room, a cheerful, encouraging, immensely competent
Dodson, an engineer to his finger-tips in his single-minded
devotion to the great engines under his care. Then aft to the
Engineers' Flat, up the companionway between the wrecked
canteen and the Police Office, out on to the upper deck. After the
heat of the boiler-room, the 100° drop in temperature, a drop that
strangled breath with the involuntary constriction of the throat
and made a skin-crawling mockery of " Arctic clothing," was
almost literally paralysing.

The starboard torpedo tubes—the only ones at the standby—
were only four paces away. The crew, huddled in the lee of the
wrecked bosun's store—the one destroyed by the *Blue Ranger's*
shells—were easily located by the stamping of frozen feet, the
uncontrollable chattering of teeth.

Vallery peered into the gloom. " L.T.O. there ? "

"Captain, sir?" Surprise, doubt in the voice.

"Yes. How are things going?"

"All right, sir." He was still off-balance, hesitant. "I think young Smith's left foot is gone, sir—frostbite."

"Take him below—at once. And organise your crew into ten minute watches : one to keep a telephone watch here, the other four in the Engineers' Flat. From now on. You understand?" He hurried away, as if to avoid the embarrassment of thanks, the murmurs of smiling gladness.

They passed the torpedo shop, where the spare torpedoes and compressed air cylinders were stored, climbed the ladder to the boat-deck. Vallery paused a moment, one hand on the boat-winch, the other holding the bloody scarf, already frozen almost solid, to mouth and nose. He could just distinguish the shadowy bulkiness of merchantmen on either side : their masts, though, were oddly visible, swinging lazily, gently against the stars as the ships rolled to a slight swell, just beginning. He shuddered, pulled his scarf higher round his neck. God, it was cold! He moved for'ard, leaning heavily on Petersen's arm. The snow, three to four inches deep, cushioned his footsteps as he came up behind an Oerlikon gun. Quietly, he laid a hand on the shoulder of the hooded gunner hunched forward in his cockpit.

"Things all right, gunner?"

No reply. The man appeared to stir, moved forward, then fell still again.

"I said, 'Are you all right?'" Vallery's voice had hardened. He shook the gunner by the shoulder, turned impatiently to Hartley.

"Asleep, Chief! At Action Stations! We're all dead from lack of sleep, I know—but his mates below are depending on him. There's no excuse. Take his name!"

"Take his name!" Nicholls echoed softly, bent over the cockpit. He shouldn't speak like this, he knew, but he couldn't help it. "Take his name," he repeated. "What for? His next of kin? This man is dead."

The snow was beginning to fall again, cold and wet and feathery, the wind lifting a perceptible fraction. Vallery felt the first icy flakes, unseen in the darkness, brushing his cheeks, heard the distant moan of the wind in the rigging, lonely and forlorn. He shivered.

" His heater's gone." Hartley withdrew an exploratory hand, straightened up. He seemed tired. " These Oerlikons have black heaters bolted to the side of the cockpit. The gunners lean against them, sir, for hours at a time. . . . I'm afraid the fuse must have blown. They've been warned against this, sir, a thousand times."

" Good God ! Good God ! " Vallery shook his head slowly. He felt old, terribly tired. " What a useless, futile way to die. . . . Have him taken to the canteen, Hartley."

" No good, sir." Nicholls straightened up also. " It'll have to wait. What with the cold and the quick onset of rigor mortis —well, it'll have to wait."

Vallery nodded assent, turned heavily away. All at once, the deck 'speaker aft of the winch blared into raucous life, a rude desecration that shattered the chilled hush of the evening.

" Do you hear there ? Do you hear there ? Captain, or notify Captain, to contact bridge immediately, please." Three times the message was repeated, then the 'speaker clicked off.

Quickly Vallery turned to Hartley.

" Where's the nearest phone, Chief ? " .

" Right here, sir." Hartley turned tack to the Oerlikon, stripped earphones and chest mouthpiece from the dead man. " That is, if the A.A. tower is still manned ? "

" What's left of it is."

" Tower ? Captain to speak to bridge. Put me through." He handed the receiver to Vallery. " Here you are, sir."

" Thank you. Bridge ? Yes, speaking. . . . Yes, yes. . . . Very good. Detail the *Sirrus*. . . . No, Commander, nothing I can do anyway—just maintain position, that's all." He took the handset off, handed it back to Hartley.

" Asdic contact from *Viking*," he said briefly. " Red 90." He turned, looked out over the dark sea, realised the futility of his instinctive action, and shrugged. " We've sent the *Sirrus* after him. Come on."

Their tour of the boat-deck gun-sites completed with a visit to the midships' pom-pom crew, bone-chilled and shaking with cold, under the command of the bearded Doyle, repectfully sulphurous in his outspoken comments on the weather, they dropped down to the main deck again. By this time Vallery was making no protest at all, not even of the most token kind, against Petersen's help and support. He was too glad of them. He blessed Brooks for his foresight and thoughtfulness, and was touched by the rare delicacy and consideration that prompted the big Norwegian to withdraw his supporting arm whenever they spoke to or passed an isolated group of men.

Inside the port screen door and just for'ard of the galley, Vallery and Nicholls, waiting as the others knocked the clamps off the hatch leading down to the stokers' mess, heard the muffled roar of distant depth-charges—there were four in all— felt the pressure waves strike the hull of the *Ulysses*. At the first report Vallery had stiffened, head cocked in attention, eyes fixed on infinity, in the immemorial manner of a man whose ears are doing the work for all the senses. He hesitated a moment, shrugged, bent his arm to hook a leg over the hatch coaming. There was nothing he could do.

In the centre of the stokers' mess was another, heavier hatch. This, too, was opened. The ladder led down to the steering position, which, as in most modern warships, was far removed from the bridge, deep in the heart of the ship below the armour-plating. Here, for a couple of minutes, Vallery talked quietly to the quartermaster, while Petersen, working in the confined space just outside, opened the massive hatch—450 lbs. of steel, actuated by a counter-balancing pulley weight—which gave access to the hold, to the very bottom of the *Ulysses*, to the Transmitting Station and No. 2 Low Power Room.

A mazing, confusing mystery of a place, this Low Power Room, confusing to the eye and ear. Round every bulkhead, interspersed with scores of switches, breakers and rheostats, were ranged tiered banks of literally hundreds of fuses, baffling to the untrained eye in their myriad complexity. Baffling, too, was the function of a score or more of low-power generators, nerve-drilling in the frenetic dissonance of their high-pitched hums. Nicholls straightened up at the foot of the ladder and shuddered involuntarily. A bad place, this. How easily could mind and nerves slide over the edge of insanity under the pounding, insistent clamour of the desynchronised cacophony !

Just then there were only two men there—an Electric Artificer and his assistant, bent over the big Sperry master gyro, making some latitude adjustment to the highly complex machinery of the compass. They looked up quickly, tired surprise melting into tired pleasure. Vallery had a few words with them—speech was difficult in that bedlam of sound—then moved over to the door of the T.S.

He had his glove on the door handle when he froze to complete stillness. Another pattern had exploded, much closer this time, two cable lengths distant, at most. Depth-charges, they knew, but only because reason and experience told them : deep down in the heart of an armour-plated ship there is no sense of explosion, no roar of eruption from a detonating depth-charge. Instead, there is a tremendous, metallic clang, peculiarly tinny in calibre, as if some giant with a giant sledge had struck the ship's side and found the armour loose.

The pattern was followed almost immediately by another two explosions, and the *Ulysses* was still shuddering under the impact of the second when Vallery turned the handle and walked in. The others filed in after the Captain, Petersen closing the door softly behind him. At once the clamour of the electric motors died gratefully away in the hushed silence of the T.S.

The T.S., fighting heart of the ship, lined like the Low Power Room though it was by banks of fuses, was completely dominated by the two huge electronic computing tables occupying almost half the floor space. These, the vital links between the Fire Control Towers and the turrets, were generally the scene of intense, controlled activity : but the almost total destruction of the towers that morning had made them all but useless, and the undermanned T.S. was strangely quiet. Altogether, there were only eight ratings and an officer manning the tables.

The air in the T.S., a T.S. prominently behung with "No Smoking" notices, was blue with tobacco smoke hanging in a flat, lazily drifting cloud near the deckhead—a cloud which spiralled thinly down to smouldering cigarette ends. For Nicholls there was something oddly reassuring in these burning cigarettes : in the unnatural bow-taut stillness, in the inhuman immobility of the men, it was the only guarantee of life.

He looked, in a kind of detached curiosity at the rating nearest him. A thin, dark-haired man, he was sitting hunched forward, his elbow on the table, the cigarette clipped between his fingers a bare inch from his half-open mouth. The smoke was curling up, lacing its smarting path across vacant, sightless eyes oblivious to the irritation, the ash on the cigarette itself almost two inches in length, drooping slightly. Vaguely, Nicholls wondered how long he had been sitting there motionless, utterly motionless . . . and why ?

Expectancy, of course. That was it—expectancy. It was too obvious. Waiting, just waiting. Waiting for what ? For the first time it struck Nicholls, struck him with blinding clarity, what it was to wait, to wait with the bowstring of the nerves strung down at inhuman tension, strung down far beyond quivering to the tautened immobility of snapping point, to wait for the torpedo that would send them crashing into oblivion. For the first time he realised why it was that men who could, invariably it seemed, find something complainingly humorous in any place and every place, never joked about the T.S. A death trap is not funny. That T.S. was twenty feet below water level : for'ard of it was " B " magazine, aft of it " A " boiler-room, on either side of it were fuel tanks, and below it was the unprotected bottom, prime target for acoustic mines and torpedoes. They were ringed, surrounded, by the elements, the threat of death, and it needed only a flash, a wandering spark, to trigger off the annihilating reality. . . . And above them, in the one in a thousand chance of survival, was a series of hatches which could all too easily warp and lock solid under the metal-twisting shock of an explosion. Besides, the primary idea was that the hatches, deliberately heavy in construction, should *stay* shut in the event of damage, to seal off the flooded compartments below. The men in the T.S. knew this.

" Good evening. Everything all right down here ? " Vallery's voice, quiet and calm as ever, sounded unnaturally loud. Startled faces, white and strained, twisted round, eyes opening in astonishment : the depth-charging, Nicholls realised, had masked their approach.

"Wouldn't worry too much about the racket outside," Vallery went on reassuringly. "A wandering U-boat, and the *Sirrus* is after him. You can thank your stars you're here and not in that sub."

No one else had spoken. Nicholls, watching them, saw their eyes flickering back from Vallery's face to the forbidden cigarettes, understood their discomfort, their embarrassment at being caught red-handed by the Captain.

"Any reports from the main tower, Brierley ? " he asked the officer in charge. He seemed unaware of the strain.

"No, sir. Nothing at all. All quiet above."

"Fine ! " Vallery sounded positively cheerful. "No news is good news." He brought his hand out from his pocket, proffered his cigarette case to Brierley. "Smoke ? And you, Nicholls ? " He took one himself, replaced the case, absently picked up a box of matches lying in front of the nearest gunner ; and if he noticed the gunner's startled disbelief, the slow beginnings of a smile, the tired shoulders slumping fractionally in a long, soundless sigh of relief, he gave no sign.

The thunderous clanging of more depth-charges drowned the rasping of the hatch, drowned Vallery's harsh, convulsive coughing as the smoke reached his lungs. Only the reddening of the sodden hand-towel betrayed him. As the last vibration died away, he looked up, concern in his eyes.

"Good God ! Does it always sound like that down here ? "

Brierley smiled faintly. "More or less, sir. Usually more."

Vallery looked slowly round the men in the T.S., nodded for'ard.

" ' B ' magazine there, isn't it ? "

"Yes, sir."

"And nice big fuel tanks all around you ? "

Brierley nodded. Every eye was on the captain.

"I see. Frankly, I'd rather have my own job—wouldn't have yours for a pension. . . . Nicholls, I think we'll spend a few minutes down here, have our smoke in peace. Besides "—he grinned—" think of the increased fervour with which we'll count our blessings when we get out of here ! "

He stayed five minutes, talking quietly to Brierley and his men. Finally, he stubbed out his cigarette, took his leave and started for the door.

" Sir." The voice stopped him on the threshhold, the voice of the thin dark gunner whose matches he had borrowed.

" Yes, what is it ? "

" I thought you might like this." He held out a clean, white towel. " That one you've got is—well, sir, I mean it's——"

" Thank you." Vallery took the towel without any hesitation. " Thank you very much."

Despite Petersen's assistance, the long climb up to the upper deck left Vallery very weak. His feet were dragging heavily.

" Look, sir, this is madness ! " Nicholls was desperately anxious. " Sorry, sir, didn't mean that, but—well, come and see Commander Brooks. Please ! "

" Certainly." The reply was a husky whisper. " Our next port of call anyway."

Half a dozen paces took them to the door of the Sick Bay. Vallery insisted on seeing Brooks alone. When he came out of the surgery after some time, he seemed curiously refreshed, his step lighter. He was smiling, and so was Brooks. Nicholls lagged behind as the Captain left.

" Give him anything, sir ? " he asked. " Honest to God, he's killing himself ! "

" He took something, not much." Brooks smiled softly. " I know he's killing himself, so does he. But he knows why, and I know why, and he knows I know why. Anyway, he feels better. Not to worry, Johnny ! "

Nicholls waited at the top of the ladder outside the Sick Bay, waited for the Captain and others to come up from the telephone exchange and No. 1 Low Power Room. He stood aside as they climbed the coaming, but Vallery took his arm, walked him slowly for'ard past the Torpedo Office, nodding curtly to Carslake, in nominal charge of a Damage Control party. Carslake, face still swathed in white, looked back with eyes wild and staring and strange, his gaze almost devoid of recognition. Vallery hesitated, shook his head, then turned to Nicholls, smiling.

" B.M.A. in secret session, eh ? " he queried. " Never mind, Nicholls, and don't worry. *I'm* the one who should be worrying."

" Indeed, sir ? Why ? "

Vallery shook his head again. " Rum in the gun turrets, cigarettes in the T.S., and now a fine old whisky in a ' Lysol ' bottle. Thought Commander Brooks was going to poison me— and what a glorious death ! Excellent stuff, and the Surgeon Commander's apologies to you for broaching your private supplies."

Nicholls flushed darkly, began to stammer an apology, but Vallery cut him off.

" Forget it, boy, forget it. What does it matter ? But it makes me wonder what we're going to find next. An opium den in the Capstan Flat, perhaps, or dancing girls in ' B ' turret ? "

But they found nothing in these or any other places, except cold, misery and hunger-haunted exhaustion. As ever, Nicholls saw, they—or rather, Vallery—left the men the better of their coming. But they themselves were now in a pretty bad state, Nicholls realised. His own legs were made of rubber, he was exhausted by continuous shivering : where Vallery found the strength to carry on, he couldn't even begin to imagine. Even Petersen's great strength was flagging, not so much from half-carrying Vallery as from the ceaseless hammering of clips frozen solid on doors and hatches.

Leaning against a bulkhead, breathing heavily after the ascent from " A " magazine, Nicholls looked hopefully at the Captain. Vallery saw the look, interpreted it correctly, and shook his head, smiling.

" Might as well finish it, boy. Only the Capstan Flat. Nobody there anyway, I expect, but we might as well have a look."

They walked slowly round the heavy machinery in the middle of the Capstan Flat, for'ard past the Battery Room and Sailmaker's Shop, past the Electrical Workshop and cells to the locked door of the Painter's Shop, the most for'ard compartment in the ship.

Vallery reached his hand forward, touched the door symbolically, smiled tiredly and turned away. Passing the cell door, he casually flicked open the inspection port, glanced in perfunctorily and moved on. Then he stopped dead, wheeled round and flung open the inspection port again.

" What in the name of—Ralston! What on earth are you doing here ? " he shouted.

Ralston smiled. Even through the thick plate glass it wasn't a pleasant smile and it never touched the blue eyes. He gestured to the barred grille, indicating that he could not hear.

Impatiently, Vallery twisted the grille handle.

" What are you doing here, Ralston ? " he demanded. The brows were drawn down heavily over blazing eyes. " In the cells—and at this time ! Speak up, man ! Tell me ! " Nicholls looked at Vallery in slow surprise. The old man—angry ! It was unheard of ! Shrewdly, Nicholls decided that he'd rather not be the object of Vallery's fury.

" I was locked up here, sir." The words were innocuous enough, but their tone said, " What a damned silly question." Vallery flushed faintly.

" .When ? "

" At 1030 this morning, sir."

" And by whom, may I inquire ? "

" By the Master-At-Arms, sir."

" On whose authority ? " Vallery demanded furiously.

Ralston looked at him a long moment without speaking. His face was expressionless. " On yours, sir."

" Mine ! " Vallery was incredulous. " I didn't tell him to lock you up ! "

" You never told him not to," said Ralston evenly. Vallery winced : the oversight, the lack of consideration was his, and that hurt badly.

" Where's your night Action Station ? " he asked sharply.

" Port tubes, sir." That, Vallery realised, explained why only the starboard crew had been closed up.

" And why—why have you been left here during Action Stations ? Don't you know it's forbidden, against all regulations ? "

" Yes, sir." Again the hint of the wintry smile. " I know.

But does the Master-At-Arms know ? " He paused a second, smiled again. " Or maybe he just forgot," he suggested.

" Hartley ! " Vallery was on balance again, his tone level and grim. " The Master-At-Arms here, immediately : see that he brings his keys ! " He broke into a harsh bout of coughing, spat some blood into the towel, looked at Ralston again.

" I'm sorry about this, my boy," he said slowly. " Genuinely sorry."

" How's the tanker ? " Ralston asked softly.

" What ? What did you say ? " Vallery was unprepared for the sudden switch. " What tanker ? "

" The one that was damaged this morning, sir ? "

" Still with us." Vallery was puzzled. " Still with us, but low in the water. Any special reason for asking ? "

" Just interested, sir." The smile was wry, but this time it was a smile. " You see——"

He stopped abruptly as a deep, muffled roar crashed through the silent night, the pressure blast listing the *Ulysses* sharply to starboard. Vallery lurched, staggered and would have fallen but for Petersen's sudden arm. He braced himself against the righting roll, looked at Nicholls in sudden dismay. The sound was all too familiar.

Nicholls gazed back at him, sorry to his heart for this fresh burden for a dying man, and nodded slowly, in reluctant agreement with the unspoken thought in Vallery's eyes.

" Afraid you're right, sir. Torpedo. Somebody's stopped a packet."

" Do you hear there ! " The capstan flat speaker was hurried, intense, unnaturally loud in the aftermath of silence. " Do you hear there ! Captain on the bridge : urgent. Captain on the bridge : urgent. Captain on the bridge : urgent. . . ."

CHAPTER ELEVEN

FRIDAY EVENING

BENT ALMOST double, Captain Vallery clutched the handrail of the port ladder leading up to the fo'c'sle deck. Desperately, he tried to look out over the darkened water, but he could see nothing. A mist, a dark and swirling and roaring mist flecked with blood, a mist shot through with dazzling light swam before his eyes and he was blind. His breath came in great whooping gasps that racked his tortured lungs : his lower ribs were clamped in giant pincers, pincers that were surely crushing him. That stumbling, lurching run from the forepeak, he dimly realised, had all but killed him. Close, too damn' close, he thought. I must be more careful in future. . . .

Slowly his vision cleared, but the brilliant light remained. Heavens above, Vallery thought, a blind man could have seen all there was to see here. For there was nothing to be seen but the tenebrous silhouette, so faint as to be almost imagined, of a tanker deep, deep in the water—and a great column of flame, hundreds of feet in height, streaking upwards from the heart of the dense mushroom of smoke that obscured the bows of the torpedoed ship. Even at the distance of half a mile, the roaring of the flames was almost intolerable. Vallery watched, appalled. Behind him he could hear Nicholls swearing, softly, bitterly, continuously.

Vallery felt Petersen's hand on his arm. " Does the Captain wish to go up to the bridge ? "

" In a moment, Petersen, in a moment. Just hang on." His mind was functioning again, his eyes, conditioned by forty years' training, automatically sweeping the horizon. Funny, he thought, you can hardly see the tanker—the *Vytura*, it must be—she's shielded by that thick pall of smoke, probably; but the other ships in the convoy, white, ghost-like, sharply etched against the indigo blue of the sky, were bathed in that deadly glare. Even the stars had died.

He became aware that Nicholls was no longer swearing in repetitious monotony, that he was talking to him.

"A tanker, isn't it, sir? Hadn't we better take shelter? Remember what happened to that other one!"

"What one?" Vallery was hardly listening.

"The *Cochella*. A few days ago, I think it was. Good God, no! It was only this morning!"

"When tankers go up, they go up, Nicholls." Vallery seemed curiously far away. "If they just burn, they may last long enough. Tankers die hard, terribly hard, my boy: they live where any other ship would sink."

"But—but she must have a hole the size of a house in her side!" Nicholls protested.

"No odds," Vallery replied. He seemed to be waiting, watching for something. "Tremendous reserve buoyancy in these ships. Maybe 27 sealed tanks, not to mention cofferdams, pump-rooms, engine-room. . . . Never heard of the Nelson device for pumping compressed air into a tanker's oil tanks to give it buoyancy, to keep it afloat? Never heard of Captain Dudley Mason and the *Ohio*? Never heard of . . ." He broke off suddenly, and when he spoke again, the dreaming lethargy of the voice was gone.

"I thought so!" he exclaimed, his voice sharp with excitement "I thought so! The *Vytura's* still under way, still under command! Good God, she must still be doing almost 15 knots! The bridge, quick!"

Vallery's feet left the deck, barely touched it again till Petersen set him down carefully on the duckboards in front of the startled Commander. Vallery grinned faintly at Turner's astonishment, at the bushy eyebrows lifting over the dark, lean buccaneer's face, leaner, more recklessly chiselled than ever in the glare of the blazing tanker. If ever a man was born 400 years too late, Vallery thought inconsequentially; but what a man to have around!

" It's all right, Commander." He laughed shortly. " Brooks thought I needed a Man Friday. That's Stoker Petersen. Over-enthusiastic, maybe a trifle apt to take orders too literally. . . . But he was a Godsend to me to-night. . . . But never mind me." He jerked his thumb towards the tanker, blazing even more whitely now, difficult to look at, almost, as the noonday sun. " How about him ? "

" Makes a bloody fine lighthouse for any German ship or plane that happens to be looking for us," Turner growled. " Might as well send a signal to Trondheim giving our lat. and long."

" Exactly," Vallery nodded. " Besides setting up some beautiful targets for the sub that got the *Vytura* just now. A dangerous fellow, Commander. That was a brilliant piece of work—in almost total darkness, too."

" Probably a scuttle somebody forgot to shut. We haven't the ships to keep checking them all the time. And it wasn't so damned brilliant, at least not for him. The *Viking's* in contact right now, sitting over the top of him. . . . I sent her right away."

" Good man ! " Vallery said warmly. He turned to look at the burning tanker, looked back at Turner, his face set. " She'll have to go, Commander."

Turner nodded slowly. " She'll have to go," he echoed.

" It *is* the *Vytura*, isn't it ? "

" That's her. Same one that caught it this morning."

" Who's the master ? "

" Haven't the foggiest," Turner confessed. " Number One, Pilot ? Any idea where the sailing list is ? "

" No, sir." The Kapok Kid was hesitant, oddly unsure of himself. " Admiral had them, I know. Probably gone, now."

" What makes you think that ? " Vallery asked sharply.

" Spicer, his pantry steward, was almost choked with smoke this afternoon, found him making a whacking great fire in his bath," the Kapok Kid said miserably. " Said he was burning vital documents that must not fall into enemy hands. Old newspapers, mostly, but I think the list must have been among them. It's nowhere else."

" Poor old . . ." Turner remembered just in time that he was speaking of the Admiral, broke off, shook his head in compassionate wonder. " Shall I send a signal to Fletcher on the *Cape Hatteras* ? "

" Never mind." Vallery was impatient. " There's no time. Bentley—to the master, *Vytura* : ' Please abandon ship immediately : we are going to sink you.' "

Suddenly Vallery stumbled, caught hold of Turner's arm.

" Sorry," he apologised. " I'm afraid my legs are going. Gone, rather." He smiled up wryly at the anxious faces. " No good pretending any longer, is there ? Not when your legs start a mutiny on their own. Oh, dear God, I'm done ! "

" And no bloody wonder ! " Turner swore. " I wouldn't treat a mad dog the way you treat yourself ! Come on, sir. Admiral's chair for you—now. If you don't, I'll get Petersen to you," he threatened, as Vallery made to protest. The protest died in a smile, and Vallery meekly allowed himself to be helped into a chair. He sighed deeply, relaxed into the God-sent support of the back and arms of the chair. He felt ghastly, powerless, his wasted body a wide sea of pain, and deadly cold ; all these things, but also proud and grateful—Turner had never even suggested that he go below.

He heard the gate crash behind him, the murmur of voices, then Turner was at his side.

" The Master-At-Arms, sir. Did you send for him ? "

" I certainly did." Vallery twisted in his chair, his face grim. " Come here, Hastings ! "

The Master-At-Arms stood at attention before him. As always, his face was a mask, inscrutable, expressionless, almost inhuman in that fierce light.

" Listen carefully." Vallery had to raise his voice above the roar of the flames : the effort even to speak was exhausting. " I have no time to talk to you now. I will see you in the morning. Meantime, you will release Leading Seaman Ralston immediately. You will then hand over your duties, your papers and your keys to Regulating Petty Officer Perrat. Twice, now, you have overstepped the limits of your authority : that is insolence, but it can be overlooked. But you have also kept a man locked in cells during Action Stations. The prisoner would have died like a rat in a trap. You are no longer Master-At-Arms of the *Ulysses*. That is all."

For a couple of seconds Hastings stood rigidly in shocked, unbelieving silence, then the iron discipline snapped. He stepped forward, arms raised in appeal, the mask collapsed in contorted bewilderment.

"Relieved of my duties? Relieved of my duties! But, sir, you can't do that! You can't . . ."

His voice broke off in a gasp of pain as Turner's iron grip closed over his elbow.

"Don't say ' can't ' to the Captain," he whispered silkily in his ear. "You heard him? Get off the bridge!"

The gate clicked behind him. Carrington said, conversationally : "Somebody's using his head aboard the *Vytura*—fitted a red filter to his Aldis. Couldn't see it otherwise."

Immediately the tension eased. All eyes were on the winking red light, a hundred feet aft of the flames, and even then barely distinguishable. Suddenly it stopped.

"What does he say, Bentley?" Vallery asked quickly.

Bentley coughed apologetically. "Message reads : ' Are you hell. Try it and I will ram you. Engine intact. We can make it.' "

Vallery closed his eyes for a moment. He was beginning to appreciate how old Giles must have felt. When he looked up again, he had made his decision.

"Signal : ' You are endangering entire convoy. Abandon ship at once. Repeat, at once.' " He turned to the Commander, his mouth bitter. "I take off my hat to him. How would *you* like to sit on top of enough fuel to blow you to Kingdom Come. . . . Must be oil in some of his tanks. . . . God, how I hate to have to threaten a man like that!"

"I know, sir," Turner murmured. "I know how it is. . . . Wonder what the *Viking's* doing out there? Should be hearing from her now?"

"Send a signal," Vallery ordered. "Ask for information." He peered aft, searched briefly for the Torpedo Lieutenant. "Where's Marshall?"

"Marshall?" Turner was surprised. "In the Sick Bay, of course. Still on the injured list, remember—four ribs gone?"

"Of course, of course!" Vallery shook his head tiredly, angry with himself. "And the Chief Torpedo Gunner's Mate—Noyes, isn't it?—he was killed yesterday in Number 3. How about Vickers?"

"He was in the F.D.R."

"In the F.D.R.," Vallery repeated slowly. He wondered why his heart didn't stop beating. He was long past the stage of chilled bone and coagulating blood. His whole body was a great block of ice. . . . He had never known that such cold could exist. It was very strange, he thought, that he was no longer shivering. . . .

"I'll do it myself, sir," Turner interrupted his wandering. "I'll take over the bridge Torpedo Control—used to be the worst Torps. officer on the China Station." He smiled faintly. "Perhaps the hand has not lost what little cunning it ever possessed!"

"Thank you." Vallery was grateful. "You just do that."

"We'll have to take him from starboard," Turner reminded him. "Port control was smashed this morning—foremast didn't do it any good. . . . I'll go check the Dumaresq.[1] . . . Good God!" His hand gripped Vallery's shoulder with a strength that made him wince. "It's the Admiral, sir! He's coming on to the bridge!"

Incredulously, Vallery twisted round in his chair. Turner was right. Tyndall was coming through the gate, heading purposefully towards him. In the deep shadow cast by the side of the bridge, he seemed disembodied. The bare head, sparsely covered with thin, straggling wisps of white, the grey, pitifully-shrunken face, the suddenly stooped shoulders, unaccountably thin under black oilskins, all these were thrown into harsh relief by the flames. Below, nothing was visible. Silently, Tyndall padded his way across the bridge, stood waiting at Vallery's side.

Slowly, leaning on Turner's ready arm, Vallery climbed down. Unsmiling, Tyndall looked at him, nodded gravely, hoisted himself into his seat. He picked up the binoculars from the ledge before him, slowly quartered the horizon.

It was Turner who noticed it first.

[1] The Dumaresq was a miniature plotting table on which such relevant factors as corresponding speeds and courses were worked out to provide firing tracks for the torpedoes.

" Sir ! You've no gloves on, sir ! "

" What ? What did you say ? " Tyndall replaced the glasses, looked incuriously at his blood-stained, bandaged hands. " Ah ! Do you know, I _knew_ I had forgotten something. That's the second time. Thank you, Commander." He smiled courteously, picked up the binoculars again, resumed his quartering of the horizon. All at once Vallery felt another, deadlier chill pass through him, and it had nothing to do with the bitter chill of the Arctic night.

Turner hesitated helplessly for a second, then turned quickly to the Kapok Kid.

" Pilot ! Haven't I seen gauntlets hanging in your chart-house ? "

" Yes, sir. Right away ! " The Kapok Kid hurried off the bridge.

Turner looked up at the Admiral again.

" Your head, sir—you've nothing on. Wouldn't you like a duffel coat, a hood, sir ? "

" A hood ? " Tyndall was amused. " What in the world for ? I'm not cold. . . . If you'll excuse me, Commander ? " He turned the binoculars full into the glare of the blazing _Vytura_. Turner looked at him again, looked at Vallery, hesitated, then walked aft.

Carpenter was on his way back with the gloves when the W.T. loudspeaker clicked on.

" W.T.—bridge. W.T.—bridge. Signal from _Viking_ : ' Lost contact. Am continuing search.' "

" Lost contact ! " Vallery exclaimed. Lost contact—the worst possible thing that could have happened ! A U-boat out there, loose, unmarked, and the whole of FR77 lit up like a fairground. A fairground, he thought bitterly, clay pipes in a shooting gallery and with about as much chance of hitting back once contact had been lost. Any second now. . . .

He wheeled round, clutched at the binnacle for support. He had forgotten how weak he was, how the tilting of the shattered bridge affected balance.

" Bentley ! No reply from the _Vytura_ yet ? "

" No, sir." Bentley was as concerned as the Captain, as aware

of the desperate need for speed. " Maybe his power's gone—
no, no, no, there he is now, sir ! "

" Captain, sir."

Vallery looked round. " Yes, Commander, what is it ? Not
more bad news, I hope ? "

" 'Fraid so, sir. Starboard tubes won't train—jammed solid."

" Won't train," Vallery snapped irritably. " That's nothing
new, surely. Ice, frozen snow. Chip it off, use boiling water,
blowlamps, any old——"

" Sorry, sir." Turner shook his head regretfully. " Not that.
Rack and turntable buckled. Must have been either the shell that
got the bosun's store or Number 3 Low Power Room—immediately below. Anyway—kaput ! "

" Very well, then ! " Vallery was impatient. " It'll have to
be the port tubes."

" No bridge control left, sir," Turner objected. " Unless we
fire by local control ? "

" No reason why not, is there ? " Vallery demanded. " After
all, that's what torpedo crews are trained for. Get on to the port
tubes—I assume the communication line there is still intact—tell
them to stand by."

" Yes, sir."

" And Turner ? "

" Sir ? "

" I'm sorry." He smiled crookedly. " As old Giles used to
say of himself, I'm just a crusty old curmudgeon. Bear with me,
will you ? "

Turner grinned sympathetically, then sobered quickly. He
jerked his head forward.

" How is he, sir ? "

Vallery looked at the Commander for a long second, shook
his head, almost imperceptibly. Turner nodded heavily and was
gone.

" Well, Bentley ? What does he say ? "

" Bit confused, sir," Bentley apologised. " Couldn't get it
all. Says he's going to leave the convoy, proceed on his own.
Something like that, sir."

Proceed on his own ! That was no solution, Vallery knew.

He might still burn for hours, a dead give-away, even on a different course. But to proceed on his own ! An unprotected, crippled, blazing tanker—and a thousand miles to Murmansk, the worst thousand miles in all the world ! Vallery closed his eyes. He felt sick to his heart. A man like that, and a ship like that— and he had to destroy them both !

Suddenly Tyndall spoke.

" Port 30 ! " he ordered. His voice was loud, authoritative. Vallery stiffened in dismay. Port 30 ! They'd turn into the *Vytura*.

There was a couple of seconds' silence, then Carrington, Officer of the Watch, bent over the speaking-tube, repeated : " Port 30." Vallery started forward, stopped short as he saw Carrington gesturing at the speaking-tube. He'd stuffed a gauntlet down the mouthpiece.

" Midships ! "

" Midships, sir ! "

" Steady ! Captain ? "

" Sir ? "

" That light hurts my eyes," Tyndall complained. " Can't we put that fire out ? "

" We'll try, sir." Vallery walked across, spoke softly. " You look tired, sir. Wouldn't you like to go below ? "

" What ? Go below ! Me ! "

" Yes, sir. We'll send for you if we need you," he added persuasively.

Tyndall considered this for a moment, shook his head firmly.

" Won't do, Dick. Not fair to you. . . ." His voice trailed away and he muttered something that sounded like ' Admiral Tyndall,' but Vallery couldn't be sure.

" Sir ? I didn't catch—— "

" Nothing ? " Tyndall was very abrupt. He looked away towards the *Vytura*, exclaimed in sudden pain, flung up an arm to protect his eyes. Vallery, too, started back, eyes screwed up to shut out the sudden blinding flash of flame from the *Vytura*.

The explosion crashed in their ears almost simultaneously, the blast of the pressure wave sent them reeling. The *Vytura* had been torpedoed again, right aft, close to her engine-room, and was heavily on fire there. Only the bridge island, amidships, was miraculously free from smoke and flames. Even in the moment of shock, Vallery thought, " She must go now. She can't last much longer." But he knew he was deluding himself, trying to avoid the inevitable, the decision he must take. Tankers, as he'd told Nicholls, died hard, terribly hard. Poor old Giles, he thought unaccountably, poor old Giles.

He moved aft to the port gate. Turner was shouting angrily into the telephone.

" You'll damn' well do what you're told, do you hear ? Get them out immediately ! Yes, I said ' immediately ! ' "

Vallery touched his arm in surprise. " What's the matter, Commander ? "

" Of all the bloody insolence ! " Turner snorted. " Telling *me* what to do ! "

" Who ? "

" The L.T.O. on the tubes. Your friend Ralston ! " said Turner wrathfully.

" Ralston ! Of course ! " Vallery remembered now. " He told me that was his night Action Stations. What's wrong ? "

" What's wrong : Says he doesn't think he can do it. Doesn't like to, doesn't wish to do it, if you please. Blasted insubordination ! " Turner fumed.

Vallery blinked at him. " Ralston—are you sure ? But of course you are. . . . I wonder. . . . That boy's been through a very private hell, Turner. Do you think—— "

" I don't know what to think ! " Turner lifted the phone again. " Tubes nine-oh ? At last ! . . . What ? What did you say ? . . . Why don't we . . . Gunfire ! Gunfire ! " He hung up the receiver with a crash, swung round on Vallery.

" Asks me, pleads with me, for gunfire instead of torpedoes ! He's mad, he must be ! But mad or not, I'm going down there to knock some sense into that mutinous young devil ! " Turner was angrier than Vallery had ever seen him. " Can you get Carrington to man this phone, sir ? "

" Yes, yes, of course ! " Vallery himself had caught up some of Turner's anger. " Whatever his sentiments, this is no time to express them ! " he snapped. " Straighten him up. . . . Maybe

I've been too lenient, too easy, perhaps he thinks we're in his debt, at some psychological disadvantage, for the shabby treatment he's received. . . . All right, all right, Commander !" Turner's mounting impatience was all too evident. " Off you go. Going in to attack in three or four minutes." He turned abruptly, passed in to the compass platform.

" Bentley ! "

" Sir ? "

" Last signal——"

" Better have a look, sir," Carrington interrupted. " He's slowing up."

Vallery stepped forward, peered over the windscreen. The *Vytura*, a roaring mass of flames, was falling rapidly astern.

" Clearing the davits, sir ! " the Kapok Kid reported excitedly. " I think—yes, yes, I can see the boat coming down ! "

" Thank God for that ! " Vallery whispered. He felt as though he had been granted a new lease of life. Head bowed, he clutched the screen with both hands—reaction had left him desperately weak. After a few seconds he looked up.

" W.T. code signal to *Sirrus*," he ordered quietly. " Circle well astern. Pick up survivors from the *Vytura's* lifeboat.' "

He caught Carrington's quick look and shrugged. " It's a better than even risk, Number One, so to hell with Admiralty orders. God," he added with sudden bitterness, " wouldn't I love to see a boatload of the ' no-survivors-will-be-picked-up' Whitehall warriors drifting about in the Barents Sea ! " He turned away, caught sight of Nicholls and Petersen.

" Still, here, are you, Nicholls ? Hadn't you better get below ? "

" If you wish, sir." Nicholls hesitated, nodded forward towards Tyndall.

" I thought, perhaps——"

" Perhaps you're right, perhaps you're right." Vallery shook his head in weary perplexity. " We'll see. Just wait a bit, will you ? " He raised his voice. " Pilot ! "

" Sir ? "

" Slow ahead both ! "

" Slow ahead both, sir ! "

Gradually, then more quickly, way fell off the *Ulysses* and she dropped slowly astern of the convoy. Soon, even the last ships in the lines were ahead of her, thrashing their way to the north-east. The snow was falling more thickly now, but still the ships were bathed in that savage glare, frighteningly vulnerable in their naked helplessness.

Seething with anger, Turner brought up short at the port torpedoes. The tubes were out, their evil, gaping mouths, high-lighted by the great flames, pointing out over the intermittent refulgence of the rolling swell. Ralston, perched high on the unprotected control position above the central tube, caught his eye at once.

" Ralston ! " Turner's voice was harsh, imperious. " I want to speak to you ! "

Ralston turned round quickly, rose, jumped on to the deck. He stood facing the Commander. They were of a height, their eyes on a level, Ralston's still, blue, troubled, Turner's dark and stormy with anger.

" What the hell's the matter with you, Ralston ? " Turner ground out. " Refusing to obey orders, is that it ? "

" No, sir." Ralston's voice was quiet, curiously strained. " That's not true."

" Not true ! " Turner's eyes were narrowed, his fury barely in check. " Then what's all this bloody claptrap about not wanting to man the tubes ? Are you thinking of emulating Stoker Riley ? Or have you just taken leave of your senses—if any ? "

Ralston said nothing.

The silence, a silence all too easily interpreted as dumb insolence infuriated Turner. His powerful hands reached out, grasped Ralston's duffel coat. He pulled the rating towards him, thrust his face closed to the other's.

" I asked a question, Ralston," he said softly. " I haven't had an answer. I'm waiting. What *is* all this ? "

" Nothing, sir." Distress in his eyes, perhaps, but no fear. " I—I just don't want to, sir. I hate to do it—to send one of our own ships to the bottom ! " The voice was pleading, now, blurred with overtones of desperation : Turner was deaf to them. " Why does she have to go, sir ! " he cried. " Why ? Why ? Why ? "

" None of your bloody business—but as it so happens she's endangering the entire convoy ! " Turner's face was still within inches of Ralston's. " You've got a job to do, orders to obey. Just get up there and obey them ! Go on ! " he roared, as Ralston hesitated. " Get up there ! " He fairly spat the words out.

Ralston didn't move.

" There are other L.T.O.s, sir ! " His arms lifted high in appeal, something in the voice cut through Turner's blind anger : he realised, almost with shock, that this boy was desperate. " Couldn't *they*—— ? "

" Let someone else do the dirty work, eh ? That's what you mean, isn't it ? " Turner was bitingly contemptuous. " Get them to do what you won't do yourself, you—you contemptible young bastard ! Communications Number ? Give me your set. I'll take over from the bridge." He took the phone, watched Ralston climb slowly back up and sit hunched forward, head bent over the Dumaresq.

" Number One ? Commander speaking. All set here. Captain there ? "

" Yes, sir. I'll call him." Carrington put down the phone, walked through the gate.

" Captain, sir. Commander's on the——"

" Just a moment ! " The upraised hand, the tenseness of the voice stopped him. " Have a look, No. 1. What do you think ? " Vallery pointed towards the *Vytura*, past the oilskinned figure of the Admiral. Tyndall's head was sunk on his chest, and he was muttering incoherently to himself.

Carrington followed the pointing finger. The lifeboat, dimly visible through the thickening snow, had slipped her falls while the *Vytura* was still under way. Crammed with men, she was dropping quickly astern under the great twisting column of flame—dropping far too quickly astern as the First Lieutenant suddenly realised. He turned round, found Vallery's eyes, bleak and tired and old, on his own. Carrington nodded slowly.

" She's picking up, sir. Under way, under command. . . . What are you going to do, sir ? "

"God help me, I've no choice. Nothing from the *Viking*, nothing from the *Sirrus*, nothing from our Asdic—and that U-boat's still out there. . . . Tell Turner what's happened. Bentley ! "

" Sir ? "

" Signal the *Vytura*." The mouth, whitely compressed, belied the eyes—eyes dark and filled with pain. " ' Abandon ship. Torpedoing you in three minutes. Last signal.' Port 20, Pilot ! "

" Port 20 it is, sir."

The *Vytura* was breaking off tangentially, heading north. Slowly, the *Ulysses* came round, almost paralleling her course, now a little astern of her.

" Half-ahead, Pilot ! "

" Half-ahead it is, sir."

" Pilot ? "

" Sir ? "

" What's Admiral Tyndall saying ? Can you make it out ? "

Carpenter bent forward, listened, shook his head. Little flurries of snow fell off his fur helmet.

" Sorry, sir. Can't make him out—too much noise from the *Vytura*. . . . I think he's humming, sir."

" Oh, God ! " Vallery bent his head, looked up again, slowly, painfully. Even so slight an effort was labour intolerable.

He looked across to the *Vytura*, stiffened to attention. The red Aldis was winking again. He tried to read it, but it was too fast : or perhaps his eyes were just too old, or tired : or perhaps he just couldn't think any more. . . . There was something weirdly hypnotic about that tiny crimson light flickering between these fantastic curtains of flame, curtains sweeping slowly, ominously together, majestic in their inevitability. And then the little red light had died, so unexpectedly, so abruptly, that Bentley's voice reached him before the realisation.

" Signal from the *Vytura*, sir."

Vallery tightened his grip on the binnacle. Bentley guessed the nod, rather than saw it.

" Message reads : ' Why don't you —— off. Nuts to the Senior Service. Tell him I send all my love.' " The voice died softly away, and there was only the roaring of the flames, the lost pinging of the Asdic.

" All my love." Vallery shook his head in silent wonderment. " All my love ! He's crazy ! He must be. ' All my love,' and I'm going to destroy him. . . . Number One ! "

" Sir ? "

" Tell the Commander to stand by ! "

Turner repeated the message from the bridge, turned to Ralston.

" Stand by, L.T.O. ! " He looked out over the side, saw that the *Vytura* was slightly ahead now, that the *Ulysses* was still angling in on an interception course. " About two minutes now, I should say." He felt the vibration beneath his feet dying away, knew the *Ulysses* was slowing down. Any second now, and she'd start slewing away to starboard. The receiver crackled again in his ear, the sound barely audible above the roaring of the flames. He listened, looked up. " ' X ' and ' Y ' only. Medium settings. Target 11 knots." He spoke into the phone. " How long ? "

" How long, sir ? " Carrington repeated.

" Ninety seconds," Vallery said huskily. " Pilot—starboard 10." He jumped, startled, as he heard the crash of falling binoculars, saw the Admiral slump forward, face and neck striking cruelly on the edge of the windscreen, the arms dangling loosely from the shoulders.

" Pilot ! "

But the Kapok Kid was already there. He slipped an arm under Tyndall, took most of the dead weight off the biting edge of the screen.

" What's the matter, sir ? " His voice was urgent, blurred with anxiety. " What's wrong ? "

Tyndall stirred slightly, his cheek lying along the edge of the screen.

" Cold, cold, cold," he intoned. The quavering tones were those of an old, a very old man.

" What ? What did you say, sir ? " the Kapok Kid begged.

" Cold. I'm cold. I'm terribly cold ! My feet, my feet ! " The old voice wandered away, and the body slipped into a corner of the bridge, the grey face upturned to the falling snow.

Intuition, an intuition amounting to a sudden sick certainty, sent the Kapok Kid plunging to his knees. Vallery heard the muffled exclamation, saw him straighten up and swing round, his face blank with horror.

" He's—he's got nothing on, sir," he said unsteadily. " He's barefoot! They're frozen—frozen solid!"

" Barefoot?" Vallery repeated unbelievingly. " Barefeet! It's not possible!"

" And pyjamas, sir! That's all he's wearing!"

Vallery lurched forward, peeling off his gloves. He reached down, felt his stomach turn over in shocked nausea as his fingers closed on ice-chilled skin. Bare feet! And pyjamas! Bare feet— no wonder he'd padded so silently across the duckboards! Numbly, he remembered that the last temperature reading had shown 35° of frost. And Tyndall, feet caked in frozen snow and slush, had been sitting there for almost five minutes! . . . He felt great hands under his armpits, felt himself rising effortlessly to his feet. Petersen. It *could* only be Petersen, of course. And Nicholls behind him.

" Leave this to me, sir. Right, Petersen, take him below." Nicholls's brisk, assured voice, the voice of a man competent in his own element, steadied Vallery, brought him back to the present, and the demands of the present, more surely than anything else could have done. He became aware of Carrington's clipped, measured voice, reeling off course, speed, directions, saw the *Vytura* 50° off the port bow, dropping slowly, steadily aft. Even at that distance, the blast of heat was barely tolerable—what in the name of heaven was it like on the bridge of the *Vytura*?

" Set course, Number One," he called. " Local control."

" Set course, local control." Carrington might have been on a peace-time exercise in the Solent.

" Local control," Turner repeated. He hung up the set, looked round. " You're on your own, Ralston," he said softly.

There was no reply. The crouched figure on the control position, immobile as graved stone, gave no sign that he had heard.

" Thirty seconds!" Turner said sharply. " All lined up?"

" Yes, sir." The figure stirred. " All lined up." Suddenly,

he swung round, in desperate, final appeal. " For God's sake, sir ! Is there no other——"

" Twenty seconds ! " Turner said viciously. " Do you want a thousand lives on your lily-livered conscience ? And if you miss . . ."

Ralston swung slowly back. For a mere breath of time, his face was caught full in the harsh glare of the *Vytura* : with sudden shock, Turner saw that the eyes were masked with tears. Then he saw the lips move. " Don't worry, sir. I won't miss." The voice was quite toneless, heavy with nameless defeat.

Perplexed, now, rather than angry, and quite uncomprehending, Turner saw the left sleeve come up to brush the eyes, saw the right hand stretch forward, close round the grip of " X " firing lever. Incongruously, there sprang to Turner's mind the famous line of Chaucer, " In goon the spears full sadly in arrest." In the closing of that hand there was the same heart-stopping decision, the same irrevocable finality.

Suddenly, so suddenly that Turner started in spite of himself, the hand jerked convulsively back. He heard the click of the tripping lever, the muffled roar in the explosion chamber, the hiss of compressed air, and the torpedo was gone, its evil sleekness gleaming fractionally in the light of the flames before it crashed below the surface of the sea. It was hardly gone before the tubes shuddered again and the second torpedo was on its way.

For five, ten seconds Turner stared out, fascinated, watching the arrowing wakes of bubbles vanish in the distance. A total of 1,500 lbs. of Amatol in these warheads—God help the poor bastards aboard the *Vytura*. . . . The deck speaker clicked on.

" Do you hear there ? Do you hear there ? Take cover immediately ! Take cover immediately ! " Turner stirred, tore his eyes away from the sea, looked up, saw that Ralston was still crouched in his seat.

" Come down out of there, you young fool ! " he shouted. " Want to be riddled when the *Vytura* goes up ? Do you hear me ? "

Silence. No word, no movement, only the roaring of the flames.

" Ralston ! "

" I'm all right, sir." Ralston's voice was muffled : he did not even trouble to turn his head.

Turner swore, leapt up on the tubes, dragged Ralston from his seat, pulled him down to the deck and into shelter. Ralston offered no resistance : he seemed sunk in a vast apathy, an uncaring indifference.

Both torpedoes struck home. The end was swift, curiously unspectacular. Listeners—there were no watchers—on the *Ulysses* tensed themselves for the shattering detonation, but the detonation never came. Broken-backed and tired of fighting, the *Vytura* simply collapsed in on her stricken midships, lay gradually, wearily over on her side and was gone.

Three minutes later, Turner opened the door of the Captain's shelter, pushed Ralston in before him.

" Here you are, sir," he said grimly. " Thought you might like to see what a conscientious objector looks like ! "

" I certainly do ! " Vallery laid down the log-book, turned a cold eye on the torpedoman, looked him slowly up and down. " A fine job, Ralston, but it doesn't excuse your conduct. Just a minute, Commander."

He turned back to the Kapok Kid. " Yes, that seems all right, Pilot. It'll make good reading for their lordships," he added bitterly. " The ones the Germans don't get, we finish off for them. . . . Remember to signal the *Hatteras* in the morning, ask for the name of the master of the *Vytura*."

" He's dead. . . . You needn't trouble yourself ! " said Ralston bitterly, then staggered as the Commander's open hand smashed across his face. Turner was breathing heavily, his eyes dark with anger.

" You insolent young devil ! " he said softly. " That was just a little too much from you."

Ralston's hand came up slowly, fingered the reddening weal on his cheek.

" You misunderstand me, sir." There was no anger, the voice was a fading murmur, they had to strain to catch his words. " The master of the *Vytura*—I can tell you his name. It's Ralston. Captain Michael Ralston. He was my father."

CHAPTER TWELVE

SATURDAY

To ALL things an end, to every night its dawn; even to the longest night when dawn never comes, there comes at last the dawn. And so it came for FR77, as grey, as bitter, as hopeless as the night had been long. But it came.

It came to find the convoy some 350 miles north of the Arctic Circle, steaming due east along the 72nd parallel of latitude, half-way between Jan Mayen and the North Cape. 8° 45' east, the Kapok Kid reckoned, but he couldn't be sure. In heavy snow and with ten-tenth cloud, he was relying on dead reckoning: he had to, for the shell that had destroyed the F.D.R. had wrecked the Automatic Plot. But roughly 600 nautical miles to go. 600 miles, 40 hours, and the convoy—or what would be left of it by that time—would be in the Kola Inlet, steaming up-river to Polyarnoe and Murmansk . . . 40 hours.

It came to find the convoy—14 ships left in all—scattered over three square miles of sea and rolling heavily in the deepening swell from the NNE.: 14 ships, for another had gone in the deepest part of the night. Mine, torpedo? Nobody knew, nobody ever would know. The *Sirrus* had stopped, searched the area for an hour with hooded ten-inch signalling lamps. There had been no survivors. Not that Commander Orr had expected to find any—not with the air temperature 6° below zero.

It came after a sleepless night of never-ending alarms, of continual Asdic contacts, of constant depth-charging that achieved nothing. Nothing, that is, from the escorts' point of view: but for the enemy, it achieved a double-edged victory. It kept exhausted men at Action Stations all night long, blunting, irreparably perhaps, the last vestiges of the knife-edged vigilance on

which the only hope—it was never more—of survival in the
Arctic depended. More deadly still, it had emptied the last depth-
charge rack in the convoy. . . . It was a measure of the intensity
of the attack, of the relentlessness of the persecution, that this had
never happened before. But it had happened now. There was
not a single depth-charge left—not one. The fangs were drawn,
the defences were down. It was only a matter of time before the
wolf-packs discovered that they could strike at will. . . .

And with the dawn, of course, came dawn Action Stations,
or what would have been dawn stations had the men not already
been closed up for fifteen hours, fifteen endless hours of intense
cold and suffering, fifteen hours during which the crew of the
Ulysses had been sustained by cocoa and one bully-beef sandwich,
thin-sliced and stale, for there had been no time to bake the
previous day. But dawn stations were profoundly significant in
themselves : they prolonged the waiting another interminable
two hours—and to a man rocking on his feet from unimaginable
fatigue, literally holding convulsively jerking eyelids apart with
finger and thumb while a starving brain, which is less a brain
than a well of fine-drawn agony, begs him to let go, let go just
for a second, just this once and never again, even a minute is
brutal eternity : and they were still more important in that they
were recognised as the Ithuriel hour of the Russian Convoys, the
testing time when every man stood out clearly for what he was.
And for the crew of a mutiny ship, for men already tried and
condemned, for physically broken and mentally scourged men
who neither could nor would ever be the same again in body or
mind, the men of the *Ulysses* had no need to stand in shame.
Not all, of course, they were only human ; but many had found,
or were finding, that the point of no return was not necessarily
the edge of the precipice: it could be the bottom of the valley,
the beginning of the long climb up the far slope, and when a
man had once begun that climb he never looked back to that
other side.

For some men, neither precipice nor valley ever existed. Men
like Carrington, for instance. Eighteen consecutive hours on the
bridge now, he was still his own indestructible self, alert with that
relaxed watchfulness that never flagged, a man of infinite en_

durance, a man who could never crack, who you knew could never crack, for the imagination baulked at the very idea. Why he was what he was, no man could tell. Such, too, were men like Chief Petty Officer Hartley, like Chief Stoker Hendry, like Colour-Sergeant Evans and Sergeant MacIntosh; four men strangely alike, big, tough, kindly, no longer young, steeped in the traditions of the Service. Taciturn, never heard to speak of themselves, they were under no illusions as to their importance : they knew—as any Naval officer would be the first to admit— that, as the senior N.C.O.s, they, and not any officer, were the backbone of the Royal Navy ; and it was from their heavy sense of responsibility that sprung their rock-like stability. And then of course, there were men—a handful only—like Turner and the Kapok Kid and Dodson, whom dawn found as men above themselves, men revelling in danger and exhaustion, for only thus could they realise themselves, for only this had they been born. And finally, men like Vallery, who had collapsed just after midnight, and was still asleep in the shelter, and Surgeon Commander Brooks : wisdom was their sheet anchor, a clear appreciation of the relative insignificance both of themselves and the fate of FR77, a coldly intellectual appraisal of, married to an infinite compassion for, the follies and suffering of mankind.

At the other end of the scale, dawn found men—a few dozen, perhaps—gone beyond recovery. Gone in selfishness, in self-pity and in fear, like Carslake, gone because their armour, the trappings of authority, had been stripped off them, like Hastings, or gone, like Leading S.B.A. Johnson and a score of others, because they had been pushed too far and had no sheet anchor to hold them.

And between the two extremes were those—the bulk of the men—who had touched zero and found that endurance can be infinite—and found in this realisation the springboard for recovery. The other side of the valley *could* be climbed, but not without a staff. For Nicholls, tired beyond words from a long night standing braced against the operating table in the surgery, the staff was pride and shame. For Leading Seaman Doyle, crouched miserably into the shelter of the for'ard funnel, watching the pinched agony, the perpetual shivering of his young midships pom-pom crew, it was pity ; he would, of course, have denied this, blasphemously. For young Spicer, Tyndall's devoted pantry-boy, it was pity, too—pity and a savage grief for the dying man in the Admiral's cabin. Even with both legs amputated below the knee, Tyndall should not have been dying. But the fight, the resistance was gone, and Brooks knew old Giles would be glad to go. And for scores, perhaps for hundreds, for men like the tubercular-ridden McQuater, chilled to death in sodden clothes, but no longer staggering drunkenly round the hoist in " Y " turret, for the heavy rolling kept the water on the move : like Petersen, recklessly squandering his giant strength in helping his exhausted mates : like Chrysler, whose keen young eyes, invaluable now that Radar was gone, never ceased to scan the horizons : for men like these, the staff was Vallery, the tre-mendous respect and affection in which he was held, the sure knowledge that they could never let him down.

These, then, were the staffs, the intangible sheet anchors that held the *Ulysses* together that bleak and bitter dawn—pride, pity, shame, affection, grief—and the basic instinct for self-preservation although the last, by now, was an almost negligible factor. Two things were never taken into the slightest account as the springs of endurance : never mentioned, never even considered, they did not exist for the crew of the *Ulysses* : two things the senti-mentalists at home, the gallant leader writers of the popular press, the propagandising purveyors of nationalistic claptrap would have had the world believe to be the source of inspiration and en-durance—hatred of the enemy, love of kinsfolk and country.

There was no hatred of the enemy. Knowledge is the prelude to hate, and they did not know the enemy. Men cursed the enemy, respected him, feared him and killed him if they could : if they didn't, the enemy would kill them. Nor did men see themselves as fighting for King and country : they saw the necessity for war, but objected to camouflaging this necessity under a spurious cloak of perfervid patriotism : they were just doing what they were told, and if they didn't, they would be stuck against a wall and shot. Love of kinsfolk—that had some validity, but not much. It was natural to want to protect your kin, but this was an equation where the validity varied according to the factor of distance. It was a trifle difficult for a man crouched in his ice-coated Oerlikon cockpit off the shores of Bear Island to visualise himself as protecting that rose-covered cottage in the Cotswolds. . . . But for the rest, the synthetic national hatreds and the carefully cherished myth of King and country, these are nothing and less than nothing when mankind stands at the last frontier of hope and endurance : for only the basic, simple human emotions, the positive ones of love and grief and pity and distress, can carry a man across that last frontier.

Noon, and still the convoy, closed up in tight formation now, rolled eastwards in the blinding snow. The alarm half-way through dawn stations, had been the last that morning. Thirty-six hours to go, now, only thirty-six hours. And if this weather continued, the strong wind and blinding snow that made flying impossible, the near-zero visibility and heavy seas that would blind any periscope . . . there was always that chance. Only thirty-six hours.

Admiral John Tyndall died a few minutes after noon. Brooks, who had sat with him all morning, officially entered the cause of death as "post-operative shock and exposure." The truth was that Giles had died because he no longer wished to live. His professional reputation was gone : his faith, his confidence in himself were gone, and there was only remorse for the hundreds of men who had died : and with both legs gone, the only life he had ever known, the life he had so loved and cherished and to which he had devoted forty-five glad and unsparing years, that life, too, was gone for ever. Giles died gladly, willingly. Just on noon he recovered consciousness, looked at Brooks and Vallery with a smile from which every trace of madness had vanished. Brooks winced at that grey smile, mocking shadow of the famous guffaw of the Giles of another day. Then he closed his eyes and muttered something about his family—Brooks knew he had no family. His eyes opened again, he saw Vallery as if for the first time, rolled his eyes till he saw Spicer. " A chair for the Captain, my boy." Then he died.

He was buried at two o'clock, in the heart of a blizzard. The Captain's voice, reading the burial service, was shredded away by snow and wind : the Union flag was flapping emptily on the

tilted board before men knew he was gone : the bugle notes were
broken and distant and lost, far away and fading like the horns of
Elfland : and then the men, two hundred of them at least, turned
silently away and trudged back to their frozen mess-decks.

Barely half an hour later, the blizzard had died, vanished as
suddenly as it had come. The wind, too, had eased, and though
the sky was still dark and heavy with snow, though the seas were
still heavy enough to roll 15,000-ton ships through a 30° arc, it
was clear that the deterioration in the weather had stopped. On
the bridge, in the turrets, in the mess-decks, men avoided each
other's eyes and said nothing.

Just before 1500, the *Vectra* picked up an Asdic contact.
Vallery received the report, hesitated over his decision. If he sent
the *Vectra* to investigate, and if the *Vectra* located the U-boat
accurately and confined herself, as she would have to do, to
describing tight circles above the submarine, the reason for this
freedom from depth-charging would occur to the U-boat captain
within minutes. And then it would only be a matter of time—
until he decided it was safe to surface and use his radio—that
every U-boat north of the Circle would know that FR77 could
be attacked with impunity. Further, it was unlikely that any
torpedo attack would be made under such weather conditions.
Not only was periscope observation almost impossible in the
heavy seas, but the U-boat itself would be a most unstable firing
platform : wave motion is not confined to the surface of the water
—the effects can be highly uncomfortable and unstablising thirty,
forty, fifty feet down—and are appreciable, under extreme conditions, at a depth of almost a hundred feet. On the other hand,
the U-boat captain might take a 1,000-1 chance, might strike
home with a lucky hit. Vallery ordered the *Vectra* to investigate.

He was too late. The order would have been too late anyway.
The *Vectra* was still winking acknowledgment of the signal, had
not begun to turn, when the rumble of a heavy explosion reached
the bridge of the *Ulysses*. All eyes swept round a full circle of the
horizon, searching for smoke and flame, for the canted deck and
slewing ship that would show where the torpedo had gone home.
They found no sign, none whatsoever, until almost half a minute

had passed. Then they noticed, almost casually, that the *Electra*, leading ship in the starboard line, was slowing up, coming to a powerless stop, already settling in the water on an even keel, with no trace of tilt either for'ard or aft. Almost certainly, she had been holed in the engine-room.

The Aldis on the *Sirrus* had begun to flash. Bentley read the message, turned to Vallery.

" Commander Orr requests permission to go alongside, port side, take off survivors."

" Port, is it ? " Turner nodded. " The sub's blind side. It's a fair chance, sir—in a calm sea. As it is . . ." He looked over at the *Sirrus*, rolling heavily in the beam sea, and shrugged. " Won't do her paintwork any good."

" Her cargo ? " Vallery asked. " Any idea ? Explosives ? " He looked round, saw the mute headshakes, turned to Bentley.

" Ask *Electra* if she's carrying any explosives as cargo."

Bentley's Aldis chattered, fell silent. After half a minute, it was clear that there was going to be no reply.

" Power gone, perhaps, or his Aldis smashed," the Kapok Kid ventured. " How about one flag for explosives, two for none ? "

Vallery nodded in satisfaction. " You heard, Bentley ? "

He looked over the starboard quarter as the message went out. The *Vectra* was almost a mile distant, rolling one minute, pitching the next as she came round in a tight circle. She had found the killer—and her depth-charge racks were empty.

Vallery swung back, looked across to the *Electra*. Still no reply, nothing. . . . Then he saw two flags fluttering up to the yardarm.

" Signal the *Sirrus*," he ordered. " 'Go ahead : exercise extreme care.' "

Suddenly, he felt Turner's hand on his arm.

" Can you hear 'em ? " Turner asked.

" Hear what ? " Vallery demanded.

" Lord only knows. It's the *Vectra*. Look ! "

Vallery followed the pointing finger. At first, he could see nothing, then all at once he saw little geysers of water leaping up in the *Vectra's* wake, geysers swiftly extinguished by the heavy seas. Then, faintly, his straining ear caught the faraway murmur of underwater explosions, all but inaudible against the wind.

" What the devil's the *Vectra* doing ? " Vallery demanded. " And what's she using ? "

" Looks like fireworks to me," Turner grunted. " What do you think, Number One ? "

" Scuttling charges—25-pounders," Carrington said briefly.

" He's right, sir," Turner admitted. " Of course that's what they are. Mind you, he might as well be using fireworks," he added disparagingly.

But the Commander was wrong. A scuttling charge has less than a tenth part of the disruptive power of a depth-charge—but one lodged snugly in the conning-tower or exploding alongside a steering plane could be almost as lethal. Turner had hardly finished speaking when a U-boat—the first the *Ulysses* had seen above water for almost six months—porpoised high above the surface of the sea, hung there for two or three seconds, then crashed down on even keel, wallowing wickedly in the troughs between the waves.

The dramatic abruptness of her appearance—one moment the empty sea, the next a U-boat rolling in full view of the entire convoy—took every ship by surprise—including the *Vectra*. She was caught on the wrong foot, moving away on the outer leg of a figure-of-eight turn. Her pom-pom opened up immediately, but the pom-pom, a notoriously inaccurate gun in the best of circumstances, is a hopeless proposition on the rolling, heeling desk of a destroyer making a fast turn in heavy weather : the Oerlikons registered a couple of hits on the conning-tower, twin Lewises peppered the hull with as much effect as a horde of angry hornets ; but by the time the *Vectra* was round, her main armament coming to bear, the U-boat had disappeared slowly under the surface.

In spite of this, the *Vectra's* 4.7s opened up, firing into the sea where the U-boat had submerged, but stopping almost immediately when two shells in succession had ricocheted off the water and whistled dangerously through the convoy. She steadied on course, raced over the position of the submerged U-boat : watchers on the *Ulysses*, binoculars to their eyes, could just distinguish duffel-coated figures on the *Vectra's* poop-deck hurling more scuttling charges over the side. Almost at once, the *Vectra's* helm went hard over and she clawed her way back south again, guns at maximum depression pointing down over her starboard side.

The U-boat must have been damaged, more severely this time, by either the shells or the last charges. Again she surfaced, even more violently than before, in a seething welter of foam, and again the *Vectra* was caught on the wrong foot, for the submarine had surfaced off her port bow, three cable-lengths away.

And this time, the U-boat was up to stay. Whatever Captain and crew lacked, it wasn't courage. The hatch was open, and men were swarming over the side of the conning-tower to man the gun, in a token gesture of defiance against crushing odds.

The first two men over the side never reached the gun— breaking, sweeping waves, waves that towered high above the submarine's deck, washed them over the side and they were gone. But others flung themselves forward to take their place, frantically training their gun through a 90° arc to bear on the onrushing bows of the *Vectra*. Incredibly—for the seas were washing over the decks, seas which kept tearing the men from their posts, and the submarine was rolling with impossible speed and violence— their first shell, fired over open sights, smashed squarely into the bridge of the *Vectra*. The first shell and the last shell, for the crew suddenly crumpled and died, sinking down by the gun or pitching convulsively over the side.

It was massacre. The *Vectra* had two Bolton-Paul Defiant night-fighter turrets, quadruple hydraulic turrets complete with astrodome, bolted to her fo'c'sle, and these had opened up simultaneously, firing, between them, something like a fantastic total of 300 shells every ten seconds. That often misused cliché "hail of lead" was completely accurate here. It was impossible for a man to live two seconds on the exposed deck of that U-boat, to hope to escape that lethal storm. Man after man kept flinging himself over the coaming in suicidal gallantry, but none reached the gun.

Afterwards, no one aboard the *Ulysses* could say when they

first realised that the *Vectra*, pitching steeply through the heavy seas, was going to ram the U-boat. Perhaps her Captain had never intended to do so. Perhaps he had expected the U-boat to submerge, had intended to carry away conning tower and periscope standard, to make sure that she could not escape again. Perhaps he had been killed when that shell had struck the bridge. Or perhaps he had changed his mind at the last second, for the *Vectra*, which had been arrowing in on the conning-tower, suddenly slewed sharply to starboard.

For an instant, it seemed that she might just clear the U-boat's bows, but the hope died the second it was born. Plunging heavily down the sheering side of a gaping trough, the *Vectra's* forefoot smashed down and through the hull of the submarine, some thirty feet aft of the bows, slicing through the toughened steel of the pressure hull as if it were cardboard. She was still plunging, still driving down, when two shattering explosions, so close together as to be blurred into one giant blast, completely buried both vessels under a sky-rocketing mushroom of boiling water and twisted steel. The why of the explosion was pure conjecture ; but what had happened was plain enough. Some freak of chance must have triggered off the T.N.T.—normally an extremely stable and inert disruptive—in a warhead in one of the U-boat's tubes : and then the torpedoes in the storage racks behind and possibly, probably even, the for'ard magazine of the *Vectra* had gone up in sympathetic detonation.

Slowly, deliberately almost, the great clouds of water fell back into the sea, and the *Vectra* and the U-boat—or what little was left of them—came abruptly into view. To the watchers on the *Ulysses*, it was inconceivable that either of them should still be afloat. The U-boat was very deep in the water, seemed to end abruptly just for'ard of the gun platform : the *Vectra* looked as if some great knife had sheared her athwartships, just for'ard of the bridge. The rest was gone, utterly gone. And throughout the convoy unbelieving minds were still wildly rejecting the evidence of their eyes when the shattered hull of the *Vectra* lurched into the same trough as the U-boat, rolled heavily, wearily, over on top of her, bridge and mast cradling the conning-tower of the submarine. And then the water closed over them and they were gone, locked together to the bottom of the sea.

The last ships in the convoy were two miles away now, and in the broken seas, at that distance, it was impossible to see whether there were any survivors. It did not seem likely. And if there were, if there were men over there, struggling, swimming, shouting for help in the murderous cold of that glacial sea, they would be dying already. And they would have been dead long before any rescue ship could even have turned round. The convoy steamed on, beating steadily east. All but two, that is— the *Electra* and the *Sirrus*.

The *Electra* lay beam on to the seas, rolling slowly, sluggishly, dead in the water. She had now a list of almost 15° to port. Her decks, fore and aft of the bridge, were lined with waiting men. They had given up their attempt to abandon ship by lifeboat when they had seen the *Sirrus* rolling up behind them, fine on the port quarter. A boat had been swung out on its davits, and with the listing of the *Electra* and the rolling of the sea it had proved impossible to recover it. It hung now far out from the ship's side, swinging wildly at the end of its davits about twenty feet above the sea. On his approach, Orr had twice sent angry signals, asking the falls to be cut. But the lifeboat remained there, a menacing pendulum in the track of the *Sirrus* : panic, possibly, but more likely winch brakes jammed solid with ice. In either event, there was no time to be lost : another ten minutes and the *Electra* would be gone.

The *Sirrus* made two runs past in all—Orr had no intention of stopping alongside, of being trampled under by the 15,000-ton deadweight of a toppling freighter. On his first run he steamed slowly by at five knots, at a distance of twenty feet—the nearest he dared go with the set of the sea rolling both ships towards each other at the same instant.

As the *Sirrus's* swinging bows slid up past the bridge of the *Electra*, the waiting men began to jump. They jumped as the *Sirrus* fo'c'sle reared up level with their deck, they jumped as it plunged down fifteen, twenty feet below. One man carrying a suitcase and Burberry stepped nonchalantly across both sets of guard-rails during the split second that they were relatively motionless to each other : others crashed sickeningly on to the ice-coated steel deck far below, twisting ankles, fracturing legs and thighs, dislocating hip-joints. And two men jumped and missed ; above the bedlam of noise, men heard the blood-chilling, bubbling scream of one as the swinging hulls crushed the life out of him, the desperate, terror-stricken cries of the other as the great, iron wall of the *Electra* guided him into the screws of the *Sirrus*.

It was just then that it happened and there could be no possible reflection on Commander Orr's seamanship : he had handled the *Sirrus* brilliantly. But even his skill was helpless against these two successive freak waves, twice the size of the others. The first flung the *Sirrus* close in to the *Electra*, then passing under the *Electra*, lurched her steeply to port as the second wave heeled the *Sirrus* far over to starboard. There was a grinding, screeching crash. The *Sirrus's* guard-rails and upper side plates buckled and tore along a 150-foot length : simultaneously, the lifeboat smashed endwise into the front of the bridge, shattering into a thousand pieces. Immediately, the telegraphs jangled, the water boiled whitely at the *Sirrus's* stern—shocked realisation of its imminence and death itself must have been only a merciful hair's-breadth apart for the unfortunate man in the water—and then the destroyer was clear, sheering sharply away from the *Electra*.

In five minutes the *Sirrus* was round again. It was typical of Orr's ice-cold, calculating nerve and of the luck that never deserted him that he should this time choose to rub the *Sirrus's* shattered starboard side along the length of the *Electra*—she was too low in the water now to fall on him—and that he should do so in a momentary spell of slack water. Willing hands caught men as they jumped, cushioned their fall. Thirty seconds and the destroyer was gone again and the decks of the *Electra* were deserted. Two minutes later and a muffled roar shook the sinking ship—her boilers going. And then she toppled slowly over on her side : masts and smokestack lay along the surface of the sea, dipped and vanished : the straight-back of bottom and keel gleamed fractionally, blackly, against the grey of sea and sky, and was gone. For a minute, great gouts of air rushed turbulently to the surface. By and by the bubbles grew smaller and smaller and then there were no more.

The *Sirrus* steadied on course, crowded decks throbbing as she began to pick up speed, to overtake the convoy. Convoy No. FR77. The convoy the Royal Navy would always want to forget. Thirty-six ships had left Scapa and St. John's. Now there were twelve, only twelve. And still almost thirty-two hours to the Kola Inlet. . . .

Moodily, even his tremendous vitality and zest temporarily subdued, Turner watched the *Sirrus* rolling up astern. Abruptly he turned away, looked furtively, pityingly at Captain Vallery, no more now than a living skeleton driven by God only knew what mysterious force to wrest hour after impossible hour from death. And for Vallery now, death, even the hope of it, Turner suddenly realised, must be infinitely sweet. He looked, and saw the shock and sorrow in that grey mask, and he cursed, bitterly, silently. And then these tired, dull eyes were on him and Turner hurriedly cleared his throat.

" How many survivors does that make in the *Sirrus* now ? " he asked.

Vallery lifted weary shoulders in the ghost of a shrug.

" No idea, Commander. A hundred, possibly more. Why ? "

" A hundred," Turner mused. " And no-survivors-will-be-picked-up. I'm just wondering what old Orr's going to say when he dumps that little lot in Admiral Starr's lap when we get back to Scapa Flow ! "

CHAPTER THIRTEEN

SATURDAY AFTERNOON

THE *Sirrus* was still a mile astern when her Aldis started flickering. Bentley took the message, turned to Vallery.

" Signal, sir. ' Have 25-30 injured men aboard. Three very serious cases, perhaps dying. Urgently require doctor.' "

" Acknowledge," Vallery said. He hesitated a moment, then : " My compliments to Surgeon-Lieutenant Nicholls. Ask him to come to the bridge." He turned to the Commander, grinned faintly. " I somehow don't see Brooks at his athletic best in a breeches buoy on a day like this. It's going to be quite a crossing."

Turner looked again at the *Sirrus*, occasionally swinging through a 40° arc as she rolled and crashed her way up from the west.

" It'll be no picnic," he agreed. " Besides, breeches buoys aren't made to accommodate the likes of our venerable chief surgeon." Funny, Turner thought, how matter-of-fact and off-hand everyone was : nobody had as much as mentioned the *Vectra* since she'd rammed the U-boat.

The gate creaked. Vallery turned round slowly, acknowledged Nicholls's sketchy salute.

" The *Sirrus* needs a doctor," he said without preamble. " How do you fancy it ? "

Nicholls steadied himself against the canted bridge and the rolling of the cruiser. Leave the *Ulysses*—suddenly, he hated the thought, was amazed at himself for his reaction. He, Johnny Nicholls, unique, among the officers anyway, in his thorough-going detestation and intolerance of all things naval—to feel like that ! Must be going soft in the head. And just as suddenly he knew that his mind wasn't slipping, knew why he wanted to stay. It was not a matter of pride or principle or sentiment: it was just that—well, just that he belonged. The feeling of belonging —even to himself he couldn't put it more accurately, more clearly than that, but it affected him strangely, powerfully. Suddenly he became aware that curious eyes were on him, looked out in confusion over the rolling sea.

"Well?" Vallery's voice was edged with impatience.

"I don't fancy it at all," Nicholls said frankly. "But of course I'll go, sir. Right now?"

"As soon as you can get your stuff together," Vallery nodded.

"That's now. We have an emergency kit packed all the time." He cast a jaundiced eye over the heavy sea again. "What am I supposed to do, sir—jump?"

"Perish the thought!" Turner clapped him on the back with a large and jovial hand. "You haven't a thing to worry about," he boomed cheerfully, "you positively won't feel a thing —these, if I recall rightly, were your exact words to me when you extracted that old molar of mine two-three weeks back." He winced in painful recollection. "Breeches buoy, laddie, breeches buoy!"

"Breeches buoy!" Nicholls protested. "Haven't noticed the weather, have you? I'll be going up and down like a blasted yo-yo!"

"The ignorance of youth." Turner shook his head sadly. "We'll be turning into the sea, of course. It'll be like a ride in a Rolls, my boy! We're going to rig it now." He turned away. "Chrysler—get on to Chief Petty Officer Hartley. Ask him to come up to the bridge."

Chrysler gave no sign of having heard. He was in his usual, favourite position these days—gloved hands on the steam pipes, the top half of his face crushed into the rubber eyepiece of the powerful binoculars on the starboard searchlight control. Every few seconds a hand would drop, revolve the milled training rack a fraction. Then again the complete immobility.

"Chrysler!" Turner roared. "Are you deaf?"

Three, four, five more seconds passed in silence. Every eye was on Chrysler when he suddenly jerked back, glanced down at the bearing indicator, then swung round. His face was alive with excitement.

"Green one-double-oh!" he shouted. "Green one-double-oh! Aircraft. Just on the horizon!" He fairly flung himself back at his binoculars. "Four, seven—no, *ten*! Ten aircraft!" he yelled.

"Green one-double-oh?" Turner had his glasses to his eyes. "Can't see a thing! Are you sure, boy?" he called anxiously.

"Still the same, sir." There was no mistaking the agitated conviction in the young voice.

Turner was through the gate and beside him in four swift steps. "Let me have a look," he ordered. He gazed through the glasses, twisted the training rack once or twice, then stepped back slowly, heavy eyebrows lowering in anger.

"There's something bloody funny here, young man!" he growled. "Either your eyesight or your imagination? And if you ask me——"

"He's right," Carrington interrupted calmly. "I've got 'em, too."

"So have I, sir!" Bentley shouted.

Turner wheeled back to the mounted glasses, looked through them briefly, stiffened, looked round at Chrysler.

"Remind me to apologise some day!" he smiled, and was back on the compass platform before he had finished speaking.

"Signal to convoy," Vallery was saying rapidly. "Code H. Full ahead, Number One. Bosun's mate? Broadcaster: stand by all guns. Commander?"

"Sir?"

"Independent targets, independent fire all A.A. guns? Agreed? And the turrets?"

"Couldn't say yet. . . . Chrysler, can you make out——"

"Condors, sir," Chrysler anticipated him.

"Condors!" Turner stared in disbelief. "A dozen Condors! Are you sure that . . . Oh, all right, all right!" he broke off hastily. "Condors they are." He shook his head in wonderment, turned to Vallery. "Where's my bloody tin hat? Condors, he says!"

"So Condors they are," Vallery repeated, smiling. Turner marvelled at the repose, the unruffled calm.

"Bridge targets, independent fire control for all turrets?" Vallery went on.

"I think so, sir." Turner looked at the two communication ratings just aft of the compass platform—one each on the group phones to the for'ard and after turrets. "Ears pinned back, you two. And hop to it when you get the word."

Vallery beckoned to Nicholls.

"Better get below, young man," he advised. "Sorry your little trip's been postponed."

"I'm not," Nicholls said bluntly.

"No?" Vallery was smiling. "Scared?"

"No, sir," Nicholls smiled back. "Not scared. And you know I wasn't."

"I know you weren't," Vallery agreed quietly. "I know—and thank you."

He watched Nicholls walk off the bridge, beckoned to the W.T. messenger, then turned to the Kapok Kid.

"When was our last signal to the Admiralty, Pilot? Have a squint at the log."

"Noon yesterday," said the Kapok Kid readily.

"Don't know what I'll do without you," Vallery murmured. "Present position?"

"72.20 north, 13.40 east."

"Thank you." He looked at Turner. "No point in radio silence now, Commander?"

Turner shook his head.

"Take this message," Vallery said quickly. "To D.N.O., London. . . . How are our friends doing, Commander?"

"Circling well to the west, sir. Usual high altitude gambit from the stern, I suppose," he added morosely. "Still," he brightened, "cloud level's barely a thousand feet."

Vallery nodded. "'FR77. 1600. 72.20, 13.40. Steady on 090. Force 5, north, heavy swell: Situation desperate. Deeply regret Admiral Tyndall died 1200 to-day. Tanker *Vytura* torpedoed last night, sunk by self. *Washington State* sunk 0145 to-day. *Vectra* sunk 1515, collision U-boat. *Electra* sunk 1530.

Am being heavily attacked by twelve, minimum twelve, Focke
wulf 200s.' A reasonable assumption, I think, Commander,"
he said wryly, " and it'll shake their Lordships. They're of the
opinion there aren't so many Condors in the whole of Norway.
' Imperative send help. Air cover essential. Advise immediately.'
Get that off at once, will you ? "

" Your nose, sir ! " Turner said sharply.

" Thank you." Vallery rubbed the frostbite, dead white in
the haggard grey and blue of his face, gave up after a few seconds :
the effort was more trouble than it was worth, drained away too
much of his tiny reserves of strength. " My God, it's bitter,
Commander ! " he murmured quietly.

Shivering, he pulled himself to his feet, swept his glasses over
FR77. Code H was being obeyed. The ships were scattered over
the sea apparently at random, broken out from the two lines
ahead which would have made things far too simple for bomb-
aimers in aircraft attacking from astern. They would have to
aim now for individual targets. Scattered, but not too scattered
—close enough together to derive mutual benefit from the
convoy's concerted barrage. Vallery nodded to himself in
satisfaction and twisted round, his glasses swivelling to the west.

There was no mistaking them now, he thought—they were
Condors, all right. Almost dead astern now, massive wing-tips
dipping, the big four-engined planes banked slowly, ponderously
to starboard, then straightened on a 180° overtaking course. And
they were climbing, steadily climbing.

Two things were suddenly clear to Vallery, two things the
enemy obviously knew. They had known where to find FR77—
the Luftwaffe was not given to sending heavy bombers out over
the Arctic on random hazard : they hadn't even bothered to send
Charlie on reconnaissance. For a certainty, some submarine had
located them earlier on, given their position and course : at any
distance at all, their chance of seeing a periscope in that heavy
sea had been remote. Further, the Germans *knew* that the
Ulysses's radar was gone. The Focke-Wulfs were climbing to
gain the low cloud, would break cover only seconds before it
was time to bomb. Against radar-controlled fire, at such close
range, it would have been near suicide. But they *knew* it was safe.

Even as he watched, the last of the labouring Condors climbed through the low, heavy ceiling, was completely lost to sight. Vallery shrugged wearily, lowered his binoculars.

" Bentley ? "

" Sir ? "

" Code R. Immediate."

The flags fluttered up. For fifteen, twenty seconds—it seemed ten times as long as that to the impatient Captain—nothing happened. And then, like rolling toy marionettes under the hand of a master puppeteer, the bows of every ship in the convoy began to swing round—those to the port of the *Ulysses* to the north, those to the starboard to the south. When the Condors broke through—two minutes, at the most, Vallery reckoned, they would find beneath them only the empty sea. Empty, that is, except for the *Ulysses* and the *Stirling*, ships admirably equipped to take care of themselves. And then the Condors would find themselves under heavy cross-fire from the merchant ships and destroyers, and too late—at that low altitude, much too late— to alter course for fore-and-aft bombing runs on the freighters. Vallery smiled wryly to himself. As a defensive tactic, it was little enough, but the best he could do in the circumstances. . . . He could hear Turner barking orders through the loudspeaker, was more than content to leave the defence of the ship in the Commander's competent hands. If only he himself didn't feel so tired. . . .

Ninety seconds passed, a hundred, two minutes—and still no sign of the Condors. A hundred eyes stared out into the cloud-wrack astern : it remained obstinately, tantalisingly grey and featureless.

Two and a half minutes passed. Still there was nothing.

" Anybody seen anything ? " Vallery asked anxiously. His eyes never left that patch of cloud astern. " Nothing ? Nothing at all ? " The silence remained, oppressive, unbroken.

Three minutes. Three and a half. Four. Vallery looked away to rest his straining eyes, caught Turner looking at him, caught the growing apprehension, the slow dawn and strengthening of surmise in the lean face. Wordlessly, at the same instant, they swung round, staring out into the sky ahead.

"That's it!" Vallery said quickly. "You're right, Commander, you must be!" He was aware that everyone had turned now, was peering ahead as intently as himself. "They've by-passed us, they're going to take us from ahead. Warn the guns! Dear God, they almost had us!" he whispered softly.

"Eyes skinned, everyone!" Turner boomed. The apprehension was gone, the irrepressible joviality, the gratifying anticipation of action was back again. "And I mean everyone! We're all in the same boat together. No joke intended. Fourteen days' leave to the first man to sight a Condor!"

"Effective as from when?" the Kapok Kid asked dryly.

Turner grinned at him. Then the smile died, the head lifted sharply in sudden attention.

"Can you hear 'em?" he asked. His voice was soft, almost as if he feared the enemy might be listening. "They're up there, somewhere—damned if I can tell where, though. If only that wind——"

The vicious, urgent thudding of the boat-deck Oerlikons stopped him dead in mid-sentence, had him whirling round and plunging for the broadcast transmitter in one galvanic, concerted movement. But even then he was too late—he would have been too late anyway. The Condors—the first three, in line ahead, were already visible—were already through the cloud, 500 feet up and barely half a mile away—dead astern. *Astern.* The bombers must have circled back to the west as soon as they had reached the cloud, completely fooled them as to their intentions. . . . Six seconds—six seconds is time and to spare for even a heavy bomber to come less than half a mile in a shallow dive. There was barely time for realisation, for the first bitter welling of mortification and chagrin when the Condors were on them.

It was almost dusk, now, the weird half-light of the Arctic twilight. Tracers, glowing hot pinpoints of light streaking out through the darkening sky, were clearly seen, at first swinging erratically, fading away to extinction in the far distance, then steadying, miraculously dying in the instant of birth as they sunk home into the fuselages of the swooping Condors. But time was too short—the guns were on target for a maximum of two seconds —and these giant Focke-Wulfs had a tremendous capacity for absorbing punishment. The leading Condor levelled out about three hundred feet, its medium 250-kilo bombs momentarily parallelling its line of flight, then arching down lazily towards the *Ulysses*. At once the Condor pulled its nose up in maximum climb, the four great engines labouring in desynchronised clamour, as it sought the protection of the clouds.

The bombs missed. They missed by about thirty feet, exploding on contact with the water just abaft the bridge. For the men in the T.S., engine- and boiler-rooms, the crash and concussion must have been frightful—literally ear-shattering. Waterspouts, twenty feet in diameter at their turbulent bases, streaked up whitely into the twilight, high above the truncated masts, hung there momentarily, then collapsed in drenching cascades on the bridge and boat-deck aft, soaking, saturating, every gunner on the pom-pom and in the open Oerlikon cockpits. The temperature stood at 2° above zero—30° of frost.

More dangerously, the blinding sheets of water completely unsighted the gunners. Apart from a lone Oerlikon on a sponson below the starboard side of the bridge, the next Condor pressed home its attack against a minimum of resistance. The approach was perfect, dead fore-and-aft on the centre line; but the pilot overshot, probably in his anxiety to hold course. Three bombs this time: for a second, it seemed that they must miss, but the first smashed into the fo'c'sle between the breakwater and the capstan, exploding in the flat below, heaving up the deck in a tangled wreckage of broken steel. Even as the explosion died, the men on the bridge could hear a furious, clanking rattle: the explosion must have shattered the fo'c'sle capstan and Blake stopper simultaneously, and sheared the retaining shackle on the anchor cable, and the starboard anchor, completely out of control, was plummeting down to the depths of the Arctic.

The other bombs fell into the sea directly ahead, and from the *Stirling*, a mile ahead, it seemed that the *Ulysses* disappeared under the great column of water. But the water subsided, and the *Ulysses* steamed on, apparently unharmed. From dead ahead, the sweeping lift of the bows hid all damage, and there was neither flame nor smoke—hundreds of gallons of water, falling from the sky and pouring in through the great jagged holes in the deck,

had killed any fire there was. The *Ulysses* was still a lucky ship.
. . . And then, at last, after twenty months of the fantastic escapes,
the fabulous good fortune that had made her a legend, a byword
for immunity throughout all the north, the luck of the *Ulysses*
ran out.

Ironically, the *Ulysses* brought disaster on herself. The main
armament, the 5.25s aft, had opened up now, was pumping its
100-lb. shells at the diving bombers, at point-blank range and
over the equivalent of open sights. The very first shell from " X "
turret sheared away the starboard wing of the third Condor
between the engines, tore it completely away to spin slowly like
a fluttering leaf into the darkly-rolling sea. For a fraction of a
second the Folke-Wulf held on course, then abruptly the nose
tipped over and the giant plane screamed down in an almost
vertical dive, her remaining engines inexplicably accelerating to
a deafening crescendo as she hurtled arrow-straight for the deck
of the *Ulysses*.

There was no time to take any avoiding action, no time to
think, no time even to hope. A cluster of jettisoned bombs
crashed in to the boiling wake—the *Ulysses* was already doing
upwards of thirty knots—and two more crashed through the
poop-deck, the first exploding in the after seamen's mess-deck,
the other in the marines' mess-deck. One second later, with a
tremendous roar and in a blinding sheet of gasoline flame, the
Condor itself, at a speed of upwards of three hundred m.p.h.,
crashed squarely into the front of " Y " turret.

Incredibly, that was the last attack on the *Ulysses*—incredibly,
because the *Ulysses* was defenceless now, wide open to any air
attack from astern. " Y " turret was gone, " X " turret, still
magically undamaged, was half-buried under the splintered
wreckage of the Condor, blinded by the smoke and leaping flame.
The boat-deck Oerlikons, too, had fallen silent. The gunners,
half-drowned under the deluge of less than a minute ago, were
being frantically dragged from their cockpits : a difficult enough
task at any time, it was almost impossible with their clothes already
frozen solid, their duffels cracking and crackling like splintering
matchwood as the men were dragged over the side of their
cockpits. With all speed, they were rushed below, thrust into

the galley passage to thaw, literally to thaw : agony, excruciating agony, but the only alternative to the quick and certain death which would have come to them in their ice-bound cockpits.

The remaining Condors had pulled away in a slow, climbing turn to starboard. They were surrounded, bracketed fore and aft and on either side, by scores of woolly, expanding puffs of exploding A.A. shells, but they flew straight through these, charmed, unhurt. Already, they were beginning to disappear into the clouds, to settle down on a south-cast course for home. Strange, Vallery thought vaguely, one would have expected them to hammer home their initial advantage of surprise, to concentrate on the crippled *Ulysses*: certainly, thus far the Condor crews had shown no lack of courage. . . . He gave it up, turned his attention to more immediate worries. And there was plenty to worry about.

The *Ulysses* was heavily on fire aft—a deck and mess-deck fire, admittedly, but potentially fatal for all that—" X " and " Y " magazines were directly below. Already, dozens of men from the damage control parties were running aft, stumbling and falling on the rolling ice-covered deck, unwinding the hose drums behind them, occasionally falling flat on their faces as two ice-bound coils locked together, the abruptly tightening hose jerking them off their feet. Others stumbled past them, carrying the big, red foam-extinguishers on their shoulders or under their arms. One unfortunate seaman—A.B. Ferry, who had left the Sick Bay in defiance of strict orders—running down the port alley past the shattered canteen, slipped and fell abreast " X " turret: the port wing of the Condor, even as it had sheared off and plunged into the sea, had torn away the guard-rails here, and Ferry, hands and feet scrabbling frantically at the smooth ice of the deck, his broken arm clawing uselessly at one of the remaining stanchions, slid slowly, inevitably over the side and was gone. For a second, the high-pitched, fear-stricken shriek rose thin and clear above the roaring of the flames, died abruptly as the water closed over him. The propellers were almost immediately below.

The men with the extinguishers were the first into action, as, indeed, they had to be when fighting a petrol fire—water would only have made matters worse, have increased the area of the fire by washing the petrol in all directions, and the petrol, being lighter than water, immiscible and so floating to the top, would have burned as furiously as ever. But the foam-extinguishers were of only limited efficiency, not so much because several release valves had jammed solid in the intense cold as because of the intense white heat which made close approach almost impossible, while the smaller carbon-tet. extinguishers, directed against electrical fires below, were shockingly ineffective : these extinguishers had never been in action before and the crew of the *Ulysses* had known for a long time of the almost magical properties of the extinguisher liquid for removing the most obstinate stains and marks in clothes. You may convince a W.T. rating of the lethal nature of 2,000 volts : you may convince a gunner of the madness of matches in a magazine : you may convince a torpedo-man of the insanity of juggling with fulminate of mercury : but you will never convince any of them of the criminal folly of draining off just a few drops of carbon-tetrachloride. . . . Despite stringent periodical checks, most of the extinguishers were only half-full. Some were completely empty.

The hoses were little more effective. Two were coupled up to the starboard mains and the valves turned : the hoses remained lifeless, empty. The starboard salt-water line had frozen solid—common enough with fresh-water systems, this, but not with salt. A third hose on the port side was coupled up, but the release valve refused to turn : attacked with hammers and crowbars, it sheered off at the base—at extremely low temperatures, molecular changes occur in metals, cut tensile strength to a fraction—the high-pressure water drenching everyone in the vicinity. Spicer, the dead Admiral's pantry-boy, a stricken-eyed shadow of his former cheerful self, flung away his hammer and wept in anger and frustration. The other port valve worked, but it took an eternity for the water to force its way through the flattened frozen hose.

Gradually, the deck fire was brought under control—less through the efforts of the firefighters than the fact that there was little inflammable material left after the petrol had burnt off. Hoses and extinguishers were then directed through the great jagged rents on the poop to the fires roaring in the mess-decks below, while two asbestos-suited figures clambered over and struggled through the red-hot, jangled mass of smoking wreckage on the poop. Nicholls had one of the suits, Leading Telegraphist Brown, a specialist in rescue work, the other.

Brown was the first on the scene. Picking his way gingerly, he climbed up to the entrance of " Y " turret. Watchers in the port and starboard alleyways saw him pause there, fighting to tie back the heavy steel door—it had been crashing monotonously backwards and forwards with the rolling of the cruiser. Then they saw him step inside. Less than ten seconds later they saw him appear at the door again, on his knees and clutching desperately at the side for support. His entire body was arching convulsively and he was being violently sick into his oxygen mask.

Nicholls saw this, wasted time neither on " Y " turret nor on the charred skeletons still trapped in the incinerated fuselage of the Condor. He climbed quickly up the vertical steel ladders to " X " gun-deck, moved round to the back and tried to open the door. The clips were jammed, immovable—whether from cold or metal distortion by blast he did not know. He looked round for some lever, stepped aside as he saw Doyle, duffel coat smouldering, haggard face set and purposeful under the beard, approaching with a sledge in his hand. A dozen, heavy, well-directed blows—the clanging, Nicholls thought, must be almost intolerable inside the hollow amplifier of the turret—and the door was open. Doyle secured it, stepped aside to let Nicholls enter.

Nicholls climbed inside. There had been no need to worry about that racket outside, he thought wryly. Every man in the turret was stone dead. Colour-Sergeant Evans was sitting bolt upright in his seat, rigid and alert in death as he had been in life : beside him lay Foster, the dashing, fiery Captain of Marines, whom death became so ill. The rest were all sitting or lying quietly at their stations, apparently unharmed and quite unmarked except for an occasional tiny trickle of blood from ear and mouth, trickles already coagulated in the intense cold—the speed of the *Ulysses* had carried the flames aft, away from the turret. The concussion must have been tremendous, death instantaneous. Heavily, Nicholls bent over the communications number, gently detached his headset, and called the bridge.

Vallery himself took the message, turned back to Turner. He looked old, defeated.

" That was Nicholls," he said. Despite all he could do, the shock and sorrow showed clearly in every deeply-etched line in that pitiably wasted face. " ' Y ' turret is gone—no survivors. ' X ' turret seems intact—but everyone inside is dead. Concussion, he says. Fires in the after mess-deck still not under control. . . . Yes, boy, what is it ? "

" ' Y ' magazine, sir," the seaman said uncertainly. " They want to speak to the gunnery officer."

" Tell them he's not available," Vallery said shortly. " We haven't time . . ." He broke off, looked up sharply. " Did you say ' Y ' magazine ? Here, let me have that phone."

He took the receiver, pushed back the hood of his duffel coat.

" Captain speaking, ' Y ' magazine. What is it ? . . . What ? Speak up man, I can't hear you. . . . Oh, damn ! " He swung round on the bridge L.T.O. " Can you switch this receiver on to the relay amplifier ? I can't hear a . . . Ah, that's better."

The amplifier above the chart-house crackled into life—a peculiarly throaty, husky life, doubly difficult to understand under the heavy overlay of a slurred Glasgow accent.

" Can ye hear me now ? " the speaker boomed.

" I can hear you." Vallery's own voice echoed loudly over the amplifier. " McQuater, isn't it ? "

" Aye, it's me, sir. How did ye ken ? " Even through the 'speaker, the surprise was unmistakable. Shocked and exhausted though he was, Vallery found himself smiling.

" Never mind that now, McQuater. Who's in charge down there—Gardiner, isn't it ? "

" Yes, sir. Gardiner."

" Put him on, will you ? " There was a pause.

" Ah canna, sir. Gardiner's deid."

" Dead ! " Vallery was incredulous. " Did you say ' dead,' McQuater ? "

" Aye, and he's no' the only one." The voice was almost truculent, but Vallery's ear caught the faint tremor below. " Ah was knocked oot masel', but Ah'm fine now."

Vallery paused, waited for the boy's bout of hoarse, harsh coughing to pass.

" But—but—what happened ? "

" How should Ah know—Ah mean, Ah dinna ken—Ah don't know, sir. A helluva bang and then—ach, Ah'm no sure whit happened. . . . Gardiner's mooth's all blood."

" How—how many of you are left ? "

" Just Barker, Williamson and masel', sir. Naebody else—just us."

" And—and they're all right, McQuater ? "

" Ach, they're fine. But Barker thinks he's deein'. He's in a gey bad wey. Ah think he's gone clean aff his trolley, sir."

" He's *what* ? "

" Loony, sir," McQuater explained patiently. " Daft. Some bluidy nonsense aboot goin' to meet his Maker, and him wi' naething behind him but a lifetime o' swindlin' his fellow-man." Vallery heard Turner's sudden chuckle, remembered that Barker was the canteen manager. " Williamson's busy shovin' cartridges back into the racks—floors littered with the bluidy things."

" McQuater ! " Vallery's voice was sharp, automatic in reproof.

" Aye, Ah'm sorry, sir. Ah clean forgot. . . . Whit's to be done, sir ? "

" Done about what ? " Vallery demanded impatiently.

" This place, sir. ' Y ' magazine. Is the boat on fire ootside ? It's bilin' in here—hotter than the hinges o' hell ! "

" What ! What did you say ? " Vallery shouted. This time he forgot to reprimand McQuater. " Hot, did you say ? How hot ? Quickly, boy ! "

" Ah canna touch the after bulkheid, sir," McQuater answered simply. " It 'ud tak' the fingers aff me."

" But the sprinklers—what's the matter with them ? " Vallery shouted. " Aren't they working ? Good God, boy, the magazine will go up any minute ! "

" Aye." McQuater's voice was noncommittal. " Aye, Ah kinna thought that might be the wey o' it. No, sir, the sprinklers arena workin'—and it's already 20° above the operatin' temperature, sir."

" Don't just stand there," Vallery said desperately. " Turn them on by hand ! The water in the sprinklers can't possibly be frozen if it's as hot as you say it is. Hurry, man, hurry. If the mag. goes up, the *Ulysses* is finished. For God's sake, hurry ! "

" Ah've tried them, sir," McQuater said softly. " It's nae bluidy use. They're solid ! "

" Then break them open ! There must be a tommy bar lying about somewhere. Smash them open, man ! Hurry ! "

" Aye, richt ye are, sir. But—but if Ah do that, sir, how am Ah to shut the valves aff again ? " There was a note almost of quiet desperation in the boy's voice—some trick of reproduction in the amplifier, Vallery guessed.

" You can't ! It's impossible ! But never mind that ! " Vallery said impatiently, his voice ragged with anxiety. " We'll pump it all out later. Hurry, McQuater, hurry ! "

There was a brief silence followed by a muffled shout and a soft thud, then they heard a thin metallic clanging echoing through the amplifier, a rapid, staccato succession of strokes. McQuater must have been raining a veritable hail of blows on the valve handles. Abruptly, the noise ceased.

Vallery waited until he heard the phone being picked up, called anxiously : " Well, how is it ? Sprinklers all right ? "

" Goin' like the clappers, sir." There was a new note in his voice, a note of pride and satisfaction. " Ah've just crowned Barker wi' the tommy bar," he added cheerfully.

" You've *what* ? "

" Laid oot old Barker," said McQuater distinctly. " He tried to stop me. Windy auld bastard. . . . Ach, he's no worth mentionin'. . . . My, they sprinklers are grand things, sir. Ah've never seen them workin' before. Place is ankle deep a'ready. And the steam's fair sizzlin' aff the after bulkheid ! "

" That's enough ! " Vallery's voice was sharp. " Get out at once—and make sure that you take Barker with you."

" Ah saw a picture once. In the Paramount in Glasgow, Ah think. Ah must've been flush." The tone was almost conversational, pleasurably reminiscent. Vallery exchanged glances with Turner, saw that he too, was fighting off the feeling of unreality. " *Rain*, it was cried. But it wisnae hauf as bad as this. There certainly wisnae hauf as much bluidy steam ! Talk aboot the hot-house in the Botanic Gardens ! "

" McQuater ! " Vallery roared. " Did you hear me ? Leave at once, I say ! At once, do you hear ? "

" Up to me knees a'ready ! " McQuater said admiringly. " It's gey cauld. . . . Did you say somethin', sir ? "

" I said, ' Leave at once ! ' " Vallery ground out. " Get out ! "

" Aye, Ah see. ' Get oot.' Aye. Ah thought that was what ye said. Get oot. Well, it's no that easy. As a matter o' fact, we canna. Hatchway's buckled and the hatch-cover, too—jammed deid solid, sir."

The echo from the speaker boomed softly over the shattered bridge, died away in frozen silence. Unconsciously, Vallery lowered the telephone, his eyes wandering dazedly over the bridge. Turner, Carrington, the Kapok Kid, Bentley, Chrysler and the others—they were all looking at him, all with the same curiously blank intensity blurring imperceptibly into the horror of understanding—and he knew that their eyes and faces only mirrored his own. Just for a second, as if to clear his mind, he screwed his eyes tightly shut, then lifted the phone again.

" McQuater ! McQuater ! Are you still there ? "

" Of course Ah'm here ! " Even through the speaker, the voice was peevish, the asperity unmistakable. " Where the hell—— ? "

" Are you sure it's jammed, boy ? " Vallery cut in desperately. " Maybe if you took a tommy-bar to the clips—— "

" Ah could take a stick o' dynamite to the bluidy thing and it 'ud make no difference," McQuater said matter-of-factly. " Ony-wey, it's just aboot red-hot a'ready—the hatch, Ah mean. There must be a bluidy great fire directly ootside it."

" Hold on a minute," Vallery called. He turned round. " Commander, have Dodson send a stoker to the main magazine flooding valve aft : stand by to shut off."

He crossed over to the nearest communication number.

" Are you on to the poop phone just now ? Good ! Give it to me. . . . Hallo, Captain here. Is—ah, it's you, Hartley. Look, give me a report on the state of the mess-deck fires. It's desperately urgent. There are ratings trapped in ' Y ' magazine, the sprinklers are on and the hatch-cover's jammed. . . . Yes, yes, I'll hold on."

He waited impatiently for the reply, gloved hand tapping mechanically on top of the phone box. His eyes swept slowly over the convoy, saw the freighters steaming in to make up position again. Suddenly he stiffened, eyes unseeing.

" Yes, Captain speaking. . . . Yes. . . . Yes. Half an hour, maybe an hour. . . . Oh, God, no ! You're quite certain ? . . . No, that's all."

He handed the receiver back, looked up slowly, his face drained of expression.

" Fire in the seamens' mess is under control," he said dully. " The marines' mess is an inferno—directly on top of ' Y ' magazine. Hartley says there isn't a chance of putting it out for an hour at least. . . . I think you'd better get down there, Number One."

A whole minute passed, a minute during which there was only the pinging of the Asdic, the regular crash of the sea as the *Ulysses* rolled in the heavy troughs.

" Maybe the magazine's cool enough now," the Kapok Kid suggested at length. " Perhaps we could shut off the water long enough . . ." His voice trailed away uncertainly.

" Cool enough ? " Turner cleared his throat noisily. " How do we know ? Only McQuater could tell us . . ." He stopped abruptly, as he realised the implications of what he was saying.

" We'll ask him," Vallery said heavily. He picked up the phone again. " McQuater ? "

" Hallo ! "

" Perhaps we could shut off the sprinklers outside, if it's safe. Do you think the temperature . . . ? "

He broke off, unable to complete the sentence. The silence stretched out, taut and tangible, heavy with decision. Vallery wondered numbly what McQuater was thinking, what he himself would have thought in McQuater's place.

" Hing on a minute," the speaker boomed abruptly. " Ah'll have a look up top."

Again that silence, again that tense unnatural silence lay heavily over the bridge. Vallery started as the speaker boomed again.

" Jings, Ah'm b——d. Ah couldna climb that ladder again for twenty-four points in the Treble Chance. . . . Ah'm on the ladder now, but Ah'm thinkin' Ah'll no be on it much longer."

" Never mind . . ." Vallery checked himself, aghast at what he had been about to say. If McQuater fell off, he'd drown like a rat in that flooded magazine.

" Oh, aye. The magazine." In the intervals between the racked bouts of coughing, the voice was strangely composed. " The shells up top are just aboot meltin'. Worse than ever, sir."

" I see." Vallery could think of nothing else to say. His eyes were closed and he knew he was swaying on his feet. With an effort, he spoke again. " How's Williamson ? " It was all he could think of.

" Near gone. Up to his neck and hangin' on to the racks." McQuater coughed again. " Says he's a message for the Commander and Carslake."

" A—a message ? "

" Uh-huh ? Tell old Blackbeard to take a turn to himself and lay off the bottle," he said with relish. The message for Carslake was unprintable.

Vallery didn't even feel shocked.

" And yourself, McQuater ? " he said. " No message, nothing you would like . . ." He stopped, conscious of the grotesque inadequacy, the futility of what he was saying.

" Me ? Ach, there's naething Ah'd like . . . Well, maybe a transfer to the *Spartiate*, but Ah'm thinking maybe it's a wee bit ower late for that.[1] Williamson ! " The voice had risen to a sudden urgent shout. " Williamson ! Hing on, boy, Ah'm coming ! " They heard the booming clatter in the speaker as McQuater's phone crashed against metal, and then there was only the silence.

" McQuater ! " Vallery shouted into the phone. " McQuater ! Answer me, man. Can you hear me ? McQuater ! " But the speaker above him remained dead, finally, irrevocably dead. Vallery shivered in the icy wind. That magazine, that flooded magazine . . . less than twenty-four hours since he had been there.

[1] H.M.S. *Spartiate* was a shore establishment, Naval H.Q. for the West of Scotland. It was at St. Enoch's Hotel, Glasgow.

He could see it now, see it as clearly as he had seen it last night. Only now he saw it dark, cavernous with only the pin-points of emergency lighting, the water welling darkly, slowly up the sides, saw that little, pitifully wasted Scots boy with the thin shoulders and pain-filled eyes, struggling desperately to keep his mate's head above that icy water, exhausting his tiny reserves of strength with the passing of every second. Even now, the time must be running out and Vallery knew hope was gone. With a sudden clear certainty he knew that when those two went down, they would go down together. McQuater would never let go. Eighteen years old, just eighteen years old. Vallery turned away, stumbled blindly through the gate on to the shattered compass platform. It was beginning to snow again and the darkness was falling all around them.

CHAPTER FOURTEEN

SATURDAY EVENING I

THE *Ulysses* rolled on through the Arctic twilight. She rolled heavily, awkwardly, in seas of the wrong critical length, a strange and stricken sight with both masts gone, with all boats and rafts gone, with shattered fore-and-aft superstructure, with a crazily tilted bridge and broken, mangled after turret, half-buried in the skeleton of the Condor's fuselage. But despite all that, despite, too, the great garish patches of red lead and gaping black holes in fo'c'sle and poop—the latter welling with dark smoke laced with flickering lances of flame—she still remained uncannily ghost-like and graceful, a creature of her own element, inevitably at home in the Arctic. Ghost-like, graceful, and infinitely enduring . . . and still deadly. She still had her guns—and her engines. Above all, she had these great engines, engines strangely blessed with endless immunity. So, at least, it seemed . . .

Five minutes dragged themselves interminably by, five minutes during which the sky grew steadily darker, during which reports from the poop showed that the firefighters were barely holding their own, five minutes during which Vallery recovered something of his normal composure. But he was now terribly weak.

A bell shrilled, cutting sharply through the silence and the gloom. Chrysler answered it, turned to the bridge.

" Captain, sir. After engine-room would like to speak to you."

Turner looked at the Captain, said quickly : " Shall I take it, sir ? "

" Thank you." Vallery nodded his head gratefully. Turner nodded in turn, crossed to the phone.

" Commander speaking. Who is it ? . . . Lieutenant Grierson. What is it, Grierson ? Couldn't be good news for a change ? "

For almost a minute Turner remained silent. The others on the bridge could hear the faint crackling of the earpiece, sensed rather than saw the taut attention, the tightening of the mouth.

" Will it hold ? " Turner asked abruptly. " Yes, yes, of course. . . . Tell him we'll do our best up here. . . . Do that. Half-hourly, if you please."

" It never rains, et cetera," Turner growled, replacing the phone. " Engine running rough, temperature hotting up. Distortion in inner starboard shaft. Dodds himself is in the shaft tunnel right now. Bent like a banana, he says."

Vallery smiled faintly. " Knowing Dodson, I suppose that means a couple of thou out of alignment."

" Maybe." Turner was serious. " What does matter is that the main shaft bearing's damaged and the lubricating line fractured."

" As bad as that ? " Vallery asked softly.

" Dodson is pretty unhappy. Says the damage isn't recent— thinks it began the night we lost our depth-charges." Turner shook his head. " Lord knows what stresses that shaft's undergone since. . . . I suppose to-night's performance brought it to a head. . . . The bearing will have to be lubricated by hand. Wants engine revs. at a minimum or engine shut off altogether. They'll keep us posted."

" And no possibility of repair," Vallery asked wryly.

" No, sir. None."

" Very well, then. Convoy speed. And Commander ? "

" Sir ? "

" Hands to stations all night. You needn't tell 'em so—but, well, I think it would be wise. I have a feeling——"

" What's that ! " Turner shouted. " Look ! What the hell's she doing ? " His finger was stabbing towards the last freighter in the starboard line : her guns were blazing away at some unseen target, the tracers lancing whitely through the twilight sky. Even as he dived for the broadcaster, he caught sight of the *Viking's* main armament belching smoke and jagged flame.

" All guns ! Green 110 ! Aircraft ! Independent fire, independent targets! Independent fire, independent targets!" He heard Vallery ordering starboard helm, knew he was going to bring the for'ard turrets to bear.

They were too late. Even as the *Ulysses* began to answer her helm, the enemy planes were pulling out of their approach dives. Great, clumsy shapes, these planes, forlorn and insubstantial in the murky gloom, but identifiable in a sickening flash by the clamour of suddenly racing engines. Condors, without a shadow of doubt. Condors that had outguessed them again, that had departed only to return, that had made a slow gliding approach, throttles cut right back, the muted roar of the engines drifting downwind, away from the convoy. Their timing, their judgment of distance, had been superb.

The freighter was bracketed twice, directly hit by at least seven bombs : in the near-darkness, it was impossible to see the bombs going home, but the explosions were unmistakable. And as each plane passed over, the decks were raked by savage bursts of machine-gun fire. Every gun position on the freighter was wide open, lacking all but the most elementary frontal protection : The Dems, Naval Ratings on the L.A. guns, Royal Marine Artillerymen on the H.A. weapons, were under no illusions as to their life expectancy when they joined the merchant ships on the Russian run. . . . For such few gunners as survived the bombing, the vicious stuttering of these machine-guns was almost certainly their last sound on earth.

As the bombs plummetted down on the next ship in line, the first freighter was already a broken-backed mass of licking, twisting flames. Almost certainly, too, her bottom had been torn out : she had listed heavily, and now slowly and smoothly broke apart just aft of the bridge as if both parts were hinged below the water-line and was gone before the clamour of the last aero engine had died away in the distance.

Tactical surprise had been complete. One ship gone, a second slewing wildly to an uncontrolled stop, deep in the water by the head, and strangely disquieting and ominous in the entire absence of smoke, flame or any movement at all, a third heavily damaged but still under command. Not one Condor had been lost.

Turner ordered the cease-fire—some of the gunners were still firing blindly into the darkness : trigger-happy, perhaps, or just that the imagination plays weird tricks on woolly minds and sunken blood-red eyes that had known no rest for more hours and days than Turner could remember. And then, as the last Oerlikon fell silent, he heard it again—the drone of heavy aero engines, the sound welling then ebbing again like breakers on a distant shore, as the wind gusted and died.

There was nothing anyone could do about it. The Focke-Wulf, although lost in the low cloud, was making no attempt to conceal its presence : the ominous drone was never lost for long. Clearly, it was circling almost directly above.

" What do you make of it, sir ? " Turner asked.

" I don't know," Vallery said slowly. " I just don't know at all. No more visits from the Condors, I'm sure of that. It's just that little bit too dark—and they know they won't catch us again. Tailing us, like as not."

" Tailing us ! It'll be black as tar in half an hour ! " Turner disagreed. " Psychological warfare, if you ask me."

" God knows." Vallery sighed wearily. " All I know is that I'd give all my chances, here and to come, for a couple of Corsairs, or radar, or fog, or another such night as we had in the Denmark Straits." He laughed shortly, broke down in a fit of coughing. " Did you hear me ? " he whispered. " I never thought I'd ask for that again. . . . How long since we left Scapa, Commander ? "

Turner thought briefly. " Five—six days, sir."

" Six days ! " He shook his head unbelievingly. " Six days. And—and thirteen ships—we have thirteen ships now."

" Twelve," Turner corrected quietly. " Another's almost gone. Seven freighters, the tanker and ourselves. Twelve . . . I wish they'd have a go at the old *Stirling* once in a while," he added morosely.

Vallery shivered in a sudden flurry of snow He bent forward, head bent against the bitter wind and slanting snow, sunk in unmoving thought. Presently he stirred.

" We will be off the North Cape at dawn," he said absently. " Things may be a little difficult, Commander. They'll throw in everything they've got."

" We've been round there before," Turner conceded.

" Fifty-fifty on our chances." Vallery did not seem to have heard him, seemed to be talking to himself. " *Ulysses* and the Sirens—' it may be that the gulfs will wash us down.' . . . I wish you luck, Commander."

Turner stared at him. " What do you mean—— ? "

" Oh, myself too." Vallery smiled, his head lifting up. " I'll need all the luck, too." His voice was very soft.

Turner did what he had never done before, never dreamed he would do. In the near-darkness he bent over the Captain, pulled his face round gently and searched it with troubled eyes. Vallery made no protest, and after a few seconds Turner straightened up.

" Do me a favour, sir," he said quietly. " Go below. I can take care of things—and Carrington will be up before long. They're gaining control aft."

" No, not to-night." Vallery was smiling, but there was a curious finality about the voice. " And it's no good dispatching one of your minions to summon old Socrates to the bridge. Please, Commander. I want to stay here—I want to see things out to-night."

" Yes, yes, of course." Suddenly, strangely, Turner no longer wished to argue. He turned away. " Chrysler ! I'll give you just ten minutes to have a gallon of boiling coffee in the Captain's shelter. . . . And you're going to go in there for half an hour," he said firmly, turning to Vallery, " and drink the damned stuff, or—or——"

" Delighted ! " Vallery murmured. " Laced with your incomparable rum, of course ? "

" Of course ! Eh—oh, yes, damn that Williamson ! " Turner growled irritably. He paused, went on slowly : " Shouldn't have said that. . . . Poor bastards, they'll have had it by this time. . . ." He fell silent, then cocked his head listening. " I wonder how long old Charlie means to keep stooging around up there," he murmured.

Vallery cleared his throat, coughed, and before he could speak the W.T. broadcaster clicked on.

" W.T.—bridge. W.T.—bridge. Two messages."

" One from the dashing Orr, for a fiver," Turner grunted.

" First from the *Sirrus*. ' Request permission to go alongside, take off survivors. As well hung for a sheep as a lamb.' "

Vallery stared through the thinly falling snow, through the darkness of the night and over the rolling sea.

" In *this* sea ? " he murmured. " And as near dark as makes no difference. He'll kill himself ! "

" That's nothing to what old Starr's going to do to him when he lays hands on him ! " Turner said cheerfully.

" He hasn't a chance. I—I could never ask a man to do that. There's no justification for such a risk. Besides, the merchant-man's been badly hit. There can't be many left alive aboard."

Turner said nothing.

" Make a signal," Vallery said clearly. " ' Thank you. Permission granted. Good luck.' And tell W.T. to go ahead."

There was a short silence, then the 'speaker crackled again.

" Second signal from London for Captain. Decoding. Messenger leaving for bridge immediately."

" Tell him to read it out," Vallery ordered.

" To Officer Commanding, 14 A.C.S., FR77," the 'speaker boomed after a few seconds. " ' Deeply distressed at news. Imperative maintain 090. Battle squadron steaming SSE. at full speed on interception course. Rendezvous approx. 1400 to-morrow. Their Lordships expressly command best wishes Rear-Admiral, repeat Rear-Admiral Vallery.' D.N.O., London."

The speaker clicked off and there was only the lost pinging of the Asdic, the throbbing monotony of the prowling Condor's engines, the lingering memory of the gladness in the broadcaster's voice.

" Uncommon civil of their Lordships," murmured the Kapok Kid, rising to the occasion as usual. " Downright decent, one might almost say."

" Bloody long overdue," Turner growled. " Congratulations, sir," he added warmly. " Signs of grace at last along the banks of the Thames." A murmur of pleasure ran round the bridge : discipline or not, no one made any attempt to hide his satisfaction.

" Thank you, thank you." Vallery was touched, deeply

touched. Promise of help at long, long last, a promise which might hold—almost certainly held—for each and every member of his crew the difference between life and death—and they could only think to rejoice in his promotion ! Dead men's shoes, he thought, and thought of saying it, but dismissed the idea immediately : a rebuff, a graceless affront to such genuine pleasure.

" Thank you very much," he repeated. " But, gentlemen, you appear to have missed the only item of news of any real significance——"

" Oh, no, we haven't," Turner growled. " Battle squadron— ha ! Too —— late as usual. Oh, to be sure, they'll be in at the death—or shortly afterwards, anyway. Perhaps in time for a few survivors. I suppose the *Illustrious* and the *Furious* will be with them ? "

" Perhaps. I don't know." Vallery shook his head, smiling. " Despite my recent—ah—elevation, I am not yet in their Lordships' confidence. But there'll be some carriers, and they could fly off a few hours away, give us air cover from dawn."

" Oh, no, they won't," said Turner prophetically. " The weather will break down, make flying off impossible. See if I'm not right."

" Perhaps, Cassandra, perhaps," Vallery smiled. " We'll see. . . . What was that, Pilot ? I didn't quite . . ."

The Kapok Kid grinned.

" It's just occurred to me that to-morrow's going to be a big day for our junior doctor—he's convinced that no battleship ever puts out to sea except for a Spithead review in peacetime."

" That reminds me," Vallery said thoughtfully. " Didn't we promise the *Sirrus*——"

" Young Nicholls is up to his neck in work," Turner cut in. " Doesn't love us—the Navy rather—overmuch, but he sure loves his job. Borrowed a fire-fighting suit, and Carrington says he's already . . ." He broke off, looked up sharply into the thin, driving snow. " Hallo ! Charlie's getting damned nosy, don't you think ? "

The roar of the Condor's engines was increasing every second : the sound rose to a clamouring crescendo as the bomber roared directly overhead, barely a couple of hundred feet above the broken masts, died away to a steady drone as the plane circled round the convoy.

"W.T. to escorts ! " Vallery called quickly. " Let him go—don't touch him ! No starshells—nothing. He's trying to draw us out, to have us give away our position. . . . It's not likely that the merchant ships . . . Oh, God ! The fools, the fools ! Too late, too late ! "

A merchantman in the port line had opened up—Oerlikons or Bofors, it was difficult to say. They were firing blind, completely blind : and in a high wind, snow and darkness, the chance of locating a plane by sound alone was impossibly remote.

The firing did not last long—ten, fifteen seconds at the outside. But long enough—and the damage was done. Charlie had pulled off, and straining apprehensive ears caught the sudden deepening of the note of the engines as the boosters were cut in for maximum climb.

"What do you make of it, sir ? " Turner asked abruptly.

"Trouble." Vallery was quiet but certain. " This has never happened before—and it's not psychological warfare, as you call it, Commander : he doesn't even rob us of our sleep—not when we're this close to the North Cape. And he can't hope to trail us long : a couple of quick course alterations and—ah ! " He breathed softly. " What did I tell you, Commander ? "

With a suddenness that blocked thought, with a dazzling glare that struck whitely, cruelly at cringing eyeballs, night was transformed into day. High above the *Ulysses* a flare had burst into intense life, a flare which tore apart the falling snow like filmy, transparent gauze. Swinging wildly under its parachute with the gusting of the wind, the flare was drifting slowly seawards, towards a sea no longer invisible but suddenly black as night, towards a sea where every ship, in its glistening sheath of ice and snow, was silhouetted in dazzling whiteness against the inky backdrop of sea and sky.

"Get that flare ! " Turner was barking into the transmitter. " All Oerlikons, all pom-poms, get that flare ! " He replaced the transmitter. " Might as well throw empty beer bottles at it with the old girl rolling like this," he muttered. " Lord, gives you a funny feeling, this ! "

" I know," the Kapok Kid supplied. " Like one of these dreams where you're walking down a busy street and you suddenly realise that all you're wearing is a wrist-watch. ' Naked and defenceless ' is the accepted term, I believe. For the non-literary, ' caught with the pants down.' " Absently he brushed the snow off the quilted kapok, exposing the embroidered " J " on the breast pocket, while his apprehensive eyes probed into the circle of darkness outside the pool of light. " I don't like this at all," he complained.

" Neither do I." Vallery was unhappy. " And I don't like Charlie's sudden disappearance either."

" He hasn't disappeared," Turner said grimly. " Listen ! " They listened, ears straining intently, caught the intermittent, distant thunder of the heavy engines. " He's 'way astern of us, closing."

Less than a minute later the Condor roared overhead again, higher this time, lost in the clouds. Again he released a flare, higher, much higher than the last, and this time squarely over the heart of the convoy.

Again the roar of the engines died to a distant murmur, again the desynchronised clamour strengthened as the Condor overtook the convoy a second time. Glimpsed only momentarily in the inverted valleys between the scudding clouds, it flew wide, this time, far out on the port hand, riding clear above the pitiless glare of the sinking flares. And, as it thundered by, flares exploded into blazing life—four of them, just below cloud level, at four-second intervals. The northern horizon was alive with light, glowing and pulsating with a fierce flame that threw every tiny detail into the starkest relief. And to the south there was only the blackness : the rim of the pool of light stopped abruptly just beyond the starboard line of ships.

It was Turner who first appreciated the significance, the implications of this. Realisation struck at him with the galvanic effect of sheer physical shock. He gave a hoarse cry, fairly flung himself at the broadcast transmitter : there was no time to await permission.

" ' B ' turret ! " he roared. " Starshells to the south. Green 90, green 90. Urgent ! Urgent ! Starshells, green 90. Maximum elevation 10. Close settings. Fire when you are ready ! " He looked quickly over his shoulder. " Pilot ! Can you see——"

" ' B ' turret training, sir."

" Good, good ! " He lifted the transmitter again. " All guns ! All guns ! Stand by to repel air attack from starboard. Probable bearing green 90. Hostiles probably torpedo-bombers." Even as he spoke, he caught sight of the intermittent flashing of the fighting lights on the lower yardarm : Vallery was sending out an emergency signal to the convoy.

" You're right, Commander," Vallery whispered. In the gaunt pallor, in the skin taut stretched across the sharp and fleshless bones, his face, in that blinding glare, was a ghastly travesty of humanity ; it was a death's-head, redeemed only by the glow of the deep-sunken eyes, the sudden flicker of bloodless lids as the whip-lash crash of " B " turret shattered the silence. " You must be," he went on slowly. " Every ship silhouetted from the north—and a maximum run-in from the south under cover of darkness." He broke off suddenly as the shells exploded in great overlapping globules of light, two miles to the south. ". You *are* right," he said gently. " Here they come."

They came from the south, wing-tip to wing-tip, flying in three waves with four or five planes in each wave. They were coming in at about 500 feet, and even as the shells burst their noses were already dipping into the plane of the shallow attack dive of the torpedo-bomber. And as they dived, the bombers fanned out, as if in search of individual targets—or what seemed, at first sight, to be individual targets. But within seconds it became obvious that they were concentrating on two ships and two ships alone—the *Stirling* and the *Ulysses*. Even the ideal double target of the crippled merchantman and the destroyer *Sirrus*, almost stopped alongside her, was strictly ignored. They were flying under orders.

" B " turret pumped out two more starshells at minimum settings, reloaded with H.E. By this time, every gun in the convoy had opened up, the barrage was intense : the torpedo-bombers—curiously difficult to identify, but looking like Heinkels

—had to fly through a concentrated lethal curtain of steel and high explosive. The element of surprise was gone : the starshells of the *Ulysses* had gained a priceless twenty seconds.

Five bombers were coming at the *Ulysses* now, fanned out to disperse fire, but arrowing in on a central point. They were levelling off, running in on firing tracks almost at wave-top height, when one of them straightened up a fraction too late, brushed lightly against a cresting wave-top, glanced harmlessly off, then catapulted crazily from wave-top to wave-top—they were flying at right angles to the set of the sea—before disappearing in a trough. Misjudgment of distance or the pilot's windscreen suddenly obscured by a flurry of snow—it was impossible to say.

A second later the leading plane in the middle disintegrated in a searing burst of flame—a direct hit on its torpedo warhead. A third plane, behind and to the west, sheered off violently to the left to avoid the hurtling debris, and the subsequent dropping of its torpedo was no more than an empty gesture. It ran half a cable length behind the *Ulysses*, spent itself in the empty sea beyond.

Two bombers left now, pressing home their attack with suicidal courage, weaving violently from side to side to avoid destruction. Two seconds passed, three, four—and still they came on, through the falling snow and intensely heavy fire, miraculous in their immunity. Theoretically, there is no target so easy to hit as a plane approaching directly head on : in practice, it never worked out that way. In the Arctic, the Mediterranean, the Pacific, the relative immunity of the torpedo-bombers, the high percentage of successful attacks carried out in the face of almost saturation fire, never failed to confound the experts. Tension, over-anxiety, fear—these were part of the trouble, at least : there are no half measures about a torpedo-bomber—you get him or he gets you. And there is nothing more nerve-racking —always, of course, with the outstanding exception of the screaming, near-vertical power-dive of the gull-winged Stuka dive-bomber—than to see a torpedo-bomber looming hugely, terrifyingly over the open sights of your gun and know that you have just five inexorable seconds to live. . . . And with the *Ulysses*, of course, the continuous rolling of the cruiser in the heavy cross-sea made accuracy impossible.

These last two bombers came in together, wing-tip to wing-tip. The plane nearer the bows dropped its torpedo less than two hundred yards away, pulled up in a maximum climbing turn to starboard, a fusillade of light cannon and machine-gun shells smashing into the upper works of the bridge : the torpedo hit the water obliquely, porpoised high into the air, then crashed back again nose first into a heavy wave, diving steeply into the sea : it passed under the *Ulysses*.

But seconds before that the last torpedo-bomber had made its attack—made its attack and failed and died. It had come roaring in less than ten feet above the waves, had come straight on without releasing its torpedo, without gaining an inch in height, until the crosses on the upper sides of the wings could be clearly seen, until it was less than a hundred yards away. Suddenly, desperately, the pilot had begun to climb : it was immediately obvious that the torpedo release mechanism had jammed, either through mechanical failure or icing in the intense cold : obviously, too, the pilot had intended to release the torpedo at the last minute, had banked on the sudden decrease of weight to lift him over the *Ulysses*.

The nose of the bomber smashed squarely into the for'ard funnel, the starboard wing shearing off like cardboard as it scythed across the after leg of the tripod mast. There was an instantaneous, blinding sheet of gasoline flame, but neither smoke nor explosion. A moment later the crumpled, shattered bomber, no longer a machine but a torn and flaming crucifix, plunged into the hissing sea a dozen yards away. The water had barely closed over it when a gigantic underwater explosion heeled the *Ulysses* far over to starboard, a vicious hammer-blow that flung men off their feet and shattered the lighting system on the port side of the cruiser.

Commander Turner hoisted himself painfully to his feet, shook his head to clear it of the cordite fumes and the dazed confusion left by cannon shells exploding almost at arm's length. The shock of the detonating torpedo hadn't thrown him to the duckboards—he'd hurled himself there five seconds previously as the flaming guns of the other bomber had raked the bridge from point-blank range.

His first thought was for Vallery. The Captain was lying on his side, crumpled strangely against the binnacle. Dry-mouthed, cold with a sudden chill that was not of that Polar wind, Turner bent quickly, turned him gently over.

Vallery lay still, motionless, lifeless. No sign of blood, no gaping wound—thank God for that ! Turner peeled off a glove, thrust a hand below duffel coat and jacket, thought he detected a faint, a very faint beating of the heart. Gently he lifted the head off the frozen slush, then looked up quickly. The Kapok Kid was standing above him.

" Get Brooks up here, Pilot," he said swiftly. " It's urgent ! "

Unsteadily, the Kapok Kid crossed over the bridge. The communication rating was leaning over the gate, telephone in his hand.

" The Sick Bay, quickly ! " the Kapok Kid ordered. " Tell the Surgeon Commander . . ." He stopped suddenly, guessed that the man was still too dazed to understand. " Here, give me that phone ! " Impatiently, he stretched out his hand and grabbed the telephone, then stiffened in horror as the man slipped gradually backwards, extended arms trailing stiffly over the top of the gate until they disappeared. Carpenter opened the gate, stared down at the dead man at his feet : there was a hole the size of his gloved fist between the shoulder-blades.

He lay alongside the Asdic cabinet, a cabinet, the Kapok Kid now saw for the first time, riddled and shattered with machine-gun bullets and shells. His first thought was the numbing appreciation that the set must be smashed beyond recovery, that their last defence against the U-boats was gone. Hard on the heels of that came the sickening realisation that there had been an Asdic operator inside there. . . . His eyes wandered away, caught sight of Chrysler rising to his feet by the torpedo control. He, too, was staring at the Asdic cabinet, his face drained of expression. Before the Kapok Kid could speak, Chrysler lurched forward, fists battering frantically, blindly at the jammed door of the cabinet. Like a man in a dream, the Kapok Kid heard him sobbing. . . . And then he remembered. The Asdic operator—his name was

Chrysler too. Sick to his heart, the Kapok Kid lifted the phone again. . . .

Turner pillowed the Captain's head, moved across to the starboard corner of the compass platform. Bentley, quiet, unobtrusive as always, was sitting on the deck, his back wedged between two pipes, his head pillowed peacefully on his chest. His hand under Bentley's chin, Turner gazed down into the sightless eyes, the only recognisable feature of what had once been a human face. Turner swore in savage quiet, tried to prise the dead fingers locked round the hand-grip of the Aldis, then gave up. The barred beam shone eerily across the darkening bridge.

Methodically, Turner searched the bridge-deck for further casualties. He found three others and it was no consolation at all that they must have died unknowing. Five dead men for a three-second burst—a very fair return, he thought bitterly. Standing on the after ladder, his face stilled in unbelief as he realised that he was staring down into the heart of the shattered for'ard funnel. More he could not see : the boat deck was already blurring into featureless anonymity in the dying glare of the last of the flares. He swung on his heel, returned to the compass platform.

At least, he thought grimly, there was no difficulty in seeing the *Stirling*. What was it that he had said—said less than ten minutes ago ? ' I wish they'd have a go at the *Stirling* once in a while.' Something like that. His mouth twisted. They'd had a go, all right. The *Stirling*, a mile ahead, was slewing away to starboard, to the south-east, her for'ard superstructure enveloped in a writhing cocoon of white flame. He stared through his night glasses, tried to assess the damage ; but a solid wall of flame masked the superstructure, from the fo'c'sle deck clear abaft the bridge. He could see nothing there, just nothing—but he could see, even in that heavy swell, that the *Stirling* was listing to starboard. It was learned later that the *Stirling* had been struck twice : she had been torpedoed in the for'ard boiler-room, and seconds later a bomber had crashed into the side of her bridge, her torpedo still slung beneath the belly of her fuselage : almost certainly, in the light of the similar occurrence on the *Ulysses*, severe icing had jammed the release mechanism. Death must have been instantaneous for every man on the bridge and the decks below ; among the dead were Captain Jefferies, the First Lieutenant and the Navigator.

The last bomber was hardly lost in the darkness when Carrington replaced the poop phone, turned to Hartley.

" Think you can manage, now, Chief ? I'm wanted on the bridge."

" I think so, sir." Hartley, blackened and stained with smoke and extinguisher foam, passed his sleeve wearily across his face. " The worst is over. . . . Where's Lieutenant Carslake ? Shouldn't he——"

" Forget him," Carrington interrupted brusquely. " I don't know where he is, nor do I care. There's no need for us to beat about the bush, Chief—we're better without him. If he returns, *you're* still in charge. Look after things."

He turned away, walked quickly for'ard along the port alley. On the packed snow and ice, the pad of his rubber seaboots was completely soundless.

He was passing the shattered canteen when he saw a tall, shadowy figure standing in the gap between the snow-covered lip of the outer torpedo tube and the end stanchion of the guard-rails, trying to open a jammed extinguisher valve by striking it against the stanchion. A second later, he saw another blurred form detach itself stealthily from the shadows, creep up stealthily behind the man with the extinguisher, a heavy bludgeon of wood or metal held high above his head.

" Look out ! " Carrington shouted. " Behind you ! "

It was all over in two seconds—the sudden, flailing rush of the attacker, the crash as the victim, lightning fast in his reactions, dropped his extinguisher and fell crouched to his knees, the thin piercing scream of anger and terror as the attacker catapulted over the stooping body and through the gap between tubes and rails, the splash—and then the silence.

Carrington ran up to the man on the deck, helped him to his feet. The last flare had not yet died, and it was still light enough for him to see who it was—Ralston, the L.T.O. Carrington gripped his arms, looked at him anxiously.

" Are you all right ? Did he get you ? Good God, who on earth——? "

" Thank you, sir." Ralston was breathing quickly, but his face was almost expressionless again. " That was too close ! Thank you very much, sir."

" But who on earth——? " Carrington repeated in wonder.

" Never saw him, sir." Ralston was grim. " But I know who it was—Sub-Lieutenant Carslake. He's been following me around all night, never let me out of his sight, not once. Now I know why."

It took much to disturb the First Lieutenant's iron equanimity, but now he shook his head in slow disbelief.

" I knew there was bad blood ! " he murmured. " But that it should come to this ! What the Captain will say to this I just——"

" Why tell him ? " Ralston said indifferently. " Why tell any-one ? Perhaps Carslake had relations. What good will it do to hurt them, to hurt anyone. Let anyone think what they like." He laughed shortly. " Let them think he died a hero's death fire-fighting, fell over the side, anything." He looked down into the dark, rushing water, then shivered suddenly. " Let him go, sir, please. He's paid."

For a long second Carrington, too, stared down over the side, looked back at the tall boy before him. Then he clapped his arm, nodded slowly and turned away.

Turner heard the clanging of the gate, lowered the binoculars to find Carrington standing by his side, gazing wordlessly at the burning cruiser. Just then Vallery moaned softly, and Carrington looked down quickly at the prone figure at his feet.

" My God ! The Old Man ! Is he hurt badly, sir ? "

" I don't know, Number One. If not, it's a bloody miracle," he added bitterly. He stooped down, raised the dazed Captain to a sitting position.

" Are you all right, sir ? " he asked anxiously. " Do you— have you been hit ? "

Vallery shuddered in a long, exhausting paroxysm of cough-ing, then shook his head feebly.

" I'm all right," he whispered weakly. He tried to grin, a pitiful, ghastly travesty of a smile in the reflected light from the burning Aldis. " I dived for the deck, but I think the binnacle got in my way." He rubbed his forehead, already bruised and discoloured. " How's the ship, Commander ? "

" To hell with the ship ! " Turner said roughly. He passed an arm round Vallery, raised him carefully to his feet. " How are things aft, Number One ? "

" Under control. Still burning, but under control. I left Hartley in charge." He made no mention of Carslake.

" Good ! Take over. Radio *Stirling*, *Sirrus*, see how they are. Come on, sir. Shelter for you ! "

Vallery protested feebly, a token protest only, for he was too weak to stand. He checked involuntarily as he saw the snow falling whitely through the barred beam of the Aldis, slowly followed the beam back to its source.

" Bentley ? " he whispered. " Don't tell me . . ." He barely caught the Commander's wordless nod, turned heavily away. They passed by the dead man stretched outside the gate, then stopped at the Asdic cabinet. A sobbing figure was crouched into the angle between the shelter and the jammed and shattered door of the hut, head pillowed on the forearm resting high against the door. Vallery laid a hand on the shaking shoulder, peered into the averted face.

" What is it ? Oh, it's you, boy." The white face had been lifted towards him. " What's the matter, Chrysler ? "

" The door, sir ! " Chrysler's voice was muffled, quivering. " The door—I can't open it."

For the first time, Vallery looked at the cabinet, at the gashed and torn metal. His mind was still dazed, exhausted, and it was almost by a process of association that he suddenly, horrifyingly thought of the gashed and mangled operator that must lie behind that locked door.

" Yes," he said quietly. " The door's buckled. . . . There's nothing anyone can do, Chrysler." He looked more closely at the grief-dulled eyes. " Come on, my boy, there's no need——"

" My brother's in there, sir." The words, the hopeless despair, struck Vallery like a blow. Dear God ! He had forgotten.

. . . Of course—Leading Asdic Operator Chrysler. . . . He stared down at the dead man at his feet, already covered with a thin layer of snow.

" Have that Aldis unplugged, Commander, will you ? " he asked absently. " And Chrysler ? "

" Yes, sir." A flat monotone.

" Go below and bring up some coffee, please."

" Coffee, sir ! " He was bewildered, uncomprehending. " Coffee ! But—but—my—my brother——"

" I know," Vallery said gently. " I know. Bring some coffee, will you ? "

Chrysler stumbled off. When the shelter door closed behind them, clicking on the light, Vallery turned to the Commander.

" Cue for moralising on the glories of war," he murmured quietly. " *Dulce et decorum,* and the proud privilege of being the sons of Nelson and Drake. It's not twenty-four hours since Ralston watched his father die. . . . And now this boy. Perhaps——"

" I'll take care of things," Turner nodded. He hadn't yet forgiven himself for what he had said and done to Ralston last night, in spite of Ralston's quick friendliness, the ready acceptance of his apologies. " I'll keep him busy, out of the way till we open up the cabinet. . . . Sit down, sir. Have a swig of this." He smiled faintly. " Friend Williams having betrayed my guilty secret. . . . Hallo ! Company."

The light clicked off and a burly figure bulked momentarily against the grey oblong of the doorway. The door shut, and Brooks stood blinking in the sudden light, red of face and gasping for breath. His eyes focused on the bottle in Turner's hand.

" Ha ! " he said at length. " Having a bottle party, are we ? All contributions gratefully received, I have no doubt." He opened his case on a convenient table, was rummaging inside when someone rapped sharply on the door.

" Come in," Vallery called.

A signalman entered, handed a note to Vallery. " From London, sir. Chief says there may be some reply."

" Thank you. I'll phone down."

The door opened and closed again. Vallery looked up at an empty-handed Turner.

" Thanks for removing the guilty evidence so quickly," he smiled. Then he shook his head. " My eyes—they don't seem so good. Perhaps you would read the signal, Commander ? "

" And perhaps *you* would like some decent medicine," Brooks boomed, " instead of that filthy muck of Turner's." He fished in his bag, produced a bottle of amber liquid. " With all the resources of modern medicine—well, practically all, anyway—at my disposal, I can find nothing to equal this."

" Have you told Nicholls ? " Vallery was stretched out on the settee now, eyes closed, the shadow of a smile on his bloodless lips.

" Well, no," Brooks confessed. " But plenty of time. Have some ? "

" Thanks. Let's have the good news, Turner."

" Good news ! " The sudden deadly quiet of the Commander's voice fell chilly over the waiting men. " No, sir, it's not good news."

" ' Rear-Admiral Vallery, Commanding 14 A.C.S., FR77.' " The voice was drained of all tone and expression. " ' *Tirpitz*, escorting cruisers, destroyers, reported moving out Alta Fjord sunset. Intense activity Alta Fjord airfield. Fear sortie under air cover. All measures avoid useless sacrifice Merchant, Naval ships. D.N.O., London.' " With deliberate care Turner folded the paper, laid it on the table. " Isn't that just wonderful," he murmured. " Whatever next ? "

Vallery was sitting bolt upright on the settee, blind to the blood trickling down crookedly from one corner of his mouth. His face was calm, unworried.

" I think I'll have that glass, now, Brooks, if you don't mind," he said quietly. The *Tirpitz*. The *Tirpitz*. He shook his head tiredly, like a man in a dream. The *Tirpitz*—the name that no man mentioned without a far-off echo of awe and fear, the name that had completely dominated North Atlantic naval strategy during the past two years. Moving out at last, an armoured Colossus, sister-ship to that other Titan that had destroyed the *Hood* with one single, savage blow—the *Hood*, the darling of the

Royal Navy, the most powerful ship in the world—or so men had thought. What chance had *their* tiny cockle-shell cruiser. . . . Again he shook his head, angrily this time, forced himself to think of the present.

"Well, gentlemen, I suppose time bringeth all things—even the *Tirpitz*. It had to come some day. Just our ill luck—the bait was too close, too tempting."

"My young colleague is going to be just delighted," Brooks said grimly. "A *real* battleship at long, long last."

"Sunset," Turner mused. "Sunset. My God!" he said sharply, "even allowing for negotiating the fjord they'll be on us in four hours on this course!"

"Exactly," Vallery nodded. "And it's no good running north. They'd overtake us before we're within a hundred miles of them."

"Them? Our big boys up north?" Turner scoffed. "I hate to sound like a gramophone record, but you'll recall my earlier statement about them—too —— late as usual!" He paused, swore again. "I hope that old bastard Starr's satisfied at last!" he finished bitterly.

"Why all the gloom?" Vallery looked up quizzically, went on softly. "We can still be back, safe and sound in Scapa in forty-eight hours. 'Avoid useless sacrifice Merchant, Naval ships,' he said. The *Ulysses* is probably the fastest ship in the world to-day. It's simple, gentlemen."

"No, no!" Brooks moaned. "Too much of an anti-climax. I couldn't stand it!"

"Do another PQ17?"[1] Turner smiled, but the smile never

[1] PQ17, a large mixed convoy—it included over 30 British, American and Panamanian ships—left Iceland for Russia under the escort of half a dozen destroyers and perhaps a dozen smaller craft, with a mixed Anglo-American cruiser and destroyer squadron in immediate support. A shadow covering force—again Anglo-American—comprising one aircraft carrier, two battleships, three cruisers and a flotilla of destroyers, lay to the north. As with FR77, they formed the spring of the trap that closed too late.

The time was midsummer, 1942, a suicidal season for the attempt, for in June and July, in these high latitudes, there is no night. About longitude 20° east, the convoy was heavily attacked by U-boats and aircraft.

On the same day as the attacks began—4th July—the covering cruiser squadron was radioed that the *Tirpitz* had just sailed from Alta Fjord. (This was not the case: the *Tirpitz* did make a brief, abortive sortie on the afternoon of the 5th, but turned back the same evening: rumour had it that she had been damaged by touched his eyes. "The Royal Navy could never stand it: Captain—Rear-Admiral Vallery would never permit it; and speaking for myself and, I'm fairly certain, this bunch of cut-throat mutineers of ours—well, I don't think we'd ever sleep so sound o' nights again."

"Gad!" Brooks murmured. "The man's a poet!"

"You're right, Turner." Vallery drained his glass, lay back exhausted. "We don't seem to have much option. . . . What if we receive orders for a—ah—high-speed withdrawal?"

"You can't read," Turner said bluntly. "Remember, you just said your eyes are going back on you."

"'Souls that have toiled and wrought and fought with me,'" Vallery quoted softly. "Thank you, gentlemen. You make things very easy for me." He propped himself on an elbow, his mind made up. He smiled at Turner, and his face was almost boyish again.

"Inform all merchant ships, all escorts. Tell them to break north."

Turner stared at him.

"North? Did you say 'north?' But the Admiralty——"

"North, I said," Vallery repeated quietly. "The Admiralty can do what they like about it. We've played along long enough.

---

torpedoes from a Russian submarine.) The support squadron and convoy escorts immediately withdrew to the west at high speed, leaving PQ17 to their fate, leaving them to scatter and make their unescorted way to Russia as best they could. The feelings of the crews of the merchant ships at this save-their-own-skins desertion and betrayal by the Royal Navy can be readily imagined. Their fears, too, can be readily imagined, but even their darkest forebodings never conceived the dreadful reality: 23 merchant ships were sent to the bottom—by U-boats and aircraft. The *Tirpitz* was not seen, never came anywhere near the convoy; but even the threat had driven the naval squadrons to flight.

The author does not know all the facts concerning PQ17, nor does he seek to interpret those he does know: still less does he presume to assign blame. Curiously enough, the only definite conclusion is that no blame can be attached to the actual commander of the squadron, Admiral Hamilton. He had no part of the decision to withdraw—the order came from the Admiralty, and was imperative. But one does not envy him.

It was a melancholy and bitter incident, all the more unpalatable in that it ran so directly counter to the traditions of a great Service. One wonders what Sir Philip Sydney would have thought, or, in more modern times, Kennedy of the *Rawalpindi* or Fegen of the *Jervis Bay*. But there was no doubt what the Merchant Navy thought, what they still think. From most of the few survivors, there can be no hope of forgiveness. They will, probably, always remember: the Royal Navy would desperately like to forget. It is difficult to blame either.

We've sprung the trap. What more can they want ? This way
there's a chance—an almost hopeless chance, perhaps, but a
fighting chance. To go east is suicide." He smiled again, almost
dreamily. " The end is not all-important," he said softly. " I
don't think I'll have to answer for this. Not now—not ever."

Turner grinned at him, his face lit up. " North, you said."

" Inform C.-in-C.," Vallery went on. " Ask Pilot for an
interception course. Tell the convoy we'll tag along behind, give
'em as much cover as we can, as long as we can. . . . As long as
we can. Let us not delude ourselves. 1,000 to 1 at the outside.
. . . Nothing else we can do, Commander ? "

" Pray," Turner said succinctly.

" And sleep," Brooks added. " Why don't you have half an
hour, sir ? "

" Sleep ! " Vallery seemed genuinely amused. " We'll have
all the time in the world to sleep, just by and by."

" You have a point," Brooks conceded. " You are very
possibly right."

CHAPTER FIFTEEN

SATURDAY EVENING II

MESSAGES WERE pouring in to the bridge now, messages from the merchant ships, messages of dismayed unbelief asking for confirmation of the *Tirpitz* breakout : from the *Stirling*, replying that the superstructure fire was now under control and that the engine-room watertight bulkheads were holding ; and one from Orr of the *Sirrus*, saying that his ship was making water to the capacity of the pumps—he had been in heavy collision with the sinking merchantman—that they had taken off forty-four survivors, that the *Sirrus* had already done her share and couldn't she go home ? The signal had arrived after the *Sirrus's* receipt of the bad news. Turner grinned to himself : no inducement on earth, he knew, could have persuaded Orr to leave now.

The messages kept pouring in, by visual signal or W.T. There was no point in maintaining radio silence to outwit enemy monitor positions ; the enemy knew where they were to a mile. Nor was there any need to prohibit light signalling—not with the *Stirling* still burning furiously enough to illumine the sea for a mile around. And so the messages kept on coming—messages of fear and dismay and anxiety. But, for Turner, the most disquieting message came neither by lamp nor by radio.

Fully quarter of an hour had elapsed since the end of the attack, and the *Ulysses* was rearing and pitching through the head seas on her new course of 350°, when the gate of the bridge crashed open and a panting, exhausted man stumbled on to the compass platform. Turner, back on the bridge again, peered closely at him in the red glare from the *Stirling*, recognised him as a stoker. His face was masked in sweat, the sweat already caking to ice in the intense cold. And in spite of that cold, he was hatless, coatless, clad only in a pair of thin dungarees. He was shivering violently, shivering from excitement and not because of the icy wind—he was oblivious to such things.

Turner seized him by the shoulder.

" What is it, man ? " he demanded anxiously. The stoker was still too breathless to speak. " What's wrong ? Quickly ! "

" The T.S., sir ! " The breathing was so quick, so agonised, that the words blurred into a gasping exhalation. " It's full of water ! "

" The T.S. ! " Turner was incredulous. " Flooded ! When did this happen ? "

" I'm not sure, sir." He was still gasping for breath. " But there was a bloody awful explosion, sir, just about amid——"

" I know ! I know ! " Turner interrupted impatiently. " Bomber carried away the for'ard funnel, exploded in the water, port side. But that was fifteen minutes ago, man ! Fifteen minutes ! Good God, they would have——"

" T.S. switchboard's gone, sir." The stoker was beginning to recover, to huddle against the wind, but frantic at the Commander's deliberation and delay, he straightened up and grasped Turner's duffel without realising what he was doing. The note of urgency deepened still further. " All the power's gone, sir. And the hatch is jammed ! The men can't get out ! "

" The hatch-cover jammed ! " Turner's eyes narrowed in concern. " What happened ? " he rapped out. " Buckled ? "

" The counter-weight's broken off, sir. It's on top of the hatch. We can only get it open an inch. You see, sir——"

" Number One ! " Turner shouted.

" Here, sir." Carrington was standing just behind him. " I heard. . . . Why can't you open it ? "

" It's the *T.S.* hatch ! " the stoker cried desperately. " A quarter of a bloody ton if it's an ounce, sir. You know—the one below the ladder outside the wheelhouse. Only two men can get at it at the same time. We've tried. . . . Hurry, sir. *Please*."

" Just a minute." Carrington was calm, unruffled, infuriatingly so. " Hartley ? No, still fire-fighting. Evans, MacIntosh—dead." He was obviously thinking aloud. " Bellamy, perhaps ? "

"What is it, Number One ? " Turner burst out. He himself had caught up the anxiety, the impatience of the stoker. " What are you trying—— ? "

" Hatch-cover plus pulley—1,000 lbs.," Carrington murmured. " A special man for a special job."

" Petersen, sir ! " The stoker had understood immediately. " Petersen ! "

" Of course ! " Carrington clapped gloved hands together. " We're on our way, sir. Acetylene ? No time ! Stoker—crowbars, sledges. . . . Perhaps if you would ring the engine-room, sir ? "

But Turner already had the phone in his hand.

Aft on the poop-deck, the fire was under control, all but in a few odd corners where the flames were fed by a fierce through draught. In the mess-decks, bulkheads, ladders, mess partitions, lockers had been twisted and buckled into strange shapes by the intense heat : on deck, the gasoline-fed flames, incinerating the two and three-quarter inch deck planking and melting the caulking as by some gigantic blow-torch, had cleanly stripped all covering and exposed the steel deck-plates, plates dull red and glowing evilly, plates that hissed and spat as heavy snowflakes drifted down to sibilant extinction.

On and below decks, Hartley and his crews, freezing one moment, reeling in the blast of heat the next, toiled like men insane. Where their wasted, exhausted bodies found the strength God only knew. From the turrets, from the Master-At-Arms's office, from mess-decks and emergency steering position, they pulled out man after man who had been there when the Condor had crashed : pulled them out, looked at them, swore, wept and plunged back into the aftermath of that holocaust, oblivious of pain and danger, tearing aside wreckage, wreckage still burning, still red-hot, with charred and broken gloves : and when the gloves fell off, they used their naked hands.

As the dead were ranged in the starboard alleyway, Leading Seaman Doyle was waiting for them. Less than half an hour previously, Doyle had been in the for'ard galley passage, rolling in silent agony as frozen body and clothes thawed out after the drenching of his pom-pom. Five minutes later, he had been back

on his gun, rock-like, unflinching, as he pumped shell after shell
over open sights into the torpedo bombers. And now, steady and
enduring as ever, he was on the poop. A man of iron, and a face
of iron, too, that night, the bearded leonine head still and impassive as he picked up one dead man after the other, walked to
the guard-rail and dropped his burden gently over the side. How
many times he repeated that brief journey that night, Doyle never
knew : he had lost count after the first twenty or so. He had no
right to do this, of course : the navy was very strong on decent
burial, and this was not decent burial. But the sailmaker was dead
and no man would or could have sewn up these ghastly charred
heaps in the weighted and sheeted canvas. The dead don't care,
Doyle thought dispassionately—let them look after themselves.
So, too, thought Carrington and Hartley, and they made no move
to stop him.

Beneath their feet, the smouldering mess-decks rang with
hollow reverberating clangs as Nicholls and Leading Telegraphist
Brown, still weirdly garbed in their white asbestos suits, swung
heavy sledges against the securing clips of " Y " magazine hatch.
In the smoke and gloom and their desperate haste, they could
hardly see each other, much less the clips : as often as not
they missed their strokes and the hammers went spinning out of
numbed hands into the waiting darkness.

Time yet, Nicholls thought desperately, perhaps there is time.
The main flooding valve had been turned off five minutes ago :
it was possible, barely possible, that the two trapped men inside
were clinging to the ladder, above water level.

One clip, one clip only was holding the hatch-cover now.
With alternate strokes of their sledges, they struck it with vicious
strength. Suddenly, unexpectedly, it sheared off at its base and
the hatch-cover crashed open under the explosive up-surge of the
compressed air beneath. Brown screamed in agony, a single
coughing shout of pain, as the bone-crashing momentum of the
swinging hatch crashed into his right hip, then fell to the deck
where he lay moaning quietly.

Nicholls did not even spare him a glance. He leant far through
the hatch, the powerful beam of his torch stabbing downwards

into the gloom. And he could see nothing, nothing at all—not what he wanted to see. All he saw was the water, dark and viscous and evil, water rising and falling, water flooding and ebbing in eerie oilbound silence as the *Ulysses* plunged and lifted in the heavy seas.

" Below ! " Nicholls called loudly. The voice, a voice, he noted impersonally, cracked and shaken with strain, boomed and echoed terrifyingly down the iron tunnel. " Below ! " he shouted again. " Is there anybody there ? " He strained his ears for the least sound, for the faintest whisper of an answer, but none came.

" McQuater ! " He shouted a third time. " Williamson ! Can you hear me ? " Again he looked, again he listened, but there was only the darkness and the muffled whisper of the oil-slicked water swishing smoothly from side to side. He stared again down the light from the torch, marvelled that any surface could so quickly dissipate and engulf the brilliance of that beam. And beneath that surface. . . . He shivered. The water—even the water seemed to be dead, old and evil and infinitely horrible. In sudden anger, he shook his head to clear it of these stupid, primitive fears : his imagination—he'd have to watch it. He stepped back, straightened up. Gently, carefully, he closed the swinging hatch. The mess-deck echoed as his sledge swung down on the clips, again and again and again.

Engineer-Commander Dodson stirred and moaned. He struggled to open his eyes but his eyelids refused to function. At least, he thought that they did for the blackness around remained as it was, absolute, impenetrable, almost palpable.

He wondered dully what had happened, how long he had been there, what had happened. And the side of his head—just below the ear—that hurt abominably. Slowly, with clumsy deliberation, he peeled off his glove, reached up an exploratory hand. It came away wet and sticky : his hair, he realised with mild surprise, was thickly matted with blood. It must be blood —he could feel it trickling slowly, heavily down the side of his cheek.

And that deep, powerful vibration, a vibration overlain with an indefinable note of strain that set his engineer's teeth on edge

—he could hear it, almost feel it, immediately in front of him. His bare hand reached out, recoiled in instant reflex as it touched something smooth and revolving—and burning hot.

The shaft tunnel! Of course. That's where he was—the shaft tunnel. They'd discovered fractured lubricating pipes on the port shafts too, and he'd decided to keep this engine turning. He knew they'd been attacked. Down here in the hidden bowels of the ship, sound did not penetrate : he had heard nothing of the aircraft engines : he hadn't even heard their own guns firing—but there had been no mistaking the jarring shock of the 5.25s surging back on their hydraulic recoils. And then—a torpedo perhaps, or a near miss by a bomb. Thank God he'd been sitting facing inboard when the *Ulysses* had lurched. The other way round and it would have been curtains for sure when he'd been flung across the shaft coupling and wrapped round. . . .

The shaft! Dear God, the shaft! It was running almost red-hot on dry bearings! Frantically, he pawed around, picked up his emergency lamp and twisted its base. There was no light. He twisted it again with all his strength, reached up, felt the jagged edges of broken screen and bulb, and flung the useless lamp to the deck. He dragged out his pocket torch : that, too, was smashed. Desperate now, he searched blindly around for his oil can : it was lying on its side, the patent spring top beside it. The can was empty.

No oil, none. Heaven only knew how near that over-stressed metal was to the critical limit. He didn't. He admitted that : even to the best engineers, metal fatigue was an incalculable unknown. But, like all men who had spent a lifetime with machines, he had developed a sixth sense for these things—and, right now, that sixth sense was jabbing at him, mercilessly, insistently. Oil—he would have to get oil. But he knew he was in bad shape, dizzy, weak from shock and loss of blood, and the tunnel was long and slippery and dangerous—and unlighted. One slip, one stumble against or over that merciless shaft. . . . Gingerly, the Engineer Commander stretched out his hand again, rested his hand for an instant on the shaft, drew back sharply in sudden pain. He lifted his hand to his cheek, knew that it was not friction that had flayed and burnt the skin off the tips of his fingers. There was no choice. Resolutely, he gathered his legs under him, swayed dizzily to his feet, his back bent against the arching convexity of the tunnel.

It was then that he noticed it for the first time—a light, a swinging, tiny pinpoint of light, imponderably distant in the converging sides of that dark tunnel, although he knew it could be only yards away. He blinked, closed his eyes and looked again. The light was still there, advancing steadily, and he could hear the shuffling of feet now. All at once he felt weak, light-headed : gratefully he sank down again, his feet safely braced once more against the bearing block.

The man with the light stopped a couple of feet away, hooked the lamp on to an inspection bracket, lowered himself carefully and sat beside Dodson. The rays of the lamp fell full on the dark heavy face, the jagged brows and prognathous jaw : Dodson stiffened in sudden surprise.

" Riley ! Stoker Riley ! " His eyes narrowed in suspicion and conjecture. " What the devil are you doing here ? "

" I've brought a two-gallon drum of lubricating oil," Riley growled. He thrust a Thermos flask into the Engineer-Commander's hands. " And here's some coffee. I'll 'tend to this— you drink that. . . . Suffering Christ ! This bloody bearing's red-hot ! "

Dodson set down the Thermos with a thump.

" Are you deaf ? " he asked harshly. " Why are *you* here ? Who sent you ? Your station's in ' B ' boiler-room ! "

" Grierson sent me," Riley said roughly. His dark face was impassive. " Said he couldn't spare his engine-room men—too bloody valuable. . . . Too much ? " The oil, thick, viscous, was pouring slowly on to the overheated bearing.

" *Lieutenant* Grierson ! " Dodson was almost vicious, his voice a whip-lash of icy correction. " And that's a damned lie, Riley ! Lieutenant Grierson never sent you : I suppose you told *him* that somebody else had sent you ? "

" Drink your coffee," Riley advised sourly. " You're wanted in the engine-room."

The Engineer-Commander clenched his fist, restrained himself with difficulty.

" You damned insolent bastard ! " he burst out. Abruptly, control came back and he said evenly : " Commander's Defaulters in the morning. You'll pay for this, Riley ! "

" No, I won't." Confound him, Dodson thought furiously, he's actually grinning, the insolent . . .

He checked his thought.

" Why not ? " he demanded dangerously.

" Because you won't report me." Riley seemed to be enjoying himself hugely.

" Oh, so that's it ! " Dodson glanced swiftly round the darkened tunnel, and his lips tightened as he realised for the first time how completely alone they were : in sudden certainty he looked back at Riley, big and hunched and menacing. Smiling yet, but no smile, Dodson thought, could ever transform that ugly brutal face. The smile on the face of the tiger. . . . Fear, exhaustion, never-ending strain—these did terrible things to a man and you couldn't blame him for what he had become, or for what he was born. . . . But his, Dodson's, first responsibility was to himself. Grimly, he remembered how Turner had berated him, called him all sorts of a fool for refusing to have Riley sent to prison.

" So that's it, eh ? " he repeated softly. He turned himself, feet thrusting solidly against the block. " Don't be so sure, Riley. I can give you twenty-five years, but——"

" Oh, for Christ's sake ! " Riley burst out impatiently. " What are you talking about, sir ? Drink your coffee—please. You're wanted in the engine-room, I tell you ! " he repeated impatiently.

Uncertainly, Dodson relaxed, unscrewed the cap of the Thermos. He had a sudden, peculiar feeling of unreality, as if he were a spectator, some bystander in no way involved in this scene, this fantastic scene. His head, he realised, still hurt like hell.

" Tell me, Riley," he asked softly. " What makes you so sure I won't report you ? "

" Oh, you can report me all right." Riley was suddenly cheerful again. " But I won't be at the Commander's table to-morrow morning."

" No ? " It was half-challenge, half-question.

" No," Riley grinned. " 'Cos there'll *be* no Commander *and* no table to-morrow morning." He clasped his hands luxuriously behind his head. " In fact, there'll be no nothin'."

Something in the voice, rather than in the words, caught and held Dodson's attention. He knew, with instant conviction, that though Riley might be smiling, he wasn't joking. Dodson looked at him curiously, but said nothing.

" Commander's just finished broadcastin'," Riley continued. " The *Tirpitz* is out—we have four hours left."

The bald, flat statement, the complete lack of histrionics, of playing for effect, left no possible room for doubt. The *Tirpitz*—out. The *Tirpitz*—out. Dodson repeated the phrase to himself, over and over again. Four hours, just four hours to go. . . . He was surprised at his own reaction, his apparent lack of concern.

" Well ? " Riley was anxious now, restive. " Are you goin' or aren't you ? I'm not kiddin', sir—you're wanted—urgent ! "

" You're a liar," Dodson said pleasantly. " Why did you bring the coffee ? "

" For myself." The smile was gone, the face set and sullen. " But I thought you needed it—you don't look so good to me. . . . They'll fix you up back in the engine-room."

" And that's just where you're going, right now ! " Dodson said evenly.

Riley gave no sign that he had heard.

" On your way, Riley," Dodson said curtly. " That's an order ! "

"—— off ! " Riley growled. " I'm stayin'. You don't require to have three —— great gold stripes on your sleeve to handle a bloody oil can," he finished derisively.

" Possibly not." Dodson braced against a sudden, violent pitch, but too late to prevent himself lurching into Riley. " Sorry, Riley. Weather's worsening, I'm afraid. Well, we—ah—appear to have reached an impasse."

" What's that ? " Riley asked suspiciously.

" A dead-end. A no-decision fight. . . . Tell me, Riley," he asked quietly. " What brought you here ? "

" I told you ! " Riley was aggrieved. " Grierson—*Lieutenant* Grierson sent me."

" What brought you here ? " Dodson persisted. It was as if Riley had not spoken.

" That's my —— business ! " Riley answered savagely.

" What brought you here ? "

" Oh, for Christ's sake leave me alone ! " Riley shouted. His voice echoed loudly along the dark tunnel. Suddenly he turned round full-face, his mouth twisted bitterly. " You know bloody well why I came."

" To do me in, perhaps ? "

Riley looked at him a long second, then turned away. His shoulders were hunched, his head held low.

" You're the only bastard in this ship that ever gave me a break," he muttered. " The only bastard I've ever *known* who ever gave me a chance," he amended slowly. " Bastard," Dodson supposed, was Riley's accolade of friendship, and he felt suddenly ashamed of his last remark. " If it wasn't for you," Riley went on softly, " I'd 'a' been in cells the first time, in a civvy jail the second. Remember, sir ? "

Dodson nodded. " You were rather foolish, Riley," he admitted.

" Why did you do it ? " The big stoker was intense, worried. " God, everyone knows what I'm like—— "

" Do they ? I wonder. . . . I thought you had the makings of a better man than you—— "

" Don't give me that bull ! " Riley scoffed. " *I* know what I'm like. I know what I am. I'm no —— good ! Everybody says I'm no —— good ! And they're right. . . ." He leaned forward. " Do you know somethin' ? I'm a Catholic. Four hours from now . . ." He broke off. " I should be on my knees, shouldn't I ? " he sneered. " Repentance, lookin' for—what do they call it ? "

" Absolution ? "

" Aye. That's it. Absolution. And do you know what ? " he spoke slowly, emphatically. " I don't give a single, solitary damn ! "

" Maybe you don't have to," Dodson murmured. " For the last time, get back to that engine-room ! "

" No ! "

The Engineer-Commander sighed, picked up the Thermos.

" In that case, perhaps you would care to join me in a cup of coffee ? "

Riley looked up, grinned, and when he spoke it was in a very creditable imitation of Colonel Chinstrap of the famous ITMA radio programme.

" Ectually, I don't mind if I do ! "

Vallery rolled over on his side, his legs doubled up, his hand automatically reaching for the towel. His emaciated body shook violently, and the sound of the harsh, retching cough beat back at him from the iron walls of his shelter. God, he thought, oh, God, it's never been as bad as this before. Funny, he thought, it doesn't hurt any more, not even a little bit. The attack eased. He looked at the crimson, sodden towel, flung it in sudden disgust and with what little feeble strength was left him into the darkest corner of the shelter.

" You carry this damned ship on your back ! " Unbidden, old Socrates's phrase came into his mind and he smiled faintly. Well, if ever they needed him, it was now. And if he waited any longer, he knew he would never be able to go.

He sat up, sweating with the effort, swung his legs carefully over the side. As his feet touched the deck, the *Ulysses* pitched suddenly, steeply, and he fell forward against a chair, sliding helplessly to the floor. It took an eternity of time, an infinite effort to drag himself to his feet again : another effort like that, he knew, would surely kill him.

And then there was the door—that heavy, steel door. Somehow he had to open it, and he knew he couldn't. But he laid hold of the handle and the door opened, and suddenly, miraculously, he was outside, gasping as the cruel, sub-zero wind seared down through his throat and wasted lungs.

He looked fore and aft. The fires were dying, he saw, the fires on the *Stirling* and on his own poop-deck. Thank God for that at least. Beside him, two men had just finished levering the door off the Asdic cabinet, were flashing a torch inside. But he couldn't bear to look : he averted his head, staggered with outstretched hands for the gate of the compass platform.

Turner saw him coming, hurried to meet him, helped him slowly to his chair.

" You've no right to be here," he said quietly. He looked at Vallery for a long moment. " How are you feeling, sir ? "

" I'm a good deal better, now, thanks," Vallery replied. He smiled and went on : " We Rear-Admirals have our responsibilities, you know, Commander : it's time I began to earn my princely salary."

" Stand back, there ! " Carrington ordered curtly. " Into the wheelhouse or up on the ladder—all of you. Let's have a look at this."

He looked down at the great, steel hatch-cover. Looking at it, he realised he'd never before appreciated just how solid, how massive that cover was. The hatch-cover, open no more than an inch, was resting on a tommy-bar. He noticed the broken, stranded pulley, the heavy counterweight lying against the sill of the wheelhouse. So that's off, he thought : thank the Lord for that, anyway.

" Have you tried a block and tackle ? " he asked abruptly.

" Yes, sir," the man nearest him replied. He pointed to a tangled heap in a corner. " No use, sir. The ladder takes the strain all right, but we can't get the hook under the hatch, except sideways—and then it slips off all the time." He gestured to the hatch. " And every clip's either bent—they were opened by sledges—or at the wrong angle. . . . I think I know how to use a block and tackle, sir."

" I'm sure you do," Carrington said absently. " Here, give me a hand, will you ? "

He hooked his fingers under the hatch, took a deep breath. The seaman at one side of the cover—the other side was hard against the after bulkhead—did the same. Together they strained, thighs and backs quivering under the strain. Carrington felt his face turning crimson with effort, heard the blood pounding in his ears, and relaxed. They were only killing themselves and that damned cover hadn't shifted a fraction—someone had done remarkably well to open it even that far. But even though they were tired and anything but fit, Carrington thought, two men should have been able to raise an edge of that hatch. He suspected that the hinges were jammed—or the deck buckled. If that were so, he mused, even if they could hook on a tackle, it would be of little help. A tackle was of no use when a sudden, immediate application of force was required ; it always yielded that fraction before tightening up.

He sank to his knees, put his mouth to the edge of the hatch. "Below there ! " he called. " Can you hear me ? "

" We can hear you." The voice was weak, muffled. " For God's sake get us out of here. We're trapped like rats ! "

" Is that you, Brierley ? Don't worry—we'll get you out. How's the water down there ? "

" Water ? More bloody oil than water ! There must be a fracture right through the port oil tank. I think the ring main passage must be flooded, too."

" How deep is it ? "

" Three-quarters way up already ! We're standing on generators, hanging on to switchboards. One of our boys is gone already—we couldn't hold him." Even muffled by the hatch, the strain, the near-desperation in the voice was all too obvious. " For pity's sake, hurry up ! "

" I said we'd get you out ! " Carrington's voice was sharp, authorative. The confidence was in his voice only, but he knew how quickly panic could spread down there. " Can you push from below at all ? "

" There's room for only one on the ladder," Brierley shouted. " It's impossible to get any pressure, any leverage upwards." There was a sudden silence, then a series of muffled oaths.

" What's up ? " Carrington called sharply.

" It's difficult to hang on," Brierley shouted. " There are waves two feet high down there. One of the men was washed off there. . . . I think he's back again. It's pitch dark down here."

Carrington heard the clatter of heavy footsteps above him, and straightened up. It was Petersen. In that narrow space, the blond Norwegian stoker looked gigantic. Carrington looked at him, looked at the immense span of shoulder, the great depth of chest, one enormous hand hanging loosely by his side, the other negligently holding three heavy crowbars and a sledge as if they were so many lengths of cane. Carrington looked at him, looked at the still, grave eyes so startlingly blue under the flaxen hair, and all at once he felt oddly confident, reassured.

"We can't open this, Petersen," Carrington said baldly. "Can you?"

"I will try, sir." He laid down his tools, stooped, caught the end of the tommy-bar projecting beneath the corner of the cover. He straightened quickly, easily : the hatch lifted a fraction, then the bar, putty-like in its apparent malleability, bent over almost to a right angle.

"I think the hatch is jammed." Petersen wasn't even breathing heavily. "It will be the hinges, sir."

He walked round the hatch, peered closely at the hinges, then grunted in satisfaction. Three times the heavy sledge, swung with accuracy and all the power of these great shoulders behind them, smashed squarely into the face of the outer hinge. On the third stroke the sledge snapped. Petersen threw away the broken shaft in disgust, picked up another, much heavier crowbar.

Again the bar bent, but again the hatch-cover lifted—an inch this time. Petersen picked up the two smaller sledges that had been used to open the clips, hammered at the hinges till these sledges, too, were broken and useless.

This time he used the last two crowbars together, thrust under the same corner of the hatch. For five, ten seconds he remained bent over them, motionless. He was breathing deeply, quickly, now, then suddenly the breathing stopped. The sweat began to pour off his face, his whole body to quiver under the titanic strain : then slowly, incredibly, both crowbars began to bend.

Carrington watched, fascinated. He had never seen anything remotely like this before : he was sure no one else had either. Neither of these bars, he would have sworn, would have bent under less than half a ton of pressure. It was fantastic, but it was happening : and as the giant straightened, they were bending more and more. Then suddenly, so unexpectedly that everyone jumped, the hatch sprang open five or six inches and Petersen crashed backwards against the bulkhead, the bars falling from his hand and splashing into the water below.

Petersen flung himself back at the hatch, tigerish in his ferocity. His fingers hooked under the edge, the great muscles of his arms and shoulders lifted and locked as he tugged and pulled at that massive hatch-cover. Three times he heaved, four times, then on the fifth the hatch almost literally leapt up with a screech of tortured metal and smashed shudderingly home into the retaining latch of the vertical stand behind. The hatch was open. Petersen just stood there smiling—no one had seen Petersen smile for a long time—his face bathed in sweat, his great chest rising and falling rapidly as his starved lungs sucked in great draughts of air.

The water level in the Low Power Room was within two feet of the hatch : sometimes, when the *Ulysses* plunged into a heavy sea, the dark, oily liquid splashed over the hatch coaming into the flat above. Quickly, the trapped men were hauled up to safety. Soaked in oil from head to foot, their eyes gummed and blinded, they were men overcome by reaction, utterly spent and on the verge of collapse, so far gone that even their fear could not overcome their exhaustion. Three, in particular, could do no more than cling helplessly to the ladder, would almost certainly have slipped back into the surging blackness below; but Petersen bent over and plucked them clean out of the Low Power Room as if they had been little children.

" Take these men to the Sick Bay at once ! " Carrington ordered. He watched the dripping, shivering men being helped up the ladder, then turned to the giant stoker with a smile. " We'll all thank you later, Petersen. We're not finished yet. This hatch must be closed and battened down."

" It will be difficult, sir," Petersen said gravely.

" Difficult or not, it *must* be done." Carrington was emphatic. Regularly, now, the water was spilling over the coaming, was lapping the sill of the wheelhouse. " The emergency steering position is gone : if the wheelhouse is flooded, we're finished."

Petersen said nothing. He lifted the retaining latch, pulled the protesting hatch-cover down a foot. Then he braced his shoulder against the ladder, planted his feet on the cover and straightened his back convulsively : the cover screeched down to 45°. He paused, bent his back like a bow, his hands taking his weight on the ladder, then pounded his feet again and again on the edge of the cover. Fifteen inches to go.

" We need heavy hammers, sir," Petersen said urgently.

" No time ! " Carrington shook his head quickly. " Two more minutes and it'll be impossible to shut the hatch-cover against the water pressure. Hell ! " he said bitterly. " If it were only the other way round—closing from below. Even I could lever it shut ! "

Again Petersen said nothing. He squatted down by the side of the hatch, gazed into the darkness beneath his feet.

" I have an idea, sir," he said quickly. " If two of you would stand on the hatch, push against the ladder. Yes, sir, that way— but you could push harder if you turned your back to me."

Carrington laid the heels of his hands against the iron step of the ladder, heaved with all his strength. Suddenly he heard a splash, then a metallic clatter, whirled round just in time to see a crowbar clutched in an enormous hand disappear below the edge of the hatch. There was no sign of Petersen. Like many big, powerful men, he was lithe and cat-like in his movements : he'd gone down over the edge of that hatch without a sound.

" Petersen ! " Carrington was on his knees by the hatch. " What the devil do you think you're doing ? Come out of there, you bloody fool ! Do you want to drown ? "

There was no reply. Complete silence below, a silence deepened by the gentle sussuration of the water. Suddenly the quiet was broken by the sound of metal striking against metal, then by a jarring screech as the hatch dropped six inches. Before Carrington had time to think, the hatch-cover dropped farther still. Desperately, the First Lieutenant seized a crowbar, thrust it under the hatch-cover : a split second later the great steel cover thudded down on top of it. Carrington had his mouth to the gap now.

" In the name of God, Petersen," he shouted. " Are you sane ? Open up, open up at once, do you hear ? "

" I can't." The voice came and went as the water surged over the stoker's head. " I won't. You said yourself . . . there is no time . . . this was the only way."

" But I never meant——"

" I know. It does not matter . . . it is better this way." It was almost impossible to make out what he was saying. " Tell Captain Vallery that Petersen says he is very sorry. . . . I tried to tell the Captain yesterday."

" Sorry ! Sorry for what ? " Madly, Carrington flung all his strength against the iron bar : the hatch-cover did not even quiver.

" The dead marine in Scapa Flow. . . . I did not mean to kill him, I could never kill any man. . . . But he angered me," the big Norwegian said simply. " He killed my friend."

For a second, Carrington stopped straining at the bar. Petersen ! Of course—who but Petersen could have snapped a man's neck like that. Petersen, the big, laughing Scandinavian, who had so suddenly changed overnight into a grave, unsmiling giant, who stalked the deck, the mess-decks and alleyways by day and by night, who was never seen to smile or sleep. With a sudden flash of insight, Carrington saw clear through into the tortured mind of that kind and simple man.

" Listen, Petersen," he begged. " I don't give a damn about that. Nobody shall ever know, I promise you. Please, Petersen, just——"

" It is better this way." The muffled voice was strangely content. " It is not good to kill a man . . . it is not good to go on living. . . . I know. . . . Please, it is important—you will tell my Captain—Petersen is sorry and filled with shame. . . . I do this for my Captain." Without warning, the crowbar was plucked from Carrington's hand. The cover clanged down in position. For a minute the wheelhouse flat rang to a succession of muffled, metallic blows. Suddenly the clamour ceased and there was only the rippling surge of the water outside the wheelhouse and the creak of the wheel inside as the *Ulysses* steadied on course.

The clear sweet voice soared high and true above the subdued roar of the engine-room fans, above the whine of a hundred electric motors and the sound of the rushing of the waters. Not even the metallic impersonality of the loudspeakers could detract from the beauty of that singing voice. . . . It was a favourite device of Vallery's, when the need for silence was not paramount, to pass the long, dark hours by coupling up the record-player to the broadcast system.

Almost invariably, the musical repertoire was strictly classical —or what is more often referred to, foolishly and disparagingly, as the popular classics. Bach, Beethoven, Tchaikovski, Lehar, Verdi, Delius—these were the favourites. " No. 1 in B flat minor," " Air on a G string," " Moonlight on the Alster," " Claire de Lune," " The Skater's Waltz "—the crew of the *Ulysses* could never have enough of these. " Ridiculous," " impossible "—it is all too easy to imagine the comments of those who equate the matelot's taste in music with the popular conception of his ethics and morals ; but those same people have never heard the hushed, cathedral silence in the crowded hangar of a great aircraft carrier in Scapa Flow as Yehudi Menuhin's magic bow sang across the strings of the violin, swept a thousand men away from the harsh urgencies of reality, from the bitter memories of the last patrol or convoy, into the golden land of music.

But now a girl was singing. It was Deanna Durbin, and she was singing " Beneath the Lights of Home," that most heartbreakingly nostalgic of all songs. Below decks and above, bent over the great engines or huddled by their guns, men listened to the lovely voice as it drifted through the darkened ship and the falling snow, and turned their minds inwards and thought of home, thought of the bitter contrast and the morning that would not come. Suddenly, half-way through, the song stopped.

" Do you hear there ? " the 'speakers boomed. " Do you hear there ? This—this is the Commander speaking." The voice was deep and grave and hesitant : it caught and held the attention of every man in the ship.

" I have bad news for you." Turner spoke slowly, quietly. " I am sorry—I . . ." He broke off, then went on more slowly still. " Captain Vallery died five minutes ago." For a moment the 'speaker was silent, then crackled again. " He died on the bridge, in his chair. He knew he was dying and I don't think he suffered at all. . . . He insisted—he insisted that I thank you for the way you all stood by him. ' Tell them '—these were his words, as far as I remember—' tell them,' he said, ' that I couldn't have carried on without them, that they are the best crew that God ever gave a Captain.' Then he said—it was the last thing he said : ' Give them my apologies.   After all they've done for me—well, well, tell them I'm terribly sorry to let them down like this.' That was all he said—just ' Tell them I'm sorry.' And then he died."

CHAPTER SIXTEEN

SATURDAY NIGHT

RICHARD VALLERY was dead. He died grieving, stricken at the thought that he was abandoning the crew of the *Ulysses*, leaving them behind, leaderless. But it was only for a short time, and he did not have to wait long. Before the dawn, hundreds more, men in the cruisers, the destroyers and the merchantmen, had died also. And they did not die as he had feared under the guns of the *Tirpitz*—another grim parallel with PQ17, for the *Tirpitz* had not left Alta Fjord. They died, primarily, because the weather had changed.

Richard Vallery was dead, and with his death a great change had come over the men of the *Ulysses*. When Vallery died, other things died also, for he took these things with him. He took with him the courage, the kindliness, the gentleness, the unshakable faith, the infinitely patient and understanding endurance, all these things which had been so peculiarly his own. And now these things were gone and the *Ulysses* was left without them and it did not matter. The men of the *Ulysses* no longer needed courage and all the adjuncts of courage, for they were no longer afraid. Vallery was dead and they did not know how much they respected and loved that gentle man until he was gone. But then they knew. They knew that something wonderful, something that had become an enduring part of their minds and memories, something infinitely fine and good, was gone and they would never know it again, and they were mad with grief. And, in war, a grief-stricken man is the most terrible enemy there is. Prudence, caution, fear, pain—for the grief-stricken man these no longer exist. He lives only to lash out blindly at the enemy, to destroy, if he can, the author of his grief. Rightly or wrongly, the *Ulysses* never thought to blame the Captain's death on any but the enemy. There was only, for them, the sorrow and the blind hate. Zombies, Nicholls had called them once, and the *Ulysses* was more than ever a ship manned by living zombies, zombies who prowled restlessly, incessantly, across the snow and ice of the heaving decks, automatons living only for revenge.

The weather changed just before the end of the middle watch. The seas did not change—FR77 was still butting into the heavy, rolling swell from the north, still piling up fresh sheets of glistening ice on their labouring fo'c'sles. But the wind dropped, and almost at once the snowstorm blew itself out, the last banks of dark, heavy cloud drifting away to the south. By four o'clock the sky was completely clear.

There was no moon that night, but the stars were out, keen and sharp and frosty as the icy breeze that blew steadily out of the north.

Then, gradually, the sky began to change. At first there was only a barely perceptible lightening on the northern rim then, slowly, a pulsating, flickering band of light began to broaden and deepen and climb steadily above the horizon, climbing higher to the south with the passing of every minute. Soon that pulsating ribbon of light was paralleled by others, streamers in the most delicate pastel shades of blue and green and violet, but always and predominantly white. And always, too, these lanes of multi-coloured light grew higher and stronger and brighter: at the climax, a great band of white stretched high above the convoy, extending from horizon to horizon. . . . These were the Northern Lights, at any time a spectacle of beauty and wonder, and this night surpassingly lovely : down below, in ships clearly illumined against the dark and rolling seas, the men of FR77 looked up and hated them.

On the bridge of the *Ulysses*, Chrysler—Chrysler of the uncanny eyesight and super-sensitive hearing, was the first to hear it. Soon everyone else heard it too, the distant roar, throbbing and intermittent, of a Condor approaching from the south. After a time they became aware that the Condor was no longer approaching, but sudden hope died almost as it was born. There was no mistaking it now—the deeper, heavier note of a Focke-Wulf in maximum climb. The Commander turned wearily to Carrington.

"It's Charlie, all right," he said grimly. "The bastard's spotted us. He'll already have radioed Alta Fjord and a hundred to one in anything you like that he's going to drop a marker flare at 10,000 feet or so. It'll be seen fifty miles away."

"Your money's safe." The First Lieutenant was withering. "I never bet against dead certs. . . . And then, by and by, maybe a few flares at a couple of thousand?"

"Exactly!" Turner nodded. "Pilot, how far do you reckon we're from Alta Fjord—in flying time, I mean?"

"For a 200-knot plane, just over an hour," the Kapok Kid said quietly. His ebullience was gone: he had been silent and dejected since Vallery had died two hours previously.

"An hour!" Carrington exclaimed. "And they'll *be* here. My God, sir," he went on wonderingly, "they're really out to get us. We've never been bombed nor torpedoed at night before. We've never had the *Tirpitz* after us before. We never——"

"The *Tirpitz*," Turner interrupted. "Just where the hell *is* that ship? She's had time to come up with us. Oh, I know it's dark and we've changed course," he added, as Carrington made to object, "but a fast destroyer screen would have picked us—Preston!" He broke off, spoke sharply to the Signal Petty Officer. "Look alive, man! That ship's flashing us."

"Sorry, sir." The signalman, swaying on his feet with exhaustion, raised his Aldis, clacked out an acknowledgment. Again the light on the merchantman began to wink furiously.

"'Transverse fracture engine bedplate,'" Preston read out. "'Damage serious: shall have to moderate speed.'"

"Acknowledge," said Turner curtly. "What ship is that, Preston?"

"The *Ohio Freighter*, sir."

"The one that stopped a tin fish a couple of days back?"

"That's her, sir."

"Make a signal. 'Essential maintain speed and position.'" Turner swore. "What a time to choose for an engine breakdown. . . . Pilot, when do we rendezvous with the Fleet?"

"Six hours' time, sir; exactly."

"Six hours." Turner compressed his lips. "Just six hours—perhaps!" he added bitterly.

"Perhaps?" Carrington murmured.

"Perhaps," Turner affirmed. "Depends entirely on the weather. C.-in-C. won't risk capital ships so near the coast unless he can fly off fighter cover against air attack. And, if you ask me, that's why the *Tirpitz* hasn't turned up yet—some wandering U-boat's tipped him off that our Fleet Carriers are steaming south. He'll be waiting on the weather. . . . What's he saying now, Preston?" The *Ohio's* signal lamp had flashed briefly, then died.

"'Imperative slow down,'" Preston repeated. "'Damage severe. Am slowing down.'"

"He is, too," Carrington said quietly. He looked up at Turner, at the set face and dark eyes, and knew the same thought was in the Commander's mind as was in his own. "He's a goner, sir, a dead duck. He hasn't a chance. Not unless——"

"Unless what?" Turner asked harshly. "Unless we leave him an escort? Leave what escort, Number One? The *Viking*—the only effective unit we've left?" He shook his head in slow decision. "The greatest good of the greatest number: that's how it has to be. They'll know that. Preston, send 'Regret cannot leave you standby. How long to effect repairs?'"

The flare burst even before Preston's hand could close on the trigger. It burst directly over FR77. It was difficult to estimate the height—probably six to eight thousand feet—but at that altitude it was no more than an incandescent pinpoint against the great band of the Northern Lights arching majestically above. But it was falling quickly, glowing more brightly by the sound: the parachute, if any, could have been only a steadying drogue.

The crackling of the W.T. 'speaker broke through the stuttering chatter of the Aldis.

"W.T.—bridge. W.T.—bridge. Message from *Sirrus*: 'Three survivors dead. Many dying or seriously wounded. Medical assistance urgent, repeat urgent.'" The 'speaker died, just as the *Ohio* started flickering her reply.

"Send for Lieutenant Nicholls," Turner ordered briefly. "Ask him to come up to the bridge at once."

Carrington stared down at the dark broad seas, seas flecked with milky foam : the bows of the *Ulysses* were crashing down heavily, continuously.

"You're going to risk it, sir ? "

"I must. You'd do the same, Number One. . . . What does the *Ohio* say, Preston ? "

"'I understand. Too busy to look after the Royal Navy anyway. We will make up on you. Au revoir ! '"

"We will make up on you. Au revoir." Turner repeated softly. "He lies in his teeth, and he knows it. By God ! " he burst out. "If anyone ever tells me the Yankee sailors have no guts—I'll push his perishing face in. Preston, send : ' Au revoir. Good luck.' . . . Number One, I feel like a murderer." He rubbed his hand across his forehead, nodded towards the shelter where Vallery lay stretched out, and strapped to his settee. "Month in, month out, he's been taking these decisions. It's no wonder . . ." He broke off as the gate creaked open.

"Is that you, Nicholls ? There is work for you, my boy. Can't have you medical types idling around uselessly all day long." He raised his hand. "All right, all right," he chuckled. "I know. . . . How are things on the surgical front ? " he went on seriously.

"We've done all we can, sir. There was very little left for us to do," Nicholls said quietly. His face was deeply lined, haggard to the point of emaciation. "But we're in a bad way for supplies. Hardly a single dressing left. And no anæsthetics at all—except what's left in the emergency kit. The Surgeon Commander refuses to touch those."

"Good, good," Turner murmured. "How do you feel, laddie ? "

"Awful."

"You look it," Turner said candidly. "Nicholls—I'm terribly sorry, boy—I want you to go over to the *Sirrus*."

"Yes, sir." There was no surprise in the voice : it hadn't been difficult to guess why the Commander had sent for him. "Now ? "

Turner nodded without speaking. His face, the lean strong features, the heavy brows and sunken eyes were quite visible now in the strengthening light of the plunging flare. A face to remember, Nicholls thought.

" How much kit can I take with me, sir ? "

" Just your medical gear. No more. You're not travelling by Pullman, laddie ! "

" Can I take my camera, my films ? "

" All right." Turner smiled briefly. " Looking forward keenly to photographing the last seconds of the *Ulysses*, I suppose. . . . Don't forget that the *Sirrus* is leaking like a sieve. Pilot—get through to the W.T. Tell the *Sirrus* to come alongside, prepare to receive medical officer by breeches buoy."

The gate creaked again. Turner looked at the bulky figure stumbling wearily on to the compass platform. Brooks, like every man in the crew, was dead on his feet ; but the blue eyes burned as brightly as ever.

" My spies are everywhere," he announced. " What's this about the *Sirrus* shanghaiing young Johnny here ? "

" Sorry, old man," Turner apologised. " It seems things are pretty bad on the *Sirrus*."

" I see." Brooks shivered. It might have been the thin threnody of the wind in the shattered rigging, or just the ice-laden wind itself. He shivered again, looked upwards at the sinking flare. " Pretty, very pretty," he murmured. " What are the illuminations in aid of ? "

" We are expecting company," Turner smiled crookedly. " An old world custom, O Socrates—the light in the window and what have you." He stiffened abruptly, then relaxed, his face graven in granitic immobility. " My mistake," he murmured. " The company has already arrived."

The last words were caught up and drowned in the rumbling roar of a heavy explosion. Turner had known it was coming—he'd seen the thin stilletto of flame stabbing skywards just for'ard of the *Ohio Freighter's* bridge. The sound had taken five or six seconds to reach them—the *Ohio* was already over a mile distant on the starboard quarter, but clearly visible still under the luminance of the Northern Lights—the Northern Lights that had betrayed her, almost stopped in the water, to a wandering U-boat.

The *Ohio Freighter* did not remain visible for long. Except for the moment of impact, there was neither smoke, nor flame, nor sound. But her back must have been broken, her bottom torn out—and she was carrying a full cargo of nothing but tanks and ammunition. There was a curious dignity about her end— she sank quickly, quietly, without any fuss. She was gone in three minutes.

It was Turner who finally broke the heavy silence on the bridge. He turned away and in the light of the flare his face was not pleasant to see.

" Au revoir," he muttered to no one in particular. " Au revoir. That's what he said, the lying . . ." He shook his head angrily, touched the Kapok Kid on the arm. " Get through to W.T.," he said sharply. " Tell the *Viking* to sit over the top of that sub till we get clear."

" Where's it all going to end ? " Brooks's face was still and heavy in the twilight.

" God knows ! How I hate those murdering bastards ! " Turner ground out. " Oh, I know, I know, we do the same— but give me something I can see, something I can fight, some- thing——"

" You'll be able to see the *Tirpitz* all right," Carrington interrupted dryly. " By all accounts, she's big enough."

Turner looked at him, suddenly smiled. He clapped his arm, then craned his head back, staring up at the shimmering loveliness of the sky. He wondered when the next flare would drop.

" Have you a minute to spare, Johnny ? " The Kapok Kid's voice was low. " I'd like to speak to you."

" Sure." Nicholls looked at him in surprise. " Sure, I've a minute, ten minutes—until the *Sirrus* comes up. What's wrong, Andy ? "

" Just a second." The Kapok Kid crossed to the Commander. " Permission to go to the charthouse, sir ? "

" Sure you've got your matches ? " Turner smiled. " O.K. Off you go."

The Kapok Kid smiled faintly, said nothing. He took Nicholls by the arm, led him into the charthouse, flicked on the lights and produced his cigarettes. He looked steadily at Nicholls as he dipped his cigarette into the flickering pool of flame.

"Know something, Johnny?" he said abruptly. "I reckon I must have Scotch blood in me."

"Scots," Nicholls corrected. "And perish the very thought."

"I'm feeling—what's the word?—fey, isn't it? I'm feeling fey to-night, Johnny." The Kapok Kid hadn't even heard the interruption. He shivered. "I don't know why—I've never felt this way before."

"Ah, nonsense! Indigestion, my boy," Nicholls said briskly. But he felt strangely uncomfortable.

"Won't wash this time." Carpenter shook his head, half-smiling. "Besides, I haven't eaten a thing for two days. I'm on the level, Johnny." In spite of himself, Nicholls was impressed. Emotion, gravity, earnestness—these were utterly alien to the Kapok Kid.

"I won't be seeing you again," the Kapok Kid continued softly. "Will you do me a favour, Johnny?"

"Don't be so bloody silly," Nicholls said angrily. "How the hell do you——?"

"Take this with you." The Kapok Kid pulled out a slip of paper, thrust it into Nicholls's hands. "Can you read it?"

"I can read it." Nicholls had stilled his anger. "Yes, I can read it." There was a name and address on the sheet of paper, a girl's name and a Surrey address. "So that's her name," he said softly. "Juanita . . . Juanita." He pronounced it carefully, accurately, in the Spanish fashion. "My favourite song and my favourite name," he murmured.

"Is it?" the Kapok Kid asked eagerly. "Is it indeed? And mine, Johnny." He paused. "If, perhaps—well, if I don't— well, you'll go to see her, Johnny?"

"What are you talking about, man?" Nicholls felt embarrassed. Half-impatiently, half-playfully, he tapped him on the chest. "Why, with that suit on, you could *swim* from here to Murmansk. You've said so yourself, a hundred times."

The Kapok Kid grinned up at him. The grin was a little crooked.

" Sure, sure, I know, I know—will you go, Johnny ? "

" Dammit to hell, yes ! " Nicholls snapped. " I'll go—and it's high time I was going somewhere else. Come on I " He snapped off the lights, pulled back the door, stopped with his foot half-way over the sill. Slowly, he stepped back inside the charthouse, closed the door and flicked on the light. The Kapok Kid hadn't moved, was gazing quietly at him.

" I'm sorry, Andy," Nicholls said sincerely. " I don't know what made me——"

" Bad temper," said the Kapok Kid cheerfully. " You always did hate to think that I was right and you were wrong ! "

Nicholls caught his breath, closed his eyes for a second. Then he stretched out his hand.

" All the best, Vasco." It was an effort to smile. " And don't worry. I'll see her if—well, I'll see her, I promise you. Juanita. . . . But if I find *you* there," he went on threateningly, " I'll——"

" Thanks, Johnny. Thanks a lot." The Kapok Kid was almost happy. " Good luck, boy. . . . Vaya con Dios. That's what she always said to me, what she said before I came away. ' Vaya con Dios.' "

Thirty minutes later, Nicholls was operating aboard the *Sirrus*.

The time was 0445. It was bitterly cold, with a light wind blowing steadily from the north. The seas were heavier than ever, longer between the crests, deeper in their gloomy troughs, and the damaged *Sirrus*, labouring under a mountain of ice, was making heavy weather of it. The sky was still clear, a sky of breath-taking purity, and the stars were out again, for the Northern Lights were fading. The fifth successive flare was drifting steadily seawards.

It was at 0445 that they heard it—the distant rumble of gun-fire far to the south—perhaps a minute after they had seen the incandescent brilliance of a burning flare on the rim of the far horizon. There could be no doubt as to what was happening. The *Viking*, still in contact with the U-boat, although powerless to do anything about it, was being heavily attacked. And the attack must have been short, sharp and deadly, for the firing ceased soon after it had begun. Ominously, nothing came through on the W.T. No one ever knew what had happened to the *Viking*, for there were no survivors.

The last echo of the *Viking's* guns had barely died away before they heard the roar of the engines of the Condor, at maximum throttle in a shallow dive. For five, perhaps ten seconds—it seemed longer than that, but not long enough for any gun in the convoy to begin tracking him accurately—the great Focke-Wulf actually flew beneath his own flare, and then was gone. Behind him, the sky opened up in a blinding coruscation of flame, more dazzling, more hurtful, than the light of the noonday sun. So intense, so extraordinary the power of those flares, so much did pupils contract and eyelids narrow in instinctive self-protection, that the enemy bombers were through the circle of light and upon them before anyone fully realised what was happening. The timing, the split-second co-operation between marker plane and bombers, was magnificent.

There were twelve planes in the first wave. There was no concentration on one target, as before : not more than two attacked any ship. Turner, watching from the bridge, watching them swoop down steeply and level out before even the first gun in the *Ulysses* had opened up, caught his breath in sudden dismay. There was something terribly familiar about the speed, the approach, the silhouette of these planes. Suddenly he had it— Heinkels, by God ! Heinkel IIIs. And the Heinkel III, Turner knew, carried that weapon he dreaded above all others—the glider bomb.

And then, as if he had touched a master switch, every gun on the *Ulysses* opened up. The air filled with smoke, the pungent smell of burning cordite : the din was indescribable. And all at once, Turner felt fiercely, strangely happy. . . . To hell with them and their glider bombs, he thought. This was war as he liked to fight it : not the cat-and-mouse, hide-and-seek frustration of trying to outguess the hidden wolf-packs, but war out in the open, where he could see the enemy and hate him and love him for fighting as honest men should and do his damndest to destroy

him. And, Turner knew, if they could at all, the crew of the
Ulysses would destroy him. It needed no great sensitivity to
direct the sea-change that had overtaken his men—yes, his men
now : they no longer cared for themselves : they had crossed
the frontier of fear and found that nothing lay beyond it and
they would keep on feeding their guns and squeezing their
triggers until the enemy overwhelmed them.

The leading Heinkel was blown out of the sky, and fittingly
enough it was " X " turret¡ that destroyed it—" X " turret, the
turret of dead marines, the turret that had destroyed the Condor,
and was now manned by a scratch marine crew. The Heinkel
behind lifted sharply to avoid the hurtling fragments of fuselage
and engines, dipped, flashed past the cruiser's bows less than a
boat-length away, banked steeply to port under maximum power,
and swung back in on the Ulysses. Every gun on the ship was
caught on the wrong foot, and seconds passed before the first
one was brought to bear—time and to spare for the Heinkel to
angle in at 60°, drop his bomb and slew frantically away as the
concentrated fire of the Oerlikons and pom-poms closed in on
him. Miraculously, he escaped.

The winged bomb was high, but not high enough. It wavered,
steadied, dipped, then glided forwards and downwards through
the drifting smoke of the guns to strike home with a tremendous,
deafening explosion that shook the Ulysses to her keel and almost
shattered the eardrums of those on deck.

To Turner, looking aft from the bridge, it seemed that the
Ulysses could never survive this last assault. An ex-torpedo
officer and explosives expert himself, he was skilled in assessing
the disruptive power of high explosive : never before had he
been so close to so powerful, so devastating an explosion. He
had dreaded these glider bombs, but even so he had under-
estimated their power : the concussion had been double, treble
what he had been expecting.

What Turner did not know was that what he had heard had
been not one explosion but two, but so nearly simultaneous as
to be indistinguishable. The glider bomb, by a freakish chance,
had crashed directly into the port torpedo tubes. There had been
only one torpedo left there—the other two had sent the Vytura

to the bottom—and normally Amatol, the warhead explosive, is extremely stable and inert, even when subjected to violent shock : but the bursting bomb had been too close, too powerful : sympathetic detonation had been inevitable.

Damage was extensive and spectacular : it was severe, but not fatal. The side of the *Ulysses* had been ripped open, as by a giant can-opener, almost to the water's edge : the tubes had vanished : the decks were holed and splintered : the funnel casing was a shambles, the funnel itself tilting over to port almost to fifteen degrees ; but the greatest energy of the explosion had been directed aft, most of the blast expending itself over the open sea, while the galley and canteen, severely damaged already, were no more than a devil's scrapyard.

Almost before the dust and debris of the explosion had settled, the last of the Heinkels was disappearing, skimming the waves, weaving and twisting madly in evasive action, pursued and harried by a hundred glowing streams of tracer. Then, magically, they were gone, and there was only the sudden deafening silence and the flares, drooping slowly to extinction, lighting up the pall above the *Ulysses*, the dark clouds of smoke rolling up from the shattered *Stirling* and a tanker with its after superstructure almost gone. But not one of the ships in FR77 had faltered or stopped ; and they had destroyed five Heinkels. A costly victory, Turner mused, if it could be called a victory ; but he knew the Heinkels would be back. It was not difficult to imagine the fury, the hurt pride of the High Command in Norway : as far as Turner knew, no Russian Convoy had ever sailed so far south before.

Riley eased a cramped leg, stretched it gently so as to avoid the great spinning shaft. Carefully, he poured some oil on to the bearing, carefully, so as not to disturb the Engineer Commander, propped in sleep between the tunnel wall and Riley's shoulder. Even as Riley drew back, Dodson stirred, opened heavy, gummed lids.

"Good God above ! " he said wearily. "You still here, Riley? " It was the first time either of them had spoken for hours.

"It's a ―― good job I *am* here," Riley growled. He nodded towards the bearing. " Bloody difficult to get a firehose down to this place, I should think ! " That was unfair, Riley knew : he and Dodson had been taking it in half-hour turns to doze and feed the bearing. But he felt he had to say something : he was finding it increasingly difficult to keep on being truculent to the Engineer Commander.

Dodson grinned to himself, said nothing. Finally, he cleared his throat, murmured casually : " The *Tirpitz* is taking its time about making its appearance, don't you think ? "

" Yes, sir." Riley was uncomfortable. " Should 'a' been here long ago, damn her ! "

" Him," Dodson corrected absently. " *Admiral von Tirpitz*, you know. . . . Why don't you give up this foolishness, Riley ? "

Riley grunted, said nothing. Dodson sighed, then brightened.
" Go and get some more coffee, Riley. I'm parched ! "

" No." Riley was blunt. " *You* get it."

" As a favour, Riley." Dodson was very gentle. " I'm damned thirsty ! "

" Oh, all right." The big stoker swore, climbed painfully to his feet. " Where'll I get it ? "

" Plenty in the engine-room. If it's not iced water they're swigging, it's coffee. But no iced water for me." Dodson shivered.

Riley gathered up the Thermos, stumbled along the passage. He had only gone a few feet when they felt the *Ulysses* shudder under the recoil of the heavy armament. Although they did not know it, it was the beginning of the air attack.

Dodson braced himself against the wall, saw Riley do the same, pause a second then hurry away in an awkward, stumbling run. There was something grotesquely familiar in that awkward run, Dodson thought. The guns surged back again and the figure scuttled even faster, like a giant crab in a panic. . . . *Panic*, Dodson thought : that's it, panic-stricken. Don't blame the poor bastard—I'm beginning to imagine things myself down here. Again the whole tunnel vibrated, more heavily this time—that must be " X " turret, almost directly above. No, I don't blame him. Thank God he's gone. He smiled quietly to himself. I won't be seeing friend Riley again—he isn't all that of a reformed character. Tiredly, Dodson settled back against the wall. On my own at last, he murmured to himself, and waited for the feeling of relief. But it never came. Instead, there was only a vexation and loneliness, a sense of desertion and a strangely empty disappointment.

Riley was back inside a minute. He came back with that same awkward, crab-like run, carrying a three-pint Thermos jug and two cups, cursing fluently and often as he slipped against the wall. Panting, wordlessly, he sat down beside Dodson, poured out a cup of steaming coffee.

" Why the hell did you have to come back ? " Dodson demanded harshly. " I don't want you and——"

" You wanted coffee," Riley interrupted rudely. " You've got the bloody stuff. Drink it."

At that instant, the explosion and the vibration from the explosion in the port tubes echoed weirdly down the dark tunnel, the shock flinging the two men heavily against each other. His whole cup of coffee splashed over Dodson's leg : his mind was so tired, his reactions so slow, that his first realisation was of how damnably cold he was, how chill that dripping tunnel. The scalding coffee had gone right through his clothes, but he could feel neither warmth nor wetness : his legs were numbed, dead below the knees. Then he shook his head, looked up at Riley.

" What in God's name was that ? What's happening ? Did you—— ? "

" Haven't a clue. Didn't stop to ask." Riley stretched himself luxuriously, blew on his steaming coffee. Then a happy thought struck him, and a broad cheerful grin came as near to transforming that face as would ever be possible.

" It's probably the *Tirpitz*," he said hopefully.

Three times more during that terrible night, the German squadrons took off from the airfield at Alta Fjord, throbbed their way nor'-nor'-west through the bitter Arctic night, over the heaving Arctic sea, in search of the shattered remnants of FR77. Not that the search was difficult—the Folke-Wulf Condor stayed with them all night, defied their best attempts to shake him off. He seemed to have an endless supply of these deadly flares, and might very well have been—in fact, almost certainly was—carrying nothing else. And the bombers had only to steer for the flares.

The first assault—about 0545—was an orthodox bombing attack, made from about 3,000 feet. The planes seemed to be Dorniers, but it was difficult to be sure, because they flew high above a trio of flares sinking close to the water level. As an attack, it was almost but not quite abortive, and was pressed home with no great enthusiasm. This was understandable : the barrage was intense. But there were two direct hits—one on a merchantman, blowing away most of the fo'c'sle, the other on the *Ulysses*. It sheered through the flag deck and the Admiral's day cabin, and exploded in the heart of the Sick Bay. The Sick Bay was crowded with the sick and dying, and, for many, that bomb must have come as a God-sent release, for the *Ulysses* had long since run out of anæsthetics. There were no survivors. Among the dead was Marshall, the Torpedo Officer, Johnson, the Leading S.B.A., the Master-At-Arms who had been lightly wounded an hour before by a splinter from the torpedo tubes, Burgess, strapped helplessly in a strait-jacket—he had suffered concussion on the night of the great storm and gone insane. Brown, whose hip had been smashed by the hatch-cover of " Y " magazine, and Brierley, who was dying anyway, his lungs saturated and rotted away with fuel oil. Brooks had not been there.

The same explosion had also shattered the telephone exchange: barring only the bridge-gun phones, and the bridge-engine phones and speaking-tubes, all communication lines in the *Ulysses* were gone.

The second attack, at 7 a.m., was made by only six bombers— Heinkels again, carrying glider-bombs. Obviously flying strictly under orders, they ignored the merchantmen and concentrated their attack solely on the cruisers. It was an expensive attack : the enemy lost all but two of their force in exchange for a single hit aft on the *Stirling*, a hit which, tragically, put both after guns out of action.

Turner, red-eyed and silent, bareheaded in that sub-zero wind, and pacing the shattered bridge of the *Ulysses*, marvelled that the *Stirling* still floated, still fought back with everything she had.

And then he looked at his own ship, less a ship, he thought wearily, than a floating shambles of twisted steel still scything impossibly through these heavy seas, and marvelled all the more. Broken, burning cruisers, cruisers ravaged and devastated to the point of destruction, were nothing new for Turner : he had seen the *Trinidad* and the *Edinburgh* being literally battered to death on these same Russian convoys. But he had never seen any ship, at any time, take such inhuman, murderous punishment as the *Ulysses* and the obsolete *Stirling* and still live. He would not have believed it possible.

The third attack came just before dawn. It came with the grey half-light, an attack carried out with great courage and the utmost determination by fifteen Heinkel III glider-bombers. Again the cruisers were the sole targets, the heavier attack by far being directed against the *Ulysses*. Far from shrinking the challenge and bemoaning their ill-luck the crew of the *Ulysses*, that strange and selfless crew of walking zombies whom Nicholls had left behind, welcomed the enemy gladly, even joyfully, for how can one kill an enemy if he does not come to you ? Fear, anxiety, the near-certainty of death—these did not exist. Home and country, families, wives and sweethearts, were names, only names : they touched a man's mind, these thoughts, touched it and lifted and were gone as if they had never been. " Tell them," Vallery had said ; " tell them they are the best crew God ever gave a captain." Vallery. *That* was what mattered, that and what Vallery had stood for, that something that had been so inseparably a part of that good and kindly man that you never saw it because it *was* Vallery. And the crew hoisted the shells, slammed the breeches and squeezed their triggers, men uncaring, men oblivious of anything and everything, except the memory of the man who had died apologising because he had let them down, except the sure knowledge that they could not let Vallery down. Zombies, but inspired zombies, men above themselves, as men commonly are when they know the next step, the inevitable step has them clear to the top of the far side of the valley. . . .

The first part of the attack was launched against the *Stirling*. Turner saw two Heinkels roaring in in a shallow dive, improbably surviving against heavy, concentrated fire at point-blank range.

The bombs, delayed action and armour-piercing, struck the *Stirling* amidships, just below deck level, and exploded deep inside, in the boiler-room and engine-room. The next three bombers were met with only pom-pom and Lewis fire : the main armament for'ard had fallen silent. With sick apprehension, Turner realised what had happened : the explosion had cut the power to the turrets.[1] Ruthlessly, contemptuously almost, the bombers brushed aside the puny opposition : every bomb went home. The *Stirling*, Turner saw, was desperately wounded. She was on fire again, and listing heavily to starboard.

The suddenly lifting crescendo of aero engines spun Turner round to look to his own ship. There were five Heinkels in the first wave, at different heights and approach angles so as to break up the pattern of A.A. fire, but all converging on the after end of the *Ulysses*. There was so much smoke and noise that Turner could only gather confused, broken impressions. Suddenly, it seemed, the air was filled with glider-bombs and the tearing, staccato crash of the German cannon and guns. One bomb exploded in mid-air, just for'ard of the after funnel and feet away from it : a maiming, murderous storm of jagged steel scythed across the boat-deck, and all Oerlikons and the pom-poms fell immediately silent, their crews victim to shrapnel or concussion. Another plunged through the deck and Engineers' Flat and turned the W.T. office into a charnel house. The remaining two that struck were higher, smashing squarely into "X" gun-deck and "X" turret. The turret was split open around the top and down both sides as by a giant cleaver, and blasted off its mounting, to lie grotesquely across the shattered poop.

Apart from the boat-deck and turret gunners, only one other man lost his life in that attack, but that man was virtually irreplaceable. Shrapnel from the first bomb had burst a compressed

[1] It is almost impossible for one single explosion, or even several in the same locality, to destroy or incapacitate all the dynamos in a large naval vessel, or to sever all the various sections of the Ring Main, which carries the power around the ship. When a dynamo or its appropriate section of the Ring Main suffered damage, the interlinking fuses automatically blew, isolating the damaged section. Theoretically, that is. In practice, it does not always happen that way—the fuses may not rupture and the entire system breaks down. Rumour—very strong rumour—had it that at least one of H.M. capital ships was lost simply because the Dynamo Fuse Release Switches—fuses of the order of 800 amps—failed to blow, leaving the capital ship powerless to defend itself.

air cylinder in the torpedo workshop, and Hartley, the man who, above all, had become the backbone of the *Ulysses* had taken shelter there, only seconds before. . . .

The *Ulysses* was running into dense black smoke, now—the *Stirling* was heavily on fire, her fuel tanks gone. What happened in the next ten minutes, no one ever knew. In the smoke and flame and agony, they were moments borrowed from hell and men could only endure. Suddenly, the *Ulysses* was out in the clear, and the Heinkels, all bombs gone, were harrying her, attacking her incessantly with cannon and machine-gun, ravening wolves with their victim on its knees, desperate to finish it off. But still, here and there, a gun fired on the *Ulysses*.

Just below the bridge, for instance—there was a gun firing there. Turner risked a quick glance over the side, saw the gunner pumping his tracers into the path of a swooping Heinkel. And then the Heinkel opened up, and Turner flung himself back, knocking the Kapok Kid to the deck. Then the bomber was gone and the guns were silent. Slowly, Turner hoisted himself to his feet, peered over the side: the gunner was dead, his harness cut to ribbons.

He heard a scuffle behind him, saw a slight figure fling off a restraining hand, and climb to the edge of the bridge. For an instant, Turner saw the pale, staring face of Chrysler, Chrysler who had neither smiled nor even spoken since they had opened up the Asdic cabinet; at the same time he saw three Heinkels forming up to starboard for a fresh attack.

"Get down, you young fool!" Turner shouted. "Do you want to commit suicide?"

Chrysler looked at him, eyes wide and devoid of recognition, looked away and dropped down to the sponson below. Turner lifted himself to the edge of the bridge and looked down.

Chrysler was struggling with all his slender strength, struggling in a strange and frightening silence, to drag the dead man from his Oerlikon cockpit. Somehow, with a series of convulsive, despairing jerks, he had him over the side, had laid him gently to the ground, and was climbing into the cockpit. His hand, Turner saw, was bare and bleeding, stripped to the raw flesh—then out of the corner of his eyes he saw the flame of the Heinkel's guns and flung himself backward.

One second passed, two, three—three seconds during which cannon shells and bullets smashed against the reinforced armour of the bridge—then, as a man in a daze, he heard the twin Oerlikons opening up. The boy must have held his fire to the very last moment. Six shots the Oerlikon fired—only six, and a great, grey shape, stricken and smoking, hurtled over the bridge barely at head height, sheared off its port wing on the Director Tower and crashed into the sea on the other side.

Chrysler was still sitting in the cockpit. His right hand was clutching his left shoulder, a shoulder smashed and shattered by a cannon shell, trying hopelessly to stem the welling arterial blood. Even as the next bomber straightened out on its strafing run, even as he flung himself backwards, Turner saw the mangled, bloody hand reach out for the trigger grip again.

Flat on the duckboards beside Carrington and the Kapok Kid, Turner pounded his fist on the deck in terrible frustration of anger. He thought of Starr, the man who had brought all this upon them, and hated him as he would never have believed he could hate anybody. He could have killed him then. He thought of Chrysler, of the excruciating hell of that gun-rest pounding into that shattered shoulder, of brown eyes glazed and shocked with pain and grief. If he himself lived, Turner swore, he would recommend that boy for the Victoria Cross. Abruptly, the firing ceased and a Heinkel swung off sharply to starboard, smoke pouring from both its engines.

Quickly, together with the Kapok Kid, Turner scrambled to his feet, hoisted himself over the side of the bridge. He did it without looking, and he almost died then. A burst of fire from the third and last Heinkel—the bridge was always the favourite target—whistled past his head and shoulders : he felt the wind of their passing fan his cheek and hair. Then, winded from the convulsive back-thrust that had sent him there, he was stretched full length on the duckboards again. They were only inches from his eyes, these duckboards, but he could not see them. All he could see was the image burned into his mind in a searing fraction of a second, the image of Chrysler, a gaping wound the size of a man's hand in his back, slumped forward across the Oerlikons, the weight of his body tilting the barrels grotesquely skywards. Both barrels had still been firing, were still firing, would keep on firing until the drums were empty, for the dead boy's hand was locked across the trigger.

Gradually, one by one, the guns of the convoy fell silent, the clamour of the aero engines began to fade in the distance. The attack was over.

Turner rose to his feet, slowly and heavily this time. He looked over the side of the bridge, stared down into the Oerlikon gunpit, then looked away, his face expressionless.

Behind him, he heard someone coughing. It was a strange, bubbling kind of cough. Turner whirled round, then stood stock-still, his hands clenched tightly at his sides.

The Kapok Kid, with Carrington kneeling helplessly at his side, was sitting quietly on the boards, his back propped against the legs of the Admiral's chair. From left groin to right shoulder through the middle of the embroidered " J " on the chest, stretched a neat, straight, evenly-spaced pattern of round holes, stitched in by the machine-gun of the Heinkel. The blast of the shells must have hurled him right across the bridge.

Turner stood absolutely still. The Kid, he knew with sudden sick certainty, had only seconds to live : he felt that any sudden move on his part would snap the spun-silk thread that held him on to life.

Gradually, the Kapok Kid became aware of his presence, of his steady gaze, and looked up tiredly. The vivid blue of his eyes was dulled already, the face white and drained of blood. Idly, his hand strayed up and down the punctured kapok, fingering the gashes. Suddenly he smiled, looked down at the quilted suit.

" Ruined," he whispered. " Bloody well ruined ! " Then the wandering hand slipped down to his side, palm upward, and his head slumped forward on his chest. The flaxen hair stirred idly in the wind.

CHAPTER SEVENTEEN

SUNDAY MORNING

THE *Stirling* died at dawn. She died while still under way, still plunging through the heavy seas, her mangled, twisted bridge and superstructure glowing red, glowing white-hot as the wind and sundered oil tanks lashed the flames into an incalescent holocaust. A strange and terrible sight, but not unique : thus the *Bismarck* had looked, whitely incandescent, just before the *Shropshire's* torpedoes had sent her to the bottom.

The *Stirling* would have died anyway—but the Stukas made siccar. The Northern Lights had long since gone : now, too, the clear skies were going, and dark cloud was banking heavily to the north. Men hoped and prayed that the cloud would spread over FR77, and cover it with blanketing snow. But the Stukas got there first.

The Stukas—the dreaded gull-winged Junkers 87 dive-bombers—came from the south, flew high over the convoy, turned, flew south again. Level with, and due west of the *Ulysses*, rear ship in the convoy, they started to turn once more : then, abruptly, in the classic Stuka attack pattern, they peeled off in sequence, port wings dipping sharply as they half-rolled, turned, and fell out of the sky, plummetting arrow-true for their targets.

Any plane that hurtles down in undeviating dive on waiting gun emplacements has never a chance. Thus spoke the pundits, the instructors in the gunnery school of Whale Island, and proceeded to prove to their own satisfaction the evident truth of their statement, using A.A. guns and duplicating the situation which would arise insofar as it lay within their power. Unfortunately, they couldn't duplicate the Stuka.

"Unfortunately," because, in actual battle, the Stuka was the only factor in the situation that really mattered. One had only to crouch behind a gun, to listen to the ear-piercing, screaming whistle of the Stuka in its near-vertical dive, to flinch from its hail of bullets as it loomed larger and larger in the sights, to know that nothing could now arrest the flight of that underslung bomb, to appreciate the truth of that. Hundreds of men alive to-day—the lucky ones who endured and survived a Stuka attack—will readily confirm that the war produced nothing quite so nerve-rending, quite so demoralising as the sight and sound of those Junkers with the strange dihedral of the wings in the last seconds before they pulled out of their dive.

But one time in a hundred, maybe one time in a thousand, when the human factor of the man behind the gun ceased to operate, the pundits could be right. This was the thousandth time, for fear was a phantom that had vanished in the night: ranged against the dive-bombers were only one multiple pom-pom and half a dozen Oerlikons—the for'ard turrets could not be brought to bear—but these were enough, and more, in the hands of men inhumanly calm, ice-cool as the Polar wind itself, and filled with an almost dreadful singleness of purpose. Three Stukas in almost as many seconds were clawed out of the sky, two to crash harmlessly in the sea, a third to bury itself with tremendous impact in the already shattered day cabin of the Admiral.

The chances against the petrol tanks not erupting in searing flame or of the bomb not exploding, were so remote as not to exist: but neither happened. It hardly seemed to call for comment—in extremity, courage becomes routine—when the bearded Doyle abandoned his pom-pom, scrambled up to the fo'c'sle deck, and flung himself on top of the armed bomb rolling heavily in scuppers awash with 100 per cent octane petrol. One tiny spark from Doyle's boot or from the twisted, broken steel of the Stuka rubbing and grinding against the superstructure would have been trigger enough: the contact fuse in the bomb was still undamaged, and as it slipped and skidded over the ice-bound deck, with Doyle hanging desperately on, it seemed animistically determined to smash its delicate percussion nose against a bulkhead or stanchion.

If Doyle thought of these things, he did not care. Coolly, almost carelessly, he kicked off the only retaining clip left on a broken section of the guard-rail, slid the bomb, fins first, over the edge, tipped the nose sharply to clear the detonator. The bomb fell harmlessly into the sea.

It fell into the sea just as the first bomb sliced contemptuously through the useless one-inch deck armour of the *Stirling* and crashed into the engine-room. Three, four, five, six other bombs buried themselves in the dying heart of the cruiser, the lightened Stukas lifting away sharply to port and starboard. From the bridge of the *Ulysses*, there seemed to be a weird, unearthly absence of noise as the bombs went home. They just vanished into the smoke and flame, engulfed by the inferno.

No one blow finished the *Stirling*, but a mounting accumulation of blows. She had taken too much and she could take no more. She was like a reeling boxer, a boxer overmatched against an unskilled but murderous opponent, sinking under an avalanche of blows.

Stony-faced, bitter beyond words at his powerlessness, Turner watched her die. Funny, he thought tiredly, she's like all the rest. Cruisers, he mused in a queerly detached abstraction, must be the toughest ships in the world. He'd seen many go, but none easily, cleanly, spectacularly. No sudden knock-out, no *coup de grace* for them—always, always, they had to be battered to death. . . . Like the *Stirling*. Turner's grip on the shattered windscreen tightened till his forearms ached. To him, to all good sailors, a well-loved ship was a well-loved friend : for fifteen months, now, the old and valiant *Stirling* had been their faithful shadow, had shared the burden of the *Ulysses* in the worst convoys of the war : she was the last of the old guard, for only the *Ulysses* had been longer on the blackout run. It was not good to watch a friend die : Turner looked away, stared down at the ice-covered duck-boards between his feet, his head sunk between hunched shoulders.

He could close his eyes, but he could not close his ears. He winced, hearing the monstrous, roaring hiss of boiling water and steam as the white-hot superstructure of the *Stirling* plunged deeply into the ice-chilled Arctic. For fifteen, twenty seconds that dreadful, agonised sibilation continued, then stopped in an instant, the sound sheared off as by a guillotine. When Turner looked up, slowly, there was only the rolling, empty sea ahead, the big oil-slicked bubbles rising to the top, bubbles rising only to be punctured as they broke the surface by the fine rain falling back into the sea from the great clouds of steam already condensing in that bitter cold.

The *Stirling* was gone, and the battered remnants of FR77 pitched and plunged steadily onwards to the north. There were seven ships left now—the four merchantmen, including the Commodore's ship, the tanker, the *Sirrus* and the *Ulysses*. None of them was whole : all were damaged, heavily damaged, but none so desperately hurt as the *Ulysses*. Seven ships, only seven : thirty-six had set out for Russia.

At 0800 Turner signalled the *Sirrus* : " W.T. gone. Signal C.-in-C. course, speed, position. Confirm 0930 as rendezvous. Code."

The reply came exactly an hour later. " Delayed heavy seas. Rendezvous approx 1030. Impossible fly off air cover. Keep coming. C.-in-C."

" Keep coming ! " Turner repeated savagely. " Would you listen to him ! ' Keep coming,' he says ! What the hell does he expect us to do—scuttle ourselves ? " He shook his head in angry despair. " I hate to repeat myself," he said bitterly. " But I must. Too bloody late as usual ! "[1]

Dawn and daylight had long since come, but it was growing darker again. Heavy grey clouds, formless and menacing, blotted out the sky from horizon to horizon. They were snow clouds, and, please God, the snow would soon fall : that could save them now, that and that alone.

But the snow did not come—not then. Once more, there

[1] It is regrettable but true—the Home Fleet squadron was almost always too late. The Admiralty could not be blamed—the capital ships were essential for the blockade of the *Tirpitz*, and they did not dare risk them close inshore against land-based bombers. The long awaited trap *did* eventually snap shut; but it caught only the heavy cruiser *Scharnhorst* and not the *Tirpitz*. It never caught that great ship. She was destroyed at her anchorage in Alta Fjord by Lancaster bombers of the Royal Air Force.

came instead the Stukas, the roar of their engines rising and falling as they methodically quartered the empty sea in search of the convoy—Charlie had left at dawn. But it was only a matter of time before the dive-bomber squadron found the tiny convoy ; ten minutes from the time of the first warning of their approach, the leading Junkers 87 tipped over its wing and dropped out of the sky.

Ten minutes—but time for a council and plan of desperation. When the Stukas came, they found the convoy stretched out in line abreast, the tanker *Varella* in the middle, two merchantmen in close line ahead on either side of it, the *Sirrus* and the *Ulysses* guarding the flanks. A suicidal formation in submarine waters— a torpedo from port or starboard could hardly miss them all. But weather conditions were heavily against submarines, and the formation offered at least a fighting chance against the Stukas. If they approached from the stern—their favourite attack technique —they would run into the simultaneous massed fire of seven ships: if they approached from the sides, they must first attack the escorts, for no Stuka would present its unprotected underbelly to the guns of a warship. . . . They elected to attack from either side, five from the east, four from the west. This time, Turner noted, they were carrying long-range fuel tanks.

Turner had no time to see how the *Sirrus* was faring. Indeed, he could hardly see how his own ship was faring, for thick acrid smoke was blowing back across the bridge from the barrels of " A " and " B " turrets. In the gaps of sound between the crash of the 5.25s, he could hear the quick-fire of Doyle's midship pom-pom, the vicious thudding of the Oerlikons.

Suddenly, startling in its breath-taking unexpectedness, two great beams of dazzling white stabbed out through the mirk and gloom. Turner stared, then bared his teeth in fierce delight. The 44-inch searchlights ! Of course ! The great searchlights, still on the official secret list, capable of lighting up an enemy six miles away ! What a fool he had been to forget them—Vallery had used them often, in daylight and in dark, against attacking aircraft. No man could look into those terrible eyes, those flaming arcs across the electrodes and not be blinded.

Blinking against the eye-watering smoke, Turner peered aft

to see who was manning the control position. But he knew who it was before he saw him. It could only be Ralston—searchlight control, Turner remembered, was his day action station : besides, he could think of no one other than the big, blond torpedoman with the gumption, the quick intelligence to burn the lamps on his own initiative.

Jammed in the corner of the bridge by the gate, Turner watched him. He forgot his ship, forgot even the bombers—he personally could do nothing about them anyway—as he stared in fascination at the man behind the controls.

His eyes were glued to the sights, his face expressionless, absolutely ; but for the gradual stiffening of back and neck as the sights dipped in docile response to the delicate caress of his fingers on the wheel, he might have been carved from marble : the immobility of the face, the utter concentration was almost frightening.

There was not a flicker of feeling or emotion : never a flicker as the first Stuka weaved and twisted in maddened torment, seeking to escape that eye-searing flame, not even a flicker as it swerved violently in its dive, pulled out too late and crashed into the sea a hundred yards short of the *Ulysses*.

What was the boy thinking of? Turner wondered. His mother, his sisters, entombed under the ruins of a Croydon bungalow : of his brother, innocent victim of that mutiny—how impossible that mutiny seemed now !—in Scapa Flow : of his father, dead by his son's own hand ? Turner did not know, could not even begin to guess : clairvoyantly, almost, he knew that it was too late, that no one would ever know now.

The face was inhumanly still. There wasn't a shadow of feeling as the second Stuka overshot the *Ulysses*, dropped its bomb into the open sea : not a shadow as a third blew up in mid-air : not a trace of emotion when the guns of the next Stuka smashed one of the lights . . . not even when the cannon shells of the last smashed the searchlight control, tore half his chest away. He died instantaneously, stood there a moment as if unwilling to abandon his post, then slumped back quietly on to the deck. Turner bent over the dead boy, looked at the face, the eyes upturned to the first feathery flakes of falling snow. The eyes, the face, were still the same, mask-like, expressionless. Turner shivered and looked away.

One bomb, and one only had struck the *Ulysses*. It had struck the fo'c'sle deck just for'ard of " A " turret. There had been no casualties, but some freak of vibration and shock had fractured the turret's hydraulic lines. Temporarily, at least, " B " was the only effective remaining turret in the ship.

The *Sirrus* hadn't been quite so lucky. She had destroyed one Stuka—the merchantmen had claimed another—and had been hit twice, both bombs exploding in the after mess-deck. The *Sirrus*, overloaded with survivors, was carrying double her normal complement of men, and usually that mess-deck would have been crowded : during action stations it was empty. Not a man had lost his life—not a man was to lose his life on the destroyer *Sirrus* : she was never damaged again on the Russian convoys.

Hope was rising, rising fast. Less than an hour to go, now, and the battle squadron would be there. It was dark, dark with the gloom of an Arctic storm, and heavy snow was falling, hissing gently into the dark and rolling sea. No plane could find them in this—and they were almost beyond the reach of shore-based aircraft, except, of course, for the Condors. And it was almost impossible weather for submarines.

" ' It may be we shall touch the Happy Isles.' " Carrington quoted softly.

" What ? " Turner looked up, baffled. " What did you say, Number One ? "

" Tennyson." Carrington was apologetic. " The Captain was always quoting him. . . . Maybe we'll make it yet."

" Maybe, maybe." Turner was non-committal. " Preston ! "

" Yes, sir, I see it." Preston was staring to the north where the signal lamp of the *Sirrus* was flickering rapidly.

" A ship, sir ! " he reported excitedly. " *Sirrus* says naval vessel approaching from the north ! "

" From the north ! Thank God ! Thank God ! " Turner shouted exultantly. " From the north ! It must be them ! They're ahead of time. . . . I take it all back. Can you see anything, Number One ? "

" Not a thing, sir. Too thick—but it's clearing a bit, I think.
. . . There's the *Sirrus* again."

" What does she say, Preston ? " Turner asked anxiously.

" Contact. Sub. contact. Green 30. Closing."

" Contact ! At this late hour ! " Turner groaned, then
smashed his fist down on the binnacle. He swore fiercely.

" By God, she's not going to stop us now ! Preston, signal
the *Sirrus* to stay . . ."

He broke off, looked incredulously to the north. Up there
in the snow and gloom, stilettos of white flame had lanced out
briefly, vanished again. Carrington by his side now, he stared
unwinkingly north, saw shells splashing whitely in the water
under the bows of the Commodore's ship, the *Cape Hatteras* :
then he saw the flashes again, stronger, brighter this time, flashes
that lit up for a fleeting second the bows and superstructure of
the ship that was firing.

He turned slowly, to find that Carrington, too, had turned,
was gazing at him with set face and bitter eyes. Turner, grey and
haggard with exhaustion and the sour foretaste of ultimate
defeat, looked in turn at his First Lieutenant in a long moment
of silence.

" The answer to many questions," he said softly. " That's
why they've been softening up the *Stirling* and ourselves for the
past couple of days. The fox is in among the chickens. It's our
old pal the *Hipper* cruiser come to pay us a social call."

" It is."

" So near and yet . . ." Turner shrugged. " We deserved
better than this. . . ." He grinned crookedly. " How would
you like to die a hero's death ? "

" The very idea appals me ! " boomed a voice behind him.
Brooks had just arrived on the bridge.

" Me, too," Turner admitted. He smiled : he was almost
happy again. " Have we any option, gentlemen ? "

" Alas, no," Brooks said sadly.

" Full ahead both ! " Carrington called down the speaking-
tube : it was by way of his answer.

" No, no," Turner chided gently. " Full *power*, Number One.
Tell them we're in a hurry : remind them of the boasts they

used to make about the *Abdiel* and the *Manxman* . . . Preston!
General emergency signal: ' Scatter: proceed independently to
Russian ports.' "

The upper deck was thick with freshly fallen snow, and the
snow was still falling. The wind was rising again and, after the
warmth of the canteen where he had been operating, it struck
at Johnny Nicholls's lungs with sudden, searing pain : the
temperature, he guessed, must be about zero. He buried his face
in his duffel coat, climbed laboriously, haltingly up the ladders
to the bridge. He was tired, deadly weary, and he winced in
agony every time his foot touched the deck : his splinted left
leg was shattered just above the ankle—shrapnel from the bomb
in the after mess-deck.

Peter Orr, commander of the *Sirrus* was waiting for him at
the gate of the tiny bridge.

" I thought you might like to see this, Doc." The voice was
strangely high-pitched for so big a man. " Rather I thought you
would want to see this," he corrected himself. " Look at her
go ! " he breathed. " Just look at her go ! "

Nicholls looked out over the port side. Half a mile away on
the beam, the *Cape Hatteras* was blazing furiously, slowing to a
stop. Some miles to the north, through the falling snow, he
could barely distinguish the vague shape of the German cruiser,
a shape pinpointed by the flaming guns still mercilessly pumping
shells into the sinking ship. Every shot went home : the accuracy
of their gunnery was fantastic.

Half a mile astern on the port quarter, the *Ulysses* was coming
up. She was sheeted in foam and spray, the bows leaping almost
clear of the water, then crashing down with a pistol-shot impact
easily heard, even against the wind, on the bridge of the *Sirrus*,
as the great engines thrust her through the water, faster, faster,
with the passing of every second.

Nicholls gazed, fascinated. This was the first time he'd seen
the *Ulysses* since he'd left her and he was appalled. The entire
upperworks, fore and aft, were a twisted, unbelievable shambles
of broken steel : both masts were gone, the smokestacks broken
and bent, the Director Tower shattered and grotesquely askew :

smoke was still pluming up from the great holes in fo'c'sle and poop, the after turrets, wrenched from their mountings, pitched crazily on the deck. The skeleton of the Condor still lay athwart " Y " turret, a Stuka was buried to the wings in the fo'c'sle deck, and she was, he knew, split right down to the water level abreast the torpedo tubes. The *Ulysses* was something out of a nightmare.

Steadying himself against the violent pitching of the destroyer, Nicholls stared and stared, numbed with horror and disbelief. Orr looked at him, looked away as a messenger came to the bridge.

" Rendezvous 1015," he read. " 1015 ! Good lord, 25 minutes time ! Do you hear that, Doc ? 25 minutes time ! "

" Yes, sir," Nicholls said absently : he hadn't heard him.

Orr looked at him, touched his arm, pointed to the *Ulysses*.

" Bloody well incredible, isn't it ? " he murmured.

" I wish to God I was aboard her," Nicholls muttered miserably. " Why did they send me——? Look ! What's that ? "

A huge flag, a flag twenty feet in length, was streaming out below the yardarm of the *Ulysses*, stretched out taut in the wind of its passing. Nicholls had never seen anything remotely like it : the flag was enormous, red and blue and whiter than the driving snow.

" The battle ensign," Orr murmured. " Bill Turner's broken out the battle ensign." He shook his head in wonder. " To take time off to do that *now*—well, Doc., only Turner would do that. You knew him well ? "

Nicholls nodded silently.

" Me, too," Orr said simply. " We are both lucky men."

The *Sirrus* was still doing fifteen knots, still headed for the enemy, when the *Ulysses* passed them by a cable-length away as if they were stopped in the water.

Long afterwards, Nicholls could never describe it all accurately. He had a hazy memory of the *Ulysses* no longer plunging and lifting, but battering through waves and troughs on a steady even keel, the deck angling back sharply from a rearing forefoot to the counter buried deep in the water, fifteen feet below the great boiling, tortured sea of white that arched up in seething magnificence above the shattered poop-deck. He could recall, too, that "B" turret was firing continuously, shell after shell screaming away through the blinding snow, to burst in brilliant splendour over and on the German cruiser : for "B" turret had only star-shells left. He carried, too, a vague mental picture of Turner waving ironically from the bridge, of the great ensign streaming stiffly astern, already torn and tattered at the edges. But what he could never forget, what he would hear in his heart and mind as long as he lived, was the tremendous, frightening roar of the great boiler-room intake fans as they sucked in mighty draughts of air for the starving engines. For the *Ulysses* was driving through the heavy seas under maximum power, at a speed that should have broken her shuddering back, should have burnt out the great engines. There was no doubt as to Turner's intentions : he was going to ram the enemy, to destroy him and take him with him, at a speed of just on or over forty incredible knots.

Nicholls gazed and gazed and did not know what to think : he felt sick at heart, for that ship was part of him now, his good friends, especially the Kapok Kid—for he did not know that the Kid was already dead—they, too, were part of him, and it is always terrible to see the end of a legend, to see it die, to see it going into the gulfs. But he felt, too, a strange exultation ; she was dying but what a way to die ! And if ships had hearts, had souls, as the old sailing men declared, surely the *Ulysses* would want it this way too.

She was still doing forty knots when, as if by magic, a great gaping hole appeared in her bows just above the water-line. Shell-fire, possibly, but unlikely at that angle. It must have been a torpedo from the U-boat, not yet located : a sudden dip of the bows could have coincided with the upthrust of a heavy sea forcing a torpedo to the surface. Such things had happened before : rarely, but they happened. . . . The *Ulysses* brushed aside the torpedo, ignored the grievous wound, ignored the heavy shells crashing into her and kept on going.

She was still doing forty knots, driving in under the guns of the enemy, guns at maximum depression, when "A" magazine blew up, blasted off the entire bows in one shattering detonation. For a second, the lightened fo'c'sle reared high into the air : then it plunged down, deep down, into the shoulder of a rolling sea. She plunged down and kept on going down, driving down to the black floor of the Arctic, driven down by the madly spinning screws, the still thundering engines her own executioners.

CHAPTER EIGHTEEN

EPILOGUE

THE AIR was warm and kind and still. The sky was blue, a deep and wonderful blue, with little puffs of cotton-wool cloud drifting lazily to the far horizon. The street-gardens, the hanging birdcage flower-baskets, spilled over with blue and yellow and red and gold, all the delicate pastel shades and tints he had almost forgotten had ever existed : every now and then an old man or a hurrying housewife or a young man with a laughing girl on his arm would stop to admire them, then walk on again, the better for having seen them. The nesting birds were singing, clear and sweet above the distant roar of the traffic, and Big Ben was booming the hour as Johnny Nicholls climbed awkwardly out of the taxi, paid off the driver and hobbled slowly up the marble steps.

His face carefully expressionless, the sentry saluted, opened the heavy swing door. Nicholls passed inside, looked around the huge hall, saw that both sides were lined with heavy, imposing doors : at the far end, beneath the great curve of the stairs and overhanging the widely convex counter of the type usually found in banks, hung a sign : "Typist Pool : Inquiries."

The tip-tap of the crutches sounded unnaturally loud on the marble floor as he limped over to the counter. Very touching and melodramatic, Nicholls, he thought dispassionately : trust the audience are having their money's worth. Half a dozen typists had stopped work as if by command, were staring at him in open curiosity, hands resting limply on their machines. A trim young Wren, red-haired and shirt-sleeved, came to the counter.

"Can I help you, sir ? " The quiet voice, the blue eyes were soft with concern. Nicholls, catching a glimpse of himself in a mirror behind her, a glimpse of a scuffed uniform jacket over a

314

grey fisherman's jersey, of blurred, sunken eyes and gaunt, pale cheeks, admitted wryly to himself that he couldn't blame her. He didn't have to be a doctor to know that he was in pretty poor shape.

"My name is Nicholls, Surgeon-Lieutenant Nicholls. I have an appointment——"

"Lieutenant Nicholls. . . . H.M.S. *Ulysses* !" The girl drew in her breath sharply. "Of course, sir. They're expecting you." Nicholls looked at her, looked at the Wrens sitting motionless in their chairs, caught the intense, wondering expression in their eyes, the awed gaze with which one would regard beings from another planet. It made him feel vaguely uncomfortable.

"Upstairs, I suppose ? " He hadn't meant to sound so brusque.

"No, sir." The Wren came quietly round the counter. "They —well, they heard you'd been wounded, sir," she murmured apologetically. "Just across the hall here, please." She smiled at him, slowed her step to match his halting walk.

She knocked, held open the door, announced him to someone he couldn't see, and closed the door softly behind him when he had passed through.

There were three men in the room. The one man he recognised, Vice-Admiral Starr, came forward to meet him. He looked older, far older, far more tired than when Nicholls had last seen him—hardly a fortnight previously.

"How are you, Nicholls ? " he asked. "Not walking so well, I see." Under the assurance, the thin joviality so flat and misplaced, the harsh edge of strain burred unmistakably. "Come and sit down."

He led Nicholls across to the table, long, big and covered with leather. Behind the table, framed against huge wall-maps, sat two men. Starr introduced them. One, big, beefy, red of face, was in full uniform, the sleeves ablaze with the broad band and four stripes of an Admiral of the Fleet : the other was a civilian, a small, stocky man with iron-grey hair, eyes still and wise and old. Nicholls recognised him immediately, would have known anyway from the deference of both the Admirals. He reflected wryly that the Navy was indeed doing him proud : such re-

ceptions were not for all. . . . But they seemed reluctant to begin
the reception, Nicholls thought—he had forgotten the shock his
appearance must give. Finally, the grey-haired man cleared his
throat.

" How's the leg, boy ? " he asked. " Looks pretty bad to
me." His voice was low, but alive with controlled authority.

" Not too bad, thank you, sir," Nicholls answered. " Two,
three weeks should see me back on the job."

" You're taking two months, laddie," said the grey-haired
man quietly. " More if you want it." He smiled faintly. " If
anyone asks, just tell 'em I said so. Cigarette ? "

He flicked the big table-lighter, sat back in his chair. Temporarily, he seemed at a loss as to what to say next. Then he
looked up abruptly.

" Had a good trip home ? "

" Very fair, sir. V.I.P. treatment all the way. Moscow,
Teheran, Cairo, Gib." Nicholls's mouth twisted. " Much more
comfortable than the trip out." He paused, inhaled deeply on his
cigarette, looked levelly across the table. " I would have preferred
to come home in the *Sirrus*."

" No doubt," Starr broke in acidly. " But we cannot afford
to cater for the personal prejudices of all and sundry. We were
anxious to have a first-hand account of FR77—and particularly
the *Ulysses*—as soon as possible."

Nicholls's hands clenched on the edge of his chair. The anger
had leapt in him like a flame, and he knew that the man opposite
was watching closely. Slowly he relaxed, looked at the grey-
haired man, interrogative eyebrows mutely asking confirmation.

The grey-haired man nodded.

" Just tell us all you know," he said kindly. " Everything—
about everything. Take your time."

" From the beginning ? " Nicholls asked in a low voice.

" From the beginning."

Nicholls told them. He would have liked to tell the story,
right as it fell out, from the convoy before FR77 straight through
to the end. He did his best, but it was a halting story, strangely
lacking in conviction. The atmosphere, the surroundings were

wrong—the contrast between the peaceful warmth of these rooms and the inhuman cold and cruelty of the Arctic was an immense gulf that could be bridged only by experience and understanding. Down here, in the heart of London, the wild, incredible tale he had to tell fell falsely, incredibly even on his own ears. Half-way through, he looked at his listeners, almost gave up. Incredulity? No, it wasn't that—at least, not with the grey-haired man and the Admiral of the Fleet. Just a baffled incomprehension, an honest failure to understand.

It wasn't so bad when he stuck to the ascertainable facts, the facts of carriers crippled by seas, of carriers mined, stranded and torpedoed : the facts of the great storm, of the desperate struggle to survive : the facts of the gradual attrition of the convoy, of the terrible dying of the two gasoline tankers, of the U-boats and bombers sent to the bottom, of the *Ulysses*, battering through the snowstorm at 40 knots, blown up by the German cruiser, of the arrival of the battle squadron, of the flight of the cruiser before it could inflict further damage, of the rounding-up of the scattered convoy, of the curtain of Russian fighters in the Barents Sea, of the ultimate arrival in the Kola Inlet of the battered remnants of FR77—five ships in all.

It was when he came to less readily ascertainable facts, to statements that could never be verified at all, that he sensed the doubt, the something more than wonder. He told the story as calmly, as unemotionally as he could : the story of Ralston, Ralston of the fighting lights and the searchlights, of his father and family : of Riley, the ringleader of the mutiny and his refusal to leave the shaft tunnel : of Petersen, who had killed a marine and gladly given his own life : of McQuater and Chrysler and Doyle and a dozen others.

For a second, his own voice broke uncertainly as he told the story of the half-dozen survivors from the *Ulysses*, picked up by the *Sirrus* soon afterwards. He told how Brooks had given his lifejacket to an ordinary seaman, who amazingly survived fifteen minutes in that water : how Turner, wounded in head and arm, had supported a dazed Spicer till the *Sirrus* came plunging alongside, had passed a bowline round him, and was gone before anything could be done : how Carrington, that enduring man of

iron, a baulk of splintered timber under his arms, had held two
men above water till rescue came. Both men—Preston was one—
had died later; Carrington had climbed the rope unaided,
clambered over the guard-rails dangling a left leg with the foot
blown off above the ankle. Carrington would survive: Carrington
was indestructible. Finally, Doyle, too, was gone: they had
thrown him a rope, but he had not seen it, for he was blind.

But what the three men really wanted to know, Nicholls
realised, was how the *Ulysses* had been, how a crew of mutineers
had borne themselves. He had told them, he knew, things of
wonder and of splendour, and they could not reconcile these
with men who would take up arms against their own ship, in
effect, against their own King.

So Nicholls tried to tell them, then knew, as he tried, that he
could never tell them. For what was there to tell? That Vallery
had spoken to the men over the broadcast system: how he had
gone among them and made them almost as himself, on that
grim, exhausting tour of inspection: how he had spoken of them
as he died: and how, most of all, his death had made them men
again? For that was all that there was to tell, and these things
were just nothing at all. With sudden insight, Nicholls saw that
the meaning of that strange transformation of the men of the
Ulysses, a transformation of bitter, broken men to men above
themselves, could neither be explained nor understood, for all
the meaning was in Vallery, and Vallery was dead.

Nicholls felt tired, now, desperately so. He knew he was far
from well. His mind was cloudy, hazy in retrospect, and he was
mixing things up: his sense of chronological time was gone, he
was full of hesitations and uncertainties. Suddenly he was overwhelmed by the futility of it all, and he broke off slowly, his voice
trailing into silence.

Vaguely, he heard the grey-haired man ask something in a
quiet voice, and he muttered aloud, unthinking.

"What was that? What did you say?" The grey-haired man
was looking at him strangely. The face of the Admiral behind the
table was impassive. Starr's, he saw, was open in disbelief.

"I only said, 'They were the best crew God ever gave a
Captain,'" Nicholls murmured.

" I see." The old, tired eyes looked at him steadily, but there was no other comment. Fingers drumming on the table, he looked slowly at the two Admirals, then back to Nicholls again.

" Take things easy for a minute, boy. . . . If you'll just excuse us . . ."

He rose to his feet, walked slowly over to the big, bay windows at the other end of the long room, the others following. Nicholls made no move, did not even look after them : he sat slumped in the chair, looking dejectedly, unseeingly, at the crutches on the floor between his feet.

From time to time, he could hear a murmur of voices. Starr's high-pitched voice carried most clearly. " Mutiny ship, sir . . . never the same again . . . better this way." There was a murmured reply, too low to catch, then he heard Starr saying, ". . . finished as a fighting unit." The grey-haired man said something rapidly, his tone sharp with disagreement, but the words were blurred. Then the deep, heavy voice of the Fleet Admiral said something about " expiation," and the grey-haired man nodded slowly. Then Starr looked at him over his shoulder, and Nicholls knew they were talking about him. He thought he heard the words " not well " and " frightful strain," but perhaps he was imagining it.

Anyway, he no longer cared. He was anxious for one thing only, and that was to be gone. He felt an alien in an alien land, and whether they believed him or not no longer mattered. He did not belong here, where everything was so sane and commonplace and real—and withal a world of shadows.

He wondered what the Kapok Kid would have said had he been here, and smiled in fond reminiscence : the language would have been terrible, the comments rich and barbed and pungent. Then he wondered what Vallery would have said, and he smiled again at the simplicity of it all, for Vallery would have said : " Do not judge them, for they do not understand."

Gradually, he became aware that the murmuring had ceased, that the three men were standing above him. His smile faded, and he looked up slowly to see them looking down strangely at him, their eyes full of concern.

" I'm damnably sorry, boy," the grey-haired man said

sincerely. " You're a sick man and we've asked far too much of you. A drink, Nicholls ? It was most remiss——"

" No, thank you, sir." Nicholls straightened himself in his chair. " I'll be perfectly all right." He hesitated. " Is—is there anything else ? "

" No, nothing at all." The smile was genuine, friendly. " You've been a great help to us, Lieutenant, a great help. And a fine report. Thank you very much indeed."

A liar and a gentleman, Nicholls thought gratefully. He struggled to his feet, reached out for his crutches. He shook hands with Starr and the Admiral of the Fleet, and said good-bye. The grey-haired man accompanied him to the door, his hand beneath Nicholls's arm.

At the door Nicholls paused.

" Sorry to bother you but—when do I begin my leave, sir ? "

" As from now," the other said emphatically. " And have a good time. God knows you've earned it, my boy. . . . Where are you going ? "

" Henley, sir."

" Henley ! I could have sworn you were Scots."

" I am, sir—I have no family."

" Oh. . . . A girl, Lieutenant ? "

Nicholls nodded silently.

The grey-haired man clapped him on the shoulder, and smiled gently.

" Pretty, I'll be bound ? "

Nicholls looked at him, looked away to where the sentry was already holding open the street doors, and gathered up his crutches.

" I don't know, sir," he said quietly. " I don't know at all. I've never seen her."

He tip-tapped his way across the marble flags, passed through the heavy doors and limped out into the sunshine.

THE END

FORCE TEN
FROM NAVARONE

To Lewis and Caroline

CHAPTER I

Prelude: Thursday
0000-0600

Commander Vincent Ryan, RN, Captain (Destroyers) and commanding officer of His Majesty's latest S-class destroyer *Sirdar*, leaned his elbows comfortably on the coaming of his bridge, brought up his night-glasses and gazed out thoughtfully over the calm and silvered waters of the moonlit Aegean.

He looked first of all due north, straight out over the huge and smoothly sculpted and whitely phosphorescent bow-wave thrown up by the knife-edged forefoot of his racing destroyer: four miles away, no more, framed in its backdrop of indigo sky and diamantine stars, lay the brooding mass of a darkly cliff-girt island: the island of Kheros, for months the remote and beleaguered outpost of two thousand British troops who had expected to die that night, and who would now not die.

Ryan swung his glasses through 180° and nodded approvingly. This was what he liked to see. The four destroyers to the south were in such perfect line astern that the hull of the leading vessel, a gleaming bone in its teeth, completely obscured the hulls of the three ships behind. Ryan turned his binoculars to the east.

It was odd, he thought inconsequentially, how unimpressive, even how disappointing, the aftermath of either natural or man-made disaster could be. Were it not for that dull red glow and wisping smoke that emanated from the upper part of the cliff and lent the scene a vaguely Dantean aura of primeval

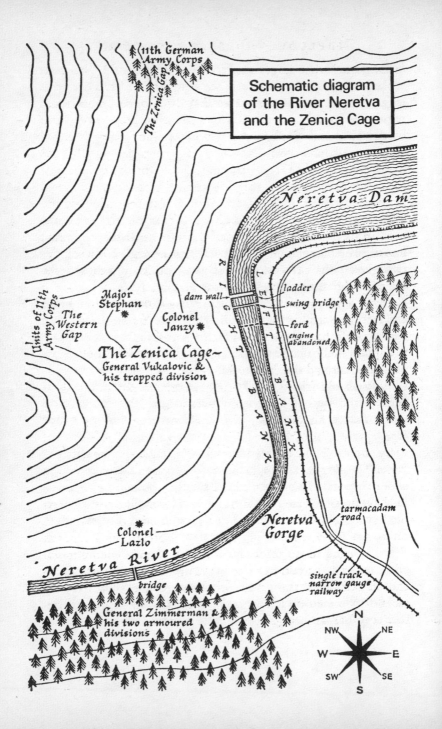

Schematic diagram of the River Neretva and the Zenica Cage

(11th German Army Corps

The Zenica Gap

Neretva Dam

Units of 11th Army Corps

The Western Gap

Major Stephan

dam wall

RIGHT BANK

LEFT BANK

ladder

swing bridge

ford

engine abandoned

Colonel Janzy

The Zenica Cage ~ General Vukalovic & his trapped division

tarmacadam road

Colonel Lazlo

Neretva Gorge

Neretva River

bridge

single track narrow gauge railway

General Zimmerman & his two armoured divisions

N
NW   NE
W   E
SW   SE
S

menace and foreboding, the precipitous far wall of the harbour looked as it might have done in the times of Homer. That great ledge of rock that looked from that distance so smooth and regular and somehow inevitable could have been carved out by the wind and weather of a hundred million years: it could equally well have been cut away fifty centuries ago by the masons of Ancient Greece seeking marble for the building of their Ionian temples: what was almost inconceivable, what almost passed rational comprehension, was the fact that ten minutes ago that ledge had not been there at all, that there had been in its place tens of thousands of tons of rock, the most impregnable German fortress in the Aegean and, above all, the two great guns of Navarone, now all buried for ever three hundred feet under the sea. With a slow shake of his head Commander Ryan lowered his binoculars and turned to look at the men responsible for achieving more in five minutes than nature could have done in five million years.

Captain Mallory and Corporal Miller. That was all he knew of them, that and the fact that they had been sent on this mission by an old friend of his, a naval captain by the name of Jensen who, he had learnt only twenty-four hours previously —and that to his total astonishment—was the Head of Allied Intelligence in the Mediterranean. But that was all he knew of them and maybe he didn't even know that. Maybe their names weren't Mallory and Miller. Maybe they weren't even a captain and a corporal. They didn't look like any captain or corporal he'd ever seen. Come to that, they didn't look like any soldiers he'd ever seen. Clad in salt-water- and blood-stained German uniforms, filthy, unshaven, quiet and watchful and remote, they belonged to no category of men he'd ever encountered: all he could be certain of as he gazed at the blurred and blood-shot sunken eyes, the gaunt and trenched and stubbled-grey faces of two men no longer young, was that he had never before seen human beings so far gone in total exhaustion.

9

'Well, that seems to be about it,' Ryan said. 'The troops on Kheros waiting to be taken off, our flotilla going north to take them off and the guns of Navarone no longer in any position to do anything about our flotilla. Satisfied, Captain Mallory?'

'That was the object of the exercise,' Mallory agreed.

Ryan lifted his glasses again. This time, almost at the range of night vision, he focused on a rubber dinghy closing in on the rocky shore-line to the west of Navarone harbour. The two figures seated in the dinghy were just discernible, no more. Ryan lowered his glasses and said thoughtfully:

'Your big friend—and the lady with him—doesn't believe in hanging about. You didn't—ah—introduce me to them, Captain Mallory.'

'I didn't get the chance to. Maria and Andrea. Andrea's a colonel in the Greek army: 19th Motorized Division.'

'Andrea *was* a colonel in the Greek army,' Miller said. 'I think he's just retired.'

'I rather think he has. They were in a hurry, Commander, because they're both patriotic Greeks, they're both islanders and there is much for both to do in Navarone. Besides, I understand they have some urgent and very personal matters to attend to.'

'I see.' Ryan didn't press the matter, instead he looked out again over the smoking remains of the shattered fortress. 'Well, that seems to be that. Finished for the evening, gentlemen?'

Mallory smiled faintly. 'I think so.'

'Then I would suggest some sleep.'

'What a wonderful word that is.' Miller pushed himself wearily off the side of the bridge and stood there swaying as he drew an exhausted forearm over blood-shot, aching eyes. 'Wake me up in Alexandria.'

'Alexandria?' Ryan looked at him in amusement. 'We won't be there for thirty hours yet.'

'That's what I meant,' Miller said.

Miller didn't get his thirty hours. He had, in fact, been asleep for just over thirty minutes when he was wakened by the slow realization that something was hurting his eyes: after he had moaned and feebly protested for some time he managed to get one eye open and saw that that something was a bright overhead light let into the deck-head of the cabin that had been provided for Mallory and himself. Miller propped himself up on a groggy elbow, managed to get his second eye into commission and looked without enthusiasm at the other two occupants of the cabin: Mallory was seated by a table, apparently transcribing some kind of message, while Commander Ryan stood in the open doorway.

'This is outrageous,' Miller said bitterly. 'I haven't closed an eye all night.'

'You've been asleep for thirty-five minutes,' Ryan said. 'Sorry. But Cairo said this message for Captain Mallory was of the greatest urgency.'

'It is, is it?' Miller said suspiciously. He brightened. 'It's probably about promotions and medals and leave and so forth.' He looked hopefully at Mallory who had just straightened after decoding the message. 'Is it?'

'Well, no. It starts off promisingly enough, mind you, warmest congratulations and what-have-you, but after that the tone of the message deteriorates a bit.'

Mallory re-read the message: SIGNAL RECEIVED WARMEST CONGRATULATIONS MAGNIFICENT ACHIEVEMENT. YOU BLOODY FOOLS WHY YOU LET ANDREA GET AWAY? ESSENTIAL CONTACT HIM IMMEDIATELY. WILL EVACUATE BEFORE DAWN UNDER DIVERSIONARY AIR ATTACK AIR STRIP ONE MILE SOUTH-EAST MANDRAKOS. SEND CE VIA SIRDAR. URGENT 3 REPEAT URGENT 3. BEST LUCK. JENSEN.

Miller took the message from Mallory's outstretched hand,

moved the paper to and fro until he had brought his bleary eyes into focus, read the message in horrified silence, handed it back to Mallory and stretched out his full length on his bunk. He said, 'Oh, my God!' and relapsed into what appeared to be a state of shock.

'That about sums it up,' Mallory agreed. He shook his head wearily and turned to Ryan. 'I'm sorry, sir, but we must trouble you for three things. A rubber dinghy, a portable radio transmitter and an immediate return to Navarone. Please arrange to have the radio lined up on a pre-set frequency to be constantly monitored by your WT room. When you receive a CE signal, transmit it to Cairo.'

'CE?' Ryan asked.

'Uh-huh. Just that.'

'And that's all?'

'We could do with a bottle of brandy,' Miller said. 'Something—anything—to see us through the rigours of the long night that lies ahead.'

Ryan lifted an eyebrow. 'A bottle of five-star, no doubt, Corporal?'

'Would you,' Miller asked morosely, 'give a bottle of three-star to a man going to his death?'

As it happened, Miller's gloomy expectations of an early demise turned out to be baseless—for that night, at least. Even the expected fearful rigours of the long night ahead proved to be no more than minor physical inconveniences.

By the time the *Sirdar* had brought them back to Navarone and as close in to the rocky shores as was prudent, the sky had become darkly overcast, rain was falling and a swell was beginning to blow up from the south-west so that it was little wonder to either Mallory or Miller that by the time they had paddled their dinghy within striking distance of the shore, they were in a very damp and miserable condition indeed: and it was even less wonder that by the time they had reached the boulder-strewn beach itself, they were soaked to the skin, for a breaking wave flung their dinghy against a sloping shelf of rock, over-turning their rubber craft and precipitating them both into the sea. But this was of little enough account in itself: their Schmeisser machine-pistols, their radio, their torches were securely wrapped in waterproof bags and all of those were safely salvaged. All in all, Mallory reflected, an almost perfect three-point landing compared to the last time they had come to Navarone by boat, when their Greek caique, caught in the teeth of a giant storm, had been battered to pieces against the jaggedly vertical—and supposedly unclimbable—South Cliff of Navarone.

Slipping, stumbling and with suitably sulphuric comments, they made their way over the wet shingle and massively rounded boulders until their way was barred by a steeply-angled slope that soared up into the near-darkness above. Mallory unwrapped a pencil torch and began to quarter the face of the slope with its narrow, concentrated beam. Miller touched him on the arm.

'Taking a bit of a chance, aren't we? With that thing, I mean?'

'No chance,' Mallory said. 'There won't be a soldier left on guard on the coasts tonight. They'll all be fighting the fires in the town. Besides, who is left for them to guard against? We are the birds and the birds, duty done, have flown. Only a mad-man would come back to the island again.'

'I know what we are,' Miller said with feeling. 'You don't have to tell me.'

Mallory smiled to himself in the darkness and continued his search. Within a minute he had located what he had been hop-ing to find—an angled gully in the slope. He and Miller scram-bled up the shale- and rock-strewn bed of the gully as fast as the treacherous footing and their encumbrances would permit:

within fifteen minutes they had reached the plateau above and paused to take their breath. Miller reached inside the depths of his tunic, a discreet movement that was at once followed by a discreet gurgling.

'What are you doing?' Mallory enquired.

'I thought I heard my teeth chattering. What's all this "urgent 3 repeat urgent 3" business in the message, then?'

'I've never seen it before. But I know what it means. Some people, somewhere, are about to die.'

'I'll tell you two for a start. And what if Andrea won't come? He's not a member of our armed forces. He doesn't have to come. *And* he said he was getting married right away.'

Mallory said with certainty: 'He'll come.'

'What makes you so sure?'

'Because Andrea is the one completely responsible man I've ever met. He has two great responsibilities—one to others, one to himself. That's why he came back to Navarone—because he knew the people needed him. And that's why he'll leave Navarone when he sees this "urgent 3" signal, because he'll know that someone, in some other place, needs him even more.'

Miller retrieved the brandy bottle from Mallory and thrust it securely inside his tunic again. 'Well, I can tell you this. The future Mrs Andrea Stavros isn't going to be very happy about it.'

'Neither is Andrea Stavros and I'm not looking forward to telling him,' Mallory said candidly. He peered at his luminous watch and swung to his feet. 'Mandrakos in half an hour.'

In precisely thirty minutes, their Schmeissers removed from their waterproof bags and now shoulder-slung at hip level, Mallory and Miller moved swiftly but very quietly from shadow to shadow through the plantations of carob trees on the outskirts of the village of Mandrakos. Suddenly, from directly ahead, they heard the unmistakable clink of glasses and bottle-necks.

For the two men a potentially dangerous situation such as this was so routine as not even to warrant a glance at each other. They dropped silently to their hands and knees and crawled forward, Miller sniffing the air appreciatively as they advanced: the Greek resinous spirit *ouzo* has an extraordinary ability to permeate the atmosphere for a considerable distance around it. Mallory and Miller reached the edge of a clump of bushes, sank prone and looked ahead.

From their richly-befrogged waistcoats, cummerbunds and fancy headgear, the two characters propped against the bole of a plane tree in the clearing ahead were obviously men of the island: from the rifles across their knees, their role appeared to be that of guards of some kind: from the almost vertical angle at which they had to tip the *ouzo* bottle to get at what little was left of its contents, it was equally apparent that they weren't taking their duties too seriously, nor had been for some considerable time past.

Mallory and Miller withdrew somewhat less stealthily than they had advanced, rose and glanced at each other. Suitable comment seemed lacking. Mallory shrugged and moved on, circling around to his right. Twice more, as they moved swiftly into the centre of Mandrakos, flitting from the shadow of carob grove to carob grove, from the shadow of plane tree to plane tree, from the shadow of house to house, they came upon but easily avoided other ostensible sentries, all busy interpreting their duties in a very liberal fashion. Miller pulled Mallory into a doorway.

'Our friends back there,' he said. 'What were they celebrating?'

'Wouldn't you? Celebrate, I mean. Navarone is useless to the Germans now. A week from now and they'll all be gone.'

'All right. So why are they keeping a watch?' Miller nodded

to a small, whitewashed Greek Orthodox church standing in
the centre of the village square. From inside came a far from
subdued murmur of voices. Also from inside came a great deal
of light escaping through very imperfectly blacked-out windows. 'Could it be anything to do with that?'

Mallory said: 'Well, there's one sure way to find out.'

They moved quietly on, taking advantage of all available
cover and shadow until they came to a still deeper shadow
caused by two flying buttresses supporting the wall of the
ancient church. Between the buttresses was one of the few
more successfully blacked-out windows with only a tiny chink
of light showing along the bottom edge. Both men stooped
and peered through the narrow aperture.

The church appeared even more ancient inside than on the
outside. The high unpainted wooden benches, adze-cut oak
from centuries long gone, had been blackened and smoothed
by untold generations of church-goers, the wood itself cracked
and splintered by the ravages of time: the whitewashed walls
looked as if they required buttresses within as well as without,
crumbling to an extinction that could not now be long delayed:
the roof appeared to be in imminent danger of falling in at any
moment.

The now even louder hum of sound came from islanders of
almost every age and sex, many in ceremonial dress, who occupied nearly every available seat in the church: the light came
from literally hundreds of guttering candles, many of them
ancient and twisted and ornamented and evidently called out
for this special occasion, that lined the walls, the central aisle
and the altar: by the altar itself, a priest, a bearded patriarch in
Greek Orthodox robes, waited impassively.

Mallory and Miller looked interrogatively at each other and
were on the point of standing upright when a very deep and
very quiet voice spoke behind them.

'Hands behind the necks,' it said pleasantly. 'And straighten

16

very slowly. I have a Schmeisser machine-pistol in my hands.'

Slowly and carefully, just as the voice asked, Mallory and Miller did as they were told.

'Turn round. Carefully, now.'

So they turned round, carefully. Miller looked at the massive dark figure who indeed had, as he'd claimed, a machine-pistol in his hands, and said irritably: 'Do you mind? Point that damned thing somewhere else.'

The dark figure gave a startled exclamation, lowered the gun to his side and bent forward; the dark, craggy, lined face expressing no more than a passing flicker of surprise. Andrea Stavros didn't go in very much for registering unnecessary emotional displays and the recovery of his habitual composure was instantaneous.

'The German uniforms,' he explained apologetically. 'They had me fooled.'

'You could have fooled me, too,' Miller said. He looked incredulously at Andrea's clothes, at the unbelievably baggy black trousers, the black jackboots, the intricately ornamented black waistcoat and violently purple cummerbund, shuddered and closed his eyes in pain. 'Been visiting the Mandrakos pawn-shop?'

'The ceremonial dress of my ancestors,' Andrea said mildly. 'You two fall overboard?'

'Not intentionally,' Mallory said. 'We came back to see you.'

'You could have chosen a more convenient time.' He hesitated, glanced at a small lighted building across the street and took their arms. 'We can talk in here.'

He ushered them in and closed the door behind him. The room was obviously, from its benches and Spartan furnishings, some sort of communal meeting-place, a village hall: illumination came from three rather smoky oil-lamps, the light from which was most hospitably reflected by the scores of bottles of spirit and wine and beer and glasses that took up almost every available inch of two long trestle tables. The haphazardly un-aesthetic layout of the refreshments bespoke a very im-promptu and hastily improvised preparation for a celebration: the serried rows of bottles heralded the intention of compen-sating for lack of quality by an excess of quantity.

Andrea crossed to the nearest table, picked up three glasses and a bottle of *ouzo*, and began to pour drinks. Miller fished out his brandy and offered it, but Andrea was too preoccupied to notice. He handed them the *ouzo* glasses.

'Health.' Andrea drained his glass and went on thought-fully: 'You did not return without a good reason, my Keith.'

Silently, Mallory removed the Cairo radio message from its waterproof oilskin wallet and handed it to Andrea, who took it half-unwillingly, then read it, scowling blackly.

He said: 'Urgent 3 means what I think it means?'

Again Mallory remained silent, merely nodding as he watch-ed Andrea unwinkingly.

'This is most inconvenient for me.' The scowl deepened. '*Most* inconvenient. There are many things for me to do in Navarone. The people will miss me.'

'It's also inconvenient for me,' Miller said. 'There are many things *I* could profitably be doing in the West End of London. They miss me, too. Ask any barmaid. But that's hardly the point.'

Andrea regarded him for an impassive moment, then looked at Mallory. '*You* are saying nothing.'

'I've nothing to say.'

The scowl slowly left Andrea's face, though the brooding frown remained. He hesitated, then reached again for the bottle of *ouzo*. Miller shuddered delicately.

'Please.' He indicated the bottle of brandy.

Andrea smiled, briefly and for the first time, poured some of Miller's five-star into their glasses, re-read the message and handed it back to Mallory. 'I must think it over. I have some business to attend to first.'

Mallory looked at him thoughtfully. 'Business?'

'I have to attend a wedding.'

'A wedding?'' Miller said politely.

'Must you two repeat everything I say? A wedding.'

'But who do *you* know?' Miller asked. 'And at this hour of night.'

'For some people in Navarone,' Andrea said drily, 'the night is the only safe time.' He turned abruptly, walked away, opened the door and hesitated.

Mallory said curiously: 'Who's getting married?'

Andrea made no reply. Instead he walked back to the nearest table, poured and drained a half-tumbler of the brandy, ran a hand through his thick dark hair, straightened his cummerbund, squared his shoulders and walked purposefully towards the door. Mallory and Miller stared after him, then at the door that closed behind him: then they stared at each other.

Some fifteen minutes later they were still staring at each other, this time with expressions which alternated between the merely bemused and slightly stunned.

They were seated in the back seat of the Greek Orthodox church—the only part of any pew in the entire church not now occupied by islanders. From where they sat, the altar was at least sixty feet away but as they were both tall men and sitting by the central aisle, they had a pretty fair view of what was going on up there.

There was, to be accurate, nothing going on up there any more. The ceremony was over. Gravely, the Orthodox priest bestowed his blessing and Andrea and Maria, the girl who had shown them the way into the fortress of Navarone, turned with the slow dignity becoming the occasion, and walked down the aisle. Andrea bent over, tenderness and solicitousness both in

19

expression and manner, and whispered something in her ear, but his words, it would have seemed, bore little relation to the way in which they were expressed for half-way down the aisle a furious altercation broke out between them. Between, perhaps, is not the right word: it was less an altercation than a very one-sided monologue. Maria, her face flushed and dark eyes flashing, gesticulating and clearly mad through, was addressing Andrea in far from low tones of not even barely-controlled fury: Andrea, for his part, was deprecatory, placatory, trying to hush her up with about the same amount of success as Canute had in holding back the tide, and looking apprehensively around. The reaction of the seated guests varied from disbelief through open-mouthed astonishment and bafflement to downright horror: clearly all regarded the spectacle as a highly unusual aftermath to a wedding ceremony.

As the couple approached the end of the aisle opposite the pew where Mallory and Miller were seated, the argument, if such it could be called, raged more furiously than ever. As they passed by the end pew, Andrea, hand over his mouth, leaned over towards Mallory.

'This,' he said, *sotto voce*, 'is our first married quarrel.'

He was given time to say no more. An imperative hand siezed his arm and almost literally dragged him through the church doorway. Even after they had disappeared from sight, Maria's voice, loud and clear, could still be heard by everyone within the church. Miller turned from surveying the empty doorway and looked thoughtfully at Mallory.

'Very high-spirited girl, that. I wish I understood Greek. What was she saying there?'

Mallory kept his face carefully expressionless. 'What about my honeymoon?'

'Ah!' Miller's face was equally dead-pan. 'Don't you think we'd better follow them?'

'Why?'

'Andrea can take care of most people.' It was the usual masterly Miller understatement. 'But he's stepped out of his class this time.'

Mallory smiled, rose and went to the door, followed by Miller, who was in turn followed by an eager press of guests understandably anxious to see the second act of this unscheduled entertainment: but the village square was empty of life.

Mallory did not hesitate. With the instinct born from the experience of long association with Andrea, he headed across the square to the communal hall where Andrea had made the earlier of his two dramatic statements. His instincts hadn't betrayed him. Andrea, with a large glass of brandy in his hand and moodily fingering a spreading patch of red on his cheek, looked up as Mallory and Miller entered.

He said moodily: 'She's gone home to her mother.'

Miller glanced at his watch. 'One minute and twenty-five seconds,' he said admiringly. 'A world record.'

Andrea glowered at him and Mallory moved in hastily.

'You're coming, then.'

'Of course I'm coming,' Andrea said irritably. He surveyed without enthusiasm the guests now swarming into the hall and brushing unceremoniously by as they headed, like the camel for the oasis, towards the bottle-laden tables. 'Somebody's got to look after you two.'

Mallory looked at his watch. 'Three and a half hours yet before that plane is due. We're dead on our feet, Andrea. Where can we sleep—a safe place to sleep. Your perimeter guards are drunk.'

'They've been that way ever since the fortress blew up,' Andrea said. 'Come, I'll show you.'

Miller looked around the islanders, who, amid a loud babel of cheerful voices, were already quite exceptionally busy with bottles and glasses. 'How about your guests?'

'How about them, then?' Andrea surveyed his compatriots morosely. 'Just look at that lot. Ever known a wedding reception yet where anybody paid any attention to the bride and groom? Come.'

They made their way southwards through the outskirts of Mandrakos to the open countryside beyond. Twice they were challenged by guards, twice a scowl and growl from Andrea sent them back hurriedly to their *ouzo* bottles. It was still raining heavily, but Mallory's and Miller's clothes were already so saturated that a little more rain could hardly make any appreciable difference to the way they felt, while Andrea, if anything, seemed even more oblivious of it. Andrea had the air of a man who had other things on his mind.

After fifteen minutes' walk, Andrea stopped before the swing doors of a small, dilapidated and obviously deserted roadside barn.

'There's hay inside,' he said. 'We'll be safe here.'

Mallory said: 'Fine. A radio message to the *Sirdar* to send her CE message to Cairo and—'

'CE?' Andrea asked. 'What's that?'

'To let Cairo know we've contacted you and are ready for pick-up . . . And after that, three lovely long hours' sleep.'

Andrea nodded. 'Three hours it is.'

'Three *long* hours,' Mallory said meditatively.

A smile slowly broke on Andrea's craggy face as he clapped Mallory on the shoulder.

'In three long hours,' he said, 'a man like myself can accomplish a great deal.'

He turned and hurried off through the rain-filled night. Mallory and Miller looked after him with expressionless faces, looked at each other, still with the same expressionless faces, then pushed open the swing doors of the barn.

The Mandrakos airfield would not have received a licence from

22

any Civil Air Board anywhere in the world. It was just over half a mile long, with hills rising steeply at both ends of the alleged runway, not more than forty yards wide and liberally besprinkled with a variety of bumps and potholes virtually guaranteed to wreck any undercarriage in the aviation business. But the RAF had used it before so it was not impossible that they might be able to use it at least once again.

To the south, the airstrip was lined with groves of carob trees. Under the pitiful shelter afforded by one of those, Mallory, Miller and Andrea sat waiting. At least Mallory and Miller did, hunched, miserable and shivering violently in their still sodden clothes. Andrea, however, was stretched out luxuriously with his hands behind his head, oblivious of the heavy drips of rain that fell on his upturned face. There was about him an air of satisfaction, of complacency almost, as he gazed at the first greyish tinges appearing in the sky to the east over the black-walled massif of the Turkish coast.

Andrea said: 'They're coming now.'

Mallory and Miller listened for a few moments, then they too heard it—the distant, muted roar of heavy aircraft approaching. All three rose and moved out to the perimeter of the airstrip. Within a minute, descending rapidly after their climb over the mountains to the south and at a height of less than a thousand feet, a squadron of eighteen Wellingtons, as much heard as seen in the light of early dawn, passed directly over the airstrip, heading for the town of Navarone. Two minutes later, the three watchers both heard the detonations and saw the brilliant orange mushrooming of light as the Wellingtons unloaded their bombs over the shattered fortress to the north. Sporadic lines of upward-flying tracer, obviously exclusively small-arm, attested to the ineffectuality, the weakness of the ground defences. When the fortress had blown up, so had all the anti-aircraft batteries in the town. The attack was short and sharp: less than two minutes after the bombardment

23

had started it ceased as abruptly as it had begun and then there was only the fading dying sound of de-synchronized engines as the Wellingtons pulled away, first to the north and then the west, across the still-dark waters of the Aegean.

For perhaps a minute the three watchers stood silent on the perimeter of the Mandrakos airstrip, then Miller said wonderingly: 'What makes us so important?'

'I don't know,' Mallory said. 'But I don't think you're going to enjoy finding out.'

'And that won't be long now.' Andrea turned round and looked towards the mountains to the south. 'Hear it?'

Neither of the others heard it, but they did not doubt that, in fact, there was something to hear. Andrea's hearing was on a par with his phenomenal eyesight. Then, suddenly, they could hear it, too. A solitary bomber—also a Wellington—came sinking in from the south, circled the perimeter area once as Mallory blinked his torch upwards in rapidly successive flashes, lined up its approach, landed heavily at the far end of the airstrip and came taxiing towards them, bumping heavily across the atrocious surface of the airfield. It halted less than a hundred yards from where they stood: then a light started winking from the flight-deck.

Andrea said: 'Now, don't forget. I've promised to be back in a week.'

'Never make promises,' Miller said severely. 'What if we aren't back in a week? What if they're sending us to the Pacific?'

'Then when we get back I'll send you in first to explain.'

Miller shook his head. 'I don't really think I'd like that.'

'We'll talk about your cowardice later on,' Mallory said. 'Come on. Hurry up.'

The three men broke into a run towards the waiting Wellington.

The Wellington was half an hour on the way to its destination, wherever its destination was, and Andrea and Miller, coffee-mugs in hand, were trying, unsuccessfully, to attain a degree of comfort on the lumpy palliasses on the fuselage floor when Mallory returned from the flight-deck. Miller looked up at him in weary resignation, his expression characterized by an entire lack of enthusiasm and the spirit of adventure.

'Well, what did you find out?' His tone of voice made it abundantly clear that what he had expected Mallory to find out was nothing short of the very worst. 'Where to, now? Rhodes? Beirut? The flesh-pots of Cairo?'

'Termoli, the man says.'

'Termoli, is it? Place I've always wanted to see.' Miller paused. 'Where the hell's Termoli?'

'Italy, so I believe. Somewhere on the south Adriatic coast.'

'Oh, no!' Miller turned on his side and pulled a blanket over his head. 'I *hate* spaghetti.'

CHAPTER 2

Thursday
1400-2330

The landing on Termoli airfield, on the Adriatic coast of Southern Italy, was every bit as bumpy as the harrowing take-off from the Mandrakos airstrip had been. The Termoli fighter air-base was officially and optimistically listed as newly-constructed but in point of fact was no more than half-finished and felt that way for every yard of the excruciating touch-down and the jack-rabbit run-up to the prefabricated control-tower at the eastern end of the field. When Mallory and Andrea swung down to terra firma neither of them looked particularly happy: Miller, who came a very shaky last, and who was widely known to have an almost pathological loathing and detestation of all conceivable forms of transport, looked very ill indeed.

Miller was given time neither to seek nor receive commiseration. A camouflaged British 5th Army jeep pulled up alongside the plane, and the sergeant at the wheel, having briefly established their identity, waved them inside in silence, a silence which he stonily maintained on their drive through the shambles of the war-torn streets of Termoli. Mallory was unperturbed by the apparent unfriendliness. The driver was obviously under the strictest instructions not to talk to them, a situation which Mallory had encountered all too often in the past. There were not, Mallory reflected, very many groups of untouchables, but his, he knew, was one of them: no one, with two or three rare exceptions, was ever permitted to talk to them. The process, Mallory knew, was perfectly understand-

able and justifiable, but it was an attitude that did tend to become increasingly wearing with the passing of the years. It
tended to make for a certain lack of contact with one's fellowmen.

After twenty minutes, the jeep stopped below the broad-
flagged steps of a house on the outskirts of the town. The jeep
driver gestured briefly to an armed sentry on the top of the
steps who responded with a similarly perfunctory greeting.
Mallory took this as a sign that they had arrived at their
destination and, not wishing to violate the young sergeant's
vow of silence, got out without being told. The others followed and the jeep at once drove off.

The house—it looked more like a modest palace—was a
rather splendid example of late Renaissance architecture, all
colonnades and columns and everything in veined marble, but
Mallory was more interested in what was inside the house than
what it was made of on the outside. At the head of the steps
their path was barred by the young corporal sentry armed with
a Lee-Enfield .303. He looked like a refugee from high school.

'Names, please.'

'Captain Mallory.'

'Identity papers? Pay-books?'

'Oh, my God,' Miller moaned. 'And me feeling so sick, too.'

'We have none,' Mallory said gently. 'Take us inside, please.'

'My instructions are—'

'I know, I know,' Andrea said soothingly. He leaned across,
effortlessly removed the rifle from the corporal's desperate
grasp, ejected and pocketed the magazine and returned the
rifle. 'Please, now.'

Red-faced and furious, the youngster hesitated briefly,
looked at the three men more carefully, turned, opened the
door behind him and gestured for the three to follow him.

Before them stretched a long, marble-flagged corridor, tall
leaded windows on one side, heavy oil paintings and the oc-

27

casional set of double-leather doors on the other. Half-way down the passage Andrea tapped the corporal on the shoulder and handed the magazine back without a word. The corporal took it, smiling uncertainly, and inserted it into his rifle without a word. Another twenty paces and he stopped before the last pair of leather doors, knocked, heard a muffled acknowledgment and pushed open one of the doors, standing aside to let the three men pass him. Then he moved out again, closing the door behind him.

It was obviously the main drawing-room of the house—or palace—furnished in an almost medieval opulence, all dark oak, heavily brocaded silk curtains, leather upholstery, leather-bound books, what were undoubtedly a set of Old Masters on the walls and a flowing sea of dull bronze carpeting from wall to wall. Taken all in all, even a member of the old-pre-war Italian nobility wouldn't have turned up his nose at it.

The room was pleasantly redolent with the smell of burning pine, the source of which wasn't difficult to locate: one could have roasted a very large ox indeed in the vast and crackling fireplace at the far end of the room. Close by this fireplace stood three young men who bore no resemblance whatsoever to the rather ineffectual youngster who had so recently tried to prevent their entry. They were, to begin with, a good few years older, though still young men. They were heavily-built, broad-shouldered characters and had about them a look of tough and hard-bitten competence. They were dressed in the uniform of that élite of combat troops, the Marine Commandos, and they looked perfectly at home in those uniforms.

But what caught and held the unwavering attention of Mallory and his two companions was neither the rather splendidly effete decadence of the room and its furnishings nor the wholly unexpected presence of the three commandos: it was the fourth figure in the room, a tall, heavily built and commanding figure who leaned negligently against a table in the centre of the room. The deeply-trenched face, the authoritative expression, the splendid grey beard and the piercing blue eyes made him a prototype for the classic British naval captain, which, as the immaculate white uniform he wore indicated, was precisely what he was. With a collective sinking of their hearts, Mallory, Andrea and Miller gazed again, and with a marked lack of enthusiasm, upon the splendidly piratical figure of Captain Jensen, RN, Chief of Allied Intelligence, Mediterranean, and the man who had so recently sent them on their suicidal mission to the island of Navarone. All three looked at one another and shook their heads in slow despair.

Captain Jensen straightened, smiled his magnificent sabre-toothed tiger's smile and strode forward to greet them, his hand outstretched.

'Mallory! Andrea! Miller!' There was a dramatic five-second pause between the words. 'I don't know what to say! I just don't know what to say! A magnificent job, a magnificent—' He broke off and regarded them thoughtfully. 'You—um—don't seem all that surprised to see me, Captain Mallory?'

'I'm not. With respect, sir, whenever and wherever there's dirty work afoot, one looks to find—'

'Yes, yes, yes. Quite, quite. And how are you all?'

'Tired,' Miller said firmly. 'Terribly tired. We need a rest. At least, I do.'

Jensen said earnestly: 'And that's exactly what you're going to have, my boy. A rest. A long one. A *very* long one.'

'A *very* long one?' Miller looked at him in frank incredulity.

'You have my word.' Jensen stroked his beard in momentary diffidence. 'Just as soon, that is, as you get back from Yugoslavia.'

'Yugoslavia!' Miller stared at him.

'Tonight.'

'Tonight!'

'By parachute.'

'By *parachute*!'

Jensen said with forbearance: 'I am aware, Corporal Miller, that you have had a classical education and are, moreover, just returned from the Isles of Greece. But we'll do without the Ancient Greek Chorus bit, if you don't mind.'

Miller looked moodily at Andrea. 'Bang goes your honeymoon.'

'What was that?' Jensen asked sharply.

'Just a private joke, sir.'

Mallory said in mild protest: 'You're forgetting, sir, that none of us has ever made a parachute jump.'

'I'm forgetting nothing. There's a first time for everything. What do you gentlemen know about the war in Yugoslavia?'

'What war?' Andrea said warily.

'Precisely.' There was satisfaction in Jensen's voice.

'I heard about it,' Miller volunteered. 'There's a bunch of what-do-you-call-'em—Partisans, isn't it—offering some kind of underground resistance to the German occupation troops.'

'It is probably as well for you,' Jensen said heavily, 'that the Partisans cannot hear you. They're not underground, they're very much over ground and at the latest count there were 350,000 of them tying down twenty-eight German and Bulgarian divisions in Yugoslavia.' He paused briefly. 'More, in fact, than the combined Allied armies are tying down here in Italy.'

'Somebody should have told me,' Miller complained. He brightened. 'If there's 350,000 of them around, what would they want us for?'

Jensen said acidly: 'You must learn to curb your enthusiasm, Corporal. The fighting part of it you may leave to the Partisans —and they're fighting the cruellest, hardest, most brutal war in Europe today. A ruthless, vicious war with no quarter and no surrender on either side. Arms, munitions, food, clothes—

the Partisans are desperately short of all of those. But they have those twenty-eight divisions pinned down.'

'I don't want any part of that,' Miller muttered.

Mallory said hastily: 'What do you want us to do, sir?'

'This.' Jensen removed his glacial stare from Miller. 'Nobody appreciates it yet, but the Yugoslavs are our most important Allies in Southern Europe. Their war is our war. And they're fighting a war they can never hope to win. Unless—'

Mallory nodded. 'The tools to finish the job.'

'Hardly original, but true. The tools to finish the job. We are the *only* people who are at present supplying them with rifles, machine-guns, ammunition, clothing and medical supplies. And those are not getting through.' He broke off, picking up a cane, walked almost angrily across the room to a large wall-map hanging between a couple of Old Masters and rapped the tip of the bamboo against it. 'Bosnia-Herzegovina, gentlemen. West-Central Yugoslavia. We've sent in four British Military Missions in the past two months to liaise with the Yugoslavs— the Partisan Yugoslavs. The leaders of all four missions have disappeared without trace. Ninety per cent of our recent airlift supplies have fallen into German hands. They have broken all our radio codes and have established a network of agents in Southern Italy here with whom they are apparently able to communicate as and when they wish. Perplexing questions, gentlemen. Vital questions. I want the answers. Force 10 will get me the answers.'

'Force 10?' Mallory said politely.

'The code name for your operation.'

'Why that particular name?' Andrea asked.

'Why not? Ever heard of *any* code name that had *any* bearing on the operation on hand? It's the whole essence of it, man.'

'It wouldn't, of course,' Mallory said woodenly, 'have anything to do with a frontal attack on something, a storming of

31

some vital place.' He observed Jensen's total lack of reaction and went on in the same tone: 'On the Beaufort Scale, Force 10 means a storm.'

'A storm!' It is very difficult to combine an exclamation and a moan of anguish in the same word, but Miller managed it without any difficulty. 'Oh my God, and all I want is a flat calm, and that for the rest of my life.'

'There are limits to my patience, Corporal Miller,' Jensen said. 'I may—I say *may*—have to change my mind about a recommendation I made on your behalf this morning.'

'On my behalf?' Miller said guardedly.

'For the Distinguished Conduct Medal.'

'*That* should look nice on the lid of my coffin,' Miller muttered.

'What was that?'

'Corporal Miller was just expressing his appreciation.' Mallory moved closer to the wall-map and studièd it briefly. 'Bosnia-Herzegovina—well, it's a fair-sized area, sir.'

'Agreed. But we can pin-point the spot—the approximate location of the disappearances—to within twenty miles.'

Mallory turned from the map and said slowly: 'There's been a lot of homework on this one. That raid this morning on Navarone. The Wellington standing by to take us here. All preparations—I infer this from what you've said—laid on for tonight. Not to mention—'

'We've been working on this for almost two months. You three were supposed to have come here some days ago. But—ah—well, you know.'

'We know.' The threatened withholding of his DCM had left Miller unmoved. 'Something else came up. Look, sir, why us? We're saboteurs, explosive experts, combat troops—this is a job for undercover espionage agents who speak Serbo-Croat or whatever.'

'You must allow me to be the best judge of that.' Jensen gave them another flash of his sabre-toothed smile. 'Besides, you're lucky.'

'Luck deserts tired men,' Andrea said. 'And we are very tired.'

'Tired or not, I can't find another team in Southern Europe to match you for resource, experience and skill.' Jensen smiled again. 'And luck. I have to be ruthless, Andrea. I don't like it, but I have to. But I take the point about your exhaustion. That's why I have decided to send a back-up team with you.'

Mallory looked at the three young soldiers standing by the hearth, then back to Jensen, who nodded.

'They're young, fresh and just raring to go. Marine Commandos, the most highly trained combat troops we have today. Remarkable variety of skills, I assure you. Take Reynolds, here.' Jensen nodded to a very tall, dark sergeant in his late twenties, a man with a deeply-tanned aquiline face. 'He can do anything from underwater demolition to flying a plane. And he will be flying a plane tonight. And, as you can see, he'll come in handy for carrying any heavy cases you have.'

Mallory said mildly: 'I've always found that Andrea makes a pretty fair porter, sir.'

Jensen turned to Reynolds. 'They have their doubts. Show them you can be of some use.'

Reynolds hesitated, then stooped, picked up a heavy brass poker and proceeded to bend it between his hands. Obviously, it wasn't an easy poker to bend. His face turned red, the veins stood out on his forehead and the tendons in his neck, his arms quivered with the strain, but slowly, inexorably, the poker was bent into a figure 'U'. Smiling almost apologetically, Reynolds handed the poker over to Andrea. Andrea took it reluctantly. He hunched his shoulders, his knuckles gleamed white but the poker remained in its 'U' shape. Andrea looked up at Reynolds, his expression thoughtful, then quietly laid the poker down.

'See what I mean?' Jensen said. 'Tired. Or Sergeant Groves

33

here. Hot-foot from London, via the Middle East. Ex-air navigator, with all the latest in sabotage, explosives and electrics. For booby-traps, time-bombs and concealed microphones, a human mine-detector. And Sergeant Saunders here —a top-flight radio-operator.'

Miller said morosely to Mallory: 'You're a toothless old lion and you're over the hill.'

'Don't talk rubbish, Corporal!' Jensen's voice was sharp. 'Six is the ideal number. You'll be duplicated in every department, and those men are *good*. They'll be invaluable. If it's any salve to your pride, they weren't originally picked to go with you: they were picked as a reserve team in case you—um— well—'

'I see.' The lack of conviction in Miller's voice was total.

'All clear, then?'

'Not quite,' Mallory said. 'Who's in charge?'

Jensen said in genuine surprise: 'You are, of course.'

'So.' Mallory spoke quietly and pleasantly. 'I understand the training emphasis today—especially in the Marine Commandos—is on initiative, self-reliance, independence in thought and action. Fine—if they happen to be caught out on their own.' He smiled, almost deprecatingly. 'Otherwise I shall expect immediate, unquestioning and total compliance with orders. My orders. Instant and total.'

'And if not?' Reynolds asked.

'A superfluous question, Sergeant. You know the wartime penalty for disobeying an officer in the field.'

'Does that apply to your friends, too?'

'No.'

Reynolds turned to Jensen. 'I don't think I like that, sir.'

Mallory sank wearily into a chair, lit a cigarette, nodded at Reynolds and said, 'Replace him.'

'What!' Jensen was incredulous.

'Replace him, I said. We haven't even left and already he's

34

questioning my judgment. What's it going to be like in action? He's dangerous. I'd rather carry a ticking time-bomb with me.'

'Now, look here, Mallory—'

'Replace him or replace me.'

'And me,' Andrea said quietly.

'And me,' Miller added.

There was a brief and far from companionable silence in the room, then Reynolds approached Mallory's chair.

'Sir.'

Mallory looked at him without encouragement.

'I'm sorry,' Reynolds went on. 'I stepped out of line. I will never make the same mistake twice. I *want* to go on this trip, sir.'

Mallory glanced at Andrea and Miller. Miller's face registered only his shock at Reynolds's incredibly foolhardy enthusiasm for action. Andrea, impassive as ever, nodded almost imperceptibly. Mallory smiled and said: 'As Captain Jensen said, I'm sure you'll be a great asset."

'Well, that's it, then.' Jensen affected not to notice the almost palpable relaxation of tension in the room. 'Sleep's the thing now. But first I'd like a few minutes—report on Navarone, you know.' He looked at the three sergeants. 'Confidential, I'm afraid.'

'Yes, sir,' Reynolds said. 'Shall we go down to the field, check flight plans, weather, parachutes and supplies?'

Jensen nodded. As the three sergeants closed the double doors behind them, Jensen crossed to a side door, opened it and said: 'Come in, General.'

The man who entered was very tall, very gaunt. He was probably about thirty-five, but looked a great deal older. The care, the exhaustion, the endless privations inseparable from too many years' ceaseless struggle for survival had heavily silvered the once-black hair and deeply etched into the swarthy, sunburnt face the lines of physical and mental suffering. The eyes were dark and glowing and intense, the hypnotic eyes of a man inspired by a fanatical dedication to some as yet unrealized ideal. He was dressed in a British Army officer's uniform, bereft of insignia and badges.

Jensen said: 'Gentlemen, General Vukalovic. The general is second-in-command of the Partisan forces in Bosnia-Herze-govina. The RAF flew him out yesterday. He is here as a Partisan doctor seeking medical supplies. His true identity is known only to us. General, those are your men.'

Vukalovic looked them over severally and steadily, his face expressionless. He said: 'Those are tired men, Captain Jensen. So much depends . . . too tired to do what has to be done.'

'He's right, you know,' Miller said earnestly.

'There's maybe a little mileage left in them yet,' Jensen said mildly. 'It's a long haul from Navarone. Now then—'

'Navarone?' Vukalovic interrupted. 'These—these are the men—'

'An unlikely-looking lot, I agree.'

'Perhaps I was wrong about them.'

'No, you weren't, General,' Miller said. 'We're exhausted. We're completely—'

'Do you mind?' Jensen said acidly. 'Captain Mallory, with two exceptions the General will be the only person in Bosnia who knows who you are and what you are doing. Whether the General reveals the identity of the others is entirely up to him. General Vukalovic will be accompanying you to Yugoslavia, but not in the same plane.'

'Why not?' Mallory asked.

'Because his plane will be returning. Yours won't.'

'Ah!' Mallory said. There was a brief silence while he, Andrea and Miller absorbed the significance behind Jensen's words. Abstractedly, Andrea threw some more wood on the sinking fire and looked around for a poker: but the only poker was the one that Reynolds had already bent into a 'U'-shape.

Andrea picked it up. Absent-mindedly, effortlessly, Andrea straightened it out, poked the fire into a blaze and laid the poker down, a performance Vukalovic watched with a very thoughtful expression on his face.

Jensen went on: 'Your plane, Captain Mallory, will not be returning because your plane is expendable in the interests of authenticity.'

'Us, too?' Miller asked.

'You won't be able to accomplish very much, Corporal Miller, without actually putting your feet on the ground. Where you're going, no plane can possibly land: so you jump —and the plane crashes.'

'That sounds very authentic,' Miller muttered.

Jensen ignored him. 'The realities of total war are harsh beyond belief. Which is why I sent those three youngsters on their way—I don't want to dampen their enthusiasm.'

'Mine's water-logged,' Miller said dolefully.

'Oh, do be quiet. Now, it would be fine if, by way of a bonus, you could discover why eighty per cent of our air-drops fall into German hands, fine if you could locate and rescue our captured mission leaders. But not important. Those supplies, those agents are militarily expendable. What are not expendable are the seven thousand men under the command of General Vukalovic here, seven thousand men trapped in an area called the Zenica Cage, seven thousand starving men with almost no ammunition left, seven thousand men with no future.'

'We can help them?' Andrea asked heavily. 'Six men?'

Jensen said candidly: 'I don't know.'

'But you have a plan?'

'Not yet. Not as such. The glimmerings of an idea. No more.' Jensen rubbed his forehead wearily. 'I myself arrived from Alexandria only six hours ago.' He hesitated, then shrugged. 'By tonight, who knows? A few hours' sleep this afternoon might transform us all. But, first, the report on Navarone. It would be pointless for you three other gentlemen to wait—there are sleeping-quarters down the hall. I daresay Captain Mallory can tell me all I want to know.'

Mallory waited till the door closed behind Andrea, Miller and Vukalovic and said: 'Where shall I begin my report, sir?'

'What report?'

'Navarone, of course.'

'The hell with Navarone. That's over and done with.' He picked up his cane, crossed to the wall, pulled down two more maps. 'Now, then.'

'You—you *have* a plan,' Mallory said carefully.

'Of course I have a plan,' Jensen said coldly. He rapped the map in front of him. 'Ten miles north of here. The Gustav Line. Right across Italy along the line of the Sangro and Liri rivers. Here the Germans have the most impregnable defensive positions in the history of modern warfare. Monte Cassino here—our finest Allied divisions have broken on it, some for ever. And here—the Anzio beach-head. Fifty thousand Americans fighting for their lives. For five solid months now we've been battering our heads against the Gustav Line and the Anzio perimeter. Our losses in men and machines—incalculable. Our gains—not one solitary inch.'

Mallory said diffidently: 'You mentioned something about Yugoslavia, sir.'

'I'm coming to that,' Jensen said with restraint. 'Now, our only hope of breaching the Gustav Line is by weakening the German defensive forces and the only way we can do *that* is by persuading them to withdraw some of their front-line divisions. So we practise the Allenby technique.'

'I see.'

'You don't see at all. General Allenby, Palestine, 1918. He had an east-west line from the Jordan to the Mediterranean. He planned to attack from the west—so he convinced the

Turks the attack was coming from the east. He did this by building up in the east a huge city of army tents occupied by only a few hundred men who came out and dashed around like beavers whenever enemy planes came over on reconnaissance. He did this by letting the same planes see large army truck convoys pouring to the east all day long—what the Turks didn't know was that the same convoys poured back to the west all night long. He even had fifteen thousand canvas dummies of horses built. Well, we're doing the same.'

'Fifteen thousand canvas horses?'

'Very, very amusing.' Jensen rapped the map again. 'Every airfield between here and Bari is jammed with dummy bombers and gliders. Outside Foggia is the biggest military encampment in Italy—occupied by two hundred men. The harbours of Bari and Taranto are crowded with assault landing-craft, the whole lot made of plywood. All day long columns of trucks and tanks converge on the Adriatic coast. If you, Mallory, were in the German High Command, what would you make of this?'

'I'd suspect an airborne and sea invasion of Yugoslavia. But I wouldn't be sure.'

'The German reaction exactly,' Jensen said with some satisfaction. 'They're badly worried, worried to the extent that they have already transferred two divisions from Italy to Yugoslavia to meet the threat.'

'But they're not certain?'

'Not quite. But almost.' Jensen cleared his throat. 'You see, our four captured mission leaders were all carrying unmistakable evidence pointing to an invasion of Central Yugoslavia in early May.'

'They carried evidence—' Mallory broke off, looked at Jensen for a long and speculative moment, then went on quietly: 'And how *did* the Germans manage to capture them all?'

'We told them they were coming.'

'You did what!'

'Volunteers all, volunteers all,' Jensen said quickly. There were, apparently, some of the harsher realities of total war that even he didn't care to dwell on too long. 'And it will be your job, my boy, to turn near-conviction into absolute certainty.' Seemingly oblivious of the fact that Mallory was regarding him with a marked lack of enthusiasm, he wheeled round dramatically and stabbed his cane at a large-scale map of Central Yugoslavia.

'The valley of the Neretva,' Jensen said. 'The vital sector of the main north-south route through Yugoslavia. Whoever controls this valley controls Yugoslavia—and no one knows this better than the Germans. If the blow falls, they know it must fall here. They are fully aware that an invasion of Yugoslavia is on the cards, they are terrified of a link-up between the Allies and the Russians advancing from the east and they *know* that any such link-up must be along this valley. They already have two armoured divisions along the Neretva, two divisions that, in the event of invasion, could be wiped out in a night. From the north—here—they are trying to force their way south to the Neretva with a whole army corps—but the only way is through the Zenica Cage here. And Vukalovic and his seven thousand men block the way.'

'Vukalovic knows about this?' Mallory asked. 'About what you really have in mind, I mean?'

'Yes. And the Partisan command. They know the risks, the odds against them. They accept them.'

'Photographs?' Mallory asked.

'Here.' Jensen pulled some photographs from a desk drawer, selected one and smoothed it out on the table. 'This is the Zenica Cage. Well-named: a perfect cage, a perfect trap. To the north and west, impassable mountains. To the east, the Neretva dam and the Neretva gorge. To the south, the Neretva river.

To the north of the cage here, at the Zenica gap, the German 11th Army Corps is trying to break through. To the west here—they call it the West Gap—more units of the 11th trying to do the same. And to the south here, over the river and hidden in the trees, two armoured divisions under a General Zimmermann.'

'And this?' Mallory pointed to a thin black line spanning the river just north of the two armoured divisions.

'That,' Jensen said thoughtfully, 'is the bridge at Neretva.'

Close-up, the bridge at Neretva looked vastly more impressive than it had done in the large-scale photograph: it was a massively cantilevered structure in solid steel, with a black asphalt roadway laid on top. Below the bridge rushed the swiftly-flowing Neretva, greenish-white in colour and swollen with melting snow. To the south there was a narrow strip of green meadowland bordering the river and, to the south of this again, a dark and towering pine forest began. In the safe concealment of the forest's gloomy depths, General Zimmermann's two armoured divisions crouched, waiting.

Parked close to the edge of the wood was the divisional command radio truck, a bulky and very long vehicle so beautifully camouflaged as to be invisible at more than twenty paces.

General Zimmermann and his ADC, Captain Warburg, were at that moment inside the truck. Their mood appeared to match the permanent twilight of the woods. Zimmermann had one of those high-foreheaded, lean and aquiline and intelligent faces which so rarely betray any emotion, but there was no lack of emotion now, no lack of anxiety and impatience as he removed his cap and ran his hand through his thinning grey hair. He said to the radio-operator seated behind the big transceiver:

'No word yet? Nothing?'

'Nothing, sir.'

41

'You are in constant touch with Captain Neufeld's camp?'
'Every minute, sir.'
'And his operator is keeping a continuous radio watch?'
'All the time, sir. Nothing. Just nothing.'

Zimmermann turned and descended the steps, followed by Warburg. He walked, head down, until he was out of earshot of the truck, then said: 'Damn it! Damn it! God damn it all!'

'You're as sure as that, sir.' Warburg was tall, good-looking, flaxen-haired and thirty, and his face at the moment reflected a nice balance of apprehension and unhappiness. 'That they're coming?'

'It's in my bones, boy. One way or another it's coming, coming for all of us.'

'You can't be *sure*, sir,' Warburg protested.

'True enough.' Zimmermann sighed. 'I can't be sure. But I'm sure of this. If they do come, if the 11th Army Group can't break through from the north, if we can't wipe out those damned Partisans in the Zenica Cage—'

Warburg waited for him to continue, but Zimmermann seemed lost in reverie. Apparently apropos of nothing, Warburg said: 'I'd like to see Germany again, sir. Just once more.'

'Wouldn't we all, my boy, wouldn't we all.' Zimmermann walked slowly to the edge of the wood and stopped. For a long time he gazed out over the bridge at Neretva. Then he shook his head, turned and was almost at once lost to sight in the dark depths of the forest.

The pine fire in the great fireplace in the drawing-room in Termoli was burning low. Jensen threw on some more logs, straightened, poured two drinks and handed one to Mallory.

Jensen said: 'Well?'

'That's the plan?' No hint of his incredulity, of his near-despair, showed in Mallory's impassive face. 'That's *all* of the plan?'

'Yes.'

'Your health.' Mallory paused. 'And mine.' After an even longer pause he said reflectively: 'It should be interesting to watch Dusty Miller's reaction when he hears about this little lot this evening.'

As Mallory had said, Miller's reactions were interesting, even if wholly predictable. Some six hours later, clad now, like Mallory and Andrea, in British Army uniform, Miller listened in visibly growing horror as Jensen outlined what he considered should be their proposed course of action in the next twenty-four hours or so. When he had finished, Jensen looked directly at Miller and said: 'Well? Feasible?'

'Feasible?' Miller was aghast. 'It's suicidal!'

'Andrea?'

Andrea shrugged, lifted his hands palms upwards and said nothing.

Jensen nodded and said: 'I'm sorry, but I'm fresh out of options. We'd better go. The others are waiting at the airstrip.'

Andrea and Miller left the room, began to walk down the long passage-way. Mallory hesitated in the doorway, momentarily blocking it, then turned to face Jensen who was watching him with a surprised lift of the eyebrows.

Mallory said in a low voice: 'Let me tell Andrea, at least.'

Jensen looked at him for a considering moment or two, shook his head briefly and brushed by into the corridor.

Twenty minutes later, without a further word being spoken, the four men arrived at the Termoli airstrip to find Vukalovic and two sergeants waiting for them: the third, Reynolds, was already at the controls of his Wellington, one of two standing at the end of the airstrip, propellers already turning. Ten minutes later both planes were airborne, Vukalovic in one, Mallory, Miller, Andrea, and the three sergeants in the other, each plane bound for its separate destination.

Jensen, alone on the tarmac, watched both planes climbing, his straining eyes following them until they disappeared into the overcast darkness of the moonless sky above. Then, just as General Zimmermann had done that afternoon, he shook his head in slow finality, turned and walked heavily away.

CHAPTER 3

Friday

0030-0200

Sergeant Reynolds, Mallory reflected, certainly knew how to handle a plane, especially this one. Although his eyes showed him to be always watchful and alert, he was precise, competent, calm and relaxed in everything he did. No less competent was Groves: the poor light and cramped confines of his tiny plotting-table clearly didn't worry him at all and as an air navigator he was quite clearly as experienced as he was proficient. Mallory peered forward through the windscreen, saw the white-capped waters of the Adriatic rushing by less than a hundred feet beneath their fuselage, and turned to Groves.

'The flight-plan calls for us to fly as low as this?'

'Yes. The Germans have radar installations on some of the outlying islands off the Yugoslav coast. We start climbing when we reach Dalmatia.'

Mallory nodded his thanks, turned to watch Reynolds again. He said, curiously: 'Captain Jensen was right about you. As a pilot. How on earth does a Marine Commando come to learn to drive one of those things?'

'I've had plenty of practice,' Reynolds said. 'Three years in the RAF, two of them as sergeant-pilot in a Wellington bomber squadron. One day in Egypt I took a Lysander up without permission. People did it all the time—but the crate I'd picked had a defective fuel gauge.'

'You were grounded?'

'With great speed.' He grinned. 'There were no objections

45

when I applied for a service transfer. I think they felt I wasn't somehow quite right for the RAF.'

Mallory looked at Groves. 'And you?'

Groves smiled broadly. 'I was his navigator in that old crate. We were fired on the same day.'

Mallory said consideringly: 'Well, I should think that might be rather useful.'

'What's useful?' Reynolds asked.

'The fact that you're used to this feeling of disgrace. It'll enable you to act your part all the better when the time comes. If the time comes.'

Reynolds said carefully: 'I'm not quite sure—'

'Before we jump, I want you—all of you—to remove every distinguishing badge or emblem of rank on your clothes.' He gestured to Andrea and Miller at the rear of the flight-deck to indicate that they were included as well, then looked at Reynolds again. 'Sergeants' stripes, regimental flashes, medal ribbons—the lot.'

'Why the hell should I?' Reynolds, Mallory thought, had the lowest boiling-point he'd come across in quite some time. 'I *earned* those stripes, those ribbons, that flash. I don't see—'

Mallory smiled. 'Disobeying an officer on active service?'

'Don't be so damned touchy,' Reynolds said.

'Don't be so damned touchy, *sir*.'

'Don't be so damned touchy, *sir*.' Reynolds suddenly grinned. 'OK, so who's got the scissors?'

'You see,' Mallory explained, 'the last thing we want to happen is to fall into enemy hands.'

'Amen,' Miller intoned.

'But if we're to get the information we want we're going to have to operate close to or even inside their lines. We might get caught. So we have our cover story.'

Groves said quietly: 'Are we permitted to know just what that cover story is, sir?'

46

'Of course you are,' Mallory said in exasperation. He went on earnestly: 'Don't you realize that, on a mission like this, survival depends on one thing and one thing only—complete and mutual trust? As soon as we start having secrets from each other—we're finished.'

In the deep gloom at the rear of the flight-deck, Andrea and Miller glanced at each other and exchanged their wearily cynical smiles.

As Mallory left the flight-deck for the fuselage, his right hand brushed Miller's shoulder. After about two minutes Miller yawned, stretched and made his way aft. Mallory was waiting towards the rear of the fuselage. He had two pieces of folded paper in his hand, one of which he opened and showed to Miller, snapping on a flash-light at the same time. Miller stared at it for some moments, then lifted an eyebrow.

'And what is this supposed to be?'

'It's the triggering mechanism for a 1,500-pound submersible mine. Learn it by heart.'

Miller looked at it without expression, then glanced at the other paper Mallory held.

'And what have you there?'

Mallory showed him. It was a large-scale map, the central feature of which appeared to be a winding lake with a very long eastern arm which bent abruptly at right-angles into a very short southern arm, which in turn ended abruptly at what appeared to be a dam wall. Beneath the dam, a river flowed away through a winding gorge.

Mallory said: 'What does it look like to you? Show them both to Andrea and tell him to destroy them.'

Mallory left Miller engrossed in his homework and moved forward again to the flight-deck. He bent over Groves's chart table.

'Still on course?'

47

'Yes, sir. We're just clearing the southern tip of the island of Hvar. You can see a few lights on the mainland ahead.' Mallory followed the pointing hand, located a few clusters of lights, then reached out a hand to steady himself as the Wellington started to climb sharply. He glanced at Reynolds.

'Climbing now, sir. There's some pretty lofty stuff ahead. We should pick up the Partisan landing lights in about half an hour.'

'Thirty-three minutes,' Groves said. 'One-twenty, near enough.'

For almost half an hour Mallory remained on a jump-seat in the flight-deck, just looking ahead. After a few minutes Andrea disappeared and did not reappear. Miller did not return. Groves navigated, Reynolds flew, Saunders listened in to his portable transceiver and nobody talked at all. At one-fifteen Mallory rose, touched Saunders on the shoulders, told him to pack up his gear and headed aft. He found Andrea and a thoroughly miserable-looking Miller with their parachute snap-catches already clipped on to the jumping wire. Andrea had the door pulled back and was throwing out tiny pieces of shredded paper which swirled away in the slipstream. Mallory shivered in the suddenly intense cold. Andrea grinned, beckoned him to the open doorway and pointed downwards. He yelled in Mallory's ear: 'There's a lot of snow down there.'

There was indeed a lot of snow down there. Mallory understood now Jensen's insistence on not landing a plane in those parts. The terrain below was rugged in the extreme, consisting almost entirely of a succession of deep and winding valleys and steep-sided mountains. Maybe half of the landscape below was covered in dense forests of pine trees: all of it was covered in what appeared to be a very heavy blanket of snow. Mallory drew back into the comparative shelter of the Wellington's fuselage and glanced at his watch.

'One-sixteen.' Like Andrea, he had to shout.

'Your watch is a little fast, maybe?' Miller bawled unhappily. Mallory shook his head, Miller shook his. A bell rang and Mallory made his way to the flight-deck, passing Saunders going the other way. As Mallory entered, Reynolds looked briefly over his shoulder, then pointed directly ahead. Mallory bent over his shoulder and peered forwards and downwards. He nodded.

The three lights, in the form of an elongated V, were still some miles ahead, but quite unmistakable, Mallory turned, touched Groves on the shoulder and pointed aft. Groves rose and left. Mallory said to Reynolds: 'Where are the red and green jumping lights?'

Reynolds indicated them.

'Press the red light. How long?'

'Thirty seconds. About.'

Mallory looked ahead again. The lights were less than half as distant as they had been when first he'd looked. He said to Reynolds: 'Automatic pilot. Close the fuel switches.'

'Close the—for all the petrol that's left—'

'Shut off the bloody tanks! And get aft. Five seconds.'

Reynolds did as he was told. Mallory waited, briefly made a last check of the landing lights ahead, pressed the green light button, rose and made his way swiftly aft. By the time he reached the jump door, even Reynolds, the last of the first five, was gone. Mallory clipped on his snap-catch, braced his hands round the edge of the doorway and launched himself out into the bitter Bosnian night.

The sudden jarring impact from the parachute harness made him look quickly upwards: the concave circle of a fully open parachute was a reassuring spectacle. He glanced downwards and saw the equally reassuring spectacle of another five open parachutes, two of which were swaying quite wildly across the sky—just as was his own. There were some things, he reflected, about which he, Andrea and Miller had a great deal

49

to learn. Controlling parachute descents was one of those things.

He looked up and to the east to see if he could locate the Wellington, but it was no longer visible. Suddenly, as he looked and listened, both engines, almost in perfect unison, cut out. Long seconds passed when the only sound was the rush of the wind in his ears, then there came an explosively metallic sound as the bomber crashed either into the ground or into some unseen mountainside ahead. There was no fire or none that he could see: just the crash, then silence. For the first time that night, the moon broke through.

Andrea landed heavily on an uneven piece of ground, rolled over twice, rose rather experimentally to his feet, discovered he was still intact, pressed the quick-release button of his parachute, then automatically, instinctively—Andrea had a built-in computer for assuring survival—swung through a complete 360° circle. But no immediate danger threatened, or none that he could see. Andrea made a more leisurely survey of their landing spot.

They had, he thought grimly, been most damnably lucky. Another hundred yards to the south and they'd have spent the rest of the night, and for all he knew, the rest of the war, clinging to the tops of the most impossibly tall pine trees he had ever seen. As it was, luck had been with them and they had landed in a narrow clearing which abutted closely on the rocky scarp of a mountainside.

Or rather, all but one. Perhaps fifty yards from where Andrea had landed, an apex of the forest elbowed its way into the clearing. The outermost tree in this apex had come between one of the parachutists and terra firma. Andrea's eyebrows lifted in quizzical astonishment, then he broke into an ambling run.

The parachutist who had come to grief was dangling from the lowermost bough of the pine. He had his hands twisted in the shrouds, his legs bent, knees and ankles close together in the classic landing position, his feet perhaps thirty inches from the ground. His eyes were screwed tightly shut. Corporal Miller seemed acutely unhappy.

Andrea came up and touched him on the shoulder, gently. Miller opened his eyes and glanced at Andrea, who pointed downwards. Miller followed his glance and lowered his legs, which were then four inches from the ground. Andrea produced a knife, sliced through the shreds and Miller completed the remainder of his journey. He straightened his jacket, his face splendidly impassive, and lifted an enquiring elbow. Andrea, his face equally impassive, pointed down the clearing. Three of the other four parachutists had already landed safely: the fourth, Mallory, was just touching down.

Two minutes later, just as all six were coming together some little distance away from the most easterly landing flare, a shout announced the appearance of a young soldier running towards them from the edge of the forest. The parachutists' guns came up and were almost immediately lowered again: this was no occasion for guns. The soldier was trailing his by the barrel, excitedly waving his free hand in greeting. He was dressed in a faded and tattered near-uniform that had been pillaged from a variety of armies, had long flowing hair, a cast to his right eye and a straggling ginger beard. That he was welcoming them, was beyond doubt. Repeating some incomprehensible greeting over and over again, he shook hands all round and then a second time, the huge grin on his face reflecting his delight.

Within thirty seconds he'd been joined by at least a dozen others, all bearded, all dressed in the same nondescript uniforms, no two of which were alike, all in the same almost festive mood. Then, as at a signal almost, they fell silent and drew slightly apart as the man who was obviously their leader appeared from the edge of the forest. He bore little resemblance to his men. He differed in that he was completely shaven and wore a uniform, a British battledress, which appeared to be all of one piece. He differed in that he was not smiling: he had about him the air of one who was seldom if ever given to smiling. He also differed from the others in that he was a hawk-faced giant of a man, at least six feet four inches in height, carrying no fewer than four wicked-looking Bowie-type knives in his belt—an excess of armament that on another man might have looked incongruous or even comical but which on this man provoked no mirth at all. His face was dark and sombre and when he spoke it was in English, slow and stilted, but precise.

'Good evening.' He looked round questioningly. 'I am Captain Droshny.'

Mallory took a step forward. 'Captain Mallory.'

'Welcome to Yugoslavia, Captain Mallory—Partisan Yugoslavia.' Droshny nodded towards the dying flare, his face twitched in what may have been an attempt at a smile, but he made no move to shake hands. 'As you can see, we were expecting you.'

'Your lights were a great help,' Mallory acknowledged.

'Thank you.' Droshny stared away to the east, then back to Mallory, shaking his head. 'A pity about the plane.'

'All war is a pity.'

Droshny nodded. 'Come. Our headquarters is close by.'

No more was said. Droshny, leading, moved at once into the shelter of the forest. Mallory, behind him, was intrigued by the footprints, clearly visible in the now bright moonlight, left by Droshny in the deep snow. They were, thought Mallory, most peculiar. Each sole left three V-shaped marks, the heel one: the right-hand side of the leading V on the right sole had a clearly defined break in it. Unconsciously, Mallory filed away this little oddity in his mind. There was no reason why he should have done so other than that the Mallorys of this world always observe and record the unusual. It helps them to stay alive.

The slope steepened, the snow deepened and the pale moonlight filtered thinly down through the spreading, snow-laden branches of the pines. The light wind was from the east: the cold was intense. For almost ten minutes no voice was heard, then Droshny's came, softly but clearly and imperative in its staccato urgency.

'Be still.' He pointed dramatically upward. 'Be still! Listen!' They stopped, looked upward and listened intently. At least, Mallory and his men looked upward and listened intently, but the Yugoslavs had other things on their minds: swiftly, efficiently and simultaneously, without either spoken or gestured command being given, they rammed the muzzles of their machine-guns and rifles into the sides and backs of the six parachutists with a force and uncompromising authority that rendered any accompanying orders quite superfluous.

The six men reacted as might have been expected. Reynolds, Groves and Saunders, who were rather less accustomed to the vicissitudes of fate than their three older companions, registered a very similar combination of startled anger and open-mouthed astonishment. Mallory looked thoughtful. Miller lifted a quizzical eyebrow. Andrea, predictably, registered nothing at all: he was too busy exhibiting his usual reaction to physical violence.

His right hand, which he had instantly lifted half-way to his shoulder in an apparent token of surrender, clamped down on the barrel of the rifle of the guard to his left, forcing it away from him, while his left elbow jabbed viciously into the solar plexus of the guard to his left, who gasped in pain and staggered back a couple of paces. Andrea, with both hands now on the rifle of the other guard, wrenched it effortlessly free, lifted it high and brought the barrel down in one continuous blur of movement. The guard collapsed as if a bridge had

53

fallen on him. The winded guard to the left, still bent and whooping in agony, was trying to line up his rifle when the butt of Andrea's rifle struck him in the face: he made a brief coughing sound and fell senseless to the forest floor.

It took all of the three seconds that this action had lasted for the Yugoslavs to release themselves from their momentary thrall of incredulity. Half-a-dozen soldiers flung themselves on Andrea, bearing him to the ground. In the furious, rolling struggle that followed, Andrea laid about him in his usual willing fashion, but when one of the Yugoslavs started pounding him on the head with the barrel of a pistol, Andrea opted for discretion and lay still. With two guns in his back and four hands on either arm Andrea was dragged to his feet: two of his captors already looked very much the worse for wear.

Droshny, his eyes bleak and bitter, came up to Andrea, unsheathed one of his knives and thrust its point against Andrea's throat with a force savage enough to break the skin and draw blood that trickled on to the gleaming blade. For a moment it seemed that Droshny would push the knife home to the hilt, then his eyes moved sideways and downwards to look at the two huddled men lying in the snow. He nodded to the nearest man.

'How are they?'

A young Yugoslav dropped to his knees, looked first at the man who had been struck by the rifle-barrel, touched his head briefly, examined the second man, then stood up. In the filtered moonlight, his face was unnaturally pale.

'Josef is dead. I think his neck is broken. And his brother— he's breathing—but his jaw seems to be—' The voice trailed away uncertainly.

Droshny transferred his gaze back to Andrea. His lips drew back, he smiled the way a wolf smiles and leaned a little harder on the knife.

'I *should* kill you now. I *will* kill you later.' He sheathed his knife, held up his clawed hands in front of Andrea's face, and shouted: 'Personally. With those hands.'

'With those hands.' Slowly, meaningfully, Andrea examined the four pairs of hands pinioning his arms, then looked contemptuously at Droshny. He said: 'Your courage terrifies me.'

There was a brief and unbelieving silence. The three young sergeants stared at the tableau before them with faces reflecting various degrees of consternation and incredulity. Mallory and Miller looked on impassively. For a moment or two, Droshny looked as if he hadn't heard aright, then his face twisted in savage anger as he struck Andrea back-handed across the face. Immediately a trickle of blood appeared at the right-hand corner of Andrea's mouth but Andrea himself remained unmoving, his face without expression.

Droshny's eyes narrowed. Andrea smiled again, briefly. Droshny struck again, this time with the back of the other hand. The effect was as before, with the exception that this time the trickle of blood came from the left-hand corner of the mouth. Andrea smiled again but to look into his eyes was to look into an open grave. Droshny wheeled and walked away, then halted as he approached Mallory.

'You *are* the leader of those men, Captain Mallory?'

'I am.'

'You're a very—*silent* leader, Captain?'

'What am I to say to a man who turns his guns on his friends and allies?' Mallory looked at him dispassionately. 'I'll talk to your commanding officer, not to a madman.'

Droshny's face darkened. He stepped forward, his arm lifted to strike. Very quickly, but so smoothly and calmly that the movement seemed unhurried, and totally ignoring the two rifle-muzzles pressing into his side, Mallory lifted his Luger and pointed it at Droshny's face. The click of the Luger safety-catch being released came like a hammer-blow in the suddenly unnatural intensity of silence.

And unnatural intensity of silence there was. Except for one little movement, so slow as to be almost imperceptible, both Partisans and parachutists had frozen into a tableau that would have done credit to the frieze on an Ionic temple. The three sergeants, like most of the Partisans, registered astonished incredulity. The two men guarding Mallory looked at Droshny with questioning eyes. Droshny looked at Mallory as if he were mad. Andrea wasn't looking at anyone, while Miller wore that look of world-weary detachment which only he could achieve. But it was Miller who made that one little movement, a movement that now came to an end with his thumb resting on his Schmeisser's safety-release. After a moment or two he removed his thumb: there would come a time for Schmeissers, but this wasn't it.

Droshny lowered his hand in a curious slow-motion gesture and took two paces backwards. His face was still dark with anger, the dark eyes cruel and unforgiving, but he had himself well in hand. He said: 'Don't you know we have to take precautions? Till we are satisfied with your identity?'

'How should I know that?' Mallory nodded at Andrea. 'Next time you tell your men to take precautions with my friend here, you might warn them to stand a little further back. He reacted the only way he knows how. And I know why.'

'You can explain later. Hand over your guns.'

'No.' Mallory returned the Luger to its holster.

'Are you mad? I can take them from you.'

'That's so,' Mallory said reasonably. 'But you'd have to kill us first, wouldn't you? I don't think you'd remain a captain very long, my friend.'

Speculation replaced anger in Droshny's eyes. He gave a sharp order in Serbo-Croat and again his soldiers levelled their guns at Mallory and his five companions. But they made no attempt to remove the prisoners' guns. Droshny turned, ges-

tured and started moving up the steeply-sloping forest floor
again. Droshny wasn't, Mallory reflected, a man likely to be
given to taking too many chances.

For twenty minutes they scrambled awkwardly up the slippery hillside. A voice called out from the darkness ahead and
Droshny answered without breaking step. They passed by two
sentries armed with machine-carbines and, within a minute,
were in Droshny's HQ.

It was a moderately-sized military encampment—if a wide
circle of rough-hewn adze-cut cabins could be called an encampment—set in one of those very deep hollows in the forest
floor that Mallory was to find so characteristic of the Bosnian
area. From the base of this hollow grew two concentric rings
of pines far taller and more massive than anything to be found
in western Europe, massive pines whose massive branches
interlocked eighty to a hundred feet above the ground, forming a snow-shrouded canopy of such impenetrable density
that there wasn't even a dusting of snow on the hard-packed
earth of the camp compound: by the same token, the same
canopy also effectively prevented any upward escape of light:
there was no attempt at any black-out in several illuminated
cabin windows and there were even some oil-lamps suspended
on outside hooks to illuminate the compound itself. Droshny
stopped and said to Mallory:

'You come with me. The rest of you stay here.'

He led Mallory towards the door of the largest hut in the
compound. Andrea, unbidden, slipped off his pack and sat on
it, and the others, after various degrees of hesitation, did the
same. Their guards looked them over uncertainly, then withdrew to form a ragged but watchful semi-circle. Reynolds
turned to Andrea, the expression on his face registering a
complete absence of admiration and goodwill.

'You're crazy.' Reynolds's voice came in a low, furious
whisper. 'Crazy as a loon. You could have got yourself killed.

57

You could have got all of us killed. What are you, shell-shocked or something?'

Andrea did not reply. He lit one of his obnoxious cigars and regarded Reynolds with mild speculation or as near an approach to mildness as it was possible for him to achieve.

'Crazy isn't half the word for it.' Groves, if anything, was even more heated than Reynolds. 'Or didn't you *know* that was a Partisan you killed? Don't you *know* what that means? Don't you *know* people like that must always take precautions?'

Whether he knew or not, Andrea wasn't saying. He puffed at his cigar and transferred his peaceable gaze from Reynolds to Groves.

Miller said soothingly: 'Now, now. Don't be like that. Maybe Andrea *was* a mite hasty but—'

'God help us all,' Reynolds said fervently. He looked at his fellow-sergeants in despair. 'A thousand miles from home and help and saddled with a trigger-happy bunch of has-beens.' He turned back to Miller and mimicked: ' "Don't be like that." '

Miller assumed his wounded expression and looked away.

The room was large and bare and comfortless. The only concession to comfort was a pine fire crackling in a rough hearthplace. The only furniture consisted of a cracked deal table, two chairs and a bench.

Those things Mallory noted only subconsciously. He didn't even register when he heard Droshny say: 'Captain Mallory. This is my commanding officer.' He seemed to be too busy staring at the man seated behind the table.

The man was short, stocky and in his mid-thirties. The deep lines around eyes and mouth could have been caused by weather or humour or both: just at that moment he was smiling slightly. He was dressed in the uniform of a captain in the German Army and wore an Iron Cross at his throat.

CHAPTER 4

Friday
0200-0330

The German captain leaned back in his chair and steepled his fingers. He had the air of a man enjoying the passing moment.

'Hauptmann Neufeld, Captain Mallory.' He looked at the places on Mallory's uniform where the missing insignia should have been. 'Or so I assume. You are surprised to see me?'

'I am *delighted* to meet you, Hauptmann Neufeld.' Mallory's astonishment had given way to the beginnings of a long, slow smile and now he sighed in deep relief. 'You just can't imagine *how* delighted.' Still smiling, he turned to Droshny, and at once the smile gave way to an expression of consternation. 'But who *are* you? Who is this man, Hauptmann Neufeld? Who in the name of God are those men out there? They must be—they must be—'

Droshny interrupted heavily: 'One of his men killed one of my men tonight.'

'What!' Neufeld, the smile now in turn vanishing from his face, stood abruptly: the backs of his legs sent his chair crashing to the floor. Mallory ignored him, looked again at Droshny.

'*Who are you?* For God's sake, tell me!'

Droshny said slowly: 'They call us Cetniks.'

'Cetniks? Cetniks? What on earth are Cetniks?'

'You will forgive me, Captain, if I smile in weary disbelief.' Neufeld was back on balance again, and his face had assumed a curiously wary impassivity, an expression in which only the eyes were alive: things, Mallory reflected, unpleasant things could happen to people misguided enough to underrate

Hauptmann Neufeld. 'You? The leader of a special mission to this country and you haven't been well enough briefed to know that the Cetniks are our Yugoslav allies?'

'Allies? Ah!' Mallory's face cleared in understanding. 'Traitors? Yugoslav Quislings? Is that it?'

A subterranean rumble came from Droshny's throat and he moved towards Mallory, his right hand closing round the haft of a knife. Neufeld halted him with a sharp word of command and a brief downward-chopping motion of his hand.

'And what do you mean by a special mission?' Mallory demanded. He looked at each man in turn and smiled in wry understanding. 'Oh, we're special mission all right, but not in the way you think. At least, not in the way I think you think.'

'No?' Neufeld's eyebrow-raising technique, Mallory reflected, was almost on a par with Miller's. 'Then why do you think we were expecting you?'

'God only knows,' Mallory said frankly. 'We thought the Partisans were. That's why Droshny's man was killed, I'm afraid.'

'That's why Droshny's man——' Neufeld regarded Mallory with his warily impassive eyes, picked up his chair and sat down thoughtfully. 'I think, perhaps, you had better explain yourself.'

As befitted a man who had adventured far and wide in the West End of London, Miller was in the habit of using a napkin when at meals, and he was using one now, tucked into the top of his tunic, as he sat on his rucksack in the compound of Neufeld's camp and fastidiously consumed some indeterminate goulash from a mess-tin. The three sergeants, seated near by, briefly observed this spectacle with open disbelief, then resumed a low-voiced conversation. Andrea, puffing the inevitable nostril-wrinkling cigar and totally ignoring half-a-dozen watchful and understandably apprehensive guards, strolled un-

concernedly about the compound, poisoning the air wherever
he went. Clearly through the frozen night air came the distant
sound of someone singing a low-voiced accompaniment to
what appeared to be guitar music. As Andrea completed his
circuit of the compound, Miller looked up and nodded in the
direction of the music.

'Who's the soloist?'

Andrea shrugged. 'Radio, maybe.'

'They want to buy a new radio. My trained ear—'

'Listen.' Reynolds's interrupting whisper was tense and urgent. 'We've been talking.'

Miller performed some fancy work with his napkin and said
kindly: 'Don't. Think of the grieving mothers and sweethearts
you'd leave behind you.'

'What do you mean?'

'About making a break for it is what I mean,' Miller said.
'Some other time, perhaps?'

'Why not now?' Groves was belligerent. 'They're off
guard—'

'Are they now.' Miller sighed. 'So young, so young. Take
another look. You don't think Andrea *likes* exercise, do you?'

The three sergeants took another look, furtively, surrep-
titiously, then glanced interrogatively at Andrea.

'Five dark windows,' Andrea said. 'Behind them, five dark
men. With five dark machine-guns.'

Reynolds nodded and looked away.

'Well, now.' Neufeld, Mallory noted, had a great propensity
for steepling his fingers: Mallory had once known a hanging
judge with exactly the same propensity. 'This *is* a most remarkably odd story you have to tell us, my dear Captain Mallory.'

'It is,' Mallory agreed. 'It would have to be, wouldn't it, to
account for the remarkably odd position in which we find ourselves at this moment.'

'A point, a point.' Slowly, deliberately, Neufeld ticked off other points on his fingers. 'You have for some months, you claim, been running a penicillin and drug-running ring in the south of Italy. As an Allied liaison officer you found no difficulty in obtaining supplies from American Army and Air Force bases.'

'We found a little difficulty towards the end,' Mallory admitted.

'I'm coming to that. Those supplies, you also claim, were funnelled through to the Wehrmacht.'

'I wish you wouldn't keep using the word "claim" in that tone of voice,' Mallory said irritably. 'Check with Field-Marshal Kesselring's Chief of Military Intelligence in Padua.'

'With pleasure.' Neufeld picked up a phone, spoke briefly in German and replaced the receiver.

Mallory said in surprise: 'You have a direct line to the outside world? From *this* place?'

'I have a direct line to a hut fifty yards away where we have a very powerful radio transmitter. So. You further claim that you were caught, court-martialled and were awaiting the confirmation of your death sentence. Right?'

'If your espionage system in Italy is all we hear it is, you'll know about it tomorrow,' Mallory said drily.

'Quite, quite. You then broke free, killed your guards and overheard agents in the briefing-room being briefed on a mission to Bosnia.' He did some more finger-steepling. 'You may be telling the truth at that. What did you say their mission was?'

'I didn't say. I didn't really pay attention. It had something to do with locating missing British mission leaders and trying to break your espionage set-up. I'm not sure. We had more important things to think about.'

'I'm sure you had,' Neufeld said distastefully. 'Such as your skins. What happened to your epaulettes, Captain? The medal ribbons? The buttons?'

'You've obviously never attended a British court-martial, Hauptmann Neufeld.'

Neufeld said mildly: 'You could have ripped them off yourself.'

'And then, I suppose, emptied three-quarters of the fuel from the tanks before we stole the plane?'

'Your tanks were only a quarter full?' Mallory nodded. 'And your plane crashed without catching fire?'

'We didn't mean to crash,' Mallory said in weary patience. 'We meant to land. But we were out of fuel—and, as we know now, at the wrong place.'

Neufeld said absently: 'Whenever the Partisans put up landing flares we try a few ourselves—*and* we knew that you—or someone—were coming. No petrol, eh?' Again Neufeld spoke briefly on the telephone, then turned back to Mallory. 'All very satisfactory—if true. There just remains to explain the death of Captain Droshny's man here.'

'I'm sorry about that. It was a ghastly blunder. But surely you can understand. The last thing we wanted was to land among you, to make direct contact with you. We've heard what happens to British parachutists dropping over German territory.'

Neufeld steepled his fingers again. 'There is a state of war. Proceed.'

'Our intention was to land in Partisan territory, slip across the lines and give ourselves up. When Droshny turned his guns on us we thought the Partisans were on to us, that they had been notified that we'd stolen the plane. And that could mean only one thing for us.'

'Wait outside. Captain Droshny and I will join you in a moment.'

Mallory left. Andrea, Miller and the three sergeants were

63

sitting patiently on their rucksacks. From the distance there still came the sound of distant music. For a moment M. 'lory cocked his head to listen to it, then walked across to join the others. Miller patted his lips delicately with his napkin and looked up at Mallory.

'Had a cosy chat?'

'I spun him a yarn. The one we talked about in the plane.' He looked at the three sergeants. 'Any of you speak German?'

All three shook their heads.

'Fine. Forget you speak English too. If you're questioned you know nothing.'

'If I'm not questioned,' Reynolds said bitterly, 'I still don't know anything.'

'All the better,' Mallory said encouragingly. 'Then you can never tell anything, can you?'

He broke off and turned round as Neufeld and Droshny appeared in the doorway. Neufeld advanced and said: 'While we're waiting for some confirmation, a little food and wine, perhaps.' As Mallory had done, he cocked his head and listened to the singing. 'But first of all, you must meet our minstrel boy.'

'We'll settle for just the food and wine,' Andrea said.

'Your priorities are wrong. You'll see. Come.'

The dining-hall, if it could be dignified by such a name, was about forty yards away. Neufeld opened the door to reveal a crude and makeshift hut with two rickety trestle tables and four benches set on the earthen floor. At the far end of the room the inevitable pine fire burnt in the inevitable stone hearth-place. Close to the fire, at the end of the farther table, three men—obviously, from their high-collared coats and guns propped by their sides, some kind of temporarily off-duty guards—were drinking coffee and listening to the quiet singing coming from a figure seated on the ground by the fire.

The singer was dressed in a tattered anorak type jacket, an even more incredibly tattered pair of trousers and a pair of knee boots that gaped open at almost every possible seam. There was little to be seen of his face other than a mass of dark hair and a large pair of rimmed dark spectacles.

Beside him, apparently asleep with her head on his shoulder, sat a girl. She was clad in a high-collared British Army greatcoat in an advanced state of dilapidation, so long that it completely covered her tucked-in legs. The uncombed platinum hair spread over her shoulders would have done justice to any Scandinavian, but the broad cheekbones, dark eyebrows and long dark lashes lowered over very pale cheeks were unmistakably Slavonic.

Neufeld advanced across the room and stopped by the fireside. He bent over the singer and said: 'Petar, I want you to meet some friends.'

Petar lowered his guitar, looked up, then turned and touched the girl on the arm. Instantly, the girl's head lifted and her eyes, great dark sooty eyes, opened wide. She had the look, almost, of a hunted animal. She glanced around her, almost wildly, then jumped quickly to her feet, dwarfed by the greatcoat which reached almost to her ankles, then reached down to help the guitarist to his feet. As he did so, he stumbled: he was obviously blind.

'This is Maria,' Neufeld said. 'Maria, this is Captain Mallory.'

'Captain Mallory.' Her voice was soft and a little husky: she spoke in almost accentless English. 'You are English, Captain Mallory?'

It was hardly, Mallory thought, the time or the place for proclaiming his New Zealand ancestry. He smiled. 'Well, sort of.'

Maria smiled in turn. 'I've always wanted to meet an Englishman.' She stepped forward towards Mallory's outstretched

65

hand, brushed it aside and struck him, open-handed and with all her strength, across the face.

'Maria!' Neufeld stared at her. 'He's on our side.'

'An Englishman *and* a traitor!' She lifted her hand again but the swinging arm was suddenly arrested in Andrea's grip. She struggled briefly, futilely, then subsided, dark eyes glowing in an angry face. Andrea lifted his free hand and rubbed his own cheek in fond recollection.

He said admiringly: 'By heavens, she reminds me of my own Maria,' then grinned at Mallory. 'Very handy with their hands, those Yugoslavs.'

Mallory rubbed his cheek ruefully with his hand and turned to Neufeld. 'Perhaps Petar—that's his name—'

'No.' Neufeld shook his head definitely. 'Later. Let's eat now.' He led the way across to the table at the far end of the room, gestured the others to seats, sat down himself and went on: 'I'm sorry. That was my fault. I should have known better.'

Miller said delicately: 'Is she—um—all right?'

'A wild animal, you think?'

'She'd make a rather dangerous pet, wouldn't you say?'

'She's a graduate of the University of Belgrade. Languages. With honours, I'm told. Some time after graduation she returned to her home in the Bosnian mountains. She found her parents and two small brothers butchered. She—well, she's been like this ever since.'

Mallory shifted in his seat and looked at the girl. Her eyes, dark and unmoving and unwinking, were fixed on him and their expression was less than encouraging. Mallory turned back to Neufeld.

'Who did it? To her parents, I mean.'

'The Partisans,' Droshny said savagely. 'Damn their black souls, the Partisans. Maria's people were our people. Cetniks.'

'And the singer?' Mallory asked.

66

'Her elder brother.' Neufeld shook his head. 'Blind from birth. Wherever they go, she leads him by the hand. She is his eyes: she is his life.'

They sat in silence until food and wine were brought in. If an army marched on its stomach, Mallory thought, this one wasn't going to get very far: he had heard that the food situation with the Partisans was close to desperate, but, if this were a representative sample, the Cetniks and Germans appeared to be in little better case. Unenthusiastically, he spooned—it would have been impossible to use a fork—a little of the greyish stew, a stew in which little oddments of indefinable meat floated forlornly in a mushy gravy of obscure origin, glanced across at Andrea and marvelled at the gastronomic fortitude that lay behind the already almost empty plate. Miller averted his eyes from the plate before him and delicately sipped the rough red wine. The three sergeants, so far, hadn't even looked at their food: they were too occupied in looking at the girl by the fireside. Neufeld saw their interest, and smiled.

'I do agree, gentlemen, that I've never seen a more beautiful girl and heaven knows what she'd look like if she had a wash. But she's not for you, gentlemen. She's not for any man. She's wed already.' He looked at the questioning faces and shook his head. 'Not to any man. To an ideal—if you can call death an ideal. The death of the Partisans.'

'Charming,' Miller murmured. There was no other comment, for there was none to make. They ate in a silence broken only by the soft singing from the fireside, the voice was melodious enough, but the guitar sounded sadly out of tune. Andrea pushed away his empty plate, looked irritably at the blind musician and turned to Neufeld.

'What's that he's singing?'

'An old Bosnian love-song, I've been told. Very old and very sad. In English you have it too.' He snapped his fingers, 'Yes, that's it. "The girl I left behind me".'

67

'Tell him to sing something else,' Andrea muttered. Neufeld looked at him, puzzled, then looked away as a German sergeant entered and bent to whisper in his ear. Neufeld nodded and the sergeant left.

'So.' Neufeld was thoughtful. 'A radio report from the patrol that found your plane. The tanks *were* empty. I hardly think we need await confirmation from Padua, do you, Captain Mallory?'

'I don't understand.'

'No matter. Tell me, have you ever heard of a General Vukalovic?'

'General which?'

'Vukalovic.'

'He's not on our side,' Miller said positively. 'Not with a name like that.'

'You must be the only people in Yugoslavia who *don't* know him. Everybody else does. Partisans, Cetniks, Germans, Bulgarians, everyone. He is one of their national heroes.'

'Pass the wine,' Andrea said.

'You'd do better to listen.' Neufeld's tone was sharp. 'Vukalovic commands almost a division of Partisan infantry who have been trapped in a loop of the Neretva river for almost three months. Like the men he leads, Vukalovic is insane. They have no shelter, none. They are short of weapons, have almost no ammunition left and are close to starvation. Their army is dressed in rags. They are finished.'

'Then why don't they escape?' Mallory asked.

'Escape is impossible. The precipices of the Neretva cut them off to the east. To the north and west are impenetrable mountains. The only conceivable way out is to the south, over the bridge at Neretva. And we have two armoured divisions waiting there.'

'No gorges?' Mallory asked. 'No passes through the mountains?'

'Two. Blocked by our best combat troops.'

'Then why don't they give up?' Miller asked reasonably. 'Has no one told them the rules of war?'

'They're insane, I tell you,' Neufeld said. 'Quite insane.'

At that precise moment in time, Vukalovic and his Partisans were proving to some other Germans just how extraordinary their degree of insanity was.

The Western Gap was a narrow, tortuous, boulder-strewn and precipitously walled gorge that afforded the only passage through the impassable mountains that shut off the Zenica Cage to the east. For three months now German infantry units —units which had recently included an increasing number of highly-skilled Alpine troops—had been trying to force the pass: for three months they had been bloodily repulsed. But the Germans never gave up trying and on this intensely cold night of fitful moonlight and gently, intermittently falling snow, they were trying again.

The Germans carried out their attack with the coldly professional skill and economy of movement born of long and harsh experience. They advanced up the gorge in three fairly even and judiciously spaced lines: the combination of white snow-suits, of the utilization of every scrap of cover and of confining their brief forward rushes to those moments when the moon was temporarily obscured made it almost impossible to see them. There was, however, no difficulty in locating them: they had obviously ammunition and to spare for machine-pistols and rifles alike and the fire-flashes from those muzzles were almost continuous. Almost as continuous, but some distance behind them, the sharp flat cracks of fixed mountain pieces pin-pointed the source of the creeping artillery barrage that preceded the Germans up the boulder-strewn slope of that narrow defile.

The Yugoslav Partisans waited at the head of the gorge, entrenched behind a redoubt of boulders, hastily piled stones and splintered tree-trunks that had been shattered by German artillery fire. Although the snow was deep and the east wind full of little knives, few of the Partisans wore greatcoats. They were clad in an extraordinary variety of uniforms, uniforms that had belonged in the past to members of British, German, Italian, Bulgarian and Yugoslav armies: the one identifying feature that all had in common was a red star sewn on to the right-hand side of their forage caps. The uniforms, for the most part, were thin and tattered, offering little protection against the piercing cold, so that the men shivered almost continuously. An astonishing proportion of them appeared to be wounded: there were splinted legs, arms in slings and bandaged heads everywhere. But the most common characteristic among this rag-tag collection of defenders was their pinched and emaciated faces, faces where the deeply etched lines of starvation were matched only by the calm and absolute determination of men who have no longer anything to lose.

Near the centre of the group of defenders, two men stood in the shelter of the thick bole of one of the few pines still left standing. The silvered black hair, the deeply trenched—and now even more exhausted—face of General Vukalovic was unmistakable. But the dark eyes glowed as brightly as ever as he bent forward to accept a cigarette and light from the officer sharing his shelter, a swarthy, hook-nosed man with at least half of his black hair concealed under a blood-stained bandage. Vukalovic smiled.

'Of course I'm insane, my dear Stephan. You're insane—or you would have abandoned this position weeks ago. We're all insane. Didn't you know?'

'I know this.' Major Stephan rubbed the back of his hand across a week-old growth of beard. 'Your parachute landing, an hour ago. That was insane. Why, you—' He broke off as a rifle fired only feet away, moved across to where a thin youngster, not more than seventeen years of age, was peering down into the white gloom of the gorge over the sights of a Lee-Enfield. 'Did you get him?'

The boy twisted and looked up. A child, Vukalovic thought despairingly, no more than a child: he should still have been at school. The boy said: 'I'm not sure, sir.'

'How many shells have you left. Count them.'

'I don't have to. Seven.'

'Don't fire till you are sure.' Stephan turned back to Vukalovic. 'God above, General, you were almost blown into German hands.'

'I'd have been worse off without the parachute,' Vukalovic said mildly.

'There's so little time.' Stephan struck a clenched fist against a palm. 'So little time left. You were crazy to come back. They need you far more—' He stopped abruptly, listened for a fraction of a second, threw himself at Vukalovic and brought them both crashing heavily to the ground as a whining mortar shell buried itself among loose rocks a few feet away, exploding on impact. Close by, a man screamed in agony. A second mortar shell landed, then a third and a fourth, all within thirty feet of one another.

'They've got the range now, damn them.' Stephan rose quickly to his feet and peered down the gorge. For long seconds he could see nothing, for a band of dark cloud had crossed the face of the moon: then the moon broke through and he could see the enemy all too clearly. Because of some almost certainly prearranged signal, they were no longer making any attempt to seek cover: they were pounding straight up the slope with all the speed they could muster, machine-carbines and rifles at the ready in their hands—and as soon as the moon broke through they squeezed the triggers of those guns. Stephan threw himself behind the shelter of a boulder.

71

'Now!' he shouted. 'Now!'

The first ragged Partisan fusillade lasted for only a few seconds, then a black shadow fell over the valley. The firing ceased.

'Keep firing,' Vukalovic shouted. 'Don't stop now. They're closing in.' He loosed off a burst from his own machine-pistol and said to Stephan, 'They know what they are about, our friends down there.'

'They should.' Stephan armed a stick grenade and spun it down the hill. 'Look at all the practice we've given them.'

The moon broke through again. The leading German infantry were no more than twenty-five yards away. Both sides exchanged hand-grenades, fired at point-blank range. Some German soldiers fell, but many more came on, flinging themselves on the redoubt. Matters became temporarily confused. Here and there bitter hand-to-hand fighting developed. Men shouted at each other, cursed each other, killed each other. But the redoubt remained unbroken. Suddenly, dark heavy clouds again rolled over the moon, darkness flooded the gorge and everything slowly fell quiet. In the distance the thunder of artillery and mortar fire fell away to a muted rumble, then finally died.

'A trap?' Vukalovic said softly to Stephan. 'You think they will come again?'

'Not tonight.' Stephan was positive. 'They're brave men, but—'

'But not insane?'

'But not insane.'

Blood poured down over Stephan's face from a re-opened wound in his face, but he was smiling. He rose to his feet and turned as a burly sergeant came up and delivered a sketchy salute.

'They've gone, Major. We lost seven of ours this time, and fourteen wounded.'

'Set pickets two hundred metres down,' Stephan said. 'He turned to Vukalovic. 'You heard, sir? Seven dead. Fourteen hurt.'

'Leaving how many?'

'Two hundred. Perhaps two hundred and five.'

'Out of four hundred.' Vukalovic's mouth twisted. 'Dear God, out of four hundred.'

'And sixty of those are wounded.'

'At least you can get them down to the hospital now.'

'There is no hospital,' Stephan said heavily. 'I didn't have time to tell you. It was bombed this morning. Both doctors killed. All our medical supplies—poof! Like that.'

'Gone? All gone?' Vukalovic paused for a long moment. 'I'll have some sent up from HQ. The walking wounded can make their own way to HQ.'

'The wounded won't leave, sir. Not any more.'

Vukalovic nodded in understanding and went on: 'How much ammunition?'

'Two days. Three, if we're careful.'

'Sixty wounded.' Vukalovic shook his head in slow disbelief. 'No medical help whatsoever for them. Ammunition almost gone. No food. No shelter. And they won't leave. Are they insane, too?'

'Yes, sir.'

'I'm going down to the river,' Vukalovic said. 'To see Colonel Lazlo at HQ.'

'Yes, sir.' Stephan smiled faintly. 'I doubt if you'll find his mental equilibrium any better than mine.'

'I don't suppose I will,' Vukalovic said.

Stephan saluted and turned away, mopping blood from his face, walked a few short swaying steps then knelt down to comfort a badly wounded man. Vukalovic looked after him

73

expressionlessly, shaking his head: then he, too, turned and left.

Mallory finished his meal and lit a cigarette. He said. 'So what's going to happen to the Partisans in the Zenica Cage, as you call it?'

'They're going to break out,' Neufeld said. 'At least, they're going to try to.'

'But you've said yourself that's impossible.'

'Nothing is too impossible for those mad Partisans to try. I wish to heaven,' Neufeld said bitterly, 'that we were fighting a normal war against normal people, like the British or Americans. Anyway, we've had information—reliable information—that an attempted break-out is imminent. Trouble is, there are those two passes—they might even try to force the bridge at Neretva—and we don't know where the break-out is coming.'

'This is very interesting.' Andrea looked sourly at the blind musician who was still giving his rendering of the same old Bosnian love-song. 'Can we get some sleep, now?'

'Not tonight, I'm afraid.' Neufeld exchanged a smile with Droshny. '*You* are going to find out for us where this break-out is coming.'

'We are?' Miller drained his glass and reached for the bottle. 'Infectious stuff, this insanity.'

Neufeld might not have heard him. 'Partisan HQ is about ten kilometres from here. You are going to report there as the bona-fide British mission that has lost its way. Then, when you've found out their plans, you tell them that you are going to their main HQ at Drvar, which, of course, you don't. You come back here instead. What could be simpler?'

'Miller's right,' Mallory said with conviction. 'You *are* mad.'

'I'm beginning to think there's altogether too much talk of

this madness.' Neufeld smiled. 'You would prefer, perhaps, that Captain Droshny here turned you over to his men. I assure you, they are most unhappy about their—ah—late comrade.'

'You can't ask us to do this!' Mallory was hard-faced in anger. 'The Partisans are bound to get a radio message about us. Sooner or later. And then—well, you know what then. You just can't ask this of us.'

'I can and I will.' Neufeld looked at Mallory and his five companions without enthusiasm. 'It so happens that I don't care for dope-peddlers and drug-runners.'

'I don't think your opinion will carry much weight in certain circles,' Mallory said.

'And that means?'

'Kesselring's Director of Military Intelligence isn't going to like this at all.'

'If you don't come back, they'll never know. If you do—' Neufeld smiled and touched the Iron Cross at his throat—'they'll probably give me an oak leaf to this.'

'Likeable type, isn't he?' Miller said to no one in particular.

'Come, then.' Neufeld rose from the table. 'Petar?'

The blind singer nodded, slung his guitar over his shoulder and rose to his feet, his sister rising with him.

'What's this, then?' Mallory asked.

'Guides.'

'*Those* two?'

'Well,' Neufeld said reasonably, 'you can't very well find your own way there, can you? Petar and his sister—well, his sister—know Bosnia better than the foxes.'

'But won't the Partisans—' Mallory began, but Neufeld interrupted.

'You don't know your Bosnia. These two wander wherever they like and no one will turn them from their door. The Bosnians believe, and God knows with sufficient reason, that they are accursed and have the evil eye on them. This is a land of superstition, Captain Mallory.'

'But—but how will they know where to take us?'

'They'll know.' Neufeld nodded to Droshny, who talked rapidly to Maria in Serbo-Croat: she in turn spoke to Petar, who made some strange noises in his throat.

'That's an odd language,' Miller observed.

'He's got a speech impediment,' Neufeld said shortly. 'He was born with it. He can sing, but not talk—it's not unknown. Do you wonder people think they are cursed?' He turned to Mallory. 'Wait outside with your men.'

Mallory nodded, gestured to the others to precede him. Neufeld, he noted, was immediately engaged in a short, low-voiced discussion with Droshny, who nodded, summoned one of his Cetniks and dispatched him on some errand. Once outside, Mallory moved with Andrea slightly apart from the others and murmured something in his ear, inaudible to all but Andrea, whose nodded acquiescence was almost imperceptible.

Neufeld and Droshny emerged from the hut, followed by Maria who was leading Petar by the hand. As they approached Mallory's group, Andrea walked casually towards them, smoking the inevitable noxious cigar. He planted himself in front of a puzzled Neufeld and arrogantly blew smoke into his face.

'I don't think I care for you very much, Hauptmann Neufeld,' Andrea announced. He looked at Droshny. 'Nor for the cutlery salesman here.'

Neufeld's face immediately darkened, became tight in anger. But he brought himself quickly under control and said with restraint: 'Your opinion of me is of no concern to me.' He nodded to Droshny. 'But do not cross Captain Droshny's path, my friend. He is a Bosnian and a proud one—and the best man in the Balkans with a knife.'

'The best man—' Andrea broke off with a roar of laughter,

76

and blew smoke into Droshny's face. 'A knife-grinder in a comic opera.'

Droshny's disbelief was total but of brief duration. He bared his teeth in a fashion that would have done justice to any Bosnian wolf, swept a wickedly-curved knife from his belt and threw himself on Andrea, the gleaming blade hooking viciously upwards, but Andrea, whose prudence was exceeded only by the extraordinary speed with which he could move his vast bulk, was no longer there when the knife arrived. But his hand was. It caught Droshny's knife wrist as it flashed upwards and almost at once the two big men crashed heavily to the ground, rolling over and over in the snow while they fought for possession of the knife.

So unexpected, so wholly incredible the speed with which the fight had developed from nowhere that, for a few seconds, no one moved. The three young sergeants, Neufeld and the Cetniks registered nothing but utter astonishment. Mallory, who was standing close beside the wide-eyed girl, rubbed his chin thoughtfully while Miller, delicately tapping the ash off the end of his cigarette, regarded the scene with a sort of weary interest.

Almost at the same instant, Reynolds, Groves and two Cetniks flung themselves upon the struggling pair on the ground and tried to pull them apart. Not until Saunders and Neufeld lent a hand did they succeed. Droshny and Andrea were pulled to their feet, the former with contorted face and hatred in his eyes, Andrea calmly resuming the smoking of the cigar which he'd somehow picked up after they had been separated.

'You madman!' Reynolds said savagely to Andrea. 'You crazy maniac. You—you're a bloody psychopath. You'll get us all killed.'

'That wouldn't surprise me at all,' Neufeld said thoughtfully. 'Come. Let us have no more of this foolishness.'

He led the way from the compound, and as he did so they

77

were joined by a group of half-a-dozen Cetniks, whose apparent leader was the youth with the straggling ginger beard and cast to his eye, the first of the Cetniks to greet them when they had landed.

'Who are they and what are they for?' Mallory demanded of Neufeld. 'They're not coming with us.'

'Escort,' Neufeld explained. 'For the first seven kilometres only.'

'Escorts? What would we want with escorts? We're in no danger from you, nor, according to what you say, will we be from the Yugoslav Partisans.'

'We're not worried about you,' Neufeld said drily. 'We're worried about the vehicle that is going to take you most of the way there. Vehicles are very few and very precious in this part of Bosnia—and there are many Partisan patrols about.'

Twenty minutes later, in a now moonless night and with snow falling, they reached a road, a road which was little more than a winding track running through a forested valley floor. Waiting for them there was one of the strangest four-wheeled contraptions Mallory or his companions had ever seen, an incredibly ancient and battered truck which at first sight, from the vast clouds of smoke emanating from it, appeared to be on fire. It was, in fact, a very much pre-war wood-burning truck, of a type at one time common in the Balkans. Miller regarded the smoke-shrouded truck in astonishment and turned to Neufeld.

'You call this a vehicle?'

'You call it what you like. Unless you'd rather walk.'

'Ten kilometres? I'll take my chance on asphyxiation.' Miller climbed in, followed by the others, till only Neufeld and Droshny remained outside.

Neufeld said: 'I shall expect you back before noon.'

'If we ever come back,' Mallory said. 'If a radio message has come through—'

'You can't make an omelette without breaking eggs,' Neufeld said indifferently.

With a great rattling and shaking and emission of smoke and steam, all accompanied by much red-eyed coughing from the canvas-covered rear, the truck jerked uncertainly into motion and moved off slowly along the valley floor, Neufeld and Droshny gazing after it. Neufeld shook his head. 'Such clever little men.'

'Such *very* clever little men,' Droshny agreed. 'But I want the big one, Captain.'

Neufeld clapped him on the shoulder. 'You shall have him, my friend. Well, they're out of sight. Time for you to go.'

Droshny nodded and whistled shrilly between his fingers. There came the distant whirr of an engine starter, and soon an elderly Fiat emerged from behind a clump of pines and approached along the hard-packed snow of the road, its chains clanking violently, and stopped beside the two men. Droshny climbed into the front passenger seat and the Fiat moved off in the wake of the truck.

CHAPTER 5

Friday
0330-0500

For the fourteen people jammed on the narrow side benches under the canvas-hooped roof, the journey could hardly be called pleasurable. There were no cushions on the seats just as there appeared to be a total absence of springs on the vehicle, and the torn and badly fitting hood admitted large quantities of icy night air and eye-smarting smoke in about equal proportions. At least, Mallory thought, it all helped considerably to keep them awake.

Andrea was sitting directly opposite him, seemingly oblivious of the thick choking atmosphere inside the truck, a fact hardly surprising considering that the penetrating power and the pungency of the smoke from the truck was of a lower order altogether than that emanating from the black cheroot clamped between Andrea's teeth. Andrea glanced idly across and caught Mallory's eye. Mallory nodded once, a millimetric motion of the head that would have gone unremarked by even the most suspicious. Andrea dropped his eyes until his gaze rested on Mallory's right hand, lying loosely on his knee. Mallory sat back and sighed, and as he did his right hand slipped until his thumb was pointing directly at the floor. Andrea puffed out another Vesuvian cloud of acrid smoke and looked away indifferently.

For some kilometres the smoke-enshrouded truck clattered and screeched its way along the valley floor, then swung off to the left, on to an even narrower track, and began to climb. Less than two minutes later, with Droshny sitting impassively in the front passenger seat, the pursuing Fiat made a similar turn off.

The slope was now so steep and the spinning driving wheels losing so much traction on the frozen surface of the track that the ancient wood-burning truck was reduced to little more than walking pace. Inside the truck, Andrea and Mallory were as watchful as ever, but Miller and the three sergeants seemed to be dozing off, whether through exhaustion or incipient asphyxiation it was difficult to say. Maria and Petar, hand in hand, appeared to be asleep. The Cetniks, on the other hand, could hardly have been more wide awake, and were making it clear for the first time that the rents and holes in the canvas cover had not been caused by accident: Droshny's six men were now kneeling on the benches with the muzzles of their machine-pistols thrust through the apertures in the canvas. It was clear that the truck was now moving into Partisan territory, or, at least, what passed for no-man's-land in that wild and rugged territory.

The Cetnik furthest forward in the truck suddenly withdrew his face from a gap in the canvas and rapped the butt of his gun against the driver's cab. The truck wheezed to a grateful halt, the ginger-bearded Cetnik jumped down, checked swiftly for any signs of ambush, then gestured the others to disembark, the repeatedly urgent movements of his hand making it clear that he was less than enamoured of the idea of hanging around that place for a moment longer than necessity demanded. One by one Mallory and his companions jumped down on to the frozen snow. Reynolds guided the blind singer down to the ground, then reached up a hand to help Maria as she clambered over the tail-board. Wordlessly, she struck his hand aside and leapt nimbly to the ground: Reynolds stared at her in hurt astonishment.

The truck, Mallory observed, had stopped opposite a small clearing in the forest. Backing and filling and issuing denser clouds of smoke than ever, it used this space to turn around in a remarkably short space of time and clanked its way off down the forest path at a considerably higher speed than it had made the ascent. The Cetniks gazed impassively from the back of the departing truck, made no gesture of farewell.

Maria took Petar's hand, looked coldly at Mallory, jerked her head and set off up a tiny footpath leading at right-angles from the track. Mallory shrugged and set off, followed by the three sergeants. For a moment or two Andrea and Miller remained where they were, gazing thoughtfully at the corner round which the truck had just disappeared. Then they, too, set off, talking in low tones to each other.

The ancient wood-burning truck did not maintain its initial impetus for any lengthy period of time. Less than four hundred yards after rounding the corner which blocked it from the view of Mallory and his companions it braked to a halt. Two Cetniks, the ginger-bearded leader of the escort and another black-bearded man, jumped over the tail-board and moved at once into the protective covering of the forest. The truck rattled off once more, its belching smoke hanging heavily in the freezing night air.

A kilometre further down the track, an almost identical scene was taking place. The Fiat slid to a halt, Droshny scrambled from the passenger's seat and vanished among the pines. The Fiat reversed quickly and moved off down the track.

The track up through the heavily wooded slope was very narrow, very winding: the snow was no longer hard-packed, but soft and deep and making for very hard going. The moon was quite gone now, the snow, gusted into their faces by the east wind, was becoming steadily heavier and the cold was intense. The path frequently arrived at a V-shaped branch but Maria, in the lead with her brother, never hesitated: she knew,

or appeared to know, exactly where she was going. Several
times she slipped in the deep snow, on the last occasion so
heavily that she brought her brother down with her. When it
happened yet again, Reynolds moved forward and took the
girl by the arm to help her. She struck out savagely and drew
her arm away. Reynolds stared at her in astonishment, then
turned to Mallory.

'What the devil's the matter with—I mean, I was only trying
to help—'

'Leave her alone,' Mallory said. 'You're one of them.'

'I'm one of—'

'You're wearing a British uniform. That's all the poor kid
understands. Leave her be.'

Reynolds shook his head uncomprehendingly. He hitched
his pack more securely on his shoulders, glanced back down
the trail, made to move on, then glanced backwards again. He
caught Mallory by the arm and pointed.

Andrea had already fallen thirty yards behind. Weighed
down by his rucksack and Schmeisser and weight of years, he
was very obviously making heavy weather of the climb and was
falling steadily behind by the second. At a gesture and word
from Mallory the rest of the party halted and peered back down
through the driving snow, waiting for Andrea to make up on
them. By this time Andrea was beginning to stumble almost
drunkenly and clutched at his right side as if in pain. Reynolds
looked at Groves: they both looked at Saunders: all three
slowly shook their heads. Andrea came up with them and a
spasm of pain flickered across his face.

'I'm sorry.' The voice was gasping and hoarse. 'I'll be all
right in a moment.'

Saunders hesitated, then advanced towards Andrea. He
smiled apologetically, then reached out a hand to indicate the
rucksack and Schmeisser.

'Come on, Dad. Hand them over.'

For the minutest fraction of a second a flicker of menace, more imagined than seen, touched Andrea's face, then he shrugged off his rucksack and wearily handed it over. Saunders accepted it and tentatively indicated the Schmeisser.

'Thanks.' Andrea smiled wanly. 'But I'd feel lost without it.'

Uncertainly, they resumed their climb, looking back frequently to check on Andrea's progress. Their doubts were well-founded. Within thirty seconds Andrea had stopped, his eyes screwed up and bent almost double in pain. He said, gaspingly: 'I must rest . . . Go on. I'll catch up with you.'

Miller said solicitously: 'I'll stay with you.'

'I don't need anybody to stay with me,' Andrea said surlily. 'I can look after myself.'

Miller said nothing. He looked at Mallory and jerked his head in an uphill direction. Mallory nodded, once, and gestured to the girl. Reluctantly, they moved off, leaving Andrea and Miller behind. Twice, Reynolds looked back over his shoulder, his expression an odd mixture of worry and exasperation: then he shrugged his shoulders and bent his back to the hill.

Andrea, scowling blackly and still clutching his ribs, remained bent double until the last of the party had rounded the nearest uphill corner, then straightened effortlessly, tested the wind with a wetted forefinger, established that it was moving up-trail, produced a cigar, lit it and puffed in deep and obvious contentment. His recovery was quite astonishing, but it didn't appear to astonish Miller, who grinned and nodded downhill. Andrea grinned in return, made a courteous gesture of precedence.

Thirty yards down-trail, at a position which gave them an uninterrupted view of almost a hundred yards of the track below them they moved into the cover of the bole of a giant pine. For about two minutes they stood there, staring downhill and listening intently, then suddenly Andrea nodded, stooped and carefully laid his cigar in a sheltered dried patch of ground behind the bole of the pine.

They exchanged no words: there was need of none. Miller crawled round to the downhill-facing front of the pine and carefully arranged himself in a spread-eagled position in the deep snow, both arms outflung, his apparently sightless face turned up to the falling snow. Behind the pine, Andrea reversed his grip on his Schmeisser, holding it by the barrel, produced a knife from the recesses of his clothing and stuck it in his belt. Both men remained as motionless as if they had died there and frozen solid over the long and bitter Yugoslav winter.

Probably because his spread-eagled form was sunk so deeply in the soft snow as to conceal most of his body, Miller saw the two Cetniks coming quite some time before they saw him. At first they were no more than two shapeless and vaguely ghost-like forms gradually materializing from the falling snow: as they drew nearer, he identified them as the Cetnik escort leader and one of his men.

They were less than thirty yards away before they saw Miller. They stopped, stared, remained motionless for at least five seconds, looked at each other, unslung their machine-pistols and broke into a stumbling uphill run. Miller closed his eyes. He didn't require them any more, his ears gave him all the information he wanted, the closing sound of crunching footsteps in the snow, the abrupt cessation of those, the heavy breathing as a man bent over him.

Miller waited until he could actually feel the man's breath in his face, then opened his eyes. Not twelve inches from his own were the eyes of the ginger-bearded Cetnik. Miller's outflung arms curved upwards and inwards, his sinewy fingers hooked deeply into the throat of the startled man above him.

Andrea's Schmeisser had already reached the limit of its backswing as he stepped soundlessly round the bole of the pine. The black-bearded Cetnik was just beginning to move to help

85

his friend when he caught sight of Andrea from the corner of one eye, and flung up both arms to protect himself. A pair of straws would have served him as well. Andrea grimaced at the sheer physical shock of the impact, dropped the Schmeisser, pulled out his knife and fell upon the other Cetnik still struggling desperately in Miller's stranglehold.

Miller rose to his feet and he and Andrea stared down at the two dead men. Miller looked in puzzlement at the ginger-bearded man, then suddenly stooped, caught the beard and tugged. It came away in his hand, revealing beneath it a clean-shaven face and a scar which ran from the corner of a lip to the chin.

Andrea and Miller exchanged speculative glances, but neither made comment. They dragged the dead men some little way off the path into the concealment of some under-growth. Andrea picked up a dead branch and swept away the drag-marks in the snow and, by the base of the pine, all traces of the encounter: inside the hour, he knew, the brush-marks he had made would have vanished under a fresh covering of snow. He picked up his cigar and threw the branch deep into the woods. Without a backward glance, the two men began to walk briskly up the hill.

Had they given this backward glance, it was barely possible that they might have caught a glimpse of a face peering round the trunk of a tree further downhill. Droshny had arrived at the bend in the track just in time to see Andrea complete his brushing operations and throw the branch away: what the meaning of this might be he couldn't guess.

He waited until Andrea and Miller had disappeared from his sight, waited another two minutes for good measure and safety, then hurried up the track, the expression on his swarthy brigand's face nicely balanced between puzzlement and sus-picion. He reached the pine where the two Cetniks had been ambushed, briefly quartered the area, then followed the line of brush-marks leading into the woods, the puzzlement on his face giving way first to pure suspicion, then the suspicion to complete certainty.

He parted the bushes and peered down at the two Cetniks lying half-buried in a snow-filled gully with that curiously huddled shapelessness that only the dead can achieve. After a few moments he straightened, turned and looked uphill in the direction in which Andrea and Miller had vanished: his face was not pleasant to look upon.

Andrea and Miller made good time up the hill. As they approached one of the innumerable bends in the trail they heard up ahead the sound of a softly-played guitar, curiously muffled and softened in tone by the falling snow. Andrea slowed up, threw away his cigar, bent forward and clutched his ribs. Solicitously, Miller took his arm.

The main party, they saw, was less than thirty yards ahead. They, too, were making slow time: the depth of snow and the increasing slope of the track made any quicker movement impossible. Reynolds glanced back—Reynolds was spending a great deal of his time in looking over his shoulder, he appeared to be in a highly apprehensive state—caught sight of Andrea and Miller and called out to Mallory who halted the party and waited for Andrea and Miller to make up with them. Mallory looked worriedly at Andrea.

'Getting worse?'

'How far to go?' Andrea asked hoarsely.

'Must be less than a mile.'

Andrea said nothing, he just stood there breathing heavily and wearing the stricken look of a sick man contemplating the prospect of another upward mile through deep snow. Saunders, already carrying two rucksacks, approached Andrea diffidently, tentatively. He said: 'It would help, you know, if—'

'I know.' Andrea smiled painfully, unslung his Schmeisser and handed it to Saunders. 'Thanks, son.'

Petar was still softly plucking the strings of his guitar, an indescribably eerie sound in those dark and ghostly pine woods. Miller looked at him and said to Mallory: 'What's the music while we march for?'

'Petar's password, I should imagine.'

'Like Neufeld said? Nobody touches our singing Cetnik?'

'Something like that.'

They moved on up the trail. Mallory let the others pass by until he and Andrea were bringing up the rear. Mallory glanced incuriously at Andrea, his face registering no more than a mild concern for the condition of his friend. Andrea caught his glance and nodded fractionally: Mallory looked away.

Fifteen minutes later they were halted, at gun-point, by three men, all armed with machine-pistols, who simply appeared to have materialized from nowhere, a surprise so complete that not even Andrea could have done anything about it —even if he had had his gun. Reynolds looked urgently at Mallory, who smiled and shook his head.

'It's all right. Partisans—look at the red star on their forage caps. Just outposts guarding one of the main trails.'

And so it proved. Maria talked briefly to one of the soldiers, who listened, nodded and set off up the path, gesturing to the party to follow him. The other two Partisans remained behind, both men crossing themselves as Petar again strummed gently on his guitar. Neufeld, Mallory reflected, hadn't exaggerated about the degree of awed respect and fear in which the blind singer and his sister were held.

They came to Partisan HQ inside another ten minutes, an HQ curiously similar in appearance and choice of location to Hauptmann Neufeld's camp: the same rough circle of crude huts set deep in the same *jamba*—depression—with similar massive pines towering high above. The guide spoke to Maria and she turned coldly to Mallory, the disdain on her face making it very plain how much against the grain it went for her to speak to him at all.

'We are to go to the guest hut. You are to report to the commandant. This soldier will show you.'

The guide beckoned in confirmation. Mallory followed him across the compound to a fairly large, fairly well-lit hut. The guide knocked, opened the door and waved Mallory inside, he himself following.

The commandant was a tall, lean, dark man with that aquiline, aristocratic face so common among the Bosnian mountainmen. He advanced towards Mallory with outstretched hand and smiled.

'Major Broznik, and at your service. Late, late hours, but as you see we are still up and around. Although I must say I did expect you before this.'

'I don't know what you're talking about.'

'You don't know—you *are* Captain Mallory, are you not?'

'I've never heard of him.' Mallory gazed steadily at Broznik, glanced briefly sideways at the guide, then looked back to Broznik again. Broznik frowned for a moment, then his face cleared. He spoke to the guide, who turned and left. Mallory put out his hand.

'Captain Mallory, at your service. I'm sorry about that, Major Broznik, but I insist we must talk alone.'

'You trust no one? Not even in *my* camp?'

'No one.'

'Not even your own men?'

'I don't trust them not to make mistakes. I don't trust myself not to make mistakes. I don't trust *you* not to make mistakes.'

'Please?' Broznik's voice was as cold as his eyes.

'Did you ever have two of your men disappear, one with ginger hair, the other with black, the ginger-haired man with a cast to his eye and a scar running from mouth to chin?'

Broznik came closer. 'What do you know about those men?'

'Did you? Know them, I mean?'

Broznik nodded and said slowly: 'They were lost in action. Last month.'

'You found their bodies?'

'No.'

'There were no bodies to be found. They had deserted—gone over to the Cetniks.'

'But they *were* Cetniks—converted to our cause.'

'They'd been re-converted. They followed us tonight. On the orders of Captain Droshny. I had them killed.'

'You—had—them—killed?'

'Think, man,' Mallory said wearily. 'If they had arrived here —which they no doubt intended to do a discreet interval after our arrival—we wouldn't have recognized them and you'd have welcomed them back as escaped prisoners. They'd have reported our every movement. Even if we had recognized them after they had arrived here and done something about it, you may have *other* Cetniks here who would have reported back to their masters that we had done away with their watchdogs. So we disposed of them very quietly, no fuss, in a very remote place, then hid them.'

'There are no Cetniks in my command, Captain Mallory.'

Mallory said drily: 'It takes a very clever farmer, Major, to see two bad apples on the top of the barrel and be quite certain that there are none lower down. No chances. None. Ever.' Mallory smiled to remove any offence from his words and went on briskly: 'Now, Major, there's some information that Hauptmann Neufeld wants.'

To say that the guest hut hardly deserved so hospitable a title would have been a very considerable understatement. As a shelter for some of the less-regarded domesticated animals it might have been barely acceptable: as an overnight accommodation for human beings it was conspicuously lacking in what our modern effete European societies regard as the minimum essentials for civilized living. Even the Spartans of ancient Greece would have considered it as too much of a good thing. One rickety trestle table, one bench, a dying fire and lots of hard-packed earthen floor. It fell short of being a home from home.

There were six people in the hut, three standing, one sitting, two stretched out on the lumpy floor. Petar, for once without his sister, sat on the floor, silent guitar clasped in his hands, gazing sightlessly into the fading embers. Andrea, stretched in apparently luxurious ease in a sleeping-bag, peacefully puffed at what, judging from the frequent suffering glances cast in his direction, appeared to be a more than normally obnoxious cigar. Miller, similarly reclining, was reading what appeared to be a slender volume of poetry. Reynolds and Groves, unable to sleep, stood idly by the solitary window, gazing out abstractedly into the dimly-lit compound: they turned as Saunders removed his radio transmitter from its casing and made for the door.

With some bitterness Saunders said: 'Sleep well.'

'Sleep well?' Reynolds raised an eyebrow. 'And where are you going?'

'Radio hut across there. Message to Termoli. Mustn't spoil your beauty sleep when I'm transmitting.'

Saunders left. Groves went and sat by the table, cradling a weary head in his hands. Reynolds remained by the window, watched Saunders cross the compound and enter a darkened hut on the far side. Soon a light appeared in the window as Saunders lit a lamp.

Reynolds's eyes moved in response to the sudden appearance of an oblong of light across the compound. The door to Major Broznik's hut had opened and Mallory stood momentarily framed there, carrying what appeared to be a sheet of paper in

91

his hand. Then the door closed and Mallory moved off in the direction of the radio hut.

Reynolds suddenly became very watchful, very still. Mallory had taken less than a dozen steps when a dark figure detached itself from the even darker shadow of a hut and confronted him. Quite automatically, Reynolds's hand reached for the Luger at his belt, then slowly withdrew. Whatever this confrontation signified for Mallory it certainly wasn't danger, for Maria, Reynolds knew, did not carry a gun. And unquestionably it was Maria who was now in such apparent close conversation with Mallory.

Bewildered now, Reynolds pressed his face close against the glass. For almost two minutes he stared at this astonishing spectacle of the girl who had slapped Mallory with such venom, who had lost no opportunity of displaying an animosity bordering on hatred, now talking to him not only animatedly but also clearly very amicably. So total was Reynolds's baffled incomprehension at this inexplicable turn of events that his mind moved into a trance-like state, a spell that was abruptly snapped when he saw Mallory put a reassuring arm around her shoulder and pat her in a way that might have been comforting or affectionate or both but which in any event clearly evoked no resentment on the part of the girl. This was still inexplicable: but the only interpretation that could be put upon it was an uncompromisingly sinister one. Reynolds whirled round and silently and urgently beckoned Groves to the window. Groves rose quickly, moved to the window and looked out, but by the time he had done so there was no longer any sign of Maria: Mallory was alone, walking across the compound towards the radio hut, the paper still in his hand. Groves glanced questioningly at Reynolds.

'They were together,' Reynolds whispered. 'Mallory and Maria. I saw them! They were talking?'

'What? You sure?'

'God's my witness. I *saw* them, man. He even had his arm around—Get away from this window—Maria's coming.'

Without haste, so as to arouse no comment from Andrea or Miller, they turned and walked unconcernedly towards the table and sat down. Seconds later, Maria entered and, without looking at or speaking to anyone, crossed to the fire, sat by Petar and took his hand. A minute or so later Mallory entered, and sat on a palliasse beside Andrea, who removed his cigar and glanced at him in mild enquiry. Mallory casually checked to see that he wasn't under observation, then nodded. Andrea returned to the contemplation of his cigar.

Reynolds looked uncertainly at Groves, then said to Mallory: 'Shouldn't we be setting a guard, sir?'

'A guard?' Mallory was amused. 'Whatever for? This is a Partisan camp, Sergeant. Friends, you know. And, as you've seen, they have their own excellent guard system.'

'You never know—'

'*I* know. Get some sleep.'

Reynolds went on doggedly: 'Saunders is alone over there. I don't like—'

'He's coding and sending a short message for me. A few minutes, that's all.'

'But—'

'Shut up,' Andrea said. 'You heard the captain?'

Reynolds was by now thoroughly unhappy and uneasy, an unease which showed through in his instantly antagonistic irritation.

'Shut up? Why should I shut up? I don't take orders from you. And while we're telling each other what to do, you might put out that damned stinking cigar.'

Miller wearily lowered his book of verse.

'I quite agree about the damned cigar, young fellow. But do bear in mind that you are talking to a ranking colonel in the army.'

93

Miller reverted to his book. For a few moments Reynolds and Groves stared open-mouthed at each other, then Reynolds stood up and looked at Andrea.

'I'm extremely sorry, sir. I—I didn't realize—'

Andrea waved him to silence with a magnanimous hand and resumed his communion with his cigar. The minutes passed in silence. Maria, before the fire, had her head on Petar's shoulder, but otherwise had not moved: she appeared to be asleep. Miller shook his head in rapt admiration of what appeared to be one of the more esoteric manifestations of the poetic muse, closed his book reluctantly and slid down into his sleeping-bag. Andrea ground out his cigar and did the same. Mallory seemed to be already asleep. Groves lay down and Reynolds, leaning over the table, rested his forehead on his arms. For five minutes, perhaps longer, Reynolds remained like this, uneasily dozing off, then he lifted his head, sat up with a jerk, glanced at his watch, crossed to Mallory and shook him by the shoulder. Mallory stirred.

'Twenty minutes,' Reynolds said urgently. 'Twenty minutes and Saunders isn't back yet.'

'All right, so it's twenty minutes,' Mallory said patiently. 'He could take that long to make contact, far less transmit the message.'

'Yes, sir. Permission to check, sir?'

Mallory nodded wearily and closed his eyes. Reynolds picked up his Schmeisser, left the hut and closed the door softly behind him. He released the safety-catch on his gun and ran across the compound.

The light still burned in the radio hut. Reynolds tried to peer through the window but the frost of that bitter night had made it completely opaque. Reynolds moved around to the door. It was slightly ajar. He set his finger to the trigger and opened the door in the fashion in which all Commandos were trained to open doors—with a violent kick of his right foot.

There was no one in the radio hut, no one, that is, who could bring him to any harm. Slowly, Reynolds lowered his gun and walked in in a hesitant, almost dream-like fashion, his face masked in shock.

Saunders was leaning tiredly over the transmitting table, his head resting on it at an unnatural angle, both arms dangling limply towards the ground. The hilt of a knife protruded between his shoulder-blades: Reynolds noted, almost subconsciously, that there was no trace of blood: death had been instantaneous. The transmitter itself lay on the floor, a twisted and mangled mass of metal that was obviously smashed beyond repair. Tentatively, not knowing why he did so, he reached out and touched the dead man on the shoulder: Saunders seemed to stir, his cheek slid along the table and he toppled to one side, falling heavily across the battered remains of the transmitter. Reynolds stooped low over him. Grey parchment now, where a bronzed tan had been, sightless, faded eyes uselessly guarding a mind now flown. Reynolds swore briefly, bitterly, straightened and ran from the hut.

Everyone in the guest hut was asleep, or appeared to be. Reynolds crossed to where Mallory lay, dropped to one knee and shook him roughly by the shoulder. Mallory stirred, opened weary eyes and propped himself up on one elbow. He gave Reynolds a look of unenthusiastic enquiry.

'Among friends, you said!' Reynolds voice was low, vicious, almost a hissing sound. 'Safe, you said. Saunders will be all right, you said. You *knew*, you said. You bloody well knew.'

Mallory said nothing. He sat up abruptly on his palliasse, and the sleep was gone from his eyes. He said: 'Saunders?'

Reynolds said: 'I think you'd better come with me.'

In silence the two men left the hut, in silence they crossed the deserted compound and in silence they entered the radio hut. Mallory went no further than the doorway. For what was

95

probably no more than ten seconds but for what seemed to Reynolds to be an unconscionably long time, Mallory stared at the dead man and the smashed transmitter, his eyes bleak, his face registering no emotional reaction. Reynolds mistook the expression, or lack of it, for something else, and could suddenly no longer contain his pent-up fury.

'Well, aren't you bloody well going to do something about it instead of standing there all night?'

'Every dog's entitled to his one bite,' Mallory said mildly. 'But don't talk to me like that again. Do what, for instance?'

'Do what?' Reynolds visibly struggled for his self-control. 'Find the nice gentleman who did this.'

'Finding him will be very difficult.' Mallory considered. 'Impossible, I should say. If the killer came from the camp here, then he'll have gone to earth in the camp here. If he came from outside, he'll be a mile away by this time and putting more distance between himself and us every second. Go and wake Andrea and Miller and Groves and tell them to come here. Then go and tell Major Broznik what's happened.'

'I'll tell them what's happened,' Reynolds said bitterly. 'And I'll also tell them it never *would* have happened if you'd listened to me. But oh no, you wouldn't listen, would you?'

'So you were right and I was wrong. Now do as I ask you.'

Reynolds hesitated, a man obviously on the brink of outright revolt. Suspicion and defiance alternated in the angry face. Then some strange quality in the expression in Mallory's face tipped the balance for sanity and compliance and he nodded in sullen antagonism, turned and walked away.

Mallory waited until he had rounded the corner of the hut, brought out his torch and started, not very hopefully, to quarter the hard-packed snow outside the door of the radio hut. But almost at once he stopped, stooped, and brought the head of the torch close to the surface of the ground.

It was a very small portion of footprint indeed, only the

front half of the sole of a right foot. The pattern showed two
V-shaped marks, the leading V with a cleanly-cut break in it.
Mallory, moving more quickly now, followed the direction
indicated by the pointed toe-print and came across two more
similar indentations, faint but unmistakable, before the frozen
snow gave way to the frozen earth of the compound, ground
so hard as to be incapable of registering any footprints at all.
Mallory retraced his steps, carefully erasing all three prints
with the toe of his boot and reached the radio hut only seconds
before he was joined by Reynolds, Andrea, Miller and Groves.
Major Broznik and several of his men joined them soon after.

They searched the interior of the radio hut for clues as to
the killer's identity, but clues there were none. Inch by inch
they searched the hard-packed snow surrounding the hut, with
the same completely negative results. Reinforced, by this time,
by perhaps sixty or seventy sleepy-eyed Partisan soldiers, they
carried out a simultaneous search of all the buildings and of the
woods surrounding the encampment: but neither the encampment nor the surrounding woods had any secrets to yield.

'We may as well call it off,' Mallory said finally. 'He's got
clean away.'

'It looks that way,' Major Broznik agreed. He was deeply
troubled and bitterly angry that such a thing should have happened in his encampment. 'We'd better double the guards for
the rest of the night.'

'There's no need for that,' Mallory said. 'Our friend won't
be back.'

'There's no need for that,' Reynolds mimicked savagely.
'There was no need for that for poor Saunders, you said. And
where's Saunders now? Sleeping comfortably in his bed? Is he
hell! No need—'

Andrea muttered warningly and took a step nearer Reynolds,
but Mallory made a brief conciliatory movement of his right
hand. He said: 'It's entirely up to you, of course, Major. I'm

97

sorry that we have been responsible for giving you and your men so sleepless a night. See you in the morning.' He smiled wryly. 'Not that that's so far away.' He turned to go, found his way blocked by Sergeant Groves, a Groves whose normally cheerful countenance now mirrored the tight hostility of Reynolds's.

'So he's got clear away, has he? Away to hell and gone. And that's the end of it, eh?'

Mallory looked at him consideringly. 'Well, no. I wouldn't quite say that. A little time. We'll find him.'

'A little time? Maybe even before he dies of old age?'

Andrea looked at Mallory. 'Twenty-four hours?'

'Less.'

Andrea nodded and he and Mallory turned and walked away towards the guest hut. Reynolds and Groves, with Miller slightly behind them, watched the two men as they went, then looked at each other, their faces still bleak and bitter.

'Aren't they a nice warm-hearted couple now? Completely broken up about old Saunders.' Groves shook his head. 'They don't care. They just don't care.'

'Oh, I wouldn't say that,' Miller said diffidently. 'It's just that they don't *seem* to care. Not at all the same thing.'

'Faces like wooden Indians,' Reynolds muttered. 'They never even said they were *sorry* that Saunders was killed.'

'Well,' Miller said patiently, 'it's a cliché, but different people react in different ways. Okay, so grief and anger is the natural reaction to this sort of thing, but if Mallory and Andrea spent their time in reacting in that fashion to all the things that have happened to *them* in their lifetimes, they'd have come apart at the seams years ago. So they don't react that way any more. They *do* things. Like they're going to do things to your friend's killer. Maybe you didn't get it, but you just heard a death sentence being passed.'

'How do *you* know?' Reynolds said uncertainly. He nodded

in the direction of Mallory and Andrea who were just entering the guest hut. 'And how did *they* know? Without talking, I mean.'

'Telepathy.'

'What do you mean—"telepathy"?'

'It would take too long,' Miller said wearily. 'Ask me in the morning.'

CHAPTER 6

Friday
0800-1000

Crowning the tops of the towering pines, the dense, interlocking snow-laden branches formed an almost impenetrable canopy that effectively screened Major Broznik's camp, huddled at the foot of the *jamba*, from all but the most fleeting glimpses of the sky above. Even at high noon on a summer's day, it was never more than a twilit dusk down below: on a morning such as this, an hour after dawn with snow falling gently from an overcast sky, the quality of light was such as to be hardly distinguishable from a starlit midnight. The interior of the dining hut, where Mallory and his company were at breakfast with Major Broznik, was gloomy in the extreme, the darkness emphasized rather than alleviated by the two smoking oil-lamps which formed the only primitive means of illumination.

The atmosphere of gloom was significantly deepened by the behaviour and expression of those seated round the breakfast table. They ate in a moody silence, heads lowered, for the most part not looking at one another: the events of the previous night had clearly affected them all deeply but none so deeply as Reynolds and Groves in whose faces was still unmistakably reflected the shock caused by Saunders's murder. They left their food untouched.

To complete the atmosphere of quiet desperation, it was clear that the reservations held about the standard of the Partisan early-morning cuisine were of a profound and lasting

nature. Served by two young *partisankas*—women members of
Marshal Tito's army—it consisted of *polenta* a highly un-
appetizing dish made from ground corn, and *raki*, a Yugoslav
spirit of unparalleled fierceness. Miller spooned his breakfast
with a marked lack of enthusiasm.

'Well,' he said to no one in particular, 'it makes a change, I'll
say that.'

'It's all we have,' Broznik said apologetically. He laid down
his spoon and pushed his plate away from him. 'And even that
I can't eat. Not this morning. Every entrance to the *jamba* is
guarded, yet there was a killer loose in my camp last night.
But maybe he *didn't* come in past the guards, maybe he was
already inside. Think of it—a traitor in my own camp. And if
there is, I can't even find him. I can't even believe it!'

Comment was superfluous, nothing could be said that hadn't
been said already, nobody as much as looked in Broznik's
direction: his acute discomfort, embarrassment and anger
were apparent to everyone in his tone of voice. Andrea, who
had already emptied his plate with apparent relish, looked at
the two untouched plates in front of Reynolds and Groves and
then enquiringly at the two sergeants themselves, who shook
their heads. Andrea reached out, brought their plates before
him and set to with every sign of undiminished appetite.
Reynolds and Groves looked at him in shocked disbelief,
possibly awed by the catholicity of Andrea's tastes, more probably astonished by the insensitivity of a man who could eat so
heartily only a few hours after the death of one of his comrades.
Miller, for his part, looked at Andrea in near horror, tried
another tiny portion of his *polenta* and wrinkled his nose in
delicate distaste. He laid down his spoon and looked morosely
at Petar who, guitar slung over his shoulder, was awkwardly
feeding himself.

Miller said irritably: 'Does he *always* wear that damned
guitar?'

'Our lost one,' Broznik said softly. 'That's what we call him. Our poor blind lost one. Always he carries it or has it by his side. Always. Even when he sleeps—didn't you notice last night? That guitar means as much to him as life itself. Some weeks ago, one of our men, by way of a joke, tried to take it from him: Petar, blind though he is, almost killed him.'

'He must be stone tone deaf,' Miller said wonderingly. 'It's the most god-awful guitar I ever heard.'

Broznik smiled faintly. 'Agreed. But don't you understand? He can feel it. He can touch it. It's his own. It's the only thing left to him in the world, a dark and lonely and empty world. Our poor lost one.'

'He could at least tune it,' Miller muttered.

'You are a good man, my friend. You try to take our minds off what lies ahead this day. But no man can do that.' He turned to Mallory. 'Any more than you can hope to carry out your crazy scheme of rescuing your captured agents and breaking up the German counter-espionage network here. It is insanity. Insanity!'

Mallory waved a vague hand. 'Here you are. No food. No artillery. No transport. Hardly any guns—and practically no ammunition for those guns. No medical supplies. No tanks. No planes. No hope—and you keep on fighting. That makes you sane?'

'Touché.' Broznik smiled, pushed across the bottle of *raki*, waited until Mallory had filled his glass. 'To the madmen of this world.'

'I've just been talking to Major Stephan up at the Western Gap,' General Vukalovic said. 'He thinks we're all mad. Would you agree, Colonel Lazlo?'

The man lying prone beside Vukalovic lowered his binoculars. He was a burly, sun-tanned, thick-set, middle-aged man with a magnificent black moustache that had every appearance of being waxed. After a moment's consideration, he said: 'Without a doubt, sir.'

'Even you?' Vukalovic said protestingly. 'With a Czech father?'

'He came from the High Tatra,' Lazlo explained. 'They're all mad there.'

Vukalovic smiled, settled himself more comfortably on his elbows, peered downhill through the gap between two rocks, raised his binoculars and scanned the scene to the south of him, slowly raising his glasses as he did so.

Immediately in front of where he lay was a bare, rocky hillside, dropping gently downhill for a distance of about two hundred feet. Beyond its base it merged gradually into a long flat grassy plateau, no more than two hundred yards wide at its maximum, but stretching almost as far as the eye could see on both sides, on the right-hand side stretching away to the west, on the left curving away to the east, north-east and finally north.

Beyond the edge of the plateau, the land dropped abruptly to form the bank of a wide and swiftly flowing river, a river of that peculiarly Alpine greenish-white colour, green from the melting ice-water of spring, white from where it foamed over jagged rocks and overfalls in the bed of the river. Directly to the south of where Vukalovic and Lazlo lay, the river was spanned by a green-and-white-painted and very solidly-constructed cantilevered steel bridge. Beyond the river, the grassy bank on the far side rose in a very easy slope for a distance of about a hundred yards to the very regularly defined limit of a forest of giant pines which stretched away into the southern distance. Scattered through the very outermost of the pines were a few dully metallic objects, unmistakably tanks. In the farthest distance, beyond the river and beyond the pines, towering, jagged mountains dazzled in their brilliant covering of snow and above that again, but more to the south-east, an equally white and dazzling sun shone from an incongruously blue patch in an otherwise snow-cloud-covered sky.

Vukalovic lowered his binoculars and sighed.

'No idea at all how many tanks are across in the woods there?'

'I wish to heaven I knew.' Lazlo lifted his arms in a small, helpless gesture. 'Could be ten. Could be two hundred. We've no idea. We've sent scouts, of course, but they never came back. Maybe they were swept away trying to cross the Neretva.' He looked at Vukalovic, speculation in his eyes. 'Through the Zenica Gap, through the Western Gap or across that bridge there—you don't know where the attack is coming from, do you, sir?'

Vukalovic shook his head.

'But you expect it soon?'

'Very soon.' Vukalovic struck the rocky ground with a clenched fist. 'Is there *no* way of destroying that damned bridge?'

'There have been five RAF attacks,' Lazlo said heavily. 'To date, twenty-seven planes lost—there are two hundred AA guns along the Neretva and the nearest Messerschmitt station only ten minutes flying time away. The German radar picks up the British bombers crossing our coast—and the Messerschmitts are here, waiting, by the time they arrive. And don't forget that the bridge is set in rock on either side.'

'A direct hit or nothing?'

'A direct hit on a target seven metres wide from three thousand metres. It is impossible. And a target so camouflaged that you can hardly see it five hundred metres away on land. Doubly impossible.'

'And impossible for us,' Vukalovic said bleakly.

'Impossible for us. We made our last attempt two nights ago.'

'You made—I told you not to.'

'You *asked* us not to. But of course I, Colonel Lazlo, knew better. They started firing star-shells when our troops were halfway across the plateau, God knows how they knew they were coming. Then the searchlights—'

'Then the shrapnel shells,' Vukalovic finished. 'And the Oerlikons. Casualties?'

'We lost half a battalion.'

'Half a battalion! And tell me, my dear Lazlo, what would have happened in the unlikely event of your men reaching the bridge?'

'They had some amatol blocks, some hand-grenades—'

'No fireworks?' Vukalovic asked in heavy sarcasm. 'That might have helped. That bridge is built of steel set in re-inforced concrete, man! You were mad even to try.'

'Yes, sir,' Lazlo looked away. 'Perhaps you ought to relieve me.'

'I think I should.' Vukalovic looked closely at the exhausted face. 'In fact I would. But for one thing.'

'One thing?'

'All my other regimental commanders are as mad as you are. And if the Germans do attack—maybe even tonight?'

'We stand here. We are Yugoslavs and we have no place to go. What else can we do?'

'What else? Two thousand men with pop-guns, most of them weak and starving and lacking ammunition, against what may perhaps be two first-line German armoured divisions. And you stand here. You could always surrender, you know.'

Lazlo smiled. 'With respect, General, this is no time for facetiousness.'

Vukalovic clapped his shoulder. 'I didn't think it funny, either. I'm going up to the dam, to the north-eastern redoubt. I'll see if Colonel Janzy is as mad as you are. And Colonel?'

'Sir?'

'If the attack comes, I may give the order to retreat.'

'Retreat!'

'Not surrender. Retreat. Retreat to what, one hopes, may be victory.'

'I am sure the General knows what he is talking about.'

'The General isn't.' Oblivious to possible sniper fire from across the Neretva, Vukalovic stood up in readiness to go. 'Ever heard of a man called Captain Mallory. Keith Mallory, a New Zealander?'

'No.' Lazlo said promptly. He paused, then went on: 'Wait a minute, though. Fellow who used to climb mountains?'

'That's the one. But he has also, I'm given to understand, other accomplishments.' Vukalovic rubbed a stubbly chin. 'If all I hear about him is true, I think you could quite fairly call him a rather gifted individual.'

'And what about this gifted individual?' Lazlo asked curiously.

'Just this.' Vukalovic was suddenly very serious, even sombre. 'When all things are lost and there is no hope left, there is always, somewhere in the world, one man you can turn to. There may be only that one man. More often than not there *is* only that one man. But that one man is always there.' He paused reflectively. 'Or so they say.'

'Yes, sir,' Lazlo said politely. 'But about this Keith Mallory—'

'Before you sleep tonight, pray for him. I will.'

'Yes, sir. And about us? Shall I pray for us, too?'

'That,' said Vukalovic, 'wouldn't be at all a bad idea.'

The sides of the *jamba* leading upwards from Major Broznik's camp were very steep and very slippery and the ascending cavalcade of men and ponies were making very heavy going of it. Or most of them were. The escort of dark stocky Bosnian Partisans, to whom such terrain was part and parcel of existence, appeared quite unaffected by the climb: and it in no way appeared to interfere with Andrea's rhythmic puffing of his usual vile-smelling cigar. Reynolds noticed this, a fact which fed fresh fuel to the already dark doubts and torments in his mind.

He said sourly: 'You seem to have made a remarkable recovery in the night-time, Colonel Stavros, sir.'

'Andrea.' The cigar was removed. 'I have a heart condition. It comes and it goes.' The cigar was replaced.

'I'm sure it does,' Reynolds muttered. He glanced suspiciously, and for the twentieth time, over his shoulder. 'Where the hell is Mallory?'

'Where the hell is *Captain* Mallory,' Andrea chided.

'Well, where?'

'The leader of an expedition has many responsibilities,' Andrea said. 'Many things to attend to. Captain Mallory is probably attending to something at this very moment.'

'You can say that again,' Reynolds muttered.

'What was that?'

'Nothing.'

Captain Mallory was, as Andrea had so correctly guessed, attending to something at that precise moment. Back in Broznik's office, he and Broznik were bent over a map spread out on the trestle table. Broznik pointed to a spot near the northern limit of the map.

'I agree. This *is* the nearest possible landing-strip for a plane. But it is very high up. At this time of year there will still be almost a metre of snow up there. There are other places, better places.'

'I don't doubt that for a moment.' Mallory said. 'Faraway fields are always greener, maybe even faraway airfields. But I

107

haven't the time to go to them.' He stabbed his forefinger on the map. 'I want a landing-strip here and only here by nightfall. I'd be most grateful if you'd send a rider to Konjic within the hour and have my request radioed immediately to your Partisan HQ at Drvar.'

Broznik said drily: 'You are accustomed to asking for instant miracles, Captain Mallory?'

'This doesn't call for miracles. Just a thousand men. The feet of a thousand men. A small price for seven thousand lives?' He handed Broznik a slip of paper. 'Wavelength and code. Have Konjic transmit it as soon as possible.' Mallory glanced at his watch. 'They have twenty minutes on me already. I'd better hurry.'

'I suppose you'd better,' Broznik said hurriedly. He hesitated, at a momentary loss for words, then went on awkwardly: 'Captain Mallory, I—I—'

'I know. Don't worry. The Mallorys of this world never make old bones anyway. We're too stupid.'

'Aren't we all, aren't we all?' Broznik gripped Mallory's hand. 'Tonight, I make a prayer for you.'

Mallory remained silent for a moment, then nodded.

'Make it a long one.'

The Bosnian scouts, now, like the remainder of the party, mounted on ponies, led the winding way down through the gentle slopes of the thickly-forested valley, followed by Andrea and Miller riding abreast, then by Petar, whose pony's bridle was in the hand of his sister. Reynolds and Groves, whether by accident or design, had fallen some little way behind and were talking in soft tones.

Groves said speculatively: 'I wonder what Mallory and the Major are talking about back there?'

Reynolds's mouth twisted in bitterness. 'It's perhaps as well we don't know.'

'You may be right at that. I just don't know.' Groves paused, went on almost pleadingly: 'Broznik is on the up-and-up. I'm sure of it. Being what he is, he *must* be.'

'That's as maybe. Mallory too, eh?'

'*He* must be, too.'

'Must?' Reynolds was savage. 'God alive, man, I tell you I saw him with my own eyes.' He nodded towards Maria, some twenty yards ahead, and his face was cruel and hard. 'That girl hit him—and *how* she hit him—back in Neufeld's camp and the next thing I see is the two of them having a cosy little lovey-dovey chat outside Broznik's hut. Odd, isn't it? Soon after, Saunders was murdered. Coincidence, isn't it? I tell you, Groves, Mallory could have done it himself. The girl *could* have had time to do it before she met Mallory—except that it would have been physically impossible for her to drive a six-inch knife home to the hilt. But Mallory could have done it all right. He'd time enough—and opportunity enough—when he handed that damned message into the radio hut.'

Groves said protestingly: 'Why in God's name should he do that?'

'Because Broznik had given him some urgent information. Mallory *had* to make a show of passing this information back to Italy. But maybe sending that message was the last thing he wanted. Maybe he stopped it in the only way he knew how— and smashed the transmitter to make sure no one else could send a message. Maybe that's why he stopped me from mounting a guard or going to see Saunders—to prevent me from discovering the fact that Saunders was already dead—in which case, of course, because of the time factor, suspicion would have automatically fallen on him.'

'You're imagining things.' Despite his discomfort, Groves was reluctantly impressed by Reynolds's reasoning.

109

'You think so? That knife in Saunders's back—did I imagine that too?'

Within half an hour, Mallory had rejoined the party. He jogged past Reynolds and Groves, who studiously ignored him, past Maria and Petar, who did the same, and took up position behind Andrea and Miller.

It was in this order, for almost an hour, that they passed through the heavily-wooded Bosnian valleys. Occasionally, they came to clearings in the pines, clearings that had once been the site of human habitation, small villages or hamlets. But now there were no humans, no habitations, for the villages had ceased to exist. The clearings were all the same, chillingly and depressingly the same. Where the hard-working but happy Bosnians had once lived in their simple but sturdy homes, there were now only the charred and blackened remains of what had once been thriving communities, the air still heavy with the acrid smell of ancient smoke, the sweet-sour stench of corruption and death, mute testimony to the no-quarter viciousness and total ruthlessness of the war between the Germans and the Partisan Yugoslavs. Occasionally, here and there, still stood a few small, stone-built houses which had not been worth the expenditure of bombs or shells or mortars or petrol: but few of the larger buildings had escaped complete destruction. Churches and schools appeared to have been the primary targets: on one occasion, as evidenced by some charred steel equipment that could have come only from an operating theatre, they passed by a small cottage hospital that had been so razed to the ground that no part of the resulting ruins was more than three feet high. Mallory wondered what would have happened to the patients occupying the hospital at the time: but he no longer wondered at the hundreds of thousands of Yugoslavs—350,000 had been the figure quoted by Captain Jensen, but, taking women and children into account, the number must have been at least a million—who had rallied under the banner of Marshal Tito. Patriotism apart, the burning desire for liberation and revenge apart, there was no place else left for them to go. They were a people, Mallory realized, with literally nothing left, with nothing to lose but their lives which they apparently held of small account, but with everything to gain by the destruction of the enemy: were he a German soldier, Mallory reflected, he would not have felt particularly happy about the prospect of a posting to Yugoslavia. It was a war which the Wehrmacht could never win, which the soldiers of no Western European country could ever have won, for the peoples of the high mountains are virtually indestructible.

The Bosnian scouts, Mallory observed, looked neither to left nor right as they passed through the lifeless shattered villages of their countrymen, most of whom were now almost certainly dead. They didn't *have* to look, he realized: they had their memories, and even their memories would be too much for them. If it were possible to feel pity for an enemy, then Mallory at that moment felt pity for the Germans.

By and by they emerged from the narrow winding mountain track on to a narrow, but comparatively wide road, wide enough, at least, for single-file vehicular traffic. The Bosnian scout in the lead threw up his hand and halted his pony.

'Unofficial no-man's-land, it would seem,' Mallory said. 'I think this is where they turfed us off the truck this morning.'

Mallory's guess appeared to be correct. The Partisans wheeled their horses, smiled widely, waved, shouted some unintelligible words of farewell and urged their horses back the way they had come.

With Mallory and Andrea in the lead and the two sergeants bringing up the rear, the seven remaining members of the party moved off down the track. The snow had stopped now, the clouds above had cleared away and the sunlight was filtering

down between the now thinning pines. Suddenly Andrea, who
had been peering to his left, reached out and touched Mallory
on the arm. Mallory followed the direction of Andrea's pointing hand. Downhill, the pines petered out less than a hundred
yards away and through the trees could be glimpsed some
distant object, a startling green in colour. Mallory swung
round in his saddle.

'Down there. I want to take a look. *Don't* move below the
tree-line.'

The ponies picked their delicate sure-footed way down the
steep and slippery slope. About ten yards from the tree-line
and at a signal from Mallory, the riders dismounted and advanced cautiously on foot, moving from the cover of one pine
to the next. The last few feet they covered on hands and knees,
then finally stretched out flat in the partial concealment of the
boles of the lowermost pines. Mallory brought out his binoculars, cleared the cold-clouded lenses and brought them to his
eyes.

The snow-line, he saw, petered out some three or four
hundred yards below them. Below that again was a mixture of
fissured and eroded rock-faces and brown earth and beyond
that again a belt of sparse and discouraged-looking grass.
Along the lower reaches of this belt of grass ran a tarmacadam
road, a road which struck Mallory as being, for that area, in
remarkably good condition: the road was more or less exactly
paralleled, at a distance of about a hundred yards, by a single-
track and extremely narrow-gauge railway: a grass-grown and
rusted line that looked as if it hadn't been used for many years.
Just beyond the line the land dropped in a precipitous cliff to
a narrow winding lake, the further margin of which was marked by far more towering precipices leading up without break
and with hardly any variation in angle to rugged snow-capped
mountains.

From where he lay Mallory was directly overlooking a right-angled bend in the lake, a lake which was almost incredibly beautiful. In the bright clear sparkling sunlight of that spring morning it glittered and gleamed like the purest of emeralds. The smooth surface was occasionally ruffled by errant catspaws of wind, catspaws which had the effect of deepening the emerald colour to an almost translucent aquamarine. The lake itself was nowhere much more than a quarter of a mile in width, but obviously miles in length: the long right-hand arm, twisting and turning between the mountains, stretched to the east almost as far as the eye could see: to the left, the short southern arm, hemmed in by increasingly vertical walls which finally appeared almost to meet overhead, ended against the concrete ramparts of a dam. But what caught and held the attention of the watchers was the incredible mirrored gleam of the far mountains in that equally incredible emerald mirror.

'Well, now,' Miller murmured, 'that *is* nice.' Andrea gave him a long expressionless look, then turned his attention to the lake again.

Groves's interest momentarily overcame his animosity.

'What lake is that, sir?'

Mallory lowered the binoculars. 'Haven't the faintest idea. Maria?' She made no answer. 'Maria! What—lake—is—that?'

'That's the Neretva dam,' she said sullenly. 'The biggest in Yugoslavia.'

'It's important, then?'

'It is important. Whoever controls that controls Central Yugoslavia.'

'And the Germans control it, I suppose?'

'They control it. *We* control it.' There was more than a hint of triumph in her smile. 'We—the Germans—have got it completely sealed off. Cliffs on both sides. To the east there—the upper end—they have a boom across a gorge only ten yards wide. And that boom is patrolled night and day. So is the dam

113

wall itself. The only way in is by a set of steps—ladders, rather —fixed to the cliff face just below the dam.'

Mallory said drily: 'Very interesting information—for a parachute brigade. But we've other and more urgent fish to fry. Come on.' He glanced at Miller, who nodded and began to ease his way back up the slope, followed by the two sergeants, Maria and Petar. Mallory and Andrea lingered for a few moments longer.

'I wonder what it's like,' Mallory murmured.

'What's what like?' Andrea asked.

'The other side of the dam.'

'And the ladder let into the cliff?'

'And the ladder let into the cliff.'

From where General Vukalovic lay, high on a cliff-top on the right-hand or western side of the Neretva gorge, he had an excellent view of the ladder let into the cliff: he had, in fact, an excellent view of the entire outer face of the dam wall and of the gorge which began at the foot of the wall and extended southwards for almost a mile before vanishing from sight round an abrupt right-hand corner.

The dam wall itself was quite narrow, not much more than thirty yards in width, but very deep, stretching down in a slightly V-formation from between overhanging cliff-faces to the greenish-white torrent of water foaming from the outlet pipes at the base. On top of the dam, at the eastern end and on a slight eminence, were the control station and two small huts, one of which, judging from the clearly visible soldiers patrolling the top of the wall, was almost certainly a guard-room. Above those buildings the walls of the gorge rose quite vertically for about thirty feet, then jutted out in a terrifying overhang.

From the control-room, a zig-zag, green-painted iron ladder, secured by brackets to the rock-face, led down to the floor of the gorge. From the base of the ladder a narrow path extended down the gorge for a distance of about a hundred yards, ending abruptly at a spot where some ancient landslide had gouged a huge scar into the side of the gorge. From here a bridge spanned the river to another path on the right-hand bank.

As bridges go, it wasn't much, an obviously very elderly and rickety wooden swing bridge which looked as if its own weight would be enough to carry it into the torrent at any moment: what was even worse, it seemed, at first glance, as if its site had been deliberately picked by someone with an unhinged mind, for it lay directly below an enormous boulder some forty feet up the landslide, a boulder so clearly in a highly precarious state of balance that none but the most foolhardy would have lingered in the crossing of the bridge. In point of fact, no other site would have been possible.

From the western edge of the bridge, the narrow, boulder-strewn path followed the line of the river, passing by what looked like an extremely hazardous ford, and finally curving away from sight with the river.

General Vukalovic lowered his binoculars, turned to the man at his side and smiled.

'All quiet on the eastern front, eh, Colonel Janzy?'

'All quiet on the eastern front,' Janzy agreed. He was a small, puckish, humorous-looking character with a youthful face and incongruous white hair. He twisted round and gazed to the north. 'But not so quiet on the northern front, I'm afraid.'

The smile faded from Vukalovic's face as he turned, lifted his binoculars again and gazed to the north. Less than three miles away and clearly visible in the morning sunlight, lay the heavily wooded Zenica Gap, for weeks a hotly contested strip of territory between Vukalovic's northern defensive forces, under the command of Colonel Janzy, and units of the investing German 11th Army Corps. At that moment frequent puffs

of smoke could be seen, to the left a thick column of smoke
spiralled up to form a dark pall against the now cloudless blue
of the sky, while the distant rattle of small-arms fire, punctuated by the occasional heavier boom of artillery, was almost
incessant. Vukalovic lowered his glasses and looked thoughtfully at Janzy.

'The softening-up before the main attack?'

'What else? The final assault.'

'How many tanks?'

'It's difficult to be sure. Collating reports, my staff estimate
a hundred and fifty.'

'One hundred and fifty!'

'That's what they make it—and at least fifty of those are
Tiger tanks.'

'Let's hope to heaven your staff can't count.' Vukalovic
rubbed a weary hand across his bloodshot eyes: he'd had no
sleep during the night just gone, no sleep during the night
previous to that. 'Let's go and see how many *we* can count.'

Maria and Petar led the way now, with Reynolds and Groves,
clearly in no mood for other company, bringing up the rear
almost fifty yards behind. Mallory, Andrea and Miller rode
abreast along the narrow road. Andrea looked at Mallory, his
eyes speculative.

'Saunders's death? Any idea?'

Mallory shook his head. 'Ask me something else.'

'The message you'd given him to send. What was it?'

'A report of our safe arrival in Broznik's camp. Nothing
more.'

'A psycho,' Miller announced. 'The handy man with the
knife, I mean. Only a psycho would kill for that reason.'

'Maybe he didn't kill for that reason,' Mallory said mildly.
'Maybe he thought it was some other kind of message.'

'Some other kind of message?' Miller lifted an eyebrow in the way that only he knew how. 'Now what kind—' He caught Andrea's eye, broke off and changed his mind about saying anything more. Both he and Andrea gazed curiously at Mallory who seemed to have fallen into a mood of intense introspection.

Whatever its reason, the period of deep preoccupation did not last for long. With the air of a man who has just arrived at a conclusion about something, Mallory lifted his head and called to Maria to stop, at the same time reining in his own pony. Together they waited until Reynolds and Groves had made up on them.

'There are a good number of options open to us,' Mallory said, 'but for better or worse this is what I have decided to do.' He smiled faintly. 'For better, I think, if for no other reason than that this is the course of action that will get us out of here fastest. I've talked to Major Broznik and found out what I wanted. He tells me—'

'Got your information for Neufeld, then, have you?' If Reynolds was attempting to mask the contempt in his voice he made a singularly poor job of it.

'The hell with Neufeld,' Mallory said without heat. 'Partisan spies have discovered where the four captured Allied agents are being held.'

'They have?' Reynolds said. 'Then why don't the Partisans do something about it?'

'For a good enough reason. The agents are held deep in German territory. In an impregnable block-house high up in the mountains.'

'And what are *we* going to do about the Allied agents held in this impregnable block-house?'

'Simple.' Mallory corrected himself. 'Well, in theory it's simple. We take them out of there and make our break tonight.'

Reynolds and Groves stared at Mallory, then at each other in

117

frank disbelief and consternation. Andrea and Miller carefully avoided looking at each other or at anyone else.

'You're mad!' Reynolds spoke with total conviction.

'You're mad, *sir*,' Andrea said reprovingly.

Reynolds looked uncomprehendingly at Andrea, then turned back to Mallory again.

'You must be!' he insisted. 'Break? Break for where, in heaven's name?'

'For home. For Italy.'

'Italy!' It took Reynolds all of ten seconds to digest this startling piece of information, then he went on sarcastically: 'We're going to fly there, I suppose?'

'Well, it's a long swim across the Adriatic, even for a fit youngster like you. How else?'

'Flying?' Groves seemed slightly dazed.

'Flying. Not ten kilometres from here is a high—a very high mountain plateau, mostly in Partisan hands. There'll be a plane there at nine o'clock tonight.'

In the fashion of people who have failed to grasp something they have just heard, Groves repeated the statement in the form of a question. 'There'll be a plane there at nine o'clock tonight? You've just arranged this?'

'How could I? We've no radio.'

Reynolds's distrustful face splendidly complemented the scepticism in his voice. 'But *how* can you be sure—well, at nine o'clock?'

'Because, starting at six o'clock this evening, there'll be a Wellington bomber over the airstrip every three hours for the next week if necessary.'

Mallory kneed his pony and the party moved on, Reynolds and Groves taking up their usual position well to the rear of the others. For some time Reynolds, his expression alternating between hostility and speculation, stared fixedly at Mallory's back: then he turned to Groves.

'Well, well, well. Isn't that very convenient indeed. We just *happen* to be sent to Broznik's camp. He just *happens* to know where the four agents are held. It just *happens* that an airplane will be over a certain airfield at a certain time—and it also so happens that I know for an absolute certainty that there are no airfields up in the high plateau. Still think everything clean and above-board?'

It was quite obvious from the unhappy expression on Groves's face that he thought nothing of the kind. He said: 'What in God's name are we going to do?'

'Watch our backs.'

Fifty yards ahead of them Miller cleared his throat and said delicately to Mallory: 'Reynolds seems to have lost some of his —um—earlier confidence in you, sir.'

Mallory said drily: 'It's not surprising. He thinks I stuck that knife in Saunders's back.'

This time Andrea and Miller did exchange glances, their faces registering expressions as close to pure consternation as either of those poker-faced individuals was capable of achieving.

CHAPTER 7

Friday

1000-1200

Half a mile from Neufeld's camp they were met by Captain Droshny and some half-dozen of his Cetniks. Droshny's welcome was noticeably lacking in cordiality but at least he managed, at what unknown cost, to maintain some semblance of inoffensive neutrality.

'So you came back?'

'As you can see,' Mallory agreed.

Droshny looked at the ponies. 'And travelling in comfort.'

'A present from our good friend Major Broznik.' Mallory grinned. 'He thinks we're heading for Konjic on them.'

Droshny didn't appear to care very much what Major Broznik had thought. He jerked his head, wheeled his horse and set off at a fast trot for Neufeld's camp.

When they had dismounted inside the compound, Droshny immediately led Mallory into Neufeld's hut. Neufeld's welcome, like Droshny's, was something less than ecstatic, but at least he succeeded in imparting a shade more benevolence to his neutrality. His face held, also, just a hint of surprise, a reaction which he explained at once.

'Candidly, Captain, I did not expect to see you again. There were so many—ah—imponderables. However, I am delighted to see you—you would not have returned without the information I wanted. Now then, Captain Mallory, to business.'

Mallory eyed Neufeld without enthusiasm. 'You're not a very business-like partner, I'm afraid.'

'I'm not?' Neufeld said politely. 'In what way?'

'Business partners don't tell lies to each other. Sure you said Vukalovic's troops are massing. So they are indeed. But not, as you said, to break out. Instead, they're massing to defend themselves against the final German attack, the assault that is to crush them once and for all, and this assault they believe to be imminent.'

'Well, now, you surely didn't expect me to give away our military secrets—which you might, I say just might, have relayed to the enemy—before you had proved yourselves,' Neufeld said reasonably. 'You're not that naïve. About this proposed attack. Who gave you the information.'

'Major Broznik.' Mallory smiled in recollection. 'He was very expansive.'

Neufeld leaned forward, his tension reflected in the sudden stillness of his face, in the way his unblinking eyes held Mallory's. 'And did they say where they expected this attack to come?'

'I only know the name. The bridge at Neretva.'

Neufeld sank back into his chair, exhaled a long soundless sigh of relief and smiled to rob his next words of any offence. 'My friend, if you weren't British, a deserter, a renegade and a dope-peddler, you'd get the Iron Cross for this. By the way,' he went on, as if by casual afterthought, 'you've been cleared from Padua. The bridge at Neretva? You're sure of this?'

Mallory said irritably: 'If you doubt my word—'

'Of course not, of course not. Just a manner of speaking.' Neufeld paused for a few moments, then said softly: 'The bridge at Neretva.' The way he spoke them, the words sounded almost like a litany.

Droshny said softly: 'This fits in with all we suspected.'

'Never mind what you suspected,' Mallory said rudely. 'To *my* business now, if you don't mind. We have done well, you

121

would say? We have fulfilled your request, got the precise information you wanted?' Neufeld nodded. 'Then get us the hell out of here. Fly us deep into some German-held territory. Into Austria or Germany itself, if you like—the further away from here the better. You know what will happen to us if we ever again fall into British or Yugoslav hands?'

'It's not hard to guess,' Neufeld said almost cheerfully. 'But you misjudge us, my friend. Your departure to a place of safety has already been arranged. A certain Chief of Military Intelligence in northern Italy would very much like to make your personal acquaintance. He has reason to believe that you can be of great help to him.'

Mallory nodded his understanding.

General Vukalovic trained his binoculars on the Zenica Gap, a narrow and heavily-wooded valley floor lying between the bases of two high and steep-shouldered mountains, mountains almost identical in both shape and height.

The German 11th Army Corps tanks among the pines were not difficult to locate, for the Germans had made no attempt either to camouflage or conceal them, measure enough, Vukalovic thought grimly, of the Germans' total confidence in themselves and in the outcome of the battle that lay ahead. He could clearly see soldiers working on some stationary vehicles: other tanks were backing and filling and manoeuvring into position as if making ready to take up battle formation for the actual attack: the deep rumbling roar of the heavy engines of Tiger tanks was almost incessant.

Vukalovic lowered his glasses, jotted down a few more pencil marks on a sheet of paper already almost covered with similar pencil marks, performed a few exercises in addition, laid paper and pencil aside with a sigh and turned to Colonel Janzy, who was similarly engaged.

Vukalovic said wryly: 'My apologies to your staff, Colonel. They can count just as well as I can.'

For once, Captain Jensen's piratical swagger and flashing, confident smile were not very much in evidence: at that moment, in fact, they were totally absent. It would have been impossible for a face of Jensen's generous proportions ever to assume an actually haggard appearance, but the set, grim face displayed unmistakable signs of strain and anxiety and sleeplessness as he paced up and down the 5th Army Operations Headquarters in Termoli in Italy.

He did not pace alone. Beside him, matching him step for step, a burly grey-haired officer in the uniform of a lieutenant-general in the British Army accompanied him backwards and forwards, the expression on his face an exact replica of that on Jensen's. As they came to the further end of the room, the General stopped and glanced interrogatively at a head-phone-wearing sergeant seated in front of a large RCA transceiver. The sergeant slowly shook his head. The two men resumed their pacing.

The General said abruptly: 'Time is running out. You do appreciate, Jensen, that once you launch a major offensive you can't possibly stop it?'

'I appreciate it,' Jensen said heavily. 'What are the latest reconnaissance reports, sir?'

'There is no shortage of reports, but God alone knows what to make of them all.' The General sounded bitter. 'There's intense activity all along the Gustav Line, involving—as far as we can make out—two Panzer divisions, one German infantry division, one Austrian infantry division and two Jaeger battalions—their crack Alpine troops. They're not mounting an offensive, that's for sure—in the first place, there's no possibility of their making an offensive from the area in which they are manœuvring and in the second place if they *were* contemplating an offensive they'd take damn good care to keep all their preparations secret.'

'All this activity, then? If they're not planning an attack.'

The General sighed. 'Informed opinion has it that they're making all preparations for a lightning pull-out. Informed opinion! All that concerns me is that those blasted divisions are still in the Gustav Line. Jensen, *what has gone wrong?*'

Jensen lifted his shoulders in a gesture of helplessness. 'It was arranged for a radio rendezvous every two hours from four a.m.—'

'There have been no contacts whatsoever.'

Jensen said nothing.

The General looked at him, almost speculatively. 'The best in Southern Europe, you said.'

'Yes, I did say that.'

The General's unspoken doubts as to the quality of the agents Jensen had selected for operation Force 10 would have been considerably heightened if he had been at that moment present with those agents in the guest hut in Hauptmann Neufeld's camp in Bosnia. They were exhibiting none of the harmony, understanding and implicit mutual trust which one would have expected to find among a team of agents rated as the best in the business. There was, instead, tension and anger in the air, an air of suspicion and mistrust so heavy as to be almost palpable. Reynolds, confronting Mallory, had his anger barely under control.

'I want to know now!' Reynolds almost shouted the words.

'Keep your voice down,' Andrea said sharply.

'I want to know now,' Reynolds repeated. This time his voice was little more than a whisper, but none the less demanding and insistent for that.

'You'll be told when the time comes.' As always, Mallory's

voice was calm and neutral and devoid of heat. 'Not till then. What you don't know, you can't tell.'

Reynolds clenched his fists and advanced a step. 'Are you damn well insinuating that—'

Mallory said with restraint: 'I'm insinuating nothing. I was right, back in Termoli, Sergeant. You're no better than a ticking time-bomb.'

'Maybe.' Reynolds's fury was out of control now. 'But at least there's something honest about a bomb.'

'Repeat that remark,' Andrea said quietly.

'What?'

'Repeat it.'

'Look, Andrea—'

'Colonel Stavros, sonny.'

'Sir.'

'Repeat it and I'll guarantee you a minimum of five years for insubordination in the field.'

'Yes, sir.' Reynolds's physical effort to bring himself under control was apparent to everyone. 'But *why* should he *not* tell us his plans for this afternoon and at the same time let us all know that we'll be leaving from this Ivenici place tonight?'

'Because our plans are something the Germans can do something about,' Andreas said patiently. 'If they find out. If one of us talked under duress. But they can't do anything about Ivenici—that's in Partisan hands.'

Miller pacifically changed the subject. He said to Mallory: 'Seven thousand feet up, you say. The snow must be thigh-deep up there. How in God's name does anyone hope to clear all that lot away?'

'I don't know,' Mallory said vaguely. 'I suspect somebody will think of something.'

And, seven thousand feet up on the Ivenici plateau, somebody had indeed thought of something.

The Ivenici plateau was a wilderness in white, a bleak and desolate and, for many months of the year, a bitterly cold and howling and hostile wilderness, totally inimical to human life, totally intolerant of human presence. The plateau was bounded to the west by a five-hundred-foot-high cliff-face, quite vertical in some parts, fractured and fissured in others. Scattered along its length were numerous frozen waterfalls and occasional lines of pine trees, impossibly growing on impossibly narrow ledges, their frozen branches drooped and laden with the frozen snow of six long months gone by. To the east the plateau was bounded by nothing but an abrupt and sharply defined line marking the top of another cliff-face which dropped away perpendicularly into the valleys below.

The plateau itself consisted of a smooth, absolutely level, unbroken expanse of snow, snow which at that height of 2,000 metres and in the brilliant sunshine gave off a glare and dazzling reflection which was positively hurtful to the eyes. In length, it was perhaps half a mile: in width, nowhere more than a hundred yards. At its southern end, the plateau rose sharply to merge with the cliff-face which here tailed off and ran into the ground.

On this prominence stood two tents, both white, one small, the other a large marquee. Outside the small tent stood two men, talking. The taller and older man, wearing a heavy greatcoat and a pair of smoked glasses, was Colonel Vis, the commandant of a Sarajevo-based brigade of Partisans: the younger, slighter figure was his adjutant, a Captain Vlanovich. Both men were gazing out over the length of the plateau.

Captain Vlanovich said unhappily: 'There must be easier ways of doing this, sir.'

'You name it, Boris, my boy, and I'll do it.' Both in appearance and voice Colonel Vis gave the impression of immense calm and competence. 'Bull-dozers, I agree, would help. So would snow-ploughs. But you will agree that to drive either of them up vertical cliff-faces in order to reach here would call for considerable skill on the part of the drivers. Besides, what's an army for, if not for marching?'

'Yes, sir,' Vlanovich said, dutifully and doubtfully.

Both men gazed out over the length of the plateau to the north.

To the north, and beyond, for all around a score of encircling mountain peaks, some dark and jagged and sombre, others rounded and snow-capped and rose-coloured, soared up into the cloudless washed-out pale blue of the sky. It was an immensely impressive sight.

Even more impressive was the spectacle taking place on the plateau itself. A solid phalanx of a thousand uniformed soldiers, perhaps half in the buff grey of the Yugoslav army, the rest in a motley array of other countries' uniforms, were moving, at a snail-pace, across the virgin snow.

The phalanx was fifty people wide but only twenty deep, each line of fifty linked arm-in-arm, heads and shoulders bowed forward as they laboriously trudged at a painfully slow pace through the snow. That the pace was so slow was no matter for wonder, the leading line of men were ploughing their way through waist-deep snow, and already the signs of strain and exhaustion were showing in their faces. It was killingly hard work, work which, at that altitude, doubled the pulse rate, made a man fight for every gasping breath, turned a man's legs into leaden and agonized limbs where only the pain could convince him that they were still part of him.

And not only men. After the first five lines of soldiers, there were almost as many women and girls in the remainder of the phalanx as there were men, although everyone was so muffled against the freezing cold and biting winds of those high altitudes that it was impossible almost to tell man from woman. The last two lines of the phalanx were composed entirely of *partisankas* and it was significantly ominous of the murderous labour still to come that even they were sinking knee-deep in the snow.

It was a fantastic sight, but a sight that was far from unique in wartime Yugoslavia. The airfields of the lowlands, completely dominated by the armoured divisions of the Wehrmacht, were permanently barred to the Yugoslavs and it was thus that the Partisans constructed many of their airstrips in the mountains. In snow of this depth and in areas completely inaccessible to powered mechanical aids, there was no other way open to them.

Colonel Vis looked away and turned to Captain Vlanovich.

'Well, Boris, my boy, do you think you're up here for the winter sports? Get the food and soup kitchens organized. We'll use up a whole week's rations of hot food and hot soup in this one day.'

'Yes, sir.' Vlanovich cocked his head, then removed his ear-flapped fur cap the better to listen to the newly-begun sound of distant explosions to the north. 'What on earth is that?'

Vis said musingly: 'Sound does carry far in our pure Yugoslavian mountain air, does it not?'

'Sir? Please?'

'That, my boy,' Vis said with considerable satisfaction, 'is the Messerschmitt fighter base at Novo Derventa getting the biggest plastering of its lifetime.'

'Sir?'

Vis sighed in long-suffering patience. 'I'll make a soldier of you some day. Messerschmitts, Boris, are fighters, carrying all sorts of nasty cannons and machine-guns. What, at this moment, is the finest fighter target in Yugoslavia?'

'What is—' Vlanovich broke off and looked again at the trudging phalanx. 'Oh!'

' "Oh," indeed. The British Air Force have diverted six of their best Lancaster heavy bomber squadrons from the Italian front just to attend to our friends at Novo Derventa.' He in turn removed his cap, the better to listen. 'Hard at work, aren't they? By the time they're finished there won't be a Messerschmitt able to take off from that field for a week. If, that is to say, there are any left to take off.'

'If I might venture a remark, sir?'

'You may so venture, Captain Vlanovich.'

'There are other fighter bases.'

'True.' Vis pointed upwards. 'See anything?'

Vlanovich craned his neck, shielded his eyes against the brilliant sun, gazed into the empty blue sky and shook his head.

'Neither do I,' Vis agreed. 'But at seven thousand metres— and with their crews even colder than we are—squadrons of Beaufighters will be keeping relief patrol up there until dark.'

'Who—who *is* he, sir? Who can ask for all our soldiers down here, for squadrons of bombers and fighters?'

'Fellow called Captain Mallory, I believe.'

'A *captain*? Like me?'

'A captain. I doubt, Boris,' Vis went on kindly, 'whether he's quite like you. But it's not the rank that counts. It's the name. Mallory.'

'Never heard of him.'

'You will, my boy, you will.'

'But—but this man Mallory. What does he want all this *for*?'

'Ask him when you see him tonight.'

'When I—he's coming here tonight?'

'Tonight. If,' Vis added sombrely, 'he lives that long.'

Neufeld, followed by Droshny, walked briskly and confidently into his radio hut, a bleak, ramshackle lean-to furnished with a table, two chairs, a large portable transceiver and nothing else. The German corporal seated before the radio looked up enquiringly at their entrance.

'The Seventh Armoured Corps HQ at the Neretva bridge,'

129

Neufeld ordered. He seemed in excellent spirits. 'I wish to speak to General Zimmermann personally.'

The corporal nodded acknowledgment, put through the call-sign and was answered within seconds. He listened briefly, looked up at Neufeld. 'The General is coming now, sir.'

Neufeld reached out a hand for the ear-phones, took them and nodded towards the door. The corporal rose and left the hut while Neufeld took the vacated seat and adjusted the head-phones to his satisfaction. After a few seconds he automatically straightened in his seat as a voice came crackling over the ear-phones.

'Hauptmann Neufeld here, Herr General. The Englishmen have returned. Their information is that the Partisan division in the Zenica Cage is expecting a full-scale attack from the south across the Neretva bridge.'

'Are they now?' General Zimmermann, comfortably seated in a swivel chair in the back of the radio truck parked on the tree-line due south of the Neretva bridge, made no attempt to conceal the satisfaction in his voice. The canvas hood of the truck was rolled back and he removed his peaked cap the better to enjoy the pale spring sunshine. 'Interesting, very interesting. Anything else.'

'Yes,' Neufeld's voice crackled metallically over the loud-speaker. 'They've asked to be flown to sanctuary. Deep behind our lines, even to Germany. They feel—ah—unsafe here.'

'Well, well, well. Is that how they feel.' Zimmermann paused, considered, then continued. 'You are fully informed of the situation, Hauptmann Neufeld? You are aware of the delicate balance of—um—niceties involved?'

'Yes, Herr General.'

'This calls for a moment's thought. Wait.'

Zimmermann swung idly to and fro in his swivel chair as he pondered his decision. He gazed thoughtfully but almost un-seeingly to the north, across the meadows bordering the south bank of the Neretva, the river spanned by the iron bridge, then the meadows on the far side rising steeply to the rocky redoubt which served as the first line of defence for Colonel Lazlo's Partisan defenders. To the east, as he turned, he could look up the green-white rushing waters of the Neretva, the meadows on either side of it narrowing until, curving north, they disappeared suddenly at the mouth of the cliff-sided gorge from which the Neretva emerged. Another quarter turn and he was gazing into the pine forest to the south, a pine forest which at first seemed innocuous enough and empty of life— until, that was, one's eyes became accustomed to the gloom and scores of large rectangular shapes, effectively screened from both observation from the air and from the northern bank of the Neretva by camouflage canvas, camouflage nets and huge piles of dead branches. The sight of those camouflaged spearheads of his two Panzer divisions somehow helped Zimmermann to make up his mind. He picked up the microphone.

'Hauptmann Neufeld? I have decided on a course of action and you will please carry out the following instructions precisely . . .'

Droshny removed the duplicate pair of ear-phones that he had been wearing and said doubtfully to Neufeld: 'Isn't the General asking rather a lot of us?'

Neufeld shook his head reassuringly. 'General Zimmermann *always* knows what he is doing. His psychological assessment of the Captain Mallorys of this world is invariably a hundred per cent right.'

'I hope so.' Droshny was unconvinced. 'For our sakes, I hope so.'

They left the hut. Neufeld said to the radio-operator: 'Captain Mallory in my office, please. And Sergeant Baer.'

Mallory arrived in the office to find Neufeld, Droshny and Baer already there. Neufeld was brief and business-like.

'We've decided on a ski-plane to fly you out—they're the only planes that can land in those damned mountains. You'll have time for a few hours sleep—we don't leave till four. Any questions?'

'Where's the landing-strip?'

'A clearing. A kilometre from here. Anything else?'

'Nothing. Just get us out of here, that's all.'

'You need have no worry on that score,' Neufeld said emphatically. 'My one ambition is to see you safely on your way. Frankly, Mallory, you're just an embarrassment to me and the sooner you're on your way the better.'

Mallory nodded and left. Neufeld turned to Baer and said: 'I have a little task for you, Sergeant Baer. Little but very important. Listen carefully.'

Mallory left Neufeld's hut, his face pensive, and walked slowly across the compound. As he approached the guest hut, Andrea emerged and passed wordlessly by, wreathed in cigar smoke and scowling. Mallory entered the hut where Petar was again playing the Yugoslavian version of 'The girl I left behind me.' It seemed to be his favourite song. Mallory glanced at Maria, Reynolds and Groves, all sitting silently by, then at Miller who was reclining in his sleeping-bag with his volume of poetry.

Mallory nodded toward the doorway. 'Something's upset our friend.'

Miller grinned and nodded in turn towards Petar. 'He's playing Andrea's tune again.'

Mallory smiled briefly and turned to Maria. 'Tell him to stop playing. We're pulling out late this afternoon and we all need all the sleep we can get.'

'We can sleep in the plane,' Reynolds said sullenly. 'We can sleep when we arrive at our destination—wherever that may be.'

'No, sleep now.'

'Why now?'

'Why now?' Mallory's unfocused eyes gazed into the far distance. He said in a quiet voice: 'For now is all the time there may be.'

Reynolds looked at him strangely. For the first time that day his face was empty of hostility and suspicion. There was puzzled speculation in his eyes, and wonder and the first faint beginnings of understanding.

On the Ivenici plateau, the phalanx moved on, but they moved no more like human beings. They stumbled along now in the advanced stages of exhaustion, automatons, no more, zombies resurrected from the dead, their faces twisted with pain and unimaginable fatigue, their limbs on fire and their minds benumbed. Every few seconds someone stumbled and fell and could not get up again and had to be carried to join scores of others already lying in an almost comatose condition by the side of the primitive runway, where *partisankas* did their best to revive their frozen and exhausted bodies with mugs of hot soup and liberal doses of *raki*.

Captain Vlanovich turned to Colonel Vis. His face was distressed, his voice low and deeply earnest.

'This is madness, Colonel, madness! It's—it's impossible, you can see it's impossible. We'll never—look, sir, two hundred and fifty dropped out in the first two hours. The altitude, the cold, sheer physical exhaustion. It's madness.'

'All war is madness,' Vis said calmly. 'Get on the radio. We require five hundred more men.'

CHAPTER 8

Friday
1500-2115

Now it had come, Mallory knew. He looked at Andrea and
Miller and Reynolds and Groves and knew that they knew it
too. In their faces he could see very clearly reflected what lay
at the very surface of his own mind, the explosive tension,
the hair-trigger alertness straining to be translated into equally
explosive action. Always it came, this moment of truth that
stripped men bare and showed them for what they were. He
wondered how Reynolds and Groves would be: he suspected
they might acquit themselves well. It never occurred to him
to wonder about Miller and Andrea, for he knew them too
well: Miller, when all seemed lost, was a man above himself,
while the normally easy-going, almost lethargic Andrea was
transformed into an unrecognizable human being, an impossible combination of an icily calculating mind and berserker
fighting machine entirely without the remotest parallel in Mallory's knowledge or experience. When Mallory spoke his voice
was as calmly impersonal as ever.

'We're due to leave at four. It's now three. With any luck
we'll catch them napping. Is everything clear?'

Reynolds said wonderingly, almost unbelievingly: 'You
mean if anything goes wrong we're to shoot our way out?'

'You're to shoot and shoot to kill. That, Sergeant, is an
order.'

'Honest to God,' Reynolds said, 'I just don't know what's
going on.' The expression on his face clearly indicated that

134

he had given up all attempts to understand what was going on.

Mallory and Andrea left the hut and walked casually across the compound towards Neufeld's hut. Mallory said: 'They're on to us, you know.'

'I know. Where are Petar and Maria?'

'Asleep, perhaps? They left the hut a couple of hours ago. We'll collect them later.'

'Later may be too late ... They are in great peril, my Keith.'

'What can a man do, Andrea? I've thought of nothing else in the past ten hours. It's a crucifying risk to have to take, but I have to take it. They are expendable, Andrea. You know what it would mean if I showed my hand now.'

'I know what it would mean,' Andrea said heavily. 'The end of everything.'

They entered Neufeld's hut without benefit of knocking. Neufeld, sitting behind his desk with Droshny by his side, looked up in irritated surprise and glanced at his watch.

He said curtly: 'Four o'clock, I said, not three.'

'Our mistake,' Mallory apologized. He closed the door. 'Please do not be foolish.'

Neufeld and Droshny were not foolish, few people would have been while staring down the muzzles of two Lugers with perforated silencers screwed to the end: they just sat there, immobile, the shock slowly draining from their faces. There was a long pause then Neufeld spoke, the words coming almost haltingly.

'I have been seriously guilty of underestimating—'

'Be quiet. Broznik's spies have discovered the whereabouts of the four captured Allied agents. We know roughly where they are. You know precisely where they are. You will take us there. Now.'

'You're mad,' Neufeld said with conviction.

'We don't require you to tell us that.' Andrea walked round behind Neufeld and Droshny, removed their pistols from their holsters, ejected the shells and replaced the pistols. He then crossed to a corner of the hut, picked up two Schmeisser machine-pistols, emptied them, walked back round to the front of the table and placed the Schmeissers on its top, one in front of Neufeld, one in front of Droshny.

'There you are, gentlemen,' Andrea said affably. 'Armed to the teeth.'

Droshny said viciously: 'Suppose we decide not to come with you?'

Andrea's affability vanished. He walked unhurriedly round the table and rammed the Luger's silencer with such force against Droshny's teeth that he gasped in pain. 'Please—' Andrea's voice was almost beseeching—'*please* don't tempt me.'

Droshny didn't tempt him. Mallory moved to the window and peered out over the compound. There were, he saw, at least a dozen Cetniks within thirty feet of Neufeld's hut, all of them armed. Across the other side of the compound he could see that the door to the stables was open indicating that Miller and the two sergeants were in position.

'You will walk across the compound to the stables,' Mallory said. 'You will talk to nobody, warn nobody, make no signals. We will follow about ten yards behind.'

'Ten yards behind. What's to prevent us making a break for it. You wouldn't dare hold a gun on us out there.'

'That's so,' Mallory agreed. 'From the moment you open this door you'll be covered by three Schmeissers from the stables. If you try anything—*anything*—you'll be cut to pieces. That's why we're keeping well behind you—we don't want to be cut to pieces too.'

At a gesture from Andrea, Neufeld and Droshny slung their empty Schmeissers in angry silence. Mallory looked at them consideringly and said: 'I think you'd better do something about your expressions. They're a dead giveaway that something is wrong. If you open that door with faces like that, Miller will cut you down before you reach the bottom step. Please try to believe me.'

They believed him and by the time Mallory opened the door had managed to arrange their features into a near enough imitation of normality. They went down the steps and set off across the compound to the stables. When they had reached half-way Andrea and Mallory left Neufeld's hut and followed them. One or two glances of idle curiosity came their way, but clearly no one suspected that anything was amiss. The crossing to the stables was completely uneventful.

So also, two minutes later, was their departure from the camp. Neufeld and Droshny, as would have been proper and expected, rode together in the lead, Droshny in particular looking very warlike with his Schmeisser, pistol and the wickedly-curved knives at his waist. Behind them rode Andrea, who appeared to be having some trouble with the action of his Schmeisser, for he had it in his hands and was examining it closely: he certainly wasn't looking at either Droshny or Neufeld and the fact that the gun-barrel, which Andrea had sensibly pointed towards the ground, had only to be lifted a foot and the trigger pressed to riddle the two men ahead was a preposterous idea that would not have occurred to even the most suspicious. Behind Andrea, Mallory and Miller rode abreast: like Andrea, they appeared unconcerned, even slightly bored. Reynolds and Groves brought up the rear, almost but not quite attaining the degree of nonchalance of the other three: their still faces and restlessly darting eyes betrayed the strain they were under. But their anxiety was needless for all seven passed from the camp not only unmolested but without as much as even an enquiring glance being cast in their direction

They rode for over two and a half hours, climbing nearly all the time, and a blood-red sun was setting among the

137

thinning pines to the west when they came across a clearing set on, for once, a level stretch of ground. Neufeld and Droshny halted their ponies and waited until the others came up with them. Mallory reined in and gazed at the building in the middle of the clearing, a low, squat, immensely strong-looking blockhouse, with narrow, heavily barred windows and two chimneys, from one of which smoke was coming.

'This the place?' Mallory asked.

'Hardly a necessary question.' Neufeld's voice was dry, but the underlying resentment and anger unmistakable. 'You think I spent all this time leading you to the wrong place?'

'I wouldn't put it past you,' Mallory said. He examined the building more closely. 'A hospitable-looking place.'

'Yugoslav Army ammunition dumps were never intended as first-class hotels.'

'I dare say not,' Mallory agreed. At a signal from him they urged their ponies forward into the clearing, and as they did so two metal strips in the facing wall of the block-house slid back to reveal a pair of embrasures with machine-pistols protruding. Exposed as they were, the seven mounted men were completely at the mercy of those menacing muzzles.

'Your men keep a good watch,' Mallory acknowledged to Neufeld. 'You wouldn't require many men to guard and hold a place like this. How many are there?'

'Six,' Neufeld said reluctantly.

'Seven and you're a dead man,' Andrea warned.

'Six.'

As they approached, the guns—almost certainly because the men behind them had identified Neufeld and Droshny—were withdrawn, the embrasures closed, the heavy metal front door opened. A sergeant appeared in the doorway and saluted respectfully, his face registering a certain surprise.

'An unexpected pleasure, Hauptmann Neufeld,' the sergeant said. 'We had no radio message informing us of your arrival.'

'It's out of action for the moment.' Neufeld waved them inside but Andrea gallantly insisted on the German officer taking precedence, reinforcing his courtesy with a threatening hitch of his Schmeisser. Neufeld entered, followed by Droshny and the other five men.

The windows were so narrow that the burning oil-lamps were obviously a necessity, the illumination they afforded being almost doubled by a large log fire blazing in the hearth. Nothing could ever overcome the bleakness created by four rough-cut stone walls, but the room itself was surprisingly well furnished with a table, chairs, two armchairs and a sofa: there were even some pieces of carpet. Three doors led off from the room, one heavily barred. Including the sergeant who had welcomed them, there were three armed soldiers in the room. Mallory glanced at Neufeld who nodded, his face tight in suppressed anger.

Neufeld said to one of the guards: 'Bring out the prisoners.' The guard nodded, lifted a heavy key from the wall and headed for the barred door. The sergeant and the other guard were sliding the metal screens back across the embrasures. Andrea walked casually towards the nearest guard, then suddenly and violently shoved him against the sergeant. Both men cannoned into the guard who had just inserted the key into the door. The third man fell heavily to the ground: the other two, though staggering wildly, managed to retain a semblance of balance or at least remain on their feet. All three twisted round to stare at Andrea, anger and startled incomprehension in their faces, and all three remained very still, and wisely so. Faced with a Schmeisser machine-pistol at three paces, the wise man always remains still.

Mallory said to the sergeant: 'There are three other men. Where are they?'

There was no reply: the guard glared at him in defiance. Mallory repeated the question, this time in fluent German:

the guard ignored him and looked questioning at Neufeld, whose lips were tight-shut in a mask of stone.

'Are you mad?' Neufeld demanded of the sergeant. 'Can't you see those men are killers? Tell him.'

'The night guards. They're asleep.' The sergeant pointed to a door. 'That one.'

'Open it. Tell them to walk out. Backwards and with their hands clasped behind their necks.'

'Do exactly as you're told,' Neufeld ordered.

The sergeant did exactly what he was told and so did the three guards who had been resting in the inner room, who walked out as they had been instructed, with obviously no thought of any resistance in their minds. Mallory turned to the guard with the key who had by this time picked himself up somewhat shakily from the floor, and nodded to the barred door.

'Open it.'

The guard opened it and pushed the door wide. Four British officers moved out slowly and uncertainly into the outer room. Long confinement indoors had made them very pale, but apart from this prison pallor and the fact that they were rather thin they were obviously unharmed. The man in the lead, with a major's insignia and a Sandhurst moustache —and, when he spoke, a Sandhurst accent—stopped abruptly and stared in disbelief at Mallory and his men.

'Good God above! What on earth are you chaps—'

'Please.' Mallory cut him short. 'I'm sorry, but later. Collect your coats, whatever warm gear you have, and wait outside.'

'But—but where are you taking us?'

'Home. Italy. Tonight. Please hurry!'

'Italy. You're talking—'

'Hurry!' Mallory glanced in some exasperation at his watch. 'We're late already.'

As quickly as their dazed condition would allow, the four

officers collected what warm clothing they had and filed outside. Mallory turned to the sergeant again. 'You must have
ponies here, a stable.'

'Round the back of the block-house,' the sergeant said
promptly. He had obviously made a rapid readjustment to
the new facts of life.

'Good lad,' Mallory said approvingly. He looked at Groves
and Reynolds. 'We'll need two more ponies. Saddle them up,
will you?'

The two sergeants left. Under the watchful guns of Mallory
and Miller, Andrea searched each of the six guards in turn,
found nothing, and ushered them all into the cell, turning the
heavy key and hanging it up on the wall. Then, just as carefully,
Andrea searched Neufeld and Droshny: Droshny's face, as
Andrea carelessly flung his knives into a corner of the room,
was thunderous.

Mallory looked at the two men and said: 'I'd shoot you if
necessary. It's not. You won't be missed before morning.'

'They might not be missed for a good few mornings,' Miller
pointed out.

'So they're over-weight anyway,' Mallory said indifferently.
He smiled. 'I can't resist leaving you with a last little pleasant
thought, Hauptmann Neufeld. Something to think about until
someone comes and finds you.' He looked consideringly at
Neufeld, who said nothing, then went on: 'About that information I gave you this morning, I mean.'

Neufeld looked at him guardedly. 'What about the information you gave me this morning?'

'Just this. It wasn't, I'm afraid, quite accurate. Vukalovic
expects the attack from the *north*, through the Zenica Gap, *not*
across the bridge at Neretva from the south. There are, we
know, close on two hundred of your tanks massed in the
woods just to the north of the Zenica Gap—but there won't
be at two a.m. this morning when your attack is due to start.

141

Not after I've got through to our Lancaster squadrons in Italy. Think of it, think of the target. Two hundred tanks bunched in a tiny trap a hundred and fifty yards wide and not more than three hundred yards long. The RAF will be there at 1.30. By two this morning there won't be a single tank left in commission.'

Neufeld look at him for a long moment, his face very still, then said, slowly and softly: 'Damn you! Damn you! Damn you!'

'Damning is all you'll have for it,' Mallory said agreeably. 'By the time you are released—hopefully assuming that you will be released—it will be all over. See you after the war.'

Andrea locked the two men in a side room and hung the key up by the one to the cell. Then they went outside, locked the outer door, hung the key on a nail by the door, mounted their ponies—Groves and Reynolds had already two additional ones saddled—and started climbing once again, Mallory, map in hand, studying in the fading light of dusk the route they had to take.

Their route took them up alongside the perimeter of a pine forest. Not more than half a mile after leaving the block-house, Andrea reined in his pony, dismounted, lifted the pony's right foreleg and examined it carefully. He looked up at the others who had also reined in their ponies.

'There's a stone wedged under the hoof,' he announced. 'Looks bad—but not too bad. I'll have to cut it out. Don't wait for me—I'll catch you up in a few minutes.'

Mallory nodded, gave the signal to move on. Andrea produced a knife, lifted the hoof and made a great play of excavating the wedged stone. After a minute or so, he glanced up and saw that the rest of the party had vanished round a corner of the pine wood. Andrea put away his knife and led the pony, which quite obviously had no limp whatsoever, into the shelter of the wood and tethered it there, then moved on foot some way down the hill towards the block-house. He sat down behind the bole of a convenient pine and removed his binoculars from their case.

He hadn't long to wait. The head and shoulders of a figure appeared in the clearing below peering out cautiously from behind the trunk of a tree. Andrea flat in the snow now and with the icy rims of the binoculars clamped hard against his eyes, had no difficulty at all in making an immediate identification: Sergeant Baer, moon-faced, rotund and about seventy pounds overweight for his unimpressive height, had an unmistakable physical presence which only the mentally incapacitated could easily forget.

Baer withdrew into the woods, then reappeared shortly afterwards leading a string of ponies, one of which carried a bulky covered object strapped to a pannier bag. Two of the following ponies had riders, both of whom had their hands tied to the pommels of their saddles. Petar and Maria, without a doubt. Behind them appeared four mounted soldiers. Sergeant Baer beckoned them to follow him across the clearing and within moments all had disappeared from sight behind the block-house. Andrea regarded the now empty clearing thoughtfully, lit a fresh cigar and made his way uphill towards his tethered pony.

Sergeant Baer dismounted, produced a key from his pocket, caught sight of the key suspended from the nail beside the door, replaced his own, took down the other, opened the door with it and passed inside.. He glanced around, took down one of the keys hanging on the wall and opened a side door with it. Hauptmann Neufeld emerged, glanced at his watch and smiled.

'You have been very punctual, Sergeant Baer. You have the radio?'

'I have the radio. It's outside.'

'Good, good, good.' Neufeld looked at Droshny and smiled again. 'I think it's time for us to make our rendezvous with the Ivenici plateau.'

Sergeant Baer said respectfully: 'How can you be so sure that it is the Ivenici plateau, Hauptmann Neufeld?'

'How can I be so sure? Simple, my dear Baer. Because Maria —you have her with you?'

'But of course, Hauptmann Neufeld.'

'Because Maria told me. The Ivenici plateau it is.'

Night had fallen on the Ivenici plateau, but still the phalanx of exhausted soldiers was trudging out the landing-strip for the plane. The work was not by this time so cruelly and physically exacting, for the snow was now almost trampled and beaten hard and flat: but, even allowing for the rejuvenation given by the influx of another five hundred fresh soldiers, the overall level of utter weariness was such that the phalanx was in no better condition than its original members who had trudged out the first outline of the airstrip in the virgin snow.

The phalanx, too, had changed its shape. Instead of being fifty wide by twenty deep it was now twenty wide by fifty deep: having achieved a safe clearance for the wings of the aircraft, they were now trudging out what was to be as close as possible an iron-hard surface for the landing wheels.

A three-quarters moon, intensely white and luminous, rode low in the sky, with scattered bands of cloud coming drifting down slowly from the north. As the successive bands moved across the face of the moon, the black shadows swept lazily across the surface of the plateau: the phalanx, at one moment bathed in silvery moonlight, was at the next almost lost to sight in the darkness. It was a fantastic scene with a remarkably faery-like quality of eeriness and foreboding about it. In fact it was, as Colonel Vis had just unromantically mentioned to Captain Vlanovich, like something out of Dante's *Inferno*, only a hundred degrees colder. At least a hundred degrees, Vis had amended: he wasn't sure how hot it was in hell.

It was this scene which, at twenty minutes to nine in the evening, confronted Mallory and his men when they topped the brow of a hill and reined in their ponies just short of the edge of the precipice which abutted on the western edge of the Ivenici plateau. For at least two minutes they sat there on their ponies, not moving, not speaking, mesmerized by the other-world quality of a thousand men with bowed heads and bowed shoulders, shuffling exhaustedly across the level floor of the plain beneath, mesmerized because they all knew they were gazing at a unique spectacle which none of them had ever seen before and would never see again. Mallory finally broke free from the trance-like condition, looked at Miller and Andrea, and slowly shook his head in an expression of profound wonder conveying his disbelief, that his refusal to accept the reality of what his own eyes told him was real and actual beyond dispute. Miller and Andrea returned his look with almost identical negative motions of their own heads. Mallory wheeled his pony to the right and led the way along the cliff-face to the point where the cliff ran into the rising ground below.

Ten minutes later they were being greeted by Colonel Vis.

'I did not expect to see you, Captain Mallory.' Vis pumped his hand enthusiastically. 'Before God, I did not expect to see you. You—and your men—must have a remarkable capacity for survival.'

'Say that in a few hours,' Mallory said drily, 'and I would be very happy indeed to hear it.'

'But it's all over now. We expect the plane—' Vis glanced at his watch—'in exactly eight minutes. We have a bearing surface for it and there should be no difficulty in landing and taking off provided it doesn't hang around too long. You have done all that you came to do and achieved it magnificently. Luck has been on your side.'

'Say that in a few hours,' Mallory repeated.

'I'm sorry.' Vis could not conceal his puzzlement. 'You expect something to happen to the plane?'

'I don't expect anything to happen to the plane. But what's gone, what's past, is—was, rather—only the prologue.'

'The—the prologue?'

'Let me explain.'

Neufeld, Droshny and Sergeant Baer left their ponies tethered inside the woodline and walked up the slight eminence before them, Sergeant Baer making heavy weather of their uphill struggle through the snow because of the weight of the large portable transceiver strapped to his back. Near the summit they dropped to their hands and knees and crawled forward till they were within a few feet of the edge of the cliff overlooking the Ivenici plateau. Neufeld unslung his binoculars and then replaced them: the moon had just moved from behind a dark barred cloud highlighting every aspect of the scene below: the intensely sharp contrast afforded by black shadow and snow so deeply and gleamingly white as to be almost phosphorescent made the use of binoculars superfluous.

Clearly visible and to the right were Vis's command tents and, near by, some hastily erected soup kitchens. Outside the smallest of the tents could be seen a group of perhaps a dozen people, obviously, even at that distance, engaged in close conversation. Directly beneath where they lay, the three men could see the phalanx turning round at one end of the runway and beginning to trudge back slowly, so terribly slowly, so terribly tiredly, along the wide path already tramped out. As Mallory and his men had been, Neufeld, Droshny and Baer were momentarily caught and held by the weird and other-worldly dark grandeur of the spectacle below. Only by a conscious actof will could Neufeld bring himself to look away and return to the world of normality and reality.

'How very kind,' he murmured, 'of our Yugoslav friends to go to such lengths on our behalf.' He turned to Baer and indicated the transceiver. 'Get through to the General, will you?'

Baer unslung his transceiver, settled it firmly in the snow, extended the telescopic aerial, pre-set the frequency and cranked the handle. He made contact almost at once, talked briefly then handed the microphone and head-piece to Neufeld, who fitted on the phones and gazed down, still half mesmerized, at the thousand men and women moving antlike across the plain below. The head-phones cracked suddenly in his ears and the spell was broken.

'Herr General?'

'Ah. Hauptmann Neufeld.' In the ear-phones the General's voice was faint but very clear, completely free from distortion or static. 'Now then. About my psychological assessment of the English mind?'

'You have mistaken your profession, Herr General. Everything has happened exactly as you forecast. You will be interested to know, sir, that the Royal Air Force is launching a saturation bombing attack on the Zenica Gap at precisely 1.30 a.m. this morning.'

'Well, well, well,' Zimmermann said thoughtfully. 'That is interesting. But hardly surprising.'

'No, sir.' Neufeld looked up as Droshny touched him on the shoulder and pointed to the north. 'One moment, sir.'

Neufeld removed the ear-phones and cocked his head in the direction of Droshny's pointing arm. He lifted his binoculars but there was nothing to be seen. But unquestionably there was something to be heard—the distant clamour of aircraft engines, closing. Neufeld readjusted the ear-phones.

'We have to give the English full marks for punctuality, sir·
The plane is coming in now.'

'Excellent, excellent. Keep me informed.'

Neufeld eased off one ear-phone and gazed to the north.
Still nothing to be seen, the moon was now temporarily behind
a cloud, but the sound of the aircraft engines was unmistakably
closer. Suddenly, somewhere down on the plateau, came three
sharp blasts on a whistle. Immediately, the marching phalanx
broke up, men and women stumbling off the runway into the
deep snow on the eastern side of the plateau, leaving behind
them, obviously by pre-arrangement, about eighty men who
spaced themselves out on either side of the runway.

'They're organized, I'll say that for them,' Neufeld said
admiringly.

Droshny smiled his wolf's smile. 'All the better for us,
eh?'

'Everybody seems to be doing their best to help us tonight,'
Neufeld agreed.

Overhead, the dark and obscuring band of cloud drifted
away to the south and the white light of the moon raced across
the plateau. Neufeld could immediately see the plane, less than
half a mile away, its camouflaged shape sharply etched in the
brilliant moonlight as it sank down towards the end of the
runway. Another sharp blast of the whistle and at once the
men lining both sides of the runway switched on hand-lamps
—a superfluity, really, in those almost bright as day perfect
landing conditions, but essential had the moon been hidden
behind cloud.

'Touching down now,' Neufeld said into the microphone.
'It's a Wellington bomber.'

'Let's hope it makes a safe landing,' Zimmermann said.

'Let's hope so indeed, sir.'

The Wellington made a safe landing, a perfect landing considering the extremely difficult conditions. It slowed down

quickly, then steadied its speed as it headed towards the end of the runway.

Neufeld said into the microphone: 'Safely down, Herr General, and rolling to rest.'

'Why doesn't it stop?' Droshny wondered.

'You can't accelerate a plane over snow as you can over a concrete runway,' Neufeld said. 'They'll require every yard of the runway for the take-off.'

Quite obviously, the pilot of the Wellington was of the same opinion. He was about fifty yards from the end of the runway when two groups of people broke from the hundreds lining the edge of the runway, one group heading for the already opened door in the side of the bomber, the other heading for the tail of the plane. Both groups reached the plane just as it rolled to a stop at the very end of the runway, a dozen men at once flinging themselves upon the tail unit and beginning to turn the Wellington through 180°.

Droshny was impressed. 'By heavens, they're not wasting much time, are they?'

'They can't afford to. If the plane stays there any time at all it'll start sinking in the snow.' Neufeld lifted his binoculars and spoke into the microphone.

'They're boarding now, Herr General. One, two, three . . . seven, eight, nine. Nine it is.' Neufeld sighed in relief and at the relief of tension. 'My warmest congratulations, Herr General. Nine it is, indeed.'

The plane was already facing the way it had come. The pilot stood on the brakes, revved the engines up to a crescendo, then twenty seconds after it had come to a halt the Wellington was on its way again, accelerating down the runway. The pilot took no chances, he waited till the very far end of the airstrip before lifting the Wellington off, but when he did it rose cleanly and easily and climbed steadily into the night sky.

'Airborne, Herr General,' Neufeld reported. 'Everything

149

perfectly according to plan.' He covered the microphone, looked after the disappearing plane, then smiled at Droshny. 'I think we should wish them *bon voyage*, don't you?'

Mallory, one of the hundreds lining the perimeter of the airstrip, lowered his binoculars. 'And a very pleasant journey to them all.'

Colonel Vis shook his head sadly. 'All this work just to send five of my men on a holiday to Italy.'

'I dare say they needed a break,' Mallory said.

'The hell with them. How about us?' Reynolds demanded. In spite of the words, his face showed no anger, just a dazed and total bafflement. 'We should have been aboard that damned plane.'

'Ah. Well. I changed my mind.'

'Like hell you changed your mind,' Reynolds said bitterly.

Inside the fuselage of the Wellington, the moustached major surveyed his three fellow-escapees and the five Partisan soldiers, shook his head in disbelief and turned to the captain by his side.

'A rum do, what?'

'Very rum, indeed, sir,' said the captain. He looked curiously at the papers the major held in his hand. 'What have you there?'

'A map and papers that I'm to give to some bearded naval type when we land back in Italy. Odd fellow, that Mallory, what?'

'Very odd indeed, sir,' the captain agreed.

Mallory and his men, together with Vis and Vlanovich, had detached themselves from the crowd and were now standing outside Vis's command tent.

Mallory said to Vis: 'You have arranged for the ropes? We must leave at once.'

'What's all the desperate hurry, sir?' Groves asked. Like Reynolds, much of his resentment seemed to have gone to be replaced by a helpless bewilderment. 'All of a sudden, like, I mean?'

'Petar and Maria,' Mallory said grimly. 'They're the hurry.

'What about Petar and Maria?' Reynolds asked suspiciously. 'Where do they come into this?'

'They're being held captive in the ammunition block-house. And when Neufeld and Droshny get back there—'

'Get back there,' Groves said dazedly. 'What do you mean, get back there. We—we left them locked up. And how in God's name do you know that Petar and Maria are being held in the block-house. How can they be? I mean, they weren't there when we left there—and that's wasn't so long ago.'

'When Andrea's pony had a stone in its hoof on the way up here from the block-house, it didn't have a stone in its hoof. Andrea was keeping watch.'

'You see,' Miller explained, 'Andrea doesn't trust anyone.'

'He saw Sergeant Baer taking Petar and Maria there,' Mallory went on. 'Bound. Baer released Neufeld and Droshny and you can bet your last cent our precious pair were up on the cliff-side there checking that we really did fly out.'

'You don't tell us very much, do you, sir?' Reynolds said bitterly.

'I'll tell you this much,' Mallory said with certainty. 'If we don't get there soon, Maria and Petar are for the high jump. Neufeld and Droshny don't *know* yet, but by this time they must be pretty convinced that it was Maria who told me where those four agents were being kept. They've always known who we really were—Maria told them. Now they know who Maria is. Just before Droshny killed Saunders—'

'Droshny?' Reynolds's expression was that of a man who has almost given up all attempt to understand. 'Maria?'

'I made a miscalculation.' Mallory sounded tired. 'We all

151

make miscalculations, but this was a bad one.' He smiled, but the smile didn't touch his eyes. 'You will recall that you had a few harsh words to say about Andrea here when he picked that fight with Droshny outside the dining hut in Neufeld's camp?'

'Sure I remember. It was one of the craziest—'

'You can apologize to Andrea at a later and more convenient time,' Mallory interrupted. 'Andrea provoked Droshny because I asked him to. I knew that Neufeld and Droshny were up to no good in the dining hut after we had left and I wanted a moment to ask Maria what they had been discussing. She told me that they intended to send a couple of Cetniks after us into Broznik's camp—suitably disguised, of course—to report on us. They were two of the men acting as our escort in that wood-burning truck. Andrea and Miller killed them.'

'Now you tell us,' Groves said almost mechanically. 'Andrea and Miller killed them.'

'What I didn't know was that Droshny was also following us. He saw Maria and myself together.' He looked at Reynolds. 'Just as you did. I didn't know at the time that he'd seen us, but I've known for some hours now. Maria has been as good as under sentence of death since this morning. But there was nothing I could do about it. Not until now. If I'd shown my hand, we'd have been finished.'

Reynolds shook his head. 'But you've just said that Maria betrayed us—'

'Maria,' Mallory said, 'is a top-flight British espionage agent. English father, Yugoslav mother. She was in this country even before the Germans came. As a student in Belgrade. She joined the Partisans, who trained her as a radio-operator, then arranged for her defection to the Cetniks. The Cetniks had captured a radio-operator from one of the first British missions. They— the Germans, rather—trained her to imitate this operator's hand—every radio-operator has his own unmistakable style—

until their styles were quite indistinguishable. And her English, of course, was perfect. So then she was in direct contact with Allied Intelligence in both North Africa and Italy. The Germans thought they had us completely fooled: it was, in fact, the other way round.'

Miller said complainingly: 'You didn't tell me any of this, either.'

'I've so much on my mind. Anyway, she was notified direct of the arrival of the last four agents to be parachuted in. She, of course, told the Germans. And all those agents carried information reinforcing the German belief that a second front —a full-scale invasion—of Yugoslavia was imminent.'

Reynolds said slowly: 'They knew we were coming too?'

'Of course. They knew everything about us all along, what we really were. What they didn't know, of course, is that we knew they knew and though what they knew of us was true it was only part of the truth.'

Reynolds digested this. He said, hesitating: 'Sir?'

'Yes?'

'I could have been wrong about you, sir.'

'It happens,' Mallory agreed. 'From time to time, it happens. You were wrong, Sergeant, of course you were, but you were wrong from the very best motives. The fault is mine. Mine alone. But my hands were tied.' Mallory touched him on the shoulder. 'One of these days you might get round to forgiving me.'

'Petar?' Groves asked. 'He's not her brother?'

'Petar is Petar. No more. A front.'

'There's still an awful lot—' Reynolds began, but Mallory interrupted him.

'It'll have to wait. Colonel Vis, a map, please.' Captain Vlanovich brought one from the tent and Mallory shone a torch on it. 'Look. Here. The Neretva dam and the Zenica Cage. I told Neufeld that Broznik had told me that the Partisans believe that the attack is coming across the Neretva bridge from the south. But, as I've just said, Neufeld knew—he knew even before we had arrived—who and what we *really* were. So he was convinced I was lying. He was convinced that I was convinced that the attack was coming through the Zenica Gap to the north here. Good reason for believing that, mind you: there are two hundred German tanks up there.'

Vis stared at him. 'Two hundred!'

'One hundred and ninety of them are made of plywood. So the only way Neufeld—and, no doubt, the German High Command—could ensure that this useful information got through to Italy was to allow us to stage this rescue bid. Which, of course, they very gladly did, assisting us in every possible way even to the extent of gladly collaborating with us in permitting themselves to be captured. They *knew*, of course, that we had no option left but to capture them and force them to lead us to the block-house—an arrangement they had ensured by previously seizing and hiding away the only other person who could have helped us in this—Maria. And, of course, knowing this in advance, they had arranged for Sergeant Baer to come and free them.'

'I see.' It was plain to everyone that Colonel Vis did not see at all. 'You mentioned an RAF saturation attack on the Zenica Gap. This, of course, will now be switched to the bridge?'

'No. You wouldn't have us break our word to the Wehrmacht, would you? As promised, the attack comes on the Zenica Gap. As a diversion. To convince them, in case they have any last doubts left in their minds, that we have been fooled. Besides, you know as well as I do that that bridge is immune to high-level air attack. It will have to be destroyed in some other way.'

'In what way?'

'We'll think of something. The night is young. Two last things, Colonel Vis. There'll be another Wellington in at midnight and a second at 3 a.m. Let them both go. The next in, at 6 a.m., hold it against our arrival. Well, our possible arrival. With any luck we'll be flying out before dawn.'

'With any luck,' Vis said sombrely.

'And radio General Vukalovic, will you? Tell him what I've told you, the exact situation. And tell him to begin intensive small-arms fire at one o'clock in the morning.'

'What are they supposed to fire at?'

'They can fire at the moon for all I care.' Mallory swung aboard his pony. 'Come on, let's be off.'

'The moon,' General Vukalovic agreed, 'is a fair-sized target, though rather a long way off. However, if that's what our friend wants, that's what he shall have.' Vukalovic paused for a moment, looked at Colonel Janzy who was sitting beside him on a fallen log in the woods to the south of the Zenica Gap, then spoke again into the radio mouth-piece.

'Anyway, many thanks, Colonel Vis. So the Neretva bridge it is. And you think it will be unhealthy for us to remain in the immediate vicinity of this area after 1 a.m. Don't worry, we won't be here.' Vukalovic removed the head-phones and turned to Janzy. 'We pull out, quietly, at midnight. We leave a few men to make a lot of noise.'

'The ones who are going to fire at the moon?'

'The ones who are going to fire at the moon. Radio Colonel Lazlo at Neretva, will you? Tell him we'll be with him before the attack. Then radio Major Stephan. Tell him to leave just a holding force, pull out of the Western Gap and make his way to Colonel Lazlo's HQ.' Vukalovic paused for a thoughtful moment. 'We should be in for a few very interesting hours, don't you think?'

'Is there any chance in the world for this man Mallory?' Janzy's tone carried with it its own answer.

'Well, look at it this way,' Vukalovic said reasonably. 'Of

course there's a chance. There has to be a chance. It is, after all, my dear Janzy, a question of options—and there are no other options left open to us.'

Janzy made no reply but nodded several times in slow succession as if Vukalovic had just said something profound.

CHAPTER 9

Friday 2115 — Saturday 0040

The pony-back ride downhill through the thickly wooded forests from the Ivenici plateau to the block-house took Mallory and his men barely a quarter of the time it had taken them to make the ascent. In the deep snow the going underfoot was treacherous to a degree, collision with the bole of a pine was always an imminent possibility and none of the five riders made any pretence towards being an experienced horseman, with the inevitable result that slips, stumbles and heavy falls were as frequent as they were painful. Not one of them escaped the indignity of involuntarily leaving his saddle and being thrown headlong into the deep snow, but it was the providential cushioning effect of that snow that was the saving of them, that and, more often, the sure-footed agility of their mountain ponies: whatever the reason or combination of reasons, bruises and winded falls there were in plenty, but broken bones, miraculously, there were none.

The block-house came in sight. Mallory raised a warning hand, slowing them down until they were about two hundred yards distant from their objective, where he reined in, dismounted and led his pony into a thick cluster of pines, followed by the others. Mallory tethered his horse and indicated to the others to do the same.

Miller said complainingly: 'I'm sick of this damned pony but I'm sicker still of walking through deep snow. Why don't we just ride on down there?'

'Because they'll have ponies tethered down there. They'll start whinnying if they hear or see or smell other ponies approaching.'

'They might start whinnying anyway.'

'And there'll be guards on watch,' Andrea pointed out. 'I don't think, Corporal Miller, that we could make a very stealthy and unobtrusive approach on pony-back.'

'Guards. Guarding against what? As far as Neufeld and company are concerned, we're half-way over the Adriatic at this time.'

'Andrea's right,' Mallory said. 'Whatever else you may think about Neufeld, he's a first-class officer who takes no chances. There'll be guards.' He glanced up to the night sky where a narrow bar of cloud was just approaching the face of the moon. 'See that?'

'I see it,' Miller said miserably.

'Thirty seconds, I'd say. We make a run for the far gable end of the block-house—there are no embrasures there. And for God's sake, once we get there, keep dead quiet. If they hear anything, if they as much as suspect that we're outside, they'll bar the doors and use Petar and Maria as hostages. Then we'll just have to leave them.'

'"You'd do that, sir?" Reynolds asked.

'I'd do that. I'd rather cut a hand off, but I'd do that. I've no choice, Sergeant.'

'Yes, sir. I understand.'

The dark bar of cloud passed over the moon. The five men broke from the concealment of the pines and pounded downhill through the deep clogging snow, heading for the farther gable-wall of the block-house. Thirty yards away, at a signal from Mallory, they slowed down lest the sound of their crunching, running footsteps be heard by any watchers who might be keeping guard by the embrasures and completed the remaining distance by walking as quickly and quietly as possible in single file, each man using the footprints left by the man in front of him.

They reached the blank gable-end undetected, with the moon still behind the cloud. Mallory did not pause to congratulate either himself or any of the others. He at once dropped to his hands and knees and crawled round the corner of the block-house, pressing close in to the stone wall.

Four feet from the corner came the first of the embrasures. Mallory did not bother to lower himself any deeper into the snow—the embrasures were so deeply recessed in the massive stone walls that it would have been quite impossible for any watcher to see anything at a lesser distance than six feet from the embrasure. He concentrated, instead, on achieving as minimal a degree of sound as was possible, and did so with success, for he safely passed the embrasure without any alarm being raised. The other four were equally successful even although the moon broke from behind the cloud as the last of them, Groves, was directly under the embrasure. But he, too, remained undetected.

Mallory reached the door. He gestured to Miller, Reynolds and Groves to remain prone where they were: he and Andrea rose silently to their feet and pressed their ears close against the door.

Immediately they heard Droshny's voice, thick with menace, heavy with hatred.

'A traitress! That's what she is. A traitress to our cause. Kill her now!'

'Why did you do it, Maria?' Neufeld's voice, in contrast to Droshny's, was measured, calm, almost gentle.

'Why did she do it?' Droshny snarled. 'Money. That's why she did it. What else?'

'Why?' Neufeld was quietly persistent. 'Did Captain Mallory threaten to kill your brother?'

'Worse than that.' They had to strain to catch Maria's low

voice. 'He threatened to kill me. Who would have looked after my blind brother then?'

'We waste time,' Droshny said impatiently. 'Let me take them both outside.'

'No.' Neufeld's voice, still calm, admitted of no argument. 'A blind boy? A terrified girl? What are you, man?'

'A Cetnikl'

'And I'm an officer of the Wehrmacht.'

Andrea whispered in Mallory's ear: 'Any minute now and someone's going to notice our foot-tracks in the snow.'

Mallory nodded, stood aside and made a small gesturing motion of his hand. Mallory was under no illusions as to their respective capabilities when it came to bursting open doors leading into rooms filled with armed men. Andrea was the best in the business—and proceeded to prove it in his usual violent and lethal fashion.

A twist of the door handle, a violent kick with the sole of the right foot and Andrea stood framed in the doorway. The wildly swinging door had still not reached the full limit of travel on its hinges when the room echoed to the flat staccato chatter of Andrea's Schmeisser: Mallory, peering over Andrea's shoulder through the swirling cordite smoke, saw two German soldiers, lethally cursed with over-fast reactions, slumping wearily to the floor. His own machine-pistol levelled, Mallory followed Andrea into the room.

There was no longer any call for Schmeissers. None of the other soldiers in the room was carrying any weapon at all while Neufeld and Droshny, their faces frozen into expressions of total incredulity, were clearly, even if only momentarily, incapable of any movement at all, far less being capable of the idea of offering any suicidal resistance.

Mallory said to Neufeld: 'You've just bought yourself your life.' He turned to Maria, nodded towards the door, waited until she had led her brother outside, then looked again at Neufeld and Droshny and said curtly: 'Your guns.'

Neufeld managed to speak, although his lips moved in a strangely mechanical fashion. 'What in the name of God—'

Mallory was in no mind for small talk. He lifted his Schmeisser. 'Your guns.'

Neufeld and Droshny, like men in a dream, removed their pistols and dropped them to the floor.

'The keys.' Droshny and Neufeld looked at him in almost uncomprehending silence. 'The keys,' Mallory repeated. 'Now. Or the keys won't be necessary.'

For several seconds the room was completely silent, then Neufeld stirred, turned to Droshny and nodded. Droshny scowled—as well as any man can scowl when his face is still overspread with an expression of baffled astonishment and homicidal fury—reached into his pocket and produced the keys. Miller took them, unlocked and opened wide the cell door wordlessly and with a motion of his machine-pistol invited Neufeld, Droshny, Baer and the other soldiers to enter, waited until they had done so, swung shut the door, locked it and pocketed the key. The room echoed again as Andrea squeezed the trigger of his machine-pistol and destroyed the radio beyond any hope of repair. Five seconds later they were all outside, Mallory, the last man to leave, locking the door and sending the key spinning to fall yards away, buried from sight in the deep snow.

Suddenly he caught sight of the number of ponies tethered outside the block-house. Seven. Exactly the right number. He ran across to the embrasure outside the cell window and shouted: 'Our ponies are tethered two hundred yards uphill just inside the pines. Don't forget.' Then he ran quickly back and ordered the other six to mount. Reynolds looked at him in astonishment.

'You think of this, sir? At such a time?'

'I'd think of this at any time.' Mallory turned to Petar, who had just awkwardly mounted his horse, then turned to Maria. 'Tell him to take off his glasses.'

Maria looked at him in surprise, nodded in apparent understanding and spoke to her brother, who looked at her uncomprehendingly, then ducked his head obediently, removed his dark glasses and thrust them deep inside his tunic. Reynolds looked on in astonishment, then turned to Mallory.

'I don't understand, sir.'

Mallory wheeled his pony and said curtly: 'It's not necessary that you do.'

'I'm sorry, sir.'

Mallory turned his pony again and said, almost wearily: 'It's already eleven o'clock, boy, and almost already too late for what we have to do.'

'Sir.' Reynolds was deeply if obscurely pleased that Mallory should call him boy. 'I don't really want to know, sir.'

'You've asked. We'll have to go as quickly as our ponies can take us. A blind man can't see obstructions, can't balance himself according to the level of the terrain, can't anticipate in advance how he should brace himself for an unexpectedly sharp drop, can't lean in the saddle for a corner his pony knows is coming. A blind man, in short, is a hundred times more liable to fall off in a downhill gallop than we are. It's enough that a blind man should be blind for life. It's too much that we should expose him to the risk of a heavy fall with his glasses on, to expose him to the risk of not only being blind but of having his eyes gouged out and being in agony for life.'

'I hadn't thought—I mean—I'm sorry, sir.'

'Stop apologizing, boy. It's really my turn, you know—to apologize to you. Keep an eye on him, will you?'

Colonel Lazlo, binoculars to his eyes, gazed down over the

moonlit rocky slope below him towards the bridge at Neretva. On the southern bank of the river, in the meadows between the south bank and the beginning of the pine forest beyond, and, as far as Lazlo could ascertain, in the fringes of the pine forest itself, there was a disconcertingly ominous lack of movement, of any sign of life at all. Lazlo was pondering the disturbingly sinister significance of this unnatural peacefulness when a hand touched his shoulder. He twisted, looked up and recognized the figure of Major Stephan, commander of the Western Gap.

'Welcome, welcome. The General has advised me of your arrival. Your battalion with you?'

'What's left of it.' Stephan smiled without really smiling. 'Every man who could walk. And all those who couldn't.'

'God send we don't need them all tonight. The General has spoken to you of this man Mallory?' Major Stephan nodded, and Lazlo went on: 'If he fails? If the Germans cross the Neretva tonight—'

'So?' Stephan shrugged. 'We were all due to die tonight anyway.'

'A well-taken point,' Lazlo said approvingly. He lifted his binoculars and returned to his contemplation of the bridge at Neretva.

So far, and almost incredibly, neither Mallory nor any of the six galloping behind him had parted company with their ponies. Not even Petar. True, the incline of the slope was not nearly as steep as it had been from the Ivenici plateau down to the block-house, but Reynolds suspected it was because Mallory had imperceptibly succeeded in slowing down the pace of their earlier headlong gallop. Perhaps, Reynolds thought vaguely, it was because Mallory was subconsciously trying to protect the blind singer, who was riding almost abreast with him, guitar firmly strapped over his shoulder, reins abandoned and both hands clasped desperately to the pommel of his saddle. Unbidden, almost, Reynolds's thoughts strayed back to that scene inside the block-house. Moments later, he was urging his pony forwards until he had drawn alongside Mallory.

'Sir?'

'What is it?' Mallory sounded irritable.

'A word, sir. It's urgent. Really it is.'

Mallory threw up a hand and brought the company to a halt. He said curtly: 'Be quick.'

'Neufeld and Droshny, sir.' Reynolds paused in a moment's brief uncertainty, then continued. 'Do you reckon they know where you're going?'

'What's that to do with anything?'

'Please.'

'Yes, they do. Unless they're complete morons. And they're not.'

'It's a pity, sir,' Reynolds said reflectively, 'that you hadn't shot them after all.'

'Get to the point,' Mallory said impatiently.

'Yes, sir. You reckoned Sergeant Baer released them earlier on?'

'Of course.' Mallory was exercising all his restraint. 'Andrea saw them arrive. I've explained all this. They—Neufeld and Droshny—had to go up to the Ivenici plateau to check that we'd really gone.'

'I understand that, sir. So you knew that Baer was following us. How did he get into the block-house?'

Mallory's restraint vanished. He said in exasperation: 'Because I left both keys hanging outside.'

'Yes, sir. You were expecting him. But Sergeant Baer didn't know you were expecting him—and even if he did he wouldn't be expecting to find keys so conveniently to hand.'

'Good God in heaven! Duplicates!' In bitter chagrin, Mallory smacked the fist of one hand into the palm of the other.

'Imbecile! Imbecile! Of *course* he would have his own keys!'

'And Droshny,' Miller said thoughtfully, 'may know a short-cut.'

'That's not all of it.' Mallory was completely back on balance again, outwardly composed, the relaxed calmness of the face the complete antithesis of his racing mind. 'Worse still, he may make straight for his camp radio and warn Zimmermann to pull his armoured divisions back from the Neretva. You've earned your passage tonight, Reynolds. Thanks, boy. How far to Neufeld's camp, do you think, Andrea?'

'A mile.' The words came over Andrea's shoulder, for Andrea, as always in situations which he knew called for the exercise of his highly specialized talents, was already on his way.

Five minutes later they were crouched at the edge of the forest less than twenty yards from the perimeter of Neufeld's camp. Quite a number of the huts had illuminated windows, music could be heard coming from the dining hut and several Cetnik soldiers were moving about in the compound.

Reynolds whispered to Mallory: 'How do we go about it, sir?'

'We don't do anything at all. We just leave it to Andrea.'

Groves spoke, his voice low. 'One man? Andrea? We leave it to one man?'

Mallory sighed. 'Tell them, Corporal Miller.'

'I'd rather not. Well, if I have to. The fact is,' Miller went on kindly, 'Andrea is rather good at this sort of thing.'

'So are we,' Reynolds said. 'We're commandos. We've been trained for this sort of thing.'

'And very highly trained, no doubt,' said Miller approvingly. 'Another half-dozen years' experience and half a dozen of you might be just about able to cope with him. Although I doubt it very much. Before the night is out, you'll learn—I don't mean to be insulting, Sergeants—that you are little lambs to Andrea's wolf.' Miller paused and went on sombrely: 'Like whoever happens to be inside that radio hut at this moment.'

'Like whoever happens—' Groves twisted round and looked behind him. 'Andrea? He's gone. I didn't see him go.'

'No one ever does,' Miller said. 'And those poor devils won't ever see him come.' He looked at Mallory. 'Time's a-wasting.'

Mallory glanced at the luminous hands of his watch. 'Eleven-thirty. Time *is* a-wasting.'

For almost a minute there was a silence broken only by the restless movements of the ponies tethered deep in the woods behind them, then Groves gave a muffled exclamation as Andrea materialized beside him. Mallory looked upand said: 'How many?'

Andrea held up two fingers and moved silently into the woods towards his pony. The others rose and followed him, Groves and Reynolds exchanging glances which indicated more clearly than any words could possibly have done that they could have been even more wrong about Andrea than they had ever been about Mallory.

At precisely the moment that Mallory and his companions were remounting their ponies in the woods fringing Neufeld's camp, a Wellington bomber came sinking down towards a well-lit airfield—the same airfield from which Mallory and his men had taken off less than twenty-four hours previously. Termoli, Italy. It made a perfect touch-down and as it taxied along the runway an army radio truck curved in on an interception course, turning to parallel the last hundred yards of the Wellington's run down. In the left-hand front seat and in the right-hand back seat of the truck sat two immediately recognizable figures: in the front, the piratical splendidly bearded figure of Captain Jensen, in the back the British lieutenant-general with whom Jensen had recently spent so much time in pacing the Termoli Operations Room.

Plane and truck came to a halt at the same moment. Jensen, displaying a surprising agility for one of his very considerable bulk, hopped nimbly to the ground and strode briskly across the tarmac and arrived at the Wellington just as its door opened and the first of the passengers, the moustached major, swung to the ground.

Jensen nodded to the papers clutched in the major's hand and said without preamble: 'Those for me?' The major blinked uncertainly, then nodded stiffly in return, clearly irked by this abrupt welcome for a man just returned from durance vile. Jensen took the papers without a further word, went back to his seat in the jeep, brought out a flash-light and studied the papers briefly. He twisted in his seat and said to the radio-operator seated beside the General: 'Flight plan as stated. Target as indicated. Now.' The radio-operator began to crank the handle.

Some fifty miles to the south-east, in the Foggia area, the buildings and runways of the RAF heavy bomber base echoed and reverberated to the thunder of scores of aircraft engines: at the dispersal area at the west end of the main runway several squadrons of Lancaster heavy bombers were lined up ready for take-off, obviously awaiting the signal to go. The signal was not long in coming.

Half-way down the airfield, but well to one side of the main runway, was parked a jeep identical to the one in which Jensen was sitting in Termoli. In the back seat a radio-operator was crouched over a radio, ear-phones to his head. He listened intently, then looked up and said matter-of-factly: 'Instructions as stated. Now. Now. Now.'

'Instructions as stated,' a captain in the front seat repeated. 'Now. Now. Now.' He reached for a wooden box, produced 'three Very pistols, aimed directly across the runway and fired each in turn. The brilliantly arcing flares burst into incandescent life, green, red and green again, before curving slowly back to earth. The thunder at the far end of the airfield mounted to a rumbling crescendo and the first of the Lancasters began to move. Within a few minutes the last of them had taken off and was lifting into the darkly hostile night skies of the Adriatic.

'I did say, I believe,' Jensen remarked conversationally and comfortably to the General in the back seat, 'that they are the best in the business. Our friends from Foggia are on their way.'

'The best in the business. Maybe. I don't know. What I do know is that those damned German and Austrian divisions are still in position in the Gustav Line. Zero hour for the assault on the Gustav Line is—' he glanced at his watch—'in exactly thirty hours.'

'Time enough,' Jensen said confidently.

'I wish I shared this blissful confidence.'

Jensen smiled cheerfully at him as the jeep moved off, then faced forward in his seat again. As he did, the smile vanished completely from his face and his fingers beat a drum tattoo on the seat beside him.

The moon had broken through again as Neufeld, Droshny and their men came galloping into camp and reined in ponies so covered with steam from their heaving flanks and distressed breathing as to have a weirdly insubstantial appearance in the pale moonlight. Neufeld swung from his pony and turned to Sergeant Baer.

'How many ponies left in the stables?'

'Twenty. About that.'

'Quickly. And as many men as there are ponies. Saddle up.'

Neufeld gestured to Droshny and together they ran towards the radio hut. The door, ominously enough on that icy night, was standing wide open. They were still ten feet short of the door when Neufeld shouted: 'The Neretva bridge at once. Tell General Zimmermann—'

He halted abruptly in the doorway, Droshny by his shoulder. For the second time that evening the faces of both men reflected their stunned disbelief, their total uncomprehending shock.

Only one small lamp burned in the radio hut, but that one small lamp was enough. Two men lay on the floor in grotesquely huddled positions, the one lying partially across the other: both were quite unmistakably dead. Beside them, with its face-plate ripped off and interior smashed, lay the mangled remains of what had once been a transmitter. Neufeld gazed at the scene for some time before shaking his head violently as if to break the shocked spell and turned to Droshny.

'The big one,' he said quietly. 'The big one did this.'

'The big one,' Droshny agreed. He was almost smiling. 'You will remember what you promised, Hauptmann Neufeld? The big one. He's for me.'

'You shall have him. Come. They can be only minutes ahead.' Both men turned and ran back to the compound where Sergeant Baer and a group of soldiers were already saddling up the ponies.

'Machine-pistols only,' Neufeld shouted. 'No rifles. It will be close-quarter work tonight. And Sergeant Baer?'

'Hauptmann Neufeld?'

'Inform the men that we will not be taking prisoners.'

As those of Neufeld and his men had been, the ponies of Mallory and his six companions were almost invisible in the dense clouds of steam rising from their sweat-soaked bodies: their lurching gait, which could not now even be called a trot, was token enough of the obvious fact that they had reached the limits of exhaustion. Mallory glanced at Andrea, who nodded and said: 'I agree. We'd make faster time on foot now.'

'I must be getting old,' Mallory said, and for a moment he sounded that way. 'I'm not thinking very well tonight, am I?'

'I do not understand.'

'Ponies. Neufeld and his men will have fresh ponies from the stables. We should have killed them—or at least driven them away.'

'Age is not the same thing as lack of sleep. It never occurred to me, either. A man cannot think of everything, my Keith.' Andrea reined in his pony and was about to swing down when something on the slope below caught his attention. He pointed ahead.

A minute later they drew up alongside a very narrow-gauge railway line, of a type common in Central Yugoslavia. At this level the snow had petered out and the track, they could see, was over-grown and rusty, but for all that, apparently in fair enough mechanical condition: undoubtedly, it was the same track that had caught their eye when they had paused to examine the green waters of the Neretva dam on the way back from Major Broznik's camp that morning. But what simultaneously caught and held the attention of both Mallory and Miller was not the track itself, but a little siding leading on to the track—and a diminutive wood-burning locomotive that stood on the siding. The locomotive was practically a solid block of rust and looked as if it hadn't moved from its present position since the beginning of the war: in all probability, it hadn't.

Mallory produced a large-scale map from his tunic and flashed a torch on it. He said: 'No doubt of it, this is the track we saw this morning. It goes down along the Neretva for at least five miles before bearing off to the south.' He paused and went on thoughtfully: 'I wonder if we could get that thing moving.'

'What?' Miller looked at him in horror. 'It'll fall to pieces if you touch it—it's only the rust that's holding the damn thing together. And that gradient there!' He peered in dismay down the slope. 'What do you think our terminal velocity is going to be when we hit one of those monster pine trees a few miles down the track?'

'The ponies are finished,' Mallory said mildly, 'and you know how much you love walking.'

Miller looked at the locomotive with loathing. 'There must be some other way.'

'Shh!' Andrea cocked his head. 'They're coming. I can hear them coming.'

'Get the chocks away from those front wheels,' Miller shouted. He ran forward and after several violent and well-directed kicks which clearly took into no account the future state of his toes, succeeded in freeing the triangular block which was attached to the front of the locomotive by a chain: Reynolds, no less energetically, did the same for the other chock.

All of them, even Maria and Petar helping, flung all their weight against the rear of the locomotive. The locomotive remained where it was. They tried again, despairingly: the wheels refused to budge even a fraction of an inch. Groves said, with an odd mixture of urgency and diffidence: 'Sir, on a gradient like this, it would have been left with its brakes on.'

'Oh my God!' Mallory said in chagrin. 'Andrea. Quickly. Release the brake-lever.'

Andrea swung himself on to the footplate. He said complainingly: 'There are a dozen damned levers up here.'

'Well, open the dozen damned levers, then.' Mallory glanced anxiously back up the track. Maybe Andrea had heard some-

171

thing, maybe not: there was certainly no one in sight yet. But he knew that Neufeld and Droshny, who must have been released from the block-house only minutes after they had left there themselves and who knew those woods and paths better than they did, must be very close indeed by this time.

There was a considerable amount of metallic screeching and swearing coming from the cab and after perhaps half a minute Andrea said: 'That's the lot.'

'Shove,' Mallory ordered.

They shoved, heels jammed in the sleepers and backs to the locomotive, and this time the locomotive moved off so easily, albeit with a tortured squealing of rusted wheels, that most of those pushing were caught wholly by surprise and fell on their backs on the track. Moments later they were on their feet and running after the locomotive which was already perceptibly beginning to increase speed. Andrea reached down from the cab, swung Maria and Petar aboard in turn, then lent a helping hand to the others. The last, Groves, was reaching for the footplate when he suddenly braked, swung round, ran back to the ponies, unhitched the climbing ropes, flung them over his shoulder and chased after the locomotive again. Mallory reached down and helped him on to the footplate.

'It's not my day,' Mallory said sadly. 'Evening rather. First, I forget about Baer's duplicate keys. Then about the ponies. Then the brakes. Now the ropes. I wonder what I'll forget about next?'

'Perhaps about Neufeld and Droshny.' Reynolds's voice was carefully without expression.

'What about Neufeld and Droshny?'

Reynolds pointed back up the railway track with the barrel of his Schmeisser. 'Permission to fire, sir.'

Mallory swung round. Neufeld, Droshny and an indeterminate number of other pony-mounted soldiers had just appeared around a bend in the track and were hardly more than a hundred yards away.

'Permission to fire,' Mallory agreed. 'The rest of you get down.' He unslung and brought up his own Schmeisser just as Reynolds squeezed the trigger of his. For perhaps five seconds the closed metallic confines of the tiny cabin reverberated deafeningly to the crash of the two machine-pistols, then, at a nudge from Mallory, the two men stopped firing. There was no target left to fire at. Neufeld and his men had loosed off a few preliminary shots but immediately realized that the wildly swaying saddles of their ponies made an impossibly unsteady firing position as compared to the cab of the locomotive and had pulled their ponies off into the woods on either side of the track. But not all of them had pulled off in time: two men lay motionless and face down in the snow while their ponies still galloped down the track in the wake of the locomotive.

Miller rose, glanced wordlessly at the scene behind, then tapped Mallory on the arm. 'A small point occurs to me, sir. How do we stop this thing.' He gazed apprehensively through the cab window. 'Must be doing sixty already.'

'Well, we're doing at least twenty,' Mallory said agreeably. 'But fast enough to out-distance those ponies. Ask Andrea. He released the brake.'

'He released a dozen levers,' Miller corrected. 'Any one could have been the brake.'

'Well, you're not going to sit around doing nothing, are you?' Mallory asked reasonably. 'Find out how to stop the damn thing.'

Miller looked at him coldly and set about trying to find out how to stop the damn thing. Mallory turned as Reynolds touched him on the arm. 'Well?'

Reynolds had an arm round Maria to steady her on the now swaying platform. He whispered: 'They're going to get us, sir. They're going to get us for sure. Why don't we stop and

173

leave those two, sir? Give them a chance to escape into the woods?'

'Thanks for the thought. But don't be mad. With us they have a chance—a small one to be sure, but a chance. Stay behind and they'll be butchered.'

The locomotive was no longer doing the twenty miles per hour Mallory had mentioned and if it hadn't approached the figure that Miller had so fearfully mentioned it was certainly going quickly enough to make it rattle and sway to what appeared to be the very limits of its stability. By this time the last of the trees to the right of the track had petered out, the darkened waters of the Neretva dam were clearly visible to the west and the railway track was now running very close indeed to the edge of what appeared to be a dangerously steep precipice. Mallory looked back into the cab. With the exception of Andrea, everyone now wore expressions of considerable apprehension on their faces. Mallory said: 'Found out how to stop this damn thing yet?'

'Easy.' Andrea indicated a lever. 'This handle here.'

'Okay, brakeman. I want to have a look.'

To the evident relief of most of the passengers in the cab, Andrea leaned back on the brake-lever. There was an eldritch screeching that set teeth on edge, clouds of sparks flew up past the sides of the cab as some wheels or other locked solid in the lines, then the locomotive eased slowly to a halt, both the intensity of sound from the squealing brakes and the number of sparks diminishing as it did so. Andrea, duty done, leaned out of the side of the cab with all the bored aplomb of the crack loco engineer: one had the feeling that all he really wanted in life at that moment was a piece of oily waste and a whistle-cord to pull.

Mallory and Miller climbed down and ran to the edge of the cliff, less than twenty yards away. At least Mallory did. Miller made a much more cautious approach, inching forward the last few feet on hands and knees. He hitched one cautious eye over the edge of the precipice, screwed both eyes shut, looked away and just as cautiously inched his way back from the edge of the cliff: Miller claimed that he couldn't even stand on the bottom step of a ladder without succumbing to the overwhelming compulsion to throw himself into the abyss.

Mallory gazed down thoughtfully into the depths. They were, he saw, directly over the top of the dam wall, which, in the strangely shadowed half-light cast by the moon, seemed almost impossibly far below in the dizzying depths. The broad top of the dam wall was brightly lit by floodlights and patrolled by at least half a dozen German soldiers, jack-booted and helmeted. Beyond the dam, on the lower side, the ladder Maria had spoken of was invisible, but the frail-looking swing bridge, still menaced by the massive bulk of the boulder on the scree on the left bank, and, farther down, the white water indicating what might or might not have been a possible—or passable —ford were plainly in sight. Mallory, momentarily abstracted in thought, gazed at the scene below for several moments, recalled that the pursuit must be again coming uncomfortably close and hurriedly made his way back to the locomotive. He said to Andrea: 'About a mile and a half, I should think. No more.' He turned to Maria. 'You know there's a ford—or what seems to be a ford—some way below the dam. Is there a way down?'

'For a mountain goat.'

'Don't insult him,' Miller said reprovingly.

'I don't understand.'

'Ignore him,' Mallory said. 'Just tell us when we get there.'

Some five or six miles below the Neretva dam General Zimmermann paced up and down the fringe of the pine forest bordering the meadow to the south of the bridge at Neretva. Beside him paced a colonel, one of his divisional commanders.

To the south of them could just dimly be discerned the shapes of hundreds of men and scores of tanks and other vehicles, vehicles with all their protective camouflage now removed, each tank and vehicle surrounded by its coterie of attendants making last-minute and probably wholly unnecessary adjustments. The time for hiding was over. The waiting was coming to an end. Zimmermann glanced at his watch.

'Twelve-thirty. The first infantry battalions start moving across in fifteen minutes, and spread out along the north bank. The tanks at two o'clock.'

'Yes, sir.' The details had been arranged many hours ago, but somehow one always found it necessary to repeat the instructions and the acknowledgments. The Colonel gazed to the north. 'I sometimes wonder if there's *anybody* at all across there.'

'It's not the north I'm worrying about,' Zimmermann said sombrely. 'It's the west.'

'The Allies? You—you think their air armadas will come soon? It's still in your bones, Herr General?'

'Still in my bones. It's coming soon. For me, for you, for all of us.' He shivered, then forced a smile. 'Some ill-mannered lout has just walked over my grave.'

CHAPTER 10

Saturday
0040-0120

'We're coming up to it now,' Maria said. Blonde hair streaming in the passing wind, she peered out again through the cab window of the clanking, swaying locomotive, withdrew her head and turned to Mallory. 'About three hundred metres.'

Mallory glanced at Andrea. 'You heard, brakeman?'

'I heard.' Andrea leaned hard on the brake-lever. The result was as before, a banshee shrieking of locked wheels on the rusty lines and a pyrotechnical display of sparks. The locomotive came to a juddering halt as Andrea looked out his cab window and observed a V-shaped gap in the edge of the cliff directly opposite where they had come to a stop. 'Within the yard, I should say?'

'Within the yard,' Mallory agreed. 'If you're unemployed after the war, there should always be a place for you in a shunter's yard.' He swung down to the side of the track, lent a helping hand to Maria and Petar, waited until Miller, Reynolds and Groves had jumped down, then said impatiently to Andrea: 'Well, hurry up, then.'

'Coming,' Andrea said peaceably. He pushed the hand-brake all the way off, jumped down, and gave the locomotive a shove: the ancient vehicle at once moved off, gathering speed as it went. 'You never know,' Andrea said wistfully. 'It might hit somebody somewhere.'

They ran towards the cut in the edge of the cliff, a cut which obviously represented the beginning of some prehistoric land-slide down to the bed of the Neretva, a maelstrom of white water far below, the boiling rapids resulting from scores of huge boulders which had slipped from this landslide in that distant aeon. By some exercise of the imagination, that scar in the side of the cliff-face might just perhaps have been called a gully, but it was in fact an almost perpendicular drop of scree and shale and small boulders, all of it treacherous and unstable to a frightening degree, the whole dangerous sweep broken only by a small ledge of jutting rock about half-way down. Miller took one brief glance at this terrifying prospect, stepped hurriedly back from the edge of the cliff and looked at Mallory in a silently dismayed incredulity.

'I'm afraid so,' Mallory said.

'But this is terrible. Even when I climbed the south cliff in Navarone—'

'You didn't climb the south cliff in Navarone,' Mallory said unkindly. 'Andrea and I pulled you up at the end of a rope.'

'Did you? I forget. But this—this is a climber's nightmare.'

'So we don't have to climb it. Just lower ourselves down. You'll be all right—as long as you don't start rolling.'

'I'll be all right as long as I don't start rolling,' Miller repeated mechanically. He watched Mallory join two ropes together and pass them around the bole of a stunted pine. 'How about Petar and Maria?'

'Petar doesn't have to see to make this descent. All he has to do is to lower himself on this rope—and Petar is as strong as a horse. Somebody will be down there before him to guide his feet on to the ledge. Andrea will look after the young lady here. Now hurry. Neufeld and his men will be up with us any minute here—and if they catch us on this cliff-face, well that's that. Andrea, off you go with Maria.'

Immediately, Andrea and the girl swung over the edge of the gully and began to lower themselves swiftly down the rope. Groves watched them, hesitated, then moved towards Mallory.

'I'll go last, sir, and take the rope with me.'

Miller took his arm and led him some feet away. He said, kindly: 'Generous, son, generous, but it's just not on. Not as long as Dusty Miller's life depends on it. In a situation like this, I must explain, all our lives depend upon the anchor-man. The Captain, I am informed, is the best anchor-man in the world.'

'He's what?'

'It's one of the non-coincidences why he was chosen to lead this mission. Bosnia is known to have rocks and cliffs and mountains all over it. Mallory was climbing the Himalayas, laddie, before you were climbing out of your cot. Even you are not too young to have heard of him.'

'*Keith* Mallory? The New Zealander?'

'Indeed. Used to chase sheep around, I gather. Come on, your turn.'

The first five made it safely. Even the last but one, Miller, made the descent to the ledge without incident, principally by employing his favourite mountain-climbing technique of keeping his eyes closed all the time. Then Mallory came last, coiling the rope with him as he came, moving quickly and surely and hardly ever seeming to look where he put his feet but at the same time not as much as disturbing the slightest pebble or piece of shale. Groves observed the descent with a look of almost awed disbelief in his eyes.

Mallory peered over the edge of the ledge. Because of a slight bend in the gorge above, there was a sharp cut-off in the moonlight just below where they stood so that while the phosphorescent whiteness of the rapids was in clear moonlight, the lower part of the slope beneath their feet was in deep shadow. Even as he watched, the moon was obscured by a shadow, and all the dimly-seen detail in the slope below vanished. Mallory knew that they could never afford to wait until the moon reappeared, for Neufeld and his men could well have arrived by then. Mallory belayed a rope round an outcrop of rock and said to Andrea and Maria: 'This one's really dangerous. Watch for loose boulders.'

Andrea and Maria took well over a minute to make their invisible descent, a double tug on the rope announcing their safe arrival at the bottom. On the way down they had started several small avalanches, but Mallory had no fears that the next man down would trigger off a fall of rock that would injure or even kill Andrea and Maria; Andrea had lived too long and too dangerously to die in so useless and so foolish a fashion—and he would undoubtedly warn the next man down of the same danger. For the tenth time Mallory glanced up towards the top of the slope they had just descended but if Neufeld, Droshny and his men had just arrived they were keeping very quiet about it and being most circumspect indeed: it was not a difficult conclusion to arrive at that, after the events of the past few hours, circumspection would be the last thing in their minds.

The moon broke through again as Mallory finally made his descent. He cursed the exposure it might offer if any of the enemy suddenly appeared on the cliff-top, even although he knew that Andrea would be guarding against precisely that danger; on the other hand it afforded him the opportunity of descending at twice the speed he could have made in the earlier darkness. The watchers below watched tensely as Mallory, without any benefit of rope, made his perilous descent: but he never even looked like making one mistake. He descended safely to the boulder-strewn shore and gazed out over the rapids.

He said to no one in particular: 'You know what's going to happen if they arrive at the top and find us half-way across here and the moon shining down on us?' The ensuing silence left no doubt but that they all knew what was going to happen. 'Now is all the time. Reynolds, you think you can make it?' Reynolds nodded. 'Then leave your gun.'

Mallory knotted a bowline round Reynolds's waist, taking the strain, if one were to arise, with Andrea and Groves. Reynolds launched himself bodily into the rapids, heading for the first of the rounded boulders which offered so treacherous a hold in that seething foam. Twice he was knocked off his feet, twice he regained them, reached the rock, but immediately beyond it was washed away off balance and swept down-river. The men on the bank hauled him ashore again, coughing and spluttering and fighting mad. Without a word to or look at anybody Reynolds again hurled himself into the rapids, and this time so determined was the fury of his assault that he succeeded in reaching the far bank without once being knocked off his feet.

He dragged himself on to the stony beach, lay there for some moments recovering from his exhaustion, then rose, crossed to a stunted pine at the base of the cliff rising on the other side, undid the rope round his waist and belayed it securely round the bole of the tree. Mallory, on his side, took two turns round a large rock and gestured to Andrea and the girl.

Mallory glanced upwards again to the top of the gully. There were still no signs of the enemy. Even so, Mallory felt that they could afford to wait no longer, that they had already pushed their luck too far. Andrea and Maria were barely half-way across when he told Groves to give Petar a hand across the rapids. He hoped to God the rope would hold, but hold it did for Andrea and Maria made it safely to the far bank. No sooner had they grounded than Mallory sent Miller on his way, carrying a pile of automatic arms over his left shoulder.

Groves and Petar also made the crossing without incident. Mallory himself had to wait until Miller reached the far bank, for he knew the chances of his being carried away were high and if he were, then Miller too would be precipitated into the water and their guns rendered useless.

Mallory waited until he saw Andrea give Miller a hand into the shallow water on the far bank and waited no longer. He unwound the rope from the rock he had been using as a belay, fastened a bowline round his own waist and plunged into the water. He was swept away at exactly the same point where Reynolds had been on his first attempt and was finally dragged ashore by his friends on the far bank with a fair amount of the waters of the Neretva in his stomach but otherwise unharmed.

'Any injuries, any cracked bones or skulls?' Mallory asked. He himself felt as if he had been over Niagara in a barrel. 'No? Fine.' He looked at Miller. 'You stay here with me. Andrea, take the others up round the first corner there and wait for us.'

'Me?' Andrea objected mildly. He nodded towards the gully. 'We've got friends that might be coming down there at any moment.'

Mallory took him some little way aside. 'We also have friends,' he said quietly, 'who might just possibly be coming down-river from the dam garrison.' He nodded at the two sergeants, Petar and Maria. 'What would happen to them if they ran into an Alpenkorps patrol, do you think?'

'I'll wait for you round the corner.'

Andrea and the four others made their slow way up-river, slipping and stumbling over the wetly slimy rocks and boulders. Mallory and Miller withdrew into the protection and concealment of two large boulders and stared upwards.

Several minutes passed. The moon still shone and the top of the gully was still innocent of any sign of the enemy. Miller said uneasily: 'What do you think has gone wrong? They're taking a damned long time about turning up.'

'No, I think that it's just that they are taking a damned long time in turning back.'

'Turning back?'

'They don't *know* where we've gone.' Mallory pulled out his map, examined it with a carefully hooded pencil-torch. 'About three-quarters of a mile down the railway track, there's a sharp turn to the left. In all probability the locomotive would have left the track there. Last time Neufeld and Droshny saw us we were aboard that locomotive and the logical thing for them to have done would have been to follow the track till they came to where we had abandoned the locomotive, expecting to find us somewhere in the vicinity. When they found the crashed engine, they would know at once what would have happened—but that would have given them another mile and a half to ride—and half of that uphill on tired ponies.'

'That must be it. I wish to God,' Miller went on grumblingly, 'that they'd hurry up.'

'What is this?' Mallory queried. 'Dusty Miller yearning for action?'

'No, I'm not,' Miller said definitely. He glanced at his watch. 'But time is getting very short.'

'Time,' Mallory agreed soberly, 'is getting terribly short.'

And then they came. Miller, glancing upward, saw a faint metallic glint in the moonlight as a head peered cautiously over the edge of the gully. He touched Mallory on the arm.

'I see him,' Mallory murmured. Together both men reached inside their tunics, pulled out their Lugers and removed their waterproof coverings. The helmeted head gradually resolved itself into a figure standing fully silhouetted in the moonlight against the sharply etched skyline. He began what was obviously meant to be a cautious descent, then suddenly flung up both arms and fell backwards and outwards. If he cried out, from where Mallory and Miller were the cry could not have been heard above the rushing of the waters. He struck

183

the ledge half-way down, bounced off and outwards for a quite incredible distance, then landed spread-eagled on the stony river bank below, pulling down a small avalanche behind him.

Miller was grimly philosophical. 'Well, you said it was dangerous.'

Another figure appeared over the lip of the precipice to make the second attempt at a descent, and was followed in short order by several more men. Then, for the space of a few minutes, the moon went behind a cloud, while Mallory and Miller stared across the river until their eyes ached, anxiously and vainly trying to pierce the impenetrable darkness that shrouded the slope on the far side.

The leading climber, when the moon did break through, was just below the ledge, cautiously negotiating the lower slope. Mallory took careful aim with his Luger, the climber stiffened convulsively, toppled backwards and fell to his death. The following figure, clearly oblivious of the fate of his companion, began the descent of the lower slope. Both Mallory and Miller sighted their Lugers but just then the moon was suddenly obscured again and they had to lower their guns. When the moon again reappeared, four men had already reached the safety of the opposite bank, two of whom, linked together by a rope, were just beginning to venture the crossing of the ford.

Mallory and Miller waited until they had safely completed two thirds of the crossing of the ford. They formed a close and easy target and at that range it was impossible that Mallory and Miller should miss, nor did they. There was a momentary reddening of the white waters of the rapids, as much imagined as seen, then, still lashed together they were swept away down the gorge. So furiously were their bodies tumbled over and over by the rushing waters, so often did cartwheeling arms and legs break surface, that they might well have given the appearance of men who, though without hope, were still desperately struggling for their lives. In any event, the two men left standing on the far bank clearly did not regard the accident as being significant of anything amiss in any sinister way. They stood and watched the vanishing bodies of their companions in perplexity, still unaware of what was happening. A matter of two or three seconds later and they would never have been aware of anything else again but once more a wisp of errant dark cloud covered the moon and they still had a little time, a very little time, to live. Mallory and Miller lowered their guns.

Mallory glanced at his watch and said irritably: 'Why the hell don't they start firing? It's five past one.'

'Why don't who start firing?' Miller asked cautiously.

'You heard. You were there. I asked Vis to ask Vukalovic to give us sound cover at one. Up by the Zenica Gap there, less than a mile away. Well, we can't wait any longer. It'll take—' He broke off and listened to the sudden outburst of rifle fire, startlingly loud even at that comparatively close distance, and smiled. 'Well, what's five minutes here or there. Come on. I have the feeling that Andrea must be getting a little anxious about us.'

Andrea was. He emerged silently from the shadows as they rounded the first bend in the river. He said reproachfully: 'Where have you two been? You had me worried stiff.'

'I'll explain in an hour's time—if we're all still around in an hour's time,' Mallory amended grimly. 'Our friends the bandits are two minutes behind. I think they'll be coming in force—although they've lost four already—six including the two Reynolds got from the locomotive. You stop at the next bend up-river and hold them off. You'll have to do it by yourself. Think you can manage?'

'This is no time for joking,' Andrea said with dignity. 'And then?'

'Groves and Reynolds and Petar and his sister come with us

185

up-river, Reynolds and Groves as nearly as possible to the dam, Petar and Maria wherever they can find some suitable shelter, possibly in the vicinity of the swing bridge—as long as they're well clear of that damned great boulder perched above it.'

'Swing bridge, sir?' Reynolds asked. 'A boulder?'

'I saw it when we got off the locomotive to reconnoitre.'

'*You* saw it. Andrea didn't.'

'I mentioned it to him,' Mallory went on impatiently. He ignored the disbelief in the sergeant's face and turned to Andrea. 'Dusty and I can't wait any longer. Use your Schmeisser to stop them.' He pointed north-westwards towards the Zenica Gap, where the rattle of musketry was now almost continuous. 'With all that racket going on, they'll never know the difference.'

Andrea nodded, settled himself comfortably behind a pair of large boulders and slid the barrel of his Schmeisser into the V between them. The remainder of the party moved up-stream, scrambling awkwardly around and over the slippery boulders and rocks that covered the right-hand bank of the Neretva, until they came to a rudimentary path that had been cleared among the stones. This they followed for perhaps a hundred yards, till they came to a slight bend in the gorge. By mutual consent and without any order being given, all six stopped and gazed upwards.

The towering breath-taking ramparts of the Neretva dam wall had suddenly come into full view. Above the dam on either side precipitous walls of rock soared up into the night sky, at first quite vertical then both leaning out in an immense overhang which seemed to make them almost touch at the top, although this, Mallory knew from the observation he had made from above, was an optical illusion. On top of the dam wall itself the guard-houses and radio huts were clearly visible, as were the pigmy shapes of several patrolling German soldiers.

From the top of the eastern side of the dam, where the huts were situated, an iron ladder—Mallory knew it was painted green, but in the half-shadow cast by the dam wall it looked black—fastened by iron supports to the bare rock face, zig-zagged downwards to the foot of the gorge, close by where foaming white jets of water boiled from the outlet pipes at the base of the dam wall. Mallory tried to estimate how many steps there would be in that ladder. Two hundred, perhaps two hundred and fifty, and once you started to climb or descend you just had to keep on going, for nowhere was there any platform or back-rest to afford even the means for a temporary respite. Nor did the ladder at any point afford the slightest scrap of cover from watchers on the bridge. As an assault route, Mallory mused, it was scarcely the one he would have chosen: he could not conceive of a more hazardous one.

About half-way between where they stood and the foot of the ladder on the other side, a swing bridge spanned the boiling waters of the gorge. There was little about its ancient, rickety and warped appearance to inspire any confidence: and what little confidence there might have been could hardly have survived the presence of an enormous boulder, directly above the eastern edge of the bridge, which seemed in imminent danger of breaking loose from its obviously insecure footing in the deep scar in the cliff-side.

Reynolds assimilated all of the scene before him, then turned to Mallory. He said quietly: 'We've been very patient, sir.'

'You've been very patient, Sergeant—and I'm grateful. You know, of course, that there is a Yugoslav division trapped in the Zenica Cage—that's just behind the mountains to our left, here. You know, too, that the Germans are going to launch two armoured divisions across the Neretva bridge at two a.m. this morning and that if once they do get across—and normally there would be nothing to stop them—the Yugoslavs, armed with only their pop-guns and with hardly any ammunition left,

187

would be cut to pieces. You know the only way to stop them is to destroy the Neretva bridge? You know that this counter-espionage and rescue mission was only a cover for the real thing?'

Reynolds said bitterly: 'I know that—now.' He pointed down the gorge. 'And I also know that the bridge lies that way.'

'And so it does. I also know that even if we could approach it—which would be quite impossible—we couldn't blow that bridge up with a truckload of explosives; steel bridges anchored in reinforced concrete take a great deal of destroying.' He turned and looked at the dam. 'So we do it another way. See that dam wall there—there's thirty million tons of water behind it—enough to carry away the Sydney bridge, far less the one over the Neretva.'

Groves said in a low voice: 'You're crazy,' and then, as an afterthought, 'sir.'

'Don't we know it? But we're going to blow up that dam all the same. Dusty and I.'

'But—but all the explosives we have are a few hand-grenades,' Reynolds said, almost desperately. 'And in that dam wall there must be ten- to twenty-feet thicknesses of reinforced concrete. Blow it up? How?'

Mallory shook his head. 'Sorry.'

'Why, you close-mouthed—'

'Be quiet! Dammit, man, will you never, *never* learn. Even up to the very last minute you could be caught and made to tell—and then what would happen to Vukalovic's division trapped in the Zenica Cage? What you don't know, you can't tell.'

'But you know.' Reynolds's voice was thick with resentment. 'You and Dusty and Andrea—Colonel Stavros—*you* know. Groves and I knew all along that you knew, and *you* could be made to talk.'

Mallory said with considerable restraint: 'Get Andrea to talk? Perhaps you might—if you threatened to take away his cigars. Sure, Dusty and I could talk—but *someone* had to know.'

Groves said in the tone of a man reluctantly accepting the inevitable: 'How do you get behind that dam wall—you can't blow it up from the front, can you?'

'Not with the means at present available to us,' Mallory agreed. 'We get behind it. We climb up there.' Mallory pointed to the precipitous gorge wall on the other side.

'We climb up there, eh?' Miller asked conversationally. He looked stunned.

'Up the ladder. But not all the way. Three-quarters of the way up the ladder we leave it and climb vertically up the cliff-face till we're about forty feet above the top of the dam wall, just where the cliff begins to overhang there. From there, there's a ledge—well, more of a crack, really—'

'A crack!' Miller said hoarsely. He was horror-stricken.

'A crack. It stretches about a hundred and fifty feet clear across the top of the dam wall at an ascending angle of maybe twenty degrees. We go that way.'

Reynolds looked at Mallory in an almost dazed incredulity. 'It's madness!'

'Madness!' Miller echoed.

'I wouldn't do it from choice,' Mallory admitted. 'Nevertheless, it's the only way in.'

'But you're bound to be seen,' Reynolds protested.

'Not bound to be.' Mallory dug into his rucksack and produced from it a black rubber frogman's suit, while Miller reluctantly did the same from his. As both men started to pull their suits on, Mallory continued: 'We'll be like black flies against a black wall.'

'He hopes,' Miller muttered.

'Then with any luck we expect them to be looking the other way when the RAF start in with the fireworks. And if we do seem in any danger of discovery—well, that's where you and Groves come in. Captain Jensen was right—as things have turned out, we couldn't have done this without you.'

'Compliments?' Groves said to Reynolds. 'Compliments from the Captain? I've a feeling there's something nasty on the way.'

'There is,' Mallory admitted. He had his suit and hood in position now and was fixing into his belt some pitons and a hammer he had extracted from his rucksack. 'If we're in trouble, you two create a diversion.'

'What kind of diversion?' Reynolds asked suspiciously.

'From somewhere near the foot of the dam you start firing up at the guards atop the dam wall.'

'But—but we'll be completely exposed.' Groves gazed across at the rocky scree which composed the left bank at the base of the dam and at the foot of the ladder. 'There's not an ounce of cover. What kind of chance will we have?'

Mallory secured his rucksack and hitched a long coil of rope over his shoulder. 'A very poor one, I'm afraid.' He looked at his luminous watch. 'But then, for the next forty-five minutes you and Groves are expendable. Dusty and I are not.'

'Just like that?' Reynolds said flatly. 'Expendable.'

'Just like that.'

'Want to change places?' Miller said hopefully. There was no reply for Mallory was already on his way. Miller, with a last apprehensive look at the towering rampart of rock above, gave a last hitch to his rucksack and followed. Reynolds made to move off, but Groves caught him by the arm and signed to Maria to go ahead with Petar. He said to her: 'We'll wait a bit and bring up the rear. Just to be sure.'

'What is it?' Reynolds asked in a low voice.

'This. Our Captain Mallory admitted that he has already made four mistakes tonight. I think he's making a fifth now.'

'I'm not with you.'

'He's putting all our eggs in one basket and he's overlooked certain things. For instance, asking the two of us to stand by at the base of the dam wall. If we have to start a diversion, one burst of machine-gun fire from the top of the dam wall will get us both in seconds. One man can create as successful a diversion as two—and where's the point in the two of us getting killed? Besides, with one of us left alive, there's always the chance that something can be done to protect Maria and her brother. I'll go to the foot of the dam while you—'

'Why should you be the one to go? Why not—'

'Wait, I haven't finished yet. I also think Mallory's very optimistic if he thinks that Andrea can hold off that lot coming up the gorge. There must be at least twenty of them and they're not out for an evening's fun and games. They're out to kill us. So what happens if they do overwhelm Andrea and come up to the swing bridge and find Maria and Petar there while we are busy being sitting targets at the base of the dam wall? They'll knock them both off before you can bat an eyelid.'

'Or maybe not knock them off,' Reynolds muttered. 'What if Neufeld were to be killed before they reached the swing bridge? What if Droshny were the man in charge—Maria and Petar might take some time in dying.'

'So you'll stay near the bridge and keep our backs covered? With Maria and Petar in shelter somewhere near?'

'You're right, I'm sure you're right. But I don't like it,' Reynolds said uneasily. 'He gave us his orders and he's not a man who likes having his orders disobeyed.'

'He'll never know—even if he ever comes back, which I very much doubt, he'll never know. *And* he's started to make mistakes.'

'Not this kind of mistake.' Reynolds was still more than vaguely uneasy.

'Am I right or not?' Groves demanded.

'I don't think it's going to matter a great deal at the end

of the day,' Reynolds said wearily. 'Okay, let's do it your way.'

The two sergeants hurried off after Maria and Petar.

Andrea listened to the scraping of heavy boots on stones, the very occasional metallic chink of a gun striking against a rock, and waited, stretched out flat on his stomach, the barrel of his Schmeisser rock-steady in the cleft between the boulders. The sounds heralding the stealthy approach up the river bank were not more than forty yards away when Andrea raised himself slightly, squinted down the barrel and squeezed the trigger.

The reply was immediate. At once three or four guns, all of them, Andrea realized, machine-pistols, opened up. Andrea stopped firing, ignored the bullets whistling above his head and ricocheting from the boulders on either side of him, carefully lined up on one of the flashes issuing from a machine-pistol and fired a one-second burst. The man behind the machine-pistol straightened convulsively, his up-flung right arm sending his gun spinning, then slowly toppled sideways in the Neretva and was carried away in the whitely swirling waters. Andrea fired again and a second man twisted round and fell heavily among the rocks. There came a suddenly barked order and the firing down-river ceased.

There were eight men in the down-river group and now one of them detached himself from the shelter of a boulder and crawled towards the second man who had been hit: as he moved, Droshny's face revealed his usual wolfish grin, but it was clear that he was feeling very far from smiling. He bent over the huddled figure in the stones, and turned him on his back: it was Neufeld, with blood streaming down from a gash in the side of the head. Droshny straightened, his face vicious in anger, and turned round as one of his Cetniks touched his arm.

'Is he dead?'

'Not quite. Concussed and badly. He'll be unconscious for hours, maybe days. I don't know, only a doctor can tell.' Droshny beckoned to two other men. 'You three—get him across the ford and up to safety. Two stay with him, the other come back. And for God's sake tell the others to hurry up and get here.'

His face still contorted with anger and for the moment oblivious of all danger, Droshny leapt to his feet and fired a long continuous burst upstream, a burst which apparently left Andrea completely unmoved, for he remained motionless where he was, resting peacefully with his back to his protective boulder, watching with mild interest but apparent unconcern as ricochets and splintered fragments of rock flew off in all directions.

The sound of the firing carried clearly to the ears of the guards patrolling the top of the dam. Such was the bedlam of small-arms fire all around and such were the tricks played on the ears by the baffling variety of echoes that reverberated up and down the gorge and over the surface of the dam itself, that it was quite impossible precisely to locate the source of the recent bursts of machine-pistol fire: what was significant, however, was that it *had* been machine-gun fire and up to that moment the sounds of musketry had consisted exclusively of rifle fire. And it *had* seemed to emanate from the south, from the gorge below the dam. One of the guards on the dam went worriedly to the captain in charge, spoke briefly, then walked quickly across to one of the small huts on the raised concrete platform at the eastern end of the dam wall. The hut, which had no front, only a rolled-up canvas protection, held a large radio transceiver manned by a corporal.

'Captain's orders,' the sergeant said. 'Get through to the bridge at Neretva. Pass a message to General Zimmermann that we—the captain, that is—is worried. Tell him that there's

193

a great deal of small-arms fire all around us and that some of it seems to be coming from down-river.'

The sergeant waited impatiently while the operator put the call through and even more impatiently as the ear-phones crackled two minutes later and the operator started writing down the message. He took the completed message from the operator and handed it to the captain, who read it out aloud.

'General Zimmermann says, "There is no cause at all for anxiety, the noise is being made by our Yugoslav friends up by the Zenica Gap who are whistling in the dark because they are momentarily expecting an all-out assault by units of the 11th Army Corps. And it will be a great deal noisier later on when the RAF starts dropping bombs in all the wrong places. But they won't be dropping them near you, so don't worry."' The captain lowered the paper. 'That's good enough for me. If the General says we are not to worry, then that's good enough for me. You know the General's reputation, sergeant?'

'I know his reputation, sir.' Some distance away and from some unidentifiable direction, came several more bursts of machine-pistol fire. The sergeant stirred unhappily.

'You are still troubled by something?' the captain asked.

'Yes, sir. I know the general's reputation, of course, and trust him implicitly.' He paused then went on worriedly: 'I could have *sworn* that that last burst of machine-pistol fire came from down the gorge there.'

'You're becoming just an old woman, sergeant,' the captain said kindly, 'and you must report to our divisional surgeon soon. Your ears need examining.'

The sergeant, in fact, was not becoming an old woman and his hearing was in considerably better shape than that of the officer who had reproached him. The current burst of machine-pistol firing was, as he'd thought, coming from the gorge, where Droshny and his men, now doubled in numbers, were moving forward, singly or in pairs, but never more than two at a time, in a series of sharp but very short rushes, firing as they went. Their firing, necessarily wildly inaccurate as they stumbled and slipped on the treacherous going underfoot, elicited no response from Andrea, possibly because he felt himself in no great danger, probably because he was conserving his ammunition. The latter supposition seemed the more likely as Andrea had slung his Schmeisser and was now examining with interest a stick-grenade which he had just withdrawn from his belt.

Farther up-river, Sergeant Reynolds, standing at the eastern edge of the rickety wooden bridge which spanned the narrowest part of the gorge where the turbulent, racing, foaming waters beneath would have offered no hope of life at all to any person so unfortunate as to fall in there, looked unhappily down the gorge towards the source of the machine-pistol firing and wondered for the tenth time whether he should take a chance, re-cross the bridge and go to Andrea's aid: even in the light of his vastly revised estimate of Andrea, it seemed impossible, as Groves had said, that one man could for long hold off twenty others bent on vengeance. On the other hand, he had promised Groves to remain there to look after Petar and Maria. There came another burst of firing from down-river. Reynolds made his mind up. He would offer his gun to Maria to afford herself and Petar what protection it might, and leave them for as little time as might be necessary to give Andrea what help he required.

He turned to speak to her, but Maria and Petar were no longer there. Reynolds looked wildly around, his first reaction was that they had both fallen into the rapids, a reaction that he at once dismissed as ridiculous. Instinctively he gazed up the bank towards the base of the dam, and, even although the moon was then obscured by a large bank of cloud, he saw them at once, making their way towards the foot of the iron ladder, where Groves was standing. For a brief moment he puzzled why they should have moved upstream without permission, then remembered that neither he nor Groves had, in fact, remembered to give them instructions to remain by the bridge. Not to worry, he thought, Groves will soon send them back down to the bridge again and when they arrived he would tell them of his decision to return to Andrea's aid. He felt vaguely relieved at the prospect, not because he entertained fears of what might possibly happen to him when he rejoined Andrea and faced up to Droshny and his men but because it postponed, if even only briefly, the necessity of implementing a decision which could be only marginally justifiable in the first place.

Groves, who had been gazing up the seemingly endless series of zig-zags of that green iron ladder so precariously, it seemed, attached to that vertical cliff-face, swung round at the soft grate of approaching footsteps on the shale and stared at Maria and Petar, walking, as always, hand in hand. He said angrily: 'What in God's name are you people doing here? You've no right to be here—can't you see, the guards have only to look down and you'll be killed? Go on. Go back and rejoin Sergeant Reynolds at the bridge. Now!'

Maria said softly: 'You are kind to worry, Sergeant Groves. But we don't want to go. We want to stay here.'

'And what in hell's name good can you do by staying here?' Groves asked roughly. He paused, then went on, almost kindly: 'I know who you are now, Maria. I know what you've done, how good you are at your own job. But this is not your job. Please.'

'No.' She shook her head. 'And I *can* fire a gun.'

'You haven't got one to fire. And Petar here, what right have you to speak for him. Does he know where he is?'

Maria spoke rapidly to her brother in incomprehensible

Serbo-Croat: he responded by making his customary odd sounds in his throat. When he had finished, Maria turned to Groves.

'He says he knows he is going to die tonight. He has what you people call the second sight and he says there is no future beyond tonight. He says he is tired of running. He says he will wait here till the time comes.'

'Of all the stubborn, thick-headed—'

'Please, Sergeant Groves.' The voice, though still low, was touched by a new note of asperity. 'His mind is made up, and you can never change it.'

Groves nodded in acceptance. He said: 'Perhaps I can change yours.'

'I do not understand.'

'Petar cannot help us anyway, no blind man could. But you can. If you would.'

'Tell me.'

'Andrea is holding off a mixed force of at least twenty Cetniks and German troops.' Groves smiled wryly. 'I have recent reason to believe that Andrea probably has no equal anywhere as a guerilla fighter, but one man cannot hold off twenty for ever. When he goes, then there is only Reynolds left to guard the bridge—and if he goes, then Droshny and his men will be through in time to warn the guards, almost certainly in time to save the dam, certainly in time to send a radio message through to General Zimmermann to pull his tanks back on to high ground. I think, Maria, that Reynolds may require your help. Certainly, you can be of no help here— but if you stand by Reynolds you *could* make all the difference between success and failure. And you did say you can fire a gun.'

'And as *you* pointed out, I haven't got a gun.'

'That was then. You have now.' Groves unslung his

Schmeisser and handed it to her along with some spare ammunition.

'But—' Maria accepted gun and ammunition reluctantly. 'But now *you* haven't a gun.'

'Oh yes I have.' Groves produced his silenced Luger from his tunic. 'This is all I want tonight. *I* can't afford to make any noise tonight, not so close to the dam as this.'

'But I *can't* leave my brother.'

'Oh, I think you can. In fact, you're going to. No one on earth can help your brother any more. Not now. Please hurry.'

'Very well.' She moved off a few reluctant paces, stopped, turned and said: 'I suppose you think you're very clever, Sergeant Groves?'

'I don't know what you're talking about,' Groves said woodenly. She looked at him steadily for a few moments, then turned and made her way down-river. Groves smiled to himself in the near-darkness.

The smile vanished in the instant of time that it took for the gorge to be suddenly flooded with bright moonlight as a black, sharply-edged cloud moved away from the face of the moon. Groves called softly, urgently to Maria: 'Face down on the rocks and keep still,' saw her at once do what he ordered, then looked up the green ladder, his face registering the strain and anxiety in his mind.

About three-quarters of the way up the ladder, Mallory and Miller, bathed in the brilliant moonlight, clung to the top of one of the angled sections as immobile as if they had been carved from the rock itself. Their unmoving eyes, set in equally unmoving faces, were obviously fixed on—or transfixed by—the same point in space.

That point was a scant fifty feet away, above and to their left, where two obviously very jumpy guards were leaning anxiously over the parapet at the top of the dam: they were gazing into the middle distance, down the gorge, towards the location of what seemed to be the sound of firing. They had only to move their eyes downwards and discovery for Groves and Maria was certain: they had only to shift their gaze to the left and discovery for Mallory and Miller would have been equally certain. And death for all inevitable.

CHAPTER II

Saturday
0120-0135

Like Mallory and Miller, Groves, too, had caught sight of the two German sentries leaning out over the parapet at the top of the dam and staring anxiously down the gorge. As a situation for conveying a feeling of complete nakedness, exposure and vulnerability, it would, Groves felt, take a lot of beating. And if he felt like that, how must Mallory and Miller, clinging to the ladder and less than a stone's throw from the guards, be feeling? Both men, Groves knew, carried silenced Lugers, but their Lugers were inside their tunics and their tunics encased in their zipped-up frogmen's suits, making them quite inaccessible. At least, making them quite inaccessible without, clinging as they were to that ladder, performing a variety of contortionist movements to get at them—and it was certain that the least untoward movement would have been immediately spotted by the two guards. How it was that they hadn't already been seen, even without movement, was incomprehensible to Groves: in that bright moonlight, which cast as much light on the dam and in the gorge as one would have expected on any reasonably dull afternoon, any normal peripheral vision should have picked them all up immediately. And it was unlikely that any front-line troops of the Wehrmacht had less than standard peripheral vision. Groves could only conclude that the intentness of the guards' gaze did not necessarily mean that they were looking intently: it could have been that all their being was at that moment concentrated on their hearing, straining to locate the source of the desultory machine-pistol

fire down the gorge. With infinite caution Groves eased his
Luger from his tunic and lined it up. At that distance, even
allowing for the high muzzle-velocity of the gun, he reckoned
his chances of getting either of the guards to be so remote
as to be hardly worth considering: but at least, as a gesture,
it was better than nothing.

Groves was right on two counts. The two sentries on the
parapet, far from being reassured by General Zimmermann's
encouraging reassurance, were in fact concentrating all their
being on listening to the down-river bursts of machine-pistol
fire, which were becoming all the more noticeable not only
because they seemed—as they were—to be coming closer, but
also because the ammunition of the Partisan defenders of the
Zenica Gap was running low and their fire was becoming more
sporadic. Groves had been right, too, about the fact that
neither Mallory nor Miller had made any attempt to get at
their Lugers. For the first few seconds, Mallory, like Groves,
had felt sure that any such move would be bound to attract
immediate attention, but, almost at once and long before the
idea had occurred to Groves, Mallory had realized that the
men were in such a trance-like state of listening that a hand
could almost have passed before their faces without their being
aware of it. And now, Mallory was certain, there would be
no need to do anything at all because, from his elevation, he
could see something that was quite invisible to Groves from
his position at the foot of the dam: another dark band of
cloud was almost about to pass across the face of the moon.

Within seconds, a black shadow flitting across the waters
of the Neretva dam turned the colour from dark green to the
deepest indigo, moved rapidly across the top of the dam wall,
blotted out the ladder and the two men clinging to it, then
engulfed the gorge in darkness. Groves sighed in soundless
relief and lowered his Luger. Maria rose and made her way
down-river towards the bridge. Petar moved his unseeing gaze

201

around in the sightless manner of the blind. And, up above, Mallory and Miller at once began to climb again.

Mallory now abandoned the ladder at the top of one of its zigs and struck vertically up the cliff-face. The rock-face, providentially, was not completely smooth, but such hand- and footholds as it afforded were few and small and awkwardly situated, making for a climb that was as arduous as it was technically difficult: normally, had he been using the hammer and pitons that were stuck in his belt, Mallory would have regarded it as a climb of no more than moderate difficulty: but the use of pitons was quite out of the question. Mallory was directly opposite the top of the dam wall and no more than 35 feet from the nearest guard: one tiny chink of hammer on metal could not fail to register on the hearing of the most inattentive listener: and, as Mallory had just observed, inattentive listening was the last accusation that could have been levelled against the sentries on the dam. So Mallory had to content himself with the use of his natural talents and the vast experience gathered over many years of rock-climbing and continue the climb as he was doing, sweating profusely inside the hermetic rubber suit, while Miller, now some forty feet below, peered upwards with such tense anxiety on his face that he was momentarily oblivious of his own precarious perch on top of one of the slanted ladders, a predicament which would normally have sent him into a case of mild hysterics.

Andrea, too, was at that moment peering at something about fifty feet away, but it would have required a hyper-active imagination to detect any signs of anxiety in that dark and rugged face. Andrea, as the guards on the dam had so recently been doing, was listening rather than looking. From his point of view all he could see was a dark and shapeless jumble of wetly glistening boulders with the Neretva rushing whitely alongside. There was no sign of life down there, but that only meant that Droshny, Neufeld and his men, having learnt their lessons the hard way—for Andrea could not know at this time that Neufeld had been wounded—were inching their way forward on elbows and knees, not once moving out from one safe cover until they had located another.

A minute passed, then Andrea heard the inevitable: a barely discernible 'click', as two pieces of stone knocked together. It came, Andrea estimated, from about thirty feet away. He nodded as if in satisfaction, armed the grenade, waited two seconds, then gently lobbed it downstream, dropping flat behind his protective boulder as he did so. There was the typically flat crack of a grenade explosion, accompanied by a briefly white flash of light in which two soldiers could be seen being flung bodily sideways.

The sound of the explosion came clearly to Mallory's ear. He remained still, allowing only his head to turn slowly till he was looking down on top of the dam wall, now almost twenty feet beneath him. The same two guards who had been previously listening so intently stopped their patrol a second time, gazed down the gorge again, looked at each other uneasily, shrugged uncertainly, then resumed their patrol. Mallory resumed his climb.

He was making better time now. The former negligible finger and toe holds had given way, occasionally, to small fissures in the rock into which he was able to insert the odd piton to give him a great deal more leverage than would have otherwise been possible. When next he stopped climbing and looked upwards he was no more than six feet below the longitudinal crack he had been looking for—and, as he had said to Miller earlier, it *was* no more than a crack. Mallory made to begin again, then paused, his head cocked towards the sky.

Just barely audible at first above the roaring of the waters of the Neretva and the sporadic small-arms fire from the direction of the Zenica Gap, but swelling in power with the passing of every second, could be heard a low and distant thunder, a sound unmistakable to all who had ever heard it during the war, a sound that heralded the approach of squadrons, of a fleet of heavy bombers. Mallory listened to the rapidly approaching clamour of scores of aero engines and smiled to himself.

Many men smiled to themselves that night when they heard the approach from the west of those squadrons of Lancasters. Miller, still perched on his ladder and still exercising all his available will-power not to look down, managed to smile to himself, as did Groves at the foot of the ladder and Reynolds by the bridge. On the right bank of the Neretva, Andrea smiled to himself, reckoned that the roar of those fast-approaching engines would make an excellent cover for any untoward sound and picked another grenade from his belt. Outside a soup tent high up in the biting cold of the Ivenici plateau, Colonel Vis and Captain Vlanovich smiled their delight at each other and solemnly shook hands. Behind the southern redoubts of the Zenica Cage, General Vukalovic and his three senior officers, Colonel Janzy, Colonel Lazlo and Major Stephan, for once removed the glasses through which they had been so long peering at the Neretva bridge and the menacing woods beyond and smiled their incredulous relief at one another. And, most strangely of all, already seated in his command truck just inside the woods to the south of the Neretva bridge, General Zimmermann smiled perhaps the most broadly of all.

Mallory resumed his climb, moving even more quickly now, reached the longitudinal crack, worked his way up above it, pressed a piton into a convenient crack in the rock, withdrew his hammer from his belt and prepared to wait. Even now, he was not much more than forty feet above the dam wall, and the piton that Mallory now wanted to anchor would require not one blow but a dozen of them, and powerful ones at that: the idea that, even above the approaching thunder of the

Lancasters' engines, the metallic hammering would go unremarked was preposterous. The sound of the heavy aero
engines was now deepening by the moment.

Mallory glanced down directly beneath him. Miller was
gazing upward, tapping his wristwatch as best a man can when
he has both arms wrapped round the same rung of a ladder,
and making urgent gestures. Mallory, in turn, shook his head
and made a downward restraining motion with his free hand.
Miller shook his own head in resignation.

The Lancasters were on top of them now. The leader
arrowed in diagonally across the dam, lifted slightly as it came
to the high mountains on the other side and then the earth
shook and ripples of dark waters shivered their erratic way
across the surface of the Neretva dam before the first explosion
reached their ears, as the first stick of 1,000-pound bombs
crashed squarely into the Zenica Gap. From then on the sound
of the explosions of the bombs raining down on the Gap were
so close together as to be almost continuous: what little time-
lapse there was between some of the explosions was bridged
by the constantly rumbling echoes that rumbled through the
mountains and valleys of central Bosnia.

Mallory had no longer any need to worry about sound any
more, he doubted he could even have heard himself speak,
for most of those bombs were landing in a concentrated area
less than a mile from where he clung to the side of the cliff,
their explosions making an almost constant white glare that
showed clearly above the mountains to the west. He hammered
home his piton, belayed a rope around it, and dropped the
rope to Miller, who immediately seized it and began to climb:
he looked, Mallory thought, uncommonly like one of the
early Christian martyrs. Miller was no mountaineer, but, no
mistake, he knew how to climb a rope: in a remarkably short
time he was up beside Mallory, feet firmly wedged into the
longitudinal crack, both hands gripping tightly to the piton.

'Think you can hang on that piton?' Mallory asked. He almost had to shout to make himself heard above the still undiminished thunder of the falling bombs.

'Just try to prise me away.'

'I won't,' Mallory grinned.

He coiled up the rope which Miller had used for his ascent, hitched it over his shoulder and started to move quickly along the longitudinal crack. 'I'll take this across the top of the dam, belay it to another piton. Then you can join me. Right?'

Miller looked down into the depths and shuddered. 'If you think I'm going to stay here, you must be mad.'

Mallory grinned again and moved away.

To the south of the Neretva bridge, General Zimmermann, with an aide by his side, was still listening to the sounds of the aerial assault on the Zenica Gap. He glanced at his watch.

'Now,' he said. 'First-line assault troops into position.'

At once heavily armed infantry, bent almost double to keep themselves below parapet level, began to move quickly across the Neretva bridge: once on the other side, they spread out east and west along the northern bank of the river, concealed from the Partisans by the ridge of high ground abutting on the river bank. Or they thought they were concealed: in point of fact a Partisan scout, equipped with night-glasses and field telephone, lay prone in a suicidally positioned slit-trench less than a hundred yards from the bridge itself, sending back a constant series of reports to Vukalovic.

Zimmermann glanced up at the sky and said to his aide: 'Hold them. The moon's coming through again.' Again he looked at his watch. 'Start the tank engines in twenty minutes.'

'They've stopped coming across the bridge, then?' Vukalovic said.

'Yes, sir.' It was the voice of his advance scout. 'I think it's because the moon is about to break through in a minute or two.'

'I think so too,' Vukalovic said. He added grimly: 'And I suggest you start working your way back before it does break through or it will be the last chance you'll ever have.'

Andrea, too, was regarding the night sky with interest. His gradual retreat had now taken him into a particularly unsatisfactory defensive position, practically bereft of all cover: a very unhealthy situation to be caught in, he reflected, when the moon came out from behind the clouds. He paused for a thoughtful moment, then armed another grenade and lobbed it in the direction of a cluster of dimly seen boulders about fifty feet away. He did not wait to see what effect it had, he was already scrambling his way up-river before the grenade exploded. The one certain effect it did have was to galvanize Droshny and his men into immediate and furious retaliation, at least half a dozen machine-pistols loosing off almost simultaneous bursts at the position Andrea had so recently and prudently vacated. One bullet plucked at the sleeve of his tunic, but that was as near as anything came. He reached another cluster of boulders without incident and took up a fresh defensive position behind them: when the moon did break through it would be Droshny and his men who would be faced with the unpalatable prospect of crossing that open stretch of ground.

Reynolds, crouched by the swing bridge with Maria now by his side, heard the flat crack of the exploding grenade and guessed that Andrea was now no more than a hundred yards downstream on the far bank. And like so many people at that precise instant, Reynolds, too, was gazing up at what could be seen of the sky through the narrow north-south gap between the precipitous walls of the gorge.

Reynolds had intended going to Andrea's aid as soon as Groves had sent Petar and Maria back to him, but three factors had inhibited him from taking immediate action. In the first place, Groves had been unsuccessful in sending back Petar: secondly, the frequent bursts of machine-pistol firing down the gorge, coming steadily closer, were indication enough that Andrea was making a very orderly retreat and was still in fine fighting fettle: and thirdly, even if Droshny and his men did get Andrea, Reynolds knew that by taking up position behind the boulder directly above the bridge, he could deny Droshny and his men the crossing of the bridge for an indefinite period.

But the sight of the large expanse of starlit sky coming up behind the dark clouds over the moon made Reynolds forget the tactically sound and cold-blooded reasons for remaining where he was. It was not in Reynolds's nature to regard any other man as an expendable pawn and he suspected strongly that when he was presented with a sufficiently long period of moonlight Droshny would use it to make the final rush that would overwhelm Andrea. He touched Maria on the shoulder.

'Even the Colonel Stavroses of this world need a hand at times. Stay here. We shouldn't be long.' He turned and ran across the swaying swing bridge.

Damn it, Mallory thought bitterly, damn it, damn it and damn it all. Why couldn't there have been heavy dark cloud covering the entire sky? Why couldn't it have been raining? Or snowing? Why hadn't they chosen a moonless night for this operation? But he was, he knew, only kicking against the pricks. No one had had any choice, for tonight was the only time there was. But still, that damnable moon.

Mallory looked to the north, where the northern wind, driving banded cloud across the moon, was leaving behind it a large expanse of starlit sky. Soon the entire dam and gorge would be bathed in moonlight for a considerable period: Mallory thought wryly that he could have wished himself to be in a happier position for that period.

By this time, he had traversed about half the length of the longitudinal crack. He glanced to his left and reckoned he had still between thirty and forty feet to go before he was well clear of the dam wall and above the waters of the dam itself. He glanced to his right and saw, not to his surprise, that Miller was still where he had left him, clinging to the piton with both hands as if it were his dearest friend on earth, which at that moment it probably was. He glanced downwards: he was directly above the dam wall now, some fifty feet above it, forty feet above the roof of the guardhouse. He looked at the sky again: a minute, no more, and the moon would be clear. What was it that he had said to Reynolds that afternoon? Yes, that was it. For now is all the time there may be. He was beginning to wish he hadn't said that. He was a New Zealander, but only a second-generation New Zealander: all his forebears were Scots and everyone knew how the Scots indulged in those heathenish practices of second sight and peering into the future. Mallory briefly indulged in the mental equivalent of a shoulder shrug and continued on his traverse.

At the foot of the iron ladder, Groves, to whom Mallory was now no more than a half-seen, half-imagined dark shape against a black cliff-face, realized that Mallory was soon going to move out of his line of sight altogether, and when that happened he would be in no position to give Mallory any covering fire at all. He touched Petar on the shoulder and with the pressure of his hand indicated that he should sit down at the foot of the ladder. Petar looked at him sightlessly, uncomprehendingly, then suddenly appeared to gather what was expected of him, for he nodded obediently and sat down.

Groves thrust his silenced Luger deep inside his tunic and began to climb.

A mile to the west, the Lancasters were still pounding the Zenica Gap. Bomb after bomb crashed down with surprising accuracy into that tiny target area, blasting down trees, throwing great eruptions of earth and stones into the air, starting all over the area scores of small fires which had already incinerated nearly all the German plywood tanks. Seven miles to the south, Zimmermann still listened with interest and still with satisfaction to the continuing bombardment to the north. He turned to the aide seated beside him in the command car.

'You will have to admit that we must give the Royal Air Force full marks for industry, if for nothing else. I hope our troops are well clear of the area?'

'There's not a German soldier within two miles of the Zenica Gap, Herr General.'

'Excellent, excellent.' Zimmermann appeared to have forgotten about his earlier forebodings. 'Well, fifteen minutes. The moon will soon be through, so we'll hold our infantry. The next wave of troops can go across with the tanks.'

Reynolds, making his way down the right bank of the Neretva towards the sound of firing, now very close indeed, suddenly became very still indeed. Most men react the same way when they feel the barrel of a gun grinding into the side of their necks. Very cautiously, so as not to excite any nervous triggerfingers, Reynolds turned both eyes and head slightly to the right and realized with a profound sense of relief that this was one instance where he need have no concern about jittery nerves.

'You had your orders,' Andrea said mildly. 'What are you doing here?'

'I—I thought you might need some help.' Reynolds rubbed the side of his neck. 'Mind you, I could have been wrong.'

'Come on. It's time we got back and crossed the bridge.' For good measure and in very quick succession, Andrea spun another couple of grenades down-river, then made off quickly up the river bank, closely followed by Reynolds.

The moon broke through. For the second time that night, Mallory became absolutely still, his toes jammed into the longitudinal crack, his hands round the piton which he had thirty seconds earlier driven into the rock and to which he had secured the rope. Less than ten feet from him Miller, who with the aid of the rope had already safely made the first part of the traverse, froze into similar immobility. Both men stared down on to the top of the dam wall.

There were six guards visible, two at the farther or western end, two at the middle and the remaining two almost directly below Mallory and Miller. How many more there might have been inside the guard-house neither Mallory nor Miller had any means of knowing. All they could know for certain was that their exposed vulnerability was complete, their position desperate.

Three-quarters of the way up the iron ladder, Groves, too, became very still. From where he was, he could see Mallory, Miller and the two guards very clearly indeed. He knew with a sudden conviction that this time there would be no escape, they could never be so lucky again. Mallory, Miller, Petar or himself—who would be the first to be spotted? On balance, he thought he himself was the most likely candidate. Slowly, he wrapped his left arm round the ladder, pushed his right hand inside his tunic, withdrew his Luger and laid the barrel along his left forearm.

The two guards on the eastern end of the dam wall were restless, apprehensive, full of nameless fears. As before, they both leaned out over the parapet and stared down the valley. They can't help but see me, Groves thought, they're *bound* to see me, good God, I'm almost directly in their line of sight. Discovery must be immediate.

It was, but not for Groves. Some strange instinct made one of the guards glance upwards and to his left and his mouth fell open at the astonishing spectacle of two men in rubber suits clinging like limpets to the sheer face of the cliff. It took him several interminable seconds before he could recover himself sufficiently to reach out blindly and grab his companion by the arm. His companion followed the other guard's line of sight, then his jaw, too, dropped in an almost comical fashion. Then, at precisely the same moment, both men broke free from their thrall-like spell and swung their guns, one a Schmeisser, the other a pistol, upwards to line up on the two men pinned helplessly to the cliff-face.

Groves steadied his Luger against both his left arm and the side of the ladder, sighted unhurriedly along the barrel and squeezed the trigger. The guard with the Schmeisser dropped the weapon, swayed briefly on his feet and started to fall outwards. Almost three seconds passed before the other guard, startled and momentarily quite uncomprehending, reached out to grab his companion, but he was far too late, he never even succeeded in touching him. The dead man, moving in an almost grotesquely slow-motion fashion, toppled wearily over the edge of the parapet and tumbled head over heels into the depths of the gorge beneath.

The guard with the pistol leaned far out over the parapet, staring in horror after his falling comrade. It was quite obvious that he was momentarily at a total loss to understand what had happened, for he had heard no sound of a shot. But realization came within the second as a piece of concrete chipped away inches from his left elbow and a spent bullet ricocheted its whistling way into the night sky. The guard's eyes lifted and widened in shock, but this time the shock had no inhibiting effect on the speed of his reactions. More in blind hope than in any real expectation of success, he loosed off two quick snap-shots and bared his teeth in satisfaction as he heard Groves cry out and saw the right hand, the forefinger still holding the Luger by the trigger-guard, reach up to clutch the shattered left shoulder.

Groves's face was dazed and twisted with pain, the eyes already clouded by the agony of the wound, but those responsible for making Groves a commando sergeant had not picked him out with a pin, and Groves was not quite finished yet. He brought his Luger down again. There was something terribly wrong with his vision now, he dimly realized, he thought he had a vague impression that the guard on the parapet was leaning far out, pistol held in both hands to make sure of his killing shot, but he couldn't be sure. Twice Groves squeezed the trigger of his Luger and then he closed his eyes, for the pain was gone and he suddenly felt very sleepy.

The guard by the parapet pitched forward. He reached out desperately to grab the coaming of the parapet, but to pull himself back to safety he had to swing his legs up to retain his balance and he found he could no longer control his legs, which slid helplessly over the edge of the parapet. His body followed his legs almost of its own volition, for the last vestiges of strength remain for only a few seconds with a man through whose lungs two Luger bullets have just passed. For a moment of time his clawed hands hooked despairingly on to the edge of the parapet and then his fingers opened.

Groves seemed unconscious now, his head lolling on his chest, the left-hand sleeve and left-hand side of his uniform already saturated with blood from the terrible wound in his shoulder. Were it not for the fact that his right arm was jammed between a rung of the ladder and the cliff-face behind it, he must certainly have fallen. Slowly, the fingers of his right hand opened and the Luger fell from his hand.

Seated at the foot of the ladder, Petar started as the Luger struck the shale less than a foot from where he was sitting. He looked up instinctively, then rose, made sure that the inevitable guitar was firmly secured across his back, reached out for the ladder and started climbing.

Mallory and Miller stared down, watching the blind singer climb up towards the wounded and obviously unconscious Groves. After a few moments, as if by telepathic signal, Mallory glanced across at Miller who caught his eyes almost at once. Miller's face was strained, almost haggard. He freed one hand momentarily from the rope and made an almost desperate gesture in the direction of the wounded sergeant. Mallory shook his head.

Miller said hoarsely: 'Expendable, huh?'

'Expendable.'

Both men looked down again. Petar was now not more than ten feet below Groves, and Groves, though Mallory and Miller could not see this, had his eyes closed and his right arm was beginning to slip through the gap between the rung and the rock. Gradually, his right arm began to slip more quickly, until his elbow was free, and then his arm came free altogether and slowly, so very slowly, he began to topple outwards from the wall. But Petar got to him first, standing on the step beneath Groves and reaching out an arm to encircle him and press him back against the ladder. Petar had him and for the moment Petar could hold him. But that was all he could do.

The moon passed behind a cloud.

Miller covered the last ten feet separating him from Mallory. He looked at Mallory and said: 'They're both going to go, you know that?'

'I know that.' Mallory sounded even more tired than he looked. 'Come on. Another thirty feet and we should be in position.' Mallory, leaving Miller where he was, continued his traverse along the crack. He was moving very quickly now, taking risks that no sane cragsman would ever have contemplated, but he had no option now, for time was running out. Within a minute he had reached a spot where he judged that he had gone far enough, hammered home a piton and securely belayed the rope to it.

He signalled to Miller to come and join him. Miller began the last stage of the traverse, and as he was on his way across, Mallory unhitched another rope from his shoulders, a sixty-foot length of climbers' rope, knotted at fifteen-inch intervals. One end of this he fastened to the same piton as held the rope that Miller was using for making his traverse: the other end he let fall down the cliff-side. Miller came up and Mallory touched him on the shoulder and pointed downwards.

The dark waters of the Neretva dam were directly beneath them.

CHAPTER 12

Saturday
0135-0200

Andrea and Reynolds lay crouched among the boulders at the western end of the elderly swing bridge over the gorge. Andrea looked across the length of the bridge, his gaze travelling up the steep gully behind it till it came to rest on the huge boulder perched precariously at the angle where the steep slope met the vertical cliff-face behind it. Andrea rubbed a bristly chin, nodded thoughtfully and turned to Reynolds.

'You cross first. I'll give you covering fire. You do the same for me when you get to the other side. Don't stop, don't look round. Now.'

Reynolds made for the bridge in a crouching run, his footsteps seeming to him abnormally loud as he reached the rotting planking of the bridge itself. The palms of his hands gliding lightly over the hand ropes on either side he continued without check or diminution of speed, obeying Andrea's instructions not to risk a quick backward glance, and feeling a very strange sensation between his shoulder-blades. To his mild astonishment he reached the far bank without a shot being fired, headed for the concealment and shelter offered by a large boulder a little way up the bank, was startled momentarily to see Maria hiding behind the same boulder, then whirled round and unslung his Schmeisser.

On the far bank there was no sign of Andrea. For a brief moment Reynolds experienced a quick stab of anger, thinking Andrea had used this ruse merely to get rid of him, then smiled to himself as he heard two flat explosive sounds some little way down the river on the far bank. Andrea, Reynolds remembered, had still had two grenades left and Andrea was not the man to let such handy things rust from disuse. Besides, Reynolds realized, it would provide Andrea with extra valuable seconds to make good his escape, which indeed it did for Andrea appeared on the far bank almost immediately and, like Reynolds, effected the crossing of the bridge entirely without incident. Reynolds called softly and Andrea joined them in the shelter of the boulder.

Reynolds said in a low voice: 'What's next?'

'First things first.' Andrea produced a cigar from a waterproof box, a match from another waterproof box, struck the match in his huge cupped hands and puffed in immense satisfaction. When he removed the cigar, Reynolds noticed that he held it with the glowing end safely concealed in the curved palm of his hand. 'What's next? I tell you what's next. Company coming to join us across the bridge, and coming very soon, too. They've taken crazy risks to try to get me—and paid for them—which shows they are pretty desperate. Crazy men don't hang about for long. You and Maria here move fifty or sixty yards nearer the dam and take cover there—and keep your guns on the far side of the bridge.'

'You staying here?' Reynolds asked.

Andrea blew out a noxious cloud of cigar smoke. 'For the moment, yes.'

'Then I'm staying, too.'

'If you want to get killed, it's all right by me,' Andrea said mildly. 'But this beautiful young lady here wouldn't look that way any more with the top of her head blown off.'

Reynolds was startled by the crudeness of the words. He said angrily: 'What the devil do you mean?'

'I mean this.' Andrea's voice was no longer mild. 'This boulder gives you perfect concealment from the bridge. But

217

Droshny and his men can move another thirty or forty yards farther up the bank on their side. What concealment will you have then?'

'I never thought of that,' Reynolds said.

'There'll come a day when you say that once too often,' Andrea said sombrely, 'and then it will be too late to think of anything again.'

A minute later they were in position. Reynolds was hidden behind a huge boulder which afforded perfect concealment both from the far side of the bridge and from the bank on the far side up to the point where it petered out: it did not offer concealment from the dam. Reynolds looked to his left where Maria was crouched farther in behind the rock. She smiled at him, and Reynolds knew he had never seen a braver girl, for the hands that held the Schmeisser were trembling. He moved out a little and peered down-river, but there appeared to be no signs of life whatsoever at the western edge of the bridge. The only signs of life at all, indeed, were to be seen behind the huge boulder up in the gully, where Andrea, completely screened from anyone at or near the far side of the bridge, was industriously loosening the foundations of rubble and earth round the base of the boulder.

Appearances, as always, were deceptive. Reynolds had judged there to be no life at the western end of the bridge but there was, in fact, life and quite a lot of it, although admittedly there was no action. Concealed in the massive boulders about twenty feet back from the bridge, Droshny, a Cetnik sergeant and perhaps a dozen German soldiers and Cetniks lay in deep concealment among the rocks.

Droshny had binoculars to his eyes. He examined the ground in the neighbourhood of the far side of the swing bridge, then traversed to his left up beyond the boulder where Reynolds and Maria lay hidden until he reached the dam wall. He lifted the glasses, following the dimly-seen zig-zag outline of the iron ladder, checked, adjusted the focus as finely as possible, then stared again. There could be no doubt: there were two men clinging to the ladder, about three-quarters of the way up towards the top of the dam.

'Good God in heaven!' Droshny lowered the binoculars, the gaunt craggy features registering an almost incredulous horror, and turned to the Cetnik sergeant by his side. 'Do you know what they mean to do?'

'The dam!' The thought had not occurred to the sergeant until that instant but the stricken expression on Droshny's face made the realization as immediate as it was inevitable. 'They're going to blow up the dam!' It did not occur to either man to wonder *how* Mallory could possibly blow up the dam: as other men had done before them, both Droshny and the sergeant were beginning to discover in Mallory and his *modus operandi* an extraordinary quality of inevitability that transformed remote possibilities into very likely probabilities.

'General Zimmermann!' Droshny's gravelly voice had become positively hoarse. 'He must be warned! If that dam bursts while his tanks and troops are crossing—'

'Warn him? Warn him? How in God's name can we warn him?'

'There's a radio up on the dam.'

The sergeant stared at him. He said: 'It might as well be on the moon. There'll be a rear-guard, they're bound to have left a rear-guard. Some of us are going to get killed crossing that bridge, captain.'

'You think so?' Droshny glanced up sombrely at the dam. 'And just what do you think is going to happen to us all down here if *that* goes?'

Slowly, soundlessly and almost invisibly, Mallory and Miller swam northwards through the dark waters of the Neretva dam, away from the direction of the dam wall. Suddenly Miller,

219

who was slightly in the lead, gave a low exclamation and stopped swimming.

'What's up?' Mallory asked.

'This is up.' With an effort Miller lifted a section of what appeared to be a heavy wire cable just clear of the water. 'Nobody mentioned this little lot.'

'Nobody did,' Mallory agreed. He reached under the water. 'And there's a steel mesh below.'

'An anti-torpedo net?'

'Just that.'

'Why?' Miller gestured to the north where, at a distance of less than two hundred yards, the dam made an abrupt right-angled turn between the towering cliff-faces. 'It's impossible for any torpedo bomber—any bomber—to get a run-in on the dam wall.'

'Someone should have told the Germans. They take no chances—and it makes things a damned sight more difficult for us.' He peered at his watch. 'We'd better start hurrying. We're late.'

They eased themselves over the wire and started swimming again, more quickly this time. Several minutes later, just after they had rounded the corner of the dam and lost sight of the dam wall, Mallory touched Miller on the shoulder. Both men trod water, turned and looked back in the direction from which they had come. To the south, not much more than two miles away, the night sky had suddenly blossomed into an incandescent and multi-coloured beauty as scores of parachute flares, red and green and white and orange, drifted slowly down towards the Neretva river.

'Very pretty, indeed,' Miller conceded. 'And what's all this in aid of?'

'It's in aid of us. Two reasons. First of all, it will take any person who looks at that—and *everyone* will look at it—at least ten minutes to recover his night-sight, which means that any odd goings-on in this part of the dam are all that less likely to be observed: and if everyone is going to be busy looking that way, then they can't be busy looking this way at the same time.'

'Very logical,' Miller approved. 'Our friend Captain Jensen doesn't miss out on very much, does he?'

'He has, as the saying goes, all his marbles about him.' Mallory turned again and gazed to the east, his head cocked the better to listen. He said: 'You have to hand it to them. Dead on target, dead on schedule. I hear him coming now.'

The Lancaster, no more than five hundred feet above the surface of the dam, came in from the east, its engine throttled back almost to stalling speed. It was still two hundred yards short of where Mallory and Miller were treading water when suddenly huge black silk parachutes bloomed beneath it: almost simultaneously, engine-power was increased to maximum revolutions and the big bomber went into a steeply banking climbing turn to avoid smashing into the mountains on the far side of the dam.

Miller gazed at the slowly descending black parachutes, turned, and looked at the brilliantly burning flares to the south. 'The skies,' he announced, 'are full of things tonight.'

He and Mallory began to swim in the direction of the falling parachutes.

Petar was near to exhaustion. For long minutes now he had been holding Groves's dead weight pinned against the iron ladder and his aching arms were beginning to quiver with the strain. His teeth were clenched hard, his face, down which rivulets of sweat poured, was twisted with the effort and the agony of it all. Plainly, Petar could not hold out much longer.

It was by the light of those flares that Reynolds, still crouched with Maria in hiding behind the big boulder, first saw the predicament of Petar and Groves. He turned to glance at Maria: one look at the stricken face was enough to tell Reynolds that she had seen it, too.

Reynolds said hoarsely: 'Stay here. I must go and help them.'

'No!' She caught his arm, clearly exerting all her will to keep herself under control: her eyes, as they had been when Reynolds had first seen her, had the look of a hunted animal about them. 'Please, Sergeant, no. You must stay here.'

Reynolds said desperately: 'Your brother—'

'There are more important things—'

'Not for you there aren't.' Reynolds made to rise, but she clung to his arm with surprising strength, so that he couldn't release himself without hurting her. He said, almost gently: 'Come on, lass, let me go.'

'No! If Droshny and his men get across—' She broke off as the last of the flares finally fizzled to extinction, casting the entire gorge into what was, by momentary contrast, an almost total darkness. Maria went on simply: 'You'll have to stay now, won't you?'

'I'll have to stay now.' Reynolds moved out from the shelter of the boulder and put his night-glasses to his eyes. The swing bridge, and as far as he could tell, the far bank seemed innocent of any sign of life. He traversed up the gully and could just make out the form of Andrea, his excavations finished, resting peacefully behind the big boulder. Again, with a feeling of deep unease, Reynolds trained his glasses on the bridge. He suddenly became very still. He removed the glasses, wiped the lenses very carefully, rubbed his eyes and lifted the glasses again.

His night-sight, momentarily destroyed by the flares, was now almost back to normal and there could be no doubt or any imagination about what he was seeing—seven or eight men, Droshny in the lead, flat on their stomachs, were inching their way on elbows, hands and knees across the wooden slats of the swing bridge.

Reynolds lowered the glasses, stood upright, armed a grenade and threw it as far as he could towards the bridge. It exploded just as it landed, at least forty yards short of the bridge. That it achieved nothing but a flat explosive bang and the harmless scattering of some shale was of no account, for it had never been intended to reach the bridge: it had been intended as a signal for Andrea, and Andrea wasted no time.

He placed the soles of both feet against the boulder, braced his back against the cliff-face and heaved. The boulder moved the merest fraction of an inch. Andrea momentarily relaxed, allowing the boulder to roll back, then repeated the process: this time the forward motion of the boulder was quite perceptible. Andrea relaxed again, then pushed for the third time.

Down below on the bridge, Droshny and his men, uncertain as to the exact significance of the exploding grenade, had frozen into complete immobility. Only their eyes moved, darting almost desperately from side to side to locate the source of a danger that lay so heavily in the air as to be almost palpable.

The boulder was distinctly rocking now. With every additional heave it received from Andrea, it was rocking an additional inch farther forward, an additional inch farther backwards. Andrea had slipped farther and farther down until now he was almost horizontal on his back. He was gasping for breath and sweat was streaming down his face. The boulder rolled back almost as if it were going to fall upon him and crush him. Andrea took a deep breath, then convulsively straightened back and legs in one last titanic heave. For a moment the boulder teetered on the point of imbalance, reached the point of no return and fell away.

Droshny could most certainly have heard nothing and, in that near darkness, it was certain as could be that he had seen nothing. It could only have been an instinctive awareness of impending death that made him glance upwards in sudden conviction that this was where the danger lay. The huge boulder, just rolling gently when Droshny's horror-stricken eyes first caught sight of it, almost at once began to bound in ever-increasing leaps, hurtling down the slope directly towards them, trailing a small avalanche behind it. Droshny screamed a warning. He and his men scrambled desperately to their feet, an instinctive reaction that was no more than a useless and token gesture in the face of death, because, for most of them, it was already far too late and they had no place to go.

With one last great leap the hurtling boulder smashed straight into the centre of the bridge, shattering the flimsy woodwork and slicing the bridge in half. Two men who had been directly in the path of the boulder died instantaneously: five others were catapulted into the torrent below and swept away to almost equally immediate death. The two broken sections of the bridge, still secured to either bank by the suspension ropes, hung down into the rushing waters, their lowermost parts banging furiously against the boulder-strewn banks.

There must have been at least a dozen parachutes attached to the three dark cylindrical objects that now lay floating, though more than half submerged, in the equally dark waters of the Neretva dam. Mallory and Miller sliced those away with their knives, then joined the three cylinders in line astern, using short wire strops that had been provided for that precise purpose. Mallory examined the leading cylinder and gently eased back a lever set in the top. There was a subdued roar as compressed air violently aerated the water astern of the leading cylinder and sent it surging forward, tugging the other two cylinders behind it. Mallory closed the lever and nodded to the other two cylinders.

'These levers on the right-hand side control the flooding

valves. Open that one till you just have negative buoyancy and no more. I'll do the same on this one.'

Miller cautiously turned a valve and nodded at the leading cylinder. 'What's that for?'

'Do *you* fancy towing a ton and a half of amatol as far as the dam wall? Propulsion unit of some kind. Looks like a sawn-off section of a twenty-one-inch torpedo tube to me. Compressed air, maybe at a pressure of five thousand pounds a square inch, passing through reduction gear. Should do the job all right.'

'Just so long as Miller doesn't have to do it.' Miller closed the valve on the cylinder. 'About that?'

'About that.' All three cylinders were now just barely submerged. Again Mallory eased back the compressed air lever on the leading cylinder. There was a throaty burble of sound, a sudden flurry of bubbles streaming out astern and then all three cylinders were under way, heading down towards the angled neck of the dam, both men clinging to and guiding the leading cylinder.

When the swing bridge had disintegrated under the impact of the boulder, seven men had died: but two still lived.

Droshny and his sergeant, furiously buffeted and badly bruised by the torrent of water, clung desperately to the broken end of the bridge. At first, they could do no more than hold on, but gradually, and after a most exhausting struggle, they managed to haul themselves clear of the rapids and hang there, arms and legs hooked round broken sections of what remained of the bridge, fighting for breath. Droshny made a signal to some unseen person or persons across the rapids, then pointed upwards in the direction from which the boulder had come.

Crouched among the boulders on the far side of the river, three Cetniks—the fortunate three who had not yet moved on to the bridge when the boulder had fallen—saw the signal

225

and understood. About seventy feet above where Droshny—completely concealed from sight on that side by the high bank of the river—was still clinging grimly to what was left of the bridge, Andrea, now bereft of cover, had begun to make a precarious descent from his previous hiding-place. On the other side of the river, one of the three Cetniks took aim and fired.

Fortunately for Andrea, firing uphill in semi-darkness is a tricky business at the best of times. Bullets smashed into the cliff-face inches from Andrea's left shoulder, the whining ricochets leaving him almost miraculously unscathed. There would be a correction factor for the next burst, Andrea knew: he flung himself to one side, lost his balance and what little precarious purchase he had and slid and tumbled helplessly down the boulder-strewn slope. Bullets, many bullets, struck close by him on his way down, for the three Cetniks on the right bank, convinced now that Andrea was the only person left for them to deal with, had risen, advanced to the edge of the river and were concentrating all their fire on Andrea.

Again fortunately for Andrea, this period of concentration lasted for only a matter of a few seconds. Reynolds and Maria emerged from cover and ran down the bank, stopping momentarily to fire at the Cetniks across the river, who at once forgot all about Andrea to meet this new and unexpected threat. Just as they did so, Andrea, in the midst of a small avalanche, still fighting furiously but hopelessly to arrest his fall, struck the bank of the river with appalling force, struck the side of his head against a large stone and collapsed, his head and shoulders hanging out over the wild torrent below.

Reynolds flung himself flat on the shale of the river bank, forced himself to ignore the bullets striking to left and right of him and whining above him and took a slow and careful aim. He fired a long burst, a very long one, until the magazine of his Schmeisser was empty. All three Cetniks crumpled and died.

Reynolds rose. He was vaguely surprised to notice that his hands were shaking. He looked at Andrea, lying unconscious and dangerously near the side of the bank, took a couple of paces in his direction, then checked and turned as he heard a low moan behind him. Reynolds broke into a run.

Maria was half-sitting, half-lying on the stony bank. Both hands cradled her leg just above the right knee and the blood was welling between her fingers. Her face, normally pale enough, was ashen and drawn with shock and pain. Reynolds cursed bitterly but soundlessly, produced his knife and began to cut away the cloth around the wound. Gently, he pulled away the material covering the wound and smiled reassuringly at the girl: her lower lip was caught tightly between her teeth and she watched him steadily with eyes dimmed by pain and tears.

It was a nasty enough looking flesh wound, but, Reynolds knew, not dangerous. He reached for his medical pack, gave her a reassuring smile and then forgot all about his medical pack. The expression in Maria's eyes had given way to one of shock and fear and she was no longer looking at him.

Reynolds twisted round. Droshny had just hauled himself over the edge of the river bank, had risen to his feet and was now heading purposefully towards Andrea's prostrate body, with the obvious intention of heaving the unconscious man into the gorge.

Reynolds picked up his Schmeisser and pulled the trigger. There was an empty click—he'd forgotten the magazine had been emptied. He glanced around almost wildly in an attempt to locate Maria's gun, but there was no sign of it. He could wait no longer. Droshny was only a matter of feet from where Andrea lay. Reynolds picked up his knife and rushed along the bank. Droshny saw him coming and he saw too that

Reynolds was armed with only a knife. He smiled as a wolf would smile, took one of his wickedly-curved knives from his belt and waited.

The two men approached closely and circled warily. Reynolds had never wielded a knife in anger in his life and so had no illusions at all as to his chances: hadn't Neufeld said that Droshny was the best man in the Balkans with a knife? He certainly looked it, Reynolds thought. His mouth felt very dry.

Thirty yards away Maria, dizzy and weak with pain and dragging her wounded leg, crawled towards the spot where she thought her gun had fallen when she had been hit. After what seemed a very long time, but what was probably no more than ten seconds, she found it half-hidden among rocks. Nauseated and faint from the pain of her wounded leg, she forced herself to sit up and brought the gun to her shoulder. Then she lowered it again.

In her present condition, she realized vaguely, it would have been impossible for her to hit Droshny without almost certainly hitting Reynolds at the same time: in fact, she might well have killed Reynolds while missing Droshny entirely. For both men were now locked chest to chest, each man's knife-hand—the right—clamped in the grip of the other's left.

The girl's dark eyes, which had so recently reflected pain and shock and fear, now held only one expression—despair. Like Reynolds, Maria knew of Droshny's reputation—but, unlike Reynolds, she had seen Droshny kill with that knife and knew too well how lethal a combination that man and that knife were. A wolf and a lamb, she thought, a wolf and a lamb. After he kills Reynolds—her mind was dulled now, her thoughts almost incoherent—after he kills Reynolds I shall kill him. But first, Reynolds would have to die, for there could be no help for it. And then the despair left the dark eyes to be replaced by an almost unthinkable hope for she knew with an intuitive certainty that with Andrea by one's side hope need never be abandoned.

Not that Andrea was as yet by anyone's side. He had forced himself up to his hands and knees and was gazing down uncomprehendingly at the rushing white waters below, shaking his leonine head from side to side in an attempt to clear it. And then, still shaking his head, he levered himself painfully to his feet and he wasn't shaking his head any more. In spite of her pain, Maria smiled.

Slowly, inexorably, the Cetnik giant twisted Reynolds's knife-hand away from himself while at the same time bringing the lancet point of his own knife nearer to Reynolds's throat. Reynolds's sweat-sheened face reflected his desperation, his total awareness of impending defeat and death. He cried out with pain as Droshny twisted his right wrist almost to breaking-point, forcing him to open his fingers and drop his knife. Droshny kneed him viciously at the same time, freeing his left hand to give Reynolds a violent shove that sent him staggering to crash on his back against the stones and lie there winded and gasping in agony.

Droshny smiled his smile of wolfish satisfaction. Even although he must have known that the need for haste was paramount he yet had to take time off to carry out the execution in a properly leisurely fashion, to savour to the full every moment of it, to prolong the exquisite joy he always felt at moments like these. Reluctantly, almost, he changed to a throwing grip on his knife and slowly raised it high. The smile was broader than ever, a smile that vanished in an instant of time as he felt a knife being plucked from his own belt. He whirled round. Andrea's face was a mask of stone.

Droshny smiled again. 'The gods have been kind to me.' His voice was low, almost reverent, his tone a caressing whisper. 'I have dreamed of this. It is better that you should die this way. This will teach you, my friend—'

Droshny, hoping to catch Andrea unprepared, broke off in mid-sentence and lunged forward with cat-like speed. The smile vanished again as he looked in almost comical disbelief at his right wrist locked in the vice-like grip of Andrea's left hand.

Within seconds, the tableau was as it had been in the beginning of the earlier struggle, both knife-wrists locked in the opponents' left hands. The two men appeared to be absolutely immobile, Andrea with his face totally impassive, Droshny with his white teeth bared, but no longer in a smile. It was, instead, a vicious snarl compounded of hate and fury and baffled anger—for this time Droshny, to his evident consternation and disbelief, could make no impression whatsoever on his opponent. The impression, this time, was being made on him.

Maria, the pain in her leg in temporary abeyance, and a slowly recovering Reynolds stared in fascination as Andrea's left hand, in almost millimetric slow-motion, gradually twisted Droshny's right wrist so that the blade moved slowly away and the Cetnik's fingers began, almost imperceptibly at first, to open. Droshny, his face darkening in colour and the veins standing out on forehead and neck, summoned every last reserve of strength to his right hand: Andrea, rightly sensing that all of Droshny's power and will and concentration were centred exclusively upon breaking his crushing grip suddenly tore his own right hand free and brought his knife scything round and under and upwards with tremendous power: the knife went in under the breast-bone, burying itself to the hilt. For a moment or two the giant stood there, lips drawn far back over bared teeth smiling mindlessly in the rictus of death, then, as Andrea stepped away, leaving the knife still embedded, Droshny toppled slowly over the edge of the ravine. The Cetnik sergeant, still clinging to the shattered remains of the bridge, stared in uncomprehending horror as Droshny, the hilt of the knife easily distinguishable, fell head-first into the boiling rapids and was immediately lost to sight.

Reynolds rose painfully and shakily to his feet and smiled at Andrea. He said: 'Maybe I've been wrong about you all along. Thank you, Colonel Stavros.'

Andrea shrugged. 'Just returning a favour, my boy. Maybe I've been wrong about you, too.' He glanced at his watch. 'Two o'clock! *Two* o'clock! Where are the others?'

'God, I'd almost forgotten. Maria there is hurt. Groves and Petar are on the ladder. I'm not sure, but I think Groves is in a pretty bad way.'

'They may need help. Get to them quickly. I'll look after the girl.'

At the southern end of the Neretva bridge, General Zimmermann stood in his command car and watched the sweep-second hand of his watch come up to the top.

'Two o'clock,' Zimmermann said, his tone almost conversational. He brought his right hand down in a cutting gesture. A whistle shrilled and at once tank engines roared and treads clattered as the spearhead of Zimmermann's first armoured division began to cross the bridge at Neretva.

CHAPTER 13

Saturday

0200-0215

'Maurer and Schmidt! Maurer and Schmidt!' The captain in charge of the guard on top of the Neretva dam wall came running from the guard-house, looked around almost wildly and grabbed his sergeant by the arm. 'For God's sake, where are Maurer and Schmidt? No one seen them? No one? Get the searchlight.'

Petar, still holding the unconscious Groves pinned against the ladder, heard the sound of the words but did not understand them. Petar, with both arms round Groves, now had his forearms locked at an almost impossible angle between the stanchions and the rock-face behind. In this position, as long as his wrists or forearms didn't break, he could hold Groves almost indefinitely. But Petar's grey and sweat-covered face, the racked and twisted face, were mute testimony enough to the almost unendurable agony he was suffering.

Mallory and Miller also heard the urgently shouted commands, but, like Petar, were unable to understand what it was that was being shouted. It would be something, Mallory thought vaguely, that would bode no good for them, then put the thought from his mind: he had other and more urgently immediate matters to occupy his attention. They had reached the barrier of the torpedo net and he had the supporting cable in one hand, a knife in the other when Miller exclaimed and caught his arm.

'For God's sake, no!' The urgency in Miller's voice had

Mallory looking at him in astonishment. 'Jesus, what do I use for brains. That's not a wire.'

'It's not—'

'It's an insulated power cable. Can't you see?'

Mallory peered closely. 'Now I can.'

'Two thousand volts, I'll bet.' Miller still sounded shaken. 'Electric chair power. We'd have been frizzled alive. *And* it would have triggered off an alarm bell.'

'Over the top with them,' Mallory said.

Struggling and pushing, heaving and pulling, for there was only a foot of clear water between the wire and the surface of the water, they managed to ease the compressed air cylinder over and had just succeeded in lifting the nose of the first of the amatol cylinders on to the wire when, less than a hundred yards away, a six-inch searchlight came to life on the top of the dam wall, its beam momentarily horizontal, then dipping sharply to begin a traverse of the water close in to the side of the dam wall.

'That's all we bloody well need,' Mallory said bitterly. He pushed the nose of the amatol block back off the wire, but the wire strop securing it to the compressed air cylinder held it in such a position that it remained with its nose nine inches clear of the water. 'Leave it. Get under. Hang on to the net.'

Both men sank under the water as the sergeant atop the dam wall continued his traverse with the searchlight. The beam passed over the nose of the first of the amatol cylinders, but a black-painted cylinder in dark waters makes a poor subject for identification and the sergeant failed to see it. The light moved on, finished its traverse of the water alongside the dam, then went out.

Mallory and Miller surfaced cautiously and looked swiftly around. For the moment, there was no other sign of immediate danger. Mallory studied the luminous hands of his watch. He said: 'Hurry! For God's sake, hurry! We're almost three minutes behind schedule.'

They hurried. Desperate now, they had the two amatol cylinders over the wire inside twenty seconds, opened the compressed air valve on the leading cylinder and were alongside the massive wall of the dam inside another twenty. At that moment, the clouds parted and the moon broke through again, silvering the dark waters of the dam. Mallory and Miller were now in a helplessly exposed position but there was nothing they could do about it and they knew it. Their time had run out and they had no option other than to secure and arm the amatol cylinders as quickly as ever possible. Whether they were discovered or not could still be all-important: but there was nothing they could do to prevent that discovery.

Miller said softly: 'Forty feet apart and forty feet down, the experts say. We'll be too late.'

'No. Not yet too late. The idea is to let the tanks across first then destroy the bridge before the petrol bowsers and the main infantry battalions cross.'

Atop the dam wall, the sergeant with the searchlight returned from the western end of the dam and reported to the captain.

'Nothing, sir. No sign of anyone.'

'Very good.' The captain nodded towards the gorge. 'Try that side. You may find something there.'

So the sergeant tried the other side and he did find something there, and almost immediately. Ten seconds after he had begun his traverse with the searchlight he picked up the figures of the unconscious Groves and the exhausted Petar and, only feet below them and climbing steadily, Sergeant Reynolds. All three were hopelessly trapped, quite powerless to do anything to defend themselves: Reynolds had no longer even his gun.

On the dam wall, a Wehrmacht soldier, levelling his machine-pistol along the beam of the searchlight, glanced up in astonishment as the captain struck down the barrel of his gun.

'Fool!' The captain sounded savage. 'I want them alive. You two, fetch ropes, get them up here for questioning. We *must* find out what they have been up to.'

His words carried clearly to the two men in the water for, just then, the last of the bombing ceased and the sound of the small-arms fire died away. The contrast was almost too much to be borne, the suddenly hushed silence strangely ominous, deathly, almost, in its sinister foreboding.

'You heard?' Miller whispered.

'I heard.' More cloud, Mallory could see, thinner cloud but still cloud, was about to pass across the face of the moon. 'Fix these float suckers to the wall. I'll do the other charge.' He turned and swam slowly away, towing the second amatol cylinder behind him.

When the beam of the searchlight had reached down from the top of the dam wall Andrea had been prepared for almost instant discovery, but the prior discovery of Groves, Reynolds and Petar had saved Maria and himself, for the Germans seemed to think that they had caught all there were to be caught and, instead of traversing the rest of the gorge with the searchlights, had concentrated, instead, on bringing up to the top of the wall the three men they had found trapped on the ladder. One man, obviously unconscious—that would be Groves, Andrea thought—was hauled up at the end of a rope: the other two, with one man lending assistance to the other, had completed the journey up the ladder by themselves. All this Andrea had seen while he was bandaging Maria's injured leg, but he had said nothing of it to her.

Andrea secured the bandage and smiled at her. 'Better?'

'Better.' She tried to smile her thanks but the smile wouldn't come.

'Fine. Time we were gone.' Andrea consulted his watch. 'If we stay here any longer I have the feeling that we're going to get very, very wet.'

He straightened to his feet and it was this sudden movement that saved his life. The knife that had been intended for his back passed cleanly through his upper left arm. For a moment, almost as if uncomprehending, Andrea stared down at the tip of the narrow blade emerging from his arm then, apparently oblivious of the agony it must have cost him, turned slowly round, the movement wrenching the hilt of the knife from the hand of the man who held it.

The Cetnik sergeant, the only other man to have survived with Droshny the destruction of the swing bridge, stared at Andrea as if he were petrified, possibly because he couldn't understand why he had failed to kill Andrea, more probably because he couldn't understand how a man could suffer such a wound in silence and, in silence, still be able to tear the knife from his grasp. Andrea had now no weapon left him nor did he require one. In what seemed an almost grotesque slow motion, Andrea lifted his right hand: but there was nothing slow-motion about the dreadful edge-handed chopping blow which caught the Cetnik sergeant on the base of the neck. The man was probably dead before he struck the ground.

Reynolds and Petar sat with their backs to the guard-hut at the eastern end of the dam. Beside them lay the still unconscious Groves, his breathing now stertorous, his face ashen and of a peculiar waxed texture. From overhead, fixed to the roof of the guard-house, a bright light shone down on them, while near by was a watchful guard with his carbine trained on them. The Wehrmacht captain of the guard stood above them, an almost awestruck expression on his face.

He said incredulously but in immaculate English: 'You

hoped to blow up a dam this size with a few sticks of dynamite? You must be mad!'

'No one told us the dam was as big as this,' Reynolds said sullenly.

'No one told you—God in heaven, talk of mad dogs and Englishmen! And where is this dynamite?'

'The wooden bridge broke.' Reynolds's shoulders were slumped in abject defeat. 'We lost all the dynamite—and all our other friends.'

'I wouldn't have believed it, I just wouldn't have believed it.' The captain shook his head and turned away, then checked as Reynolds called him. 'What is it?'

'My friend here.' Reynolds indicated Groves. 'He is very ill, you can see that. He needs medical attention.'

'Later.' The captain turned to the soldier in the open transceiver cabin. 'What news from the south.'

'They have just started to cross the Neretva bridge, sir.'

The words carried clearly to Mallory, at that moment some distance apart from Miller. He had just finished securing his float to the wall and was on the point of rejoining Miller when he caught a flash of light out of the corner of his eye. Mallory remained still and glanced upward and to his right.

There was a guard on the dam wall above, leaning over the parapet as he moved along, flashing a torch downwards. Discovery, Mallory at once realized, was certain. One or both of the supporting floats were bound to be seen. Unhurriedly, and steadying himself against his float, Mallory unzipped the top of his rubber suit, reached under his tunic, brought out his Luger, unwrapped it from its waterproof cover and eased off the safety-catch.

The pool of light from the torch passed over the water, close in to the side of the dam wall. Suddenly, the beam of the torch remained still. Clearly to be seen in the centre of the light was a small, torpedo-shaped object fastened to the dam wall by suckers and, just beside it, a rubber-suited man with a gun in his hand. And the gun—it had, the sentry automatically noticed, a silencer screwed to the end of the barrel—was pointed directly at him. The sentry opened his mouth to shout a warning but the warning never came for a red flower bloomed in the centre of his forehead, and he leaned forward tiredly, the upper half of his body over the edge of the parapet, his arms dangling downwards. The torch slipped from his lifeless hand and tumbled down into the water.

The impact of the torch on the water made a flat, almost cracking sound. In the now deep silence it was bound to be heard by those above, Mallory thought. He waited tensely, the Luger ready in his hand, but after twenty seconds had passed and nothing happened Mallory decided he could wait no longer. He glanced at Miller, who had clearly heard the sound, for he was staring at Mallory, and at the gun in Mallory's hand with a puzzled frown on his face. Mallory pointed up towards the dead guard hanging over the parapet. Miller's face cleared and he nodded his understanding. The moon went behind a cloud.

Andrea, the sleeve of his left arm soaked in blood, more than half carried the hobbling Maria across the shale and through the rocks: she could hardly put her right foot beneath her. Arrived at the foot of the ladder, both of them stared upwards at the forbidding climb, at the seemingly endless zig-zags of the iron ladder reaching up into the night. With a crippled girl and his own damaged arm, Andrea thought, the prospects were poor indeed. And God only knew when the wall of the dam was due to go up. He looked at his watch. If everything was on schedule, it was due to go now: Andrea hoped to God that Mallory, with his passion for punctuality, had for once fallen behind schedule. The girl looked at him and understood.

'Leave me,' she said. 'Please leave me.'

'Out of the question,' Andrea said firmly. 'Maria would never forgive me.'

'Maria?'

'Not you.' Andrea lifted her on to his back and wound her arms round his neck. 'My wife. I think I'm going to be terrified of her.' He reached out for the ladder and started to climb.

The better to see how the final preparations for the attack were developing, General Zimmermann had ordered his command car out on to the Neretva bridge itself and now had it parked exactly in the middle, pulled close in to the right-hand side. Within feet of him clanked and clattered and roared a seemingly endless column of tanks and self-propelled guns and trucks laden with assault troops: as soon as they reached the northern end of the bridge, tanks and guns and trucks fanned out east and west along the banks of the river, to take temporary cover behind the steep escarpment ahead before launching the final concerted attack.

From time to time, Zimmermann raised his binoculars and scanned the skies to the west. A dozen times he imagined he heard the distant thunder of approaching air armadas, a dozen times he deceived himself. Time and again he told himself he was a fool, a prey to useless and fearful imaginings wholly unbecoming to a general in the Wehrmacht: but still this deep feeling of unease persisted, still he kept examining the skies to the west. It never once occurred to him, for there was no reason why it should, that he was looking in the wrong direction.

Less than half a mile to the north, General Vukalovic lowered his binoculars and turned to Colonel Janzy.

'That's it, then.' Vukalovic sounded weary and inexpressibly sad. 'They're across—or almost all across. Five more minutes. Then we counter-attack.'

'Then we counter-attack,' Janzy said tonelessly. 'We'll lose a thousand men in fifteen minutes.'

'We asked for the impossible,' Vukalovic said. 'We pay for our mistakes.'

Mallory, a long trailing lanyard in his hand, rejoined Miller. He said: 'Fixed?'

'Fixed.' Miller had a lanyard in his own hand. 'We pull those leads to the hydrostatic chemical fuses and take off?'

'Three minutes. You know what happens to us if we're still in this water after three minutes?'

'Don't even talk about it,' Miller begged. He suddenly cocked his head and glanced quickly at Mallory. Mallory, too, had heard it, the sound of running footsteps up above. He nodded at Miller. Both men sank beneath the surface of the water.

The captain of the guard, because of inclination, a certain rotundity of figure and very proper ideas as to how an officer of the Wehrmacht should conduct himself, was not normally given to running. He had, in fact, been walking, quickly and nervously, along the top of the dam wall when he caught sight of one of his guards leaning over the parapet in what he could only consider an unsoldierly and slovenly fashion. It then occurred to him that a man leaning over a parapet would normally use his hands and arms to brace himself and he could not see the guard's hands and arms. He remembered the missing Maurer and Schmidt and broke into a run.

The guard did not seem to hear him coming. The captain caught him roughly by the shoulder, then stood back aghast as the dead man slid back off the parapet and collapsed at his feet, face upwards: the place where his forehead had been was not a pretty sight. Seized by a momentary paralysis, the captain stared for long seconds at the dead man, then, by a conscious effort of will, drew out both his torch and pistol, snapped on the beam of the one and released the safety-catch of the other and risked a very quick glance over the dam parapet.

There was nothing to be seen. Rather, there was nobody to be seen, no sign of the enemy who must have killed his guard within the past minute or so. But there *was* something to be seen, additional evidence, as if he ever needed such evidence, that the enemy had been there: a torpedo-shaped object—no, *two* torpedo-shaped objects—clamped to the wall of the dam just at water level. Uncomprehendingly at first, the captain stared at those, then the significance of their presence there struck him with the violence, almost, of a physical blow. He straightened and started running towards the eastern end of the dam, shouting 'Radio! Radio!' at the top of his voice.

Mallory and Miller surfaced. The shouts—they were almost screams—of the running captain of the guard—carried clear over the now silent waters of the dam. Mallory swore.

'Damn and damn and damn again!' His voice was almost vicious in his chagrin and frustration. 'He can give Zimmermann seven, maybe eight minutes warning. Time to pull the bulk of his tanks on to the high ground.'

'So now?'

'So now we pull those lanyards and get the hell out of here.'

The captain, racing along the wall, was now less than thirty yards from the radio hut and where Petar and Reynolds sat with their backs to the guard-house.

'General Zimmermann!' he shouted. 'Get through. Tell him to pull his tanks to the high ground. Those damned English have mined the dam!'

Petar took off his dark glasses and rubbed his eyes.

'Ah, well.' Petar's voice was almost a sigh. 'All good things come to an end.'

Reynolds stared at him, his face masked in astonishment.

241

Automatically, involuntarily, his hand reached out to take the dark glasses Petar was passing him, automatically his eyes followed Petar's hand moving away again and then, in a state of almost hypnotic trance, he watched the thumb of that hand press a catch in the side of the guitar. The back of the instrument fell open to reveal inside the trigger, magazine and gleamingly-oiled mechanism of a sub-machine-gun.

Petar's forefinger closed over the trigger. The sub-machine-gun, its first shell shattering the end of the guitar, stuttered and leapt in Petar's hands. The dark eyes were narrowed, watchful and cool. And Petar had his priorities right.

The soldier guarding the three prisoners doubled over and died, almost cut in half by the first blast of shells. Two seconds later the corporal guard by the radio hut, while still desperately trying to unsling his Schmeisser, went the same way. The captain of the guard, still running, fired his pistol repeatedly at Petar, but Petar still had his priorities right. He ignored the captain, ignored a bullet which struck his right shoulder, and emptied the remainder of the magazine into the radio trans-ceiver, then toppled sideways to the ground, the smashed guitar falling from his nerveless hands, blood pouring from his shoulder and a wound on his head.

The captain replaced his still smoking revolver in his pocket and stared down at the unconscious Petar. There was no anger in the captain's face now, just a peculiar sadness, the dull acceptance of ultimate defeat. His eyes moved and caught Reynolds's: in a moment of rare understanding both men shook their heads in a strange and mutual wonder.

Mallory and Miller, climbing the knotted rope, were almost opposite the top of the dam wall when the last echoes of the firing drifted away across the waters of the dam. Mallory glanced down at Miller, who shrugged as best a man can shrug when hanging on to a rope and shook his head wordlessly.

Both men resumed their climb, moving even more quickly than before.

Andrea, too, had heard the shots, but had no idea what their significance might be. At that moment, he did not particularly care. His left upper arm felt as if it were burning in a fierce bright flame, his sweat-covered face reflected his pain and near-exhaustion. He was not yet, he knew, half-way up the ladder. He paused briefly, aware that the girl's grip around his neck was slipping, eased her carefully in towards the ladder, wrapped his left arm round her waist and continued his painfully slow and dogged climb. He wasn't seeing very well now and he thought vaguely that it must be because of the loss of blood. Oddly enough, his left arm was beginning to become numb and the pain was centring more and more on his right shoulder which all the time took the strain of their combined weights.

'Leave me!' Maria said again. 'For God's sake, leave me. You can save yourself.'

Andrea gave her a smile or what he thought was a smile and said kindly: 'You don't know what you're saying. Besides, Maria would murder me.'

'Leave me! Leave me!' She struggled and exclaimed in pain as Andrea tightened his grip. 'You're hurting me.'

'Then stop struggling,' Andrea said equably. He continued his pain-racked, slow-motion climb.

Mallory and Miller reached the longitudinal crack running across the top of the dam wall and edged swiftly along crack and rope until they were directly above the arc lights on the eaves of the guard-house some fifty feet below: the brilliant illumination from those lights made it very clear indeed just what had happened. The unconscious Groves and Petar, the two dead German guards, the smashed radio transceiver and,

243

above all, the sub-machine-gun still lying in the shattered casing of the guitar told a tale that could not be misread. Mallory moved another ten feet along the crack and peered down again: Andrea, with the girl doing her best to help by pulling on the rungs of the ladder, was now almost two-thirds of the way up, but making dreadfully slow progress of it: they'll never make it in time, Mallory thought, it is impossible that they will ever make it in time. It comes to us all, he thought tiredly, some day it's bound to come to us all: but that it should come to the indestructible Andrea pushed fatalistic acceptance beyond its limits. Such a thing was inconceivable: and the inconceivable was about to happen now.

Mallory rejoined Miller. Quickly he unhitched a rope—the knotted rope he and Miller had used to descend to the Neretva dam—secured it to the rope running above the longitudinal crack and lowered it until it touched softly on the roof of the guard-house. He took the Luger in his hand and was about to start sliding down when the dam blew up.

The twin explosions occurred within two seconds of each other: the detonation of 3,000 pounds of high explosive should normally have produced a titanic outburst of sound, but because of the depth at which they took place, the explosions were curiously muffled, felt, almost, rather than heard. Two great columns of water soared up high above the top of the dam wall, but for what seemed an eternity of time but certainly was not more than four or five seconds, nothing appeared to happen. Then, very, very slowly, reluctantly, almost, the entire central section of the dam wall, at least eighty feet in width and right down to its base, toppled outwards into the gorge: the entire section seemed to be all still in one piece.

Andrea stopped climbing. He had heard no sound, but he felt the shuddering vibration of the ladder and he knew what had happened, what was coming. He wrapped both arms around Maria and the stanchions, pressed her close to the ladder and looked over her head. Two vertical cracks made their slow appearance on the outside of the dam wall, then the entire wall fell slowly towards them, almost as if it were hinged on its base, and then was abruptly lost to sight as countless millions of gallons of greenish-dark water came boiling through the shattered dam wall. The sound of the crash of a thousand tons of masonry falling into the gorge below should have been heard miles away: but Andrea could hear nothing above the roaring of the escaping waters. He had time only to notice that the dam wall had vanished and now there was only this mighty green torrent, curiously smooth and calm in its initial stages, then pouring down to strike the gorge beneath in a seething white maelstrom of foam before the awesome torrent was upon them. In a second of time Andrea released one hand, turned the girl's terrified face and buried it against his chest for he knew that if she should impossibly live, then that battering-ram of water, carrying with it sand and pebbles and God only knew what else, would tear the delicate skin from her face and leave her forever scarred. He ducked his own head against the fury of the coming onslaught and locked his hands together behind the ladder.

The impact of the waters drove the breath from his gasping body. Buried in this great falling crushing wall of green, Andrea fought for his life and that of the girl. The strain upon him, battered and already bruising badly from the hammer-blows of this hurtling cascade of water which seemed so venomously bent upon his instant destruction, was, even without the cruel handicap of his badly injured arm, quite fantastic. His arms, it felt, were momentarily about to be torn from their sockets, it would have been the easiest thing in the world, the wisest thing in the world to unclasp his hands and let kindly oblivion take the place of the agony that seemed to be tearing limbs and muscles asunder. But Andrea did not let go and

Andrea did not break. Other things broke. Several of the
ladder supports were torn away from the wall and it seemed
that both ladder and climbers must be inevitably swept away.
The ladder twisted, buckled and leaned far out from the wall
so that Andrea was now as much lying beneath the ladder as
hanging on to it: but still Andrea did not let go, still some
remaining supports held. Then very gradually, after what
seemed to the dazed Andrea an interminable period of time,
the dam level dropped, the force of the water weakened, not
much but just perceptibly, and Andrea started to climb again.
Half a dozen times, as he changed hands on the rungs, his
grip loosened and he was almost torn away: half a dozen times
his teeth bared in the agony of effort, the great hands clamped
tight and he impossibly retained his grip. After almost a minute
of this titanic struggle he finally won clear of the worst of the
waters and could breathe again. He looked at the girl in his
arms. The blonde hair was plastered over her ashen cheeks,
the incongruously dark eyelashes closed. The ravine seemed
almost full to the top of its precipitously-sided walls with this
whitely boiling torrent of water sweeping everything before
it, its roar, as it thundered down the gorge with a speed faster
than that of an express train, a continuous series of explosions,
an insane and banshee shrieking of sound.

Almost thirty seconds elapsed from the time of the blowing
up of the dam until Mallory could bring himself to move again.
He did not know why he should have been held in thrall for
so long. He told himself, rationalizing, that it was because of
the hypnotic spectacle of the dramatic fall in the level of the
dam coupled with the sight of that great gorge filled almost to
the top with those whitely seething waters: but, without admit-
ting it to himself, he knew it was more than that, he knew he
could not accept the realization that Andrea and Maria had
been swept to their deaths, for Mallory did not know that at

that instant Andrea, completely spent and no longer knowing what he was doing, was vainly trying to negotiate the last few steps of the ladder to the top of the dam. Mallory seized the rope and slid down down recklessly, ignoring or not feeling the burning of the skin on the palms of his hands, his mind irrationally filled with murder—irrationally, because it was he who had triggered the explosion that had taken Andrea to his death.

And then, as his feet touched the roof of the guard-house, he saw the ghost—the ghosts, rather—as the heads of Andrea and a clearly unconscious Maria appeared at the top of the ladder. Andrea, Mallory noticed, did not seem to be able to go any farther. He had a hand on the top rung, and was making convulsive, jerking movements, but making no progress at all. Andrea, Mallory knew, was finished.

Mallory was not the only one who had seen Andrea and the girl. The captain of the guard and one of his men were staring in stupefaction over the awesome scene of destruction, but a second guard had whirled round, caught sight of Andrea's head and brought up his machine-pistol. Mallory, still clinging to the rope, had no time to bring his Luger to bear and release the safety-catch and Andrea should have assuredly died then: but Reynolds had already catapulted himself forward in a desperate dive and brought down the gun in the precise instant that the guard opened fire. Reynolds died instantaneously. The guard died two seconds later. Mallory lined up the still smoking barrel of his Luger on the captain and the guard.

'Drop those guns,' he said.

They dropped their guns. Mallory and Miller swung down from the guard-house roof, and while Miller covered the Germans with his guns, Mallory ran quickly across to the ladder, reached down a hand and helped the unconscious girl and the swaying Andrea to safety. He looked at Andrea's exhausted, blood-flecked face, at the flayed skin on his hands, at the left sleeve saturated in blood and said severely: 'And where the hell have you been?'

'Where have I been?' Andrea asked vaguely. 'I don't know.' He stood rocking on his feet, barely conscious, rubbed a hand across his eyes and tried to smile. 'I think I must have stopped to admire the view.'

General Zimmermann was still in his command car and his car was still parked in the right centre of the bridge at Neretva. Zimmermann had again his binoculars to his eyes, but for the first time he was gazing neither to the west nor to the north. He was gazing instead to the east, up-river towards the mouth of the Neretva gorge. After a little time he turned to his aide, his face at first uneasy, then the uneasiness giving way to apprehension, then the apprehension to something very like fear.

'You hear it?' he asked.

'I hear it, Herr General.'

'And feel it?'

'And I feel it.'

'What in the name of God almighty can it be?' Zimmermann demanded. He listened as a great and steadily increasing roar filled all the air around them. 'That's not thunder. It's far too loud for thunder. And too continuous. And that wind—that wind coming out of the gorge there.' He could now hardly hear himself speak above the almost deafening roar of sound coming from the east. 'It's the dam! The dam at Neretva! They've blown the dam! Get out of here!' he screamed at the driver. 'For God's sake get out of here!'

The command car jerked and moved forward, but it was too late for General Zimmermann, just as it was too late for his massed echelons of tanks and thousands of assault troops concealed on the banks of the Neretva by the low escarpment to the north of them and waiting to launch the devastating attack that was to annihilate the seven thousand fanatically stubborn defenders of the Zenica Gap. A mighty wall of white water, eighty feet high, carrying with it the irresistible pressure of millions of tons of water and sweeping before it a gigantic battering ram of boulders and trees, burst out of the mouth of the gorge.

Mercifully for most of the men in Zimmermann's armoured corps, the realization of impending death and death itself were only moments apart. The Neretva bridge, and all the vehicles on it, including Zimmermann's command car, were swept away to instant destruction. The giant torrent overspread both banks of the river to a depth of almost twenty feet, sweeping before its all-consuming path tanks, guns, armoured vehicles, thousands of troops and all that stood in its way: when the great flood finally subsided, there was not one blade of grass left growing along the banks of the Neretva. Perhaps a hundred or two of combat troops on both sides of the river succeeded in climbing in terror to higher ground and the most temporary of safety for they too would not have long to live, but for ninety-five per cent of Zimmermann's two armoured divisions destruction was as appallingly sudden as it was terrifyingly complete. In sixty seconds, no more, it was all over. The German armoured corps was totally destroyed. But still that mighty wall of water continued to boil forth from the mouth of the gorge.

'I pray God that I shall never see the like again.' General Vukalovic lowered his glasses and turned to Colonel Janzy, his face registering neither jubilation nor satisfaction, only an awestruck wonder mingled with a deep compassion. 'Men should not die like that, even our enemies should not die like that.' He was silent for a few moments, then stirred. 'I think a hundred or two of their infantry escaped to safety on this side, Colonel. You will take care of them?'

'I'll take care of them,' Janz ysaid sombrely. 'This is a night for prisoners, not killing, for there won't be any fight. It's as well, General. For the first time in my life I'm not looking forward to a fight.'

'I'll leave you then.' Vukalovic clapped Janzy's shoulder and smiled, a very tired smile. 'I have an appointment. At the Neretva dam—or what's left of it.

'With a certain Captain Mallory?'

'With Captain Mallory. We leave for Italy tonight. You know, Colonel, we could have been wrong about that man.'

'I never doubted him,' Janzy said firmly.

Vukalovic smiled and turned away.

Captain Neufeld, his head swathed in a blood-stained bandage and supported by two of his men, stood shakily at the top of the gully leading down to the ford in the Neretva and stared down, his face masked in shocked horror and an almost total disbelief, at the whitely boiling maelstrom, its seething surface no more than twenty feet below where he stood, of what had once been the Neretva gorge. He shook his head very, very slowly in unspeakable weariness and final acceptance of defeat, then turned to the soldier on his left, a youngster who looked as stupefied as he, Neufeld, felt.

'Take the two best ponies,' Neufeld said. 'Ride to the nearest Wehrmacht command post north of the Zenica Gap. Tell them that General Zimmermann's armoured divisions have been wiped out—we don't *know*, but they must have been. Tell them the valley of Neretva is a valley of death and that there is no one left to defend it. Tell them the Allies can send in their airborne divisions tomorrow and that there won't be a single shot fired. Tell them to notify Berlin immediately. You understand, Lindemann?'

'I understand, sir.' From the expression on Lindemann's face, Neufeld thought that Lindemann had understood very little of what he had said to him: but Neufeld felt infinitely tired and he did not feel like repeating his instructions. Lindemann mounted a pony, snatched the reins of another and spurred his pony up alongside the railway track.

Neufeld said, almost to himself: 'There's not all that hurry, boy.'

'Herr Hauptmann?' The other soldier was looking at him strangely.

'It's too late now,' Neufeld said.

Mallory gazed down the still foaming gorge, turned and gazed at the Neretva dam whose level had already dropped by at least fifty feet, then turned to look at the men and the girl behind him. He felt weary beyond all words.

Andrea, battered and bruised and bleeding, his left arm now roughly bandaged, was demonstrating once again his quite remarkable powers of recuperation: to look at him it would have been impossible to guess that, only ten minutes ago, he had been swaying on the edge of total collapse. He held Maria cradled in his arms: she was coming to, but very, very slowly. Miller finished dressing the head wound of a now sitting Petar who, though wounded in shoulder and head, seemed more than likely to survive, crossed to Groves and stooped over him. After a moment or two he straightened and stared down at the young sergeant.

'Dead?' Mallory asked.

'Dead.'

'Dead.' Andrea smiled, a smile full of sorrow. 'Dead—and you and I are alive. Because this young lad is dead.'

'He was expendable,' Miller said.

'And young Reynolds.' Andrea was inexpressibly tired. 'He was expendable too. What was it you said to him this afternoon, my Keith—for now is all the time there may be? And that was all the time there was. For young Reynolds. He saved my life tonight—twice. He saved Maria's. He saved Petar's. But he wasn't clever enough to save his own. *We* are the clever ones, the old ones, the wise ones, the knowing ones. And the old ones are alive and the young ones are dead. And so it always is. We mocked them, laughed at them, distrusted them, marvelled at their youth and stupidity and ignorance.' In a curiously tender gesture he smoothed Maria's wet blonde hair back from her face and she smiled at him. 'And in the end they were better men than we were . . .'

'Maybe they were at that,' Mallory said. He looked at Petar sadly and shook his head in wonder. 'And to think that all three of them are dead, Reynolds dead, Groves dead, Saunders dead, and not one of them ever knew that you were the head of British espionage in the Balkans.'

'Ignorant to the end.' Miller drew the back of his sleeve angrily across his eyes. 'Some people never learn. Some people just never learn.'

Epilogue

Once again Captain Jensen and the British lieutenant-general were back in the Operations Room in Termoli, but now they were no longer pacing up and down. The days of pacing were over. True, they still looked very tired, their faces probably fractionally more deeply lined than they had been a few days previously: but the faces were no longer haggard, the eyes no longer clouded with anxiety, and, had they been walking instead of sitting deep in comfortable armchairs, it was just conceivable that they might have had a new spring to their steps. Both men had glasses in their hands, large glasses.

Jensen sipped his whisky and said, smiling: 'I thought a general's place was at the head of his troops?'

'Not in these days, Captain,' the General said firmly. 'In 1944 the wise general leads from behind his troops—about twenty miles behind. Besides, the armoured divisions are going so quickly I couldn't possibly hope to catch up with them.'

'They're moving as fast as that?'

'Not quite as fast as the German and Austrian divisions that pulled out of the Gustav Line last night and are now racing for the Yugoslav border. But they're coming along pretty well.' The General permitted himself a large gulp of his drink and a smile of considerable satisfaction. 'Deception complete, break-through complete. On the whole, your men have done a pretty fair job.'

Both men turned in their chairs as a respectful rat-a-tat of knuckles preceded the opening of the heavy leather doors. Mallory entered, followed by Vukalovic, Andrea and Miller.

All four were unshaven, all of them looked as if they hadn't slept for a week. Andrea carried his arm in a sling.

Jensen rose, drained his glass, set it on a table, looked at Mallory dispassionately and said: 'Cut it a bit bloody fine, didn't you?'

Mallory, Andrea and Miller exchanged expressionless looks. There was a fairly long silence, then Mallory said: 'Some things take longer than others.'

Petar and Maria were lying side by side, hands clasped, in two regulation army beds in the Termoli military hospital when Jensen entered, followed by Mallory, Miller and Andrea.

'Excellent reports about both of you, I'm glad to hear,' Jensen said briskly. 'Just brought some—ah—friends to say goodbye.'

'What sort of hospital is this, then?' Miller asked severely. 'How about the high army moral tone, hey? Don't they have separate quarters for men and women?'

'They've been married for almost two years,' Mallory said mildly. 'Did I forget to tell you?'

'Of course you didn't forget,' Miller said disgustedly. 'It just slipped your mind.'

'Speaking of marriage—' Andrea cleared his throat and tried another tack. 'Captain Jensen may recall that back in Navarone—'

'Yes, yes.' Jensen held up a hand. 'Quite so. Quite. Quite. But I thought perhaps—well, the fact of the matter is—well, it so happens that another little job, just a tiny little job really, has just come up and I thought that seeing you were here anyway . . .'

Andrea stared at Jensen. His face was horror-stricken.

WHEN
EIGHT BELLS
TOLL

TO PAUL AND XENIA

I

Dusk Monday—3 a.m. Tuesday

The Peacemaker Colt has now been in production, without change in design, for a century. Buy one to-day and it would be indistinguishable from the one Wyatt Earp wore when he was the Marshal of Dodge City. It is the oldest hand-gun in the world, without question the most famous and, if efficiency in its designated task of maiming and killing be taken as criterion of its worth, then it is also probably the best hand-gun ever made. It is no light thing, it is true, to be wounded by some of the Peacemaker's more highly esteemed competitors, such as the Luger or Mauser: but the high-velocity, narrow-calibre, steel-cased shell from either of those just goes straight through you, leaving a small neat hole in its wake and spending the bulk of its energy on the distant landscape whereas the large and unjacketed soft-nosed lead bullet from the Colt mushrooms on impact, tearing and smashing bone and muscle and tissue as it goes and expending all its energy on you.

In short when a Peacemaker's bullet hits you in, say, the leg, you don't curse, step into shelter, roll and light a cigarette one-handed then smartly shoot your assailant between the eyes. When a Peacemaker bullet hits your leg you fall to the ground unconscious, and if it hits the thigh-bone and you are lucky enough to survive the torn arteries and shock, then you will never walk again without crutches because a totally disintegrated femur leaves the surgeon with no option but to cut your leg off. And so I stood absolutely motionless, not breathing, for the Peacemaker Colt that had prompted this unpleasant train of thought was pointed directly at my right thigh.

5

Another thing about the Peacemaker: because of the very heavy and varying trigger pressures required to operate the semi-automatic mechanism, it can be wildly inaccurate unless held in a strong and steady hand. There was no such hope here. The hand that held the Colt, the hand that lay so lightly yet purposefully on the radio-operator's table, was the steadiest hand I'd ever seen. It was literally motionless. I could see the hand very clearly. The light in the radio cabin was very dim, the rheostat of the angled table lamp had been turned down until only a faint pool of yellow fell on the scratched metal of the table, cutting the arm off at the cuff, but the hand was very clear. Rock-steady, the gun could have lain no quieter in the marbled hand of a statue. Beyond the pool of light I could half sense, half see the dark outline of a figure leaning back against the bulkhead, head slightly tilted to one side, the white gleam of unwinking eyes under the peak of a hat. My eyes went back to the hand. The angle of the Colt hadn't varied by a fraction of a degree. Unconsciously, almost, I braced my right leg to meet the impending shock. Defensively, this was a very good move, about as useful as holding up a sheet of newspaper in front of me. I wished to God that Colonel Sam Colt had gone in for inventing something else, something useful, like safety-pins.

Very slowly, very steadily, I raised both hands, palms outward, until they were level with my shoulders. The careful deliberation was so that the nervously inclined wouldn't be deceived into thinking that I was contemplating anything ridiculous, like resistance. It was probably a pretty superfluous precaution as the man behind that immobile pistol didn't seem to have any nerves and the last thought I had in my head was that of resistance. The sun was long down but the faint red after-glow of sunset still loomed on the north-west horizon and I was perfectly silhouetted against it through the cabin doorway. The lad behind the desk probably had his left hand on the rheostat switch ready to turn it up and blind me at an instant's notice. And there was that gun. I was paid to take chances. I was paid even to step, on occasion, into danger. But I wasn't paid to act the part of a congenital and

6

suicidal idiot. I hoisted my hands a couple of inches higher and tried to look as peaceful and harmless as possible. The way I felt, that was no feat.

The man with the gun said nothing and did nothing. He remained completely still. I could see the white blur of teeth now. The gleaming eyes stared unwinkingly at me. The smile, the head cocked slightly to one side, the negligent relaxation of the body— the aura in that tiny cabin of a brooding and sardonic menace was so heavy as to be almost palpable. There was something evil, something frighteningly unnatural and wrong and foreboding in the man's stillness and silence and cold-blooded cat-and-mouse indifference. Death was waiting to reach out and touch with his icy forefinger in that tiny cabin. In spite of two Scots grandparents I'm in no way psychic or fey or second-sighted, as far as extra-sensory perception goes I've about the same degree of receptive sensitivity as a lump of old lead. But I could smell death in the air.

"I think we're both making a mistake," I said. "Well, you are. Maybe we're both on the same side." The words came with difficulty, a suddenly dry throat and tongue being no aid to clarity of elocution, but they sounded all right to me, just as I wanted them to sound, low and calm and soothing. Maybe he was a nut case. Humour him. Anything. Just stay alive. I nodded to the stool at the front corner of his desk. "It's been a hard day. Okay if we sit and talk? I'll keep my hands high, I promise you."

The total reaction I got was nil. The white teeth and eyes, the relaxed contempt, that iron gun in that iron hand. I felt my own hands begin to clench into fists and hastily unclenched them again, but I couldn't do anything about the slow burn of anger that touched me for the first time.

I smiled what I hoped was a friendly and encouraging smile and moved slowly towards the stool. I faced him all the time, the cordial smile making my face ache and the hands even higher than before. A Peacemaker Colt can kill a steer at sixty yards, God only knew what it would do to me. I tried to put it out of my mind, I've only got two legs and I'm attached to them both.

7

I made it with both still intact. I sat down, hands still high, and started breathing again. I'd stopped breathing but hadn't been aware of it, which was understandable enough as I'd had other things on my mind, such as crutches, bleeding to death and such-like matters that tend to grip the imagination.

The Colt was as motionless as ever. The barrel hadn't followed me as I'd moved across the cabin, it was still pointing rigidly at the spot where I'd been standing ten seconds earlier.

I moved fast going for that gun-hand, but it was no break-neck dive. I didn't, I was almost certain, even have to move fast, but I haven't reached the advanced age in which my chief thinks he honours me by giving me all the dirtiest jobs going by ever taking a chance when I don't have to.

I eat all the right foods, take plenty of exercise and, even although no insurance company in the world will look at me, their medical men would pass me any time, but even so I couldn't tear that gun away. The hand that had looked like marble felt like marble, only colder. I'd smelled death all right, but the old man hadn't been hanging around with his scythe at the ready, he'd been and gone and left this lifeless shell behind him. I straightened, checked that the windows were curtained, closed the door noiselessly, locked it as quietly and switched on the overhead light.

There's seldom any doubt about the exact time of a murder in an old English country house murder story. After a cursory examination and a lot of pseudo-medical mumbo-jumbo, the good doctor drops the corpse's wrist and says, "The decedent deceased at 11.57 last night" or words to that effect, then, with a thin deprecatory smile magnanimously conceding that he's a member of the fallible human race, adds, "Give or take a minute or two." The good doctor outside the pages of the detective novel finds it rather more difficult. Weight, build, ambient temperature and cause of death all bear so heavily and often unpredictably on the cooling of the body that the estimated time of death may well lie in a span of several hours.

I'm not a doctor, far less a good one, and all I could tell about the man behind the desk was that he had been dead long enough for rigor mortis to set in but not long enough for it to wear off. He was stiff as a man frozen to death in a Siberian winter. He'd been gone for hours. How many, I'd no idea.

He wore four gold bands on his sleeves, so that would seem to make him the captain. The captain in the radio cabin. Captains are seldom found in the radio cabin and never behind the desk. He was slumped back in his chair, his head to one side, the back of it resting against a jacket hanging from a hook on the bulkhead, the side of it against a wall cabinet. Rigor mortis kept him in that position but he should have slipped to the floor or at least slumped forward on to the table before rigor mortis had set in.

There were no outward signs of violence that I could see but on the assumption that it would be stretching the arm of co-incidence a bit far to assume that he had succumbed from natural causes while preparing to defend his life with his Peacemaker I took a closer look. I tried to pull him upright but he wouldn't budge. I tried harder, I heard the sound of cloth ripping, then suddenly he was upright, then fallen over to the left of the table, the right arm pivoting stiffly around and upwards, the Colt an accusing finger pointing at heaven.

I knew now how he had died and why he hadn't fallen forward before. He'd been killed by a weapon that projected from his spinal column, between maybe the sixth and seventh vertebræ, I couldn't be sure, and the handle of this weapon had caught in the pocket of the jacket on the bulkhead and held him there.

My job was one that had brought me into contact with a fair number of people who had died from a fair assortment of un-natural causes, but this was the first time I'd ever seen a man who had been killed by a chisel. A half-inch wood chisel, apparently quite ordinary in every respect except that its wooden handle had been sheathed by a bicycle's rubber hand-grip, the kind that doesn't show fingerprints. The blade was imbedded to a depth of at least four inches and even allowing for an edge honed to a razor sharpness it had taken a man as powerful as he was violent to strike that blow. I tried to jerk the chisel free, but it wouldn't

9

come. It often happens that way with a knife: bone or cartilage that has been pierced by a sharp instrument locks solid over the steel when an attempt is made to withdraw it. I didn't try again. The chances were that the killer himself had tried to move it and failed. He wouldn't have wanted to abandon a handy little sticker like that if he could help it. Maybe someone had interrupted him. Or maybe he had a large supply of half-inch wood chisels and could afford to leave the odd one lying around carelessly in someone's back.

Anyway, I didn't really want it. I had my own. Not a chisel but a knife. I eased it out of the plastic sheath that had been sewn into the inner lining of my coat, just behind the neck. It didn't look so much, a four-inch handle and a little double-edged three-inch blade. But that little blade could slice through a two-inch manila with one gentle stroke and the point was the point of a lancet. I looked at it and looked at the inner door behind the radio table, the one that led to the radio-operator's sleeping cabin, then I slid a little fountain-pen torch from my breast pocket, crossed to the outer door, switched off the overhead lamp, did the same for the table lamp and stood there waiting.

How long I stood there I couldn't be sure. Maybe two minutes, maybe as long as five. Why I waited, I don't know. I told myself I was waiting until my eyes became adjusted to the almost total darkness inside the cabin, but I knew it wasn't that. Maybe I was waiting for some noise, the slightest imagined whisper of stealthy sound, maybe I was waiting for something, anything, to happen— or maybe I was just scared to go through that inner door. Scared for myself? Perhaps I was. I couldn't be sure. Or perhaps I was scared of what I would find behind that door. I transferred the knife to my left hand—I'm right-handed but ambidextrous in some things—and slowly closed my fingers round the handle of the inner door.

It took me all of twenty seconds to open that door the twelve inches that was necessary for me to squeeze through the opening. In the very last half-inch the damned hinges creaked. It was a tiny sound, a sound you wouldn't normally have heard two yards away. With my steel-taut nerves in the state they were in, a six-inch naval gun going off in my ear would have sounded muffled by contrast. I stood petrified as any graven image, the dead man by my side was no more immobile than I. I could hear the thump of my accelerating heartbeat and savagely wished the damned thing would keep quiet.

If there was anyone inside waiting to flash a torch in my face and shoot me, knife me or do a little fancy carving up with a chisel, he was taking his time about it. I treated my lungs to a little oxygen, stepped soundlessly and sideways through the opening. I held the flash at the full outstretched extent of my right arm. If the ungodly are going to shoot at a person who is shining a torch at them they generally aim in the very close vicinity of the torch as the unwary habitually hold a torch in front of them. This, as I had learnt many years previously from a colleague who'd just had a bullet extracted from the lobe of his left lung because of this very unwariness, was a very unwise thing to do. So I held the torch as far from my body as possible, drew my left arm back with the knife ready to go, hoping fervently that the reactions of any person who might be in that cabin were slower than mine, and slid forward the switch of the torch.

There was someone there all right, but I didn't have to worry about his reactions. Not any more. He'd none left. He was lying face down on the bunk with that huddled shapeless look that belongs only to the dead. I made a quick traverse of the cabin with the pencil beam. The dead man was alone. As in the radio cabin, there was no sign of a struggle.

I didn't even have to touch him to ascertain the cause of death. The amount of blood that had seeped from that half-inch incision in his spine wouldn't have filled a tea-spoon. I wouldn't have expected to find more; when the spinal column has been neatly severed the heart doesn't go on pumping long enough to matter a damn. There would have been a little more internal bleeding, but not much.

The curtains were drawn. I quartered every foot of the deck, bulkheads and furniture with my flash. I don't know what I expected to find: what I found was nothing. I went out, closed the door behind me and searched the radio cabin with the same results. There was nothing more for me here, I had found all I wanted to find, all I had never wanted to find. And I never once looked at the faces of the two dead men. I didn't have to, they were faces I knew as well as the face that looked back at me every morning out of my shaving mirror. Seven days previously they had dined with me and our chief in our favourite pub in London and they had been as cheerful and relaxed as men in their profession can ever be, their normal still watchfulness overlaid by the momentary savouring of the lighter side of life they knew could never really be for them. And I had no doubt they had gone on being as still and watchful as ever, but they hadn't been watchful enough and now they were only still. What had happened to them was what inevitably happened to people in our trade, which would inevitably happen to myself when the time came. No matter how clever and strong and ruthless you were, sooner or later you would meet up with someone who was cleverer and stronger and more ruthless than yourself. And that someone would have a half-inch wood chisel in his hand and all your hardly won years of experience and knowledge and cunning counted for nothing for you never saw him coming and you never saw him coming because you had met your match at last and then you were dead.

And I had sent them to their deaths. Not willingly, not knowingly, but the ultimate responsibility had been mine. This had all been my idea, my brain-child and mine alone, and I'd overridden all objections and fast-talked our very doubtful and highly sceptical chief into giving if not his enthusiastic approval at least his grudging consent. I'd told the two men, Baker and Delmont, that if they played it my way no harm would come to them so they'd trusted me blindly and played it my way and now they lay dead beside me. No hesitation, gentlemen, put your faith in me, only see to it that you make your wills first of all

There was nothing more to be done here now. I'd sent two men to their deaths and that couldn't be undone. It was time to be gone.

I opened that outer door the way you'd open the door to a cellar you knew to be full of cobras and black widow spiders. The way *you* would open the door, that is: were cobras and black widow spiders all I had to contend with aboard that ship, I'd have gone through that door without a second thought, they were harmless and almost lovable little creatures compared to some specimens of homo sapiens that were loose on the decks of the freighter *Nantesville* that night.

With the door opened at its fullest extent I just stood there. I stood there for a long time without moving a muscle of body or limbs, breathing shallowly and evenly, and when you stand like that even a minute seems half a lifetime. All my being was in my ears. I just stood there and listened. I could hear the slap of waves against the hull, the occasional low metallic rumble as the *Nantesville* worked against wind and tide on its moorings, the low moan of the strengthening night wind in the rigging and, once, the far-off lonely call of a curlew. Lonesome sounds, safe sounds, sounds of the night and nature. Not the sounds I was listening for. Gradually, these sounds too became part of the silence. Foreign sounds, sounds of stealth and menace and danger, there were none. No sound of breathing, no slightest scrape of feet on steel decks, no rustle of clothing, nothing. If there was anyone waiting out there he was possessed of a patience and immobility that was superhuman and I wasn't worried about superhumans that night, just about humans, humans with knives and guns and chisels in their hands. Silently I stepped out over the storm sill.

I've never paddled along the night-time Orinoco in a dug-out canoe and had a thirty-foot anaconda drop from a tree, wrap a coil around my neck and start constricting me to death and what's more I don't have to go there now to describe the experience for I know exactly what it feels like. The sheer animal power, the feral ferocity of the pair of huge hands that closed round my neck from behind was terrifying, something I'd never known of, never dreamed of. After the first moment of blind panic and shocked paralysis, there was only one thought in my mind: it comes to us all and now it has come to me, someone who is cleverer and stronger and more ruthless than I am.

I lashed back with all the power of my right foot but the man behind me knew every rule in the book. His own right foot, travelling with even more speed and power than mine, smashed into the back of my swinging leg. It wasn't a man behind me, it was a centaur and he was shod with the biggest set of horseshoes I'd ever come across. My leg didn't just feel as if it had been broken, it felt as if it had been cut in half. I felt his left toe behind my left foot and stamped on it with every vicious ounce of power left me but when my foot came down his toe wasn't there any more. All I had on my feet was a pair of thin rubber swimming moccasins and the agonising jar from the steel deck plates shot clear to the top of my head. I reached up my hands to break his little fingers but he knew all about that too for his hands were clenched into iron-hard balls with the second knuckle grinding into the carotid artery. I wasn't the first man he'd strangled and unless I did something pretty quickly I wasn't going to be the last either. In my ears I could hear the hiss of compressed air escaping under high pressure and behind my eyes the shooting lines and flashes of colour were deepening and brightening by the moment.

What saved me in those first few seconds were the folded hood and the thick rubberised canvas neck ruff of the scuba suit I was wearing under my coat. But it wasn't going to save me many seconds longer, the life's ambition of the character behind me seemed to be to make his knuckles meet in the middle of my neck. With the progress he was making that wouldn't take him too long, he was half-way there already.

I bent forward in a convulsive jerk. Half of his weight came on my back, that throttling grip not easing a fraction, and at the same time he moved his feet as far backwards as possible—the instinctive reaction to my move, he would have thought that I was making a grab for one of my legs. When I had him momentarily off-balance I swung round in a short arc till both our backs were towards the sea. I thrust backwards with all my strength, one, two, three steps, accelerating all the way. The *Nantesville* didn't boast of any fancy teak guard-rails, just small-section chain, and the small of the strangler's back took our combined charging weights on the top chain.

If I'd taken that impact I'd have broken my back or slipped enough discs to keep an orthopædic surgeon in steady employment for months. But no shouts of agony from this lad. No gasps, even. Not a whisper of sound. Maybe he was a deaf mute —I'd heard of several deaf mutes possessed of this phenomenal strength, part of nature's compensatory process, I suppose.

But he'd been forced to break his grip, to grab swiftly at the upper chain to save us both from toppling over the side into the cold dark waters of Loch Houron. I thrust myself away and spun round to face him, my back against the radio office bulkhead. I needed that bulkhead, too—any support while my swimming head cleared and a semblance of life came back into my numbed right leg.

I could see him now as he straightened up from the guard-rail. Not clearly—it was too dark for that—but I could see the white blur of face and hands and the general outline of his body.

I'd expected some towering giant of a man, but he was no giant —unless my eyes weren't focusing properly, which was likely enough. From what I could see in the gloom he seemed a compact and well enough made figure, but that was all. He wasn't even as big as I was. Not that that meant a thing—George Hackenschmidt was a mere five foot nine and a paltry fourteen stone when he used to throw the Terrible Turk through the air like a football and prance around the training ring with eight hundred pounds of cement strapped to his back just to keep him in trim. I had no compunction or false pride about running from a smaller man and as far as this character was concerned the farther and faster the better. But not yet. My right leg wasn't up to it. I reached my hand behind my neck and brought the knife down, holding it in front of me, the blade in the palm of my hand so that he couldn't see the sheen of steel in the faint starlight.

15

He came at me calmly and purposefully, like a man who knew exactly what he intended to do and was in no doubt at all as to the outcome of his intended action. God knows I didn't doubt he had reason enough for his confidence. He came at me sideways so that my foot couldn't damage him, with his right hand extended at the full stretch of his arm. A one track mind. He was going for my throat again. I waited till his hand was inches from my face then jerked my own right hand violently upwards. Our hands smacked solidly together as the blade sliced cleanly through the centre of his palm.

He wasn't a deaf mute after all. Three short unprintable words, an unjustified slur on my ancestry, and he stepped quickly backwards, rubbed the back and front of his hand against his clothes then licked it in a queer animal-like gesture. He peered closely at the blood, black as ink in the starlight, welling from both sides of his hand.

"So the little man has a little knife, has he?" he said softly. The voice was a shock. With this caveman-like strength I'd have expected a caveman-like intelligence and voice to match, but the words came in the calm, pleasant, cultured almost accentless speech of the well-educated southern Englishman. "We shall have to take the little knife from him, shan't we?" He raised his voice. "Captain Imrie?" At least, that's what the name sounded like.

"Be quiet, you fool!" The urgent irate voice came from the direction of the crew accommodation aft. "Do you want to——"

"Don't worry, Captain." The eyes didn't leave me. "I have him. Here by the wireless office. He's armed. A knife. I'm just going to take it away from him."

"You have him? You have him? Good, good, good!" It was the kind of a voice a man uses when he's smacking his lips and rubbing his hands together: it was also the kind of voice that a German or Austrian uses when he speaks English. The short guttural "gut" was unmistakable. "Be careful. This one I want alive. Jacques! Henry! Kramer! All of you. Quickly! The bridge. Wireless office."

"Alive," the man opposite me said pleasantly, "can also mean not quite dead." He sucked some more blood from the palm of his hand. "Or will you hand over the knife quietly and peaceably? I would suggest——"

I didn't wait for more. This was an old technique. You talked to an opponent who courteously waited to hear you out, not appreciating that half-way through some well-turned phrase you were going to shoot him through the middle when, lulled into a sense of temporary false security, he least expected it. Not quite cricket, but effective, and I wasn't going to wait until it took effect on me. I didn't know how he was coming at me but I guessed it would be a dive, either head or feet first and that if he got me down on the deck I wouldn't be getting up again. Not without assistance. I took a quick step forward, flashed my torch a foot from his face, saw the dazzled eyes screw shut for the only fraction of time I'd ever have and kicked him.

It wasn't as hard as it might have been, owing to the fact that my right leg still felt as if it were broken, nor as accurate, because of the darkness, but it was a pretty creditable effort in the circumstances and it should have left him rolling and writhing about the deck, whooping in agony. Instead he just stood there, unable to move, bent forward and clutching himself with his hands. He was more than human, all right. I could see the sheen of his eyes, but I couldn't see the expression in them, which was just as well as I don't think I would have cared for it very much.

I left. I remembered a gorilla I'd once seen in Basle Zoo, a big black monster who used to twist heavy truck tyres into figures of eight for light exercise. I'd as soon have stepped inside that cage as stay around that deck when this lad became more like his old self again. I hobbled forward round the corner of the radio office, climbed up a liferaft and stretched myself flat on the deck.

The nearest running figures, some with torches, were already at the foot of the companionway leading up to the bridge. I had to get right aft to the rope with the rubber-covered hook I'd swung up to swarm aboard. But I couldn't do it until the midship decks were clear. And then, suddenly, I couldn't do it at all: now that the need for secrecy and stealth was over someone had switched on the cargo loading lights and the midships and foredecks were bathed in a brilliant dazzle of white. One of the foredeck arc lamps was on a jumbo mast, just for'ard of and well above where I was lying. I felt as exposed as a fly pinned to a white ceiling. I flattened myself on that deck as if I were trying to push myself through it.

They were up the companion way and by the radio office now. I heard the sudden exclamations and curses and knew they'd found the hurt man: I didn't hear his voice so I assumed he wasn't able to speak yet.

The curt, authoritative German-accented voice took command. "You cackle like a flock of hens. Be silent. Jacques, you have your machine-pistol?"

"I have my pistol, Captain." Jacques had the quiet competent sort of voice that I would have found reassuring in certain circumstances but didn't very much care for in the present ones.

"Go aft. Stand at the entrance to the saloon and face for'ard. Cover the midships decks. We will go to the fo'c'sle and then come aft in line abreast and drive him to you. If he doesn't surrender to you, shoot him through the legs. I want him alive."

God, this was worse than the Peacemaker Colt. At least that fired only one shot at a time. I'd no idea what kind of machine-pistol Jacques had, probably it fired bursts of a dozen or more. I could feel my right thigh muscle begin to stiffen again, it was becoming almost a reflex action now.

"And if he jumps over the side, sir?"

"Do I have to tell you, Jacques?"

"No, sir."

I was just as clever as Jacques was. He didn't have to tell me either. That nasty dry taste was back in my throat and mouth again. I'd a minute left, no more, and then it would be too late. I slid silently to the side of the radio office roof, the starboard side, the side remote from the spot where Captain Imrie was issuing curt instructions to his men, lowered myself soundlessly to the deck and made my way to the wheelhouse.

I didn't need my torch in there, the backwash of light from the big arc-lamps gave me all the illumination I wanted. Crouching down, to keep below window level, I looked around and saw what I wanted right away—a metal box of distress flares.

Two quick flicks of the knife severed the lashings that secured the flare-box to the deck. One piece of rope, perhaps ten feet in all, I left secured to a handle of the box. I pulled a plastic bag from the pocket of my coat, tore off the coat and the yachtsman's rubber trousers that I was wearing over my scuba suit, stuffed them inside and secured the bag to my waist. The coat and trousers had been essential. A figure in a dripping rubber diving suit walking across the decks of the *Nantesville* would hardly have been likely to escape comment whereas in the dusk and with the outer clothing I had on I could have passed for a crewman and, indeed, had done so twice at a distance: equally important, when I'd left the port of Torbay in my rubber dinghy it had been broad daylight and the sight of a scuba-clad figure putting to sea towards evening wouldn't have escaped comment either, as the curiosity factor of the inhabitants of the smaller ports of the Western Highlands and Islands did not, I had discovered, lag noticeably behind that of their mainland brethren. Some would put it even more strongly than that.

Still crouching low, I moved out through the wheelhouse door on to the starboard wing of the bridge. I reached the outer end and stood up straight. I had to, I had to take the risk, it was now or never at all, I could hear the crew already beginning to move forward to start their search. I lifted the flare box over the side, eased it down the full length of the rope and started to swing it slowly, gently, from side to side, like a leadsman preparing to cast his lead.

The box weighed at least forty pounds, but I barely noticed the weight. The pendulum arc increased with every swing I made. It had reached an angle of about forty-five degrees on each swing now, pretty close to the maximum I could get and both time and my luck must be running out, I felt about as conspicuous as a trapeze artist under a dozen spotlights and just about as vulnerable too. As the box swung aft on its last arc I gave the rope a final thrust to achieve all the distance and momentum I could, opened my hands at the extremity of the arc and dropped down behind the canvas wind-dodger. It was as I dropped that I remembered I hadn't holed the damned box, I had no idea whether it would float or sink but I did have a very clear idea of what would happen to me if it didn't sink. One thing for sure, it was too late to worry about it now.

I heard a shout come from the main deck, some twenty or thirty feet aft of the bridge. I was certain I had been seen but I hadn't. A second after the shout came a loud and very satisfactory splash and a voice I recognised as Jacques's shouting: "He's gone over the side. Starboard abaft the bridge. A torch quick!" He must have been walking aft as ordered, seen this dark blur falling, heard the splash and come to the inevitable conclusion. A dangerous customer who thought fast, was Jacques. In three seconds he'd told his mates all they required to know: what had happened, where and what he wanted done as the necessary preliminary to shooting me full of holes.

The men who had been moving forward to start the sweep for me now came running aft, pounding along the deck directly beneath where I was crouching on the wing of the bridge.

"Can you see him, Jacques?" Captain Imrie's voice, very quick, very calm.

"Not yet, sir."

"He'll be up soon." I wished he wouldn't sound so damned confident. "A dive like that must have knocked most of the breath out of him. Kramer, two men and into the boat. Take lamps and circle around. Henry, the box of grenades. Carlo, the bridge, quick. Starboard searchlight."

I'd never thought of the boat, that was bad enough, but the grenades! I felt chilled. I knew what an underwater explosion, even a small explosion, can do to the human body, it was twenty times as deadly as the same explosion on land. And I had to, I just had to, be in that water in minutes. But at least I could do something about that searchlight, it was only two feet above my head. I had the power cable in my left hand, the knife in my right and had just brought the two into contact when my mind stopped thinking about those damned grenades and started working again. Cutting that cable would be about as clever as leaning over the wind-dodger and yelling "Here I am, come and catch me"—a dead giveaway that I was still on board. Clobbering Carlo from behind as he came up the ladder would have the same effect. And I couldn't fool them twice. Not people like these. Hobbling as fast as I could I passed through the wheelhouse on to the port wing, slid down the ladder and ran towards the forepeak. The foredeck was deserted.

I heard a shout and the harsh chatter of some automatic weapon —Jacques and his machine-pistol, for a certainty. Had he imagined he'd seen something, had the box come to the surface, had he actually seen the box and mistaken it for me in the dark waters? It must have been the last of these—he wouldn't have wasted ammunition on anything he'd definitely recognised as a box. Whatever the reason, it had all my blessing. If they thought I was floundering about down there, riddled like a Gruyère cheese, then they wouldn't be looking for me up here.

They had the port anchor down. I swung over the side on a rope, got my feet in the hawse-pipe, reached down and grabbed the chain. The international athletics board should have had their stop-watches on me that night, I must have set a new world record for shinning down anchor chains.

The water was cold but my exposure suit took care of that. It was choppy, with a heavy tide running, both of which suited me well. I swam down the port side of the *Nantesville*, underwater for ninety per cent of the time and I saw no one and no one saw me: all the activity was on the starboard side of the vessel.

My aqualung unit and weights and flippers were where I had left them, tied to the top of the rudder post—the *Nantesville* was not much more than half-way down to her marks and the top of the post not far under water. Fitting on an aqualung in choppy seas with a heavy tide running isn't the easiest of tasks but the thought of Kramer and his grenades was a considerable help. Besides, I was in a hurry to be gone for I had a long way to go and many things to do when I arrived at my destination.

I could hear the engine note of the lifeboat rising and falling as it circled off the ship's starboard side but at no time did it come within a hundred feet of me. No more shots were fired and Captain Imrie had obviously decided against using the grenades. I adjusted the weights round my waist, dropped down into the dark safety of the waters, checked my direction on my luminous wrist compass and started to swim. After five minutes I came to the surface and after another five felt my feet ground on the shore of the rocky islet where I'd cached my rubber dinghy.

I clambered up on the rocks and looked back. The *Nantesville* was ablaze with light. A searchlight was shining down into the sea and the lifeboat still circling around. I could hear the steady clanking of the anchor being weighed. I hauled the dinghy into the water, climbed in, unshipped the two stubby oars and paddled off to the south-west. I was still within effective range of the searchlight but its chances of picking up a black-clad figure in a low-silhouette black dinghy on those black waters were remote indeed.

After a mile I shipped the oars and started up the outboard. Or tried to start it up. Outboards always work perfectly for me, except when I'm cold, wet and exhausted. Whenever I really need them, they never work. So I took to the stubby oars again and rowed and rowed and rowed, but not for what seemed any longer than a month. I arrived back at the *Firecrest* at ten to three in the morning.

2

Tuesday: 3 a.m.—dawn

"Calvert?" Hunslett's voice was a barely audible murmur in the darkness.

"Yes." Standing there above me on the *Firecrest*'s deck, he was more imagined than seen against the blackness of the night sky. Heavy clouds had rolled in from the south-west and the last of the stars were gone. Big heavy drops of cold rain were beginning to spatter off the surface of the sea. "Give me a hand to get the dinghy aboard."

"How did it go?"

"Later. This first." I climbed up the accommodation ladder, painter in hand. I had to lift my right leg over the gunwale. Stiff and numb and just beginning to ache again, it could barely take my weight. "And hurry. We can expect company soon."

"So that's the way of it," Hunslett said thoughtfully. "Uncle Arthur *will* be pleased about this."

I said nothing to that. Our employer, Rear-Admiral Sir Arthur Arnford-Jason, K.C.B. and most of the rest of the alphabet, wasn't going to be pleased at all. We heaved the dripping dinghy inboard, unclamped the outboard and took them both on to the foredeck.

"Get me a couple of waterproof bags," I said. "Then start getting the anchor chain in. Keep it quiet—leave the brake pawl off and use a tarpaulin."

"We're leaving?"

"We would if we had any sense. We're staying. Just get the anchor up and down."

By the time he'd returned with the bags I'd the dinghy de-

23

flated and in its canvas cover. I stripped off my aqualung and scuba suit and stuffed them into one of the bags along with the weights, my big-dialled waterproof watch and the combined wrist-compass and depth-gauge. I put the outboard in the other bag, restraining the impulse just to throw the damn' thing overboard: an outboard motor was a harmless enough object to have aboard any boat, but we already had one attached to the wooden dinghy hanging from the davits over the stern.

Hunslett had the electric windlass going and the chain coming in steadily. An electric windlass is in itself a pretty noiseless machine: when weighing anchor all the racket comes from four sources—the chain passing through the hawse-pipe, the clacking of the brake pawl over the successive stops, the links passing over the drum itself and the clattering of the chain as it falls into the chain locker. About the first of these we could do nothing: but with the brake pawl off and a heavy tarpaulin smothering the sound from the drum and chain locker, the noise level was surprisingly low. Sound travels far over the surface of the sea, but the nearest anchored boats were almost two hundred yards away—we had no craving for the company of other boats in harbour. At two hundred yards, in Torbay, we felt ourselves uncomfortably close: but the sea-bed shelved fairly steeply away from the little town and our present depth of twenty fathoms was the safe maximum for the sixty fathoms of chain we carried.

I heard the click as Hunslett's foot stepped on the deck-switch. "She's up and down."

"Put the pawl in for a moment. If that drum slips, I'll have no hands left." I pulled the bags right for'ard, leaned out under the pulpit rail and used lengths of heaving line to secure them to the anchor chain. When the lines were secure I lifted the bags over the side and let them dangle from the chain.

"I'll take the weight," I said. "Lift the chain off the drum— we'll lower it by hand."

Forty fathoms is 240 feet of chain and letting that lot down to the bottom didn't do my back or arms much good at all, and the rest of me was a long way below par before we started. I was pretty close to exhaustion from the night's work, my neck ached fiercely, my leg only badly and I was shivering violently. I know of various ways of achieving a warm rosy glow but wearing only a set of underclothes in the middle of a cold, wet and windy autumn night in the Western Isles is not one of them. But at last the job was done and we were able to go below. If anyone wanted to investigate what lay at the foot of our anchor chain he'd need a steel articulated diving suit.

Hunslett pulled the saloon door to behind us, moved around in the darkness adjusting the heavy velvet curtains then switched on a small table lamp. It didn't give much light but we knew from experience that it didn't show up through the velvet, and advertising the fact that we were up and around in the middle of the night was the last thing I wanted to do.

Hunslett had a dark narrow saturnine face, with a strong jaw, black bushy eyebrows and thick black hair—the kind of face which is so essentially an expression in itself that it rarely shows much else. It was expressionless now and very still.

"You'll have to buy another shirt," he said. "Your collar's too tight. Leaves marks."

I stopped towelling myself and looked in a mirror. Even in that dim light my neck looked a mess. It was badly swollen and discoloured, with four wicked-looking bruises where the thumbs and forefinger joints had sunk deep into the flesh. Blue and green and purple they were, and they looked as if they would be there for a long time to come.

"He got me from behind. He's wasting his time being a criminal, he'd sweep the board at the Olympic weight-lifting. I was lucky. He also wears heavy boots." I twisted around and looked down at my right calf. The bruise was bigger than my fist and if it missed out any of the colours of the rainbow I couldn't off-hand think which one. There was a deep red gash across the middle of it and blood was ebbing slowly along its entire length. Hunslett gazed at it with interest.

"If you hadn't been wearing that tight scuba suit, you'd have most like bled to death. I better fix that for you."

25

"I don't need bandages. What I need is a Scotch. Stop wasting your time. Oh, hell, sorry, yes, you'd better fix it, we can't have our guests sloshing about ankle deep in blood."

"You're very sure we're going to have guests?"

"I half expected to have them waiting on the doorstep when I got back to the *Firecrest*. We're going to have guests, all right. Whatever our pals aboard the *Nantesville* may be, they're no fools. They'll have figured out by this time that I could have approached only by dinghy. They'll know damn' well that it was no nosey-parker local prowling about the ship—local lads in search of a bit of fun don't go aboard anchored ships in the first place. In the second place the locals wouldn't go near Beul nan Uamh—the mouth of the grave—in daylight, far less at night time. Even the *Pilot* says the place has an evil reputation. And in the third place no local lad would get aboard as I did, behave aboard as I did or leave as I did. The local lad would be dead."

"I shouldn't wonder. And?"

"So we're not locals. We're visitors. We wouldn't be staying at any hotel or boarding house—too restricted, couldn't move. Almost certainly we'll have a boat. Now, where would our boat be? Not to the north of Loch Houron for with a forecast promising a south-west Force 6 strengthening to Force 7, no boat is going to be daft enough to hang about a lee shore in that lot. The only holding ground and shallow enough sheltered anchorage in the other direction, down the Sound for forty miles, is in Torbay— and that's only four or five miles from where the *Nantesville* was lying at the mouth of Loch Houron. Where would you look for us?"

"I'd look for a boat anchored in Torbay. Which gun do you want?"

"I don't want any gun. You don't want any gun. People like us don't carry guns."

"Marine biologists don't carry guns," he nodded. "Employees of the Ministry of Agriculture and Fisheries don't carry guns. Civil Servants are above reproach. So we play it clever. You're the boss."

26

"I don't feel clever any more. And I'll take long odds that I'm not your boss any more. Not after Uncle Arthur hears what I have to tell him."

"You haven't told *me* anything yet." He finished tying the bandage round my leg and straightened. "How's that feel?"

I tried it. "Better. Thanks. Better still when you've taken the cork from that bottle. Get into pyjamas or something. People found fully dressed in the middle of the night cause eyebrows to go up." I towelled my head as vigorously as my tired arms would let me. One wet hair on my head and eyebrows wouldn't just be lifting, they'd be disappearing into hairlines. "There isn't much to tell and all of it is bad."

He poured me a large drink, a smaller one for himself, and added water to both. It tasted the way Scotch always does after you've swum and rowed for hours and damn' near got yourself killed in the process.

"I got there without trouble. I hid behind Carrara Point till it was dusk and then paddled out to the Bogha Nuadh. I left the dinghy there and swam underwater as far as the stern of the ship. It was the *Nantesville* all right. Name and flag were different, a mast was gone and the white superstructure was now stone—but it was her all right. Near as dammit didn't make it—it was close to the turn of the tide but it took me thirty minutes against that current. Must be wicked at the full flood or ebb."

"They say it's the worst on the West Coast—worse even than Coirebhreachan."

"I'd rather not be the one to find out. I had to hang on to the stern post for ten minutes before I'd got enough strength back to shin up that rope."

"You took a chance."

"It was near enough dark. Besides," I added bitterly, "there are some precautions intelligent people don't think to take about crazy ones. There were only two or three people in the after accommodation. Just a skeleton crew aboard, seven or eight, no more. All the original crew have vanished completely."

"No sign of them anywhere?"

"No sign. Dead or alive, no sign at all. I had a bit of bad luck. I was leaving the after accommodation to go to the bridge when I passed someone a few feet away. I gave a half wave and grunted something and he answered back, I don't know what. I followed him back to the quarters. He picked up a phone in the crew's mess and I heard him talking to someone, quick and urgent. Said that one of the original crew must have been hiding and was trying to get away. I couldn't stop him—he faced the door as he was talking and he had a gun in his hand. I had to move quickly. I walked to the bridge structure——"

"You what? When you knew they were on to you? Mr. Calvert, you want your bloody head examined."

"Uncle Arthur will put it less kindly. It was the only chance I'd ever have. Besides, if they thought it was only a terrified member of the original crew they wouldn't have been so worried: if this guy had seen me walking around dripping wet in a scuba suit he'd have turned me into a colander. He wasn't sure. On the way for'ard I passed another bloke without incident—he'd left the bridge superstructure before the alarm had been given, I suppose. I didn't stop at the bridge. I went right for'ard and hid behind the winchman's shelter. For about ten minutes there was a fair bit of commotion and a lot of flash-light work around the bridge island then I saw and heard them moving aft—must have thought I was still in the after accommodation.

"I went through all the officers' cabins in the bridge island. No one. One cabin, an engineer's, I think, had smashed furniture and a carpet heavily stained with dry blood. Next door, the captain's bunk had been saturated with blood."

"They'd been warned to offer no resistance."

"I know. Then I found Baker and Delmont."

"So you found them. Baker and Delmont." Hunslett's eyes were hooded, gazing down at the glass in his hand. I wished to God he'd show some expression on that dark face of his.

"Delmont must have made a last-second attempt to send a call for help. They'd been warned not to, except in emergency, so they must have been discovered. He'd been stabbed in the back with a half-inch wood chisel and then dragged into the radio officer's cabin which adjoined the radio office. Some time later Baker had come in. He was wearing an officer's clothes—some desperate attempt to disguise himself, I suppose. He'd a gun in his hand, but he was looking the wrong way and the gun was pointing the wrong way. The same chisel in the back."

Hunslett poured himself another drink. A much larger one. Hunslett hardly ever drank. He swallowed half of it in one gulp. He said: "And they hadn't all gone aft. They'd left a reception committee."

"They're very clever. They're very dangerous. Maybe we've moved out of our class. Or I have. A one-man reception committee, but when that one man was this man, two would have been superfluous. I know he killed Baker and Delmont. I'll never be so lucky again."

"You got away. Your luck hadn't run out."

And Baker's and Delmont's had. I knew he was blaming me. I knew London would blame me. I blamed myself. I hadn't much option. There was no one else to blame.

"Uncle Arthur," Hunslett said. "Don't you think——"

"The hell with Uncle Arthur. Who cares about Uncle Arthur? How in God's name do you think I feel?" I felt savage and I know I sounded it. For the first time a flicker of expression showed on Hunslett's face. I wasn't supposed to have any feelings.

"Not that," he said, "About the *Nantesville*. Now that she's been identified *as* the *Nantesville*, now we know her new name and flag—what were they, by the way?"

"*Alta Fjord*. Norwegian. It doesn't matter."

"It does matter. We radio Uncle Arthur——"

"And have our guests find us in the engine-room with earphones round our heads. Are you mad?"

"You seem damned sure they'll come."

"I *am* sure. You too. You said so."

"I agreed this is where they would come. *If* they come."

"If they come. *If* they come. Good God, man, for all that they know I was aboard that ship for hours. I may have the names and full descriptions of all of them. As it happens I couldn't identify any of them and their names may or may not mean anything. But they're not to know that. For all they know I'm on the blower right now bawling out descriptions to Interpol. The chances are at least even that some of them are on file. They're too good to be little men. Some must be known."

"In that case they'd be too late anyway. The damage would be done."

"Not without the sole witness who could testify against them."

"I think we'd better have those guns out."

"No."

"Then for God's sake let's get out of here."

"No."

"You don't blame me for trying?"

"No."

"Baker and Delmont. Think of them."

"I'm thinking of nothing else but them. You don't have to stay."

He set his glass down very carefully. He was really letting himself go to-night, he'd allowed that dark craggy face its second expression in ten minutes and it wasn't a very encouraging one. Then he picked up his glass and grinned.

"You don't know what you're saying," he said kindly. "Your neck—that's what comes from the blood supply to the brain being interrupted. You're not fit to fight off a teddy-bear. Who's going to look after you if they start playing games?"

"I'm sorry," I said. I meant it. I'd worked with Hunslett maybe ten times in the ten years I'd known him and it had been a stupid thing for me to say. About the only thing Hunslett was incapable of was leaving your side in time of trouble. "You were speaking of Uncle?"

"Yes. We know where the *Nantesville* is. Uncle could get a Navy boat to shadow her, by radar if——"

"I know where she was. She upped anchor as I left. By dawn she'll be a hundred miles away—in any direction."

30

"She's gone? We've scared them off? They're going to love this." He sat down heavily, then looked at me. "But we have her new description——"

"I said that didn't matter. By to-morrow she'll have another description. The *Hokomaru* from Yokohama, with green topsides, Japanese flag, different masts——"

"An air search. We could——"

"By the time an air search could be organised they'd have twenty thousand square miles of sea to cover. You've heard the forecast. It's bad. Low cloud—and they'd have to fly under the low cloud. Cuts their effectiveness by ninety per cent. And poor visibility and rain. Not a chance in a hundred, not one in a thousand of positive identification. And if they do locate them—if—what then? A friendly wave from the pilot? Not much else he can do."

"The Navy. They could call up the Navy——"

"Call up what Navy? From the Med? Or the Far East? The Navy has very few ships left and practically none in those parts. By the time any naval vessel could get to the scene it would be night again and the *Nantesville* to hell and gone. Even if a naval ship did catch up with it, what then? Sink it with gunfire—with maybe the twenty-five missing crew members of the *Nantesville* locked up in the hold?"

"A boarding party?"

"With the same twenty-five ex-crew members lined up on deck with pistols at their backs and Captain Imrie and his thugs politely asking the Navy boys what their next move was going to be?"

"I'll get into my pyjamas," Hunslett said tiredly. At the doorway he paused and turned. "If the *Nantesville* has gone, her crew—the new crew—have gone too and we'll be having no visitors after all. Had you thought of that?"

"No."

"I don't really believe it either."

They came at twenty past four in the morning. They came in a very calm and orderly and law-abiding and official fashion, they stayed for forty minutes and by the time they had left I still wasn't sure whether they were our men or not.

Hunslett came into my small cabin, starboard side forward, switched on the light and shook me. "Wake up," he said loudly. "Come on. Wake up."

I was wide awake. I hadn't closed an eye since I'd lain down. I groaned and yawned a bit without overdoing it then opened a bleary eye. There was no one behind him.

"What is it? What do you want?" A pause. "What the hell's up? It's just after four in the morning."

"Don't ask me what's up," Hunslett said irritably. "Police. Just come aboard. They say it's urgent."

"Police? Did you say, 'police'?"

"Yes. Come on, now. They're waiting."

"Police? Aboard our boat? What——"

"Oh, for God's sake! How many more night-caps did you have last night after I went to bed? Police. Two of them and two customs. It's urgent, they say."

"It better bloody well be urgent. In the middle of the bloody night. Who do they think we are—escaped train robbers? Haven't you told them who we are? Oh, all right, all right, all *right*! I'm coming."

Hunslett left, and thirty seconds afterwards I joined him in the saloon. Four men sat there, two police officers and two customs officials. They didn't look a very villainous bunch to me. The older, bigger policeman got to his feet. A tall, burly, brown-faced sergeant in his late forties, he looked me over with a cold eye, looked at the near-empty whisky bottle with the two unwashed glasses on the table, then looked back at me. He didn't like wealthy yachtsmen. He didn't like wealthy yachtsmen who drank too much at night-time and were bleary-eyed, bloodshot and tousle-haired at the following crack of dawn. He didn't like wealthy effete yachtsmen who wore red silk dragon Chinese dressing-gowns with a Paisley scarf to match tied negligently round the neck. I didn't like them very much myself, especially the Paisley scarf, much in favour though it was with the yachting fraternity: but I had to have something to conceal those bruises on my neck.

"Are you the owner of this boat, sir?" the sergeant inquired. An unmistakable West Highland voice and a courteous one, but it took him all his time to get his tongue round the "sir."

"If you would tell me what makes it any of your damn' business," I said unpleasantly, "maybe I'll answer that and maybe I won't. A private boat is the same as a private house, sergeant. You have to have a warrant before you shove your way in. Or don't you know the law?"

"He knows the law," one of the customs men put in. A small dark character, smooth-shaven at four in the morning, with a persuasive voice, not West Highland. "Be reasonable. This is not the sergeant's job. We got him out of bed almost three hours ago. He's just obliging us."

I ignored him. I said to the sergeant: "This is the middle of the night in a lonely Scottish bay. How would you feel if four unidentified men came aboard in the middle of the night?" I was taking a chance on that one, but a fair chance. If they were who I thought they might be and if I were who they thought I might be, then I'd never talk like that. But an innocent man would. "Any means of identifying yourselves?"

"Identifying myself?" The sergeant stared coldly at me. "I don't have to identify myself, Sergeant MacDonald. I've been in charge of the Torbay police station for eight years. Ask any man in Torbay. They all know me." If he was who he claimed to be this was probably the first time in his life that anyone had asked him for identification. He nodded to the seated policeman. "Police-Constable MacDonald."

"Your son?" The resemblance was unmistakable. "Nothing like keeping it in the family, eh, Sergeant?" I didn't know whether to believe him or not, but I felt I'd been an irate householder long enough. A degree less truculence was in order. "And customs, eh? I know the law about you, too. No search warrants for you boys. I believe the police would like your

33

powers. Go anywhere you like and ask no one's permission beforehand. That's it, isn't it?"

"Yes, sir." It was the younger customs man who answered. Medium height, fair hair, running a little to fat, Belfast acent, dressed like the other in blue overcoat, peaked hat, brown gloves, smartly creased trousers. "We hardly ever do, though. We prefer co-operation. We like to ask."

"And you'd like to ask to search this boat, is that it?" Hunslett said.

"Yes, sir."

"Why?" I asked. Puzzlement now in my voice. And in my mind. I just didn't know what I had on my hands. "If we're all going to be so courteous and co-operative, could we have any explanation?"

"No reason in the world why not, sir." The older customs man was almost apologetic. "A truck with contents valued at £12,000 was hi-jacked on the Ayrshire coast last night—night before last, that is, now. In the news this evening. From information received, we know it was transferred to a small boat. We think it came north."

"Why?"

"Sorry, sir. Confidential. This is the third port we've visited and the thirteenth boat—the fourth in Torbay—that we've been on in the past fifteen hours. We've been kept on the run, I can tell you." An easy friendly voice, a voice that said: "You don't really think we suspect you. We've a job to do, that's all."

"And you're searching all boats that have come up from the south. Or you think have come from there. Fresh arrivals, anyway. Has it occurred to you that any boat with hi-jacked goods on board wouldn't dare pass through the Crinan canal? Once you're in there, you're trapped. For four hours. So he'd have to come round the Mull of Kintyre. We've been here since this afternoon. It would take a pretty fast boat to get up here in that time."

"You've got a pretty fast boat here, sir," Sergeant MacDonald said. I wondered how the hell they managed it, from the Western Isles to the East London docks every sergeant in the country had

34

the same wooden voice, the same wooden face, the same cold eye. Must be something to do with the uniform. I ignored him.

"What are we—um—supposed to have stolen?"

"Chemicals. It was an I.C.I. truck."

"Chemicals?" I looked at Hunslett, grinned, then turned back to the customs officer. "Chemicals, eh? We're loaded with them. But not £12,000 worth, I'm afraid."

There was a brief silence. MacDonald said: "Would you mind explaining, sir?"

"Not at all." I lit a cigarette, the little mind enjoying its big moment, and smiled. "This is a government boat, Sergeant MacDonald. I thought you would have seen the flag. Ministry of Agriculture and Fisheries. We're marine biologists. Our after cabin is a floating laboratory. Look at our library here." Two shelves loaded with technical tomes. "And if you've still any doubt left I can give you two numbers, one in Glasgow, one in London, that will establish our *bona-fides*. Or phone the lockmaster in the Crinan sea-basin. We spent last night there."

"Yes, sir." The lack of impression I had made on the sergeant was total. "Where did you go in your dinghy this evening?"

"I beg your pardon, Sergeant?"

"You were seen to leave this boat in a black rubber dinghy about five o'clock this evening." I'd heard of icy fingers playing up and down one's spine but it wasn't fingers I felt then, it was a centipede with a hundred icy boots on. "You went out into the Sound. Mr. McIlroy, the postmaster, saw you."

"I hate to impugn the character of a fellow civil servant but he must have been drunk." Funny how an icy feeling could make you sweat. "I haven't got a black rubber dinghy. I've never owned a black rubber dinghy. You just get out your little magnifying glass, Sergeant, and if you can find a black rubber dinghy I'll make you a present of the brown wooden dinghy, which is the only one we have on the *Firecrest*."

The wooden expression cracked a little. He wasn't so certain now. "So you weren't out?"

"I *was* out. In our own dinghy. I was just round the corner of

35

Garve Island there, collecting some marine samples from the Sound. I can show them to you in the after cabin. We're not here on a holiday, you know."

"No offence, no offence." I was a member of the working classes now, not a plutocrat, and he could afford to thaw a little. "Mr. McIlroy's eyesight isn't what it was and everything looks black against the setting sun. You don't *look* the type, I must say, who'd land on the shores of the Sound and bring down the telephone wires to the mainland."

The centipede started up again and broke into a fast gallop. Cut off from the mainland. How very convenient for somebody. I didn't spend any time wondering who had brought the wires down—it had been no act of God, I was sure of that.

"Did you mean what I thought you to mean, Sergeant?" I said slowly. "That you suspected me——"

"We can't take chances, sir." He was almost apologetic now. Not only was I a working man, I was a man working for the Government. All men working for the Government are *ipso facto* respectable and trustworthy citizens.

"But you won't mind if we take a little look round?" The dark-haired customs officer was even more apologetic. "The lines are down and, well, you know . . ." His voice trailed off and he smiled. "If you were the hi-jackers—I appreciate now that it's a chance in a million, but still—and if we didn't search—well, we'd be out of a job to-morrow. Just a formality."

"I wouldn't want to see that happen, Mr.—ah——"

"Thomas. Thank you. Your ship's papers? Ah, thank you." He handed them to the younger man. "Let's see now. Ah, the wheelhouse. Could Mr. Durran here use the wheelhouse to make copies? Won't take five minutes."

"Certainly. Wouldn't he be more comfortable here?"

"We're modernised now, sir. Portable photo-copier. Standard on the job. Has to be dark. Won't take five minutes. Can we begin in this laboratory of yours?"

A formality, he'd said. Well, he was right there, as a search it was the least informal thing I'd ever come across. Five minutes after he'd gone to the wheelhouse Durran came aft to join us and he and Thomas went through the *Firecrest* as if they were looking for the Koh-i-noor. To begin with, at least. Every piece of mechanical and electrical equipment in the after cabin had to be explained to them. They looked in every locker and cupboard. They rummaged through the ropes and fenders in the large stern locker aft of the laboratory and I thanked God I hadn't followed my original idea of stowing the dinghy, motor and scuba gear in there. They even examined the after toilet. As if I'd be careless enough to drop the Koh-i-noor in there.

They spent most time of all in the engine-room. It was worth examining. Everything looked brand new, and gleamed. Two big 100 h.p. diesels, diesel generator, radio generator, hot and cold water pumps, central heating plant, big oil and water tanks and the two long rows of lead-acid batteries. Thomas seemed especially interested in the batteries.

"You carry a lot of reserve there, Mr. Petersen," he said. He'd learnt my name by now, even though it wasn't the one I'd been christened with. "Why all the power?"

"We haven't even got enough. Care to start those two engines by hand? We have eight electric motors in the lab.—and the only time they're used, in harbour, we can't run either the engines or generators to supply juice. Too much interference. A constant drain." I was ticking off my fingers. "Then there's the central heating, hot and cold water pumps, radar, radio, automatic steering, windlass, power winch for the dinghy, echo-sounder, navigation lights——"

"You win, you win." He'd become quite friendly by this time. "Boats aren't really in my line. Let's move forward, shall we?"

The remainder of the inspection, curiously, didn't take long. In the saloon I found that Hunslett had persuaded the Torbay police force to accept the hospitality of the *Firecrest*. Sergeant MacDonald hadn't exactly become jovial, but he was much more human than when he'd come on board. Constable MacDonald, I noticed, didn't seem so relaxed. He looked positively glum.

Maybe he didn't approve of his old man consorting with potential criminals.

If the examination of the saloon was cursory, that of the two forward cabins was positively perfunctory. Back in the saloon, I said:

"Sorry I was a bit short, gentlemen. I like my sleep. A drink before you go?"

"Well." Thomas smiled. "We don't want to be rude either. Thank you."

Five minutes and they were gone. Thomas didn't even glance at the wheelhouse—Durran had been there, of course. He had a quick look at one of the deck lockers but didn't bother about the others. We were in the clear. A civil good-bye on both sides and they were gone. Their boat, a big indeterminate shape in the darkness, seemed to have plenty of power.

"Odd," I said.

"What's odd?"

"That boat. Any idea what it was like?"

"How could I?" Hunslett was testy. He was as short of sleep as I was. "It was pitch dark."

"That's just the point. A gentle glow in their wheelhouse—you couldn't even see what that was like—and no more. No deck lights, no interior lights, no navigation lights even."

"Sergeant MacDonald has been looking out over this harbour for eight years. Do you need light to find your way about your own living-room after dark?"

"I haven't got twenty yachts and cruisers in my living-room swinging all over the place with wind and tide. And wind and tide doesn't alter my own course when I'm crossing my living-room. There are only three boats in the harbour carrying anchor lights. He'll have to use something to see where he's going."

And he did. From the direction of the receding sound of engines a light stabbed out into the darkness. A five-inch searchlight, I would have guessed. It picked up a small yacht riding at anchor less than a hundred yards ahead of it, altered to starboard, picked up another, altered to port, then swung back on course again.

" 'Odd' was the word you used," Hunslett murmured. "Quite a good word, too, in the circumstances. And what are we to think of the alleged Torbay police force?"

"You talked to the sergeant longer than I did. When I was aft with Thomas and Durran."

"I'd like to think otherwise," Hunslett said inconsequentially. "It would make things easier, in a way. But I can't. He's a genuine old-fashioned cop and a good one, too. I've met too many. So have you."

"A good cop and an honest one," I agreed. "This is not his line of country and he was fooled. It is our line of country and we were fooled. Until now, that is."

"Speak for yourself."

"Thomas made one careless remark. An off-beat remark. You didn't hear it—we were in the engine-room." I shivered, maybe it was the cold night wind. "It meant nothing—not until I saw that they didn't want their boat recognised again. He said: 'Boats aren't really in my line.' Probably thought he'd been asking too many questions and wanted to reassure me. Boats not in his line—a customs officer and boats not in his line. They only spend their lives aboard boats, examining boats, that's all. They spend their lives looking and poking in so many odd corners and quarters that they know more about boats than the designers themselves. Another thing, did you notice how sharply dressed they were? A credit to Carnaby Street."

"Customs officers don't usually go around in oil-stained overalls."

"They've been living in those clothes for twenty-four hours. This is the what—the thirteenth boat they've searched in that time. Would you still have knife-edged creases to your pants after that lot? Or would you say they'd only just taken them from the hangers and put them on?"

"What else did they say? What else did they do?" Hunslett spoke so quietly that I could hear the note of the engines of the customs' boat fall away sharply as their searchlight lit up the low-water stone pier, half a mile away. "Take an undue interest in anything?"

"They took an undue interest in everything. Wait a minute, though, wait a minute. Thomas seemed particularly intrigued by the batteries, by the large amount of reserve electrical power we had."

"Did he now? Did he indeed? And did you notice how lightly our two customs friends swung aboard their launch when leaving?"

"They'll have done it a thousand times."

"Both of them had their hands free. They weren't carrying anything. They should have been carrying something."

"The photo-copier. I'm getting old."

"The photo-copier. Standard equipment my ruddy foot. So if our fair-haired pal wasn't busy photo-copying he was busy doing something else."

We moved inside the wheelhouse. Hunslett selected the larger screw-driver from the tool-rack beside the echo-sounder and had the face-plate off our R.T./D.F. set inside sixty seconds. He looked at the interior for five seconds, looked at me for the same length of time, then started screwing the face-plate back into position. One thing was certain, we wouldn't be using that transmitter for a long time to come.

I turned away and stared out through the wheelhouse windows into the darkness. The wind was still rising, the black sea gleamed palely as the whitecaps came marching in from the south-west, the *Firecrest* snubbed sharply on her anchor chain and, with the wind and the tide at variance, she was beginning to corkscrew quite noticeably now. I felt desperately tired. But my eyes were still working. Hunslett offered me a cigarette. I didn't want one, but I took one. Who knew, it might even help me to think. And then I had caught his wrist and was staring down at his palm.

"Well, well," I said. "The cobbler should stick to his last."

"He what?"

"Wrong proverb. Can't think of the right one. A good workman uses only his own tools. Our pal with the penchant for smashing valves and condensers should have remembered that.

No wonder my neck was twitching when Durran was around. How did you cut yourself?"

"I didn't cut myself."

"I know. But there's a smear of blood on your palm. He's been taking lessons from Peter Sellers, I shouldn't wonder. Standard southern English on the *Nantesville*, northern Irish on the *Firecrest*. I wonder how many other accents he has up his sleeve—behind his larynx, I should say. And I thought he was running to a little fat. He's running to a great deal of muscle. You noticed he never took his gloves off, even when he had that drink?"

"I'm the best noticer you ever saw. Beat me over the head with a club and I'll notice anything." He sounded bitter. "Why didn't they clobber us? You, anyway? The star witness?"

"Maybe we *have* moved out of our class. Two reasons. They couldn't do anything with the cops there, genuine cops as we've both agreed, not unless they attended to the cops too. Only a madman would deliberately kill a cop and whatever those boys may lack it isn't sanity."

"But why cops in the first place?"

"Aura of respectability. Cops are above suspicion. When a uniformed policeman shoves his uniformed cap above your gunwale in the dark watches of the night, you don't whack him over the head with a marline-spike. You invite him aboard. All others you might whack, especially if we had the bad consciences we might have been supposed to have."

"Maybe. It's arguable. And the second point?"

"They took a big chance, a desperate chance, almost, with Durran. He was thrown to the wolves to see what the reaction would be, whether either of us recognised him."

"Why Durran?"

"I didn't tell you. I shone a torch in his face. The face didn't register, just a white blur with screwed-up eyes half-hidden behind an upflung hand. I was really looking lower down, picking the right spot to kick him. But they weren't to know that. They wanted to find out if we would recognise him. We didn't. If we

41

had done we'd either have started throwing the crockery at him or yelped for the cops to arrest them—if we're against them then we're with the cops. But we didn't. Not a flicker of recognition. Nobody's as good as that. I defy any man in the world to meet up again in the same night with a man who has murdered two other people and nearly murdered himself without at least twitching an eyebrow. So the immediate heat is off, the urgent necessity to do us in has become less urgent. It's a safe bet that if we didn't recognise Durran, then we recognised nobody on the *Nantesville* and so we won't be burning up the lines to Interpol."

"We're in the clear?"

"I wish to God we were. They're on to us."

"But you said——"

"I don't know how I know," I said irritably. "I know. They went through the after end of the *Firecrest* like a Treble Chance winner hunting for the coupon he's afraid he's forgotten to post. Then half-way through the engine-room search—click!—just like that and they weren't interested any more. At least Thomas wasn't. He'd found out something. You saw him afterwards in the saloon, the fore cabins and the upper deck. He couldn't have cared less."

"The batteries?"

"No. He was satisfied with my explanation. I could tell. I don't know why, I only know I'm sure."

"So they'll be back."

"They'll be back."

"I get the guns out now?"

"There's no hurry. Our friends will be sure we can't communicate with anyone. The mainland boat calls here only twice a week. It came to-day and won't be back for four days. The lines to the mainland are down and if I thought for a moment they wouldn't stay down I should be back in kindergarten. Our transmitter is out. Assuming there are no carrier pigeons in Torbay, what's the only remaining means of communication with the mainland?"

"There's the *Shangri-la*." The *Shangri-la*, the nearest craft to ours, was white, gleaming, a hundred and twenty feet long and wouldn't have left her owner a handful of change from a quarter of a million pounds when he'd bought her. "She'll have a couple of thousand quids' worth of radio equipment aboard. Then there are two, maybe three yachts big enough to carry transmitters. The rest will carry only receivers, if that."

"And how many transmitters in Torbay harbour will still be in operating condition to-morrow?"

"One."

"One. Our friends will attend to the rest. They'll have to. We can't warn anyone. We can't give ourselves away."

"The insurance companies can stand it." He glanced at his watch. "This would be a nice time to wake up Uncle Arthur."

"I can't put it off any longer." I wasn't looking forward to talking to Uncle Arthur.

Hunslett reached for a heavy coat, pulled it on, made for the door and stopped. "I thought I'd take a walk on the upper deck. While you're talking. Just in case. A second thought—I'd better have that gun now. Thomas said they'd already checked three boats in the harbour. MacDonald didn't contradict him, so it was probably true. Maybe there *are* no serviceable transmitters left in Torbay now. Maybe our friends just dumped the cops ashore and are coming straight back for us."

"Maybe. But those yachts are smaller than the *Firecrest*. Apart from us, there's only one with a separate wheelhouse. The others will carry transmitters in the saloon cabin. Lots of them sleep in their saloon cabins. The owners would have to be banged on the head first before the radios could be attended to. They couldn't do that with MacDonald around."

"You'd bet your pension on that? Maybe MacDonald didn't always go aboard."

"I'll never live to collect my pension. But maybe you'd better have that gun."

The *Firecrest* was just over three years old. The Southampton boatyard and marine-radio firm that had combined to build her

43

had done so under conditions of sworn secrecy to a design provided by Uncle Arthur. Uncle Arthur had not designed her himself although he had never said so to the few people who knew of the existence of the boat. He'd pinched the idea from a Japanese-designed Indonesian-owned fishing craft that had been picked up with engine failure off the Malaysian coast. Only one engine had failed though two were installed, but still she had been not under command, an odd circumstance that had led the alert Engineer Lieutenant on the frigate that had picked her up to look pretty closely at her: the net result of his investigations, apart from giving this splendid inspiration to Uncle Arthur, was that the crew still languished in a Singapore prisoner of war camp.

The *Firecrest*'s career had been chequered and inglorious. She had cruised around the Eastern Baltic for some time, without achieving anything, until the authorities in Memel and Leningrad, getting tired of the sight of her, had declared the *Firecrest persona non grata* and sent her back to England. Uncle Arthur had been furious, especially as he had to account to a parsimonious Under-Secretary for the considerable expenses involved. The Waterguard had tried their hand with it at catching smugglers and returned it without thanks. No smugglers. Now for the first time ever it was going to justify its existence and in other circumstances Uncle Arthur would have been delighted. When he heard what I had to tell him he would have no difficulty in restraining his joy.

What made the *Firecrest* unique was that while she had two screws and two propeller shafts, she had only one engine. Two engine casings, but only one engine, even although that one engine was a special job fitted with an underwater by-pass exhaust valve. A simple matter of disengaging the fuel pump coupling and unscrewing four bolts on top—the rest were dummies—enabled the entire head of the diesel starboard engine to be lifted clear away, together with the fuel lines and injectors. With the assistance of the seventy foot telescopic radio mast housed inside our aluminium foremast, the huge gleaming transmitter that took up eighty per cent of the space inside the starboard engine casing could have sent a signal to the moon, if need be: as Thomas had observed, we had power and to spare. As it happened I didn't want to send a signal to the moon, just to Uncle Arthur's com-binex office and home in Knightsbridge.

The other twenty per cent of space was taken up with a motley collection of material that even the Assistant Commissioner in New Scotland Yard wouldn't have regarded without a thoughtful expression on his face. There were some packages of pre-fabric-ated explosives with amatol, primer and chemical detonator combined in one neat unit with a miniature timing device that ranged from five seconds to five minutes, complete with sucker clamps. There was a fine range of burglar's house-breaking tools, bunches of skeleton keys, several highly sophisticated listening devices, including one that could be shot from a Very-type pistol, several tubes of various harmless-looking tablets which were alleged, when dropped in some unsuspecting character's drink, to induce unconsciousness for varying periods, four pistols and a box of ammunition. Anyone who was going to use that lot in one operation was in for a busy time indeed. Two of the pistols were Lugers, two were 4.25 German Lilliputs, the smallest really effective automatic pistol on the market. The Lilliput had the great advantage that it could be concealed practically anywhere on your person, even upside down in a spring-loaded clip in your lower left sleeve—if, that was, you didn't get your suits cut in Carnaby Street.

Hunslett lifted one of the Lugers from its clamp, checked the loading indicator and left at once. It wasn't that he was imagining that he could already hear stealthy footsteps on the upper deck, he just didn't want to be around when Uncle Arthur came on the air. I didn't blame him. I didn't really want to be around then either.

I pulled out the two insulated rubber cables, fitted the power-fully spring-loaded saw-toothed metal clamps on to the battery terminals, hung on a pair of earphones, turned on the set, pulled another switch that actuated the call-up and waited. I didn't have to tune in, the transmitter was permanently pre-set, and pre-set on

45

a V.H.F. frequency that would have cost the licence of any ham operator who dared wander anywhere near it for transmission purposes.

The red receiver warning light came on. I reached down and adjusted the magic eye control until the green fans met in the middle.

"This is station SPFX," a voice came. "Station SPFX."

"Good-morning. This is Caroline. May I speak to the manager, please?"

"Will you wait, please?" This meant that Uncle Arthur was in bed. Uncle Arthur was never at his best on rising. Three minutes passed and the earphones came to life again.

"Good morning, Caroline. This is Annabelle."

"Good morning. Location 481, 281." You wouldn't find those references in any Ordnance Survey Map, there weren't a dozen maps in existence with them. But Uncle Arthur had one. And so had I.

There was a pause, then: "I have you, Caroline. Proceed."

"I located the missing vessel this afternoon. Four or five miles north-west of here. I went on board to-night."

"You did what, Caroline?"

"Went on board. The old crew has gone home. There's a new crew aboard. A smaller crew."

"You located Betty and Dorothy?" Despite the fact that we both had scramblers fitted to our radio phones, making intelligible eavesdropping impossible, Uncle Arthur always insisted that we spoke in a roundabout riddle fashion and used code names for his employees and himself. Girls' names for our surnames, initials to match. An irritating foible, but one that we had to observe. He was Annabelle, I was Caroline, Baker was Betty, Delmont, Dorothy and Hunslett, Harriet. It sounded like a series of Caribbean hurricane warnings.

"I found them." I took a deep breath. "They won't be coming home again, Annabelle."

"They won't be coming home again," he repeated mechanically. He was silent for so long that I began to think that he had gone off

46

the air. Then he came again, his voice empty, remote. "I warned you of this, Caroline."

"Yes, Annabelle, you warned me of this."

"And the vessel?"

"Gone."

"Gone where?"

"I don't know. Just gone. North, I suppose."

"North, you suppose." Uncle Arthur never raised his voice, when he went on it was as calm and impersonal as ever, but the sudden disregard of his own rules about circumlocution betrayed the savage anger in his mind. "North where? Iceland? A Norwegian fjord? To effect a trans-shipment of cargo anywhere in a million square miles between the mid-Atlantic and the Barents Sea? And you lost her. After all the time, the trouble, the planning, the expense, you've lost her!" He might have spared me that bit about the planning, it had been mine all the way. "And Betty and Dorothy." The last words showed he'd taken control of himself again.

"Yes, Annabelle, I've lost her." I could feel the slow anger in myself. "And there's worse than that, if you want to listen to it."

"I'm listening."

I told him the rest and at the end of it he said: "I see. You've lost the vessel. You've lost Betty and Dorothy. And now our friends know about you, the one vital element of secrecy is gone for ever and every usefulness and effectiveness you might ever have had is completely negated." A pause. "I shall expect you in my office at nine p.m. to-night. Instruct Harriet to take the boat back to base."

"Yes, sir." The hell with his Annabelle. "I had expected that. I've failed. I've let you down. I'm being pulled off."

"Nine o'clock to-night, Caroline. I'll be waiting."

"You'll have a long wait, Annabelle."

"And what might you mean by that?" If Uncle Arthur had had a low silky menacing voice then he'd have spoken those words in a low silky menacing voice. But he hadn't, he'd only this flat level monotone and it carried infinitely more weight and authority than any carefully modulated theatrical voice that had ever graced a stage.

"There are no planes to this place, Annabelle. The mail-boat doesn't call for another four days. The weather's breaking down and I wouldn't risk our boat to try to get to the mainland. I'm stuck here for the time being, I'm afraid."

"Do you take me for a nincompoop, sir?" Now he was at it. "Go ashore this morning. An air-sea rescue helicopter will pick you up at noon. Nine p.m. at my office. Don't keep me waiting."

This, then, was it. But one last try. "Couldn't you give me another twenty-four hours, Annabelle?"

"Now you're being ridiculous. And wasting my time. Good-bye."

"I beg of you, sir."

"I'd thought better of you than that. Good-bye."

"Good-bye. We may meet again sometime. It's not likely. Good-bye."

I switched the radio off, lit a cigarette and waited. The call-up came through in half a minute. I waited another half-minute and switched on. I was very calm. The die was cast and I didn't give a damn.

"Caroline? Is that you, Caroline?" I could have sworn to a note of agitation in his voice. This was something for the record books.

"Yes."

"What did you say? At the end there?"

"Good-bye. You said good-bye. I said good-bye."

"Don't quibble with me, sir! You said——"

"If you want me aboard that helicopter," I said, "you'll have to send a guard with the pilot. An armed guard. I hope they're good. I've got a Luger, and you know I'm good. And if I have to kill anyone and go into court, then you'll have to stand there beside me because there's no single civil action or criminal charge that even you, with all your connections, can bring against me that would justify the sending of armed men to apprehend me, an innocent man. Further, I am no longer in your employ. The terms of my civil service contract state clearly that I can resign at any moment, provided that I am not actively engaged on an operation at that moment. You've pulled me off, you've recalled me to London. My resignation will be on your desk as soon as the mail can get through. Baker and Delmont weren't your friends. They were my friends. They were my friends ever since I joined the service. You have the temerity to sit there and lay all the blame for their deaths on my shoulders when you know damn' well that every operation must have your final approval, and now you have the final temerity to deny me a one last chance to square accounts. I'm sick of your damned soulless service. Good-bye."

"Now wait a moment, Caroline." There was a cautious, almost placatory note to his voice. "No need to go off half-cocked." I was sure that no one had ever talked to Rear-Admiral Sir Arthur Arnford-Jason like that before but he didn't seem particularly upset about it. He had the cunning of a fox, that infinitely agile and shrewd mind would be examining and discarding possibilities with the speed of a computer, he'd be wondering whether I was playing a game and if so how far he could play it with me without making it impossible for me to retreat from the edge of the precipice. Finally he said quietly: "You wouldn't want to hang around there just to shed tears. You're on to something."

"Yes, sir, I'm on to something." I wondered what in the name of God I was on to.

"I'll give you twenty-four hours, Caroline."

"Forty-eight."

"Forty-eight. And then you return to London. I have your word?"

"I promise."

"And Caroline?"

"Sir?"

"I didn't care for your way of talking there. I trust we never have a repetition of it."

49

"No, sir. I'm sorry, sir."

"Forty-eight hours. Report to me at noon and midnight." A click. Uncle Arthur was gone.

The false dawn was in the sky when I went on deck. Cold heavy slanting driving rain was churning up the foam-flecked sea. The *Firecrest*, pulling heavily on her anchor chain, was swinging slowly through an arc of forty degrees, corkscrewing quite heavily now on the outer arc of the swing, pitching in the centre of them. She was snubbing very heavily on the anchor and I wondered uneasily how long the lengths of heaving line securing the dinghy, outboard and scuba gear to the chain could stand up to this sort of treatment.

Hunslett was abaft the saloon, huddling in what little shelter it afforded. He looked up at my approach and said: "What do you make of that?" He pointed to the palely gleaming shape of the *Shangri-la*, one moment on our quarter, the next dead astern as we swung on our anchor. Lights were burning brightly in the fore part of her superstructure, where the wheelhouse would be.

"Someone with insomnia," I said. "Or checking to see if the anchor is dragging. What do you think it is—our recent guests laying about the *Shangri-la*'s radio installation with crow-bars? Maybe they leave lights on all night."

"Came on just ten minutes ago. And look, now—they're out. Funny. How did you get on with Uncle?"

"Badly. Fired me, then changed his mind. We have forty-eight hours."

"Forty-eight hours? What are you going to do in forty-eight hours?"

"God knows. Have some sleep first. You too. Too much light in the sky for callers now."

Passing through the saloon, Hunslett said, apropos of nothing: "I've been wondering. What did you make of P.C. MacDonald? The young one."

"What do you mean?"

"Well, glum, downcast. Heavy weight on his shoulders."

50

"Maybe he's like me. Maybe he doesn't like getting up in the middle of the night. Maybe he has girl trouble and if he has I can tell you that P.C. MacDonald's love-life is the least of my concerns. Good night."

I should have listened to Hunslett more. For Hunslett's sake.

3

I need my sleep, just like anyone else. Ten hours, perhaps only eight, and I would have been my own man again. Maybe not exuding brightness, optimism and cheerfulness, the circumstances weren't right for that, but at least a going concern, alert, perceptive, my mind operating on what Uncle Arthur would be by now regarding as its customary abysmal level but still the best it could achieve. But I wasn't given that ten hours. Nor even the eight. Exactly three hours after dropping off I was wide awake again. Well, anyway, awake. I would have had to be stone deaf, drugged or dead to go on sleeping through the bawling and thumping that was currently assailing my left ear from what appeared to be a distance of not more than twelve inches.

"Ahoy, there, *Firecrest*! Ahoy there!" Thump, thump, thump on the boat's side. "Can I come aboard? Ahoy, there! Ahoy, ahoy, ahoy!"

I cursed this nautical idiot from the depths of my sleep-ridden being, swung a pair of unsteady legs to the deck and levered myself out of the bunk. I almost fell down, I seemed to have only one leg left, and my neck ached fiercely. A glance at the mirror gave quick external confirmation of my internal decrepitude. A haggard unshaven face, unnaturally pale, and bleary bloodshot eyes with dark circles under them. I looked away hurriedly, there were lots of things I could put up with first thing in the morning, but not sights like that.

I opened the door across the passage. Hunslett was sound asleep and snoring. I returned to my own cabin and got busy with the dressing-gown and Paisley scarf again. The iron-lunged thumping character outside was still at it, if I didn't hurry he would be roaring out "avast there" any moment. I combed my hair into some sort of order and made my way to the upper deck.

It was a cold, wet and windy world. A grey, dreary, unpleasant world, why the hell couldn't they have let me sleep on. The rain was coming down in slanting sheets, bouncing inches high on the decks, doubling the milkiness of the spume-flecked sea. The lonely wind mourned through the rigging and the lower registers of sound and the steep-sided wind-truncated waves, maybe three feet from tip to trough, were high enough to make passage difficult if not dangerous for the average yacht tender.

They didn't make things in the slightest difficult or dangerous for the yacht tender that now lay alongside us. It maybe wasn't as big—it looked it at first sight—as the *Firecrest*, but it was big enough to have a glassed-in cabin for'ard, a wheelhouse that bristled and gleamed with controls and instrumentation that would have been no disgrace to a VC-10 and, abaft that, a sunken cockpit that could have sunbathed a football team without over-crowding. There were three crewmen dressed in black oilskins and fancy French navy hats with black ribbons down the back, two of them each with a boat-hook round one of the *Firecrest*'s guardrail stanchions. Half a dozen big inflated spherical rubber fenders kept the *Firecrest* from rubbing its plebeian paintwork against the whitely-varnished spotlessness of the tender alongside and it didn't require the name on the bows or the crew's hats to let me know that this was the tender that normally took up most of the after-deck space on the *Shangri-la*.

Amidships a stocky figure, clad in a white vaguely naval brass-buttoned uniform and holding above his head a golf umbrella that would have had Joseph green with envy, stopped banging his gloved fist against the *Firecrest*'s planking and glared up at me.

"Ha!" I've never actually heard anyone snort out a word but this came pretty close to it. "There you are at last. Took your time about it, didn't you? I'm soaked, man, soaked!" A few spots of rain did show up quite clearly on the white seersucker. "May I come aboard?" He didn't wait for any permission, just leaped aboard with surprising nimbleness for a man of his build and years and nipped into the *Firecrest*'s wheelhouse ahead of me, which was pretty selfish of him as he still had his umbrella and all I had was my dressing-gown. I followed and closed the door behind me.

He was a short, powerfully built character, fifty-five I would have guessed, with a heavily-tanned jowled face, close-cropped iron-grey hair with tufted eyebrows to match, long straight nose and a mouth that looked as if it had been closed with a zip-fastener. A good-looking cove, if you liked that type of looks. The dark darting eyes looked me up and down and if he was impressed by what he saw he made a heroic effort to keep his admiration in check.

"Sorry for the delay," I apologised. "Short of sleep. We had the customs aboard in the middle of the night and I couldn't get off after that." Always tell everyone the truth if there's an even chance of that truth coming out anyway, which in this case there was: gives one a reputation for forthright honesty.

"The customs?" He looked as if he intended to say "pshaw" or "fiddlesticks" or something of that order, then changed his mind and looked up sharply. "An intolerable bunch of busy-bodies. And in the middle of the night. Shouldn't have let them aboard. Sent them packing. Intolerable. What the deuce did they want?" He gave the distinct impression of having himself had some trouble with the customs in the past.

"They were looking for stolen chemicals. Stolen from some place in Ayrshire. Wrong boat."

"Idiots!" He thrust out a stubby hand, he'd passed his final judgment on the unfortunate customs and the subject was now closed. "Skouras. Sir Anthony Skouras."

"Petersen." His grip made me wince, less from the sheer power of it than from the gouging effects of the large number of thickly encrusted rings that adorned his fingers. I wouldn't have been surprised to see some on his thumbs but he'd missed out on that. I looked at him with new interest. "Sir Anthony Skouras. I've heard of you of course."

"Nothing good. Columnists don't like me because they know I despise them. A Cypriot who made his shipping millions through sheer ruthlessness, they say. True. Asked by the Greek Government to leave Athens. True. Became a naturalised British citizen and bought a knighthood. Absolutely true. Charitable works and public services. Money can buy anything. A baronetcy next but the market's not right at the moment. Price is bound to fall. Can I use your radio transmitter? I see you have one."

"What's that?" The abrupt switch had me off-balance, no great achievement the way I was feeling.

"Your radio transmitter, man! Don't you listen to the news? All those major defence projects cancelled by the Pentagon. Price of steel tumbling. Must get through to my New York broker at once!"

"Sorry. Certainly you may—but, but your own radio-telephone? Surely——"

"It's out of action." His mouth became more tight-lipped than ever and the inevitable happened: it disappeared. "It's urgent, Mr. Petersen."

"Immediately. You know how to operate this model?"

He smiled thinly, which was probably the only way he was capable of smiling. Compared to the cinema-organ job he'd have aboard the *Shangri-la*, asking him if he could operate this was like asking the captain of a transatlantic jet if he could fly a Tiger Moth. "I think I can manage, Mr. Petersen."

"Call me when you're finished. I'll be in the saloon." He'd be calling me before he'd finished, he'd be calling me before he'd even started. But I couldn't tell him. Word gets around. I went down to the saloon, contemplated a shave and decided against it. It wouldn't take that long.

It didn't. He appeared at the saloon door inside a minute, his face grim.

"Your radio is out of order, Mr. Petersen."

"They're tricky to operate, some of those older jobs," I said tactfully. "Maybe if I——"

"I say it's out of order. I mean it's out of order."

55

"Damned odd. It was working——"

"Would you care to try it, please?"

I tried it. Nothing. I twiddled everything I could lay hands on. Nothing.

"A power failure, perhaps," I suggested. "I'll check——"

"Would you be so good as to remove the face-plate, please?"

I stared at him in perplexity, switching the expression, after a suitable interval, to shrewd thoughtfulness. "What do you know, Sir Anthony, that I don't?"

"You'll find out."

So I found out and went through all the proper motions of consternation, incredulity and tight-lipped indignation. Finally I said: "You knew. How did you know?"

"Obvious, isn't it?"

"Your transmitter," I said slowly. "It's more than just out of order. You had the same midnight caller."

"And the *Orion*." The mouth vanished again. "The big blue ketch lying close in. Only other craft in the harbour apart from us with a radio transmitter. Smashed. Just come from there."

"Smashed? Theirs as well? But who in God's name—it must be the work of a madman."

"Is it? Is it the work of a madman? I know something of those matters. My first wife——" He broke off abruptly and gave an odd shake of the head, then went on slowly: "The mentally disturbed are irrational, haphazard, purposeless, aimless in their behaviour patterns. This seems an entirely irrational act, but an act with a method and a purpose to it. Not haphazard. It's planned. There's a reason. At first I thought the reason was to cut off my connection with the mainland. But it can't be that. By rendering me temporarily incommunicado nobody stands to gain, I don't stand to lose."

"But you said the New York Stock——"

"A bagatelle," he said contemptuously. "Nobody likes to lose money." Not more than a few millions anyway. "No, Mr. Petersen, I am not the target. We have here an A and a B. A

56

regards it as vital that he remains in constant communication with the mainland. B regards it as vital that A doesn't. So B takes steps. There's something damned funny going on in Torbay. And something big. I have a nose for such things."

He was no fool but then not many morons have ended up as multi-millionaires. I couldn't have put it better myself. I said: "Reported this to the police yet?"

"Going there now. After I've made a phone call or two." The eyes suddenly became bleak and cold. "Unless our friend has smashed up the two public call boxes in the main street."

"He's done better than that. He's brought down the lines to the mainland. Somewhere down the Sound. No one knows where."

He stared at me, wheeled to leave, then turned, his face empty of expression. "How did you know that?" The tone matched the face.

"Police told me. They were aboard with the customs last night."

"The police? That's damned odd. What were the police doing here?" He paused and looked at me with his cold measuring eyes. "A personal question, Mr. Petersen. No impertinence intended. A question of elimination. What are *you* doing here? No offence."

"No offence. My friend and I are marine biologists. A working trip. Not our boat—the Ministry of Agriculture and Fisheries." I smiled. "We have impeccable references, Sir Anthony."

"Marine biology, eh? Hobby of mine, you might say. Layman, of course. Must have a talk sometime." He was speaking absent-mindedly, his thoughts elsewhere. "Could you describe the policeman, Mr. Petersen?"

I did and he nodded. "That's him all right. Odd, very odd. Must have a word with Archie about this."

"Archie?"

"Sergeant MacDonald. This is my fifth consecutive season's cruising based on Torbay. The South of France and the Ægean can't hold a candle to these waters. Know quite a few of the locals pretty well by this time. He was alone?"

57

"No. A young constable. His son, he said. Melancholy sort of lad."

"Peter MacDonald. He has reason for his melancholy, Mr. Petersen. His two young brothers, sixteen years old, twins, died a few months back. At an Inverness school, lost in a late snowstorm in the Cairngorms. The father is tougher, doesn't show it so much. A great tragedy. I knew them both. Fine boys."

I made some appropriate comment but he wasn't listening.

"I must be on my way, Mr. Petersen. Put this damned strange affair in MacDonald's hands. Don't see that he can do much. Then off for a short cruise."

I looked through the wheelhouse windows at the dark skies, the white-capped seas, the driving rain. "You picked a day for it."

"The rougher the better. No bravado. I like a mill-pond as well as any man. Just had new stabilisers fitted in the Clyde—we got back up here only two days ago—and it seems like a good day to try them out." He smiled suddenly and put out his hand. "Sorry to have barged in. Taken up far too much of your time. Seemed rude, I suppose. Some say I am. You and your colleague care to come aboard for a drink to-night? We eat early at sea. Eight o'clock, say? I'll send the tender." That meant we didn't rate an invitation to dinner, which would have made a change from Hunslett and his damned baked beans, but even an invitation like this would have given rise to envious tooth-gnashing in some of the stateliest homes in the land: it was no secret that the bluest blood in England, from Royalty downwards, regarded a holiday invitation to the island Skouras owned off the Albanian coast as the conferment of the social cachet of the year or any year. Skouras didn't wait for an answer and didn't seem to expect one. I didn't blame him. It would have been many years since Skouras had discovered that it was an immutable law of human nature, human nature being what it is, that no one ever turned down one of his invitations.

"You'll be coming to tell me about your smashed transmitter and asking me what the devil I intend to do about it," Sergeant MacDonald said tiredly. "Well, Mr. Petersen, I know all about it already. Sir Anthony Skouras was here half an hour ago. Sir Anthony had a lot to say. And Mr. Campbell, the owner of the *Orion*, has just left. He'd a lot to say, too."

"Not me, Sergeant. I'm a man of few words." I gave him what I hoped looked like a self-deprecatory smile. "Except, of course, when the police and customs drag me out of bed in the middle of the night. I take it our friends have left?"

"Just as soon as they'd put us ashore. Customs are just a damn' nuisance." Like myself, he looked as if he could do with some hours' sleep. "Frankly, Mr. Petersen, I don't know what to do about the broken radio-transmitters. Why on earth—who on earth would want to do a daft vicious thing like that?"

"That's what I came to ask you."

"I can go aboard your boat," MacDonald said slowly. "I can take out my note-book, look around and see if I can't find any clues. I wouldn't know what to look for. Maybe if I knew something about fingerprinting and analysis and microscopy I might just find out something. But I don't. I'm an island police-man, not a one-man Flying Squad. This is C.I.D. work and we'd have to call in Glasgow. I doubt if they'd send a couple of detectives to investigate a few smashed radio valves."

"Old man Skouras draws a lot of water."

"Sir?"

"He's powerful. He has influence. If Skouras wanted action I'm damned sure he could get it. If the need arose and the mood struck him I'm sure he could be a very unpleasant character indeed."

"There's not a better man or a kinder man ever sailed into Torbay," MacDonald said warmly. That hard brown face could conceal practically anything that MacDonald wanted it to conceal but this time he was hiding nothing. "Maybe his ways aren't my ways. Maybe he's a hard, aye, a ruthless businessman. Maybe, as the papers hint, his private life wouldn't bear investigation. That's none of my business. But if you were to look for a man in

59

Torbay to say a word against him, you'll have a busy time on your hands, Mr. Petersen."

"You've taken me up wrongly, Sergeant," I said mildly. "I don't even know the man."

"No. But we do. See that?" He pointed through the side window of the police station to a large Swedish-style timber building beyond the pier. "Our new village hall. Town hall, they call it. Sir Anthony gave us that. Those six wee chalets up the hill there? For old folks. Sir Anthony again—every penny from his own pocket. Who takes all the schoolchildren to the Oban Games—Sir Anthony on the *Shangri-la*. Contributes to every charity going and now he has plans to build a boatyard to give employment to the young men of Torbay—there's not much else going since the fishing-boats left."

"Well, good for old Skouras," I said. "He seems to have adopted the place. Lucky Torbay. I wish he'd buy me a new radio-transmitter."

"I'll keep my eyes and ears open, Mr. Petersen. I can't do more. If anything turns up I'll let you know at once."

I told him thanks, and left. I hadn't particularly wanted to go there, but it would have looked damned odd if I hadn't turned up to add my pennyworth to the chorus of bitter complaint.

I was very glad that I had turned up.

The midday reception from London was poor. This was due less to the fact that reception is always better after dark than to the fact that I couldn't use our telescopic radio mast: but it was fair enough and Uncle's voice was brisk and businesslike and clear.

"Well, Caroline, we've found our missing friends," he said.

"How many?" I asked cautiously. Uncle Arthur's ambiguous references weren't always as clear as Uncle Arthur imagined them to be.

"All twenty-five." That made it the former crew of the *Nantesville*. "Two of them are pretty badly hurt but they'll be all right." That accounted for the blood I had found in the captain's and one of the engineers' cabins.

"Where?" I asked.

He gave me a map reference. Just north of Wexford. The *Nantesville* had sailed from Bristol, she couldn't have been more than a few hours on her way before she'd run into trouble.

"Exactly the same procedure as on the previous occasions," Uncle Arthur was saying. "Held in a lonely farmhouse for a couple of nights. Plenty to eat and drink and blankets to keep the cold out. Then they woke up one morning and found their guards had gone."

"But a different procedure in stopping the—our friend?" I'd almost said *Nantesville* and Uncle Arthur wouldn't have liked that at all.

"As always. We must concede them a certain ingenuity, Caroline. After having smuggled men aboard in port, then using the sinking fishing-boat routine, the police launch routine and the yacht with the appendicitis case aboard, I thought they would be starting to repeat themselves. But this time they came up with a new one—possibly because it's the first time they've hi-jacked a ship during the hours of darkness. Carley rafts, this time, with about ten survivors aboard, dead ahead of the vessel. Oil all over the sea. A weak distress flare that couldn't have been seen a mile away and probably was designed that way. You know the rest."

"Yes, Annabelle." I knew the rest. After that the routine was always the same. The rescued survivors, displaying a marked lack of gratitude, would whip out pistols, round up the crew, tie black muslin bags over their heads so that they couldn't identify the vessel that would appear within the hour to take them off, march them on board the unknown vessel, land them on some lonely beach during the dark then march them again, often a very long way indeed, till they arrived at their prison. A deserted farmhouse. Always a deserted farmhouse. And always in Ireland, three times in the north and now twice in the south. Meantime the prize crew sailed the hi-jacked vessel to God alone knew where and the first the world knew of the disappearance of the pirated vessel was when the original crew, released after two or three days' painless captivity, would turn up at some remote dwelling and start hollering for the nearest telephone.

"Betty and Dorothy," I said. "Were they still in safe concealment when the crew were taken off?"

"I imagine so. I don't know. Details are still coming in and I understand the doctors won't let anyone see the captain yet." Only the captain had known of the presence aboard of Baker and Delmont. "Forty-one hours now, Caroline. What have you done?"

For a moment I wondered irritably what the devil he was talking about. Then I remembered. He'd given me forty-eight hours. Seven were gone.

"I've had three hours' sleep." He'd consider that an utter waste of time, his employees weren't considered to need sleep. "I've talked to the constabulary ashore. And I've talked to a wealthy yachtsman, next boat to us here. We're paying him a social call to-night."

There was a pause. "You're doing *what* to-night, Caroline?"

"Visiting. We've been invited. Harriet and I. For drinks."

This time the pause was markedly longer. Then he said: "You have forty-one hours, Caroline."

"Yes, Annabelle."

"We assume you haven't taken leave of your senses."

"I don't know how unanimous informed opinion might be about that. I don't think I have."

"And you haven't given up? No, not that. You're too damn' stiff-necked and—and——"

"Stupid?"

"Who's the yachtsman?"

I told him. It took me some time, partly because I had to spell out names with the aid of his damned code-book, partly because I gave him a very full account of everything Skouras had said to me and everything Sergeant MacDonald had said about Skouras. When his voice came again it was cagey and wary. As Uncle Arthur couldn't see me I permitted myself a cynical grin. Even Cabinet Ministers found it difficult to make the grade as far as

Skouras's dinner-table, but the Permanent Under-Secretaries, the men with whom the real power of government lies, practically had their own initialled napkin rings. Under-Secretaries were the bane of Uncle Arthur's life.

"You'll have to watch your step very carefully here, Caroline."

"Betty and Dorothy aren't coming home any more, Annabelle. Someone has to pay. I want someone to pay. You want someone to pay. We all do."

"But it's inconceivable that a man in his position, a man of his wealth——"

"I'm sorry, Annabelle. I don't understand."

"A man like that. Dammit all, I know him well, Caroline. We dine together. First-name terms. Know his present wife even better. Ex-actress. A philanthropist like that. A man who's spent five consecutive seasons there. Would a man like that, a millionaire like that, spend all that time, all that money, just to build up a front——"

"Skouras?" I used the code name. Interrogatory, incredulous, as if it had just dawned upon me what Uncle Arthur was talking about. "I never said I suspected him, Annabelle. I have no reason to suspect him."

"Ah!" It's difficult to convey a sense of heartfelt gladness, profound satisfaction and brow-mopping relief in a single syllable, but Uncle Arthur managed it without any trouble. "Then why go?" A casual eavesdropper might have thought he detected a note of pained jealousy in Uncle Arthur's voice, and the casual eavesdropper would have been right. Uncle Arthur had only one weakness in his make-up—he was a social snob of monumental proportions.

"I want aboard. I want to see this smashed transmitter of his."

"Why?"

"A hunch, let me call it, Annabelle. No more."

Uncle Arthur was going in for the long silences in a big way to-day. Then he said: "A hunch? A *hunch*? You told me this morning you were on to something."

63

"There's something else. I want you to contact the Post Office Savings Bank, Head Office, in Scotland. After that, the Records files of some Scottish newspapers. I suggest the *Glasgow Herald*, the *Scottish Daily Express* and, most particularly, the West Highland weekly, the *Oban Times*."

"Ah!" No relief this time, just satisfaction. "This is more like it, Caroline. What do you want and why?"

So I told him what I wanted and why, lots more of the fancy code work, and when I'd finished he said: "I'll have my staff on to this straight away. I'll have all the information you want by midnight."

"Then I don't want it, Annabelle. Midnight's too late for me. Midnight's no use to me."

"Don't ask the impossible, Caroline." He muttered something to himself, something I couldn't catch, then: "I'll pull every string, Caroline. Nine o'clock."

"Four o'clock, Annabelle."

"Four o'clock this afternoon?" When it came to incredulity he had me whacked to the wide. "Four hours' time? You *have* taken leave of your senses."

"You can have ten men on it in ten minutes. Twenty in twenty minutes. Where's the door that isn't open to you? Especially the door of the Assistant Commissioner. Professionals don't kill for the hell of it. They kill because they must. They kill to gain time. Every additional hour is vital to them. And if it's vital to them, how much more so is it to us? Or do you think we're dealing with amateurs, Annabelle?"

"Call me at four," he said heavily. "I'll see what I have for you. What's your next move, Caroline?"

"Bed," I said. "I'm going to get some sleep."

"Of course. Time, as you said, is of the essence. You mustn't waste it, must you, Caroline?" He signed off. He sounded bitter. No doubt he was bitter. But then, insomnia apart, Uncle Arthur could rely on a full quota of sleep during the coming night. Which was more than I could. No certain foreknowledge, no second sight, just a hunch, but not a small one, the kind of hunch you

64

couldn't have hidden behind the Empire State Building. Just like the one I had about the *Shangri-la*.

I only just managed to catch the last fading notes of the alarm as it went off at ten minutes to four. I felt worse than I had done when we'd lain down after a miserable lunch of corned beef and reconstituted powdered potatoes—if old Skouras had had a spark of human decency, he'd have made that invitation for dinner. I wasn't only growing old, I felt old. I'd been working too long for Uncle Arthur. The pay was good but the hours and working conditions—I'd have wagered that Uncle Arthur hadn't even set eyes on a tin of corned beef since World War II—were shocking. And all this constant worrying, chiefly about life expectancy, helped wear a man down.

Hunslett came out of his cabin as I came out of mine. He looked just as old as I did. If they had to rely on a couple of ageing crocks like us, I thought morosely, the rising generation must be a pretty sorry lot.

Passing through the saloon, I wondered bitterly about the identity of all those characters who wrote so glibly about the Western Isles in general and the Torbay area in particular as being a yachtsman's paradise without equal in Europe. Obviously, they'd never been there. Fleet Street was their home and home was a place they never left, not if they could help it. An ignorant bunch of travel and advertising copy writers who regarded King's Cross as the northern limits of civilisation. Well, maybe not all that ignorant, at least they were smart enough to stay south of King's Cross.

Four o'clock on an autumn afternoon, but already it was more night than day. The sun wasn't down yet, not by a very long way, but it might as well have been for all the chance it had of penetrating the rolling masses of heavy dark cloud hurrying away to the eastwards to the inky blackness of the horizon beyond Torbay. The slanting sheeting rain that foamed whitely across the bay further reduced what little visibility there was to a limit of not more than four hundred yards. The village itself, half a mile

65

distant and nestling in the dark shadow of the steeply-rising pine-covered hills behind, might never have existed. Off to the north-west I could see the navigation lights of a craft rounding the head-land, Skouras returning from his stabiliser test run. Down in the *Shangri-la*'s gleaming galley a master chef would be preparing the sumptuous evening meal, the one to which we hadn't been invited. I tried to put the thought of that meal out of my mind, but I couldn't, so I just put it as far away as possible and followed Hunslett into the engine-room.

Hunslett took the spare earphones and squatted beside me on the deck, note-book on his knee. Hunslett was as competent in shorthand as he was in everything else. I hoped that Uncle Arthur would have something to tell us, that Hunslett's presence there would be necessary. It was.

"Congratulations, Caroline," Uncle Arthur said without pre-amble. "You really are on to something." As far as it is possible for a dead flat monotone voice to assume an overtone of warmth, then Uncle Arthur's did just that. He sounded positively friendly. More likely it was some freak of transmission or reception but at least he hadn't started off by bawling me out.

"We've traced those Post Office Savings books," he went on. He rattled off book numbers and details of times and amounts of deposits, things of no interest to me, then said: "Last deposits were on December 27th. Ten pounds in each case. Present balance is £78 14s. 6d. Exactly the same in both. And those accounts have not been closed."

He paused for a moment to let me congratulate him, which I did, then continued.

"That's nothing, Caroline. Listen. Your queries about any mysterious accidents, deaths, disappearances off the west coasts of Inverness-shire or Argyll, or anything happening to people from that area. We've struck oil, Caroline, we've really struck oil. My God, why did we never think of this before. Have your pencil handy?"

"Harriet has."

"Here we go. This seems to have been the most disastrous

sailing season for years in the west of Scotland. But first, one from last year. The *Pinto*, a well-found sea-worthy forty-five-foot motor cruiser left Kyle of Lochalsh for Oban at eight a.m. September 4th. She should have arrived that afternoon. She never did. No trace of her has ever been found."

"What was the weather at the time, Annabelle?"

"I thought you'd ask me that, Caroline." Uncle Arthur's combination of modesty and quiet satisfaction could be very trying at times. "I checked with the Met. office. Force one, variable. Flat calm, cloudless sky. Then we come to this year. April 6th and April 26th. The *Evening Star* and the *Jeannie Rose*. Two East Coast fishing boats—one from Buckie, the other from Fraserburgh."

"But both based on the west coast?"

"I wish you wouldn't try to steal my thunder," Uncle Arthur complained. "Both were based on Oban. Both were lobster boats. The *Evening Star*, the first one to go, was found stranded on the rocks off Islay. The *Jeannie Rose* vanished without trace. No member of either crew was ever found. Then again on the 17th of May. This time a well-known racing yacht, the *Cap Gris Nez*, an English built and owned craft, despite her name, highly experienced skipper, navigator and crew, all of them long-time and often successful competitors in R.O.R.C. races. That class. Left Londonderry for the north of Scotland in fine weather. Disappeared. She was found almost a month later—or what was left of her—washed up on the Isle of Skye."

"And the crew?"

"Need you ask? Never found. Then the last case, a few weeks ago—August 8th. Husband, wife, two teenage children, son and daughter. Converted lifeboat, the *Kingfisher*. By all accounts a pretty competent sailor, been at it for years. But he'd never done any night navigation, so he set out one calm evening to do a night cruise. Vanished. Boat and crew."

"Where did he set out from?"

"Torbay."

That one word made his afternoon. It made mine, too. I said:

"And do you still think the *Nantesville* is hell and gone to Iceland or some remote fjord in northern Norway?"

"I never thought anything of the kind." Uncle's human relationship barometer had suddenly swung back from friendly to normal, normal lying somewhere between cool and glacial. "The significance of the dates will not have escaped you?"

"No, Annabelle, the significance has not escaped me." The Buckie fishing-boat, the *Evening Star*, had been found washed up on Islay three days after the S.S. *Holmwood* had vanished off the south coast of Ireland. The *Jeannie Rose* had vanished exactly three days after the M.V. *Antara* had as mysteriously disappeared in the St. George's Channel. The *Cap Gris Nes*, the R.O.R.C. racer that had finally landed up on the rocks of the island of Skye had vanished the same day as the M.V. *Headley Pioneer* had disappeared somewhere, it was thought, off Northern Ireland. And the converted lifeboat, *Kingfisher*, had disappeared, never to be seen again, just two days after the S.S. *Hurricane Spray* had left the Clyde, also never to be seen again. Coincidence was coincidence and I classed those who denied its existence with intellectual giants like the twentieth-century South African president who stoutly maintained that the world was flat and that an incautious step would take you over the edge with results as permanent as they would be disastrous: but this was plain ridiculous. The odds against such a perfect matching of dates could be calculated only in astronomical terms: while the complete disappearance of the crews of four small boats that had come to grief in so very limited an area was the final nail in the coffin of coincidence. I said as much to Uncle.

"Let us not waste time by dwelling upon the obvious, Caroline," Uncle said coldly, which was pretty ungracious of him as the idea had never even entered his head until I had put it there four hours previously. "The point is—what is to be done? Islay to Skye is a pretty big area. Where does this get us?"

"How much weight can you bring to bear to secure the co-operation of the television and radio networks?"

There was a pause, then: "What do you have in mind, Caroline?" Uncle at his most forbidding.

"An insertion of an item in their news bulletins."

"Well." An even longer pause. "It was done daily during the war, of course. I believe it's been done once or twice since. Can't compel them, of course—they're a stuffy lot, both the B.B.C. and the I.T.A." His tone left little doubt as to his opinion of those die-hard reactionaries who brooked no interference, an odd reaction from one who was himself a past-master of brookmanship of this nature. "If they can be persuaded that it's completely apolitical and in the national interest there's a chance. What do you want?"

"An item that a distress signal has been received from a sinking yacht somewhere south of Skye. Exact position unknown. Signals ceased, the worst feared, an air-sea search to be mounted at first light to-morrow. That's all."

"I may manage it. Your reason, Caroline?"

"I want to look around. I want an excuse to move around without raising eyebrows."

"You're going to volunteer the *Firecrest* for this search and then poke around where you shouldn't?"

"We have our faults, Annabelle, Harriet and I, but we're not crazy. I wouldn't take this tub across the Serpentine without a favourable weather forecast. It's blowing a Force 7 outside. And a boat search would take a lifetime too long in those parts. What I had in mind was this. At the very eastern tip of Torbay Island, about five miles from the village, there's a small deserted sandy cove, semicircular and well protected by steep bluffs and pine trees. Will you please arrange to have a long-range helicopter there exactly at dawn."

"And now it's your turn to think I am crazy," Uncle Arthur said coldly. That remark about the sea-keeping qualities of his own brain-child, the *Firecrest*, would have rankled badly. "I'm supposed to snap my fingers and hey presto! a helicopter will be there at dawn."

"That's fourteen hours from now, Caroline. At five o'clock this morning you were prepared to snap your fingers and have a heli-

69

copter here by noon. Seven hours. Exactly half the time. But that was for something important, like getting me down to London to give me the bawling out of a lifetime before firing me."

"Call me at midnight, Caroline. I hope to God you know what you are doing."

I said: "Yes, sir," and hung up. I didn't mean, Yes, sir, I knew what I was doing, I meant, Yes, sir, I hoped to God I knew what I was doing.

If the carpet in the *Shangri-la*'s saloon had cost a penny under five thousand pounds, then old Skouras must have picked it up second-hand somewhere. Twenty by thirty, bronze and russet and gold, but mainly gold, it flowed across the deck like a field of ripe corn, an illusion heightened both by its depth and the impediment it offered to progress. You had to wade through the damn' thing. I'd never seen an item of furnishing like it in my life except for the curtains that covered two-thirds of the bulkhead space. The curtains made the carpet look rather shoddy. Persian or Afghanistan, with a heavy gleaming weave that gave a shimmering shot-silk effect with every little movement of the *Shangri-la*, they stretched all the way from deckhead to deck. What little of the bulkheads that could be seen were sheathed in a satiny tropical hardwood, the same wood as was used for the magnificent bar that took up most of the after bulkhead of the saloon. The opulently upholstered settees and armchairs and bar-stools, dark green leather with gold piping, would have cost another fortune, even the trade-in value of the beaten copper tables scattered carelessly about the carpet would have fed a family of five for a year. At the Savoy Grill.

On the port bulkhead hung two Cézannes, on the starboard two Renoirs. The pictures were a mistake. In that room they didn't have a chance. They'd have felt more at home in the galley.

So would I. So, I was pretty sure, would Hunslett. It wasn't merely that our sports coats and Paisley scarves clashed violently with the décor in general and the black ties and dinner jackets of our host and his other guests in particular. It wasn't even that

70

the general run of conversation might have been specifically designed to reduce Hunslett and myself to our proper status of artisans and pretty inferior artisans at that. All this talk about debentures and mergers and cross-options and takeovers and millions and millions of dollars has a pretty demoralising effect on the lower classes, but you didn't need to have the I.Q. of a genius to realise that this line of talk wasn't being aimed specifically at us; to the lads with the black ties, debentures and takeovers were the stuff and staff of life and so a principal staple of conversation. Besides, this wish to be somewhere else obviously didn't apply only to us: at least two others, a bald-headed, goatee-bearded merchant banker by the name of Henri Biscarte and a big bluff Scots lawyer by the name of MacCallum were just as uncomfortable as I felt, but showed it a great deal more.

A silent movie picture of the scene would have given no clue as to what was wrong. Everything was so very comfortable, so very civilised. The deep armchairs invited complete relaxation. A blazing if superfluous log-fire burned in the hearth. Skouras was the smiling and genial host to the life. The glasses were never empty—the press of an unheard bell brought a white-jacketed steward who silently refilled glasses and as silently departed again. All so urbane, so wealthy, so pleasantly peaceful. Until you cut in the movie sound-track, that was. That was when you wished you were in the galley.

Skouras had his glass refilled for the fourth time in the forty-five minutes we had been there, smiled at his wife sitting in the armchair across the fire from him, lifted his glass in a toast. "To you, my dear. To your patience with putting up with us all so well. A most boring trip for you, most boring. I congratulate you."

I looked at Charlotte Skouras. Everybody looked at Charlotte Skouras. There was nothing unusual in that, millions of people had looked at Charlotte Skouras when she had been the most sought-after actress in Europe. Even in those days she'd been neither particularly young nor beautiful, she didn't have to be because she'd been a great actress and not a beautiful but bone-headed movie star. Now she was even older and less good-looking and her figure was beginning to go. But men still looked at her. She was somewhere in her late thirties, but they would still be looking at her when she was in her bath-chair. She had that kind of face. A worn face, a used face, a face that had been used for living and laughing and thinking and feeling and suffering, a face with brown tired wise-knowing eyes a thousand years old, a face that had more quality and character in every little line and wrinkle—and heaven only knew there was no shortage of these—than in a whole battalion of the fringe-haired darlings of contemporary society, the ones in the glossy magazines, the ones who week after week stared out at you with their smooth and beautiful faces, with their beautiful and empty eyes. Put them in the same room as Charlotte Skouras and no one would ever have seen them. Mass-produced carbon copies of chocolate boxes are no kind of competition at all for a great painter's original in oils.

"You are very kind, Anthony." Charlotte Skouras had a deep slow slightly-foreign accented voice and, just then, a tired strained smile that accorded well with the darkness under the brown eyes. "But I am never bored. Truly. You know that."

"With this lot as guests?" Skouras's smile was as broad as ever. "A Skouras board meeting in the Western Isles instead of your blue-blooded favourites on a cruise in the Levant? Take Dollmann here." He nodded to the man by his side, a tall thin bespectacled character with receding thin dark hair who looked as if he needed a shave but didn't. John Dollmann, the managing director of the Skouras shipping lines. "Eh, John? How do you rate yourself as a substitute for young Viscount Horley? The one with sawdust in his head and fifteen million in the bank?"

"Poorly, I'm afraid, Sir Anthony." Dollmann was as urbane as Skouras himself, as apparently unconscious of anything untoward in the atmosphere. "Very poorly. I've a great deal more brains, a great deal less money and I've no pretensions to being a gay and witty conversationalist."

"Young Horley *was* rather the life and soul of the party, wasn't he? Especially when I wasn't around," Skouras added thoughtfully. He looked at me. "You know him, Mr. Petersen?"

72

"I've heard of him. I don't move in those circles, Sir Anthony."
Urbane as all hell, that was me.

"Um." Skouras looked quizzically at the two men sitting close
by myself. One, rejoicing in the good Anglo-Saxon name of
Hermann Lavorski, a big jovial twinkling-eyed man with a great
booming laugh and an inexhaustible supply of risqué stories, was,
I'd been told, his accountant and financial adviser. I'd never seen
anyone less like an accountant and finance wizard, so that probably made him the best in the business. The other, a middle-
aged, balding, Sphinx-faced character with a drooping handle-
bar moustache of the type once sported by Wild Bill Hickock and
a head that cried out for a bowler hat, was Lord Charnley, who, in
spite of his title, found it necessary to work as a broker in the
City to make ends meet. "And how would you rate our two good
friends here, Charlotte?" This with another wide and friendly
smile at his wife.

"I'm afraid I don't understand." Charlotte Skouras looked at
her husband steadily, not smiling.

"Come now, come now, of course you do understand. I'm still
talking about the poor company I provide for so young and
attractive a woman as you." He looked at Hunslett. "She *is* a
young and attractive woman, don't you think, Mr. Hunslett?"

"Well, now." Hunslett leaned back in his armchair, fingers
judiciously steepled, an urbanely sophisticated man entering into
the spirit of things. "What is youth, Sir Anthony? I don't know."
He smiled across at Charlotte Skouras. "Mrs. Skouras will never
be old. As for attractive—well, it's a bit superfluous to ask that.
For ten million European men—and for myself—Mrs. Skouras
was the most attractive actress of her time."

"*Was*, Mr. Hunslett? *Was?*" Old Skouras was leaning forward
in his chair now, the smile a shadow of its former self. "But now,
Mr. Hunslett?"

"Mrs. Skouras's producers must have employed the worst
cameramen in Europe." Hunslett's dark, saturnine face gave
nothing away. He smiled at Charlotte Skouras. "If I may be
pardoned so personal a remark."

73

If I'd had a sword in my hand and the authority to use it, I'd have knighted Hunslett on the spot. After, of course, having first had a swipe at Skouras.

"The days of chivalry are not yet over," Skouras smiled. I saw MacCallum and Biscarte, the bearded banker, stir uncomfortably in their seats. It was damnably awkward. Skouras went on: "I only meant, my dear, that Charnley and Lavorski here are poor substitutes for sparkling young company like Welshblood, the young American oil man, or Domenico, that Spanish count with the passion for amateur astronomy. The one who used to take you on the afterdeck to point out the stars in the Ægean." He looked again at Charnley and Lavorski. "I'm sorry, gentlemen, you just wouldn't do at all."

"I don't know if I'm all that insulted," Lavorski said comfortably. "Charnley and I have our points. Um—I haven't seen young Domenico around for quite some time." He'd have made an excellent stage feed man, would Lavorski, trained to say his lines at exactly the right time.

"You won't see him around for a very much longer time," Skouras said grimly. "At least not in my yacht or in any of my houses." A pause. "Or near anything I own. I promised him I'd see the colour of his noble Castilian blood if I ever clapped eyes on him again." He laughed suddenly. "I must apologise for even bringing that nonentity's name into the conversation. Mr. Hunslett. Mr. Petersen. Your glasses are empty."

"You've been very kind, Sir Anthony. We've enjoyed ourselves immensely." Bluff old, stupid old Calvert, too obtuse to notice what was going on. "But we'd like to get back. It's blowing up badly to-night and Hunslett and I would like to move the *Firecrest* into the shelter of Garve Island." I rose to a window, pulling one of his Afghanistan or whatever curtains to one side. It felt as heavy as a stage fire curtain, no wonder he needed stabilisers with all that topweight on. "That's why we left our riding and cabin lights on. To see if we'd moved. She dragged a fair bit earlier this evening."

"So soon? So soon?" He sounded genuinely disappointed.

"But of course, if you're worried——" He pressed a button, not the one for the steward, and the saloon door opened. The man who entered was a small weatherbeaten character with two gold stripes on his sleeves. Captain Black, the *Shangri-la*'s captain. He'd accompanied Skouras when we'd been briefly shown around the *Shangri-la* after arriving aboard, a tour that had included an inspection of the smashed radio transmitter. No question about it, their radio was well and truly out of action.

"Ah, Captain Black. Have the tender brought alongside at once, will you. Mr. Petersen and Mr. Hunslett are anxious to get back to the *Firecrest* as soon as possible."

"Yes, sir. I'm afraid there'll be a certain delay, Sir Anthony."

"Delay?" Old Skouras could put a frown in his voice without putting one on his face.

"The old trouble, I'm afraid," Captain Black said apologetically.

"Those bloody carburettors," Skouras swore. "You were right, Captain Black, you were right. Last tender I'll ever have with petrol engines fitted. Let me know as soon as she's all right. And detail one of the hands to keep an eye on the *Firecrest* to see that she doesn't lose position. Mr. Petersen's afraid she'll drag."

"Don't worry, sir." I didn't know whether Black was speaking to Skouras or myself. "She'll be all right."

He left. Skouras spent some time in extolling diesel engines and cursing petrol ones, pressed some more whisky on Hunslett and myself and ignored my protests, which were based less on any dislike of whisky in general or Skouras in particular than on the fact that I didn't consider it very good preparation for the night that lay ahead of me. Just before nine o'clock he pressed a button by his arm rest and the doors of a cabinet automatically opened to reveal a 23-inch TV set.

Uncle Arthur hadn't let me down. The newscaster gave quite a dramatic account of the last message received from the T.S.D.Y. *Moray Rose*, reported not under command and making water fast somewhere to the south of the Island of Skye. A full-scale air and sea search, starting at dawn the next day, was promised.

75

Skouras switched the set off. "The sea's crowded with damn' fools who should never be allowed outside a canal basin. What's the latest on the weather? Anyone know?"

"There was a Hebrides Force 8 warning on the 1758 shipping forecast," Charlotte Skouras said quietly. "South-west, they said."

"Since when did you start listening to forecasts?" Skouras demanded. "Or to the radio at all? But of course, my dear, I'd forgotten. Not so much to occupy your time these days, have you? Force 8 and south-west, eh? And the yacht would be coming down from the Kyle of Lochalsh, straight into it. They must be mad. And they have a radio—they sent a message. That makes them stark staring lunatics. Whether they didn't listen to the forecast or whether they listened and still set out, they must have been lunatics. Get them everywhere."

"Some of those lunatics may be dying, drowning now. Or already drowned," Charlotte Skouras said. The shadows under the brown eyes seemed bigger and darker than ever, but there was still life in those brown eyes.

For perhaps five seconds Skouras, face set, stared at her and I felt that if I snapped my fingers there would be a loud tinkling or crashing sound, the atmosphere was as brittle as that. Then he turned away with a laugh and said to me: "The little woman, eh, Petersen? The little mother—only she has no children. Tell me, Petersen, are you married?"

I smiled at him while debating the wisdom of throwing my whisky glass in his face or clobbering him with something heavy, then decided against it. Apart from the fact that it would only make matters worse, I didn't fancy the swim back to the *Firecrest*. So I smiled and smiled, feeling the knife under the cloak, and said: "Afraid not, Sir Anthony."

"Afraid not? Afraid not?" He laughed his hearty good-fellowship laugh, the kind I can't stand, and went on cryptically: "You're not so young to be sufficiently naïve to talk that way, come now, are you, Mr. Petersen?"

"Thirty-eight and never had a chance," I said cheerfully.

76

"The old story, Sir Anthony. The ones I'd have wouldn't have me. And vice-versa." Which wasn't quite true. The driver of a Bentley with, the doctors had estimated, certainly not less than a bottle of whisky inside him, had ended my marriage before it was two months old—and also accounted for the savagely scarred left side of my face. It was then that Uncle Arthur had prised me from my marine salvage business and since then no girl with any sense would ever have contemplated marrying me if she'd known what my job was. What made it even more difficult was the fact that I couldn't tell her in the first place. And the scars didn't help.

"You don't look a fool to me," Skouras smiled. "If I may say so without offence." That was rich, old Skouras worrying about giving offence. The zip-fastener of a mouth softened into what, in view of his next words, I correctly interpreted in advance as being a nostalgic smile. "I'm joking, of course. It's not all that bad. A man must have his fun. Charlotte?"

"Yes?" The brown eyes wary, watchful.

"There's something I want from our stateroom. Would you——?"

"The stewardess. Couldn't she——?"

"This is personal, my dear. And, as Mr. Hunslett has pointed out, at least by inference, you're a good deal younger than I am." He smiled at Hunslett to show that no offence was intended. "The picture on my dressing-table."

"What!" She suddenly sat forward in her armchair, hands reaching for the fronts of the arm rests as if about to pull herself to her feet. Something touched a switch inside Skouras and the smiling eyes went bleak and hard and cold, changing their direction of gaze fractionally. It lasted only a moment because his wife had caught it even before I did, because she sat forward abruptly, smoothing down the short sleeves of her dress over sun-tanned arms. Quick and smooth, but not quite quick enough. For a period of not more than two seconds the sleeves had ridden nearly all the way up to her shoulders—and nearly four inches below those shoulders each arm had been encircled by a ring of bluish-red bruises. A continuous ring. Not the kind of bruises that are

77

made by blows or finger pressure. The kind that are made by a rope.

Skouras was smiling again, pressing the bell to summon the steward. Charlotte Skouras rose without a further word and hurried quickly from the room. I could have wondered if I'd only imagined this momentary tableau I'd seen, but I knew damned well I hadn't. I was paid not to have an imagination of that kind.

She was back inside a moment, a picture frame maybe six by eight in her hand. She handed it to Skouras and sat down quickly in her own chair. This time she was very careful with the sleeves, without seeming to be.

"My wife, gentlemen," Skouras said. He rose from his arm-chair and handed round a photograph of a dark-eyed, dark-haired woman with a smiling face that emphasised the high Slavonic cheek-bones. "My first wife. Anna. We were married for thirty years. Marriage isn't all that bad. That's Anna, gentle-men."

If I'd a gramme of human decency left in me I should have knocked him down and trampled all over him. For a man to state openly in company that he kept the picture of his former wife by his bedside and then impose upon his present wife the final and utter humiliation and degradation of fetching it was beyond belief. That and the rope-burns on his present wife's arms made him almost too good for shooting. But I couldn't do it, I couldn't do anything about it. The old coot's heart was in his voice and his eyes. If this was acting, it was the most superb acting I had ever seen, the tear that trickled down from his right eye would have rated an Oscar any year since cinema had begun. And if it wasn't acting then it was just the picture of a sad and lonely man, no longer young, momentarily oblivious of this world, gazing desolately at the only thing in this world that he loved, that he ever had loved or ever would love, something gone beyond recall. And that was what it was.

If it hadn't been for the other picture, the picture of the still, proud, humiliated Charlotte Skouras staring sightlessly into the fire, I might have felt a lump in my own throat. As it happened,

I'd no difficulty in restraining my emotion. One man couldn't, however, but it wasn't sympathy for Skouras that got the better of him. MacCallum, the Scots lawyer, pale-faced with outrage, rose to his feet, said something in a thick voice about not feeling well, wished us good night and left. The bearded banker left on his heels. Skouras didn't see them go, he'd fumbled his way back to his seat and was staring before him, his eyes as sightless as those of his wife. Like his wife, he was seeing something in the depths of the flames. The picture lay face down on his knee. He didn't even look up when Captain Black came in and told us the tender was ready to take us back to the *Firecrest*.

When the tender had left us aboard our own boat we waited till it was half-way back to the *Shangri-la*, closed the saloon door, unbuttoned the studded carpet and pulled it back. Carefully I lifted a sheet of newspaper and there, on the thin film of flour spread out on the paper below it, were four perfect sets of footprints. We tried our two for'ard cabins, the engine-room and the after cabin, and the silk threads we'd so laboriously fitted before our departure to the *Shangri-la* were all snapped.

Somebody, two at least to judge from the footprints, had been through the entire length of the *Firecrest*. They could have had at least a clear hour for the job, so Hunslett and I spent a clear hour trying to find out why they had been there. We found nothing, no reason at all.

"Well," I said, "at least we know now why they were so anxious to have us aboard the *Shangri-la*."

"To give them a clear field here? That's why the tender wasn't ready—it was here."

"What else?"

"There's something else. I can't put my finger on it. But there's something else."

"Let me know in the morning. When you call Uncle at midnight, ask him to dig up what information he can on those characters on the *Shangri-la* and about the physician who attended the late Lady Skouras. There's a lot I want to know about the late Lady Skouras." I told him what I wanted to know. "Meantime, let's shift this boat over to Garve Island. I've got to be up at three-thirty—you've all the time for sleep in the world."

I should have listened to Hunslett. Again I should have listened to Hunslett. And again for Hunslett's sake. But I didn't know then that Hunslett was to have time for all the sleep in the world.

4

As the saying went in those parts, it was as black as the earl of hell's waistcoat. The sky was black, the woods were black, and the icy heavy driving rain reduced what little visibility there was to just nothing at all. The only way to locate a tree was to walk straight into it, the only way to locate a dip in the ground was to fall into it. When Hunslett had woken me at three-thirty with a cup of tea he told me that when he'd been speaking to Uncle Arthur at midnight—I'd been asleep—he was left in no doubt that although the helicopter had been laid on Uncle had been most un-enthusiastic and considered the whole thing a waste of time. It was a rare occasion indeed when I ever felt myself in total agree-ment with Uncle Arthur but this was one of those rare occasions.

It was beginning to look as if I'd never even find that damned helicopter anyway. I wouldn't have believed that it could have been so difficult to find one's way across five miles of wooded island at night-time. It wasn't even as if I had to contend with rivers or rushing torrents or cliffs or precipitous clefts in the ground or any kind of dense or tangled vegetation. Torbay was just a moderately wooded gently sloping island and crossing from one side to the other of it would have been only an easy Sunday afternoon stroll for a fairly active octogenarian. I was no octo-genarian, though I felt like one, but then this wasn't a Sunday afternoon.

The trouble had started from the moment I'd landed on the Torbay shore opposite Garve Island. From the moment I'd tried to land. Wearing rubber-soled shoes and trying to haul a rubber dinghy over slippery seaweed-covered rocks, some as much as six feet in diameter, to a shore-line twenty interminable yards away is, even in broad daylight, a bone-breaking job: in pitch darkness it's almost as good a way as any for a potential suicide to finish off the job with efficiency and dispatch. The third time I fell I smashed my torch. Several bone-jarring bruises later my wrist-compass went the same way. The attached depth-gauge, almost inevitably, remained intact. A depth-gauge is a great help in finding your way through a trackless wood at night.

After deflating and caching the dinghy and pump I'd set off along the shore-line remote from the village of Torbay. It was logical that if I followed this long enough I'd be bound to come to the sandy cove at the far end of the island where I was to rendez-vous with the helicopter. It was also logical that, if the tree line came right down to the shore, if that shore was heavily indented with little coves and if I couldn't see where I was going, I'd fall into the sea with a fair degree of regularity. After I'd hauled my-self out for the third time I gave up and struck inland. It wasn't because I was afraid of getting wet—as I hadn't seen much point in wearing a scuba suit for walking through a wood and sitting in a helicopter I'd left it aboard and was already soaked to the skin. Nor was it because of the possibility that the hand distress flares I'd brought along for signalling the helicopter pilot, wrapped though they were in oilskin, might not stand up to this treatment indefinitely. The reason why I was now blundering my blind and painful way through the wood was that if I'd stuck to the shore-line my rate of progress there wouldn't have brought me to the rendezvous before midday.

My only guides were the wind-lashed rain and the lie of the land. The cove I was heading for lay to the east, the near-gale force wind was almost due west, so as long as I kept that cold stinging rain on the back of my neck I'd be heading in approxim-ately the right direction: as a check on that, the Island of Torbay has a spinal hog's back, covered in pines to the top, running its east-west length and when I felt the land falling away to one side or the other it meant I was wandering. But the rain-laden wind swirled unpredictably as the wood alternately thinned and became dense again, the hog's back had offshoots and irregularities and as a result of the combination of the two I lost a great deal of time. Half an hour before dawn—by my watch, that was, it was still as black as the midnight hour—I was beginning to wonder if I could possibly make it in time.

And I was beginning to wonder if the helicopter could make it either. There was no doubt in my mind that it could land—that eastern cove was perfectly sheltered—but whether it could get there at all was another question. I had a vague idea that helicopters were unmanageable above certain wind speeds but had no idea what those wind speeds were. And if the helicopter didn't turn up, then I was faced with the long cold wet trudge back to where I had hidden the dinghy and then an even longer, colder and hungry wait until darkness fell at night and I could get out to the *Firecrest* unseen. Even now, I had only twenty-four hours left. By nightfall I would have only twelve. I began to run.

Fifteen minutes and God knows how many iron-hard tree trunks later I heard it, faint and intermittent at first, then gradually swelling in strength—the clattering roar of a helicopter engine. He was early, damn him, he was far too early, he'd land there, find the place deserted and take off for base again. It says much for my sudden desperate state of mind that it never occurred to me how he could even begin to locate, far less land in, that sandy cove in a condition of darkness that was still only a degree less than total. For a moment I even contemplated lighting a flare to let the pilot know that I was at least there or thereabouts and had the flare half-way out of my pocket before I shoved it back again. The arrangement had been that the flare would be lit only to show the landing strip in the sand: if I lit one there and then he might head for it, strike the tops of the pine trees and that would be the end of that.

I ran even faster. It had been years since I'd run more than a couple of hundred yards and my lungs were already wheezing and gasping like a fractured bellows in a blacksmith's shop. But I ran as hard as I could. I cannoned into trees, I tripped over roots, fell into gullies, had my face whipped time and again by low-spreading branches, but above all I cannoned into those damned trees. I stretched my arms before me but it did no good, I ran into them all the same. I picked up a broken branch I'd tripped over and held it in front of me but no matter how I pointed it the trees always seemed to come at me from another direction. I hit every tree in the Island of Torbay. I felt the way a bowling ball must feel after a hard season in a bowling alley, the only difference, and a notable one, being that whereas the ball knocked the skittles down, the trees knocked me down. Once, twice, three times I heard the sound of the helicopter engine disappearing away to the east, and the third time I was sure he was gone for good. But each time it came back. The sky was lightening to the east now, but still I couldn't see the helicopter: for the pilot, everything below would still be as black as night.

The ground gave way beneath my feet and I fell. I braced myself, arms outstretched, for the impact as I struck the other side of the gully. But my reaching hands found nothing. No impact. I kept on falling, rolling and twisting down a heathery slope, and for the first time that night I would have welcomed the appearance of a pine tree, any kind of tree, to stop my progress. I don't know how many trees there were on that slope, I missed the lot. If it was a gully, it was the biggest gully on the Island of Torbay. But it wasn't a gully at all, it was the end of Torbay. I rolled and bumped over a sudden horizontal grassy bank and landed on my back in soft wet sand. Even while I was whooping and gasping and trying to get my knocked-out breath back into my lungs I still had time to appreciate the fortunate fact that kindly providence and a few million years had changed the jagged rocks that must once have fringed that shore into a nice soft yielding sandy beach.

I got to my feet. This was the place, all right. There was only one such sandy bay, I'd been told, in the east of the Isle of Torbay and there was now enough light for me to see that this was indeed just that, though a lot smaller than it appeared on the chart. The helicopter was coming in again from the east, not, as far as I could judge, more than three or four hundred feet up. I ran half-way down to the water's edge, pulled a hand flare from my pocket, slid away the waterproof covering and tore off the ignition strip. It flared into life at once, a dazzling blue-white magnesium light so blinding that I had to clap my free hand over my eyes. It lasted for only thirty seconds, but that was enough. Even as it fizzled and sputtered its acrid and nostril-wrinkling way to extinction the helicopter was almost directly overhead. Two vertically-downward pointing searchlights, mounted fore and aft on the helicopter, switched on simultaneously, interlocking pools of brilliance on the pale white sand. Twenty seconds later the skids sank into the soft sand, the rackety clangour of the motor died away and the blades idled slowly to a stop. I'd never been in a helicopter in my life but I'd seen plenty: in the half-darkness this looked like the biggest one I'd ever seen.

The right-hand door opened and a torch shone in my face as I approached. A voice, Welsh as the Rhondda Valley, said: "'Morning. You Calvert?"

"Me. Can I come aboard?"

"How do I know you're Calvert?"

"I'm telling you. Don't come the hard man, laddie. You've no authority to make an identification check."

"Have you no proof? No papers?"

"Have you no sense? Haven't you enough sense to know that there are some people who *never* carry any means of identification? Do you think I just happened to be standing here, five miles from nowhere, and that I just happened to be carrying flares in my pocket? You want to join the ranks of the unemployed before sunset?" A very auspicious beginning to our association.

"I was told to be careful." He was as worried and upset as a cat snoozing on a sun-warmed wall. Still a marked lack of cordiality. "Lieutenant Scott Williams, Fleet Air Arm. Takes an admiral to sack me. Step up."

I stepped up, closed the door and sat. He didn't offer to shake hands. He flicked on an overhead light and said: "What the hell's happened to your face?"

"What's the matter with my face?"

"Blood. Hundreds of little scratches."

"Pine needles." I told him what had happened. "Why a

85

machine this size? You could ferry a battalion in this one."

"Fourteen men, to be precise. I do lots of crazy things, Calvert, but I don't fly itsy-bitsy two-bit choppers in this kind of weather. Be blown out of the sky. With only two of us, the long-range tanks are full."

"You can fly all day?"

"More or less. Depends how fast we go. What do you want from me?"

"Civility, for a start. Or don't you like early morning rising?"

"I'm an Air-Sea Rescue pilot, Calvert. This is the only machine on the base big enough to go out looking in this kind of weather. And I should be out looking, not out on some cloak-and-dagger joy-ride. I don't care how important it is, there's people maybe clinging to a life-raft fifty miles out in the Atlantic. That's my job. But I've got my orders. What do you want?"

"The *Moray Rose?*"

"You heard? Yes, that's her."

"She doesn't exist. She never has existed."

"What are you talking about? The news broadcasts——"

"I'll tell you as much as you need to know, Lieutenant. It's essential that I be able to search this area without arousing suspicion. The only way that can be done is by inventing an iron-clad reason. The foundering *Moray Rose* is that reason. So we tell the tale."

"Phoney?"

"Phoney."

"You can fix it?" he said slowly. "You can fix a news broadcast?"

"Yes."

"Maybe you could get me fired at that." He smiled for the first time. "Sorry, sir. Lieutenant Williams—Scotty to you—is now his normal cheerful willing self. What's on?"

"Know the coast-lines and islands of this area well?"

"From the air?"

"Yes."

"I've been here twenty months now. Air-Sea Rescue and in

86

between army and navy exercises and hunting for lost climbers. Most of my work is with the Marine Commandos. I know this area at least as well as any man alive."

"I'm looking for a place where a man could hide a boat. A fairly big boat. Forty feet—maybe fifty. Might be in a big boat-house, might be under over-hanging trees up some creek, might even be in some tiny secluded harbour normally invisible from the sea. Between Islay and Skye."

"Well, now, is that all. Have you any idea how many hundreds of miles of coastline there is in that lot, taking in all the islands? Maybe thousands? How long do I have for this job? A month?"

"By sunset to-day. Now, wait. We can cut out all centres of population, and by that I mean anything with more than two or three houses together. We can cut out known fishing grounds. We can cut out regular steamship routes. Does that help?"

"A lot. What are we really looking for?"

"I've told you."

"Okay, okay, so mine is not to reason why. Any idea where you'd like to start, any ideas for limiting the search?"

"Let's go due east to the mainland. Twenty miles up the coast, then twenty south. Then we'll try Torbay Sound and the Isle of Torbay. Then the islands farther west and north."

"Torbay Sound has a steamer service."

"Sorry, I should have said a daily service. Torbay has a bi-weekly service."

"Fasten your seat-belt and get on those earphones. We're going to get thrown around quite a bit to-day. I hope you're a good sailor."

"And the earphones?" They were the biggest I'd ever seen, four inches wide with inch-thick linings of what looked like sorbo rubber. A spring loaded swing microphone was attached to the headband.

"For the ears," the lieutenant said kindly. "So that you don't get perforated drums. And so you won't be deaf for a week after-wards. If you can imagine yourself inside a steel drum in the middle of a boiler factory with a dozen pneumatic chisels hammer-

87

ing outside, you'll have some idea of what the racket is like once we start up."

Even with the earphone muffs on, it sounded exactly like being in a steel drum in a boiler factory with a dozen pneumatic chisels hammering on the outside. The earphones didn't seem to have the slightest effect at all, the noise came hammering and beating at you through every facial and cranial bone, but on the one and very brief occasion when I cautiously lifted one phone to find out what the noise was like without them and if they were really doing any good at all, I found out exactly what Lieutenant Williams meant about perforated drums. He hadn't been joking. But even with them on, after a couple of hours my head felt as if it were coming apart. I looked occasionally at the dark lean face of the young Welshman beside me, a man who had to stand this racket day in, day out, the year round. He looked quite sane to me. I'd have been in a padded cell in a week.

I didn't have to be in that helicopter a week. Altogether, I spent eight hours' flying time in it and it felt like a leap year.

Our first run northwards up the mainland coast produced what was to be the first of many false alarms that day. Twenty minutes after leaving Torbay we spotted a river, a small one but still a river, flowing into the sea. We followed it upstream for a mile, then suddenly the trees, crowding down close to the banks on both sides, met in the middle where the river seemed to run through some rocky gorge.

I shouted into the microphone: "I want to see what's there."

Williams nodded. "We passed a place a quarter of a mile back. I'll set you down."

"You've got a winch. Couldn't you lower me?"

"When you know as much as I do about the effect of forty to fifty mile an hour winds in steep-sided valleys," he said, "you'll never talk about such things. Not even in a joke. I want to take this kite home again."

So he turned back and set me down without much difficulty in the shelter of a bluff. Five minutes later I'd reached the beginning

88

of the overhanging stretch. Another five minutes and I was back in the helicopter.

"What luck?" the lieutenant asked.

"No luck. An ancient oak tree right across the river, just at the entrance to the overhang."

"Could be shifted."

"It weighs two or three tons, it's imbedded feet deep in the mud and it's been there for years."

"Well, well, we can't be right first time, every time."

A few more minutes and another river mouth. It hardly looked big enough to take a boat of any size, but we turned up anyway. Less than half a mile from its mouth the river foamed whitely as it passed through rapids. We turned back.

By the time it was fully daylight we had reached the northern limit of possibility in this area. Steep-sided mountains gave way to precipitous cliffs that plunged almost vertically into the sea.

"How far does this go north?" I asked.

"Ten, twelve miles to the head of Loch Lairg."

"Know it?"

"Flown up there a score of times."

"Caves?"

"Nary a cave."

I hadn't really thought that there would be. "How about the other side?" I pointed to the west where the mountainous shore-line, not five miles away yet barely visible through the driving rain and low scudding cloud, ran in an almost sheer drop from the head of Loch Lairg to the entrance to Torbay Sound.

"Even the gulls can't find a foothold there. Believe me."

I believed him. We flew back the way we had come as far as our starting point on the coast, then continued southwards. From the Isle of Torbay to the mainland the sea was an almost unbroken mass of foaming white, big white-capped rollers marching east-wards across the darkened firth, long creamy lines of spume torn from the wave-tops veining the troughs between. There wasn't a single craft in sight, even the big drifters had stayed at home, it was as bad as that. In that buffeting gale-force wind our big helicopter was having a bad time of it now, violently shaking and swaying like an out-of-control express train in the last moments before it leaves the track: one hour's flying in those conditions had turned me against helicopters for life. But when I thought of what it would be like down there in a boat in that seething mælstrom of a firth I could feel a positive bond of attachment growing between me and that damned helicopter.

We flew twenty miles south—if the way we were being jarred and flung through the air could be called flying—but covered sixty miles in that southing. Every little sound between the islands and the mainland, every natural harbour, every sea-loch and inlet had to be investigated. We flew very low most of the time, not much above two hundred feet: sometimes we were forced down to a hundred feet—so heavy was the rain and so powerful the wind now battering against the streaming windscreen that the wipers were almost useless and we had to get as low as possible to see anything at all. As it was, I don't think we missed a yard of the coastline of the mainland or the close inshore islands. We saw everything. And we saw nothing.

I looked at my watch. Nine-thirty. The day wearing on and nothing achieved. I said: "How much more of this can the helicopter stand?"

"I've been 150 miles out over the Atlantic in weather a damn' sight worse than this." Lieutenant Williams showed no signs of strain or anxiety or fatigue, if anything he seemed to be enjoying himself. "The point is how much more can *you* stand?"

"Very little. But we'll have to. Back to where you picked me up and we'll make a circuit of the coast of Torbay. South coast first, then north up the west coast, then east past Torbay and down the southern shore of the Sound."

"Yours to command." Williams brought the helicopter round to the north-west in a swinging side-slipping movement that didn't do my stomach any good. "You'll find coffee and sandwiches in that box there." I left the sandwiches and coffee where they were.

It took us almost forty minutes to cover the twenty-five miles to the eastern tip of the Isle of Torbay, that wind took us two steps back for every three forward. Visibility was so bad that Williams flew on instruments the whole way and with that violent cross-wind blowing he should have missed our target by miles. Instead he hit that sandy cove right on the nose as if he'd been flying in on a radio beacon. I was beginning to have a very great deal of confidence in Williams, a man who knew exactly what he was doing: I was beginning to have no confidence at all in myself and to wonder if I had any idea in the world what I was doing. I thought about Uncle Arthur and quickly decided I'd rather think about something else.

"There," Williams pointed. We were about half-way along the south coast of Torbay. "A likely set-up, wouldn't you say?"

And a likely set-up it was. A large white three-storey stone-built Georgian house, set in a clearing about a hundred yards back from and thirty yards above the shore. There are dozens of such houses scattered in the most unlikely positions in some of the most barren and desolate islands in the Hebrides. Heaven only knew who built them, why or how. But it wasn't the house that was the focal point of interest in this case, it was the big boat-house on the edge of a tiny land-locked harbour. Without a further word from me Williams brought the big machine down neatly in the shelter of the trees behind the house.

I unwrapped the polythene bag I'd been carrying under my shirt. Two guns. The Luger I stuck in my pocket, the little German Lilliput I fixed to the spring clip in my left sleeve. Williams stared unconcernedly ahead and began to whistle to himself.

Nobody had lived in that house for years. Part of the roof had fallen in, years of salt air erosion had removed all paintwork and the rooms, when I looked in through the cracked and broken windows, were bare and crumbling with long strips of wall-paper lying on the floor. The path down to the little harbour was completely overgrown with moss. Every time my heel sunk into the path a deep muddy mark was left behind, the first made there for a long long time. The boatshed was big enough, at least sixty by twenty, but that was all that could be said for it. The two big doors had three hinges apiece and two huge padlocks where they met in the middle. Padlocks and hinges alike were almost eaten through by rust. I could feel the heavy tug of the Luger in my pocket and the weight made me feel faintly ridiculous. I went back to the helicopter.

Twice more in the next twenty minutes we came across almost identical situations. Big white Georgian houses with big boat-houses at their feet. I knew they would be false alarms but I had to check them both. False alarms they were. The last occupants of those houses had been dead before I'd been born. People had lived in those houses once, people with families, big families, people with money and ambition and confidence and no fear at all of the future. Not if they had built houses as big as those. And now the people were gone and all that was left were those crumbl-ing, mouldering monuments to a misplaced faith in the future. Some years previously I'd seen houses in plantations in South Carolina and Georgia, houses widely dissimilar but exactly the same, white-porticoed ante-bellum houses hemmed in by ever-green live oaks and overgrown with long grey festoons of Spanish moss. Sadness and desolation and a world that was gone for ever.

The west coast of the Isle of Torbay yielded nothing. We gave the town of Torbay and Garve Island a wide berth and flew east-wards down the southern shore of the Sound with the gale behind us. Two small hamlets, each with its disintegrating pier. Beyond that, nothing.

We reached the sandy cove again, flew north till we reached the northern shore of the Sound, then westwards along this shore. We stopped twice, once to investigate a tree-overhung land-locked harbour less than forty yards in diameter, and again to investigate a small complex of industrial buildings which had once, so Williams said, produced a fine-quality sand that had been one of the ingredients in a famous brand of toothpaste. Again, nothing.

At the last place we stopped for five minutes. Lieutenant Williams said he was hungry. I wasn't. I'd become used to the helicopter by now but I wasn't hungry. It was midday. Half our time gone and nothing accomplished. And it was beginning to look very much as if nothing was going to be accomplished. Uncle Arthur would be pleased. I took the chart from Williams.

"We have to pick and choose," I said. "We'll have to take a chance. We'll go up the Sound to Dolman Head, opposite Garve Island, then go up Loch Hynart." Loch Hynart was a seven mile long loch, winding and many-islanded, that ran more or less due east, nowhere more than half a mile wide, deep into the heart of the mountain massif. "Back to Dolman Point again then along the southern shore of the mainland peninsula again as far as Carrara Point. Then east along the southern shore of Loch Houron."

"Loch Houron," Williams nodded. "The wildest waters and the worst place for boats in the West of Scotland. Last place I'd go looking, Mr. Calvert, that's for sure. From all accounts you'll find nothing there but wrecks and skeletons. There are more reefs and skerries and underwater rocks and overfalls and whirlpools and tidal races in twenty miles there than in the whole of the rest of Scotland. Local fishermen won't go near the place." He pointed at the chart. "See this passage between Dubh Sgeir and Ballara Island, the two islands at the mouth of Loch Houron? That's the most feared spot of all. You should see the grip the fishermen get on their whisky glasses when they talk about it. Beul nan Uamh, it's called. The mouth of the grave."

"They're a cheery lot, hereabouts. It's time we were gone."

The wind blew as strongly as ever, the sea below looked as wicked as ever, but the rain had stopped and that made our search all that much easier. The stretch of the Sound from the sand quarry to Dolman Point yielded nothing. Neither did Loch Hynart. Between Loch Hynart and Carrara Point, eight miles to the west, there were only two tiny hamlets crouched against the water's edge, their backs to the barren hills behind, their inhabitants—if there were any inhabitants—subsisting on God alone knew what. Carrara Point was storm-torn desolation itself. Great jagged broken fissured cliffs, huge fanged rocks rising from the sea, massive Atlantic breakers smashing in hundred foot high spray against the cliffs, the rocks and the tiny-seeming lighthouse at the foot of the cliffs. If I were Sir Billy Butlin looking for the

93

site for my latest holiday camp, I wouldn't have spent too much time on Carrara Point.

We turned north now, then north-east, then east, along the southern shore of Loch Houron.

Many places have evil reputations. Few, at first seeing, live up to those reputations. But there are a few. In Scotland, the Pass of Glencoe, the scene of the infamous massacre, is one of them. The Pass of Brander is another. And Loch Houron was beyond all doubt another.

It required no imagination at all to see this as a dark and deadly and dangerous place. It looked dark and deadly and dangerous. The shores were black and rocky and precipitous and devoid of any form of vegetation at all. The four islands strung out in a line to the east were a splendid match for the hospitable appearance of the shores. In the far distance the northern and the southern shores of the loch came close together and vanished in a towering vertical cleft in the sinister brooding mountains. In the lee of the islands the loch was black as midnight but elsewhere it was a seething boiling white, the waters wickedly swirling, churning, spinning in evil-looking whirlpools as it passed across overfalls or forced its way through the narrow channels between the islands or between the islands and the shore. Water in torment. In the Beul nan Uamh—the mouth of the grave—between the first two islands the rushing leaping milk-white waters looked like floodwater in the Mackenzie river rapids in springtime, when the snows melt. A yachtsman's paradise. Only a madman would take his boat into these waters.

Apparently there were still a few madmen around. We'd just left the first of the islands, Dubh Sgeir, to port, when I caught sight of a narrow break in the cliffs on the southern mainland. A small rock-girt bay, if bay it could be called, about the size of a couple of tennis courts, almost completely enclosed from the sea, the entrance couldn't have been more than ten yards wide. I glanced at the chart—Little Horseshoe Bay, it was called. Not original, but very apt. There was a boat in there, a fairly big one, a converted M.F.V. by the looks of her, anchored fore and aft in the middle of the bay. Behind the bay was a little plateau, mossy or grass-covered, I couldn't tell which, and, behind that, what looked like a dried-up river bed rising steeply into the hills behind. On the little plateau were four khaki-coloured tents, with men working at them.

"This could be it?" Williams said.

"This could be it."

This wasn't it. A glance at the thin, wispy-bearded, pebble-bespectacled lad who came hurrying forward to greet me when I stepped on to the ground was all the proof I required that this was indeed not it. Another glance at the seven or eight bearded, scarved and duffel-coated characters behind him who had not, as I'd thought, been working but were struggling to prevent their tents from being blown away by the wind, was almost superfluous proof. That lot couldn't have hi-jacked a rowing boat. The M.F.V., I could see now, was down by the stern and listing heavily to starboard.

"Hallo, hallo, hallo," said the character with the wispy beard. "Good afternoon, good afternoon. By Jove, are we glad to see you!"

I looked at him, shook the outstretched hand, glanced at the listing boat and said mildly: "You may be shipwrecked, but those are hardly what I'd call desperate straits. You're not on a deserted island. You're on the mainland. Help is at hand!"

"Oh, we know where we are all right." He waved a deprecating hand. "We put in here three days ago but I'm afraid our boat was holed in a storm during the night. Most unfortunate, most inconvenient."

"Holed as she lay there? Just as she's moored now?"

"Yes, indeed."

"Bad luck. Oxford or Cambridge?"

"Oxford, of course." He seemed a bit huffed at my ignorance. "Combined geological and marine biological party."

"No shortage of rocks and sea-water hereabouts," I agreed. "How bad is the damage?"

"A holed plank. Sprung. Too much for us, I'm afraid."

95

"All right for food?"

"Of course."

"No transmitter?"

"Receiver only."

"The helicopter pilot will radio for a shipwright and engineer to be sent out as soon as the weather moderates. Good-bye."

His jaw fell about a couple of inches. "You're off? Just like that?"

"Air-Sea Rescue. Vessel reported sinking last night."

"Ah, that. We heard."

"Thought you might be it. Glad for your sakes you're not. We've a lot of ground to cover yet."

We continued eastwards towards the head of Loch Houron. Half-way there I said: "Far enough. Let's have a look at those four islands out in the loch. We'll start with the most easterly one first of all—what's it called, yes, Eilean Oran—then make our way back towards the mouth of Loch Houron again."

"You said you wanted to go all the way to the top."

"I've changed my mind."

"You're the man who pays the piper," he said equably. He was a singularly incurious character, was young Lieutenant Williams. "Northward ho for Eilean Oran."

We were over Eilean Oran in three minutes. Compared to Eilean Oran, Alcatraz was a green and lovely holiday resort. Half a square mile of solid rock and never a blade of grass in sight. But there was a house. A house with smoke coming from its chimney. And beside it a boatshed, but no boat. The smoke meant an inhabitant, at least one inhabitant, and however he earned his living he certainly didn't do it from tilling the good earth. So he would have a boat, a boat for fishing for his livelihood, a boat for transportation to the mainland, for one certain thing among the manifold uncertainties of this world was that no passenger vessel had called at Eilean Oran since Robert Fulton had invented the steamboat. Williams set me down not twenty yards from the shed.

I rounded the corner of the boat-house and stopped abruptly.

96

I always stop abruptly when I'm struck in the stomach by a battering-ram. After a few minutes I managed to whoop enough air into my lungs to let me straighten up again.

He was tall, gaunt, grey, in his middle sixties. He hadn't shaved for a week or changed his collarless shirt in a month. It wasn't a battering-ram he'd used after all, it was a gun, none of your fancy pistols, just a good old-fashioned double-barrelled twelve-bore shotgun, the kind of gun that at close range—six inches in this case—can give points even to the Peacemaker Colt when it comes to blowing your head off. He had it aimed at my right eye. It was like staring down the Mersey tunnel. When he spoke I could see he'd missed out on all those books that laud the unfailing courtesy of the Highlander.

"And who the hell are you?" he snarled.

"My name's Johnson. Put that gun away. I——"

"And what the hell do you want here?"

"How about trying the 'Ceud Mile Failte' approach?" I said. "You see it everywhere in those parts. A hundred thousand welcomes——"

"I won't ask again, mister."

"Air-Sea Rescue. There's a missing boat——"

"I haven't seen any boat. You can just get to hell of my island." He lowered his gun till it pointed at my stomach, maybe because he thought it would be more effective there or make for a less messy job when it came to burying me. "Now!"

I nodded to the gun. "You could get prison for this."

"Maybe I could and maybe I couldn't. All I know is that I don't like strangers on my island and that Donald MacEachern protects his own."

"And a very good job you make of it, too, Donald," I said approvingly. The gun moved and I said quickly: "I'm off. And don't bother saying 'haste ye back' for I won't be."

As we rose from the island Williams said: "I just caught a glimpse. That was a gun he had there?"

"It wasn't the outstretched hand of friendship they're always talking about in those parts," I said bitterly.

97

"Who is he? What is he?"

"He's an undercover agent for the Scottish Tourist Board in secret training to be their goodwill ambassador abroad. He's not any of those I'm looking for, that I know. He's not a nut case, either—he's as sane as you are. He's a worried man and a desperate one."

"You didn't look in the shed. You wanted to find out about a boat. Maybe there was someone pointing a gun at him."

"That was one of the thoughts that accounted for my rapid departure. I could have taken the gun from him."

"You could have got your head blown off."

"Guns are my business. The safety catch was in the 'On' position."

"Sorry." Williams's face showed how out of his depth he was, he wasn't as good at concealing his expression as I was. "What now?"

"Island number two to the west here." I glanced at the chart. "Craigmore."

"You'll be wasting your time going there." He sounded very positive. "I've been there. Flew out a badly injured man to a Glasgow hospital."

"Injured how?"

"He'd cut himself to the thigh-bone with a flensing knife. Infection had set in."

"A flensing knife? For whales? I'd never heard——"

"For sharks. Basking sharks. They're as common as mackerel hereabouts. Catch them for their livers—you can get a ton of liver oil from a good-sized one." He pointed to the chart, to a tiny mark on the north coast. "Craigmore village. Been abandoned, they say, from before the First World War. We're coming up to it now. Some of those old boys built their homes in the damndest places."

Some of those old boys had indeed built their homes in the damndest places. If I'd been compelled to build a home either there or at the North Pole I'd have been hard put to it to make a choice. A huddle of four small grey houses built out near the tip of a foreland, several wicked reefs that made a natural break-water, an even more wicked-looking entrance through the reefs and two fishing boats swinging and rolling wildly at anchor inside the reefs. One of the houses, the one nearest the shore, had had its entire seaward wall cut away. On the twenty or thirty feet of sloping ground that separated the house from the sea I could see three unmistakable sharks. A handful of men appeared at the open end of the house and waved at us.

"That's their flensing shed," Williams said. "Haul them from the water straight up inside."

"It's one way of making a living. Can you put me down?"

"What do you think, Mr. Calvert?"

"I don't think you can." Not unless he set his helicopter down on top of one of the little houses, that was. "You winched this sick man up?"

"Yes. And I'd rather not winch you down, if you don't mind. Not in this weather and not without a crewman to help me. Unless you're desperate."

"Not all that desperate. Would you vouch for them?"

"I'd vouch for them. They're a good bunch. I've met the boss, Tim Hutchinson, an Aussie about the size of a house, several times. Most of the fishermen on the west coast would vouch for them."

"Fair enough. The next island is Ballara."

We circled Ballara once. Once was enough. Not even a barnacle would have made his home in Ballara.

We were over the channel between Ballara and Dubh Sgeir now and the Beul nan Uamh was a sight to daunt even the stoutest-hearted fish. It certainly daunted me, five minutes in that lot whether in a boat or scuba suit and that would have been that. The ebb-tide and the wind were in head-on collision and the result was the most spectacular witches' cauldron I'd ever seen. There were no waves as such, just a bubbling swirling seething mælstrom of whirlpools, overfalls and races, running no way and every way, gleaming boiling white in the overfalls and races, dark and smooth and evil in the hearts of the whirlpools. Not a place to take Aunty

Gladys out in a row-boat for a gentle paddle in the quiet even fall.

Oddly enough, close in to the east and south coast of Dubh Sgeir, one *could* have taken Aunty Gladys out. In those tidal races between islands a common but not yet clearly understood phenomenon frequently leaves an undisturbed stretch of water close in to one or other of the shores, calm and smooth and flat, a millpond with a sharply outlined boundary between it and the foaming races beyond. So it was here. For almost a mile between the most southerly and easterly headlands of Dubh Sgeir, for a distance of two or three hundred yards out from the shore, the waters were black and still. It was uncanny.

"Sure you really want to land here?" Williams asked.

"Is it tricky?"

"Easy. Helicopters often land on Dubh Sgeir. Not mine—others. It's just that you're likely to get the same reception here as you got on Eilean Oran. There are dozens of privately owned islands off the West Coast and none of them likes uninvited visitors. The owner of Dubh Sgeir hates them."

"This world-famous Highland hospitality becomes positively embarrassing at times. The Scotsman's home is his castle, eh?"

"There *is* a castle here. The ancestral home of the Clan Dalwhinnie. I think."

"Dalwhinnie's a town, not a clan."

"Well, something unpronounceable." That was good, considering that he like as not hailed from Rhosllanerchrugog or Pontrhydfendgaid. "He's the clan chief. Lord Kirkside. Ex-Lord Lieutenant of the shire. Very important citizen but a bit of a recluse now. Seldom leaves the place except to attend Highland Games or go south about once a month to flay the Archbishop of Canterbury in the Lords."

"Must be difficult for him to tell which place he's at, at times. I've heard of him. Used to have a very low opinion of the Commons and made a long speech to that effect every other day."

"That's him. But not any more. Lost his older son—and his future son-in-law—in an air accident some time ago. Took the heart from the old boy, so they say. People in these parts think the world of him."

We were round to the south of Dubh Sgeir now and suddenly the castle was in sight. Despite its crenellated battlements, round towers and embrasures, it didn't begin to rank with the Windsors and Balmorals of this world. A pocket castle. But the site had the Windsors and Balmorals whacked to the wide. It grew straight out of the top of a hundred and fifty foot cliff and if you leaned too far out of your bedroom window the first thing to stop your fall would be the rocks a long long way down. You wouldn't even bounce once.

Below the castle and a fair way to the right of it a cliff-fall belonging to some bygone age had created an artificial foreshore some thirty yards wide. From this, obviously at the cost of immense labour, an artificial harbour had been scooped out, the boulders and rubble having been used for the construction of a horseshoe breakwater with an entrance of not more than six or seven yards in width. At the inner end of this harbour a boat-house, no wider than the harbour entrance and less than twenty feet in length, had been constructed against the cliff face. A boat-house to berth a good-sized row-boat, no more.

Williams took his machine up until we were two hundred feet above the castle. It was built in the form of a hollow square with the landward side missing. The seaward side was dominated by two crenellated towers, one topped by a twenty-foot flagpole and flag, the other by an even taller TV mast. Aesthetically, the flag-pole had it every time. Surprisingly the island was not as barren as it had appeared from the sea. Beginning some distance from the castle and extending clear to the cliff-bound northern shore of the island ran a two hundred yard wide stretch of what seemed to be flat smooth turf, not the bowling green standard but undoubtedly grass of the genuine variety as testified to by the heads down position of a handful of goats that browsed close to the castle. Williams tried to land on the grass but the wind was too strong to allow him to hold position: he finally put down in the eastern lee of the castle, close but not too close to the cliff edge.

I got out, keeping a wary eye on the goats, and was rounding the landward corner of the castle when I almost literally bumped into the girl.

I've always known what to look for in a suddenly-encountered girl in a remote Hebridean Island. A kilt, of course, a Hebridean girl without a kilt was unthinkable, a Shetland two-piece and brown brogues: and that she would be a raven-haired beauty with wild, green, fey eyes went without saying. Her name would be Deirdre. This one wasn't like that at all, except for the eyes, which were neither green nor fey but certainly looked wild enough. What little I could see of them, that was. Her blonde hair was cut in the uniform peekabo scalloped style of the day, the one where the long side hair meets under the chin and the central fringe is hacked off at eyebrow level, a coiffure which in any wind above Force 1 allows no more than ten per cent of the face to be seen at any one time. Below hair level she wore a horizontally striped blue and white sailor's jersey and faded blue denim pants that must have been fixed on with a portable sewing machine as I didn't see how else she could have got into them. Her tanned feet were bare. It was comforting to see that the civilising influence of television reached even the remoter outposts of empire.

I said: "Good afternoon, Miss—um——"

"Engine failure?" she asked coldly.

"Well, no——"

"Mechanical failure? Of any kind? No? Then this is private property. I must ask you to leave. At once, please."

There seemed to be little for me here. An outstretched hand and a warm smile of welcome and she'd have been on my list of suspects at once. But this was true to established form, the weary stranger at the gates receiving not the palm of the hand but the back of it. Apart from the fact that she lacked a blunderbuss and had a much better figure, she had a great deal in common with Mr. MacEachern. I bent forward to peer through the wind-blown camouflage of blonde hair. She looked as if she had spent most of the night and half the morning down in the castle wine-cellars. Pale face, pale lips, dark smudges under the blue-grey eyes. But clear blue-grey eyes.

"What the hell's the matter with you?" she demanded.

"Nothing. The end of a dream. Deirdre would never have talked like that. Where's your old man?"

"My old man?" The one eye I could see had the power turned up to its maximum shrivelling voltage. "You mean my father?"

"Sorry. Lord Kirkside." It was no feat to guess that she was Lord Kirkside's daughter, hired help are too ignorant to have the execrable manners of their aristocratic betters.

"I'm Lord Kirkside." I turned round to see the owner of the deep voice behind me, a tall rugged-looking character in his fifties, hawk nose, jutting grey eyebrows and moustache, grey tweeds, grey deer-stalker, hawthorn stick in hand. "What's the trouble, Sue?"

Sue. I might have known. Exit the last vestige of the Hebridean dream. I said: "My name is Johnson. Air-Sea Rescue. There was a boat, the *Moray Rose*, in bad trouble somewhere south of Skye. If she'd been not under command but still afloat she might have come drifting this way. We wondered——"

"And Sue was going to fling you over the cliff before you had a chance to open your mouth?" He smiled down affectionately at his daughter. "That's my Sue. I'm afraid she doesn't like newspapermen."

"Some do and some don't. But why pick on me?"

"When you were twenty-one could you, as the saying goes, tell a newspaperman from a human being? I couldn't. But I can now, a mile away. I can also tell a genuine Air-Sea Rescue helicopter when I see one. And so should you too, young lady. I'm sorry, Mr. Johnson, we can't help you. My men and I spent several hours last night patrolling the cliff-tops to see if we could see anything. Lights, flares, anything. Nothing, I'm afraid."

"Thank you, sir. I wish we had more voluntary co-operation of this kind." From where I stood I could see, due south, the gently rocking masts of the Oxford field expedition's boat in Little Horseshoe Bay. The boat itself and the tents beyond were hidden behind the rocky eastern arm of the bay. I said to Lord Kirkside: "But why newspapermen, sir? Dubh Sgeir isn't quite as accessible as Westminster."

"Indeed, Mr. Johnson." He smiled, not with his eyes. "You may have heard of—well, of our family tragedy. My elder boy, Jonathon, and John Rollinson—Sue's fiancé."

I knew what was coming. And after all those months she had those smudges under her eyes. She must have loved him a lot. I could hardly believe it.

"I'm no newspaperman, sir. Prying isn't my business." It wasn't my business, it was my life, the *raison d'être* for my existence. But now wasn't the time to tell him.

"The air accident. Jonathon had his own private Beechcraft." He waved towards the stretch of green turf running to the northern cliffs. "He took off from here that morning. They—the reporters —wanted on-the-spot reporting. They came by helicopter and boat—there's a landing stage to the west." Again the mirthless smile. "They weren't well received. Care for a drink? You and your pilot?" Lord Kirkside, for all the reputation Williams had given him, seemed to be cast in a different mould from his daughter and Mr. Donald MacEachern: on the other hand, as the Archbishop of Canterbury knew to his cost, Lord Kirkside was a very much tougher citizen than either his daughter or Mr. MacEachern.

"Thank you, sir. I appreciate that. But we haven't many hours of daylight left."

"Of course, of course. How thoughtless of me. But you can't have much hope left by this time."

"Frankly, none. But, well, you know how it is, sir."

"We'll cross our fingers for that one chance in a million. Good luck, Mr. Johnson." He shook my hand and turned away. His daughter hesitated then held out her hand and smiled. A fluke of the wind had blown the hair off her face, and when she smiled like that, sooty eyes or not, the end of Deirdre and the Hebridean dream didn't seem to be of so much account after all. I went back to the helicopter.

"We're getting low on both fuel and time," Williams said. "Another hour or so and we'll have the dark with us. Where now, Mr. Calvert?"

"North. Follow this patch of grass—seems it used to be used as a light aircraft runway—out over the edge of the cliff. Take your time."

So he did, taking his time as I'd asked him, then continued on a northward course for another ten minutes. After we were out of sight of watchers on any of the islands we came round in a great half circle to west and south and east and headed back for home.

The sun was down and the world below was more night than day as we came in to land on the sandy cove on the eastern side of the Isle of Torbay. I could just vaguely distinguish the blackness of the tree-clad island, the faint silvery gleam of the sand and the semicircular whiteness where the jagged reef of rocks fringed the seaward approach to the cove. It looked a very dicey approach indeed to me but Williams was as unworried as a mother at a baby-show who has already slipped the judge a five-pound note. Well, if he wasn't going to worry, neither was I: I knew nothing about helicopters but I knew enough about men to recognise a superb pilot when I sat beside one. All I had to worry about was that damned walk back through those Stygian woods. One thing, I didn't have to run this time.

Williams reached up his hand to flick on the landing lights, but the light came on a fraction of a second before his fingers touched the switch. Not from the helicopter but from the ground. A bright light, a dazzling light, at least a five-inch searchlight located between the high-water line of the cove and the tree-line beyond. For a moment the light wavered, then steadied on the cockpit of the helicopter, making the interior bright as the light from the noon-day sun. I twisted my head to one side to avoid the glare. I saw Williams throw up a hand to protect his eyes, then slump forward wearily, dead in his seat, as the white linen of his shirt turned to red and the centre of his chest disintegrated. I flung myself forwards and downwards to try to gain what illusory shelter I could from the cannonading sub-machine shells shattering the windscreen. The helicopter was out of control, dipping sharply forwards and spinning slowly on its axis. I reached out to grab the controls from the dead man's hands but even as I did the trajectory of the bullets changed, either because the man with the machine-gun had altered his aim or because he'd been caught off-balance by the sudden dipping of the helicopter. An abruptly mad cacophony of sound, the iron clangour of steel-nosed bullets smashing into the engine casing mingled with the banshee ricochet of spent and mangled shells. The engine stopped, stopped as suddenly as if the ignition had been switched off. The helicopter was completely out of control, lifeless in the sky. It wasn't going to be in the sky much longer but there was nothing I could do about it. I braced myself for the jarring moment of impact when we struck the water, and when the impact came it was not just jarring, it was shattering to a degree I would never have anticipated. We'd landed not in the water but on the encircling reef of rocks.

I tried to get at the door but couldn't make it, we'd landed nose down and facing seawards on the outside of the reefs and from the position where I'd been hurled under the instrument panel the door was above and beyond my reach. I was too dazed, too weak, to make any real effort to get at it. Icy water poured in through the smashed windscreen and the fractured floor of the fuselage. For a moment everything was as silent as the grave, the hiss of the flooding waters seemed only to emphasise the silence, then the machine-gun started again. The shells smashed through the lower after part of the fuselage behind me and went out through the top of the windscreen above me. Twice I felt angry tugs on the right shoulder of my coat and I tried to bury my head even more deeply into the freezing waters. Then, due probably to a combination of an accumulation of water in the nose and the effect of the fusillade of bullets aft, the helicopter lurched forwards, stopped momentarily, then slid off the face of the reef and fell like a stone, nose first, to the bottom of the sea.

5

Among the more ridiculous and wholly unsubstantiated fictions perpetuated by people who don't know what they are talking about is the particularly half-witted one that death by drowning is peaceful, easy and, in fact, downright pleasant. It's not. It's a terrible way to die. I know, because I was drowning and I didn't like it one little bit. My ballooning head felt as if it were being pumped full of compressed air, my ears and eyes ached savagely, my nostrils, mouth and stomach were full of sea water and my bursting lungs felt as if someone had filled them with petrol and struck a match. Maybe if I opened my mouth, maybe if to relieve that flaming agony that was my lungs I took that one great gasping breath that would be the last I would ever take, maybe then it would be quiet and pleasant and peaceful. On the form to date, I couldn't believe it.

The damned door was jammed. After the beating the fuselage had taken, first of all in smashing into the reef and then into the sea-bed, it would be a miracle if it hadn't jammed. I pushed the door, I pulled at it, I beat at it with my clenched fists. It stayed jammed. The blood roared and hissed in my ears, the flaming vice around my chest was crushing my ribs and lungs, crushing the life out of me. I braced both feet on the instrument panel, laid both hands on the door handle. I thrust with my legs and twisted with my hands, using the power and the leverage a man can use only when he knows he is dying. The door handle sheared, the thrust of my legs carried me backwards and upwards towards the after end of the fuselage and suddenly my lungs could take no more. Death couldn't be worse than this agony.

The air rushed out through my water-filled mouth and nostrils and I sucked in this one great gasping breath, this lungful of sea-water, this last I would ever take.

It wasn't a lungful of water, it was a lungful of air. Noxious compressed air laden with the fumes of petrol and oil, but air for all that. Not the tangy salt-laden air of the Western Isles, not the wine-laden air of the Ægean, the pine-laden air of Norway or the sparkling champagne air of the high Alps. All those I'd tasted and all of them put together were a thin and anæmic substitute for this marvellous mixture of nitrogen and oxygen and petrol and oil that had been trapped in an air pocket under the undamaged upper rear part of the helicopter's fuselage, the only part of the plane that hadn't been riddled by machine-gun bullets. This was air as it ought to be.

The water level was around my neck. I took half a dozen deep whooping breaths, enough to ease the fire in my lungs and the roaring and hissing and dizziness in my head to tolerable levels, then pushed myself backwards and upwards to the extreme limit of the fuselage. The water was at chest level now. I moved a hand around in the blind darkness to try to estimate the amount of air available to me. Impossible to judge accurately, but enough, I guessed, compressed as it was, to last for ten to fifteen minutes.

I moved across to the left of the fuselage, took a deep breath and pushed myself forwards and downwards. Eight feet behind the pilot's seat was the passenger door, maybe I could force that. I found it right away, not the door but the opening where the door had been. The impact that had jammed the door on the right-hand side where I'd been had burst this door open. I pushed myself back to the upper part of the fuselage again and helped myself to a few more deep breaths of that compressed air. It didn't taste quite so good as it had done the first time.

Now that I knew I could go at any time, I was in no hurry to leave. Up above, guns in hand, those men would be waiting and if there was one outstanding attribute that characterised their attitude to work on hand, it was a single-minded thoroughness. Where those lads were concerned, a job half done was no job at all.

They could only have come there by boat and that boat would have been very nearby. By this time it would be even nearer by, it would be sitting directly over the spot where the helicopter had gone down and the crew wouldn't be sitting around with drinks in their hands congratulating themselves on their success, they'd be lining the side with searchlights or flashes and waiting to see if anyone would break surface. With their guns in their hands.

If I ever got back to the *Firecrest* again, if I ever got in touch with Uncle Arthur again, I wondered dully what I would say to him. Already I'd lost the *Nantesville*, already I'd been responsible for the deaths of Baker and Delmont, already I'd given away to the unknown enemy the secret of my identity—if that hadn't been obvious after the fake customs officers had smashed our transmitter it was bitterly obvious now—and now I'd lost Lieutenant Scott Williams his life and the Navy a valuable helicopter. Of Uncle Arthur's forty-eight hours only twelve were left now, and nothing could be more certain than when Uncle Arthur had finished with me, I wouldn't be allowed even those twelve hours. After Uncle Arthur had finished with me my days as an investigator would be finished, and finished for ever; with the kind of references he'd give me I wouldn't even qualify as a store detective in a street barrow. Not that it would make any difference what Uncle Arthur thought now. Baker and Delmont and Williams were gone. There was a heavy debt that had to be paid and the matter was out of Uncle Arthur's hands now. On the form to date, I thought bleakly, there wasn't one bookmaker in the land who would have given odds of one in a thousand of that debt ever being repaid. Only a fool bets against a certainty.

I wondered vaguely how long the men up top would wait—my conviction that they would be waiting was absolute. And then I felt a dry salty taste in my mouth that had nothing to do with the steadily deteriorating quality of air. It was pretty foul by this time, but a man can survive a surprisingly long time in foul air and there was enough oxygen left in that heavily tainted atmosphere to last me for a good few minutes yet.

The question was not how long they would wait but how long I could wait. Or had I already waited too long? I could feel the panic in my throat like some solid lump in my windpipe completely obstructing my breathing and had to make a conscious physical effort to force it down.

I tried to recall all I could from my marine salvage days. How long had I been under water and how deep down was I? How long had that dive down from the surface of the sea to the bottom taken?

Under those conditions time loses all meaning. Say forty seconds. Just over half-way down I'd taken my last gulp of air before the water in the fuselage had flooded over my head. And then a minute, probably a minute and a half, fighting with that jammed door. Since then a minute to recover, half a minute to locate that open door, and then how long since? Six minutes, seven? Not less than seven. I couldn't reckon on a total of less than ten minutes. The lump was back in my throat again.

How deep was I? That was the life-or-death question. I could tell from the pressure that I was pretty deep. But how deep? Ten fathoms? Fifteen? Twenty? I tried to recall the chart of Torbay Sound. There were eighty fathoms in the deepest channel and the channel was pretty close to the southern shore at this point, so that the water was steep-to. God above, I might even be in twenty-five fathoms. If I was, well that was it. Finish. How did the decompression tables go again? At thirty fathoms a man who has been under water for ten minutes requires to spend eighteen minutes for decompression stops on the way up. When you breathe air under pressure, the excess nitrogen is stored in the tissues: when you begin to surface this nitrogen is carried by the blood-stream to the lungs and is eliminated in respiration: and if you rise too rapidly respiration can't cope with it and nitrogen bubbles form in the blood, causing the agonising and crippling diver's bends. Even at twenty fathoms I'd require a six-minute halt for decompression on the way up and if there was one certain fact in life it was that decompression stops were out for me. I'd be a broken man. What I did know for certain was that every additional second I remained there would make the bends all the more agonising and crippling when they finally struck. All at once the prospect of surfacing beneath the steady guns and the pitiless eyes of the men above seemed positively attractive compared to the alternative. I took several deep breaths to get as much oxygen as possible into my blood-stream, exhaled to the fullest extent, took a long final breath to fill every last cubic millimetre in every last nook and cranny in my lungs, dived under the water, pushed my way out through the doorway and made for the surface.

I'd lost count of time on the way down and I now lost all count of time on the way up. I swam slowly and steadily using enough power to assist my progress through the water, but not so much as prematurely to use up all the stored oxygen. Every few seconds I let a little air escape from my mouth, not much, just enough to ease the pressure in my lungs. I looked up but the waters above me were as black as ink, there could have been fifty fathoms above my head for any trace of light I could see. And then suddenly, quite some time before the air supply was exhausted and before my lungs had begun to hurt again, the water was a shade less than pitch black and my head struck something hard and un-yielding. I grabbed it, held on, surfaced, sucked in some lung-fuls of that cold, salt, wonderful air and waited for the decompression pains to start, those sharply agonising twinges in the joints of the limbs. But none came. I couldn't have been more than fifteen fathoms down and even then I should have felt something. It had probably been something nearer ten.

During the past ten minutes my mind had taken as much a beating as any other part of me but it would have to have been in very much poorer shape than it was for me not to recognise what I was clinging to. A boat's rudder, and if any confirmation had been required the milkily phosphorescent water being turned up by the two slowly turning screws a couple of feet ahead of me would have been all that was required. I'd surfaced right under their boat. I was lucky. I might have surfaced right under one of their propellers and had my head cut in half. Even now, if the man at the wheel suddenly decided to go astern I'd be sucked into the vortex of one or other of the screws and end up like something that had passed through a turnip-cutting machine. But I'd been through too much to cross any bridges before I came to them.

Off to port I could see, sharply illuminated by a couple of powerful lights from the boat's deck, the reef where we'd crashed. We were about forty yards away and, relative to the reefs, stationary in the water, the engines turning just enough to maintain the boat's position against the effect of wind and tide. Now and again a searchlight patrolled the dark waters all around. I couldn't see anything of the men on deck, but I didn't have to be told what they were doing, they were waiting and watching and the safety catches would be off. Nor could I see anything of the boat itself but I made up my mind that, even though I couldn't recognise it, I'd know it if I ever came across it again. I took out the knife from the sheath behind my neck and cut a deep vee notch in the trailing edge of the rudder.

For the first time, I heard voices. I heard four voices and I had no difficulty in the world in identifying any of them. If I lived to make Methuselah look a teenager I'd never forget any one of them.

"Nothing on your side, Quinn?" Captain Imrie, the man who had organised the manhunt for me aboard the *Nantesville*.

"Nothing on my side, Captain." I could feel the hairs rise on the nape of my neck. Quinn. Durran. The bogus customs officer. The man who had almost, but not quite, strangled me to death.

"Your side, Jacques?" Captain Imrie again.

"Nothing, sir." The machine-pistol specialist. "Eight minutes since we've been here, fifteen since they went under. A man would require pretty good lungs to stay down that long, Captain."

"Enough," Imrie said. "There'll be a bonus for all of us for this night's work. Kramer?"

"Captain Imrie?" A voice as guttural as Imrie's own.

"Full ahead. Up the Sound."

I thrust myself backwards and dived deep. The waters above my head boiled into turbulent, phosphorescent life. I stayed deep, maybe ten feet down, heading for the reef. How long I swam like that, I don't know. Certainly less than a minute, my lungs weren't what they used to be, not even what they had been fifteen minutes ago: but when I was forced to the surface, I'd my dark oilskin over my head.

I needn't have bothered. I could see the faintly shimmering outline of the disappearing wake, no more. The searchlights were extinguished; when Captain Imrie decided a job was finished, then that job was finished. Predictably, the boat was in complete darkness with neither interior nor navigation lights showing.

I turned and swam slowly towards the reef. I reached a rock and clung to it until a measure of strength returned to my aching muscles, to my exhausted body. I would not have believed that fifteen minutes could have taken so much out of a man. I stayed there for five minutes. I could have stayed there for an hour. But time was not on my side. I slipped into deep water again and made for the shore.

Three times I tried and three times I failed to pull myself up from the rubber dinghy over the gunwale of the *Firecrest*. Four feet, no more. Just four feet. A Matterhorn. A ten-year-old could have done it. But not Calvert. Calvert was an old, old man.

I called out for Hunslett, but Hunslett did not come. Three times I called, but he did not come. The *Firecrest* was dark and still and lifeless. Where the hell was he? Asleep? Ashore? No, not ashore, he'd promised to stay aboard in case word came through at any time from Uncle Arthur. Asleep, then, asleep in his cabin. I felt the blind unreasoning anger rise. This was too much, after what I had been through this was too much. Asleep. I shouted at the top of my voice and hammered feebly on the steel hull with the butt of my Luger. But he didn't come.

The fourth time I made it. It was touch and go, but I made it. For a few seconds, dinghy painter in hand, I teetered on my stomach on the edge of the gunwale then managed to drag myself aboard. I secured the painter and went in search of Hunslett. There were words I wished to have with Hunslett.

I never used them. He wasn't aboard. I searched the *Firecrest* from forepeak to the after stowage locker, but no Hunslett. No signs of a hasty departure, no remnants of a meal on the saloon table or unwashed dishes in the galley, no signs of any struggle, everything neat and in good order. Everything as it ought to have been. Except that there was no Hunslett.

For a minute or two I sat slumped in the saloon settee trying to figure out a reason for his absence, but only for a minute or two. I was in no condition to figure out anything. Wearily I made my way out to the upper deck and brought dinghy and outboard over the side. No fancy tricks about securing them to the anchor chain this time: apart from the fact that it was, the way I felt, physically impossible, the time for that was past. I deflated the dinghy and stowed it, along with the outboard, in the after locker. And if someone came aboard and started looking? If someone came aboard and started looking he'd get a bullet through him. I didn't care if he claimed to be a police superintendent or an assistant commissioner or the top customs official in the country, he'd get a bullet through him, in the arm or leg, say, and I'd listen to his explanations afterwards. If it was one of my friends, one of my friends from *Nantesville* or the reef back there, he got it through the head.

I went below. I felt sick. The helicopter was at the bottom of the sea. The pilot was down there with it, half his chest shot away by machine-gun bullets. I'd every right to feel sick. I stripped off my clothes and towelled myself dry and the very action of towelling seemed to drain away what little strength was left to me. Sure I'd had a hard time in the last hour, all this running and slipping and stumbling through the dark woods, locating and blowing up the dinghy and dragging it over those damned seaweed covered boulders had taken it out of me, but I was supposed to be fit, it shouldn't have left me like this. I was sick, but the sickness was in the heart and mind, not in the body.

I went into my cabin and laboriously dressed myself in fresh clothes, not forgetting the Paisley scarf. The rainbow coloured bruises that Quinn had left on my neck had now swollen and spread to such an extent that I had to bring the scarf right up to the lobes of my ears to hide them. I looked in the mirror. It might have been my grandfather staring back at me. My grandfather on his deathbed. My face had that drawn and waxy look .that one normally associates with approaching dissolution. Not an all-over waxiness though, there was no blood on my face now but the pine needles had left their mark, I looked like someone with galloping impetigo. I felt like someone with galloping bubonic plague.

I checked that the Luger and the little Lilliput—I'd put them both back in their waterproof covering after leaving Dubh Sgeir—were still in working order. They were. In the saloon I poured myself a stiff three fingers of whisky. It went down my throat like a ferret down a burrow after a rabbit, one moment there, the next vanished in the depths. The weary old red corpuscles hoisted themselves to their feet and started trudging around again. It seemed a reasonable assumption that if I encouraged them with some more of the same treatment they might even break into a slow gallop and I had just closed my hand around the bottle when I heard the sound of an approaching engine. I put the bottle back in the rack, switched out the saloon lights—although they would have been invisible from outside through the velvet curtains—and took up position behind the open saloon door.

I was pretty sure the precautions were unnecessary, ten to one this was Hunslett coming back from shore, but why hadn't he taken the dinghy, still slung on the davits aft? Probably someone, for what Hunslett had regarded as an excellent reason, had persuaded him to go ashore and was now bringing him back.

The motor-boat's engine slowed, went into neutral, astern, then neutral again. A slight bump, the murmur of voices, the sound of someone clambering aboard and then the engine opening up again.

The footfalls passed over my head as the visitor—there was only one set of footfalls—made his way towards the wheelhouse door. The springy confident step of a man who knew what he was about. There was only one thing wrong with that springy confident step. It didn't belong to Hunslett. I flattened myself against the bulkhead, took out the Luger, slid off the safety catch and prepared to receive my visitor in what I had now come to regard as the best traditions of the Highlands.

I heard the click as the wheelhouse door opened, the louder click as it was shut by a firm hand. A pool of light from a flash-lamp preceded the visitor down the four steps from the wheel-house to the saloon. He paused at the foot of the steps and the light moved away as he made to locate the light-switch. I stepped round the door and did three things at once—I hooked an arm around his neck, brought up a far from gentle knee into the small of his back and ground the muzzle of the Luger into his right ear. Violent stuff, but not unnecessarily violent stuff, it might have been my old friend Quinn. The gasp of pain was enough to show that it wasn't.

"This isn't a hearing aid you feel, friend. It's a Luger pistol. You're one pound pressure from a better world. Don't make me nervous."

The better world seemed to have no appeal for him. He didn't make me nervous. He made an odd gurgling noise in his throat, he was trying either to speak or breathe, but he stood motionless, head and back arched. I eased the pressure a little.

"Put that light switch on with your left hand. Slowly. Care-fully."

He was very slow, very careful. The saloon flooded with light.

"Raise your hands above your head. As high as you can reach."

He was a model prisoner, this one, he did exactly as he was told. I turned him round, propelled him into the centre of the room and told him to face me.

He was of medium height, nattily dressed in an astrakhan coat and a fur Cossack hat. He had a beautifully trimmed white beard and moustache, with a perfectly symmetrical black streak in the centre of the beard, the only one of its kind I had ever seen. The tanned face was red, either from anger or near-suffocation. From both, I decided. He lowered his hands without permission, sat on the settee, pulled out a monocle, screwed it into his right eye and stared at me with cold fury. I gave him look for look, stare for

116

stare, pocketed the Luger, poured a whisky and handed it to Uncle Arthur. Rear-Admiral Sir Arthur Arnford-Jason, K.C.B. and all the rest of the alphabet.

"You should have knocked, sir," I said reproachfully.

"I should have knocked." His voice sounded half-strangled, maybe I had exerted more pressure than had been necessary. "Do you always greet your guests this way?"

"I don't have guests, sir. I don't have friends, either. Not in these Western Isles. All I have is enemies. Anyone who comes through that door is an enemy. I didn't expect to see you here, sir."

"I hope not. In view of that performance, I hope not." He rubbed his throat, drank some whisky and coughed. "Didn't expect to be here myself. Do you know how much bullion was aboard the *Nantesville?*"

"Close on a million, I understood."

"That's what I understood. Eight millions! Think of it, eight million pounds' worth. All this gold that's being shovelled back from Europe into the vaults at Fort Knox usually goes in small lots, 108 lb. ingots at a time. For safety. For security. In case anything goes wrong. But the Bank knew that nothing could go wrong this time, they knew our agents were aboard, they were behind with their payments, so they cleverly loaded fourteen hundred and forty ingots without telling anyone. Eight million. The Bank is hopping mad. The government is hopping mad. And everyone is taking it out on me."

And he'd come up here to take it out on me. I said: "You should have let me know. That you were coming."

"I tried to. You failed to keep your noon-day schedule. The most elementary of crimes, Calvert, and the most serious. You failed to keep a schedule. You or Hunslett. Then I knew things were going from bad to worse. I knew I had to take over myself. So I came by plane and R.A.F. rescue launch." That would have been the high-speed launch I'd seen taking a bad battering in the Sound as we had headed down towards the cove. "Where's Hunslett?"

"I don't know, sir."

"You don't know?" He was using his quiet unemphatic tone, the one I didn't care for very much. "You're out of your depth in this one, Calvert, aren't you?"

"Yes, sir. I'm afraid he's been removed by force. I'm not sure how. What have you been doing in the past two hours, sir?"

"Explain yourself." I wished he'd stop screwing that damned monocle into his eye. It was no affectation, that monocle, he was nearly blind on that side, but it was an irritating mannerism. At that moment, anything would have irritated me.

"That R.A.F. launch that dropped you off here just now. It should have been here at least two hours ago. Why didn't you come aboard then?"

"I did. We almost ran the *Firecrest* down in the darkness as we came round the headland. No one here. So I went and had some dinner. Nothing but baked beans aboard this damned boat as far as I could see."

"The Columba hotel wouldn't offer you much more. Toast below the beans, if you were lucky." The Columba was Torbay's only hotel.

"I had smoked trout, filet mignon and an excellent bottle of hock. I dined aboard the *Shangri-la*." This with the slight hint of a smile. Uncle Arthur's Achilles' heel was showing again: Uncle Arthur loved a lord like nobody's business, and a knight with a seven-figure income was as good as a lord any day.

"The *Shangri-la*?" I stared at him, then remembered. "Of course. You told me. You know Lady Skouras well. No, you said you knew her very well and her husband well. How is my old Sir Anthony?"

"Very well," he said coldly. Uncle Arthur had as much humour as the next man, but discussing titled millionaires in tones of levity was not humorous.

"And Lady Skouras?"

He hesitated. "Well——"

"Not so well. Pale, drawn, unhappy, with dark smudges under

her eyes. Not unlike myself. Her husband mistreats her and mistreats her badly. Mentally and physically. He humiliated her in front of a group of men last night. And she had rope burns on her arms. Why would she have rope burns on her arms, Sir Arthur?"

"Impossible. Quite fantastic. I knew the former Lady Skouras, the one who died this year in hospital. She——"

"She was undergoing treatment in a mental hospital. Skouras as good as told me."

"No matter. She adored him. He adored her. A man can't change like that. Sir Anthony—Sir Anthony's a gentleman."

"Is he? Tell me how he made his first millions. You saw Lady Skouras, didn't you?"

"I saw her," he said slowly. "She was late. She arrived with the filet mignon." He didn't seem to find anything funny in that. "She didn't look very well and she's a bruise on her right temple. She'd fallen climbing aboard from the tender and hit her head against a guardrail."

"Hit her head against her husband's fist, more like. To get back to the first time you boarded the *Firecrest* this evening. Did you search it?"

"I searched it. All except the after cabin. It was locked. I assumed there was something in there you didn't want chance callers to see."

"There was something in there that callers, not chance, didn't want *you* to see," I said slowly. "Hunslett. Hunslett under guard. They were waiting for word of my death, then they'd have killed Hunslett or kept him prisoner. If word came through that I hadn't been killed, then they'd have waited until my return and taken me prisoner too. Or killed us both. For by then they would have known that I knew too much to be allowed to live. It takes time, a long time, to open up a strong-room and get all those tons of gold out and they know their time is running out. They're desperate now. But they still think of everything."

"They were waiting for word of your death," Uncle Arthur said mechanically. "I don't understand."

"That helicopter you laid on for me, sir. We were shot down to-night after sunset. The pilot's dead and the machine is at the bottom of the sea. They believe me to be dead also."

"I see. You go from strength to strength, Calvert." The absence of reaction was almost total, maybe he was getting punch-drunk by this time, more likely he was considering the precise phraseology that would return me to the ranks of the unemployed with economy and dispatch. He lit a long, thin and very black cheroot and puffed meditatively. "When we get back to London remind me to show you my confidential report on you."

"Yes, sir." So this was how it was coming.

"I was having dinner with the Under-Secretary just forty-eight hours ago. One of the things he asked me was which country had the best agents in Europe. Told him I'd no idea. But I told him who I thought, on the balance of probabilities, was the best agent in Europe. Philip Calvert."

"That was very kind of you, sir." If I could remove that beard, whisky, cheroot and monocle, at least three of which were obscuring his face at any given moment, his expression might have given me some faint clue as to what was going on in that devious mind. "You were going to fire me thirty-six hours ago."

"If you believe that," Uncle Arthur said calmly, "you'll believe anything." He puffed out a cloud of foul smoke and went on: "One of the comments in your report states: 'Unsuitable for routine investigation. Loses interest and becomes easily bored. Operates at his best only under extreme pressure. At this level he is unique.' It's on the files, Calvert. I don't cut off my right hand."

"No, sir. Do you know what you are, sir?"

"A Machiavellian old devil," Uncle Arthur said with some satisfaction. "You know what's going on?"

"Yes, sir."

"Pour me another whisky, my boy, a large one, and tell me what's happened, what you know and what you think you know."

So I poured him another whisky, a large one, and told him

what had happened, what I knew and as much of what I thought I knew as seemed advisable to tell him.

He heard me out, then said: "Loch Houron, you think?"

"Loch Houron it must be. I spoke to no one else, anywhere else, and to the best of my knowledge no one else saw me. Someone recognised me. Or someone transmitted my description. By radio. It must have been by radio. The boat that was waiting for Williams and myself came from Torbay or somewhere near Torbay, a boat from Loch Houron could never have made it to the eastern end of the Sound of Torbay in five times the time we took. Somewhere near here, on land or sea, is a transceiver set. Somewhere out on Loch Houron there's another."

"This University expedition boat you saw on the south shore of Loch Houron. This alleged University expedition. It would have a radio transmitter aboard."

"No, sir. Boys with beards." I rose, pulled back the saloon curtains on both sides, then sat down again. "I told you their boat was damaged and listing. She'd been riding moored fore and aft in plenty of water. They didn't hole it themselves and it wasn't holed by any act of nature. Somebody kindly obliged. Another of those odd little boating incidents that occur with such profusion up and down the west coast."

"Why did you pull those curtains back?"

"Another of those odd little boating incidents, sir. One that's about to happen. Some time to-night people will be coming aboard. Hunslett and I, those people think, are dead. At least, I'm dead and Hunslett is dead or a prisoner. But they can't leave an abandoned *Firecrest* at anchor to excite suspicion and invite investigation. So they'll come in a boat, up anchor, and take the *Firecrest* out into the Sound, followed by their own boat. Once there, they'll slice through the flexible salt-water cooling intake, open the salt-water cock, take to their own boat and lift their hats as the *Firecrest* goes down to join the helicopter. As far as the big wide innocent world is concerned, Hunslett and I will just have sailed off into the sunset."

"And the gulfs will have washed you down," Uncle Arthur nodded. "You are very sure of this, Calvert?"

"You might say I'm absolutely certain."

"Then why open those blasted curtains?"

"The scuttling party may be coming from anywhere and they may not come for hours. The best time to scuttle a boat in close waters is at slack tide, when you can be sure that it will settle exactly where you want it to settle, and slack tide is not until one o'clock this morning. But if someone comes panting hotfoot aboard soon after those curtains are opened, then that will be proof enough that the radio transmitter we're after, and our friends who are working the transmitter, are somewhere in this bay, ashore or afloat."

"How will it be proof?" Uncle Arthur said irritably. "Why should they come, as you say, panting hotfoot?"

"They know they have Hunslett. At least, I assume they have, I can't think of any other reason for his absence. They think they know I'm dead, but they can't be sure. Then they see the beckoning oil lamp in the window. What is this, they say to themselves, Calvert back from the dead? Or a third, or maybe even a third and a fourth colleague of Calvert and Hunslett that we wot not of? Whether it's me or my friends, they must be silenced. And silenced at once. Wouldn't you come panting hotfoot?"

"There's no need to treat the matter with levity," Uncle Arthur complained.

"In your own words, sir, if you can believe that, you can believe anything."

"You should have consulted me first, Calvert." Uncle Arthur shifted in his seat, an almost imperceptible motion, though his expression didn't change. He was a brilliant administrator, but the more executive side of the business, the sand-bagging and pushing of people off high cliffs, wasn't exactly in his line. "I've told you that I came to take charge."

"Sorry, Sir Arthur. You'd better change that report, hadn't you? The bit about the best in Europe, I mean."

"*Touché, touché, touché,*" he grumbled. "And they're coming at us out of the dark, is that it? On their way now. Armed men. Killers. Shouldn't we—shouldn't we be preparing to defend ourselves? Dammit, man, I haven't even got a gun."

"You won't need one. You may not agree with me." I handed him the Luger. He took it, checked the indicator and that the safety catch moved easily, then sat there holding it awkwardly in his hand.

"Shouldn't we move, Calvert? We're sitting targets here."

"They won't be here for some time. The nearest house or boat is a mile away to the east. They'll be pushing wind and tide and they daren't use a motor. Whether they're rowing a boat or paddling a rubber dinghy they have a long haul ahead of them. Time's short, sir. We have a lot to do to-night. To get back to Loch Houron. The expedition's out, they couldn't pirate a dinghy, far less five ocean-going freighters. Our friend Donald Mac-Eachern acts in a highly suspicious fashion, he's got the facilities there, he's dead worried and he might have had half a dozen guns at his back while he had his in my front. But it was all too good to be true, professionals wouldn't lay it on the line like that."

"Maybe that's how professionals would expect a fellow-professional to react. And you said he's worried."

"Maybe the fish aren't biting. Maybe he's involved, but not directly. Then there's the shark-fishers. They have the boats, the facilities and, heaven knows, they're tough enough. Against that, they've been based there for years, the place is littered with sharks—it should be easy enough to check if regular consignments of liver oil are sent to the mainland—and they're well known and well thought of along the coast. They'll bear investigating. Then there's Dubh Sgeir. Lord Kirkside and his lovely daughter Sue."

"Lady Susan," Uncle Arthur said. It's difficult to invest an impersonal, inflectionless voice with cool reproach, but he managed it without any trouble. "I know Lord Kirkside, of course"—his tone implied that it would be remarkable if he didn't—"and while I may or may not be right about Sir Anthony, and I will lay you a hundred to one, in pounds, that I am, I'm convinced that Lord Kirkside is wholly incapable of any dishonest or illegal action."

"Me, too. He's a very tough citizen, I'd say, but on the side of the angels."

"And his daughter? I haven't met her."

"Very much a girl of to-day. Dressed in the modern idiom, speaks in the modern idiom, I'm tough and I'm competent and I can take care of myself, thank you. She's not tough at all, just a nice old-fashioned girl in new-fashioned clothes."

"So that clears them." Uncle Arthur sounded relieved. "That leaves us the expedition, in spite of your sneers, or MacEachern's place, or the shark-fishers. I go for the shark-fishers myself."

I let him go for wherever he wanted to. I thought it was time I went to the upper deck and told him so.

"It won't be long now?"

"I shouldn't think so, sir. We'll put out the lights in the saloon here—it would look very odd if they peered in the windows and saw no one here. We'll put on the two sleeping-cabin lights and the stern light. That will destroy their night-sight. The after deck will be bathed in light. For'ard of that, as far as they are concerned, it will be pitch dark. We hide in the dark."

"Where in the dark?" Uncle Arthur didn't sound very confident.

"You stand inside the wheelhouse. All wheelhouse doors are hinged for'ard and open outwards. Keep your hand on the inside handle. Lightly. When you feel it begin to turn, a very slow and stealthy turn, you can bet your boots, wait till the door gives a fraction, then kick the rear edge, just below the handle, with the sole of your right foot and with all the weight you have. If you don't break his nose or knock him overboard you'll at least set him in line for a set of false teeth. I'll take care of the other or others."

"How?"

"I'll be on the saloon roof. It's three feet lower than the wheelhouse roof so they can't see me silhouetted against the loom of the stern light even if they approach from the bows."

"But what are you going to do?"

"Clobber him or them. A nice big Stilson from the engine-room with a rag round it will do nicely."

"Why don't we just dazzle them with torches and tell them to put their hands up?" Uncle Arthur clearly didn't care for my proposed *modus operandi.*

"Three reasons. These are dangerous and deadly men and you never give them warning. Not the true sporting spirit, but it helps you survive. Then there will almost certainly be night-glasses trained on the *Firecrest* at this very moment. Finally, sound carries very clearly over water and the wind is blowing towards Torbay. Shots, I mean."

He said no more. We took up position and waited. It was still raining heavily with the wind still from the west. For once the rain didn't bother me, I'd a full set of oilskins on. I just lay there, spread-eagled on the saloon coach-roof, occasionally easing the fingers of my hands, the right round the Stilson, the left round the little knife. After fifteen minutes they came. I heard the gentle scuff of rubber on our starboard side—the side of the wheelhouse door. I pulled on the cord which passed through the rear window of the wheelhouse. The cord was attached to Uncle Arthur's hand.

There were only two of them. My eyes were perfectly tuned to the dark by this time and I could easily distinguish the shape of the first man coming aboard just below where I lay. He secured a painter and waited for his mate. They moved forward together.

The leading man gave a cough of agony as the door smashed, fair and square, as we later established, into his face. I wasn't so successful, the second man had cat-like reactions and had started to drop to the deck as the Stilson came down. I caught him on back or shoulder, I didn't know which, and dropped on top of him. In one of his hands he'd have either a gun or knife and if I'd wasted a fraction of a second trying to find out which hand and what he had in it, I'd have been a dead man. I brought down my left hand and he lay still.

I passed the other man lying moaning in agony in the scuppers, brushed by Uncle Arthur, pulled the saloon curtains to and

125

switched on the lights. I then went out, half-pulled, half-lifted the moaning man through the wheelhouse door, down the saloon steps and dropped him on the carpet. I didn't recognise him. That wasn't surprising, his own mother or wife wouldn't have recognised him. Uncle Arthur was certainly a man who believed in working with a will and he'd left the plastic surgeon a very tricky job.

"Keep your gun on him, sir," I said. Uncle Arthur was looking down at his handiwork with a slightly dazed expression. What one could see of his face behind the beard seemed slightly paler than normal. "If he breathes, kill him."

"But—but look at his face, man. We can't leave——"

"You look at this, sir." I stooped and picked up the weapon that had fallen from the man's hand as I'd dropped him to the floor. "This is what is technically known to the United States' police departments as a whippet. A shot-gun with two-thirds of the barrel and two-thirds of the stock sawn off. If he'd got you first, you wouldn't have any face left at all. I mean that literally. Do you still feel like playing Florence Nightingale to the fallen hero?" That wasn't at all the way one should talk to Uncle Arthur, there would be a few more entries in the confidential report when we got back. If we got back. But I couldn't help myself, not then. I passed by Uncle Arthur and went out.

In the wheelhouse I picked up a small torch, went outside and shone it down into the water, hooding it with my hand so that the beam couldn't have been seen fifty yards away. They had a rubber dinghy, all right—and an outboard motor attached. The conquering heroes, bathed in that warm and noble glow of satisfaction that comes from the comforting realisation of a worth-while job well done, had intended to make it home the easy way.

Looping a heaving line round the outboard's cylinder head and hauling alternately on the heaving line and painter, I had both dinghy and outboard up and over in two minutes. I unclamped the outboard, lugged the dinghy round to the other side of the superstructure, the side remote from the inner harbour, and examined it carefully in the light of the torch. Apart from the manufacturer's name there was no mark on it, nothing to indicate to which craft it belonged. I sliced it to ribbons and threw it over the side.

Back in the wheelhouse, I cut a twenty-foot length from a roll of P.V.C. electric wiring cable, went outside again and lashed the outboard to the dead man's ankles. I searched his pockets. Nothing, I'd known there would be nothing, I was dealing with professionals. I hooded the torch and looked at his face. I'd never seen him before. I took from him the pistol still clutched in his right hand, undid the spring clips holding the guard-chains in place above the gunwale slots for our companion-way ladder, then eased, first the outboard, and then the man, over the side. They vanished into the dark waters of Torbay harbour without the whisper of a splash. I went inside, closing wheelhouse and saloon doors behind me.

Uncle Arthur and the injured man had reversed positions by this time. The man was on his feet now, leaning drunkenly against the bulkhead, dabbing his face with a blood-stained towel Uncle Arthur must have found, and moaning from time to time. I didn't blame him, if I'd a broken nose, most of my front teeth displaced and a jaw that might or might not have been fractured, I'd have been moaning too. Uncle Arthur, gun in one hand and some more of my Scotch in the other, was sitting on the settee and contemplating his bloody handiwork with an odd mixture of satisfaction and distaste. He looked at me as I came in, nodded towards the prisoner.

"Making a fearful mess of the carpet," he complained. "What do we do with him?"

"Hand him over to the police."

"The police? You had your reservations about the police, I thought."

"Reservations is hardly the word. We have to make the break some time."

"Our friend outside, as well?"

"Who?"

"This fellow's—ah—accomplice."

127

"I threw him over the side."

Uncle Arthur made the mess on the carpet even worse. He spilt whisky all over it. He said: "You what?"

"There's no worry." I pointed downwards. "Twenty fathoms and thirty pounds of metal attached to his ankles."

"At—at the bottom of the sea?"

"What did you expect me to do with him? Give him a state funeral? I'm sorry, I didn't tell you, he was dead. I had to kill him."

"Had to? Had to?" He seemed upset. "Why, Calvert?"

"There's no 'why.' There's no justification needed. I killed him or he killed me, and then you, and now we'd both be where he is. Do you have to justify killing men who have murdered at least three times, probably oftener? And if that particular character wasn't a murderer, he came to-night to murder. I killed him with as little thought and compunction and remorse as I'd have tramped on a black widow spider."

"But you can't go around acting like a public executioner."

"I can and I will. As long as it's a choice between them and me."

"You're right, you're right." He sighed. "I must confess that reading your reports of an operation is quite different from being with you on one. But I must also confess that it's rather comforting having you around at times like this. Well, let's put this man in cells."

"I'd like to go to the *Shangri-la* first, sir. To look for Hunslett."

"I see. To look for Hunslett. Has it occurred to you, Calvert, that if they are hostile to us, as you admit is possible, that they may not let you look for Hunslett?"

"Yes, sir. It's not my intention to go through the *Shangri-la*, a gun in each hand, searching for him. I wouldn't get five feet. I'm just going to ask for him, if anyone has seen him. Assuming they really are the bandits, don't you think it might be most instructive, sir, to observe their reactions when they see a dead man walking aboard, especially a dead man coming alongside from a boat to which they'd shortly beforehand dispatched a couple of

128

killers? And don't you think it will become more and more instructive to watch them as time passes by with no sign of First and Second Murderers entering left?"

"Assuming they are the bandits, of course."

"I'll know before we say good-bye to them."

"And how do we account for our knowing one another?"

"If they're white as the driven snow, we don't have to account to them. If they're not, they won't believe a damned word either of us say anyway."

I collected the roll of flex from the wheelhouse and led our prisoner to the after cabin. I told him to sit down with his back to one of the bulkhead generators and he did. Resistance was the last thought in his mind. I passed a few turns of flex round his waist and secured him to the generator: his feet I secured to one of the stanchions. His hands I left free. He could move, he could use the towel and the bucket of cold fresh water I left to administer first aid to himself whenever he felt like it. But he was beyond the reach of any glass or sharp instrument with which he could either free himself or do himself in. On the latter score I wasn't really worried one way or another.

I started the engines, weighed anchor, switched on the navigation lights and headed for the *Shangri-la*. Quite suddenly, I wasn't tired any more.

6

Less than two hundred yards from the *Shangri-la* the anchor clattered down into fifteen fathoms of water. I switched off the navigation lights, switched on all the wheelhouse lights, passed into the saloon and closed the door behind me.

"How long do we sit here?" Uncle Arthur asked.

"Not long. Better get into your oilskins now, sir. Next really heavy shower of rain and we'll go."

"They'll have had their night-glasses on us all the way across the bay, you think?"

"No question of that. They'll still have the glasses on us. They'll be worried stiff, wondering what the hell has gone wrong, what's happened to the two little playmates they sent to interview us. *If* they are the bandits."

"They're bound to investigate again."

"Not yet. Not for an hour or two. They'll wait for their two friends to turn up. They may think that it took them longer than expected to reach the *Firecrest* and that we'd upped anchor and left before they got there. Or they may think they'd trouble with their dinghy." I heard the sudden drumming of heavy rain on the coach-roof. "It's time to go."

We left by the galley door, felt our way aft, quietly lowered the dinghy into the water and climbed down the transom ladder into it. I cast off. Wind and tide carried us in towards the harbour. Through the driving rain we could dimly see the *Shangri-la*'s riding light as we drifted by about a hundred yards from her port side. Half-way between the *Shangri-la* and the shore I started up the outboard motor and made back towards the *Shangri-la*.

The big tender was riding at the outer end of a boom which

stretched out from the *Shangri-la*'s starboard side about ten feet for'ard of the bridge. The stern of the tender was about fifteen out from the illuminated gangway. I approached from astern, upwind, and closed in on the gangway. An oilskinned figure wearing one of the *Shangri-la*'s crew's fancy French sailor hats came running down the gangway and took the painter.

"Ah, good-evening, my man," Uncle Arthur said. He wasn't putting on the style, it was the way he talked to most people. "Sir Anthony is aboard?"

"Yes, sir."

"I wonder if I could see him for a moment?"

"If you could wait a——" The sailor broke off and peered at Sir Arthur. "Oh, it's—it's the Admiral, sir."

"Admiral Arnford-Jason. Of course—you're the fellow who ran me ashore to the Columba after dinner."

"Yes, sir. I'll show you to the saloon, sir."

"My boat will be all right here for a few moments." The unspoken implication was that I was his chauffeur.

"Perfectly, sir."

They climbed the gangway and went aft. I spent ten seconds examining the portable lead that served the gangway light, decided that it wouldn't offer much resistance to a good hefty tug, then followed the two men aft. I passed by the passage leading to the saloon and hid behind a ventilator. Almost at once the sailor emerged from the passage and made his way for'ard again. Another twenty seconds and he'd be yelling his head off about the mysteriously vanished chauffeur. I didn't care what he did in twenty seconds.

When I reached the partly open saloon door I heard Sir Arthur's voice.

"No, no, I really am most sorry to break in upon you like this. Well, yes, thank you, a small one if you will. Yes, soda, please." Uncle Arthur really was having a go at the whisky to-night. "Thank you, thank you. Your health, Lady Skouras. Your health, gentlemen. Mustn't delay you. Fact is, I wonder if you can help us. My friend and I are most anxious, really most anxious. I wonder where he is, by the way? I thought he was right behind——"

Cue for Calvert. I turned down the oilskin collar that had been obscuring the lower part of my face, removed the sou'wester that had been obscuring most of the upper part of my face, knocked politely and entered. I said: "Good evening, Lady Skouras. Good-evening, gentlemen. Please forgive the interruption, Sir Anthony."

Apart from Uncle Arthur there were six of them gathered round the fire at the end of the saloon. Sir Anthony standing, the others seated. Charlotte Skouras, Dollmann, Skouras's managing director, Lavorski, his accountant, Lord Charnley, his broker and a fifth man I didn't recognise. All had glasses in their hands.

Their reaction to my sudden appearance, as expressed by their faces, was interesting. Old Skouras showed a half-frowning, half-speculative surprise. Charlotte Skouras gave me a strained smile of welcome: Uncle Arthur hadn't been exaggerating when he spoke of that bruise, it was a beauty. The stranger's face was non-committal, Lavorski's inscrutable, Dollmann's rigid as if carved from marble and Lord Charnley's for a fleeting moment that of a man walking through a country churchyard at midnight when someone taps him on the shoulder. Or so I thought. I could have imagined it. But there was no imagination about the sudden tiny snapping sound as the stem of the glass fell soundlessly on to the carpet. A scene straight from Victorian melodrama. Our aristocratic broker friend had something on his mind. Whether the others had or not it was difficult to say. Dollmann, Lavorski and, I was pretty sure, Sir Anthony could make their faces say whatever they wanted them to say.

"Good lord, Petersen!" Skouras's tone held surprise but not the surprise of a person welcoming someone back from the grave. "I didn't know you two knew each other."

"My goodness, yes. Petersen and I have been colleagues for years, Tony. UNESCO, you know." Uncle Arthur always gave out that he was a British delegate to UNESCO, a cover that gave him an excellent reason for his frequent trips abroad. "Marine biology

132

may not be very cultural, but it's scientific and educational enough. Peterson's one of my star performers. Lecturing, I mean. Done missions for me in Europe, Asia, Africa and South America." Which was true enough, only they weren't lecture missions. "Didn't even know he was here until they told me at the hotel. But dear me, dear me, mustn't talk about ourselves. It's Hunslett. Petersen's colleague. And mine in a way. Can't find him anywhere. Hasn't been in the village. Yours is the nearest boat. Have you seen anything of him, anything at all?"

"Afraid I haven't," Skouras said. "Anybody here? No? Nobody?" He pressed a bell and a steward appeared. Skouras asked him to make inquiries aboard and the steward left. "When did he disappear, Mr. Petersen?"

"I've no idea. I left him carrying out experiments. I've been away all day collecting specimens. Jellyfish." I laughed deprecatingly and rubbed my inflamed face. "The poisonous type, I'm afraid. No sign of him when I returned."

"Could your friend swim, Mr. Petersen?" the stranger asked. I looked at him, a dark thickset character in his middle forties, with black snapping eyes deepset in a tanned face. Expressionless faces seemed to be the order of the day there, so I kept mine expressionless. It wasn't easy.

"I'm afraid not," I said quietly. "I'm afraid you're thinking along the same lines as myself. We've no guard rails aft. A careless step——" I broke off as the steward re-entered and reported that no one had seen a sign of Hunslett, then went on: "I think I should report this to Sergeant MacDonald at once."

Everybody else seemed to think so, too, so we left. The cold slanting rain was heavier than ever. At the head of the gangway I pretended to slip, flung my arms about wildly for a bit then toppled into the sea, taking the gangway wandering lead with me. What with the rain, the wind and the sudden darkness there was quite a bit of confusion and it was the better part of a minute before I was finally hauled on to the landing stage of the companionway. Old Skouras was commiseration itself and offered me a change of clothes at once but I declined politely and went back to the *Firecrest* with Uncle Arthur. Neither of us spoke on the way back.

As we secured the dinghy I said: "When you were at dinner on the *Shangri-la* you must have given some story to account for your presence here, for your dramatic appearance in an R.A.F. rescue launch."

"Yes. It was a good one. I told them a vital UNESCO conference in Geneva was being dead-locked because of the absence of a certain Dr. Spenser Freeman. It happens to be true. In all the papers to-day. Dr. Freeman is not there because it suits us not to have him there. No one knows that, of course. I told them that it was of vital national importance that he should be there, that we'd received information that he was doing field research in Torbay and that the Government had sent me here to get him back."

"Why send the launch away? That would seem odd."

"No. If he's somewhere in the wilds of Torbay I couldn't locate him before daylight. There's a helicopter, I said, standing by to fly him out. I've only to lift the phone to have it here in fifty minutes."

"And, of course, you weren't to know that the telephone lines were out of order. It might have worked—if you hadn't called at the *Firecrest* in the rescue launch *before* you went to the *Shangri-la*. You weren't to know that our friends who were locked in the after cabin when you went aboard would report back that they'd heard an R.A.F. rescue launch here at such and such a time. They might have seen it through a porthole, but even that wouldn't be necessary, the engines are unmistakable. So now our friends know you're lying like a trooper. The chances are that they've now a very shrewd idea as to who exactly you are. Congratulations, sir. You've now joined the category I've been in for years—no insurance company in the world would issue you a life policy even on a ninety-nine per cent premium."

"Our trip to the *Shangri-la* has removed your last doubts about our friends out there?"

"Yes, sir. You saw the reaction of our belted broker, Lord Charnley. And him an aristocrat to boot!"

"A small thing to base a big decision on, Calvert," Uncle Arthur said coldly.

"Yes, sir." I fished my scuba suit from the after locker and led the way below. "I didn't fall into the water by accident. By accident on purpose. I didn't mention that when I was hanging on to the boat's rudder off the reef this evening I cut a notch in it. A deep vee notch. The *Shangri-la*'s tender has a deep vee notch in it. Same notch, in fact. Same boat."

"I see. I see indeed." Uncle Arthur sat on the settee and gave me the combination of the cold blue eye and the monocle. "You forgot to give me advance notification of your intentions."

"I didn't forget." I started to change out of my soaking clothes. "I'd no means of knowing how good an actor you are, sir."

"I'll accept that. So that removed your last doubts."

"No, sir. Superfluous confirmation, really. I knew before then. Remember that swarthy character sitting beside Lavorski who asked me if Hunslett could swim. I'll bet a fortune to a penny that he wasn't at the *Shangri-la*'s dinner table earlier on."

"You would win. How do you know?"

"Because he was in command of the crew of the boat who shot down the helicopter and killed Williams and hung around afterwards waiting to have a go at me. His name is Captain Imrie. He was the captain of the prize crew of the *Nantesville*."

Uncle Arthur nodded, but his mind was on something else. It was on the scuba suit I was pulling on.

"What the hell do you think you're going to do with that thing?" he demanded.

"Advance notification of intentions, sir. Won't be long. I'm taking a little trip to the *Shangri-la*. The *Shangri-la*'s tender, rather. With a little homing device and a bag of sugar. With your permission, sir."

"Something else you forgot to tell me, hey, Calvert? Like that breaking off the *Shangri-la*'s gangway light was no accident?"

"I'd like to get there before they replace it, sir."

"I can't believe it, I can't believe it." Uncle Arthur shook his head. For a moment I thought he was referring to the dispatch with which I had made the uneventful return trip to the *Shangri-la*'s tender, but his next words showed that his mind was on higher and more important things. "That Tony Skouras should be up to his neck in this. There's something far wrong. I just *can't* believe it. Good God, do you know he was up for a peerage in the next List?"

"So soon? He told me he was waiting for the price to come down."

Uncle Arthur said nothing. Normally, he would have regarded such a statement as a mortal insult, as he himself automatically collected a life peerage on retirement. But nothing. He was as shaken as that.

"I'd like nothing better than to arrest the lot of them," I said. "But our hands are tied. We're helpless. But now that I know what we do know I wonder if you would do me a favour before we go ashore, sir. There are two things I want to know. One is whether Sir Anthony really was down at some Clyde shipyard a few days ago having stabilisers fitted—a big job that few yards would tackle in a yacht that size. Should find out in a couple of hours. People tell silly and unnecessary lies. Also I'd like to find out if Lord Kirkside has taken the necessary steps to have his dead son's title—he was Viscount somebody or other—transferred to his younger son."

"You get the set ready and I'll ask them anything you like," Uncle Arthur said wearily. He wasn't really listening to me, he was still contemplating with stunned disbelief the possibility that his future fellow peer was up to the neck in skullduggery on a vast scale. "And pass me that bottle before you go below."

At the rate Uncle Arthur was going, I reflected, it was providential that the home of one of the most famous distilleries in the Highlands was less than half a mile from where we were anchored.

I lowered the false head of the starboard diesel to the engine-room deck as if it weighed a ton. I straightened and stood there for a full minute, without moving. Then I went to the engine-room door.

"Sir Arthur?"

"Coming, coming." A few seconds and he was at the doorway, the glass of whisky in his hand. "All connected up?"

"I've found Hunslett, sir."

Uncle Arthur moved slowly forward like a man in a dream.

The transmitter was gone. All our explosives and listening devices and little portable transmitters were gone. That had left plenty of room. They'd had to double him up to get him in, his head was resting on his forearms and his arms on his knees, but there was plenty of room. I couldn't see his face. I could see no marks of violence. Half-sitting, half-lying there he seemed curiously peaceful, a man drowsing away a summer afternoon by a sun-warmed wall. A long summer afternoon because for ever was a long time. That's what I'd told him last night, he'd all the time in the world for sleep.

I touched his face. It wasn't cold yet. He'd been dead two to three hours, no more. I turned his face to see if I could find how he had died. His head lolled to one side like that of a broken rag doll. I turned and looked at Sir Arthur. The dream-like expression had gone, his eyes were cold and bitter and cruel. I thought vaguely of the tales I'd heard, and largely discounted, of Uncle Arthur's total ruthlessness. I wasn't so ready to discount them now. Uncle Arthur wasn't where he was now because he'd answered an advertisement in the *Daily Telegraph*, he'd have been hand-picked by two or three very clever men who would have scoured the country to find the one man with the extraordinary qualifications they required. And they had picked Uncle Arthur, the man with the extraordinary qualifications, and total ruthlessness must have been one of the prime requisites. I'd never really thought of it before.

He said: "Murdered, of course."

"Yes, sir."

"How?"

"His neck is broken, sir."

137

"His neck? A powerful man like Hunslett?"

"I know a man who could do it with one twist of his hands. Quinn. The man who killed Baker and Delmont. The man who almost killed me."

"I see." He paused, then went on, almost absently: "You will, of course, seek out and destroy this man. By whatever means you choose. You can reconstruct this, Calvert?"

"Yes, sir." When it came to reconstruction when it was too damn' late, I stood alone. "Our friend or friends boarded the *Firecrest* very shortly after I had left this morning. That is, before daylight. They wouldn't have dared try it after it was light. They overpowered Hunslett and kept him prisoner. Confirmation that he was held prisoner all day comes from the fact that he failed to meet the noon-day schedule. They still held him prisoner when you came aboard. There was no reason why you should suspect that there was anyone aboard—the boat that put them aboard before dawn would have gone away at once. They couldn't leave one of the *Shangri-la*'s boats lying alongside the *Firecrest* all day."

"There's no necessity to dot i's and cross t's."

"No, sir. Maybe an hour or so after you departed the *Shangri-la*'s tender with Captain Imrie, Quinn and company aboard turns up: they report that I'm dead. That was Hunslett's death warrant. With me dead they couldn't let him live. So Quinn killed him. Why he was killed this way I don't know. They may have thought shots could be heard, they may not have wanted to use knives or blunt instruments in case they left blood all over the deck. They were intending to abandon the boat till they came back at night, at midnight, to take it out to the Sound and scuttle it and someone might have come aboard in the interim. My own belief is that he was killed this way because Quinn is a psychopath and compulsive killer and liked doing it this way."

"I see. And then they said to themselves: 'Where can we hide Hunslett till we come back at midnight? Just in case someone does come aboard.' And then they said: 'Ha! We know. We'll hide him in the dummy diesel.' So they threw away the transmitter and all the rest of the stuff—or took it with them. It doesn't matter. And they put Hunslett inside." Uncle Arthur had been speaking very quietly throughout and then suddenly, for the first time I'd ever known it, his voice became a shout. "How in the name of God did they know this was a dummy diesel, Calvert? How *could* they have known?" His voice dropped to what was a comparative whisper. "Someone talked, Calvert. Or someone was criminally careless."

"No one talked, sir. Someone was criminally careless. I was. If I'd used my eyes Hunslett wouldn't be lying there now. The night the two bogus customs officers were aboard I knew that they had got on to something when we were in the engine-room here. Up to the time that they'd inspected the batteries they'd gone through the place with a tooth-comb. After that they didn't give a damn. Hunslett even suggested that it was something to do with the batteries but I was too clever to believe him." I walked to the work-bench, picked up a torch and handed it to Uncle Arthur. "Do you see anything about those batteries that would excite suspicion?"

He looked at me, that monocled eye still ice-cold and bitter, took the torch and examined the batteries carefully. He spent all of two minutes searching, then straightened.

"I see nothing," he said curtly.

"Thomas—the customs man who called himself Thomas—did. He was on to us from the start. He knew what he was looking for. He was looking for a powerful radio transmitter. Not the tuppence ha'penny job we have up in the wheelhouse. He was looking for signs of a power take-off from those batteries. He was looking for the marks left by screw clamps or by a pair of saw-toothed, powerfully spring-loaded crocodile clips."

Uncle Arthur swore, very quietly, and bent over the batteries again. This time his examination took only ten seconds.

"You make your point well, Calvert." The eyes were still bitter, but no longer glacial.

"No wonder they knew exactly what I was doing to-day," I said savagely. "No wonder they knew that Hunslett would be alone before dawn, that I'd be landing at that cove this evening. All they required was radio confirmation from someone out in Loch Houron that Calvert had been snooping around there and the destruction of the helicopter was a foregone conclusion. All this damned fol-de-rol about smashing up radio transmitters and making us think that we were the only craft left with a transmitter. God, how blind can you be?"

"I assume that there's some logical thought behind this outburst," Uncle Arthur said coldly.

"That night Hunslett and I were aboard the *Shangri-la* for drinks. I told you that when we returned we knew that we'd had visitors. We didn't know why, then. My God!"

"You've already been at pains to demonstrate the fact that I was no brighter than yourself about the battery. It's not necessary to repeat the process——"

"Let me finish," I interrupted. Uncle Arthur didn't like being interrupted. "They came down to the engine-room here. They knew there was a transmitter. They looked at that starboard cylinder head. Four bolts—the rest are dummies—with the paint well and truly scraped off. The port cylinder head bolts without a flake of paint missing. They take off this head, wire into the transceiver lines on the output side of the scrambler and lead out to a small radio transmitter hidden, like as not, behind the battery bank there. They'd have all the equipment with them for they knew exactly what they wanted to do. From then on they could listen in to our every word. They knew all our plans, everything we intended to do, and made their own plans accordingly. They figured—and how right they were—that it would be a damn' sight more advantageous for them to let Hunslett and I have our direct communication with you and so know exactly what was going on than to wreck this set and force us to find some other means of communication that they couldn't check on."

"But why—but why destroy the advantage they held by—by—" He gestured at the empty engine casing.

"It wasn't an advantage any longer," I said tiredly. "When they ripped out that set Hunslett was dead and they thought Calvert was dead. They didn't need the advantage any more."

"Of course, of course. My God, what a fiendish brew this is." He took out his monocle and rubbed his eye with the knuckles of his hand. "They're bound to know that we will find Hunslett the first time we attempt to use this radio. I am beginning to appreciate the weight of your remark in the saloon that we might find it difficult to insure ourselves. They cannot know how much we know, but they cannot afford to take chances. Not with, what is it now, a total of seventeen million pounds at stake. They will have to silence us."

"Up and off is the only answer," I agreed. "We've been down here too long already, they might even be on their way across now. Don't let that Luger ever leave your hand, sir. We'll be safe enough under way. But first we must put Hunslett and our friend in the after cabin ashore."

"Yes. Yes, we must put them ashore first."

At the best of times, weighing anchor by electric windlass is not a job for a moron, even an alert moron. Even our small windlass had a pull of over 1,400 pounds. A carelessly placed hand or foot, a flapping trouser leg or the trailing skirts of an oilskin, any of those being caught up between chain and drum and you can be minus a hand or foot before you can cry out, far less reach the deck switch which is invariably placed abaft the windlass. Doing this on a wet slippery deck is twice as dangerous. Doing it on a wet slippery deck, in total darkness, heavy rain and with a very unstable boat beneath your feet, not to mention having the brake pawl off and the winch covered by a tarpaulin, is a highly dangerous practice indeed. But it wasn't as dangerous as attracting the attention of our friends on the *Shangri-la*.

Perhaps it was because of my total absorption in the job on hand, perhaps because of the muffled clank of the anchor coming inboard, that I didn't locate and identify the sound as quickly as I might. Twice I'd thought I'd heard the far-off sound of a woman's voice, twice I'd vaguely put it down to late-night revelry on one of the smaller yachts in the bay—it would require an I.B.M. computer to work out the gallonage of gin consumed in

British yacht harbours after the sun goes down. Then I heard the voice again, much nearer this time, and I put all thought of revelry afloat out of my mind. The only cry of desperation ever heard at a yacht party is when the gin runs out: this soft cry had a different quality of desperation altogether. I stamped on the deck switch, and all sound on the fo'c'sle ceased. The Lilliput was in my hand without my knowing how it had got there.

"Help me!" The voice was low and urgent and desperate. "For God's sake, help me."

The voice came from the water, amidships on the port side. I moved back silently to where I thought the voice had come from and stood motionless. I thought of Hunslett and I didn't move a muscle. I'd no intention of helping anyone until I'd made sure the voice didn't come from some dinghy—a dinghy with two other passengers, both carrying machine-guns. One word, one incautious flash of light, a seven pound pull on a trigger and Calvert would be among his ancestors if, that was, they would have anything to do with such a bloody fool of a descendant.

"Please! Please help me! Please!"

I helped her. Not so much because the desperation in the voice was unquestionably genuine as because of the fact that it as unquestionably belonged to Charlotte Skouras.

I pushed through between the scuppers and the lowest guardrail, a rubber tyre fender that was permanently attached to one of the guard-rail stanchions and lowered it to water-level. I said: "Lady Skouras?"

"Yes, yes, it's me. Thank God, thank God!" Her voice didn't come just as easily as that, she was gasping for breath and she'd water in her mouth.

"There's a fender at the boat's side. Catch it."

A moment or two, then: "I have it."

"Can you pull yourself up?"

More splashing and gasping, then: "No. No, I can't do it."

"No matter. Wait." I turned round to go for Uncle Arthur but he was already by my side. I said softly in his ear: "Lady Skouras is down there in the water. It may be a trap. I don't think so. But if you see a light, shoot at it."

He said nothing but I felt his arm move as he took the Luger from his pocket. I stepped over the guard-rail and lowered myself till my foot came to rest on the lower part of the tyre. I reached down and caught her arm. Charlotte Skouras was no slender sylph-like figure, she had some bulky package tied to her waist, and I wasn't as fit as I'd been a long, long time ago, say about forty-eight hours, but with a helping hand from Uncle Arthur I managed to get her up on deck. Between us, we half carried her to the curtained saloon and set her down on the settee. I propped a cushion behind her head and took a good look at her.

She'd never have made the front cover of *Vogue*. She looked terrible. Her dark slacks and shirt looked as if they had spent a month in the sea instead of probably only a few minutes. The long tangled auburn hair was plastered to her head and cheeks, her face was dead-white, the big brown eyes, with the dark half-circles, were wide open and frightened and both mascara and lipstick had begun to run. And she hadn't been beautiful to start with. I thought she was the most desirable woman I'd ever seen. I must be nuts.

"My dear Lady Skouras, my dear Lady Skouras!" Uncle Arthur was back among the aristocracy and showed it. He knelt by her side, ineffectually dabbing at her face with a handkerchief. "What in God's name has happened? Brandy, Calvert, brandy! Don't just stand there, man. Brandy!"

Uncle Arthur seemed to think he was in a pub but, as it happened, I did have some brandy left. I handed him the glass and said: "If you'll attend to Lady Skouras, sir, I'll finish getting the anchor up."

"No, no!" She took a gulp of the brandy, choked on it and I had to wait until she had finished coughing before she went on. "They're not coming for at least two hours yet. I know. I heard. There's something terrible going on, Sir Arthur. I had to come, I had to come."

"Now, don't distress yourself, Lady Skouras, don't distress

yourself," Uncle Arthur said, as if she weren't distressed enough already. "Just drink this down, Lady Skouras."

"No, not that!" I got all set to take a poor view of this, it was damned good brandy, then I realised she was talking of something else. "Not Lady Skouras. Never again! Charlotte. Charlotte Meiner. Charlotte."

One thing about women, they always get their sense of priorities right. There they were on the *Shangri-la*, rigging up a home-made atom bomb to throw through our saloon windows and all she could think was to ask us to call her "Charlotte." I said: "Why did you have to come?"

"Calvert!" Uncle Arthur's voice was sharp. "Do you mind? Lady—I mean, Charlotte—has just suffered a severe shock. Let her take her time to——"

"No." She struggled to an upright sitting position and forced a wan smile, half-scared, half-mocking. "No, Mr. Petersen, Mr. Calvert, whatever your name, you're quite right. Actresses tend to over-indulge their emotions. I'm not an actress any longer." She took another sip of the brandy and a little colour came back to her face. "I've known for some time that something was very far wrong aboard the *Shangri-la*. Strange men have been aboard. Some of the old crew were changed for no reason. Several times I've been put ashore with the stewardess in hotels while the *Shangri-la* went off on mysterious journeys. My husband—Sir Anthony—would tell me nothing. He has changed terribly since our marriage—I think he takes drugs. I've seen guns. Whenever those strange men came aboard I was sent to my stateroom after dinner." She smiled mirthlessly. "It wasn't because of any jealousy on my husband's part, you may believe me. The last day or two I sensed that everything was coming to a climax. To-night, just after you were gone, I was sent to my stateroom. I left, but stayed out in the passage. Lavorski was talking. I heard him saying: 'If your admiral pal is a UNESCO delegate, Skouras, then I'm King Neptune. I know who he is. We all know who he is. It's too late in the day now and they know too much. It's them or us.' And then Captain Imrie—how I hate that man!—said:

'I'll send Quinn and Jacques and Kramer at midnight. At one o'clock they'll open the sea-cocks in the Sound.' "

"Charming friends your husband has," I murmured.

She looked at me, half-uncertainly, half-speculatively and said: "Mr. Petersen or Mr. Calvert—and I heard Lavorski call you Johnson——"

"It *is* confusing," I admitted. "Calvert. Philip Calvert."

"Well, Philip,"—she pronounced it the French way and very nice it sounded too—"you are one great bloody fool if you talk like that. You are in deadly danger."

"Mr. Calvert," Uncle Arthur said sourly—it wasn't her language he disapproved of, it was this Christian name familiarity between the aristocracy and the peasants—"is quite aware of the danger. He has unfortunate mannerisms of speech, that's all. You are a very brave woman, Charlotte." Blue-bloods first-naming each other was a different thing altogether. "You took a great risk in eavesdropping. You might have been caught."

"I was caught, Sir Arthur." The smile showed up the lines on either side of her mouth but didn't touch her eyes. "That is another reason why I am here. Even without the knowledge of your danger, yes, I would have come. My husband caught me. He took me into my stateroom." She stood up shakily, turned her back to us and pulled up the sodden dark shirt. Right across her back ran three great blue-red weals. Uncle Arthur stood stock-still, a man incapable of movement. I crossed the saloon and peered at her back. The weals were almost an inch wide and running half-way round her body. Here and there were tiny blood-spotted punctures. Lightly I tried a finger on one of the weals. The flesh was raised and puffy, a fresh weal, as lividly-genuine a weal as ever I'd clapped eyes on. She didn't move. I stepped back and she turned to face us.

"It is not nice, is it? It does not feel very nice." She smiled and again that smile. "I could show you worse than that."

"No, no, no," Uncle Arthur said hastily. "That will not be necessary." He was silent for a moment, then burst out: "My dear Charlotte, what you must have suffered. It's fiendish, absolutely fiendish. He must be—he must be inhuman. A monster. A monster, perhaps under the influence of drugs. I would never have believed it!" His face was brick-red with outrage and his voice sounded as if Quinn had him by the throat. Strangled. "No one would ever have believed it!"

"Except the late Lady Skouras," she said quietly. "I understand now why she was in and out of mental homes several times before she died." She shrugged. "I have no wish to go the same way. I am made of tougher stuff than Madeline Skouras. So I pick up my bag and run away." She nodded at the small polythene bag of clothes that had been tied to her waist. "Like Dick Whittington, is it not?"

"They'll be here long before midnight when they discover you're gone," I observed.

"It may be morning before they find out. Most nights I lock my cabin door. To-night I locked it from the outside."

"That helps," I said. "Standing about in those sodden clothes doesn't. There's no point in running away only to die of pneumonia. You'll find towels in my cabin. Then we can get you a room in the Columba Hotel."

"I had hoped for better than that." The fractional slump of the shoulders was more imagined than seen, but the dull defeat in the eyes left nothing to the imagination. "You would put me in the first place they would look for me. There is no safe place for me in Torbay. They will catch me and bring me back and my husband will take me into that stateroom again. My only hope is to run away. Your only hope is to run away. Please. Can we not run away together?"

"No."

"A man not given to evasive answers, is that it?" There was a lonely dejection, a proud humiliation about her that did very little for my self-respect. She turned towards Uncle Arthur, took both his hands in hers and said in a low voice: "Sir Arthur. I appeal to you as an English gentleman." Thumbs down on Calvert, that foreign-born peasant. "May I stay? Please?"

Uncle Arthur looked at me, hesitated, looked at Charlotte

Skouras, looked into those big brown eyes and was a lost man.

"Of course you may stay, my dear Charlotte." He gave a stiff old-fashioned bow which,I had to admit, went very well with the beard and the monocle. "Yours to command, my dear lady."

"Thank you, Sir Arthur." She smiled at me, not with triumph or satisfaction, just an anxious-to-be-friendly smile. "It would be nice, Philip, to have the consent—what do you say?—unanimous."

"If Sir Arthur wishes to expose you to a vastly greater degree of risk aboard this boat than you would experience in Torbay, that is Sir Arthur's business. As for the rest, my consent is not required. I'm a well-trained civil servant and I obey orders."

"You are gracious to a fault," Uncle Arthur said acidly.

"Sorry, sir." I'd suddenly seen the light and a pretty dazzling beam it was too. "I should not have called your judgment in question. The lady is very welcome. But I think she should remain below while we are alongside the pier, sir."

"A reasonable request and a wise precaution," Uncle Arthur said mildly. He seemed pleased at my change of heart, at my proper deference to the wishes of the aristocracy.

"It won't be for long." I smiled at Charlotte Skouras. "We leave Torbay within the hour."

"What do I care what you charge him with?" I looked from Sergeant MacDonald to the broken-faced man with the wet blood-stained towel, then back to MacDonald again. "Breaking and entering. Assault and battery. Illegal possession of a dangerous weapon with intent to create a felony—murder. Anything you like."

"Well, now. It's just not quite as easy as that." Sergeant MacDonald spread his big brown hands across the counter of the tiny police station and looked at the prisoner and myself in turn. "He didn't break and enter, you know, Mr. Petersen. He boarded. No law against that. Assault and battery? It looks as if he has been the victim and not the perpetrator. And what kind of weapon was he carrying Mr. Petersen?"

"I don't know. It must have been knocked overboard."

"I see. Knocked overboard, was it? So we have no real proof of any felonious intent."

I was becoming a little tired of Sergeant MacDonald. He was fast enough to co-operate with bogus customs officers but with me he was just being deliberately obstructive. I said: "You'll be telling me next that it's all a product of my fevered imagination You'll be telling me next that I just stepped ashore, grabbed the first passer-by I saw, hit him in the face with a four-by-two then dragged him up here inventing this tale as I went. Even you can't be so stupid as to believe that."

The brown face turned red and, on the counter, the brown knuckles turned ivory. He said softly: "You'll kindly not talk to me like that."

"If you insist on behaving like a fool I'll treat you as such. Are you going to lock him up?"

"It's only your word against his."

"No. I had a witness. He's down at the old pier now, if you want to see him. Admiral Sir Arthur Arnford-Jason. A very senior civil servant."

"You had a Mr. Hunslett with you last time I was aboard your boat."

"He's down there, too." I nodded at the prisoner. "Why don't you ask a few questions of our friend here?"

"I've sent for the doctor. He'll have to fix his face first. I can't understand a word he says."

"The state of his face doesn't help," I admitted. "But the main trouble is that he speaks in Italian."

"Italian, is it? I'll soon fix that. The owner of the Western Isles café is an Italian."

"That helps. There are four little questions he might put to our pal here. Where is his passport, how he arrived in this country, who is his employer and where does he live."

The sergeant looked at me for a long moment then said slowly: "It's a mighty queer marine biologist that you are, Mr. Petersen."

"And it's a mighty queer police sergeant that you are, Mr. MacDonald. Good night."

I crossed the dimly-lit street to the sea-wall and waited in the shadow of a phone booth. After two minutes a man with a small bag came hurrying up the street and turned into the police station. He was out again in five minutes, which wasn't surprising: there was little a G.P. could do for what was plainly a hospital job.

The station door opened again and Sergeant MacDonald came hurrying out, long black mackintosh buttoned to the neck. He walked quickly along the sea wall, looking neither to left nor right, which made it very easy for me to follow him, and turned down the old stone pier. At the end of the pier he flashed a torch, went down a flight of steps and began to haul in a small boat. I leaned over the pier wall and switched on my own torch.

"Why don't they provide you with a telephone or radio for conveying urgent messages?" I asked. "You could catch your death of cold rowing out to the *Shangri-la* on a night like this."

He straightened slowly and let the rope fall from his hands. The boat drifted out into the darkness. He came up the steps with the slow heavy tread of an old man and said quietly: "What did you say about the *Shangri-la?*"

"Don't let me keep you, Sergeant," I said affably. "Duty before the idle social chit-chat. Your first duty is to your masters. Off you go, now, tell them that one of their hirelings has been severely clobbered and that Petersen has very grave suspicions about Sergeant MacDonald."

"I don't know what you are talking about," he said emptily. "The *Shangri-la*—I'm not going anywhere near the *Shangri-la.*"

"Where are you going, then? Do tell. Fishing? Kind of forgotten your tackle, haven't you?"

"And how would you like to mind your own damn' business?" MacDonald said heavily.

"That's what I'm doing. Come off it, Sergeant. Think I give a damn about our Italian pal? You can charge him with playing tiddley-winks in the High Street for all I care. I just threw him at you, together with a hint that you yourself were up to no good, to see what the reaction would be, to remove the last doubts in my mind. You reacted beautifully."

"I'm maybe not the cleverest, Mr. Petersen," he said with dignity. "Neither am I a complete idiot. I thought you were one of them or after the same thing as them." He paused. "You're not. You're a Government agent."

"I'm a civil servant." I nodded to where the *Firecrest* lay not twenty yards away. "You'd better come to meet my boss."

"I don't take orders from Civil Servants."

"Suit yourself," I said indifferently, turned away and looked out over the sea-wall. "About your two sons, Sergeant Mac-Donald. The sixteen-year-old twins who, I'm told, died in the Cairngorms some time back."

"What about my sons?" he said tonelessly.

"Just that I'm not looking forward to telling them that their own father wouldn't lift a finger to bring them back to life again."

He just stood there in the darkness, quite still, saying nothing. He offered no resistance when I took his arm and led him towards the *Firecrest*.

Uncle Arthur was at his most intimidating and Uncle Arthur in full intimidating cry was a sight to behold. He'd made no move to rise when I'd brought MacDonald into the saloon and he hadn't asked him to sit. The blue basilisk stare, channelled and magnified by the glittering monocle, transfixed the unfortunate sergeant like a laser beam.

"So your foot slipped, Sergeant," Uncle Arthur said without preamble. He was using his cold, flat, quite uninflected voice, the one that curled your hair. "The fact that you stand here now indicates that. Mr. Calvert went ashore with a prisoner and enough rope for you to hang yourself and you seized it with both hands. Not very clever of you, Sergeant. You should not have tried to contact your friends."

"They are no friends of mine, sir," MacDonald said bitterly.

"I'm going to tell you as much as you need to know about Calvert—Petersen was a pseudonym—and myself and what we are doing." Uncle Arthur hadn't heard him. "If you ever repeat any part of what I say to anyone, it will cost you your job, your pension, any hope that you will ever again, in whatever capacity, get another job in Britain and several years in prison for contravention of the Official Secrets Act. I myself will personally formulate the charges." He paused then added in a masterpiece of superfluity: "Do I make myself clear?"

"You make yourself very clear," MacDonald said grimly.

So Uncle Arthur told him all he thought MacDonald needed to know, which wasn't much, and finished by saying: "I am sure we can now count on your hundred per cent co-operation, Sergeant."

"Calvert is just guessing at my part in this," he said dully.

"For God's sake!" I said. "You *knew* those customs officers were bogus. You *knew* they had no photo-copier with them. You *knew* their only object in coming aboard was to locate and smash that set—and locate any other we might have. You *knew* they couldn't have gone back to the mainland in that launch—it was too rough. The launch, was, in fact, the *Shangri-la*'s tender—which is why you left without lights—and no launch left the harbour after your departure. We'd have heard it. The only life we saw after that was when they switched on their lights in the *Shangri-la*'s wheelhouse to smash up their own radio—*one* of their own radios, I should have said. And how did you *know* the telephone lines were down in the Sound? You knew they were down, but why did you say the Sound? Because you *knew* they had been cut there. Then, yesterday morning, when I asked you if there was any hope of the lines being repaired, you said no. Odd. One would have thought that you would have told the customs boys going back to the mainland to contact the G.P.O. at once. But you *knew* they weren't going back there. And your two sons, Sergeant, the boys supposed to be dead, you forgot to close their accounts. Because you *knew* they weren't dead."

"I forgot about the accounts," MacDonald said slowly. "And all the other points—I'm afraid I'm not good at this sort of thing." He looked at Uncle Arthur. "I know this is the end of the road for me. They said they would kill my boys, sir."

"If you will extend us your full co-operation," Uncle Arthur said precisely, "I will personally see to it that you remain the Torbay police sergeant until you're falling over your beard. Who are 'they'?"

"The only men I've seen is a fellow called Captain Imrie and the two customs men—Durran and Thomas. Durran's real name is Quinn. I don't know the others' names. I usually meet them in my house, after dark. I've been out to the *Shangri-la* only twice. To see Imrie."

"And Sir Anthony Skouras?"

"I don't know." MacDonald shrugged helplessly. "He's a good man, sir, he really is. Or I thought so. Maybe he is mixed up in this. Anyone can fall into bad company. It's very strange, sir."

"Isn't it? And what's been your part in this?"

"There's been funny things happening in this area in the past months. Boats have vanished. People have vanished. Fishermen have had their nets torn, in harbour, and yacht engines have been mysteriously damaged, also in harbour. This is when Captain Imrie wants to prevent certain boats from going certain places at the wrong time."

"And your part is to investigate with great diligence and a total lack of success," Uncle Arthur nodded. "You must be invaluable to them, Sergeant. A man with your record and character is above suspicion. Tell me, Sergeant, what are they up to?"

"Before God, sir, I have no idea."

"You're totally in the dark?"

"Yes, sir."

"I don't doubt it. This is the way the very top men operate. And you will have no idea where your boys are being held?"

"No, sir."

"How do you know they're alive?"

"I was taken out to the *Shangri-la* three weeks ago. My sons had been brought there from God only knows where. They were well."

"And are you really so naïve as to believe that your sons will be well and will be returned alive when all this is over? Even although your boys will be bound to know who their captors are and would be available for testimony and identification if the time came for that?"

"Captain Imrie said they would come to no harm. If I co-operated. He said that only fools ever used unnecessary violence."

"You are convinced, then, they wouldn't go to the length of murder?"

"Murder! What are you talking about, sir?"

"Calvert?"

"Sir?"

"A large whisky for the sergeant."

"Yes, sir." When it came to lashing out with my private supplies Uncle Arthur was generous to a fault. Uncle Arthur paid no entertainment allowance. So I poured the sergeant a large whisky and, seeing that bankruptcy was inevitable anyway, did the same for myself. Ten seconds later the sergeant's glass was empty. I took his arm and led him to the engine-room. When we came back to the saloon in a minute's time the sergeant needed no persuading to accept another glass. His face was pale.

"I told you that Calvert carried out a helicopter reconnaissance to-day," Uncle Arthur said conversationally. "What I didn't tell you was that his pilot was murdered this evening. I didn't tell you that two other of my best agents have been killed in the last sixty hours. And now, as you've just seen, Hunslett. Do you still believe, Sergeant, that we are dealing with a bunch of gentlemanly law-breakers to whom human life is sacrosanct?"

"What do you want me to do, sir?" Colour was back in the brown cheeks again and the eyes were cold and hard and a little desperate.

"You and Calvert will take Hunslett ashore to your office. You will call in the doctor and ask for an official post-mortem—we must have an official cause of death. For the trial. The other dead men are probably beyond recovery. You will then row out to the *Shangri-la* and tell Imrie that we brought Hunslett and the other man—the Italian—to your office. You will tell them that you heard us say that we must go to the mainland for new depth-sounding equipment and for armed help and that we can't be back for two days at least. Do you know where the telephone lines are cut in the Sound?"

"Yes, sir. I cut them myself."

"When you get back from the *Shangri-la* get out there and fix them. Before dawn. Before dawn to-morrow you, your wife and son must disappear. For thirty-six hours. If you want to live. That is understood?"

"I understand what you want done. Not why you want it done."

"Just do it. One last thing. Hunslett has no relations—few of my men have—so he may as well be buried in Torbay. Knock up your local undertaker during the night and make arrangements for the funeral on Friday. Calvert and I would like to be there."

"But—but Friday? That's just the day after to-morrow."

"The day after to-morrow. It will be all over then. You'll have your boys back home."

MacDonald looked at him in long silence, then said slowly: "How can you be sure?"

"I'm not sure at all." Uncle Arthur passed a weary hand across his face and looked at me. "Calvert is. It's a pity, Sergeant, that the Secrets Act will never permit you to tell your friends that you once knew Philip Calvert. If it can be done, Calvert can do it. I think he can. I certainly hope so."

"I certainly hope so, too," MacDonald said sombrely.

Me too, more than either of them, but there was already so much despondency around that it didn't seem right to deepen it, so I just put on my confident face and led MacDonald back down to the engine-room.

7

Three of them came to kill us, not at midnight as promised, but at
10.40 p.m. that night. Had they come five minutes earlier then
they would have got us because five minutes earlier we were still
tied up to the old stone pier. And had they come and got us that
five minutes earlier, then the fault would have been mine for, after
leaving Hunslett in the police station I had insisted that Sergeant
MacDonald accompany me to use his authority in knocking up
and obtaining service from the proprietor of the only chemist's
shop in Torbay. Neither of them had been too keen on giving me
the illegal help I wanted and it had taken me a full five minutes
and the best part of my extensive repertoire of threats to extract
from the very elderly chemist the minimum of reluctant service
and a small green-ribbed bottle informatively labelled "The
Tablets." But I was lucky and I was back aboard the *Firecrest*
just after 10.30 p.m.

The west coast of Scotland doesn't go in much for golden Indian summers and that night was no exception. Apart from being
cold and windy, which was standard, it was also black as sin and
bucketing heavily, which if not quite standard was at least not so
unusual as to excite comment. A minute after leaving the pier I
had to switch on the searchlight mounted on the wheelhouse roof.
The western entrance to the Sound from Torbay harbour, between Torbay and Garve Island, is a quarter of a mile wide and I
could have found it easily on a compass course: but there were
small yachts, I knew, between the pier and the entrance and if
any of them was carrying a riding light it was invisible in that
driving rain.

The searchlight control was on the wheelhouse deckhead. I

moved it to point the beam down and ahead, then traversed it through a forty-degree arc on either side of the bows.

I picked up the first boat inside five seconds, not a yacht riding at its moorings but a rowing dinghy moving slowly through the water. It was fine on the port bow, maybe fifty yards away. I couldn't identify the man at the oars, the oars wrapped at their middle with some white cloth to muffle the sound of the rowlocks, because his back was towards me. A very broad back. Quinn. The man in the bows was sitting facing me. He wore oilskins and a dark beret and in his hand he held a gun. At fifty yards it's almost impossible to identify any weapon, but his looked like a German Schmeisser machine-pistol. Without a doubt Jacques, the machine-gun specialist. The man crouched low in the sternsheets was quite unidentifiable, but I could see the gleam of a short gun in his hand. Messrs. Quinn, Jacques and Kramer coming to pay their respects as Charlotte Skouras had said they would. But much ahead of schedule.

Charlotte Skouras was on my right in the darkened wheelhouse. She'd been there only three minutes, having spent all our time alongside in her darkened cabin with the door closed. Uncle Arthur was on my left, desecrating the clean night air with one of his cheroots. I reached up for a clipped torch and patted my right-hand pocket to see if the Lilliput was still there. It was.

I said to Charlotte Skouras: "Open the wheelhouse door. Put it back on the catch and stand clear." Then I said to Uncle Arthur: "Take the wheel, sir. Hard a-port when I call. Then back north on course again."

He took the wheel without a word. I heard the starboard wheelhouse door click on its latch. We were doing no more than three knots through the water. The dinghy was twenty-five yards away, the men in the bows and stern holding up arms to shield their eyes from our searchlight. Quinn had stopped rowing. On our present course we'd leave them at least ten feet on our port beam. I kept the searchlight steady on the boat.

Twenty yards separated us and I could see Jacques lining up his machine-pistol on our light when I thrust the throttle lever

156

right open. The note of the big diesel exhaust deepened and the *Firecrest* began to surge forward.

"Hard over now," I said.

Uncle Arthur spun the wheel. The sudden thrust of our single port screw boiled back against the port-angled rudder, pushing the stern sharply to starboard. Flame lanced from Jacques' machine-pistol, a silent flame, he'd a silencer on. Bullets ricocheted off our aluminium foremast but missed both light and wheelhouse. Quinn saw what was coming and dug his oars deep but he was too late. I shouted "Midships, now," pulled the throttle lever back to neutral and jumped out through the starboard doorway on to the deck.

We hit them just where Jacques was sitting, breaking off the dinghy's bows, capsizing it and throwing the three men into the water. The overturned remains of the boat and a couple of struggling figures came slowly down the starboard side of the *Firecrest*. My torch picked up the man closer in to our side. Jacques, with the machine-pistol held high above his head, instinctively trying to keep it dry though it must have been soaked when he had been catapulted into the water. I held gun-hand and torch-hand together, aiming down the bright narrow beam. I squeezed the Lilliput's trigger twice and a bright crimson flower bloomed where his face had been. He went down as if a shark had got him, the gun still in the stiffly-upstretched arms. It was a Schmeisser machine-pistol all right. I shifted the torch. There was only one other to be seen in the water and it wasn't Quinn, he'd either dived under the *Firecrest* or was sheltering under the upturned wreck of the dinghy. I fired twice more at the second figure and he started to scream. The screaming went on for two or three seconds, then stopped in a shuddering gurgle. I heard the sound of someone beside me on the deck being violently sick over the side. Charlotte Skouras. But I'd no time to stay and comfort Charlotte Skouras, she'd no damned right to be out on deck anyway. I had urgent matters to attend to, such as preventing Uncle Arthur from cleaving Torbay's old stone pier in half. The townspeople would not have liked it. Uncle Arthur's idea of midships differed sharply from mine, he'd brought the *Firecrest* round in a three-quarter circle. He would have been the ideal man at the helm of one of those ram-headed Phœnician galleys that specialised in cutting the opposition in two, but as a helmsman in Torbay harbour he lacked something. I jumped into the wheelhouse, pulled the throttle all the way to astern and spun the wheel to port. I jumped out again and pulled Charlotte Skouras away before she got her head knocked off by one of the barnacle-encrusted piles that fronted the pier. Whether or not we grazed the pier was impossible to say but we sure as hell gave the barnacles a nasty turn.

I moved back into the wheelhouse, taking Charlotte Skouras with me. I was breathing heavily. All this jumping in and out through wheelhouse doors took it out of a man. I said: "With all respects, sir, what the hell were you trying to do?"

"Me?" He was as perturbed as a hibernating bear in January. "Is something up, then?"

I moved the throttle to slow ahead, took the wheel from him and brought the *Firecrest* round till we were due north on a compass bearing. I said: "Keep it there, please," and did some more traversing with the searchlight. The waters around were black and empty, there was no sign even of the dinghy. I'd expected to see every light in Torbay lit up like a naval review, those four shots, even the Lilliput's sharp, light-weight cracks, should have had them all on their feet. But nothing, no sign, no movement at all. The gin bottle levels would be lower than ever. I looked at the compass: north-twenty-west. Like the honey-bee for the flower, the iron filing for the magnet, Uncle Arthur was determinedly heading straight for the shore again. I took the wheel from him, gently but firmly, and said: "You came a bit close to the pier back there, sir."

"I believe I did." He took out a handkerchief and wiped his monocle. "Damn' glass misted up just at the wrong moment. I trust, Calvert, that you weren't just firing at random out there." Uncle Arthur had become a good deal more bellicose in the past hour or so: he'd had a high regard for Hunslett.

"I got Jacques and Kramer. Jacques was the handy one with the automatic arms. He's dead. I think Kramer is too. Quinn got away." What a set-up, I thought bleakly, what a set-up. Alone with Uncle Arthur on the high seas in the darkness of the night. I'd always known that his eyesight, even in optimum conditions, was pretty poor: but I'd never suspected that, when the sun was down, he was virtually blind as a bat. But unfortunately, unlike the bat, Uncle Arthur wasn't equipped with a built-in radar which would enable him to shy clear of rocks, headlands, islands and such-like obstructions of a similarly permanent and final nature with which we might go bump in the dark. To all intents and purposes I was single-handed. This called for a radical revision in plans only I didn't see how I could radically revise anything.

"Not too bad," Uncle Arthur said approvingly. "Pity about Quinn, but otherwise not too bad at all. The ranks of the ungodly are being satisfactorily depleted. Do you think they'll come after us?"

"No. For four reasons. One, they won't know yet what has happened. Two, both their sorties this evening have gone badly and they won't be in a hurry to try any more boarding expeditions for some time. Three, they'd use the tender for this job, not the *Shangri-la* and if they get that tender a hundred yards I've lost all faith in demerara sugar. Four, there's mist or fog coming up. The lights of Torbay are obscured already. They can't follow us because they can't find us."

Till that moment the only source of illumination we'd had in the wheelhouse had come from the reflected light of the compass lamp. Suddenly the overhead light came on. Charlotte Skouras's hand was on the switch. Her face was haggard and she was staring at me as if I were the thing from outer space. Not one of those admiring affectionate looks.

"What kind of man are you, Mr. Calvert?" No "Philip" this time. Her voice was lower and huskier than ever and it had a shake in it. "You—you're not human. You kill two men and go on speaking calmly and reasonably as if nothing had happened.

What in God's name are you, a hired killer? It's—it's unnatural. Have you no feelings, no emotions, no regrets?"

"Yes, I have. I'm sorry I didn't kill Quinn too."

She stared at me with something like horror in her face, then switched her gaze to Uncle Arthur. She said to him and her voice was almost a whisper: "I saw that man, Sir Arthur. I saw his face being blown apart by the bullets. Mr. Calvert could have— could have arrested him, held him up and handed him over to the police. But he didn't. He killed him. And the other. It was slow and deliberate. Why, why, why?"

"There's no 'why' about it, my dear Charlotte." Sir Arthur sounded almost irritable. "There's no justification needed. Calvert killed them or they killed us. They came to kill us. You told us that yourself. Would you feel any compunction at killing a poisonous snake? Those men were no better than that. As for arresting them!" Uncle Arthur paused, maybe for the short laugh he gave, maybe because he was trying to recall the rest of the homily I'd delivered to him earlier that evening. "There's no intermediate stage in this game. It's kill or be killed. These are dangerous and deadly men and you never give them warning." Good old Uncle Arthur, he'd remembered the whole lecture, practically word for word.

She looked at him for a long moment, her face uncomprehending, looked at me then slowly turned and left the wheelhouse.

I said to Uncle Arthur: "You're just as bad as I am."

She reappeared again exactly at midnight, switching on the light as she entered. Her hair was combed and neat, her face was less puffy and she was dressed in one of those synthetic fibre dresses, white, ribbed and totally failing to give the impression that she stood in need of a good meal. From the way she eased her shoulders I could see that her back hurt. She gave me a faint tentative smile. She got none in return.

I said: "Half an hour ago, rounding Carrara Point, I near as dammit carried away the lighthouse. Now I hope I'm heading north of Dubh Sgeir but I may be heading straight into the middle of it. It couldn't be any blacker if you were a mile down in an abandoned coal mine, the fog is thickening, I'm a not very experienced sailor trying to navigate my way through the most dangerous waters in Britain and whatever hope we have of survival depends on the preservation of what night-sight I've slowly and painfully built up over the past hour or so. *Put out that damned light!*"

"I'm sorry." The light went out. "I didn't think."

"And don't switch on any other lights either. Not even in your cabin. Rocks are the least of my worries in Loch Houron."

"I'm sorry," she repeated. "And I'm sorry about earlier on. That's why I came up. To tell you that. About the way I spoke and leaving so abruptly, I mean. I've no right to sit on judgment on others—and I think my judgment was wrong. I was just—well, literally shocked. To see two men killed like that, no, not killed, there's always heat and anger about killing, to see two men executed like that, because it wasn't kill or be killed as Sir Arthur said, and then see the person who did it not care . . ." Her voice faded away uncertainly.

"You might as well get your facts and figures right, my dear," Uncle Arthur said. "Three men, not two. He killed one just before you came on board to-night. He had no option. But Philip Calvert is not what any reasonable man would call a killer. He doesn't care in the way you say, because if he did he would go mad. In another way, he cares very much. He doesn't do this job for money. He's miserably paid for a man of his unique talents." I made a mental note to bring this up next time we were alone. "He doesn't do it for excitement, for—what is the modern expression?—kicks: a man who devotes his spare time to music, astronomy and philosophy does not live for kicks. But he cares. He cares for the difference between right and wrong, between good and evil, and when that difference is great enough and the evil threatens to destroy the good then he does not hesitate to take steps to redress the balance. And maybe that makes him better than either you or me, my dear Charlotte."

"And that's not all of it either," I said. "I'm also renowned for my kindness to little children."

"I'm sorry, Calvert," Uncle Arthur said. "No offence and no embarrassment, I hope. But if Charlotte thought it important enough to come up here and apologise, I thought it important enough to set the record straight."

"That's not all Charlotte came up for," I said nastily. "*If* that's what she came up for in the first place. She came up here because she's consumed with feminine curiosity. She wants to know where we are going."

"Do you mind if I smoke?" she asked.

"Don't strike the match in front of my eyes."

She lit the cigarette and said: "Consumed with curiosity is right. What do you think? Not about where we're going, I know where we're going. You told me. Up Loch Houron. What I want to know is what is going on, what all this dreadful mystery is about, why all the comings and goings of strange men aboard the *Shangri-la*, what is so fantastically important to justify the deaths of three men in one evening, what you are doing here, what you are, who you are. I never really thought you were a UNESCO delegate, Sir Arthur. I know now you're not. Please. I have the right to know, I think."

"Don't tell her," I advised.

"Why ever not?" Uncle Arthur said huffily. "As she says, she is deeply involved, whether she wants it or not. She does have the right to know. Besides, the whole thing will be public knowledge in a day or two."

"You didn't think of that when you threatened Sergeant MacDonald with dismissal and imprisonment if he contravened the Official Secrets Act."

"Merely because he could ruin things by talking out of turn," he said stiffly. "Lady—I mean, Charlotte—is in no position to do so. Not, of course," he went on quickly, "that she would ever dream of doing so. Preposterous. Charlotte is an old and dear friend, a *trusted* friend, Calvert. She *shall* know."

Charlotte said quietly: "I have the feeling that our friend Mr.

162

Calvert does not care for me overmuch. Or maybe he just does not care for women."

"I care like anything," I said. "I was merely reminding the Admiral of his own dictum: Never, never, never—I forget how many nevers, I think there were four or five—tell anyone anything unless it's necessary, essential and vital. In this case it's none of the three."

Uncle Arthur lit another vile cheroot and ignored me. His dictum was not meant to refer to confidential exchanges between members of the aristocracy. He said: "This is the case of the missing ships, my dear Charlotte. Five missing ships, to be precise. Not to mention a fair scattering of very much smaller vessels, also missing or destroyed.

"Five ships, I said. On 5th April of this year the S.S. *Holmwood* disappeared off the south coast of Ireland. It was an act of piracy. The crew was imprisoned ashore, kept under guard for two or three days, then released unharmed. The *Holmwood* was never heard of again. On 24th April, the M.V. *Antara* vanished in St. George's Channel. On 17th May, the M.V. *Headley Pioneer* disappeared off Northern Ireland, on 6th August the S.S. *Hurricane Spray* disappeared after leaving the Clyde and, finally, last Saturday, a vessel called the *Nantesville* vanished soon after leaving Bristol. In all cases the crews turned up unharmed.

"Apart from their disappearances and the safe reappearances of their crews, those five vessels all had one thing in common—they were carrying extremely valuable and virtually untraceable cargoes. The *Holmwood* had two and a half million pounds of South African gold aboard, the *Antara* had a million and a half pounds' worth of uncut Brazilian diamonds for industrial use, the *Headley Pioneer* had close on two million pounds' worth of mixed cut and uncut Andean emeralds from the Muzo mines in Colombia, the *Hurricane Spray*, which had called in at Glasgow *en route* from Rotterdam to New York, had just over three million pounds' worth of diamonds, nearly all cut, and the last one, the *Nantesville*,"—Uncle Arthur almost choked over this one—"had eight

163

million pounds in gold ingots, reserves being called in by the U.S. Treasury.

"We had no idea where the people responsible for these disappearances were getting their information. Such arrangements as to the decision to ship, when, how and how much, are made in conditions of intense secrecy. They, whoever 'they' are, had impeccable sources of information. Calvert says he knows those sources now. After the disappearance of the first three ships and about six million pounds' worth of specie it was obvious that a meticulously organised gang was at work."

"Do you mean to say—do you mean to say that Captain Imrie is mixed up in this?" Charlotte asked.

"Mixed up is hardly the word," Uncle Arthur said dryly. "He may well be the directing mind behind it all."

"And don't forget old man Skouras," I advised. "He's pretty deep in the mire, too—about up to his ears, I should say."

"You've no right to say that," Charlotte said quickly.

"No right? Why ever not? What's he to you and what's all this defence of the maestro of the bull-whip? How's your back now?"

She said nothing. Uncle Arthur said nothing, in a different kind of way, then went on:

"It was Calvert's idea to hide two of our men and a radio signal transmitter on most of the ships that sailed with cargoes of bullion or specie after the *Headley Pioneer* had vanished. We had no difficulty, as you can imagine, in securing the co-operation of the various exporting and shipping companies and governments concerned. Our agents—we had three pairs working—usually hid among the cargo or in some empty cabin or machinery space with a food supply. Only the masters of the vessels concerned knew they were aboard. They delivered a fifteen-second homing signal at fixed—very precisely fixed—but highly irregular intervals. Those signals were picked up at selected receiving stations round the west coast—we limited our stations to that area for that was where the released crews had been picked up—and by a receiver aboard this very boat here. The *Firecrest*, my dear Charlotte, is a highly unusual craft in many respects." I thought he was going to boast, quietly of course, of his own brilliance in designing the *Firecrest* but he remembered in time that I knew the truth.

"Between 17th May and 6th August, nothing happened. No piracy. We believe they were deterred by the short, light nights. On 6th August, the *Hurricane Spray* disappeared. We had no one aboard that vessel—we couldn't cover them all. But we had two men aboard the *Nantesville*, the ship that sailed last Saturday. Delmont and Baker. Two of our best men. The *Nantesville* was forcibly taken just off the Bristol Channel. Baker and Delmont immediately began the scheduled transmissions. Cross-bearings gave us a completely accurate position at least every half-hour.

"Calvert and Hunslett were in Dublin, waiting. As soon——"

"That's right," she interrupted. "Mr. Hunslett. Where is he? I haven't seen——"

"In a moment. The *Firecrest* moved out, not following the *Nantesville*, but moving ahead of its predicted course. They reached the Mull of Kintyre and had intended waiting till the *Nantesville* approached there but a south-westerly gale blew up out of nowhere and the *Firecrest* had to run for shelter. When the *Nantesville* reached the Mull of Kintyre area our radio beacon fixes indicated that she was still on a mainly northerly course and that it looked as if she might pass up the Mull of Kintyre on the outside—the western side. Calvert took a chance, ran up Loch Fyne and through the Crinan Canal. He spent the night in the Crinan sea-basin. The sea-lock is closed at night. Calvert could have obtained the authority to have it opened but he didn't want to: the wind had veered to westerly late that evening and small boats don't move out of Crinan through the Dorus Mor in a westerly gusting up to Force 9. Not if they have wives and families to support—and even if they haven't.

"During the night the *Nantesville* turned out west into the Atlantic. We thought we had lost her. We think we know now why she turned out: she wanted to arrive at a certain place at a certain state of the tide in the hours of darkness, and she had time to kill. She went west, we believe, firstly because it was the

165

easiest way to ride out the westerly gale and, secondly, because she didn't want to be seen hanging around the coast all of the next day and preferred to make a direct approach from the sea as darkness was falling.

"The weather moderated a fair way overnight. Calvert left Crinan at dawn, almost at the very minute the *Nantesville* turned back east again. Radio transmissions were still coming in from Baker and Delmont exactly on schedule. The last transmission came at 1022 hours that morning: after that, nothing."

Uncle Arthur stopped and the cheroot glowed fiercely in the darkness. He could have made a fortune contracting out to the cargo shipping companies as a one-man fumigating service. Then he went on very quickly as if he didn't like what he had to say next, and I'm sure he didn't.

"We don't know what happened. They may have betrayed themselves by some careless action. I don't think so, they were too good for that. Some member of the prize crew may just have stumbled over their hiding-place. Again it's unlikely, and a man who stumbled over Baker and Delmont wouldn't be doing any more stumbling for some time to come. Calvert thinks, and I agree with him, that by the one unpredictable chance in ten thousand, the prize crew's radio-operator happened to be traversing Baker and Delmont's wave-band at the very moment they were sending their fifteen second transmission. At that range he'd about have his head blasted off and the rest was inevitable.

"A plot of the *Nantesville*'s fixes between dawn and the last transmission showed her course as 082° true. Predicted destination—Loch Houron. Estimated time of arrival—sunset. Calvert had less than a third of the *Nantesville*'s distance to cover. But he didn't take the *Firecrest* into Loch Houron because he was pretty sure that Captain Imrie would recognise a radio beacon transmitter when he saw one and would assume that we had his course. Calvert was also pretty sure that if the *Nantesville* elected to continue on that course—and he had a hunch that it would—any craft found in the entrance to Loch Houron would receive pretty short shrift, either by being run down or sunk by gunfire.

So he parked the *Firecrest* in Torbay and was skulking around the entrance to Loch Houron in a frogman's suit and with a motorised rubber dinghy when the *Nantesville* turned up. He went aboard in darkness. The name was changed, the flag was changed, one mast was missing and the superstructure had been repainted. But it was the *Nantesville*.

"Next day Calvert and Hunslett were storm-bound in Torbay but on Wednesday Calvert organised an air search for the *Nantesville* or some place where she might have been hidden. He made a mistake. He considered it extremely unlikely that the *Nantesville* would still be in Loch Houron because Imrie knew that we knew that he had been headed there and therefore would not stay there indefinitely, because the chart showed Loch Houron as being the last place in Scotland where anyone in their sane minds would consider hiding a vessel and because, after Calvert had left the *Nantesville* that evening, she'd got under way and started to move out to Carrara Point. Calvert thought she'd just stayed in Loch Houron till it was dark enough to pass undetected down the Sound of Torbay or round the south of Torbay Island to the mainland. So he concentrated most of his search on the mainland and on the Sound of Torbay and Torbay itself. He thinks now the *Nantesville* is in Loch Houron. We're going there to find out." His cheroot glowed again. "And that's it, my dear. Now, with your permission, I'd like to spend an hour on the saloon settee. Those nocturnal escapades . . ." He sighed, and finished: "I'm not a boy any longer. I need my sleep."

I liked that. I wasn't a boy any longer either and I didn't seem to have slept for months. Uncle Arthur, I knew, always went to bed on the stroke of midnight and the poor man had already lost fifteen minutes. But I didn't see what I could do about it. One of my few remaining ambitions in life was to reach pensionable age and I couldn't make a better start than by ensuring that Uncle Arthur never never laid hands on the wheel of the *Firecrest*.

"But surely that's not it," Charlotte protested. "That's not all of it. Mr. Hunslett, where's Mr. Hunslett? And you said Mr. Calvert was aboard the *Nantesville*. How on earth did he——?"

"There are some things you are better not knowing, my dear. Why distress yourself unnecessarily? Just leave this to us."

"You haven't had a good look at me recently, have you, Sir Arthur?" she asked quietly.

"I don't understand."

"It may have escaped your attention but I'm not a child any more. I'm not even young any more. Please don't treat me as a juvenile. And if you want to get to that settee to-night——"

"Very well. If you insist. The violence, I'm afraid, has not all been one-sided. Calvert, as I said, was aboard the *Nantesville*. He found my two operatives, Baker and Delmont." Uncle Arthur had the impersonal emotionless voice of a man checking his laundry list. "Both men had been stabbed to death. This evening the pilot of Calvert's helicopter was killed when the machine was shot down in the Sound of Torbay. An hour after that Hunslett was murdered. Calvert found him in the *Firecrest*'s engine-room with a broken neck."

Uncle Arthur's cheroot glowed and faded at least half a dozen times before Charlotte spoke. The shake was back in her voice. "They are fiends. Fiends." A long pause, then: "How can you cope with people like that?"

Uncle Arthur puffed a bit more then said candidly: "I don't intend to try. You don't find generals slugging it out hand-to-hand in the trenches. Calvert will cope with them. Good night, my dear."

He pushed off. I didn't contradict him. But I knew that Calvert couldn't cope with them. Not any more, he couldn't. Calvert had to have help. With a crew consisting of a myopic boss and a girl who, every time I looked at her, listened to her or thought of her, started the warning bells clanging away furiously in the back of my head, Calvert had to have a great deal of help. And he had to have it fast.

After Uncle Arthur had retired, Charlotte and I stood in silence in the darkened wheelhouse. But a companionable silence. You can always tell. The rain drummed on the wheelhouse roof. It

168

was as dark as it ever becomes at sea and the patches of white fog were increasing in density and number. Because of them I had cut down to half speed and with the loss of steerage way and that heavy westerly sea coming up dead astern I'd normally have been hard put to it to control the direction of the *Firecrest*: but I had the auto-pilot on and switched to "Fine" and we were doing famously. The auto-pilot was a much better helmsman than I was. And streets ahead of Uncle Arthur.

Charlotte said suddenly: "What is it you intend to do to-night?"

"You *are* a gourmand for information. Don't you know that Uncle Arthur—sorry, Sir Arthur—and I are engaged upon a highly secret mission? Security is all."

"And now you're laughing at me—and forgetting I'm along on this secret mission too."

"I'm glad you're along and I'm not laughing at you, because I'll be leaving this boat once or twice to-night and I have to have somebody I can trust to look after it when I'm away."

"You have Sir Arthur."

"I have, as you say, Sir Arthur. There's no one alive for whose judgment and intelligence I have greater respect. But at the present moment I'd trade in all the judgment and intelligence in the world for a pair of sharp young eyes. Going by to-night's performance, Sir Arthur shouldn't be allowed out without a white stick. How are yours?"

"Well, they're not so young any more, but I think they're sharp enough."

"So I can rely on you?"

"On me? I—well, I don't know anything about handling boats."

"You and Sir Arthur should make a great team. I saw you star once in a French film about——"

"We never left the studio. Even in the studio pool I had a stand-in."

"Well, there'll be no stand-in to-night." I glanced out through the streaming windows. "And no studio pool. This is the real stuff, the genuine Atlantic. A pair of eyes, Charlotte, that's all I require. A pair of eyes. Just cruising up and down till I come back and seeing that you don't go on the rocks. Can you do that?"

"Will I have any option?"

"Nary an option."

"Then I'll try. Where are you going ashore?"

"Eilean Oran and Craigmore. The two innermost islands in Loch Houron. If," I said thoughtfully, "I can find them."

"Eilean Oran and Craigmore." I could have been wrong, but I thought the faint French accent a vast improvement on the original Gaelic pronunciation. "It seems so wrong. So very wrong. In the middle of all this hate and avarice and killing. These names—they breathe the very spirit of romance."

"A highly deceptive form of respiration, my dear." I'd have to watch myself, I was getting as bad as Uncle Arthur. "Those islands breathe the very spirit of bare, bleak and rocky desolation. But Eilean Oran and Craigmore hold the key to everything. Of that I'm very sure."

She said nothing. I stared out through the high-speed Kent clear-view screen and wondered if I'd see Dubh Sgeir before it saw me. After a couple of minutes I felt a hand on my upper arm and she was very close to me. The hand was trembling. Wherever she'd come by her perfume it hadn't been bought in a super-market or fallen out of a Christmas cracker. Momentarily and vaguely I wondered about the grievous impossibility of ever understanding the feminine mind: before fleeing for what she had thought to be her life and embarking upon a hazardous swim in the waters of Torbay harbour, she hadn't forgotten to pack a sachet of perfume in her polythene kit-bag. For nothing was ever surer than that any perfume she'd been wearing had been well and truly removed before I'd fished her out of Torbay harbour.

"Philip?"

Well, this was better than the Mr. Calvert stuff. I was glad Uncle Arthur wasn't there to have his aristocratic feelings scandalised. I said: "Uh-huh?"

"I'm sorry." She said it as if she meant it and I supposed I should have tried to forget that she was once the best actress in

170

Europe. "I'm truly sorry. About what I said—about what I thought—earlier on. For thinking you were a monster. The men you killed, I mean. I—well, I didn't know about Hunslett and Baker and Delmont and the helicopter pilot. All your friends. I'm truly sorry, Philip. Truly."

She was overdoing it. She was also too damn' close. Too damn' warm. You'd have required a pile-driver in top condition to get a cigarette card between us. And that perfume that hadn't fallen out of a cracker—intoxicating, the ad-boys in the glossies would have called it. And all the time the warning bells were clanging away like a burglar alarm with the St. Vitus's dance. I made a manful effort to do something about it. I put my mind to higher things.

She said nothing. She just squeezed my arm a bit more and even the pile-driver would have gone on strike for piece-work rates. I could hear the big diesel exhaust thudding away behind us, a sound of desolate reassurance. The *Firecrest* swooped down the long overtaking combers then gently soared again. I was conscious for the first time of a curious meteorological freak in the Western Isles. A marked rise in temperature after midnight. And I'd have to speak to the Kent boys about their guarantee that their clear-view screen wouldn't mist up under any conditions, but maybe that wasn't fair, maybe they'd never visualised conditions like this. I was just thinking of switching off the auto-pilot to give me something to do when she said: "I think I'll go below soon. Would you like a cup of coffee first?"

"As long as you don't have to put on a light to do it. And as long as you don't trip over Uncle Arthur—I mean, Sir——"

"Uncle Arthur will do just fine," she said. "It suits him." Another squeeze of the arm and she was gone.

The meteorological freak was of short duration. By and by the temperature dropped back to normal and the Kent guarantee became operative again. I took a chance, left the *Firecrest* to its own devices and nipped aft to the stern locker. I took out my scuba diving equipment, together with air-cylinders and mask, and brought them for'ard to the wheelhouse.

It took her twenty-five minutes to make the coffee. Calor gas has many times the calorific efficiency of standard domestic coal gas and, even allowing for the difficulties of operating in darkness, this was surely a world record for slowness in making coffee at sea. I heard the clatter of crockery as the coffee was brought through the saloon and smiled cynically to myself in the darkness. Then I thought of Hunslett and Baker and Delmont and Williams, and I wasn't smiling any more.

I still wasn't smiling when I dragged myself on to the rocks of Eilean Oran, removed the scuba equipment and set the big, rectangular-based, swivel-headed torch between a couple of stones with its beam staring out to sea. I wasn't smiling, but it wasn't for the same reason that I hadn't been smiling when Charlotte had brought the coffee to the wheelhouse just over half an hour ago, I wasn't smiling because I was in a state of high apprehension and I was in a state of high apprehension because for ten minutes before leaving the *Firecrest* I'd tried to instruct Sir Arthur and Charlotte in the technique of keeping a boat in a constant position relative to a fixed mark on the shore.

"Keep her on a due west compass heading," I'd said. "Keep her bows on to the sea and wind. With the engine at 'Slow' that will give you enough steerage way to keep your head up. If you find yourselves creeping too far forwards, come round to the *south*"—if they'd come round to the north they'd have found themselves high and dry on the rocky shores of Eilean Oran— "head due east at half speed, because if you go any slower you'll broach to, come sharply round to the north then head west again at slow speed. You can see those breakers on the south shore there. Whatever you do, keep them at least two hundred yards away on the starboard hand when you're going west and a bit more when you're going east."

They had solemnly assured me that they would do just that and seemed a bit chuffed because of what must have been my patent lack of faith in them both, but I'd reason for my lack of faith for neither had shown any marked ability to make a clear distinction between shore breakers and the north-south line of the foaming tops of the waves rolling eastwards towards the mainland. In desperation I'd said I'd place a fixed light on the shore and that that would serve as a permanent guide. I just trusted to God that Uncle Arthur wouldn't emulate the part of an eighteenth-century French sloop's skipper vis-à-vis the smugglers' lamp on a rock-girt Cornish shore and run the damned boat aground under the impression that he was heading for a beacon of hope. He was a very clever man, was Uncle Arthur, but the sea was not his home.

The boatshed wasn't quite empty, but it wasn't far off it. I flashed my small torch around its interior and realised that MacEachern's boatshed wasn't the place I was after. There was nothing there but a weather-beaten, gunwale-splintered launch, with, amidships, an unboxed petrol engine that seemed to be a solid block of rust.

I came to the house. On its northern side, the side remote from the sea, a light shone through a small window. A light at half past one in the morning. I crawled up to this and hitched a wary eye over the window-sill. A neat, clean, well-cared-for small room, with lime-washed walls, mat-covered stone floor and the embers of a drift-wood fire smouldering in an ingle-nook in the corner. Donald MacEachern was sitting in a cane-bottomed chair, still unshaven, still in his month-old shirt, his head bent, staring into the dull red heart of the fire. He had the look of a man who was staring into a dying fire because that was all that was left in the world for him to do. I moved round to the door, turned the handle and went inside.

He heard me and turned around, not quickly, just the way a man would turn who knows there is nothing left on earth that can hurt him. He looked at me, looked at the gun in my hand, looked at his own twelve-bore hanging on a couple of nails on the wall then sank back into his chair again.

He said tonelessly: "Who in the name of God are you?"

"Calvert's my name. I was here yesterday." I pulled off my rubber hood and he remembered all right. I nodded to the twelve-bore. "You won't be needing that gun to-night, Mr. MacEachern. Anyway, you had the safety catch on."

"You don't miss much," he said slowly. "There were no cartridges in the gun."

"And no one standing behind you, was there?"

"I don't know what you mean," he said tiredly. "Who are you, man? What do you want?"

"I want to know why you gave me the welcome you did yesterday." I put the gun away. "It was hardly friendly, Mr. MacEachern."

"Who are you, sir?" He looked even older than he had done yesterday, old and broken and done.

"Calvert. They told you to discourage visitors, didn't they, Mr. MacEachern?" No answer. "I asked some questions tonight of a friend of yours. Archie MacDonald. The Torbay police sergeant. He told me you were married. I don't see Mrs. MacEachern."

He half rose from his cane chair. The old bloodshot eyes had a gleam to them. He sank back again and the eyes dimmed.

"You were out in your boat one night, weren't you, Mr. MacEachern? You were out in your boat and you saw too much. They caught you and they took you back here and they took Mrs. MacEachern away and they told you that if you ever breathed a word to anyone alive you would never see your wife that way again. Alive, I mean. They told you to stay here in case any chance acquaintances or strangers should call by and wonder why you weren't here and raise the alarm, and just to make sure that you wouldn't be tempted to go the mainland for help—although heaven knows I would have thought there would be no chance in the world of you being as mad as that—they immobilised your engine. Salt-water impregnated sacks, I shouldn't wonder, so that any chance caller would think it was due to neglect and disuse, not sabotage."

"Aye, they did that." He stared sightlessly into the fire, his voice the sunken whisper of a man who is just thinking aloud and hardly aware that he is speaking. "They took her away and they ruined my boat. And I had my life savings in the back room there

174

and they took that too. I wish I'd had a million pounds to give them. If only they had left my Mairi. She's five years older than myself." He had no defences left.

"What in the name of God have you been living on?"

"Every other week they bring me tinned food, not much, and condensed milk. Tea I have, and I catch a fish now and then off the rocks." He gazed into the fire, his forehead wrinkling as if he were suddenly realising that I brought a new dimension into his life. "Who are you, sir? Who are you? You're not one of them. And you're not a policeman, I know you're not a policeman. I've seen them. I've seen policemen. But you are a very different kettle of fish." There were the stirrings of life in him now, life in his face and in his eyes. He stared at me for a full minute, and I was beginning to feel uncomfortable under the gaze of those faded eyes, when he said: "I know who you are. I know who you must be. You are a Government man. You are an agent of the British Secret Service."

Well, by God, I took my hat off to the old boy. There I was, looking nondescript as anything and buttoned to the chin in a scuba suit, and he had me nailed right away. So much for the inscrutable faces of the guardians of our country's secrets. I thought of what Uncle Arthur would have said to him, the automatic threats of dismissal and imprisonment if the old man breathed a word. But Donald MacEachern didn't have any job to be dismissed from and after a lifetime on Eilean Oran even a maximum security prison would have looked like a hostelry to which Egon Ronay would have lashed out six stars without a second thought, so as there didn't seem to be much point in threatening him I said instead, for the first time in my life: "I am an agent of the Secret Service, Mr. MacEachern. I am going to bring your wife back to you."

He nodded very slowly, then said: "You will be a very brave man, Mr. Calvert, but you do not know the terrible men who will wait for you."

"If I ever earn a medal, Mr. MacEachern, it will be a case of mistaken identification, but, for the rest, I know very well what I am up against. Just try to believe me, Mr. MacEachern. It will be all right. You were in the war, Mr. MacEachern."

"You know. You were told?"

I shook my head. "Nobody had to tell me."

"Thank you, sir." The back was suddenly very straight. "I was a soldier for twenty-two years. I was a sergeant in the 51st Highland Division."

"You were a sergeant in the 51st Highland Division," I repeated. "There are many people, Mr. MacEachern, and not all of them Scots, who maintain that there was no better in the world."

"And it is not Donald MacEachern who would be disagreeing with you, sir." For the first time the shadow of a smile touched the faded eyes. "There were maybe one or two worse. You make your point, Mr. Calvert. We were not namely for running away, for losing hope, for giving up too easily." He rose abruptly to his feet. "In the name of God, what am I talking about? I am coming with you, Mr. Calvert."

I rose to my feet and touched my hands to his shoulders. "Thank you, Mr. MacEachern, but no. You've done enough. Your fighting days are over. Leave this to me."

He looked at me in silence, then nodded. Again the suggestion of a smile. "Aye, maybe you're right. I would be getting in the way of a man like yourself. I can see that." He sat down wearily in his chair.

I moved to the door. "Good night, Mr. MacEachern. She will soon be safe."

"She will soon be safe," he repeated. He looked up at me, his eyes moist, and when he spoke his voice held the same faint surprise as his face. "You know, I believe she will."

"She will. I'm going to bring her back here personally and that will give me more pleasure than anything I've ever done in my life. Friday morning, Mr. MacEachern."

"Friday morning? So soon? So soon?" He was looking at a spot about a billion light years away and seemed unaware that I was standing by the open door. He smiled, a genuine smile of delight, and the old eyes shone. "I'll not sleep a wink to-night, Mr. Calvert. Nor a wink to-morrow night either."

"You'll sleep on Friday," I promised. He couldn't see me any longer, the tears were running down his grey unshaven cheeks, so I closed the door with a quiet hand and left him alone with his dreams.

8

Thursday: 2 a.m.—4·30 a.m.

I had exchanged Eilean Oran for the island of Craigmore and I still wasn't smiling. I wasn't smiling for all sorts of reasons. I wasn't smiling because Uncle Arthur and Charlotte Skouras together made a nautical combination that terrified the life out of me, because the northern tip of Craigmore was much more exposed and reef-haunted than the south shore of Eilean Oran had been, because the fog was thickening, because I was breathless and bruised from big combers hurling me on to unseen reefs on my swim ashore, because I was wondering whether I had any chance in the world of carrying out my rash promise to Donald MacEachern. If I thought a bit more I'd no doubt I could come up with all sorts of other and equally valid reasons why I wasn't smiling, but I hadn't the time to think any more about it, the night was wearing on and I'd much to do before the dawn.

The nearest of the two fishing boats in the little natural harbour was rolling quite heavily in the waves that curled round the reef forming the natural breakwater to the west so I didn't have to worry too much about any splashing sound I might make as I hauled myself up on deck. What I did have to worry about was that damned bright light in its sealed inverted glass by the flensing shed, it was powerful enough to enable me to be seen from the other houses on shore. . . . But my worry about it was a little thing compared to my gratitude for its existence. Out in the wild blue yonder Uncle Arthur could do with every beacon of hope he could find.

It was a typical M.F.V., about forty-five feet long and with the

178

general look of a boat that could laugh at a hurricane. I went through it in two minutes. All in immaculate condition, not a thing aboard that shouldn't have been there. Just a genuine fishing boat. My hopes began to rise. There was no other direction they could go.

The second M.F.V. was the mirror image of the first, down to the last innocuous inch. It wouldn't be true to say that my hopes were now soaring, but at least they were getting up off the ground where they'd been for a long time.

I swam ashore, parked my scuba equipment above the high-water mark and made my way to the flensing shed, keeping its bulk between the light and myself as I went. The shed contained winches, steel tubs and barrels, a variety of ferocious weapons doubtless used for flensing, rolling cranes, some unidentifiable but obviously harmless machinery, the remains of some sharks and the most fearful smell I'd ever come across in my life. I left, hurriedly.

The first of the cottages yielded nothing. I flashed a torch through a broken window. The room was bare, it looked as if no one had set foot there for half a century, it was only too easy to believe Williams's statement that this tiny hamlet had been abandoned before the First World War. Curiously, the wall-paper looked as if it had been applied the previous day—a curious and largely unexplained phenomenon in the Western Isles. Your grandmother—in those days grandpa would have signed the pledge sooner than lift a finger inside the house—slapped up some wall-paper at ninepence a yard and fifty years later it was still there, as fresh as the day it had been put up.

The second cottage was as deserted as the first.

The third cottage, the one most remote from the flensing shed, was where the shark-fishers lived. A logical and very understandable choice, one would have thought, the farther away from that olfactory horror the better. Had I the option, I'd have been living in a tent on the other side of the island. But that was a purely personal reaction. The stench of that flensing shed was probably to the shark-fishers, as is the ammonia-laden, nostril-

179

wrinkling, wholly awful *mist*—liquid manure—to the Swiss farmers: the very breath of being. The symbol of success. One can pay too high a price for success.

I eased open the well-oiled—shark-liver oil, no doubt—door and passed inside. The torch came on again. Grandma wouldn't have gone very much on this front parlour but grandpa would cheerfully have sat there watching his beard turn white through the changing seasons without ever wanting to go down to the sea again. One entire wall was given up to food supplies, a miserable couple of dozen crates of whisky and scores upon scores of crates of beer. Australians, Williams had said. I could well believe it. The other three walls—there was hardly a scrap of wall-paper to be seen—was devoted to a form of art, in uninhibited detail and glorious Technicolor, of a type not usually to be found in the better-class museums and art galleries. Not grandma's cup of tea at all.

I skirted the furniture which hadn't come out of Harrods and opened the interior door. A short corridor lay beyond. Two doors to the right, three to the left. Working on the theory that the boss of the outfit probably had the largest room to himself, I carefully opened the first door to the right.

The flash-light showed it to be a surprisingly comfortable room. A good carpet, heavy curtains, a couple of good armchairs, bedroom furniture in oak, a double bed and a bookcase. A shaded electric light hung above the bed. Those rugged Australians believed in their home comforts. There was a switch beside the door. I touched it and the overhead lamp came on.

There was only one person in the double bed but even at that he was cramped in it. It's hard to gauge a man's height when he's lying down but if this lad tried to stand up in a room with a ceiling height of less than six feet four inches, he'd finish up with concussion. His face was towards me but I couldn't see much of it, it was hidden by a head of thick black hair that had fallen over his brows and the most magnificently bushy black beard I'd ever clapped eyes on. He was sound asleep.

I crossed to the bed, prodded his ribs with the gun barrel and a pressure sufficient to wake a lad of his size and said: "Wake up."

He woke up. I moved a respectful distance away. He rubbed his eyes with one hairy forearm, got his hands under him and heaved himself to a sitting position. I wouldn't have been surprised to see him wearing a bearskin, but no, he was wearing a pair of pyjamas in excellent taste, I might have chosen the colour myself.

Law-abiding citizens woken in the dark watches of the night by a gun-pointing stranger react in all sorts of ways, varying from terror to apoplectically-purple outrage. The man in the beard didn't react in any of the standard ways at all. He just stared at me from under dark overhanging cliffs of eyebrows and the expression in the eyes was that of a Bengal tiger mentally tucking in his napkin before launching himself on the thirty-foot leap that is going to culminate in lunch. I stepped back another couple of paces and said: "Don't try it."

"Put that gun away, sonny boy," he said. The deep rumbling voice seemed to come from the innermost recesses of the Carlsbad cavern. "Put it away or I'll have to get up and clobber you and take it from you."

"Don't be like that," I complained, then added politely: "If I put it away, will you clobber me?"

He considered this for a moment, then said: "No." He reached out for a big black cigar and lit it, his eyes on me all the time. The acrid fumes reached across the room and as it isn't polite for a guest in another's house to rush to open the nearest window without permission I didn't but it was a near thing. No wonder he'd never notice the stench from the flensing shed: compared to this, Uncle Arthur's cheroots came into the same category as Charlotte's perfume.

"My apologies for the intrusion. Are you Tim Hutchinson?"

"Yeah. And you, sonny boy?"

"Philip Calvert. I want to use one of your boat's transmitters to contact London. I also need your help. How urgently you can't

181

imagine. A good many lives and millions of pounds can be lost in the next twenty-four hours."

He watched a particularly noxious cloud of this Vesuvian poison gas drift up to the cringing ceiling, then bent his eyes on me again. "Ain't you the little kidder, now, sonny boy."

"I'm not kidding, you big black ape. And, while we're at it, we'll dispense with the 'sonny boy,' Timothy."

He bent forward, the deep-set, coal-black eyes, not at all as friendly as I would have liked, then relaxed with a laugh. "*Touché*, as my French governess used to say. Maybe you ain't kidding at that. What are you, Calvert?"

In for a penny, in for a pound. This man would grant his co-operation for nothing less than the truth. And he looked like a man whose co-operation would be very well worth having. So, for the second time that night and the second time in my life, I said: "I'm an agent of the British Secret Service." I was glad that Uncle Arthur was out there fighting for his life on the rolling deep, his blood pressure wasn't what it ought to have been and a thing like this, twice in one night, could have been enough to see him off.

He considered my reply for some time, then said: "The Secret Service. I guess you have to be at that. Or a nut case. But you blokes never tell."

"I had to. It would have been obvious anyway when I tell you what I have to tell you."

"I'll get dressed. Join you in the front room in two minutes. Help yourself to a Scotch there." The beard twitched and I deduced from this that he was grinning. "You should find some, somewhere."

I went out, found some somewhere and was conducting myself on the grand tour of the Craigmore art gallery when Tim Hutchinson came in. He was dressed all in black, trousers, sailor's jersey, mackinaw and seaboots. Beds were deceptive, he'd probably passed the six foot four mark when he was about twelve and had just stopped growing. He glanced at the collection and grinned.

"Who would have thought it?" he said. "The Guggenheim and Craigmore. Hotbeds of culture, both of them. Don't you think the one with the ear-rings looks indecently overdressed?"

"You must have scoured the great galleries of the world," I said reverently.

"I'm no connoisseur. Renoir and Matisse are my cup of tea." It was so unlikely that it had to be true. "You look like a man in a hurry. Just leave out all the inessentials."

I left out the inessentials, but not one of the essentials. Unlike MacDonald and Charlotte, Hutchinson got not only the truth but the whole truth.

"Well, if that isn't the most goddamned story any man ever heard. And right under our bloody noses." It was hard to tell at times whether Hutchinson was Australian or American—I learnt later that he'd spent many years tuna-fishing in Florida. "So it was you in that chopper this afternoon. Brother, you've had a day and then some. I retract that 'sonny boy' crack. One of my more ill-advised comments. What do you want, Calvert?"

So I told him what I wanted, his own personal assistance that night, the loan of his boats and crews for the next twenty-four hours and the use of a radio transmitter immediately. He nodded.

"Count on us. I'll tell the boys. You can start using that transmitter right away."

"I'd rather go out with you to our boat right away," I said, "leave you there and come back in myself to transmit."

"You lack a mite confidence in your crew, hey?"

"I'm expecting to see the bows of the *Firecrest* coming through that front door any minute."

"I can do better than that. I'll roust out a couple of the boys, we'll take the *Charmaine*—that's the M.F.V. nearest the flensing shed—out to the *Firecrest*, I'll go aboard, we'll cruise around till you get your message off, then you come aboard the *Firecrest* while the boys take the *Charmaine* back again."

I thought of the mælstrom of white breakers outside the mouth of the alleged harbour. I said: "It won't be too dangerous to take an M.F.V. out on a night like this?"

183

"What's wrong with a night like this? It's a fine fresh night. You couldn't ask for better. This is nothing, I've seen the boys take a boat out there, six o'clock in a black December evening, into a full gale."

"What kind of emergency was that?"

"A serious one, admittedly." He grinned. "We'd run out of supplies and the boys wanted to get to Torbay before the pubs shut. Straight up, Calvert."

I said no more. It was obviously going to be a great comfort to have Hutchinson around with me for the rest of the night. He turned towards the corridor and hesitated: "Two of the boys are married. I wonder——"

"There'll be no danger for them. Besides, they'll be well rewarded for their work."

"Don't spoil it, Calvert." For a man with such a deep rumbling voice he could make it very soft at times. "We don't take money for this kind of work."

"I'm not hiring you," I said tiredly. I'd quite enough people fighting me already without Tim Hutchinson joining their ranks. "There's an insurance reward. I have been instructed to offer you half."

"Ah, now, that's very different indeed. I'll be delighted to relieve the insurance companies of their excess cash at any time. But not half, Calvert, not half. Not for a day's work, not after all you've done. Twenty-five per cent to us, seventy-five per cent to you and your friends."

"Half is what you get. The other half will be used to pay compensation for those who have suffered hardship. There's an old couple on Eilean Oran, for instance, who are going to be wealthy beyond their dreams for the rest of their days."

"You get nothing?"

"I get my salary, the size of which I'd rather not discuss, as it's a sore point. Civil Servants are not permitted to accept gratuities."

"You mean to say you get beaten up, shot down, half-drowned and suffer another couple of murder attempts just for a lousy pay cheque? What makes you tick, Calvert? Why the hell do you do it?"

"That's not an original question. I ask myself the same question about twenty times a day, rather more often recently. It's time we were gone."

"I'll get the boys up. They'll be tickled pink by those gold watches or whatever the insurance boys will be handing over. Engraved, of course. We insist on that."

"The reward will be in cash, not kind. Depends how much of the stolen goods are recovered. We're pretty sure to recover all the *Nantesville*'s cargo. Chances are that we'll recover the lot. The award is ten per cent. Yours will be five. The minimum you and your boys will pick up will be four hundred thousand pounds: the maximum will be eight hundred and fifty. Thousand pounds, I mean."

"Say that in English." He looked as if the London Post Office Tower had fallen on top of him. So I said it again, and after a time he looked as if only a telegraph pole had fallen on him and said carefully: "At rates like that, a man might expect a fair bit of co-operation. Say no more. Put right out of your head any thoughts you had of advertising in the *Telegraph*. Tim Hutchinson is your man."

And Tim Hutchinson was undoubtedly my man. On a night like that, dark as doomsday, rain sluicing down and a thickening mist making it impossible—for me, at least—to tell the difference between a naturally breaking sea and a wave foaming over a reef, Tim Hutchinson was my man. Cheap at half a million.

He was one of that rare breed, that very rare breed, of naturals to whom the sea is truly home. Twenty years' daily polishing and refining in every conceivable condition a rarely-bestowed gift with which you must be born in the first place and anyone can be like this. Just as the great Grand Prix drivers, the Carraciolas and Nuvolaris and Clarks, operate on a level incomprehensible to highly competent drivers of very fast cars, so Hutchinson operated on a level incomprehensible to the finest of amateur yachtsmen. Search your ocean racing clubs and Olympic yachting teams the world over and you will not find men like this. They are to be

185

found, and even then so very seldom, only in the ranks of the professional deep-sea fishermen.

Those huge hands on throttle and wheel had the delicacy of a moth. He had the night-sight of a barn owl and an ear which could infallibly distinguish between waves breaking in the open sea, on reefs or on shores: he could invariably tell the size and direction of seas coming at him out of the darkness and mist and touch wheel or throttle as need be: he had an inbuilt computer which provided instant correlation of wind, tide, current and our own speed and always let him know exactly where he was. And I'll swear he could smell land, even on a lee shore and with the rest of us suffering olfactory paralysis from the fumes of the big black cigars which seemed to be an inseparable part of the man. It required only ten minutes beside him to realise that one's ignorance of the sea and ships was almost total. A chastening discovery.

He took the *Charmaine* out through the Scylla and Charybdis of that evil alleged harbour entrance under full throttle. Foaming white-fanged reefs reached out at us, bare feet away, on either side. He didn't seem to notice them. He certainly didn't look at them. The two "boys" he'd brought with him, a couple of stunted lads of about six foot two or thereabouts, yawned prodigiously. Hutchinson located the *Firecrest* a hundred yards before I could even begin to imagine I could see any shape at all and brought the *Charmaine* alongside as neatly as I could park my car by the kerb in broad daylight—on one of my better days, that was. I went aboard the *Firecrest* to the vast alarm of Uncle Arthur and Charlotte who'd heard no whisper of our arrival, explained the situation, introduced Hutchinson and went back aboard the *Charmaine*. Fifteen minutes later, the radio call over, I was back aboard the *Firecrest*.

Uncle Arthur and Tim Hutchinson were already thick as thieves. The bearded Australian giant was extremely courteous and respectful, calling Uncle Arthur "Admiral" every other sentence while Uncle Arthur was plainly delighted and vastly relieved to have him on board. If I felt this was a slight on my own seaman-like qualities, I was undoubtedly correct.

"Where are we off to now?" Charlotte Skouras asked. I was disappointed to see that she was just as relieved as Uncle Arthur.

"Dubh Sgeir," I said. "To pay a call on Lord Kirkside and his charming daughter."

"Dubh Sgeir!" She seemed taken aback. "I thought you said the answer lay in Eilean Oran and Craigmore?"

"So I did. The answers to some essential preliminary questions. But the end of the road lies in Dubh Sgeir. And the foot of the rainbow."

"You talk in riddles," she said impatiently.

"Not to me, he doesn't," Hutchinson said jovially. "The foot of the rainbow, ma'am. That's where the pot of gold lies."

"Here and now I'd settle for a pot of coffee," I said. "Coffee for four and I'll make it with my own fair hands."

"I think I would rather go to bed," Charlotte said. "I am very tired."

"You made me drink your coffee," I said threateningly. "Now you drink mine. Fair's fair."

"If you are quick, then."

I was quick. I'd four cups on a little tin tray in nothing flat, a powerful mixture of instant coffee, milk and sugar in all of them and a little something extra in one of them. There were no complaints about the coffee. Hutchinson drained his cup and said: "Can't see why you three shouldn't get your heads down for a little. Unless you think I need help?"

No one thought he needed help. Charlotte Skouras was the first to go, saying she felt very sleepy, which I didn't doubt. She sounded it. Uncle Arthur and I left a moment later, Tim Hutchinson promising to call me when we neared the landing stage on the west side of Dubh Sgeir. Uncle Arthur wrapped himself in a rug on the saloon settee. I went to my own cabin and lay down.

I lay for three minutes then rose, picked up a three-cornered file, softly opened my cabin door and as softly knocked on Charlotte's door. There was no reply, so I opened the door, passed in, silently closed it and switched on the lights.

She was asleep all right, she was a million miles away. She

hadn't even managed to make it to bed, she was lying on the carpet, still fully clothed. I put her on the bunk and pulled a couple of blankets over her. I pushed up a sleeve and examined the mark left by the rope burn.

It wasn't a very big cabin and it took me only a minute to find what I was looking for.

It made a pleasant change and a very refreshing one to transfer myself from the *Firecrest* to land without that damned clammy scuba suit impeding every stroke or step of the way.

How Tim Hutchinson located that old stone pier in the rain, the fog and the darkness was something that would have been for ever beyond me—if he hadn't told me later that night. He sent me to the bows with a torch in my hand and damned if the thing didn't loom out of the darkness as if he'd gone in on a radio bearing. He went into reverse, brought the bows, plunging heavily in the deep troughs, to within two feet of the pier, waited till I picked my moment to jump off then went full astern and disappeared into the fog and darkness. I tried to imagine Uncle Arthur executing that lot, but my imagination wasn't up to it. It boggled. Uncle Arthur, thank heaven, slept the sleep of the just. Drake was in his hammock and a thousand miles away, dreaming all the time of W.C.1.

The path from the landing stage to the plateau above was steep and crumbling and someone had carelessly forgotten to equip it with a handrail on the seaward side. I was in no way heavily burdened. All I was carrying apart from the weight of my own years was a torch, gun and coil of rope—I'd neither the intention nor the expectation of doing a Douglas Fairbanks on the outer battlements of the Dubh Sgeir castle, but experience had taught me that a rope was the most essential piece of equipment to carry along on a jaunt on a precipitously walled island—but even so I was breathing pretty heavily by the time I reached the top.

I turned not towards the castle but north along the grass strip that led to the cliff at the northern end of the island. The strip that Lord Kirkside's elder son had taken off from in his Beech-

188

craft on the day when he and his brother-in-law to be had died, the strip that Williams and I had flown along less than twelve hours previously after our talk with Lord Kirkside and his daughter, the strip at the abrupt northern end of which I'd imagined I'd seen what I'd wanted to see, but couldn't be sure. Now I was going to make sure.

The strip was smooth and flat and I made good time without having to use the big rubber torch I had with me. I didn't dare use it anyway, not so close to the castle. There was no light to be seen from there but that was no guarantee that the ungodly weren't maintaining a sleepless watch on the battlements. If I were the ungodly, I'd have been maintaining a sleepless watch on the battlements. I stumbled over something warm and soft and alive and hit the ground hard.

My nerves weren't what they had been forty-eight hours ago and my reactions were comparatively fast. I had the knife in my hand and was on to him before he could get to his feet. To his four feet. He had about him the pungent aroma of a refugee from Tim Hutchinson's flensing shed. Well might they say why stinks the goat on yonder hill who seems to dote on chlorophyll. I said a few conciliatory words to our four-footed friend and it seemed to work for he kept his horns to himself. I went on my way.

This humiliating sort of encounter, I'd noticed, never happened to the Errol Flynns of this world. Moreover, if Errol Flynn had been carrying a torch a little fall like that would not have smashed it. Had he been carrying only a candle it would still have kept burning brightly in the darkness. But not my torch. Not my rubber encased, rubber mounted bulb, plexi-glass guaranteed unbreakable torch. It was kaput. I fished out the little pencil torch and tried it inside my jacket. I could have spared myself the caution, a glow-worm would have sneered at it. I stuck it back in my pocket and kept going.

I didn't know how far I was from the precipitous end of the cliff and I'd no intention of finding out the hard way. I dropped to my hands and knees and crawled forward, the glow-worm leading the way. I reached the cliff edge in five minutes and found

189

what I was looking for almost at once. The deep score on the cliff edge was almost eighteen inches in width and four in depth in the centre. The mark was fresh but not too fresh. The grass had grown in again in most places. The time factor would be just about right. It was the mark that had been left by the tail fuselage of the Beechcraft plane when, with no one aboard, it had been started up, throttle opened and then the chocks removed. It hadn't had enough speed to become airborne and had fallen over the cliff edge, ripping this score in the earth as it had gone. That was all I needed, that and the holed hull of the Oxford expedition boat and the dark circles under the blue eyes of Susan Kirkside. Here was certainty.

I heard a slight noise behind me. A moderately fit five-year-old grabbing me by the ankles could have had me over the edge with nothing I could do to prevent it. Or maybe it was Billy the Kid back to wreak vengeance for the rude interruption of his night's sleep. I swung round with torch and gun at the ready. It *was* Billy the Kid, his yellow eyes staring balefully out of the night. But his eyes belied him, he was just curious or friendly or both. I moved back slowly till I was out of butting range, patted him weakly on the head and left. At this rate I'd die of heart failure before the night was out.

The rain had eased by this time and the wind fallen away quite a bit, but to compensate for this the mist was worse than ever. It swirled clammily around me and I couldn't see four feet in front of my face. I wondered grimly how Hutchinson was getting on in this lot, but put him quickly out of my mind. I'd no doubt he was a damned sight better at his job than I was at mine. I kept the wind on my right cheek and continued towards the castle. Under my rubber-canvas raincoat my last suit was sodden. The Civil Service was going to be faced with a cleaner's bill of some note.

I near as a toucher walked into the castle wall but saw its loom just in time. I didn't know whether I was to the right or the left of the entrance gate on the landward side, so I felt my way cautiously to the left to find out. After about ten feet the wall fell away at right angles to another wall. That meant I'd arrived at the left or eastern side of the gate. I began to feel my way to the right.

It was as well I had come upon the castle wall where I had done: had I arrived at the right-hand side, I'd have been upwind of the central gate and would never have smelled the tobacco smoke. It wasn't much as tobacco went, nothing like as robust as Uncle Arthur's cheroots and positively anæmic as compared to Tim Hutchinson's portable poison-gas factories, but tobacco smoke for all that. Someone at the entrance gate was smoking a cigarette. It was axiomatic that sentries should never smoke cigarettes. This I could deal with. They'd never trained me on how to handle billy goats on the edge of a precipice but on this subject they had become boringly repetitive.

I held the gun by the barrel and moved quietly forwards. He was leaning against the corner of the entrance, a hardly-seen shape, but his position outlined clearly enough by the movement of his cigarette end. I waited till he brought it to his mouth for the third time, and when it was glowing at its brightest and his night vision consequently most affected I took one step forward and brought the butt down where by extension of the curve and subsequent glow of the cigarette end the back of the head of a normal man ought to have been. Fortunately, he was a normal man.

He fell back against me. I caught him and something jabbed painfully into my ribs. I let him finish the trip down on his own and removed this item that had become stuck in my coat. A bayonet, and, what was more, a bayonet with a very nasty point to it. Attached to the bayonet was a Lee Enfield .303. Very military. It seemed unlikely that this was just a routine precaution. Our friends were becoming worried and I had no means of knowing how much they knew or guessed. Time was running very short for them, almost as short as it was for me. In a few hours it would be dawn.

I took the rifle and moved cautiously towards the edge of the cliff, the bayonet prodding the earth ahead of me as I went. By this time I was becoming quite adept at not falling over the edges of precipices and, besides, with a rifle and bayonet stretched out in advance you have five feet notification of where eternity begins. I found the edge, stepped back, reversed the rifle, made two parallel scores in the sodden turf about a foot apart and eighteen inches in length, terminating on the very edge. I wiped the butt clean and placed the rifle on the ground. When the dawn came, the sentry changed and a search made, I trusted the proper conclusions would be drawn.

I hadn't hit him as hard as I'd thought, he was beginning to stir and moan feebly by the time I got back to him. This was all to the good, the alternative would have been to carry him and I was in no fit state to carry anyone. I stuffed a handkerchief into his mouth and the moaning stopped. Bad practice, I knew, for a gagged man with a head cold or nasal obstruction can die of suffocation in four minutes, but I hadn't the facilities to carry out a sinus examination, and, more importantly, it was his health or mine.

He was up on his feet in two minutes. He didn't try to run away or offer resistance, for by this time he had his ankles on a short hobble, his hands tied securely behind his back and the barrel of an automatic pressing into the side of his neck. I told him to walk, and he walked. Two hundred yards away, at the head of the path leading down to the landing stage, I led him off to one side, tied his wrists and ankles together and left him there. He seemed to be breathing without too much difficulty.

There were no other sentries, at least not on the main gate. I crossed the hollow square of a courtyard and came to the main door. It was closed but not locked. I passed inside and said a few hard things to myself about myself for not having searched that sentry for the torch he would almost certainly have been carrying. The window curtains must have been drawn and the darkness inside that hall was total. I didn't much fancy moving around a Scottish baronial hall in total darkness, the risk of bringing down a suit of armour with a resounding metallic crash or impaling oneself on targes, claymores or a royal set of antlers must be high. I took out my pencil flash but the glow-worm inside was breathing its last, even when hard-pressed against the face of my wrist-watch it was impossible to tell the time. It was impossible to see the wrist-watch.

From the air, yesterday, I'd seen that the castle had been built in perfect symmetry round three sides of a hollow square. It was a reasonable assumption then that if the main door was in the middle of the central or seaward-facing section then the main staircase would be directly opposite. It seemed likely that the middle of the hall would offer a passage unimpeded by either claymores or antlers.

It did. The stairs were where they should have been. Ten wide shallow steps and then the stairs branched both right and left. I chose the right-hand side because above me, on that side, I could see a faint loom of light. Six steps on the second flight of stairs, another right turn, eight more steps and then I was on the landing. Twenty-four steps and never a creak. I blessed the architect who had specified marble.

The light was much stronger now. I advanced towards its source, a door no more than an inch ajar, and applied a wary eye to the crack. All I could see was the corner of a wardrobe, a strip of carpet, the corner of the foot of a bed and, on the last, a muddy boot. A low-register cacophony of sound emerged, reminiscent of a boiler factory in the middle distance. I pushed the door and walked inside.

I'd come to see Lord Kirkside, and whoever this was it wasn't Lord Kirkside, for whatever Lord Kirkside was in the habit of doing I was fairly certain that he didn't go to bed in boots, braces and cloth cap, with a bayoneted rifle lying on the blankets beside him, which was what this character had done. I couldn't see his face, because the cloth cap reached as far as his nose. On the bed-side table beside him lay a torch and a half-empty whisky bottle. No glass, but from what little I could see of him I would have judged that he was, anyhow, one of those characters whose direct and simple enjoyment of life has not been impaired by the effete conventions of modern civilisation. The faithful watchman prudently preparing himself for the rigours of the West Highland night before taking his turn at sentry-go. But he wouldn't be making it at the appointed hour for there was no one now to call him. From the look of it, he'd be lucky to make it for lunch.

It was just possible that he might wake himself up, those stentorian snores wouldn't have gone unremarked in a mortuary. He had about him the look of a man who, on regaining consciousness, would find himself in need of thirst-quenching nourishment, so I unscrewed the bottle top, dropped in half a dozen of the tablets supplied by my pharmaceutical friend in Torbay, replaced the top, took the torch and left.

Behind the next door to the left lay a bathroom. A filthy basin with, above it, a water-stained mirror, two shaving brushes covered with lather, a jar of shaving cream with the top off, two unwashed razors and, on the floor, two towels that might just possibly have been white at some distant æon in the past. The interior of the bath was immaculate. Here was where the watchman performed his rudimentary ablutions.

The next room was a bedroom as dirty and disorderly as the watchman's. It was a fair guess that this was the home of the man I'd left lying out among the gorse and stones on the hillside.

I moved across to the left-hand side of the central block—Lord Kirkside would have his room somewhere in that block. He did, but he wasn't at home. The first room beyond the sleeping warrior's was his all right, a glance at the contents of the nearest wardrobe confirmed this. But his bed hadn't been slept in.

Predictably in this symmetrically designed house, the next room was a bathroom. The watchman wouldn't have felt at all at home in here, this antiseptic cleanliness was the hallmark of an effete aristocracy. A medicine cabinet was fixed to the wall. I took out a tin of Elastoplast and covered the face of the torch till I was left with a hole no more than the size of a sixpence. I put the tin in my pocket.

The next door was locked but locks, in the days when the Dubh Sgeir Castle had been built, were pretty rudimentary affairs. I took from my pocket the best skeleton key in the world—an oblong of stiff Celluloid. I shoved it between door and jamb at bolt level, pulled the door handle back in the direction of the hinges, eased in the Celluloid, released the handle, repeated the process and stood stock-still. That click might have wakened my watchman friend, it should certainly have wakened the person inside. But I heard no sound of movement.

I opened the door a fraction of an inch and went through the stock-still standing process once more. There was a light on inside the room. I changed the torch for the gun, went on my knees, crouched low and abruptly opened the door wide. I stood up, closed and locked the door and crossed over to the bed.

Susan Kirkside wasn't snoring but she was just as deep in sleep as the man I'd just left. She had a blue silk band round her hair, and all of her face was visible, a sight that must have been rare indeed during her waking hours. Twenty-one, her father had said she was, but lying there asleep, smudged eyes and all, she looked no older than seventeen. A magazine had slipped from her hands to the floor. On the bedside table was a half-empty glass of water and beside that a bottle containing a commercial brand of Nembutal tablets. Oblivion appeared to be a pretty hard thing to come by in Dubh Sgeir and I'd no doubt Susan Kirkside found it more difficult than most.

I picked up a towel from a basin in the corner of the room, removed the worst of the moisture and dirt from head and face, combed my hair into some semblance of order and gave my kindly reassuring smile a try-out in the mirror. I looked like someone from the pages of the *Police Gazette*.

It took almost two minutes to shake her awake or, at least, to pull her up from the dark depths of oblivion to a state of semi-awareness. Full consciousness took another minute, and it was probably this that saved me from a screaming match, she had time to adjust herself to the slow realisation of the presence of a stranger in the middle of the night. Mind you, I had my kindly smile going full blast till my face ached, but I don't think it helped much.

"Who are you? Who *are* you?" Her voice was shaking, the blue eyes, still misted with sleep, wide open and scared. "Don't you touch me! Don't you—I'll scream for help—I'll——"

I took her hands just to show her that there was touching and touching. "I won't touch you, Sue Kirkside. And a fat lot of good screaming for help would do around these parts. Don't scream, there's a good girl. In fact, don't even talk above a whisper. I don't think it would be very wise or safe, do you?"

She stared at me for a few seconds, her lips moving as if she were about to speak, but the fear slowly leaving her eyes. Suddenly she sat bolt upright. "You're Mr. Johnson. The man from the helicopter."

"You should be more careful," I said reproachfully. "They'd have you arrested for that in the Folies-Bergère." Her free hand hauled the blankets up to her chin and I went on: "My name is Calvert. I work for the Government. I'm a friend. I think you need a friend, don't you, Susan? You and your old man—Lord Kirkside, that is."

"What do you want?" she whispered. "What are you doing here?"

"I'm here to end your troubles," I said. "I'm here to cadge an invitation to your wedding to the Honourable John Rollinson. Make it about the end of next month, will you? I'm due some leave, then."

"Go away from here." Her voice was low and desperate. "Go away from here or you'll ruin everything. Please, please, *please* go away. I'm begging you, I'm begging you. Go away. If you're a friend, go away. Please, oh please go away!"

It seemed that she wanted me to leave. I said: "It appears that they have you pretty well brain-washed. If you believe their promise, you'll believe anything in the world. They won't let you go, they daren't let you go, they'll destroy every shred and trace of evidence that might ever point a finger at them. That includes anyone who has ever had anything to do with them."

"They won't, they *won't*. I was with Mr. Lavorski when he promised Daddy that no one would come to any harm. He said they were businessmen, and killing was no part of business. He meant it."

"Lavorski, is it? It had to be." I looked at the earnest scared face. "He may have meant it when he said it. He wouldn't have mentioned that they've murdered four people in the last three days, or that they have tried to murder me four times in the last three days."

"You're lying! You're making this up. Things like that—things like that don't happen any more. For pity's sake leave us alone!"

"There speaks the true daughter of the old Scottish clan chieftain." I said roughly. "You're no good to me. Where's your father?"

"I don't know. Mr. Lavorski and Captain Imrie—he's another of them—came for him at eleven to-night. Daddy didn't say where he was going. He tells me nothing." She paused and snatched her hands away. Faint red patches stained her cheeks. "What do you mean, I'm no good to you?"

"Did he say when he would be back?"

"What do you mean I'm no good to you?"

"Because you're young and not very clever and you don't know too much about this world and you'll believe anything a hardened criminal will tell you. But most especially because you won't believe me. You won't believe the one person who can save you all. You're a stupid and pig-headed young fool, Miss Kirkside. If it wasn't that he was jumping from the frying-pan into the fire, I'd say the Honourable Rollinson has had a lucky escape."

"What do you mean?" It is hard for a mobile young face to be expressionless, but hers was then.

"He can't marry you when he is dead," I said brutally. "And he is going to die. He's going to die because Sue Kirkside let him die. Because she was too blind to know truth when she saw it." I had what was, for me, an inspiration. I turned down my collar and pulled my scarf away. "Like it?" I asked.

She didn't like it at all. The red faded from her cheeks. I could see myself in her dressing-table mirror and I didn't like it either. Quinn's handiwork was in full bloom. The kaleidoscope of colour now made a complete ring round my neck.

"Quinn?" she whispered.

"You know his name. You know him?"

"I know them all. Most of them, anyway. Cook said that one night, after he'd too much to drink, he'd been boasting in the kitchen about how he'd once been the strong man in a stage act. He'd an argument one night with his partner. About a woman. He killed his partner. That way." She had to make a physical effort to turn her eyes away from my neck. "I thought—I thought it was just talk."

"And do you still think our pals are unpaid missionaries for the Society for the Propagation of Christian Knowledge?" I sneered. "Do you know Jacques and Kramer?"

She nodded.

"I killed them both to-night. After they had killed a friend of mine. They broke his neck. Then they tried to kill my boss and myself. And I killed another. He came out of the dark to murder us. I think his name was Henry. Do you believe me now? Or do you still think we're all dancing round the old maypole on the village green, singing ring-a-ring-o'-roses as we go?"

The shock treatment worked almost too well. Her face wasn't pale now, it was ashen. She said: "I think I'm going to be sick."

"Later," I said coldly. What little self-regard I had was down among my shoe-laces, what I would have liked to do was to take her in my arms and say: "There, there, now, don't you worry your pretty head, just you leave everything to your old Uncle Philip and all will be well at the end of the day." In fact, it was damned hard not to do it. Instead, what I said, still in the same nasty voice, was: "We've no time for those little fol-de-rols. You want to get married, don't you? Did your father say when he would be back?"

She looked at the wash-basin in the corner of the room as if she were still making up her mind whether to be sick or not then pulled her eyes back to me and whispered: "You're just as bad as they are. You're a terrible man. You're a killer."

I caught her shoulders and shook them. I said savagely: "Did he say when he would be back?"

"No." Her eyes were sick with revulsion. It was a long time since any woman had looked at me like that. I dropped my hands.

"Do you know what those men are doing here?"

"No."

I believed her. Her old man would know, but he wouldn't have told her. Lord Kirkside was too astute to believe that their uninvited guests would just up and leave them unharmed. Maybe he was just desperately gambling that if he told his daughter nothing and if he could swear she knew nothing then they would leave her be. If that was what he thought, he was in urgent need of an alienist. But that was being unjust, if I stood in his shoes— or, more accurately, was swimming in the murky waters he was in —I'd have grabbed at any straw.

"It's obvious that you know that your fiancé is still alive," I went on. "And your elder brother. And others. They're being held here, aren't they?"

She nodded silently. I wished she wouldn't look at me like that.

"Do you know how many?"

"A dozen. More than that. And I know there are children there. Three boys and a girl."

That would be right. Sergeant MacDonald's two sons and the boy and the girl that had been aboard the converted lifeboat that had disappeared after setting off on the night cruise from Torbay. I didn't believe a word that Lavorski had said to Susan about their reverence for human life. But I wasn't surprised that the people in the boats who had accidentally stumbled across his illegal operations were still alive. There was a very good reason for this.

"Do you know where they are kept? There should be any amount of handy dungeons in Dubh Sgeir castle."

"There are cellars deep underground. I've never been allowed to go near them in the past four months."

"This is your big chance come at last. Get your clothes on and take me there."

"Go down to the cellars?" Aghast was the word for her expression. "Are you mad? Daddy tells me there are at least three men on guard duty all night long." There were only two men now, but her opinion of me was low enough already, so I kept

199

quiet. "They're armed. You *must* be mad. I'm not going!"

"I didn't think you would. You'll let your boy friend die just because you're a contemptible little coward." I could almost taste the self-loathing in my mouth. "Lord Kirkside and the Honourable Rollinson. What a lucky father. What a fortunate fiancé."

She hit me, and I knew I had won. I said without touching my face: "Don't do that. You'll waken up the guard. Get your clothes on."

I rose, sat on the footboard of the bed and contemplated the door and higher things while she changed. I was becoming tired of women telling me what a horrible character I was.

"I'm ready," she said.

She was back in her uniform of pirate's jersey and the denims she'd outgrown when she was about fifteen. Thirty seconds flat and nary a sound of a portable sewing machine. Baffling, that's what it was.

9

Thursday: 4.30 a.m.—dawn

We went down the stairs hand in hand. I may have been the last man in the world she would have elected to be alone with on a desert island, but she clung on pretty tightly all the same.

At the foot of the steps we turned right. I flicked on the torch every few yards but it wasn't really necessary, Susan knew every yard of the way. At the end of the hall we turned left along the eastern wing. Eight yards and we stopped at a door on the right-hand side.

"The pantry," she whispered. "The kitchen is beyond that."

I stooped and looked through the keyhole. Beyond was darkness. We passed through the doorway, then into an archway giving on to the kitchen. I flashed the tiny beam around the room. Empty.

There were three guards, Susan had said. The outside man, for whom I had accounted. The lad who patrolled the battlements: No, she didn't know what he did, but it was a good guess that he wasn't studying astronomy or guarding against parachutists. He'd have night glasses to his eyes and he'd be watching for fishing vessels, naval craft or fishery cruisers that might happen by and interrupt honest men at their work. He wouldn't see much on a night like this. And the third man, she said, guarded the back kitchen premises, the only entrance to the castle apart from the main gate—and the unfortunates in their cellars down below.

He wasn't in the kitchen premises, so he would be in the cellars down below.

A flight of steps led from the scullery beyond the kitchen down to a stone-flagged floor. To the right of this floor I could see the loom of light. Susan raised a finger to her lips and we made our way soundlessly down to the foot of the steps. I slid a cautious eye round the corner of this passageway.

It wasn't a passageway, it was the damnedest flight of steps I'd ever come across. They were lit by two or three far-spaced and very weak electric bulbs, the walls coming together towards the foot like a pair of railway lines disappearing into the distance. Maybe fifty feet—or seventy steps—down, where the first light was, another passageway branched off to the right. There was a stool at the corner of the small stone landing there, and sitting on the stool a man. Across his knees lay a rifle. They certainly went in for the heavy artillery.

I drew back. I murmured to Susan: "Where in hell's name do those steps lead to?"

"The boathouse, of course." A surprised whisper. "Where else?"

Where else, indeed. Brilliant work, Calvert, brilliant work. You'd skirted the south side of the Dubh Sgeir in the helicopter, you'd seen the castle, you'd seen the boathouse, you'd seen nary a handhold on the sheer cliff separating them, and you'd never raised an eyebrow at the glaring obviousness of the fact that ne'er the twain did meet.

"Those are the cellars in that passage going off to the right?" She nodded. "Why so far down? It's a long walk to collect the bubbly."

"They're not really wine-cellars. They used to be used as water reservoirs."

"No other way of getting down there?"

"No. Only this way."

"And if we take five steps down this way he shoots us full of holes with his Lee Enfield. Know who it is?"

"Harry. I don't know his other name. He's an Armenian, Daddy says. People can't pronounce his real name. He's young and smooth and greasy—and detestable."

"He had the effrontery to make a pass at the chieftain's daughter?"

"Yes. It was horrible." She touched her lips with the back of her hand. "He stank of garlic."

"I don't blame him. I'd do it myself if I didn't feel my pension creeping up on me. Call him up and make amends."

"What?"

"Tell him you're sorry. Tell him you misjudged his noble character. Tell him your father is away and this is the first chance you've had of speaking to him. Tell him anything."

"No!"

"Sue!"

"He'll never believe me," she said wildly.

"When he gets within two feet of you, he'll forget all about the reasoning why. He's a man, isn't he?"

"You're a man. And you're only six inches away." The eternal female illogic.

"I've told you how it is, it's my pension coming between us. Quickly!"

She nodded reluctantly and I disappeared into the shadows of the nearest cellar, reversed gun in hand. She called and he came a-running, his rifle at the ready. When he saw who it was, he forgot all about his rifle. Susan started to speak her lines but she might have saved her breath. Harry, if nothing else, was an impetuous young man. That wild Armenian blood. I stepped forwards, arm swinging, and lowered him to the ground. I tied him up and, as I'd run out of handkerchiefs, ripped away part of his shirt-front and used it as a gag. Susan giggled, a giggle with a note of hysteria.

"What's up?" I asked.

"Harry. He's what they call a snappy dresser. That's a silk shirt. You're no respecter of persons, Mr. Calvert."

"Not persons like Harry. Congratulations. Wasn't so bad, was it?"

"It was still horrible." Again the hand to the mouth. "He's reeking of whisky."

"Youngsters have odd tastes," I said kindly. "You'll grow

203

out of it. At least it must have been an improvement on the garlic."

The boathouse wasn't really a boathouse at all, it was a large vaulting cave formed in a cleft in a natural fault in the cliff strata. At the inner end of the cave longitudinal tunnels stretched away on either side paralleling the coastline, until they vanished beyond the reach of my torch. From the air, the boathouse in the small artificial harbour, a structure of about twenty feet by twenty, had seemed incapable of housing more than two or three fair-sized rowing boats. Inside it was big enough to berth a boat the size of the *Firecrest*, and then leave room to spare. Mooring bollards, four in number, lined the eastern side of the boathouse. There were signs of recent work where the inner end of the cave had been lengthened in the direction of the longitudinal tunnels to increase the berthing space and provide a bigger working platform, but otherwise it was as it must have been for hundreds of years. I picked up a boat-hook and tried to test the depth, but couldn't find bottom. Any vessel small enough to be accommodated inside could enter and leave at any state of the tide. The two big doors looked solid but not too solid. There was a small dry-land doorway on the eastern side.

The berth was empty, as I had expected to find it. Our friends were apprehensive and on piece-work rates. It wasn't difficult to guess what they were working at, the working platform was liberally stacked with the tools of their trade: an oil engine-driven air compressor with a steel reservoir with outlet valves, a manually-operated, two-cylinder double-acting air pump with two outlets, two helmets with attached corselets, flexible, non-collapsible air tubes with metal couplings, weighted boots, diving dresses, life-cum-telephone lines, lead weights and scuba equipment such as I had myself, with a stack of compressed air cylinders at the ready.

I felt neither surprise nor elation, I'd known this must exist for the past forty-eight hours although I'd become certain of the location only that night. I was faintly surprised, perhaps, to see all this equipment here, for this would surely be only the spares.

But I shouldn't have been even vaguely surprised. Whatever this bunch lacked, it wasn't a genius for organisation.

I didn't see that night, nor did I ever see, the cellars where the prisoners were housed. After I'd huffed and puffed three-quarters of the way up that interminable flight of steps, I turned left along the passageway where we'd first seen Harry taking his ease. After a few yards the passageway broadened out into a low damp chamber containing a table made of beer-cases, some seats of the same and, in one corner, some furniture that hadn't yet been drunk. A bottle of whisky, nearly full, stood on the table: Harry's remedy for garlic halitosis.

Beyond this chamber was a massive wooden door secured by an equally massive-looking lock with the key missing. All the Celluloid in the world wouldn't open this lot but a beehive plastic explosive would do a very efficient job indeed. I made another of the many mental notes I'd made that night and went up the stairs to rejoin Susan.

Harry had come to. He was saying something in his throat which fortunately couldn't get past his silk-shirted gag to the delicate ears of the chieftain's young daughter, his eyes, to mint a phrase, spoke volumes and he was trying as best he could to do a Houdini with the ropes round his legs and arms. Susan Kirkside was pointing a rifle in his general direction and looking very apprehensive. She needn't have bothered, Harry was trussed like a turkey.

"These people down in the cellars," I said. "They've been there for weeks, some for months. They'll be blind as bats and weak as kittens by the time they get out."

She shook her head. "I think they'll be all right. They're taken out on the landing strip there for an hour and a half every morning under guard. They can't be seen from the sea. We're not allowed to watch. Or not supposed to. I've seen them often. Daddy insisted on it. And Sir Anthony."

"Well, good old Daddy." I stared at her. "Old man Skouras. He comes here?"

"Of course." She seemed surprised at my surprise. "He's one of them. Lavorski and this man Dollmann, the men that do all the arranging, they work for Sir Anthony. Didn't you know? Daddy and Sir Anthony are friends—were friends—before this. I've been in Sir Anthony's London home often."

"But they're not friends now?" I probed keenly.

"Sir Anthony has gone off his head since his first wife died," Susan said confidently. I looked at her in wonder and tried to remember when I'd last been so authoritatively dogmatic on subjects I knew nothing about. I couldn't remember. "He married again, you know. Some French actress or other. That wouldn't have helped. She's no good. She caught him on the rebound."

"Susan," I said reverently, "you're really wonderful. I don't believe you'll ever understand what I mean by my pension coming between us. You know her well?"

"I've never met her."

"You didn't have to tell me. And poor old Sir Anthony—he doesn't know what he's doing, is that it?"

"He's all mixed up," she said defensively. "He's sweet, really he is. Or was."

"All mixed up with the deaths of four men, not to mention three of his own," I said. Sergeant MacDonald thought him a good man. Susan thought him sweet. I wondered what she would say if she saw Charlotte Skouras's back. "How do the prisoners do for food?"

"We have two cooks. They do it all. The food is brought down to them."

"What other staff?"

"No other staff. Daddy was made to sack them all four months ago."

That accounted for the state of the watchman's bathroom. I said: "My arrival in the helicopter here yesterday afternoon was duly reported by radio to the *Shangri-la*. A man with a badly scarred face. Where's the radio transmitter?"

"You know everything, don't you?"

"Know-all Calvert. Where is it?"

"Off the hall. In the room behind the stairs. It's locked."

"I have keys that'll open the Bank of England. Wait a minute." I went down to the guard's room outside the prisoners' cellar, brought the whisky bottle back up to where Susan was standing and handed it to her. "Hang on to this."

She looked at me steadily. "Do you really need this?"

"Oh my God, sweet youth," I said nastily. "Sure I need it. I'm an alcoholic."

I untied the rope round Harry's ankles and helped him to his feet. He repaid this Samaritan gesture by swinging at me with his right foot but fifteen minutes on the floor hadn't helped his circulation or reactions any and I forestalled him with the same manœuvre. When I helped him up the second time there was no fight left in him.

"Did you—did you really have to do that?" The revulsion was back in her eyes.

"Did I—did you see what he tried to do to me?" I demanded.

"You men are all the same," she said.

"Oh, shut up!" I snarled. I was old and sick and tired and I'd run right out of the last of my witty ripostes.

The transceiver was a beauty, a big gleaming metallic RCA, the latest model as used in the naval vessels of a dozen nationalities. I didn't waste any time wondering where they had obtained it, that lot were fit for anything. I sat down and started tuning the set, then looked up at Susan. "Go and fetch me one of your father's razor blades."

"You don't want me to hear, is that it?"

"Think what you like. Just get it."

If she'd been wearing a skirt she'd have flounced out of the room. With what she was wearing flouncing was out of the question. The set covered every transmission frequency from the bottom of the long wave to the top of the V.H.F. It took only two minutes to raise SPFX. It was manned night and day the year round. It really was most considerate of the ungodly to provide me with such a magnificent instrument.

Sue Kirkside was back before I started speaking. I was ten

minutes on the microphone altogether. Apart from code-names and map references I used plain English throughout. I had to, I'd no book, and time was too short anyway. I spoke slowly and clearly, giving precise instructions about the movements of men, the alignment of radio frequencies, the minutest details of the lay-out of Dubh Sgeir castle and asking all-important questions about recent happenings on the Riviera. I didn't repeat myself once, and I asked for nothing to be repeated to me, because every word was being recorded. Before I was half-way through, Susan's eyebrows had disappeared up under the blonde fringe and Harry was looking as if he had been sandbagged. I signed off, reset the tuning band to its original position and stood up.

"That's it," I said. "I'm off."

"You're *what*?" The grey-blue eyes were wide, the eyebrows still up under the fringe, but with alarm, this time, not astonish-ment. "You're leaving? You're leaving me here?"

"I'm leaving. If you think I'd stay a minute longer in this damned castle than I have to, you must be nuts. I've played my hand far enough already. Do you think I want to be around here when the guards change over or when the toilers on the deep get back here?"

"Toilers on the deep? What do you mean?"

"Skip it." I'd forgotten she knew nothing about what our friends were doing. "It's Calvert for home."

"You've got a gun," she said wildly. "You could—you could capture them, couldn't you?"

"Capture who?" The hell with the grammar.

"The guards. They're on the second floor. They'll be asleep."

"How many?"

"Eight or nine. I'm not sure."

"Eight or nine, she's not sure! Who do you think I am, Super-man? Stand aside, do you want me to get killed? And, Susan, tell nothing to anybody. Not even Daddy. Not if you want to see Johnny-boy walk down that aisle. You understand?"

She put a hand on my arm and said quietly but with the fear still in her face: "You could take me with you."

"I could. I could take you with me and ruin everything. If I as much as fired a single shot at any of the sleeping warriors up top, I'd ruin everything. Everything depends on their never knowing that anybody was here to-night. If they suspected that, just had a hint of a suspicion of that, they'd pack their bags and take off into the night. To-night. And I can't possibly do anything until to-morrow night. You understand, of course, that they wouldn't leave until after they had killed everyone in the cellar. And your father, of course. And they'd stop off at Torbay and make sure that Sergeant MacDonald would never give evidence against them. Do you want that, Susan? God knows I'd love to take you out of here, I'm not made of Portland cement, but if I take you the alarm bells will ring and then they'll pull the plug. Can't you see that? If they come back and find you gone, they'll have one thought and one thought only in their minds: our little Sue has left the island. With, of course, one thought in mind. You must not be missing."

"All right." She was calm now. "But you've overlooked something."

"I'm a great old overlooker. What?"

"Harry. He'll be missing. He'll have to be. You can't leave him to talk."

"He'll be missing. So will the keeper of the gate. I clobbered him on the way in." She started to get all wide-eyed again but I held up my hand, stripped off coat and wind-breaker, unwrapped the razor she'd brought me and nicked my forearm, not too deeply, the way I felt I needed all the blood I had, but enough to let me smear the bottom three inches of the bayonet on both sides. I handed her the tin of Elastoplast and without a word she stuck a strip across the incision. I dressed again and we left, Susan with the whisky bottle and torch, myself with the rifle, shepherding Harry in front of me. Once in the hall I relocked the door with the skeleton key I'd used to open it.

The rain had stopped and there was hardly any wind, but the mist was thicker than ever and the night had turned bitterly cold. The Highland Indian summer was in full swing. We made our way through the courtyard across to where I'd left the bayonet lying on the cliff edge, using the torch, now with the Elastoplast removed from its face, quite freely, but keeping our voices low. The lad maintaining his ceaseless vigil on the battlements couldn't have seen us five yards away with the finest night-glasses in the world, but sound in heavy mist has unpredictable qualities, it can be muffled, it can be distorted, or it can occasionally be heard with surprising clarity, and it was now too late in the day to take chances.

I located the bayonet and told Harry to lie face down in the grass; if I'd left him standing he just might have been tempted to kick me over the edge. I gouged the grass in assorted places with heel and toe, made a few more scores with the butt of a bayonet, stuck the blade of the gate-keeper's bayonet in the ground at a slight angle so that the rifle was just clear of the ground, laid Harry's down so that the blood-stained bayonet tip was also just clear of the ground, so preventing the blood from running off among the wet grass, scattered most of the contents of the whisky bottle around and carefully placed the bottle, about a quarter full now, close to one of the bayonets. I said to Susan: "And what happened here do you think?"

"It's obvious. They had a drunken fight and both of them slipped on the wet grass over the edge of the cliff."

"And what did you hear?"

"Oh! I heard the sound of two men shouting in the hall. I went on to the landing and I heard them shouting at the tops of their voices. I heard the one tell Harry to get back to his post and Harry saying, no, by God, he was going to settle it now. I'll say both men were drunk, and I won't repeat the kind of language they were using. The last I heard they were crossing the court-yard together, still arguing."

"Good girl. That's exactly what you heard."

She came with us as far as the place where I'd left the gate-keeper. He was still breathing. I used most of what rope I'd left to tie them together at the waist, a few feet apart, and wrapped the end of it in my hand. With their arms lashed behind their backs they weren't going to have much balancing power and no holding power at all on the way down that steep and crumbling path to the landing stage. If either slipped or stumbled I might be able to pull them back to safety with a sharp tug. There was going to be none of this Alpine stuff with the rope around my waist also. If they were going to step out into the darkness they were going to do it without me.

I said: "Thank you, Susan. You have been a great help. Don't take any more of those Nembutal tablets to-night. They'd think it damn' funny if you were still asleep at midday to-morrow."

"I wish it were midday the next day. I won't let you down, Mr. Calvert. Everything is going to be all right, isn't it?"

"Of course."

There was a pause, then she said: "You could have pushed these two over the edge if you wanted to, couldn't you. But you didn't. You could have cut Harry's arm, but you cut your own. I'm sorry for what I said, Mr. Calvert. About you being horrible and terrible. You do what you have to do." Another pause. "I think you're rather wonderful."

"They all come round in the end," I said, but I was talking to myself, she'd vanished into the mist. I wished drearily that I could have agreed with her sentiments, I didn't feel wonderful at all, I just felt dead tired and worried stiff for with all the best planning in the world there were too many imponderables and I wouldn't have bet a brass farthing on the next twenty-four hours. I got some of the worry and frustration out of my system by kicking the two prisoners to their feet.

We went slowly down that crumbling treacherous path in single file, myself last, torch in my left hand, rope tightly—but not too tightly—in my right hand. I wondered vaguely as we went why I *hadn't* nicked Harry instead of myself. It would have been so much more fitting, Harry's blood on Harry's bayonet.

"You had a pleasant outing, I trust?" Hutchinson asked court-eously.

"It wasn't dull. You would have enjoyed it." I watched Hutchinson as he pushed the *Firecrest* into the fog and the darkness. "Let me into a professional secret. How in the world did you find your way back into this pier to-night? The mist is twice as bad as when I left. You cruise up and down for hours, impossible to take any bearings, there's the waves, tide, fog, currents—and yet there you are, right on the nose, to the minute. It can't be done."

"It was an extraordinary feat of navigation," Hutchinson said solemnly. "There are such things as charts, Calvert, and if you look at that large-scale one for this area you'll see an eight fathom bank, maybe a cable in length, lying a cable and a half out to the west of the old pier there. I just steamed out straight into wind and tide, waited till the depth-sounder showed I was over the bank and dropped the old hook. At the appointed hour the great navigator lifts his hook and lets wind and tide drift him ashore again. Not many men could have done it."

"I'm bitterly disappointed," I said. "I'll never think the same of you again. I suppose you used the same technique on the way in?"

"More or less. Only I used a series of five banks and patches. My secrets are gone for ever. Where now?"

"Didn't Uncle Arthur say?"

"You misjudge Uncle Arthur. He says he never interferes with you in—what was it?—the execution of a field operation. 'I plan,' he says. 'I co-ordinate. Calvert finishes the job.'"

"He has his decent moments," I admitted.

"He told me a few stories about you in the past hour. I guess it's a privilege to be along."

"Apart from the four hundred thousand quid or whatever?"

"Apart, as you say, for the green men. Where to, Calvert?"

"Home. If you can find it in this lot."

"Craigmore? I can find it." He puffed at his cigar and held the end close to his eyes. "I think I should put this out. It's getting so I can't even see the length of the wheelhouse windows, far less beyond them. Uncle Arthur's taking his time, isn't he?"

"Uncle Arthur is interrogating the prisoners."

"I wouldn't say he'd get much out of that lot."

"Neither would I. They're not too happy."

"Well, it *was* a nasty jump from the pier to the foredeck. Especially with the bows plunging up and down as they were. And more especially with their arms tied behind their backs."

"One broken ankle and one broken forearm," I said. "It could have been worse. They could have missed the foredeck altogether."

"You have a point," Hutchinson agreed. He stuck his head out the side window and withdrew it again. "It's not the cigar," he announced. "No need to quit smoking. Visibility is zero, and I mean zero. We're flying blind on instruments. You may as well switch on the wheelhouse lights. Makes it all that easier to read the charts, depth-sounder and compass and doesn't affect the radar worth a damn." He stared at me as the light came on. "What the hell are you doing in that flaming awful outfit?"

"This is a dressing-gown," I explained. "I've three suits and all three are soaked and ruined. Any luck, sir?" Uncle Arthur had just come in to the wheelhouse.

"One of them passed out." Uncle Arthur wasn't looking very pleased with himself. "The other kept moaning so loudly that I couldn't make myself heard. Well, Calvert, the story."

"The story, sir? I was just going to bed. I've told you the story."

"Half a dozen quick sentences that I couldn't hear above their damned caterwauling," he said coldly. "The whole story, Calvert."

"I'm feeling weak, sir."

"I've rarely known a time when you weren't feeling weak, Calvert. You know where the whisky is."

Hutchinson coughed respectfully. "I wonder if the Admiral would permit——"

"Certainly, certainly," Uncle Arthur said in a quite different tone. "Of course, my boy." The boy was a clear foot taller than Uncle Arthur. "And while you're at it, Calvert, you might bring one for me, too, a normal-sized one." He had his nasty side to him, had Uncle Arthur.

I said "good night" five minutes later. Uncle Arthur wasn't too pleased, I'd the feeling he thought I'd missed out on the suspense and fancy descriptions, but I was as tired as the old man with the scythe after Hiroshima. I looked in on Charlotte Skouras, she was sleeping like the dead. I wondered about that chemist back in Torbay, he'd been three parts asleep, myopic as a barn owl and crowding eighty. He could have made a mistake. He could have had only a minimal experience in the prescribing of sleep-inducing drugs for those who lived in the land of the Hebridean prayer: "Would that the peats might cut themselves and the fish jump on the shore, that I upon my bed might lie, and sleep for ever more."

But I'd done the old boy an injustice. After what was, to me, our miraculous arrival in Craigmore's apology for a harbour it had taken me no more than a minute to shake Charlotte into something resembling wakefulness. I told her to get dressed—a cunning move this to make her think I didn't know she was still dressed—and come ashore. Fifteen minutes after that we were all inside Hutchinson's house and fifteen minutes still later, when Uncle Arthur and I had roughly splinted the prisoners' fractures and locked them in a room illuminated only by a sky-light that would have taken Houdini all his time to wriggle through, I was in bed in another tiny box-room that was obviously the sleeping-quarters of the chairman of the Craigmore's art gallery selection committee, for he'd kept all the best exhibits to himself. I was just dropping off to sleep, thinking that if the universities ever got around to awarding Ph.D.s to house agents, the first degree would surely go to the first man who sold a Hebridean hut within sniffing distance of a flensing shed, when the door opened and the light came on. I blinked open exhausted eyes and saw Charlotte Skouras softly closing the door behind her.

"Go away," I said. "I'm sleeping."

"May I come in?" she asked. She gazed around the art gallery

214

and her lips moved in what could have been the beginnings of a smile. "I would have thought you would have gone to sleep with the lights on to-night."

"You should see the ones behind the wardrobe doors," I boasted. I slowly opened my eyes as far as I could without mechanical aid. "Sorry, I'm tired. What can I do? I'm not at my best receiving lady callers in the middle of the night."

"Uncle Arthur's next door. You can always scream for help if you want to." She looked at a moth-eaten armchair. "May I sit down?"

She sat down. She still wore that uncrushable white dress and her hair was neatly combed, but that was about all you could say for her. Attempts at humour there might have been in her voice, but there was none in her face and none in her eyes. Those brown, wise, knowing eyes, eyes that knew all about living and loving and laughter, the eyes that had once made her the most sought-after actress of her time now held only sadness and despair. And fear. Now that she had escaped from her husband and his accomplices, there should have been no need for fear. But it was there, half-buried in the tired brown eyes, but there. Fear was an expression I knew. The lines round the eyes and mouth that looked so right, so inevitable, when she smiled or laughed—in the days when she had smiled and laughed—looked as if they had been etched by time and suffering and sorrow and despair into a face that had never known laughter and love. Charlotte Skouras's face, without the Charlotte Meiner of old behind it, no longer looked as if it belonged to her. A worn, a weary and an alien face. She must have been about thirty-five, I guessed, but she looked a deal older. And yet when she sat in that chair, almost huddled in that chair, the Craigmore art gallery no longer existed.

She said flatly: "You don't trust me, Philip."

"What on earth makes you say that? Why shouldn't I?"

"You tell me. You are evasive, you will not answer questions. No, that is wrong, you will and you do answer questions, but I know enough of men to know that the answers you give me are

215

the ones you want to give me and not the ones I should hear. Why should this be, Philip? What have I done that you should not trust me?"

"So the truth is not in me? Well, I suppose I do stretch it a bit at times, I may even occasionally tell a lie. Strictly in the line of business, of course. I wouldn't lie to a person like you." I meant it and intended not to—unless I had to do it for her sake, which was different.

"Why should you not lie to a person like me?"

"I don't know how to say it. I could say I don't usually lie to lovely and attractive women for whom I have a high regard, and then you'd cynically say I was stretching the truth till it snapped, and you'd be wrong because it is the truth, if truth lies in the eye of the beholder. I don't know if that sounds like an insult, it's never meant to be. I could say it's because I hate to see you sitting there all washed up and with no place to go and no one to turn to at the one time in your life you need some place to go and someone to turn to, but I suppose again that might sound like an insult. I could say I don't lie to my friends, but that again would be an insult, the Charlotte Skourases of this world don't make friends with government hirelings who kill for their wages. It's no good. I don't know what to say, Charlotte, except that it doesn't matter whether you believe me or not as long as you believe that no harm will come to you from me and, as long as I'm near you, no harm will come to you from anyone else either. Maybe you don't believe that either, maybe your feminine intuition has stopped working."

"It is working—what you say?—overtime. Very hard indeed." The brown eyes were still and the face without expression. "I do think I could place my life in your hands."

"You might not get it back again."

"It's not worth all that much. I might not want it back."

She looked at me for a long moment when there was no fear in her eyes, then stared down at her folded hands. She gazed at them so long that I finally looked in the same direction myself, but there was nothing wrong with her hands that I could see. Finally she

216

looked up with an almost timid half-smile that didn't belong to her at all.

"You are wondering why I came," she asked.

"No. You've told me. You want me to tell you a story. Especially the beginning and end of the story."

She nodded. "When I began as a stage actress, I played very small parts, but I knew what the play was all about. In this real-life play, I'm still playing a very small part. Only, I no longer know what the play is all about. I come on for three minutes in Act 2, but I have no idea what has gone before. I'm back for another minute in Act 4, but I've no idea in the world what's happened between Acts 2 and 4. And I cannot begin to imagine how it will all end." She half-lifted her arms, turning the palms upwards. "You cannot imagine how frustrating this can be for a woman."

"You really know nothing of what has gone before this?"

"I ask you to believe me."

I believed her. I believed her because I knew it to be true.

"Go to the front room and bring me, as they say in these parts, a refreshment," I said. "I grow weaker by the hour."

So she rose obediently and went to the front room and brought me the refreshment which gave me just enough strength to tell her what she wanted to know.

"They were a triumvirate," I said, which if not strictly accurate, was close enough to the truth for my explanation. "Sir Anthony, Lavorski, who, I gather, was not only his public and private accountant, but his overall financial director as well, and John Dollmann, the managing director of the shipping companies—they were split up for tax reasons—associated with your husband's oil companies. I thought that MacCallum, the Scots lawyer, and Jules Biscarte, the lad with the beard who owns one of the biggest merchant banks in Paris, was in with them too. But they weren't. At least not Biscarte. I think he was invited aboard ostensibly to discuss business but actually to provide our triumvirate with information that would have given them the basis for their next coup, but he didn't like the way the wind was blowing and shied off. I know nothing about MacCallum."

"I know nothing about Biscarte," Charlotte said. "Neither he nor Mr. MacCallum stayed aboard the *Shangri-la*, they were at the Columba hotel for a few days and were invited out twice for dinner. They haven't been aboard since the night you were there."

"Among other things they didn't care for your husband's treatment of you."

"I didn't care for it myself. I know what Mr. MacCallum was doing aboard. My husband was planning to build a refinery in the Clyde estuary this coming winter and MacCallum was negotiating the lease for him. My husband said that, by the end of the year, he expected to have a large amount of uncommitted capital for investment."

"I'll bet he did, that's as neat a phrase for the proceeds of grand larceny as ever I've come across. Lavorski, I think we'll find, was the instigator and guiding brain behind all this. Lavorski it would have been who discovered that the Skouras empire was badly in need of some new lifeblood in the way of hard cash and saw the way of putting matters right by using means they already had close to hand."

"But—but my husband was never short of money," Charlotte objected. "He had the best of everything, yachts, cars, houses——"

"He was never short in that sense. Neither were half the millionaires who jumped off the New York skyscrapers at the time of the stock market crash. Do be quiet, there's a good girl, you know nothing about high finance." Coming from a character who eked out a bare living from an inadequate salary, I reflected, that was very good indeed. "Lavorski struck upon the happy idea of piracy on a grand scale—vessels carrying not less than a million pounds' worth of specie at a time."

She stared at me, her lips parted. I wished I had teeth like that, instead of having had half of them knocked out by Uncle Arthur's enemies over the years. Uncle Arthur, I mused bitterly, was

218

twenty-five years older than I was and was frequently heard to boast that he'd still to lose his first tooth. She whispered: "You're making all this up."

"Lavorski made it all up. I'm just telling you, I wouldn't have the brains to think of something like that. Having thought up this splendid scheme for making money, they found themselves with three problems to solve: how to discover when and where large quantities of specie were being shipped, how to seize those ships and how to hide them while they opened the strong-room—a process which in ships fitted with the most modern strong-rooms can take anything up to a day—and removed said specie.

"Problem number one was easy. I have no doubt they may have suborned high-ranking banking officials—the fact that they tried it on with Biscarte is proof of that—but I don't think it will ever be possible to bring those men to justice. But it will be possible to arrest and very successfully indict their ace informant, their trump card, our good friend the belted broker, Lord Charnley. To make a real good-going success of piracy you require the co-operation of Lloyd's. Well, that's an actionable statement, the co-operation of someone in Lloyd's. Someone like Lord Charnley. He is, by profession, a marine underwriter at Lloyd's. Stop staring at me like that, you're putting me off.

"A large proportion of valuable marine cargoes are insured at Lloyd's. Charnley would know of at least a number of those. He would know the amount, the firm or bank of dispatch, and possibly the date of dispatch and vessel."

"But Lord Charnley is a wealthy man," she said.

"Lord Charnley gives the appearance of being a wealthy man," I corrected. "Granted, he had to prove that he was a man of substance to gain admission to the old club, but he may have backed the wrong insurance horses or played the stock market. He either needed money or wanted money. He *may* have plenty but money is like alcohol, some people can take it and some can't, and with those who can't the more money they have the more they require.

"Dollmann solved problem two—the hi-jacking of the specie. I shouldn't imagine this strained his resources too far. Your husband ships his oil into some very odd and very tough places indeed and it goes without saying that he employs some very odd and very tough people to do it. Dollmann wouldn't have recruited the hi-jacking crew himself, he probably singled out our good friend Captain Imrie, who will prove to have a very interesting history, and gave him the authority to go through the Skouras fleets and hand-pick suitable men for the job. Once the hi-jacking crew was assembled and ready, Messrs. Skouras, Lavorski and Dollmann waited till the victim was on the high seas, dumped you and the stewardess in a hotel, embarked the lads on the *Shangri-la*, intercepted the specie-carrying vessel and by one of a series of ruses I'll tell you about later, succeeded in boarding it and taking over. Then the *Shangri-la* landed the captured crew under guard while the prize crew sailed the hi-jacked vessel to the appointed hiding place."

"It can't be true, it can't be true," she murmured. It was a long time since I'd seen any woman wringing her hands but Charlotte Skouras was doing it then. Her face was quite drained of colour. She knew that what I was saying was true and she'd never heard of any of it before. "Hiding place, Philip? What hiding place?"

"Where would you hide a ship, Charlotte?"

"How should I know?" She shrugged tiredly. "My mind is not very clear to-night. Up in the Arctic perhaps, or in a lonely Norwegian fjord or some desert island. I can't think any more, Philip. There cannot be many places. A ship is a big thing."

"There are millions of places. You can hide a ship practically anywhere in the world. All you have to do is to open the bilge-valves and engine-room non-return valves to the bilges and detonate a couple of scuttling charges."

"You mean—you mean that——"

"I mean just that. You send it to the bottom. The west side of the Sound to the east of Dubh Sgeir island, a cheery stretch of water rejoicing in the name of Beul nan Uamh—the mouth of the

220

grave—must be the most densely packed marine graveyard in Europe to-day. At dead slack water the valves were opened at a very carefully selected spot in the Beul nan Uamh and down they went, all five of them, gurgle, gurgle, gurgle. Tide tables show that, coincidentally, most of them were sunk at or near midnight. Cease upon the midnight, as the poet says, only in this case with a very great deal of pain, at least for the underwriters involved. Beul nan Uamh. Odd, I never thought of it before. A very apt name indeed. The mouth of the grave. Damn' place is printed far too large in the chart, it doesn't have to be very obvious to be too obvious for Calvert."

She hadn't been listening to my meanderings. She said: "Dubh Sgeir? But—but that's the home of Lord Kirkside."

"It's not but, it's because. The hiding place was picked either by your husband, or, if someone else, then the arrangement was made through your husband. I never knew until recently that your husband was an old drinking pal of Lord Kirkside. I saw him yesterday, but he wouldn't talk. Nor would his charming daughter."

"You do move around. I've never met the daughter."

"You should. She thinks you're an old gold-digging hag. A nice kid really. But terrified, terrified for her life and those of others."

"Why on earth should she be?"

"How do you think our triumvirate got Lord Kirkside to agree to their goings-on?"

"Money. Bribery."

I shook my head. "Lord Kirkside is a Highlander and a gentleman. It's a pretty fierce combination. Old Skouras could never lay hands on enough money to bribe Lord Kirkside to pass the uncollected fares box on a bus, if he hadn't paid. A poor illustration, Lord Kirkside wouldn't recognise a bus even if it ran over him, but what I mean is, the old boy is incorruptible. So your charming friends kidnapped old Kirkside's elder son—the younger lives in Australia—and just to make sure that Susan Kirkside wouldn't be tempted to do anything silly, they kidnapped her fiancé. A guess, but a damned good one. They're supposed to be dead."

"No, no," she whispered. Her hand was to her mouth and her voice was shaking. "My God, no!"

"My God, yes. It's logical and tremendously effective. They also kidnapped Sergeant MacDonald's sons and Donald Mac-Eachern's wife for the same reason. To buy silence and co-operation."

"But—but people just can't disappear like that."

"We're not dealing with street corner boys, we're dealing with criminal master-minds. Disappearances are rigged to look like accidental death. A few other people have disappeared also, people who had the misfortune to be hanging around in small private boats while our friends were waiting for the tide to be exactly right before opening the sea-cocks on the hi-jacked ships."

"Didn't it arouse police suspicion? Having so many small boats disappear in the same place."

"They sailed or towed two of those boats fifty or more miles away and ran them on the rocks. Another could have disappeared anywhere. The fourth did set sail from Torbay and disappeared, but the disappearance of one boat is not enough to arouse suspicion."

"It must be true, I know it must be true." She shook her head as if she didn't believe it was true at all. "It all fits so well, it explains so many things and explains them perfectly. But—but what's the good of knowing all this now? They're on to you, they *know* you know that something is far wrong and that that something is in Loch Houron. They'll leave——"

"How do they know we suspect Loch Houron?"

"Uncle Arthur told me in the wheelhouse last night." Surprise in her voice. "Don't you remember?"

I hadn't remembered. I did now. I was half-dead from lack of sleep. A stupid remark. Perhaps even a give-away remark. I was glad Uncle Arthur hadn't heard that one.

"Calvert nears the sunset of his days," I said. "My mind's going. Sure they'll leave. But not for forty-eight hours yet. They will think they have plenty of time, it's less than eight hours since we instructed Sergeant MacDonald to tell them that we were going to the mainland for help."

"I see," she said dully. "And what did you do on Dubh Sgeir to-night, Philip?"

"Not much. But enough." Another little white lie. "Enough to confirm my every last suspicion. I swam ashore to the little harbour and picked the side door of the boathouse. It's quite a boathouse. Not only is it three times as big on the inside as it is from the outside, but it's stacked with diving equipment."

"Diving equipment?"

"Heaven help us all, you're almost as stupid as I am. How on earth do you think they recover the stuff from the sunken vessels? They use a diving-boat and the Dubh Sgeir boathouse is its home."

"Was—was that all you found out?"

"There was nothing more to find out. I had intended taking a look round the castle—there's a long flight of steps leading up to it from the boatyard inside the cliff itself—but there was some character sitting about three parts of the way up with a rifle in his hand. A guard of some sorts. He was drinking out of some sort of bottle, but he was doing his job for all that. I wouldn't have got within a hundred steps of him without being riddled. I left."

"Dear God," she murmured. "What a mess, what a terrible mess. And you've no radio, we're cut off from all help. What are we going to do? What *are* you going to do, Philip?"

"I'm going there in the *Firecrest* this coming night, that's what I'm going to do. I have a machine-gun under the settee of the saloon in the *Firecrest* and Uncle Arthur and Tim Hutchinson will have a gun apiece. We'll reconnoitre. Their time is running short and they'll want to be gone to-morrow at the latest. The boathouse doors are ill-fitting and if there's no light showing that will mean they still haven't finished their diving. So we wait till they have finished and come in. We'll see the light two miles away when they open the door to let the diving-boat in to load up all the stuff they've cached from the four other sunken ships. The front doors of the boathouse will be closed, of course, while they load

223

up. So we go in through the front doors. On the deck of the *Firecrest*. The doors don't look all that strong to me. Surprise is everything. We'll catch them napping. A sub-machine-gun in a small enclosed space is a deadly weapon."

"You'll be killed, you'll be killed!" She crossed to and sat on the bed-side, her eyes wide and scared. "Please, Philip! Please, *please* don't. You'll be killed, I tell you. I beg of you, don't do it!" She seemed very sure that I would be killed.

"I have to, Charlotte. Time has run out. There's no other way."

"Please." The brown eyes were full of unshed tears. This I couldn't believe. "Please, Philip. For my sake."

"No." A tear-drop fell at the corner of my mouth, it tasted as salt as the sea. "Anything else in the world. But not this."

She rose slowly to her feet and stood there, arms hanging limply by her side, tears trickling down her cheeks. She said dully: "It's the maddest plan I've ever heard in my life," turned and left the room, switching off the light as she went.

I lay there staring into the darkness. There was sense in what the lady said. It *was*, I thought, the maddest plan *I'd* ever heard in my life. I was damned glad I didn't have to use it.

IO

Thursday: noon—Friday: dawn

"Let me sleep." I said. I kept my eyes shut. "I'm a dead man."

"Come on, come on." Another violent shake, a hand like a power shovel. "Up!"

"Oh, God!" I opened the corner of one eye. "What's the time?"

"Just after noon. I couldn't let you sleep any more."

"Noon! I asked to be shaken at five. Do you know——"

"Come here." He moved to the window, and I swung my legs stiffly out of bed and followed him. I'd been operated on during my sleep, no anæsthetic required in the condition I was in, and someone had removed the bones from my legs. I felt awful. Hutchinson nodded towards the window. "What do you think of that?"

I peered out into the grey opaque world. I said irritably: "What do you expect me to see in that damn' fog?"

"The fog."

"I see," I said stupidly. "The fog."

"The two a.m. shipping forecast," Hutchinson said. He gave the impression of exercising a very great deal of patience. "It said the fog would clear away in the early morning. Well, the goddamned fog hasn't cleared away in the early morning."

The fog cleared away from my befuddled brain. I swore and jumped for my least sodden suit of clothing. It was damp and clammy and cold but I hardly noticed these things, except subconsciously, my conscious mind was frantically busy with something else. On Monday night they'd sunk the *Nantesville* at slack water but there wasn't a chance in a thousand that they would have been able to get something done that night or the Tuesday

225

night, the weather had been bad enough in sheltered Torbay harbour, God alone knew what it would have been like in Beul nan Uamh. But they could have started last night, they *had* started last night for there had been no diving-boat in the Dubh Sgeir boathouse, and reports from the *Nantesville*'s owners had indicated that the strongroom was a fairly antiquated one, not of hardened steel, that could be cut open in a couple of hours with the proper equipment. Lavorski and company would have the proper equipment. The rest of last night, even had they three divers and reliefs working all the time, they could have brought up a fair proportion of the bullion but I'd been damn' sure they couldn't possibly bring up all eighteen tons of it. Marine salvage had been my business before Uncle Arthur had taken me away. They would have required another night or at least a good part of the night, because they only dared work when the sun was down. When no one could see them. But no one could see them in dense fog like this. This was as good as another night thrown in for free.

"Give Uncle Arthur a shake. Tell him we're on our way. In the *Firecrest*."

"He'll want to come."

"He'll have to stay. He'll know damn' well he'll have to stay. Beul nan Uamh, tell him."

"Not Dubh Sgeir? Not the boathouse?"

"*You* know damn' well we can't move in against that until midnight."

"I'd forgotten," Hutchinson said slowly. "We can't move in against it until midnight."

The Beul nan Uamh wasn't living up to its fearsome reputation. At that time in the afternoon it was dead slack water and there was only the gentlest of swells running up from the south-west. We crossed over from Ballara to the extreme north of the eastern shore of Dubh Sgeir and inched our way southward with bare steerage way on. We'd cut the by-pass valve into the underwater exhaust and, even in the wheelhouse, we could barely hear the throb of the diesel. Even with both wheelhouse doors wide open, we could just hear it and no more. But we hadn't the wheelhouse doors open for the purpose of not hearing our own engine.

By this time we were almost half-way down the eastern patch of miraculously calm water that bordered the normal mill-race of Beul nan Uamh, the one that Williams and I had observed from the helicopter the previous afternoon. For the first time, Hutchinson was showing something approaching worry. He never spared a glance through the wheelhouse windows, and only a very occasional one for the compass: he was navigating almost entirely by chart and depth-sounder.

"Are you sure it'll be this fourteen-fathom ledge, Calvert?"

"It has to be. It damn' well has to be. Out to the seven fathom mark there the sea-bottom is pretty flat, but there's not enough depth to hide superstructure and masts at low tide. From there to fourteen it's practically a cliff. And beyond the fourteen fathom ledge it goes down to thirty-five fathom, steep enough to roll a ship down there. You can't operate at those depths without very special equipment indeed."

"It's a damn' narrow ledge," he grumbled. "Less than a cable. How could they be sure the scuttled ship would fetch up where they wanted it to?"

"They could be sure. In dead slack water, you can always be sure."

Hutchinson put the engine in neutral and went outside. We drifted on quietly through the greyly opaque world. Visibility didn't extend beyond our bows. The muffled beat of the diesel served only to enhance the quality of ghostly silence. Hutchinson came back into the wheelhouse, his vast bulk moving as unhurriedly as always.

"I'm afraid you're right. I hear an engine."

I listened, then I could hear it too, the unmistakable thudding of an air compressor. I said: "What do you mean afraid?"

"You know damn' well." He touched the throttle, gave the wheel a quarter turn to port and we began to move out gently into deeper water. "You're going to go down."

"Do you think I'm a nut case? Do you think I *want* to go down? I bloody well don't want to go down—and you bloody well know that I *have* to go down. And you know why. You want them to finish up here, load up in Dubh Sgeir and the whole lot to be hell and gone before midnight?"

"Half, Calvert. Take half of our share. God, man, we do nothing."

"I'll settle for a pint in the Columba Hotel in Torbay. You just concentrate on putting this tub exactly where she ought to be. I don't want to spend the rest of my life swimming about the Atlantic when I come back up from the *Nantesville*."

He looked at me, the expression in his eyes saying "if," not "when," but kept quiet. He circled round to the south of the diving-boat—we could faintly hear the compressor all the way— then slightly to the west. He turned the *Firecrest* towards the source of the sound, manœuvring with delicacy and precision. He said: "About a cable length."

"About that. Hard to judge in fog."

"North twenty-two east true. Let go the anchor."

I let go the anchor, not the normal heavy Admiralty type on the chain but a smaller CQR on the end of forty fathoms of rope. It disappeared silently over the side and the Terylene as silently slid down after it. I let out all forty fathoms and made fast. I went back to the wheelhouse and strapped the cylinders on my back.

"You won't forget, now," Hutchinson said. "When you come up, just let yourself drift. The ebb's just setting in from the nor'-nor'-east and will carry you back here. I'll keep the diesel ticking, you'll be able to hear the underwater exhaust twenty yards away. I hope to hell the mist doesn't clear. You'll just have to swim for Dubh Sgeir."

"That *will* be ducky. What happens to you if it clears?"

"I'll cut the anchor rope and take off."

"And if they come after you?"

"Come after me? Just like that? And leave two or three dead divers down inside the *Nantesville*?"

"I wish to God," I said irritably, "that you wouldn't talk about dead divers inside the *Nantesville*."

There were three divers aboard the *Nantesville*, not dead but all working furiously, or as furiously as one can work in the pressurised slow-motion world of the undersea.

Getting down there had been no trouble. I'd swum on the surface towards the diving-boat, the compressor giving me a clear bearing all the time, and dived when only three yards away. My hands touched cables, life-lines and finally an unmistakable wire hawser. The wire hawser was the one for me.

I stopped my descent on the wire when I saw the dim glow of light beneath me. I swam some distance to one side then down until my feet touched something solid. The deck of the *Nantesville*. I moved cautiously towards the source of the light.

There were two of them, standing in their weighted boots at the edge of an open hatchway. As I'd expected, they were wearing not my self-contained apparatus, but regular helmet and corselet diving gear, with air-lines and life-lines, the life-lines almost certainly with telephone wires imbedded inside them. Self-contained diving equipment wouldn't have been much use down here, it was too deep for oxygen and compressed-air stores too limited. With those suits they could stay down an hour and a half, at least, although they'd have to spend thirty to forty minutes on decompression stops on the way up. I wanted to be gone in less than that, I wanted to be gone that very moment, my heart was banging away against my chest wall like a demented pop drummer with the ague but it was only the pressure of the water, I told myself, it couldn't be fear, I was far too brave for that.

The wire rope I'd used to guide me down to the *Nantesville*, terminated in a metal ring from which splayed out four chains to the corners of a rectangular steel mesh basket. The two divers were loading this basket with wire- and wood-handled steel boxes that they were hauling up from the hold at the rate of, I guessed, about one every minute. The steel boxes were small but obviously heavy: each held four 28-lb. ingots of gold.

Each box held a fortune. There were three hundred and sixty such fortunes aboard the *Nantesville*.

I tried to calculate the overall rate of unloading. The steel basket held sixteen boxes. Sixteen minutes to load. Another ten minutes to winch up to the diving-boat, unload and lower again. Say forty an hour. In a ninety-minute stretch, about sixty. But after ninety minutes they would have to change divers. Forty minutes, including two decompression stops of, say, twelve and twenty-four minutes, to get to the surface, then twenty minutes to change over and get other divers down. An hour at least. So, in effect, they were clearing sixty boxes every two and a half hours, or twenty-four an hour. The only remaining question was, how many boxes were left in the *Nantesville*'s strongroom?

I had to find out and I had to find out at once. I'd had only the two compressed air-cylinders aboard the *Firecrest* and already their two hundred atmospheres were seriously depleted. The wire hawser jerked and the full basket started to rise, the divers guiding it clear of the superstructure with a trailing guide rope. I moved forward from the corner of the partially opened hatch remote from where they were standing and cautiously wriggled over and down. With excessive caution, I supposed: their lamp cast only a small pool of light and they couldn't possible have seen me from where I was standing.

I felt my hands—already puffed and numbed by the icy water—touch a life-line and air-line and quickly withdrew them. Below and to my right I could see another faint pool of light. A few cautious strokes and I could see the source of the light.

The light was moving. It was moving because it was attached to the helmet of a diver, angled so as to point down at an angle of forty-five degrees. The diver was inside the strongroom.

They hadn't opened that strongroom with any Yale key. They'd opened it with underwater torches cutting out a roughly rectangular section in the strongroom's side, maybe six feet by four.

I moved up to this opening and pushed my head round the side. Beyond the now stooping diver was another light suspended from

230

the deckhead. The bullion boxes were neatly stacked in racks round the side and it was a five-second job to estimate their number. Of the three hundred and sixty bullion boxes, there were about one hundred and twenty left.

Something brushed my arm, pulled past my arm. I glanced down and saw that it was a rope, a nylon line, that the diver was pulling in to attach to the handle of one of the boxes. I moved my arm quickly out of the way.

His back was towards me. He was having difficulty in fastening the rope but finally secured it with two half hitches, straightened and pulled a knife from his waist sheath. I wondered what the knife was for.

I found out what the knife was for. The knife was for me. Stooped over as he had been, he could just possibly have caught a glimpse of me from the corner of his eye: or he might have felt the sudden pressure, then release of pressure, on the nylon rope: or his sixth sense was in better working condition than mine. I won't say he whirled round, for in a heavy diving suit at that depth the tempo of movement becomes slowed down to that of a slow-motion film.

But he moved too quickly for me, It wasn't my body that was slowing down as much as my mind. He was completely round and facing me, not four feet away, and I was still where I'd been when he'd first moved, still displaying all the lightning reactions and co-ordinated activity of a bag of cement. The six-inch-bladed knife was held in his lowered hand with thumb and forefinger towards me, which is the way that only nasty people with lethal matters on their minds hold knives, and I could see his face clearly. God knows what he wanted the knife for, it must have been a reflex action, he didn't require a knife to deal with me, he wouldn't have required a knife to deal with two of me.

It was Quinn.

I watched his face with a strangely paralysed intentness. I watched his face to see if the head would jerk down to press the telephone call-up buzzer with his chin. But his head didn't move, Quinn had never required any help in his life and he didn't require any now. Instead his lips parted in a smile of almost beatific joy. My mask made it almost impossible for my face to be recognised but he knew whom he had, he knew whom he had without any doubt in the world. He had the face of a man in the moment of supreme religious ecstasy. He fell slowly forwards, his knees bending, till he was at an angle of almost forty-five degrees and launched himself forward, his right arm already swinging far behind his back.

The moment of thrall ended. I thrust off backwards from the strongroom's outer wall with my left foot, saw the air-hose come looping down towards me as Quinn came through the jagged hole, caught it and jerked down with all my strength to pull him off-balance. A sharp stinging pain burned its way upwards from my lower ribs to my right shoulder I felt a sudden jerk in my right hand. I fell backwards on to the floor of the hold and then I couldn't see Quinn any more, not because the fall had dazed me nor because Quinn had moved, but because he had vanished in the heart of an opaque, boiling, mushrooming cloud of dense air-bubbles. A non-collapsible air-hose can, and often has to, stand up to some pretty savage treatment, but it can't stand up to the wickedly slicing power of a razor-sharp knife in the hands of the strongest man I'd ever known. Quinn had cut his own air-hose, had slashed it cleanly in two.

No power on earth could save Quinn now. With a pressure of forty pounds to the square inch on that severed air-line, he would be drowning already, his suit filling up with water and weighting him down so that he could never rise again. Almost without realising what I was doing I advanced with the nylon rope still in my hands and coiled it any old way round the madly threshing legs, taking great care indeed to keep clear of those flailing arms, for Quinn could still have taken me with him, could have snapped my neck like a rotten stick. At the back of my mind I had the vague hope that when his comrades investigated, as they were bound to do immediately—those great clouds of bubbles must have already passed out through the hold on their way to the surface—they would think he'd become entangled and tried to cut himself free. I did not think it a callous action then nor do I now. I had no qualms about doing this to a dying man, and no compunction: he was doomed anyway, he was a psychopathic monster who killed for the love of it and, most of all, I had to think of the living who might die, the prisoners in the cellars of the Dubh Sgeir castle. I left him threshing there, dying there, and swam up and hid under the deck-head of the hold.

The two men who had been on deck were already on their way down, being slowly lowered on their life-lines. As soon as their air helmets sunk below my level I came up through the hatchway, located the wire hawser and made my way up. I'd been down for just under ten minutes so when my wrist depth-gauge showed a depth of two fathoms I stopped for a three-minute decompression period. By now, Quinn would be dead.

I did as Hutchinson had told me, drifted my way back to the *Firecrest*—there was no hurry now—and located it without difficulty. Hutchinson was there to help me out of the water and I was glad of his help.

"Am I glad to see you, brother," he said. "Never thought the day would come when Tim Hutchinson would die a thousand deaths, but die a thousand deaths he did. How did it go?"

"All right. We've time. Five or six hours yet."

"I'll get the hook up." Three minutes later we were on our way and three minutes after that we were out near enough in the mid-channel of the Beul nan Uamh, heading north-north-east against the gathering ebb. I could hear the helm going on auto-pilot and then Hutchinson came through the door into the lit saloon, curtains tightly if, in that fog, unnecessarily drawn, where I was rendering some first aid to myself, just beginning to tape up a patch of gauze over the ugly gash that stretched all the way from lowest rib to shoulder. I couldn't see the expression behind the darkly-luxuriant foliage of that beard, but his sudden immobility was expression enough. He said, quietly: "What happened, Calvert?"

"Quinn. I met him in the strongroom of the *Nantesville*."

He moved forward and in silence helped me to tape up the

gauze. When it was finished, and not until then, he said: "Quinn is dead." It wasn't a question.

"Quinn is dead. He cut his own air-hose." I told him what had happened and he said nothing. He didn't exchange a dozen words all the way back to Craigmore. I knew he didn't believe me. I knew he never would.

Neither did Uncle Arthur. He'd never believe me till the day he died. But his reaction was quite different, it was one of profound satisfaction. Uncle Arthur was, in his own avuncular fashion, possessed of an absolute ruthlessness. Indeed, he seemed to take half the credit for the alleged execution. "It's not twenty-four hours," he'd announced at the tea-table, "since I told Calvert to seek out and destroy this man by whatever means that came to hand. I must confess that I never thought the means would consist of the blade of a sharp knife against an air-hose. A neat touch, my boy, a very neat touch indeed."

Charlotte Skouras believed me. I don't know why, but she believed me. While she was stripping off my makeshift bandage, cleaning the wound and re-bandaging it very efficiently, a process I suffered with unflinching fortitude because I didn't want to destroy her image of a secret service agent by bellowing out loud at the top of my voice, I told her what had happened and there was no doubt that she believed me without question. I thanked her, for bandage and belief, and she smiled.

Six hours later, twenty minutes before our eleven p.m. deadline for taking off in the *Firecrest*, she was no longer smiling. She was looking at me the way women usually look at you when they have their minds set on something and can see that they are not going to get their own way: a rather less than affectionate look.

"I'm sorry, Charlotte," I said. "I'm genuinely sorry, but it's not on. You are not coming with us, and that's that." She was dressed in dark slacks and sweater, like one who had—or had had—every intention of coming with us on a midnight jaunt. "We're

234

not going picnicking on the Thames. Remember what you said yourself this morning. There will be shooting. Do you think I want to see you killed?"

"I'll stay below," she pleaded. "I'll stay out of harm's way. Please, Philip, let me come."

"No."

"You said you'd do anything in the world for me. Remember?"

"That's unfair, and you know it. Anything to help you, I meant. Not anything to get you killed. Not you, of all people."

"Of all people? You think so much of me?"

I nodded.

"I mean so much to you?"

I nodded again. She looked at me for a long time, her eyes wide and questioning, her lips moving as if about to speak and yet not speaking, then took a step forward, latched her arms around my neck and tried to break it. At least, that was the way it felt, the dead Quinn's handiwork was still with me, but it wasn't that at all, she was clinging to me as she might cling to a person who she knew she would never see again. Maybe she was fey, maybe she had second sight, maybe she could see old Calvert floating, face down, in the murky waters of the Dubh Sgeir boathouse. When I thought about it I could see it myself, and it wasn't an attractive sight at all. I was beginning to have some difficulty with my breathing when she suddenly let me go, half-led, half-pushed me from the room and closed the door behind me. I heard the key turn in the lock.

"Our friends are at home," Tim Hutchinson said. We'd circled far to the south of Dubh Sgeir, close in to the southern shore of Loch Houron and were now drifting quickly on the flood tide, engines stopped, in an east by northerly direction past the little man-made harbour of Dubh Sgeir. "You were right, Calvert. They're getting all ready for their moonlit flitting."

"Calvert is usually right," Uncle Arthur said in his best trained-him-myself voice. "And now, my boy?"

The mist had thinned now, giving maybe a hundred yards'

visibility. I looked at the T-shaped crack of light showing where the boathouse doors didn't quite meet each other in the middle and where the tops of the doors sagged away from the main structure.

"Now it is," I said. I turned to Hutchinson. "We've all of a fifteen foot beam. That entrance is not more than twenty wide. There's not a beacon or a mark on it. There's a four knot tide running. You really think it can be done—taking her through that entrance at four or five knots, fast enough to smash open those doors, without piling ourselves up on the rocks on the way in?"

"There's only one way to find out." He pressed the starter button and the warm diesel caught fire at once, its underpass exhaust barely audible. He swung her round to the south on minimum revs, continued on this course for two cables, westwards for the same distance, curved round to the north, pushed the throttle wide open and lit a cigar. Tim Hutchinson preparing for action. In the flare of the match the dark face was quiet and thoughtful, no more.

For just over a minute there was nothing to be seen, just the darkness and patches of grey mist swirling past our bows. Hutchinson was heading a few degrees west of north, making allowance for the set of the tide. All at once we could see it, slightly off the starboard bow as it had to be to correct for the tide, that big T-shaped light in the darkness, fairly jumping at us. I picked up the sub-machine-gun, opened and latched back the port wheelhouse door and stood there, gun in left hand, door-jamb in right, with one foot on the outside deck and the other still in the wheelhouse. Uncle Arthur, I knew, was similarly positioned on the starboard side. We were as firmly braced as it was possible to be. When the *Firecrest* stopped, it would stop very suddenly indeed.

Forty yards away, Hutchinson eased the throttle and gave the wheel a touch to port. That bright T was even farther round on our starboard side now, but directly in line with us and the patch of dark water to the west of the almost phosphorescently foaming whiteness that marked the point where the flood tide ripped past

236

the outer end of the eastern breakwater. Twenty yards away he pushed the throttle open again, we were heading straight for where the unseen west breakwater must be, we were far too far over to port, it was impossible now that we could avoid smashing bow first into it, then suddenly Hutchinson had the wheel spinning to starboard, the tide pushing him the same way, and we were through and not an inch of Uncle Arthur's precious paintwork had been removed. Hutchinson had the engine in neutral. I wondered briefly whether, if I practised for the rest of my life, I could effect a manœuvre like that: I knew damned well that I couldn't.

I'd told Hutchinson that the bollards were on the starboard side of the boathouse, so that the diving-boat would be tied up on that side. He angled the boat across the tiny harbour towards the right-hand crack of light, spun the wheel to port till we were angling in towards the central crack of light and put the engine full astern. It was no part of the plan to telescope the *Firecrest*'s bows against the wall of the boathouse and send it—and us—to the bottom.

As an entrance it erred, if anything, on the spectacular side. The doors, instead of bursting open at their central hasps, broke off at the hinges and we carried the whole lot before us with a thunderous crash. This took a good knot off our speed. The aluminium foremast, with Uncle Arthur's fancy telescopic aerial inside, almost tore the tabernacle clear of the deck before it sheared off, just above wheelhouse level, with a most unpleasant metallic shrieking. That took another knot off. The screw, biting deep in maximum revs astern, took off yet another knot, but we still had a fair way on when, amid a crackling, splintering of wood, partly of our planking but mainly of the doors, and the screeching of the rubber tyres on our well-fendered bows, we stopped short with a jarring shock, firmly wedged between the port quarter of the diving-boat and the port wall of the boat-house. Uncle Arthur's feelings must have been almost as bruised and lacerated as the planking of his beloved *Firecrest*. Hutchinson moved the throttle to slow ahead to keep us wedged in position and switched on the five-inch searchlight, less to illuminate the already sufficiently well-lit shed than to dazzle bystanders ashore. I stepped out on the deck with the machine-pistol in my hands.

We were confronted, as the travel books put it, with a scene of bustling activity, or, more precisely, what had been a scene of bustling activity before our entrance had apparently paralysed them all in whatever positions they had been at the time. On the extreme right three faces stared at us over the edge of the hold of the diving-boat, a typical forty-five-foot M.F.V. about the same size as the *Charmaine*. Two men on deck were frozen in the act of lifting a box across to the hold. Another two were standing upright, one with his hands stretched above his head, waiting for another box swinging gently from a rope suspended from a loading boom. That box was the only moving thing in the boathouse. The winchman himself, who bore an uncommon resemblance to Thomas, the bogus customs officer, one lever against his chest and another held in his outstretched right hand, looked as if the lavas of Vesuvius had washed over him twenty centuries ago and left him frozen there for ever. Two others, backs bent, were standing on the wall at the head of the boathouse, holding a rope attached to a very large box which two frogmen were helping to lift clear of the water. When it came to hiding specie, they had one-track minds. On the extreme left stood Captain Imrie, presumably there to supervise operations, and, beside him, his patrons, Lavorski and Dollmann. This was the big day, this was the culmination of all their dreams, and they weren't going to miss a moment of it.

Imrie, Lavorski and Dollmann were the ones for me. I moved forward until I could see the barrel of the machine-gun and until they could also see that it was pointing at them.

"Come close," I said. "Yes, you three. Captain Imrie, speak to your men. Tell them that if they move, if they try anything at all, I'll kill all three of you. I've killed four of you already. If I double the number, what then? Under the new laws you get only fifteen years. For murderous vermin, that is not enough. I'd rather you died here. Do you believe me, Captain Imrie?"

"I believe you." The guttural voice was deep and sombre. "You killed Quinn this afternoon."

"He deserved to die."

"He should have killed you that night on the *Nantesville*," Imrie said. "Then none of this would have happened."

"You will come aboard our boat one at a time," I said. "In this situation, Captain Imrie, you are without question the most dangerous man. After you, Lavorski, then——"

"Please keep very still. Terribly still." The voice behind me was totally lacking in inflection, but the gun pressed hard against my spine carried its own message, one not easily misunderstood. "Good. Take a pace forward and take your right hand away from the gun."

I took a pace forward and removed my right hand. This left me holding the machine-pistol by the barrel.

"Lay the gun on the deck."

It obviously wasn't going to be much use to me as a club, so I laid it on the deck. I'd been caught like this before, once or twice, and just to show that I was a true professional I raised my hands high and turned slowly round.

"Why, Charlotte Skouras!" I said. Again I knew what to do, how to act, the correct tone for the circumvented agent, bantering but bitter. "Fancy meeting you here. Thank you very much, my dear." She was still dressed in the dark sweater and slacks, only they weren't quite as spruce as the last time I'd seen them. They were soaking wet. Her face was dead white and without expression. The brown eyes were very still. "And how in God's name did you get here?"

"I escaped through the bedroom window and swam out. I hid in the after cabin."

"Did you indeed? Why don't you change out of those wet clothes?"

She ignored me. She said to Hutchinson: "Turn off that searchlight."

"Do as the lady says," I advised.

He did as the lady said. The light went out and we were all now

239

in full view of the men ashore. Imrie said: "Throw that gun over the side, Admiral."

"Do as the gentleman says," I advised.

Uncle Arthur threw the gun over the side. Captain Imrie and Lavorski came walking confidently towards us. They could afford to walk confidently, the three men in the hold, the two men who had suddenly appeared from behind the diving-boat's wheel-house and the winch-driver—a nice round total of six—had suddenly sprouted guns. I looked over this show of armed strength and said slowly: "You were waiting for us."

"Certainly we were waiting for you," Lavorski said jovially. "Our dear Charlotte announced the exact time of your arrival. Haven't you guessed that yet, Calvert?"

"How do you know my name?"

"Charlotte, you fool. By heavens, I believe we have been grievously guilty of over-estimating you."

"Mrs. Skouras was a plant," I said.

"A bait," Lavorski said cheerfully. I wasn't fooled by his cheerfulness, he'd have gone into hysterics of laughter when I came apart on the rack. "Swallowed hook, line, and sinker. A bait with a highly effective if tiny transmitter and a gun in a polythene bag. We found the transmitter in your starboard engine." He laughed again until he seemed in danger of going into convulsions. "We've known of every move you've made since you left Torbay. And how do you like that, Mr. Secret Agent Calvert?"

"I don't like it at all. What are you going to do with us?"

"Don't be childish. What are you going to do with us, asks he naïvely. I'm afraid you know all too well. How did you locate this place?"

"I don't talk to executioners."

"I think we'll shoot the admiral through the foot, to begin with," Lavorski beamed. "A minute afterwards through the arm, then the thigh——"

"All right. We had a radio-transmitter aboard the *Nantesville*."

"We know that. How did you pin-point Dubh Sgeir?"

"The boat belonging to the Oxford geological expedition. It is moored fore and aft in a little natural harbour south of here. It's well clear of any rock yet it's badly holed. It's impossible that it would be holed naturally where it lay. It was holed unnaturally, shall we say. Any other boat you could have seen coming from a long way off, but that boat had only to move out to be in full sight of the boathouse—and the anchored diving-boat. It was very clumsy."

Lavorski looked at Imrie, who nodded. "He would notice that. I advised against it at the time. Was there more, Calvert?"

"Donald MacEachern on Eilean Oran. You should have taken him, not his wife. Susan Kirkside—you shouldn't have allowed her out and about, when did you last see a fit young twenty-one-year-old with blue shadows that size under her eyes? A fit young twenty-one-year-old with nothing in the world to worry about, that is? And you should have disguised that mark made by the tail fuselage of the Beechcraft belonging to Lord Kirkside's elder son when you ran it over the edge of the north cliff. I saw it from the helicopter."

"That's all?" Lavorski asked. I nodded, and he looked again at Imrie.

"I believe him," Imrie said. "No one talked. That's all we need to know. Calvert first, Mr. Lavorski?" They were certainly a brisk and business-like outfit.

I said quickly: "Two questions. The courtesy of two answers. I'm a professional. I'd like to know. I don't know if you understand."

"And two minutes," Lavorski smiled. "Make it quick. We have business on hand."

"Where is Sir Anthony Skouras? He should be here."

"He is. He's up in the castle with Lord Kirkside and Lord Charnley. The *Shangri-la*'s tied up at the west landing stage."

"Is it true that you and Dollmann engineered the whole plan, that you bribed Charnley to betray insurance secrets, that you—or Dollmann, rather—selected Captain Imrie to pick his crew of cut-throats, and that you were responsible for the capture and sinking of the ships and the subsequent salvaging of the cargoes.

241

And, incidentally, the deaths, directly or indirectly, of our men?"

"It's late in the day to deny the obvious." Again Lavorski's booming laugh. "We think we did rather well, eh, John?"

"Very well indeed," Dollmann said coldly. "We're wasting time."

I turned to Charlotte Skouras. The gun was still pointing at me. I said: "I have to be killed, it seems. As you will be responsible for my death, you might as well finish the job." I reached down, caught the hand with the gun in it and placed it against my chest, letting my own hand fall away. "Please do it quickly."

There was no sound to be heard other than the soft throb of the *Firecrest*'s diesel. Every pair of eyes in that boatshed were on us, my back was to them all, but I knew it beyond any question. I wanted every pair of eyes in that boatshed to be on us. Uncle Arthur took a step inside the starboard door and said urgently: "Are you mad, Calvert? She'll kill you! She's one of them."

The brown eyes were stricken, there was no other expression for it, the eyes of one who knows her world is coming to an end. The finger came off the trigger, the hand opened slowly and the gun fell to the deck with a clatter that seemed to echo through the boatshed and the tunnels leading off on either side. I took her left arm and said: "It seems Mrs. Skouras doesn't feel quite up to it. I'm afraid you'll have to find someone else to——"

Charlotte Skouras cried out in sharp pain as her legs caught the wheelhouse sill and maybe I did shove her through that doorway with unnecessary force, but it was too late in the day to take chances now. Hutchinson had been waiting and caught her as she fell, dropping to his knees at the same time. I went through that door after her like an international rugby three-quarter diving for the line with a dozen hands reaching out for him, but even so Uncle Arthur beat me to it. Uncle Arthur had a lively sense of self-preservation. Even as I fell, my hand reached out for the loud-hailer that had been placed in position on the wheelhouse deck.

"Don't fire!" The amplified voice boomed cavernously against the rock-faces and the wooden walls of the boatshed. "If you shoot, you'll die! One shot, and you may all die. There's a

242

machine-gun lined up on the back of every man in this boat-house. Just turn round, very very slowly, and see for yourselves."

I half rose to my feet, hoisted a wary eye over the lower edge of a wheelhouse window, got the rest of the way to my feet, went outside and picked up the machine-gun on the deck.

Picking up that machine-gun was the most superfluous and unnecessary action I had performed for many a long day. If there was one thing that boathouse was suffering from at the moment it was a plethora of machine-guns. There were twelve of them in all, shoulder-slung machine-pistols, in twelve of the most remarkably steady pairs of hands I'd ever seen. The twelve men were ranged in a rough semicircle round the inner end of the boathouse, big, quiet, purposeful-looking men dressed in woollen caps, grey-and-black camouflaged smocks and trousers and rubber boots. Their hands and faces were the colour of coal. Their eyes gleamed whitely, like performers in the Black and White Minstrel show, but with that every hint of light entertainment ended.

"Lower your hands to your sides and let your guns fall." The order came from a figure in the middle of the group, a man indistinguishable from the others. "Do please be very careful. Slowly down, drop the guns, utter stillness. My men are very highly trained commandos. They have been trained to shoot on suspicion. They know only how to kill. They have not been trained to wound or cripple."

They believed him. I believed him. They dropped their guns and stood very still indeed.

"Now clasp your hands behind your necks."

They did. All but one. Lavorski. He wasn't smiling any more and his language had little to recommend it.

That they were highly trained I could believe. No word or signal passed. The commando nearest Lavorski walked towards him on soundless soles, machine-pistol held across his chest. The butt seemed to move no more than three inches. When Lavorski picked himself up the lower part of his face was covered in blood and I could see the hole where some teeth had been. He clasped his hands behind his neck.

"Mr. Calvert?" the officer asked.

"Me," I said.

"Captain Rawley, sir. Royal Marine Commandos."

"The castle, Captain?"

"In our hands."

"The *Shangri-la?*"

"In our hands."

"The prisoners?"

"Two men are on their way up, sir."

I said to Imrie: "How many guards?"

He spat and said nothing. The commando who had dealt with Lavorski moved forward, machine-pistol high. Imrie said: "Two."

I said to Rawley: "Two men enough?"

"I hope, sir, that the guards will not be so foolish as to offer resistance."

Even as he finished speaking the flat rapid-fire chatter of a sub-machine-gun came echoing down the long flight of stone steps. Rawley shrugged.

"They'll never learn to be wise now. Robinson?" This to a man with a waterproof bag over his shoulder. "Go up and open the cellar door. Sergeant Evans, line them up in two rows against the wall there, one standing, one sitting."

Sergeant Evans did. Now that there was no danger of being caught in cross-fire we landed and I introduced Uncle Arthur, full military honours and all, to Captain Rawley. Captain Rawley's salute was something to see. Uncle Arthur beamed. Uncle Arthur took over.

"Capitally done, my boy!" he said to Rawley. "Capitally. There'll be a little something for you in this New Year's List. Ah! Here come some friends."

They weren't all exactly friends, this group that appeared at the bottom of the steps. There were four tough but dispirited looking characters whom I'd never seen before, but unquestionably Imrie's men, closely followed by Sir Anthony Skouras and Lord Charnley. They, in their turn, were closely followed by four commandos with the very steady hands that were a hallmark of Rawley's men. Behind them came Lord Kirkside and his daughter. It was impossible to tell what the black-faced commandos were thinking, but the other eight had the same expression on their faces, dazed and utter bewilderment.

"My dear Kirkside! My dear fellow!" Uncle Arthur hurried forward and shook him by the hand, I'd quite forgotten that they knew one another. "Delighted to see you safe and sound, my dear chap. Absolutely delighted. It's all over now."

"What in God's name is happening?" Lord Kirkside asked. "You—you've got them? You have them all? Where is my boy? Where is Rollinson? What——?"

An explosive crack, curiously muffled, came down the flight of steps. Uncle Arthur looked at Rawley, who nodded. "Plastic explosive, sir."

"Excellent, excellent," Uncle Arthur beamed. "You'll see them any minute, Kirkside." He crossed over to where old Skouras was lined up against the wall, hands clasped behind his neck, reached up both his own, pulled Skouras's arms down and shook his right hand as if he were attempting to tear it off.

"You're lined up with the wrong team, Tony, my boy." This was one of the great moments of Uncle Arthur's life. He led him across to where Lord Kirkside was standing. "It's been a frightful nightmare, my boy, a frightful nightmare. But it's all over now."

"Why did you do it?" Skouras said dully. "Why did you do it? God, oh God, you don't know what you've done."

"Mrs. Skouras? The *real* Mrs. Skouras?" There is the ham actor in all of us, but more than most in Uncle Arthur. He pushed back his sleeve and studied his watch carefully. "She arrived in London by air from Nice just over three hours ago. She is in the London Clinic.

"What in God's name do you mean? You don't know what you are saying. My wife——"

"Your wife is in London. Charlotte here is Charlotte Meiner and always was." I looked at Charlotte. A total incomprehension

245

and the tentative beginnings of a dazed hope. "Earlier this year, blazing the trail for many kidnappings that were to follow, your friends Lavorski and Dollmann had your wife seized and hidden away to force you to act with them, to put your resources at their disposal. I think they felt aggrieved, Tony, that you should be a millionaire while they were executives: they had it all worked out, even to having the effrontery of intending to invest the proceeds in your empire. However. Your wife managed to escape, so they seized her cousin and best friend, Charlotte—a friend upon whom, shall we say, your wife was emotionally very dependent—and threatened to kill her unless they got Mrs. Skouras back again. Mrs. Skouras surrendered immediately. This gave them the bright idea of having two swords of Damocles hanging over your head, so, being men of honour, they decided to keep Charlotte as well as your imprisoned wife. Then, they knew, you would do exactly as they wanted, when and as they wanted. To have a good excuse to keep both you and Charlotte under their surveillance at the same time, and to reinforce the idea that your wife was well and truly dead, they gave out that you had been secretly married." Uncle Arthur was a kind man: no mention of the fact that it was common knowledge that, at the time of her alleged death, brain injuries sustained by Mrs. Skouras in a car crash two years previously had become steadily worse and it was known that she would never leave hospital again.

"How on earth did you guess that?" Lord Kirkside asked.

"No guess. Must give my lieutenants their due," Uncle Arthur said in his best magnanimous taught-'em-all-I-know voice. "Hunslett radioed me at midnight on Tuesday. He gave me a list of names of people about whom Calvert wanted immediate and exhaustive inquiries made. That call was tapped by the *Shangri-la* but they didn't know what Hunslett was talking about because in our radio transmissions all proper names are invariably coded. Calvert told me later that when he'd seen Sir Anthony on Tuesday night he thought Sir Anthony was putting on a bit of an act. He said it wasn't all act. He said Sir Anthony was completely broken and desolated by the thought of his dead wife. He said he believed

246

the original Mrs. Skouras was still alive, that it was totally inconceivable that a man who so patently cherished the memory of his wife should have married again two or three months later, that he could only have pretended to marry again for the sake of the one person whom he ever and so obviously loved.

"I radioed France. Riviera police dug up the grave in Beaulieu where she had been buried near the nursing home where she'd died. They found a coffin full of logs. You knew this, Tony."

Old Skouras nodded. He was a man in a dream.

"It took them half an hour to find out who had signed the death certificate and most of the rest of the day to find the doctor himself. They charged him with murder. This can be done in France on the basis of a missing body. The doctor wasted no time at all in taking them to his own private nursing home, where Mrs. Skouras was in a locked room. The doctor, matron and a few others are in custody now. Why in God's name didn't you come to us before?"

"They had Charlotte and they said they would kill my wife out of hand. What—what would you have done?"

"God knows," Uncle Arthur said frankly. "She's in fair health, Tony. Calvert got radio confirmation at five a.m." Uncle Arthur jerked a thumb upwards. "On Lavorski's big transceiver in the castle."

Both Skouras and Lord Kirkside had their mouths open. Lavorski, blood still flowing from his mouth, and Dollmann looked as if they had been sandbagged. Charlotte's eyes were the widest wide I'd ever seen. She was looking at me in a very peculiar way.

"It's true," Susan Kirkside said. "I was with him. He told me to tell nobody." She crossed to take my arm and smiled up at me. "I'm sorry again for what I said last night. I think you're the most wonderful man I've ever known. Except Rolly, of course." She turned round at the sound of footsteps coming down the stairs and promptly forgot all about the second most wonderful man she'd ever known.

247

"Rolly!" she cried. "Rolly!" I could see Rolly bracing himself. They were all there, I counted them, Kirkside's son, the Hon. Rollinson, the policeman's sons, the missing members of the small boats and, behind them all, a small brown-faced old woman in a long dark dress with a black shawl over her head. I went forward and took her arm.

"Mrs. MacEachern," I said. "I'll take you home soon. Your husband is waiting."

"Thank you, young man," she said calmly. "That will be very nice." She lifted her arm and held mine in a proprietorial fashion.

Charlotte Skouras came and held my other arm, not in quite so proprietorial a fashion, but there for everyone to see. I didn't mind. She said: "You were on to me? You were on to me all the time?"

"He was," Uncle Arthur said thoughtfully. "He just said he knew. You never quite got round to explaining that bit, Calvert."

"It wasn't difficult, sir—if you knew all the facts, that is," I added hastily. "Sir Anthony put me on to you. That visit he paid me on the *Firecrest* to allay any suspicion we might have had about our smashed radio set only served, I'm afraid, to make me suspicious. You wouldn't have normally come to me, you'd have gone ashore immediately to the police or to a phone, sir. Then, in order to get me talking about the cut telephone wires, you wondered if the radio-wrecker, to complete our isolation from the mainland, had smashed the two public call boxes. From a man of your intelligence, such a suggestion was fatuous, there must be scores of houses in Torbay with their private phone. But you thought it might sound suspicious if you suggested cut lines, so you didn't. Then Sergeant MacDonald gave me a glowing report about you, said you were the most respected man in Torbay and your public reputation contrasted so sharply with your private behaviour in the *Shangri-la* on Tuesday night—well, I just couldn't buy it.

"That nineteenth-century late Victorian melodrama act that you and Charlotte put on in the saloon that night had me fooled for all of five seconds. It was inconceivable that any man so

248

devoted to his wife could be vicious towards another obviously nice woman——"

"Thank you kindly, sir," Charlotte murmured.

"It was inconceivable that he send her for his wife's photograph, unless he had been ordered to do so. And you had been ordered to do so, by Lavorski and Dollmann. And it was inconceivable that she would have gone—the Charlotte Meiner I knew would have clobbered you over the head with a marline spike. Ergo, if you weren't what you appeared to be, neither were you, Charlotte.

"The villains, they thought, were laying a foundation for an excellent reason for your flight from the wicked baron to the *Firecrest*, where you could become their eyes and ears and keep them informed of all our plans and moves, because they'd no idea how long their secret little transmitter in the engine-room would remain undetected. After they knew we'd found Hunslett— they'd removed the transmitter by that time—it was inevitable that they would try to get you aboard the *Firecrest*. So they laid a little more groundwork by giving you a bruised eye—the dye is nearly off already—and some wicked weals across your back and dumped you into the water with your little polythene kitbag with the micro-transmitter and gun inside it. Do this, they said, or Mrs. Skouras will get it."

She nodded. "They said that."

"I have twenty-twenty eyesight. Sir Arthur hasn't—his eyes were badly damaged in the war. I had a close look at those weals on your back. Genuine weals. Also genuine pin-pricks where the hypodermic with the anæsthetic had been inserted before the lashes were inflicted. To that degree, at least, someone was humane."

"I could stand most things," Skouras said heavily. "I couldn't stand the thought of—the thought of——"

"I guessed you had insisted on the anæsthetic, sir. No, I knew. The same way that I knew that you had insisted that the crews of all those small yachts be kept alive or the hell with the consequences. Charlotte, I ran a finger-nail down one of those weals. You should have jumped through the saloon roof. You

249

never batted an eyelid. After submersion in salt water. After that, I knew.

"I have devious reasons for the things I do. You told us that you had come to warn us of our deadly danger—as if we didn't know. I told you we were leaving Torbay within the hour, so off you trotted to your little cabin and told them we were going to leave within the hour. So Quinn, Jacques and Kramer came paddling across well in advance of the time you'd told us they would be coming, trusting we would have been lulled into a sense of false security. You must love Mrs. Skouras very much, Charlotte. A clear-cut choice, she or us, and you made your choice. But I was waiting for them, so Jacques and Kramer died. I told you we were going to Eilean Oran and Craigmore, so off you trotted down to your little cabin and told them we were going to Eilean Oran and Craigmore, which wouldn't have worried them at all. Later on I told you we were going to Dubh Sgeir. So off you trotted down to your little cabin again, but before you could tell them anything you passed out on your cabin deck, possibly as a result of a little night-cap I'd put in your coffee. I couldn't have you telling your friends here that I was going to Dubh Sgeir, could I now? They would have had a reception committee all nicely organised."

"You—you were in my cabin? You said I was on the floor?"

"Don Juan has nothing on me. I flit in and out of ladies' bedrooms like anything. Ask Susan Kirkside. You were on the floor. I put you to bed. I looked at your arms, incidentally, and the rope marks were gone. They'd used rubber bands, twisted pretty tightly, just before Hunslett and I had arrived?"

She nodded. She looked dazed.

"I also, of course, found the transmitter and gun. Then, back in Craigmore, you came and pumped me for some more information. And you did try to warn me, you were about torn in half by that time. I gave you that information. It wasn't the whole truth, I regret, but it was what I wanted you to tell Lavorski and company, which," I said approvingly, "like a good little girl you did. Off you trotted to your little white-washed bedroom——"

"Philip Calvert," she said slowly, "you are the nastiest, sneak-ingest, most low-down double-crossing——"

"There are some of Lavorski's men aboard the *Shangri-la*," old Skouras interrupted excitedly. He had rejoined the human race. "They'll get away——"

"They'll get life," I said. "They're in irons, or whatever Captain Rawley's men here are in the habit of using."

"But how did you—how did you know where the *Shangri-la* was? In the darkness, in the mist, it's impossible——"

"How's the *Shangri-la*'s tender working?" I asked.

"The what? The *Shangri-la*'s—what the devil——?" He calmed down. "It's not working. Engines out of order."

"Demerara sugar has that effect upon them," I explained. "Any sugar has, in fact, when dumped in the petrol tanks, but demerara was all I could lay hands on that Wednesday night after Sir Arthur and I had left you but before we took the *Firecrest* into the pier. I went aboard the tender with a couple of pounds of the stuff. I'm afraid you'll find the valves are ruined. I also took with me a homing signal transmitter, a transistorised battery-powered job, which I attached to the inner after bulkhead of the anchor locker, a place that's not looked at once a year. So, when you hauled the incapacitated tender aboard the *Shangri-la*—well, we knew where the *Shangri-la* was."

"I'm afraid I don't follow, Calvert."

"Look at Messrs. Dollmann, Lavorski and Imrie. They follow all right. I know the exact frequency that transmitter sends on—after all, it *was* my transmitter. One of Mr. Hutchinson's skippers was given this frequency and tuned in to it. Like all M.F.V.s it has a loop aerial for direction finding, he just had to keep turning the loop till the signal was at full strength. He couldn't miss. He didn't miss."

"Mr. Hutchinson's skippers?" Skouras said carefully. "M.F.V.s you said?"

It was as well, I reflected, that I wasn't overly troubled with self-consciousness, what with Mrs. MacEachern on one hand, Charlotte on the other, and every eye, a large proportion of them hostile to a degree, bent upon me, it could have been embarrassing to a degree. "Mr. Hutchinson has two shark-fishing boats. Before I came to Dubh Sgeir last night I radioed from one of his boats asking for help—the gentlemen you see here. They said they couldn't send boats or helicopters in this weather, in almost zero visibility. I told them the last thing I wanted was their damned noisy helicopters, secrecy was everything, and not to worry about the sea transport, I knew some men for whom the phrase 'zero visibility' was only a joke. Mr. Hutchinson's skippers. They went to the mainland and brought Captain Rawley and his men back here. I didn't think they'd arrive until late at night, that's why Sir Arthur and I were afraid to move before midnight. What time did you get here, Captain Rawley?"

"Nine-thirty."

"So early? I must admit it was a bit awkward without a radio. Then ashore in your little rubber boats, through the side door, waited until the diving-boat came back—and waited and waited."

"We were getting pretty stiff, sir."

Lord Kirkside cleared his throat. Maybe he was thinking of my nocturnal assignation with his daughter.

"Tell me this, Mr. Calvert. If you radioed from Mr. Hutchinson's boat in Craigmore, why did you have to radio again from here later that night?"

"If I didn't, you'd be down among the dead men by this time. I spent the best part of fifteen minutes giving highly detailed descriptions, of Dubh Sgeir externally and of the castle and boathouse layout internally. Everything that Captain Rawley and his men have done had to be done in total darkness. You'll keep an eye on our friends, Captain Rawley? A fishery cruiser will be off Dubh Sgeir shortly after dawn."

The Marines herded them off into the left-hand cave, set three powerful lights shining into the prisoners' faces and mounted a four-man guard with machine-pistols at the ready. Our friends would undoubtedly keep until the fishery cruiser came in the morning.

Charlotte said slowly: "That was why Sir Arthur remained

252

behind this afternoon when you and Mr. Hutchinson went to the *Nantesville*? To see that I didn't talk to the guards and find out the truth?"

"Why else?"

She took her arm away and looked at me without affection. "So you put me through the hoop," she said quietly. "You let me suffer like this for thirty hours while you knew all the time."

"Fair's fair. You were doing me down, I was doing you down."

"I'm very grateful to you," she said bitterly.

"If you aren't, you damn' well ought to be," Uncle Arthur said coldly. This was one for the books, Uncle Arthur talking to the aristocracy, even if only the aristocracy by marriage, in this waspish tone. "If Calvert won't speak for himself, I will.

"Point one: if you hadn't kept on sending your little radio messages, Lavorski would have thought that there was something damned fishy going on and might well have left the last ton or two of gold in the *Nantesville* and taken off before we got here. People like Lavorski have a highly attuned sixth sense of danger. Point two: they wouldn't have confessed to their crimes unless they thought we were finished. Point three: Calvert wanted to engineer a situation where all attention was on the *Firecrest* so that Captain Rawley and his men could move into position and so eliminate all fear of unnecessary bloodshed—maybe *your* blood, my dear Charlotte. Point four, and more important: if you hadn't been in constant radio contact with them, advising them of our impending arrival right up to the moment we came through those doors—we'd even left the saloon door open so that you could clearly overhear us and know all we were doing—there would have been a pitched battle, guns firing as soon as those doors were breached, and who knows how many lives would have been lost. But they *knew* they were in control, they *knew* the trap was set, they *knew* you were aboard with that gun to spring the trap. Point five, and most important of all: Captain Rawley here was hidden almost a hundred yards away along the cross tunnel and the detachment up above were concealed in a store-room in the castle. How do you think *they* knew when to move in and move in simultaneously? Because, like all commandos, they had portable radio sets and were listening in to every word of your running commentary. Don't forget your transmitter was stolen from the *Firecrest*. It was *Calvert's* transmitter, my dear. He knew the transmitting frequency you were using and radioed that frequency to the mainland last night. That was after he had—um—given you a little something to drink and checked your transmitter before using the one up in the castle last night."

Charlotte said to me: "I think you are the most devious and detestable and untrustworthy man I've ever met." Her eyes were shining, whether from tears or whatever I didn't know. I felt acutely embarrassed and uncomfortable. She put her hand on my arm and said in a low voice: "You fool, oh, you fool! That gun might have gone off. I—I might have killed you, Philip!"

I patted her hand and said: "You don't even begin to believe that yourself." In the circumstances, I thought it better not to say that if that gun had gone off I'd never have trusted a three-cornered file again.

The grey mist was slowly clearing away and the dawn coming up on the quiet dark sea when Tim Hutchinson eased the *Firecrest* in towards Eilean Oran.

There were only four of us on the boat, Hutchinson, myself, Mrs. MacEachern and Charlotte. I'd told Charlotte to find a bed in Dubh Sgeir castle for the night, but she'd simply ignored me, helped Mrs. MacEachern on to the *Firecrest* and had made no move to go ashore again. Very self-willed, she was, and I could see that this was going to cause a lot of trouble in the years to come.

Uncle Arthur wasn't with us, a team of wild horses couldn't have dragged Uncle Arthur aboard the *Firecrest* that night. Uncle Arthur was having his foretaste of Paradise, sitting in front of a log fire in the Dubh Sgeir castle drawing-room, knocking back old Kirkside's superlative whisky and retailing his exploits to a breathless and spell-bound aristocracy. If I were lucky, maybe he'd mention my name a couple of times in the course of his recounting of the epic. On the other hand, maybe he wouldn't.

Mrs. MacEachern wasn't having her foretaste of Paradise, she was there already, a calm dark old lady with a wrinkled brown face who smiled and smiled and smiled all the way to her home on Eilean Oran. I hoped to God old Donald MacEachern had remembered to change his shirt.